White Tiger Pass

Xuemo

Tranaslated by Howard Goldblatt and Sylvia Li-chun Lin

中華國際傳媒出版集團
ZHONGHUA INTERNATIONAL MEDIA PUBLISHING GROUP

First Edition 2021

ISBN 978-988-79930-7-0
Copyright © 2021 by Xuemo
Published by Zhonghua International Media Publishing Group
Room 1003, 10 / F, Tower 1, Lippo Centre, 89 Queensway, Hong Kong
Tel:(86)13434375544
http://xuemo.cn
E-mail: xuemo1963@163.com

Contents

Chapter One

Black clouds loom over Mount Niuxin
Nine springs reflect a flash of lightning

1

Laoshun was scandalized by the scene that played out on the threshing ground.

He'd thought that an animal was sneaking leaves from bean stalks when he saw the bean stack bounce around. "Dai!" he yelled, and the movement stopped. He took a look around and saw no sign of an animal. He wondered what was going on when the stack moved again.

So he climbed onto the shed.

Mengzi was on top of the stack, a woman pinned underneath him. The sight of white buttocks pumping in the morning light stunned Laoshun.

He felt as if he'd been clubbed. His son, bad news personified, had already created a shocking sex scandal by bedding Shuangfu's wife, but that news had come to Laoshun as gossip. Seeing it with his own eyes dealt him a staggering blow, as he suddenly became conscious of the fact that his son was a grown man capable of mounting a woman, doing what he himself had so often done in the past. This both shocked and discomforted him. People said that witnessing copulation can lead to a year of bad luck, but that was not what bothered Laoshun. What he cared about was the startled and resentful look on his son's face, which projected a complex range of emotions, including embarrassment over the discovery of his appalling act and fury over his nosy father climbing onto the shed to spy on him. What was he thinking? Should he keep on doing what he felt like and not worry now that his father knew? Or should he be resentful over his father's failure to find him a wife? What else? Laoshun shook his head so hard it began to buzz, but it yielded no coherent thought.

He could only mutter: Disgusting.

The sun stuck its dismal face out from behind a sand dune in the east. Laoshun's face burned and his throat was parched, a sensation reminiscent of younger days, when he lingered outside a widow's door. Fucking weird. He was angry at himself. Why be ashamed? It wasn't him up there doing that. And doing what exactly . . . his son was old enough to screw around . . . he wasn't a gelded horse, and even if he was, he'd still rear up at the sight of a pretty mare. It can't be helped, and it doesn't matter, Laoshun told himself. Though in his heart it did matter, and damned if that didn't bother him.

It was his fault.

It really was. Why had he, a man in his fifties, decided to climb up onto the shed? And how was he to know his son would be using the bean stack as a honeymoon bed? He would have run off and hidden if he'd known. Why . . . go up . . . and stick his neck out to take a look? He should have figured that no animal sneaking food could have made the stack bounce like that.

All he recalled was how those pumping white buttocks and Mengzi's twisted face had stunned him. Momentarily dumbfounded, he coughed at the wrong time, immediately realizing how stupid that was. Now what? His head buzzed, as if a swarm of bees had taken up residence there.

When he jumped down, he forgot to step on the wall left there to make getting up and down easy, and landed on a pile of sand behind it, looking like a rabbit that's managed to elude the hunter's rifle.

"What's up, Laoshun? Practicing martial-arts leaps?" Meng Baye mocked.

Laoshun smiled uncomfortably. A quick look told him that Meng did not know why he was acting out of character, so, his mind at ease, he coughed dryly a few times and stole a look at the bean stack, the source of his awkward behavior. It stood quietly, no sound and no movement. The disgusting couple must be holding their breath, not daring to make a move. Shame on you! Carrying on like that in broad daylight, Laoshun fulminated silently.

Meng Baye wore his usual prankish, teasing smile. Affected by a guilty conscience, Laoshun nonetheless sensed something different in the smile, though he was used to his old friend acting up in ways. Could Meng have witnessed it too? If so, he would turn it into a running joke, something like: "A white ass has turned Laoshun into a rabbit. Hei, let's see how fast he can run. He's too old to be scared by a cunt, but he hasn't been around enough to see one as big as a saucer. Oh—he was scared shitless." Meng would say awful things like that regardless of where he was, which would be a huge headache for Laoshun. But another look at his friend's face eased his concern. Meng was squinting at people out in the field running around like ants.

In no mood to chat with Meng, and intending to give the couple a way out, Laoshun walked off like a sleepwalker. He was anxious for his son. It was time for fieldwork, and, with people coming and going all the time, he'd be discovered soon enough. What a loss of face that would be. He couldn't tell his son to speed it up, could he? Losing face is as easy as drinking cold water; their ancestors would jump off the sacrificial altar out of shame.

Bad news!

"It's time to find him a wife," Laoshun was thinking. "He's a grown man." This thought came as a surprise, almost as if his son had grown up overnight. His sons had grown as tall as a wall before he'd had time to react, and now he thought he could read the expression on his son's face; it said: "You won't get me a woman, and I need to get my sex somewhere." Was that it? Maybe so; no, definitely so. Laoshun sighed when he considered how Mengzi's embarrassment and fury characterized his wild, sometimes even murderous nature and willful attitude.

Laoshun walked toward the village after casting one last glance at the unmoving stack. It was time to get him a wife. Sooner or later you have to burn the hair off a sheep's head. It's just that you can't kill a man without a knife. Money was hard to come by. Marrying a son would cost twenty or thirty thousand yuan, and he had no idea where he could get that much. What little wheat they had left they could sell for four or five thousand if the family tightened their throats and ate less. So go ahead and sell it. It had to be sold eventually, if his son was ever going to be married. He'd planned to save the wheat for hard times, but why do that now? If there's drink, enjoy it today, don't worry if there's only cold water tomorrow. One day lived is two half days earned.

Laoshun lay down as soon as he was in his room. He was exhausted, tired inside and out, fatigued from top to bottom, drained of energy. Ying'er, his eldest son's widow, had taken her son to visit the grandparents, leaving the house with a bit of peace and quiet. He did not want to open his eyes or think about anything. But Mengzi's angry face and those white buttocks would not stop pumping in front of him, and his mood darkened. A rooster was chasing a hen out in the yard. Laoshun's temper flared up over the hen's coy cackling, so he clicked his tongue at them through the window. When that failed to stop them from making their flirtatious racket, with a savage spit, he jumped down to floor, took off a mud-spattered shoe, and flung it to separate the amorous pair.

The startled cackles drew his wife out of the kitchen. When she saw him hopping over to pick up his shoe, she complained:

"Why hit the chicken, she didn't stop you from eating?"

"It's you who's eating, eating shit!" Laoshun snapped as he picked up a twig to scrape chicken droppings off his shoe.

The rooster, slowly regaining its composure after being interrupted by the flying shoe, resumed its harassment of the hen. Laoshun decided to ignore them. Even roosters want to do it, he said to himself, why not people? Having no interest in bantering with his wife, he took out his pipe and lighter, and when he blew on the stem, embers arced through the air and landed in the dirt, where several chickens flocked over to peck at them. He held the smoke in his lungs as long as he could, a hissing sound escaping through his teeth.

"What's wrong?" his wife asked when she noticed his worried look. "A frown like that bothers me."

He just sucked on his pipe, releasing puff after puff of acrid smoke.

"What's wrong?" she persisted.

"Why ask me?" he barked angrily. "That young master of yours got laid in broad daylight."

"Who are you talking about?"

"Who else? That dumb-ass young master of yours."

"Mengzi?" She asked with a surprised look. "Be a father and stop making jokes about your own son."

"What do you think I'm being?" Angry smoke shot out of his nostrils as he sucked the pipe hard. "This is no joke."

"Who with?" she asked slyly as she took a look around, eyes opened wide.

Who? Laoshun stared, eyes as wide as hers. Who with? He didn't know. How could he have missed something that important? That was the big question. Who was she anyway? A young woman or somebody's wife? A girlfriend or a woman he picked up? It all came down to her identity. Laoshun knitted his brow and thought hard, going over the scene to retrieve a thread of information. But his brain was a blank, an anemic grayness. His son's face escaped him, let alone a glimpse of the woman. The white buttocks were all he could call to mind, but even they had become a blur, like the hazy reflection of the moon on rippling water. Laoshun grumbled to himself. His brain was fighting him, remembering what he should forget and forgetting what he should remember. What had just happened would disgust any father, but seeing it flash through his mind's bothered him, for his brain had drawn a blank just when he needed details to solve the puzzle. He slapped himself unhappily before finally admitting to himself that he hadn't seen her face.

"I don't know," he said, resigned to that fact.

"Then it's bullshit," his wife said. "You should break the teeth of whoever told you. People these days will spread any rumor that comes along. They like nothing more than gossip. If it had been me, I'd have broken all his teeth."

"You'd break whose teeth?" Laoshun said angrily. "Come on, break mine. No one spread any gossip about your precious young master. I saw it with my own eyes. Do you think I'd spread a rumor about my own son? You're a nuisance!"

Her eyes bulged, as if she were choking, her muscles twitched. It took her a moment to finally break out of her silence. "So what if you saw him? Why yell at me? You think you're so damned powerful. Dragons beget dragons, phoenixes beget phoenixes, and rats' offspring are only good at making holes. How dare you criticize your own son!"

Laoshun's face colored as he snorted angrily. He'd held back as long as he could, but when she brought up the past, he grabbed her by the hair with his left hand, raised his right, and slapped her sallow face hard—and more than once.

She screamed and wailed, cursing him the whole time, with increasingly colorful content.

An expert in fast-paced guerrilla warfare, Laoshun quit while he was ahead and scurried out, but not so fast he forgot his pipe on the windowsill.

2

A chill desert wind came at Laoshun as he walked out the gate, clearing his mind and softening his anger. This had become the pattern over decades. She was good with her words, he was quick with his hands. Usually she got the upper hand at first, while he reacted later, strongly enough to end the battle, and then she'd mop up with tears. Over the days that followed, she'd throw her weight around and he'd be cautious and solicitous, until finally everything smoothed out. Their fights never got out of hand, with strength pitted against weakness. Though she strutted around, she was clever enough to check to see if her grinning husband suddenly clenched his teeth.

"We're old, too old to be fighting like that." Laoshun shook his head, a sense of regret over the hard slaps sneaking up on him. She'd become little more than skin and bones since the death of their oldest son, Hantou. Not long after that, their youngest son, Lingguan, had left home, and they'd heard nothing from him since. She was always talking and worrying about him, but there was nothing they could do if he refused to contact them. Parents are devoted to their children, whose hearts are as hard as stone. Ingrates!

He was acting like a man who'd swallowed gunpowder, he thought.

It was no big deal, so why had he reacted so violently after a few words of veiled criticism? Yet it was hard not to. Too often he found he could not control his hands, or, for that matter, his head. His mind created anger, his hands vented, and there was nothing he could do about it. He wanted to smile, but a sigh escaped from between his parted lips.

His mood darkened when he recalled why he'd slapped his wife, as Mengzi's furious, embarrassed face appeared before him again. Now he was sure it had been fury and embarrassment. Mengzi had shouted the same thing the night Shuangfu returned and walked in on Mengzi and his wife, "You should have found me a wife."

Bad news.

Laoshun finally understood why his ancestors had called sons "bad news." That was so true. What was a son? A son was someone who could, without a need to justify his action and with no qualms, take money from your pocket, pluck meat from your bowl, and snatch food out of your mouth. Maybe I did owe them a debt in our previous lives, he said to himself. Take the oldest, Hantou. They'd raised him from the time he was the size of a mouse until he was as tall as the wall, then they'd found him a wife, and he'd fallen ill. Once he'd collected the debt he was owed, he'd kicked his legs out one last time and was gone forever. As if dying weren't enough, he'd left behind a pile of debts that Laoshun, the father, must pay off. If that isn't bad news, what is it?

And now it was Mengzi's turn for his payment. Laoshun was rattled when he recalled Mengzi's bare rump pumping on the bean stack, so he headed to someplace where there was a crowd. That was his usual solution, drowning out agitation with noise.

At the time, there were two places with lots of people and plenty of action: the first was the Vajravārāhī Cave, the second was White Tiger Pass. The former, a cave containing a trove of documents and cultural relics, was discovered when villagers were digging in the mountain. After they reinforced the cave, an official from the Religion Department declared it to be a site in which to perform Buddhist rites. Later on, Shuangfu put up the money for power lines and moved a dozen old houses from Liangzhou to the grounds outside the cave to attract villagers, who loved novelty.

A crowd had gathered at the cave opening, and Laoshun could tell they were talking about Queen Mother, a Daoist deity.

It was a fresh topic, concerning an old woman who'd come to the village one day and left behind a letter. Some people claimed she was the Jade Emperor's first wife, who left the celestial court secretly to save the human world from devastating calamities. According to the letter, people were wicked, the world was overrun by evildoers; no one believed in the deities or in the Buddha, deceiving Heaven above and telling lies below, so enraging Heaven that it would mete out punishments. When that happened, the sun would not rise, the moon would not be bright, rivers would flood, poisonous insects would be everywhere, plagues would spread, white bones would blanket the earth, ferocious beasts would overrun the land, people would become cannibals, houses would stand empty, garments would be rendered useless, land would lie fallow, food would go to waste, and more. It would be horrible beyond belief.

Tongues wagged in the village, with everyone predicting that the end of the world was near. They sounded like exuberant jackasses, as if hoping it would arrive soon, despite their fears. Strange, wasn't it? One of them said. A black whirlwind swallowed up the sky, like an atomic bomb, taking away the sun and the world below. No one had ever seen anything like that. In the Shaman's words, it was the end of the world.

"This is a karmic calamity," Shaman Qi said. "No one can escape it, we're doomed. You can escape the Black Sun calamity—the past—and the Red Sun calamity—the present—but not the White Sun calamity—the future. It is something everyone must experience."

"What exactly is a karmic calamity?" someone asked her.

"It is a calamity and it is karmic," she said. "Doesn't the government admit its existence? Isn't the Cultural Revolution called a Ten-Year Calamity? There's your calamity. It's like a whirlwind, sweeping up everything in its wake, like leaves, dust, paper scraps. Humans too. You want to hide from it? Sure. Just do good deeds to accumulate positive karma."

Fear of the end of the world had turned many villagers religious, including Laoshun's wife, whose belief had cost her the ability to think for herself. But not Laoshun. He was unable to come up with good reasons for his disbelief, but like a blind cat staring at a dead rat, he zeroed in on two issues and frequently said: one, "You're a religious person now, woman, so why continue to curse me with filthy words?" and two, "Didn't you claim protection from the Vajravārāhī, woman? Where is she when I slap you?" She would stare blankly, hemming and hawing until her face turned red and she had to make a scene to cover up her lack of a meaningful explanation. He would chortle and crow, "You don't understand science, like a dog chasing a train."

In his view, the end of the world could come at any time, and he was ready for it. He wouldn't be like his wife, who, like a young donkey scared by its own fart, would totter over to the cave to recite incantations and bang her head on the ground. I can flatten that sallow face of yours into a rag with a single slap, Laoshun thought, but I don't see Vajravārāhī showing up to protect you.

He had no interest in such nonsense as previous lives, future lives, and transmigration, all of which meant nothing. Why worry about the past or the future, when he couldn't get a handle on the here and now? His mind was crammed full of what was happening right under his nose, like getting Mengzi a wife, or figuring out what the hell was up with Lingguan. Both practical matters, everything else was claptrap.

Laoshun called the Shaman aside and asked her to find Mengzi a wife. The scene at the bean stack was a bone caught in his throat. The young hothead might cause serious trouble if he wasn't tied to a woman soon.

Suddenly, they heard the raspy voice of the village bachelor, Mao Dan:

"Hey—there's gold!"

"Hey—there's gold," some boys echoed.

"Is there really gold there?" Laoshun wondered with a shake of his head as he followed the crowd to White Tiger Pass.

3

A month earlier, Shuangfu had brought dozens of young men to White Tiger Pass to dig pits and build wooden enclosures, telling people they were panning for gold.

Laoshun had crinkled his nose and said, "He's so gold crazy his head has shrunken to the size of a flea. If there'd been gold here, our ancestors wouldn't have left any of it for us."

The villagers agreed, saying there couldn't be gold in this corner of the desert, a place where even wolves won't shit. They mocked Shuangfu, who met with resistance when he tried to hire village boys.

Not once in nearly six decades had Laoshun actually seen gold. He'd heard it was yellow, that it shone, and that it was heavy. He didn't see anything special in that. On the other hand, his forebears had passed down a story that by following White Tiger Pass, you could reach Mount Tianti, and from there climb to Mount Moqi, under which a gold mill turned nonstop. Put a rock into the mill and bits of gold came out. But to open up the mountain you needed to find a mountain-clutching bird and a leverage stone. He'd heard that a distant ancestor had once raised a scrawny chicken that looked half dead. But a Daoist monk from Mount Tianti said it was a mountain-clutching bird, and told the villagers to feed it beans for a hundred days before they could use it to clutch the mountain. The monk left in search of a leverage stone. The ancestor ran out of beans on the ninety-ninth day. Too impatient to wait, he set the chicken free; it flew into the great void and quickly picked up Mount Moqi, but sadly died of exhaustion without the leverage stone. An hour later, the monk showed up with a stone, but the mountain slammed shut, and no one was ever able to open it again.

The lore had been around for hundreds of years.

That's all it is, folklore, Laoshun thought. Something only children would believe. Everyone in the village was waiting to see Shuangfu make a fool of himself. To everyone's amazement, a month later, he actually produced some gold.

Water zigzagged its way from the village reservoir like a silver snake to the panning trough, where loose sand was washed away, leaving behind a thin layer of bright yellow flecks. Laoshun swallowed hard and shook his head, overcome by a dreamy sensation. So this is gold. He looked into the sky, where the sun sent down clamorous ray.

Laoshun harbored an irrational antipathy toward Shuangfu, because of the disgraceful aftermath of Mengzi's affair with Shuangfu's wife. "Heaven is shit-ass dumb. Shuangfu had obviously become the God of Fortune's favorite son. He was on television and in the papers, even said he'd take his business public and sell stock. Now he'd found gold, while the wretchedly poor men in the village could not afford a decent pair of pants." Laoshun was indignant over the injustice.

Big Head, their production team leader, arrived when he heard the news, his voice booming even when he was a hundred meters away. "You made a good bet this time, Shuangfu. I thought you'd lose for sure, because I did the math—the boys' wages alone would cost ten thousand."

"It's not like a blind donkey bumping into a haystack, you know,"

Shuangfu laughed. "I gave it a lot of thought. Since they found gold in Double Dragon Gulch upstream, there ought to be gold downstream at White Tiger Pass. So I got myself a precision instrument, and when I checked the resistance level, I knew there was gold here."

Laoshun knew nothing about resistance, but he'd seen a device used by tomb raiders to send out electromagnetic waves that penetrated deep into the ground and showed if there was copper or iron down there. That must have been how Shuangfu detected the existence of gold. Laoshun was plagued by jealousy.

After pouring the gold flecks into a tea mug, Shuangfu held a panning sieve for a boy to shovel sand into it, and then placed the sieve under running water. The sand seeped through noisily. Laoshun held his breath while his heart bobbed along with the movements of Shuangfu's hands. "I don't expect to see any gold this time," he said silently, but sparkling yellow appeared as the sand flowed away.

"Hey, gold!" Mao Dan yelled again.

"What's with all the excitement? It's his gold," Laoshun snarled.

"It may be his gold, but we're the ones who dug it out." Mao Dan grinned.

"How does digging sand make you so proud of yourself? We wouldn't survive a single day if you were our local magistrate?" Laoshun spat out.

"I'd execute anyone who refused to send me gifts if I was." Mao Dan smiled and lowered his voice: "I know you want Shuangfu to fail. But don't let that get to you. His woman was happy being screwed by Mengzi. Pluck a turnip and the hole remains."

Mao Dan had found his sore spot. Laoshun's face darkened. He spat at the man, who grinned and made a face before slinging his willow basket over his shoulder and heading down into the pit.

Laoshun had stayed away from the pit because of Mengzi's scandal.

Now that he was here, he might as well take a look. The pit, dug straight into the ground, was pitch black. He squinted for a while before he could see the bottom. To prevent the spongy wall from collapsing, they'd built a framework of wood woven with willow branches. The red willows in the desert are going to suffer, he said to himself.

A diesel engine roared at the side of the pit, pumping muddy water through a thick rubber hose. Big Head shouted down into the pit, "Be careful, don't dig into a waterway and don't drown any yellow rats."

"Watch your mouth up there," came Mao Dan's voice from below.

"All my good intentions are wasted on him." Big Head laughed before turning to Shuangfu. "Let's be clear on this now. You need to donate some of the money to the village if you find gold. That way people won't complain about me."

"Why would they?" Shuangfu smiled. "In the hundreds of years White Tiger Pass has been here, have you seen anyone pay for anything they've done here?"

"You're right, but people are going to get jealous once you find something," Big Head replied before turning to Laoshun. "Want a piece of the action? I can give you a pit too, and if you strike gold, you'll be rich."

Laoshun was tempted, but he had to ask, "What if I don't get anything?"

"Well, all you'd lose would be twenty, thirty thousand, maybe a little more."

"Right. You go ahead without me. I can get by now, but if I lost that much money, I'd have to sell my pots and pans for scrap metal and send generations of my family into the pit of poverty. I'm poor, but I feel secure."

"Keep those women away!" Beizhu shouted.

Laoshun turned to see some women coming up to the pit to see what was going on. They shrank back when they heard the shout.

"A taboo against women at a gold pit is a custom among gold prospectors. I don't see why, but that's what everyone says." Shuangfu said.

"You have to believe something like that," Big Head said, "but maybe not a hundred percent."

With a shout at each step, Mao Dan made his way up the rope ladder on the side of the pit, a basket of sand over his back. The rope swayed under his weight and made Laoshun dizzy. That didn't bother Mao Dan, though, who'd had a screw loose since he was a child. During one New Year's, when the villagers had hung a swing between two large trees, he'd walked across the pole strung between the trees, teetering and tottering as he went, eliciting gasps and screams from village women. He was the first to sign on when no one else would respond to Shuangfu's hiring call.

Laoshun left the pit and headed home, running into crowds on their way to White Tiger Pass, like operagoers. It's his gold, why run over there? Laoshun thought. He'd like to have a pit too, but gave that thought up when he considered the financial outlay. Where would he get the money? You can't depend on banks. They hand it to the rich and hide it from the poor. Even if he could scare up the money, what would he do if he failed? A secure life was still better. You can't lose by being careful.

He ran into Mengzi at the gate. Still scandalized by what he'd seen at the bean stack, he pretended not to see his son. But Mengzi stopped him:

"Have you heard, Pa? They found gold at White Tiger Pass. Let's get us a pit."

What's wrong with young people these days? Laoshun wondered. The filthy thing he'd done had no effect on him. Shameless. If this had happened a few years earlier, and to someone with thinner skin, he might have had to kill himself. The parents would have to keep an eye on him so he wouldn't hang himself or slit his own throat. And here this young man is acting like nothing happened. Laoshun grunted as he walked into the yard.

He went into the room they called the study and found his wife asleep in bed. Concerned she might be sick, he asked if she was feeling all right.

Sunlight slanted in through the thin curtain and shone down on the blanket, blurring the spot and giving it a hazy look. She was facing the window, her head under a corner of her blanket, a ridiculous look, since it wasn't particularly cold.

Laoshun had to laugh when he recalled the fight they'd just had. "Enough of that, you old hag. Don't act like a pig pretending to be an elephant by sticking a leek up your nose. You weren't born to fake a scene like this. You'll run off like your ass is on fire if you hear a pig grunt or a chicken cackle. Hei-hei."

"They can die for all I care," she fumed. "I'm tired of being a maid and I refuse to be one any longer. I waited on the masters young and old like tending pigs, and what do I get? He's got a powerful hand, all thanks to me, and he uses it on me. He's got a temper, spoiled by me, and he takes that out on me too. Now I've learned my lesson, and I'm washing my hands of all of it. I'll be a carefree mistress of the house for a few days." She finished with a violent tug of the blanket around her.

Laoshun was relieved by her response. Women can cry and raise hell, and that's fine. The worst is when they quietly stew in anger, for the more they think about things, the angrier they get, and the angrier they get, the more they think, until they can't think of anything but to take the easy way out. Her tone told him that her anger was mostly spent. He had to say, however, that it was all her fault. You never hit people in the face and you don't expose their shortcomings. She shouldn't have seized on what he said about Mengzi to criticize him. Was there ever a man who never did a few foolish things?

Chapter Two

Since you left, melons are my sole companion
I hold a melon vine, my heart a gray pall

1

Ying'er returned with her baby after visiting her parents. She called the boy Panpan, and everyone said it was a good, forward-looking name.

She was much thinner, and the rosy glow on her face was gone, as she hadn't yet recovered from the death of her husband. An affair with his brother, Lingguan, was destiny's whip, lashing at her over and over. Losing weight was inevitable.

The baby resembled Lingguan in almost every way—his big, lively eyes, straight nose, the whorls on his fingers, even the way he yawned when he woke up. He crinkled his brow and scrunched up his face to pull the facial muscles together, making seemingly pained yawning sounds, all of which sent her into a mesmerized trance. What she remembered most clearly about their trysts was the exaggerated way he'd yawned upon waking up. On the rare occasions when they could spend the night together, she'd fight to stay awake, afraid that daybreak would arrive the moment she shut her eyes. Sleep could corrupt the happiness she felt about being with him, so she decided to stay awake. With the help of faint moonlight seeping in through the curtain, she would look at his handsome, sleeping face, watching as his nostrils flared and his chest rose and fell, while a wondrous rhythm rippled through her heart. Sometimes she would lower the lantern and lay a pillow cover over the bulb to shine the dim yellow light on his face and then spend the rest of the night immersed in a uniquely beautiful sensation. Just before dawn arrived, she would sing a folk tune, "The crescent moon travels west before daybreak/ the chicks are chirping in their coop. Wake up, sleeping elder brother/it's time for you to leave." She'd then nudge him and gently bite his earlobe. Lingguan would, just like the baby, scrunch up his face as if in pain and yawn grandly and loudly, which always elicited a smile from her. Waking him up was for her an unforgettable scene. Once awake, he would hold her so tightly his arms would flatten her chest, before he mumbled, "One two three four five/metal wood water fire earth/get up hurry get up/only a donkey stays in bed." He would toss the blanket aside with a manly flair, but was barely up before falling into her arms and muttering, "I'm not getting up/I'd rather be a donkey."

These scenes remained vivid in her mind.

Ying'er could hardly believe how she'd survived the months after he left home. It was a bad dream, a prolonged, seemingly never-ending nightmare in which she was wide awake and yet unable to break it off. Day after day, she lived in a daze, her mind a blur. A water-logged whip of reason frequently lashed at her, until she was on the brink of a nervous breakdown. Everything in the room reminded her that a living body had visited the place; he had belonged to her, and she'd had total possession of him. Then he'd left, traveling to some faraway place, one beyond the reach of a heart, the farthest place in the world.

On the night before he left, Lingguan had drifted into her room like a shadow. At the time the dead Hantou filled the space and filled their hearts. The dark night seemed studded with his eyes; everywhere she looked she saw countless pairs of his sad, helpless eyes. Lingguan unquestionably saw them too. They faced each other wordlessly for a long time before he finally said, "I'm going away, I want to see the world." His voice was so flat, so cold. There was nothing she could say. If not for the baby inside her, Ying'er would have liked to see the world too. Beyond the world shown on the small TV screen, there was another world for her, bigger than the real one, and better. It must have been the same for him. She was aware that the outside world she imagined would disappear once he'd seen the real one. Nonetheless, one ought to see world outside in one's lifetime.

So he left.

Ying'er felt as if she'd seen him off. Standing on a high sand dune, she'd watched him slowly disappear into the distance, while a weighty sentiment spread and filled the air, inundating everything between heaven and earth. A viscous liquid saturated her heart, agitating her once and again, surging and powerful until it finally broke through—

Walking on and on—moving farther and farther away—

Tears—tears fill my eyes—

Tears—tears drown my heart—

Ai-li-ai-hai-yo—

Tears—tears drown my heart—

Walking on and on—moving farther and farther away—

In his bag—the food gets lighter—

In my heart—the sorrow grows heavier—

Ai-li-ai-hai-yo—

In my heart—the sorrow grows heavier—

Tears—tears drown my heart—

She felt he'd walked out of Shawan in the midst of her song. Somewhere nearby a young man was mesmerized by her singing, and the spell would not break throughout his life, drawing him to China's West, taking him off his route to Paris. He was the songwriter Wang Luobin. It was a story that rippled in her mind countless times, flitting past and turning into a totem.

What actually happened was, she did not see him off. She came back to life amid the happy yawns of her baby. It was the on-off button of happiness that never failed to intoxicate her, but it was also a rope that tugged and tore at a wound, a reminder for her to face an inescapable reality. Fits of intoxication and searing pain later, the boy was one month old and Ying'er was her former self again. Working lithely and smiling gracefully as usual, she held the baby tenderly and sang him folk tunes, with all her heart, just as she had done for Lingguan.

She sensed that the baby was smiling, and that three words came out of his gently wriggling mouth: sounds of nature. His tiny face seemed to be replaced by Lingguan's. Her heart melted when she changed the baby and touched his tender skin. She tickled him, making her little Lingguan, a hairless little mouse, giggle. She smiled, her lips pressed together. "It's strange how a handsome man like Lingguan grew up out of a hairless little mouse like this one."

Over the days following Hantou's death, it was the baby's laughter, tears, and bodily needs that filled the enormous void in the house and in her heart.

Ying'er said to herself: heaven has eyes. It makes up for what you've lost elsewhere and in equal amounts.

2

Once, when Lanlan, who liked to tease her sister-in-law, came home to see her parents, she opened her eyes extra wide to scrutinize the baby before turning her dramatic gaze to Ying'er until she was red in the face.

"Why do I think this baby reminds me of someone?" she asked.

"What do you mean?" Ying'er poked her. "Stop the nonsense, will you?"

"You don't believe me? How about I take him out and let everyone have a look?" Lanlan pretended to walk out with the baby. Ying'er pulled her by the ear. "Stop the nonsense!" She snatched the baby back, laid him on the kang, and tickled Lanlan breathless.

"You got me wrong. I just thought he looked like a movie star," Lanlan said.

It was all in good fun, and they dropped the subject to avoid the obvious. They can guess all they want, Ying'er said to herself, as long as it's not out in the open.

People weren't gossiping in public, though it was hard to say if they did so in private. But you cannot worry about what people say in private. They did adore the baby though. Whenever neighbors dropped by, they insisted on holding him, smacking their lips noisily on his tender cheeks, pouring their thoughts for Hantou onto the boy, so delighting her mother-in-law that she smiled broadly.

Lanlan spent the night with Ying'er every time she came home to visit, and they talked late into the night. The two women considered it an enormous gift from heaven that in a tiny corner of this boundless universe, with oceans of people, they could find someone to talk with so freely over several nights out of the endless passage of time. So many women had no one to confide in and went to the grave alone when their lives ended, what the villagers called "lonely ghosts."

Lanlan and Ying'er could talk about almost anything, except for topics they both knew should remain untouchable. Lanlan liked to talk about the blockhead Huaqiu, while Ying'er enjoyed anecdotes from Lingguan's childhood. More often than not, she would find a way to change the subject. Lingguan had been a naughty boy. Once he'd burned a hole in a bamboo pole with fire tongs, filled the hollow with dry dirt, put his mouth around one end, and blown a puff of dirt straight into the eye of the commune director, gaining Laoshun unwanted fame. For about a month, the commune PA system broadcast the news of Laoshun's failure to properly raise his son. Lanlan and Ying'er giggled themselves silly at the story. Ying'er looked over at the sleeping baby during their laughing fits and thought, "This karmic retribution isn't going to be easy to raise. He'll surely cause me trouble." Yet deep down she felt the billows of a squall of happiness.

Ying'er also talked about Huaqiu just to make Lanlan feel included. The romantic relationship between Lanlan and Huaqiu seemed laughable to everyone, for Huaqiu was still a boy when Lanlan was a big girl. Yet Lanlan had taken Huaqiu when she sneaked into the field to dig up soybean seeds that they then roasted to enjoy. Lanlan said the black ashes from burned wheat straw around Huaqiu's lips were telltale signs of his theft. One day after that, the word "love" escaped from between those smeared lips, sending her into a state of confusion and anxiety.

Sometimes Laoshun, who slept in the next room, would yell impatiently, "Are you two having too much gas from eating all those beans?"

Ying'er stuck her tongue out while Lanlan sneered and muttered, "Getting jealous, are you? You have no one to talk to when you feel like it."

Later on, these intimate nights would become some of the most memorable moments of their recollections.

They were oblivious, however, to the storm of destiny that was closing in on them.

Chapter Three

The bridge at Yehuqiao has fallen down
All the pretty flowers have wilted in a frost

1

Lanlan got another beating.

Bai Fu, her husband, whipped her like flogging a donkey. Her body was crisscrossed with red and purple bloody welts. When he left to go gambling, she struggled out and returned to her parents' house.

She walked in the gate, and was greeted by a yard littered with chicken droppings. So she picked up a broom and started sweeping, making her arms and legs scream from the pain. She did not need to check to know that they were badly bruised. It had been like that for some time. Ever since the death of her daughter, Yindi, she had been hot-tempered, which naturally brought on more beatings from her husband. That was the only progress her plan for divorce had achieved.

Divorce was no small matter, she knew that. Either both sides agreed to divorce or the court would intercede. The former was out of question for her, so the court was her only recourse. But the thought of a courtroom frightened Lanlan, for whom it held scary images. So it went on as usual until this latest beating led her to make up her mind to return to her parents' home. She would never go back, no matter what, she told herself. And what was so scary about the court? The worst was they'd lop off my head.

She went to draw water after sweeping the yard, two of her pre-marriage chores. Every time she came back to visit, she made sure to do what she'd always done before. Besides giving her mother a break, she derived from the work the pleasure of doing something she'd not done for a while, a mixture of innocence, purity, illusions, and passion, normally considered unique to young girls. It's better to be an unmarried girl, she thought.

Poling buckets on her shoulder, Lanlan stepped onto the narrow, dusty path. The village looked different, older and uglier, an odd appearance that had escaped her attention till now. Sand and dust covered the path, but it did not stick to her, which pleased her. At her in-law's home, the dirt liked her more than the people did and clung to her all the time; she could thump all she wanted, but she never managed to knock it off.

The air was as refreshing as cool water; a single breath washed clean her insides and brightened them up. This was the first time in days she'd felt refreshed, because of the air, but also because this was her home. The village, the houses, the small paths, and the trees, even the bird calls had been part of her life, and had left indelible marks on her.

The local pond was by a dry ditch north of the village, where people and livestock had enough water for a month each time it filled up. But she hadn't drunk pond water since her marriage; now it tasted slimy, unpleasantly earthy, and did not look clean. It was better in the winter, for in the summer, frogs took over. As soon as night fell, the frogs started their chorus, singing up a storm that kept sleep at bay.

Surprised to see Huaqiu waiting there, Lanlan felt her tongue dry up. With one hand resting on a bucket and the other holding a ladle, he looked at her with a gaze that was all too familiar.

"Say, when you got married, you gave him your heart too, didn't you? A woman's heart is like a fleeting cloud," he said.

She put down the buckets and looked at him with a gaze that could draw you into the depths of her soul. The years they'd been apart felt like lifetimes; she sought restitution for a long-standing debt through her gaze. Time stopped; the sun, the sand, the village, and everything else quietly receded, leaving only their hearts pounding violently. They had been childhood sweethearts, playing together without spending time apart, so naturally they hadn't experienced intense yearnings for one another, not then. But now, after insufferable torment, she was dizzy with happiness, like a desert trekker coming upon a fresh spring.

The sun slowly rose over their heads. The emerald green hue was gone from the pond, which returned to its original state of murky stagnation. Its ugliness was exposed, with wheat straw floating on top, sunken hoof prints, and squirming tadpoles. She saw it all, but none of it registered. Swathed in surging elation, she felt she'd skipped over all of life's adversities and returned to the old days. A sense of being a young girl was awakened, her heart raced, her face burned, and she was seized by a mysterious giddiness.

From a distance, Fengxiang, Beizhu's wife, was heading their way.

"Tonight. Same place," Huaqiu whispered. Lanlan mumbled something as she took up a ladle to fill her buckets.

After filling his buckets, Huaqiu picked up his carrying pole, hooked them on, and walked off.

"Hey, you weren't having a cozy chat, were you?" Fengxiang's mockery came on the air. "I wanted to know what you were saying, but he left as soon as I arrived. What did he say, Lanlan? Something about love and feelings, I'll bet."

"Jealous? Then go find someone for yourself," Lanlan said.

"I'm too old for that. I was so dumb back then I became a wife without knowing what was what. I had no idea what love was. Now, I'm old and worn, like the callouses on my heel. He likes the young, cute ones, don't you, Huaqiu?" she shouted.

"I like the way you flirt," Huaqiu replied from a distance.

"You rascal!" Fengxiang said with mock anger while looking around and whispering, "Are you really going to get a divorce, Lanlan?"

"Who told you that?"

"Everybody says so. They're all talking about it. It's no big deal, really; it's not like a frost has killed off all the men in the world."

Lanlan sighed. You could let a fart here, and the whole village would know about it. No wonder some people gave her funny looks, as if seeing a monster. Her in-laws must have started the rumor, since her mother-in-law told everyone she met, "That slut's head is filled with terrible ideas. She's planning to leap over the trough." Well, so be it, Lanlan said to herself. She didn't have to dodge the issue any longer. "So what if I am?"

"Don't have another baby if that's what you want. Once a karmic spawn is around, even the most spirited horse will be reined in. The way I see it, you're better off getting a divorce than living that kind of life. Short-term pain for long-term gain. It's easy now, but it would be too late if you had another baby. Once the pus is ready to pop, you have to do it."

"Is that really what you think?" Lanlan was so moved she grabbed the other woman's hand. "You don't think I'm shameless? Won't people attack me?"

"They've got mouths, they can talk all they want. You don't live for them, so why do you care what they say? Do you really think it's shameless? You're not a thief or a robber. Besides, you'll be the one leaving, not him kicking you out, so the Bai family will be the ones losing face, not you," Fengxiang said crisply, and so fast it sounded like pouring walnuts out of a clay jar.

A warm current rose inside Lanlan. With her eyes on Fengxiang, she wanted to say something, but nothing could fully express the gratitude she felt. Then she noticed a black speck next to Fengxiang's nose, so she reached out to gently wipe it off with a handkerchief. Before long, the warm current surged up and ended in her eyes, where it turned to tears. Instead of holding back, she cried, expelling from her chest the pain and suffering that had been building for too long.

2

The moon was up.

Rubbing her chest over her racing heart, Lanlan walked toward the Dasha River. All around her was a blur, the squat houses, peeling walls, and dry dust on the ground all fading into the moonlit night. She was fond of the moon. Before she was married, she used to gaze at it under the date tree by the gate. It had been brighter, fuller then, forever racing with the clouds in the boundless evening sky. The moon ran fast, quickly ducking into one puffy cloud and then another, as swift as the shuttle on a loom. It's so much better being the moon, she'd thought back then. It's free to do whatever it wants up in the sky. When she grew up, she realized that the moon was also in bondage, tethered to an invisible rope, turning around and around like her mother at the stove or a donkey at the mill. Who knew how many years it had been turning like that? And yet she still envied it, until later, that is, once marriage and the distractions of daily life drove it from her mind.

Huaqiu was always associated with the moon. They'd spread coats out on a sand dune and lain down to gaze at the moon. Moonlight shone into their hearts, along with tender words. If it was springtime, there'd be the refreshing fragrance of desert date blooms, which, with the moonlight and tender words, gave her countless memories. Later, she thought she might have squandered her happiness during those moments; happiness, like money, lasts longer if expended prudently.

Lanlan recalled a favorite song of hers back then. It had been a long time since she'd sung it, and she'd forgotten most of the lyrics, all but a few important lines: You helped me escape the yellow dog at the village entrance/you helped me out of eighteen years of worry and sorrow/ you took me on a long journey in the night/you took me to watch the sun rise in the east." It might as well have based on her life. In those days, she'd quietly unlatched the gate after her parents were asleep and headed for the Dasha River. She often heard Meng Baye's dog growl like muffled thunder. It was a smart dog and would, at the slightest sound or movement, raise its head to bark at the sky. Her fear of ghosts disappeared when she heard the barks; a gloomy, scary forest path would be filled with tenderness, a feeling that lasted until the day her mother asked her to marry Bai Fu so her brother could have Bai Fu's sister for a wife.

She sighed at the thought of her marriage, which always soured her mood. The Dasha River was a much better subject.

Back then, water still ran in the river; there were water plants and clean rocks that could be fished out and dried in the sun to show off their different patterns. She had collected many rocks and enjoyed looking at them when she had nothing else to do. Besides the rocks, the water was fine too, clear and cool, not a speck of impurity. She had heard it was snowmelt from Qilian Mountains flowing through endless time and space to form a bend here, where it supported the livelihood of an entire village, before meandering northward to who knows where. Waves of sand wriggled along the riverbanks and rose higher and higher to crest into an ocean of sand.

Then Lanlan changed, from a limpid young girl to a drab woman. Much like the Dasha River, whose water dried up, whose plants died, and whose trees thinned out. The stand of desert date trees was all that remained the same. Sturdy and hardy, unlike more delicate trees, they sank roots deep into the ground and, with tiny leaves and a modest need for water, they survived. When she was little, she had staved off hunger by gathering desert dates. She and Huaqiu had come here often with other village children to cut green feed for pigs, knock down dates, and collect cow dung. Her mother had assigned the children each with a task, and those who failed to complete it would get a taste of her shoe on their backsides. Sharp eyes and quick hands were essential in swatting down dates. One of them would climb up a tree and swat them down with a switch, sending the others scrambling after them. Her mother did not care much about the dates, so it didn't matter how many she got. Cow dung was a different matter. It was their fuel, without which they could not boil water or cook a meal. The children often got into fights over it, until a rule was set that whoever spotted it got to keep it. Huaqiu, who had sharp eyes, often yelled, "The black yak-ox is raising its tail—I spotted that one for Lanlan." She would run over, scoop it up, and toss it into her basket.

She recalled that Huaqiu had stuck close to her ever since he was little. Maybe there was a karmic attraction, but if so, why hadn't it lasted forever?

Unlike other rivers, the Dasha had a low river bed and was surrounded by towering sand hills. Her heart softened at the thought of the river, the swaying shadows of the trees, and the pleasing fragrance of the date flowers.

According to her mother, this was a clean river that invoked bright, upbeat thoughts day or night, unlike the Bianwan River, which always had an eerie feel, even on a hot day. "The Dasha River is wonderful, clean, and no ghosts," her mother had once said. Sure, the river was without ghosts, Lanlan thought, but not her mind. Something was going on there. She smiled at the thought.

She clapped her hands, a secret signal, when she got there.

There was no response. Huaqiu was late again. Leaning against a date tree, she looked into the sky, where an enormous moon hung amid sparse stars, the Milky Way barely visible. Clusters of stars merged to form a large river across the sky in the same direction as the Dasha River. On one end was the Cowherd Boy and the other the Weaving Girl, just like Huaqiu and her. On the seventh day of the seventh month, the celestial lovers walked across a bridge made of magpie feathers to have their yearly reunion. That had been going on for a thousand years, and she envied them. The Queen Mother wasn't a bad mother, she thought, for she didn't force the Weaving Girl to marry, and the girl was lucky not to get married for her brother's sake.

They had fared better because they were immortals. Lanlan sighed.

On the night before her wedding, she recalled, she'd hardened her heart and missed their tryst. It was better not to see him; otherwise, her tears would crush her resolve. Her parents' life had been hard and so had Hantou's, so Huaqiu had to suffer. Yet tears flowed freely in her chest and broke out whenever she was alone, though naturally she put on a smile for her parents.

It felt truly like a dream.

She had been in that dream for several years. Dreamily, she got married, became someone's wife, had a child, fought her mother-in-law, and got beaten by her husband like a donkey. She was no longer the Lanlan of years past, turning from a limpid young girl into a drab peasant woman. It felt like a dream, but her dream was gone; a dreamless life betrayed its ugliness as reality destroyed everything. She remembered a line from *Waterloo Bridge*, "War destroys everything." But out here war was not needed for that; or, put differently, they were born into a war. Life bared its sharp teeth and, with a few nips, bit away her innate femininity and covered her body with bruises, not a spot spared.

Only in occasional reveries did she recall that she'd once been young, had enjoyed dreams, and had longed for rosy stories. But all these resembled the images in a water-stained painting. Huaqiu and the date trees receded into the distance like the halo around the moon, exposing moldy smells typical of events from long ago. She was forever looking for excuses to talk herself into accepting her fate.

Until this night, when she refused to take it any longer, and many of her feelings came alive, like a snake emerging from hibernation.

She clapped again: slap-slap—slap—slap-slap.

What she should have heard from him would be: slap—slap-slap—slap.

A barking dog gave the only response. She was about to duck when Huaqiu appeared from behind a tree. "Silly thing," she chided happily as she ran up and he took her into his arms. Lanlan liked the way he held and kissed her, passionate the way a man should be, but with his frenzied manner. Her heart pounded like a startled fawn, a sensation that had all but disappeared since her wedding, for her senses had been dulled and her heart coated in a thick layer of dust. Everything in her life had turned murky, curdling her inborn aspirations. One cannot live without them; you strain to pass each day, like making herbal medicine, boiled in bitter water, soaked in medicinal liquid, and fried by the fire from life's brazier, but they are no longer the same aspirations. As if tethered to a millstone, she lived a colorless life, turning around and around along a set track and listening to the sad, monotonous sound of stone grinding against stone. Her youth vanished as the meter-thick mill stone was ground down; her black hair turned white as crane feathers, her rosy glow disappeared beneath wrinkles, her tenderness was driven away by sandy wind, and her romantic vision was swallowed up by poverty and hardships. A voice kept intoning in her mind, "Accept your fate!"

Tears wetted her face as a warm current rose up inside. For several days now, she'd longed to cry, to rest her head against his shoulder and cry her heart out. Something had been lodged in her throat; if she spit it out in front of her father, he'd only sigh, in front of her mother, she'd shed tears; she was in no mood to share it with anyone else, and the rumors would fly. She'd often seen old village women go into people's houses to curse them for leading their daughters-in-law astray. That happened so frequently that she turned inward; she'd rather keep everything inside, even if it stank, than reveal it to anyone. Yet the emotion simmered and gathered. Some women went to cry at their parents' grave. Lanlan was not so lucky, and could only fantasize about Huaqiu's shoulder.

"Go ahead, cry. Cry all you want, you'll feel better," Huaqiu said.

She dried her tears instead. They saw each other so seldom she ought to smile, she told herself. But the thing was still lodged inside, and she could only sigh. "I can't go on like this any longer."

"Get a divorce."

"What do I do after that?"

"Get married, of course."

She sighed again. What he said made sense but sounded unconvincing. A smoky fog appeared before her eyes, sticky as glue, and she could not break free of its hold, no matter how she tried. So, she looked into the sky and at the moon through half-opened eyes, reminiscing about dreams in younger days. It was an immense pleasure to be thinking about them in his arms. She shut her eyes to quietly savor the wind, the moonlight, her racing heart, and the sweet dizzying sensation until she was intoxicated.

"Wouldn't it be wonderful if we didn't have to grow up? We'd be carefree, living in our dreams. Once we grow up, all the ugliness is exposed, and I feel like I've been lied to."

"It's all the same. The girls in my class were as pretty as flowers, and they wrote about youth and aspirations in their essays. After they were married, their aspirations were as worthless as pig shit. I often see them carrying buckets of slop, holding a paddle, and calling to the pigs—sooey-sooey—to feed them. What little culture they learned in school reeks from manure. Let's not talk about this; it's meaningless. That's life. What can you do about it? You shut your eyes and grit your teeth and your life is over. You'll only age faster if you think too much."

She sighed. He was right. Every time she looked at herself in the mirror, she was saddened by the sight: the rosy glow of youth was gone, replaced by a sallow hue. Crow's feet were stealing up into the corners of her eyes. She refused to accept it. Her youth was gone before she'd made much of her life. And her husband—the person she'd longed for as a young woman turned out to be—to be—worthless. All this—she refused to accept it. She wanted something better.

"I've made up my mind this time. I don't care if I bump up against a wall and break my head." She clenched her teeth.

"I agree. We're only here for a few decades, and we'll be old in the blink of an eye. If you die without trying to live, you'll become an unhappy ghost."

Dew settled in, its cool moisture seeping through their clothes. With their arms around each other, they were deep in the delirium typical of lovers. The village blurred in the distant night; everything faded around them. Their sorrows became a thread floating in the poetic night air, affording them a different kind of pleasure. Everything felt elegiac, the moon, the wind, the chill the wind brought, as well as their racing hearts and sweaty palms.

"I wish this could last forever," she murmured. "No wind, rain or sun, just the Dasha River, the date tress, the moon, and you."

"We'll also need a sack of potatoes." He laughed. "Then we can roast them when we're hungry."

"I don't care if we don't have potatoes." She said. "We'd just be ghosts if we died of hunger. It'd be wonderful, coming and going like the wind. Living like this is terrible. I feel empty, I have nothing to hold on to and nothing to look forward to. I'm just biding my time. It's terrifying. How is it any different from death?"

The night was cool, refreshing, not chilling. A gentle breeze blew over, a warm wind from the desert, carrying its unique smell, soft and light. It was more evening air than wind. Yes, it was the undercurrent of night air, surging in her heart. Lanlan felt like crying.

He gently caressed her face. She teared up silently, not wanting her sobs to disturb the serenity and charm of the moment. Lightly she dried her tears and leaned her head against his chest; she could feel the powerful thumping of his heart. It truly felt like a dream.

Yes, the village blurred in the distant night, and everything faded around them. Their sorrows turned into a thread floating in the poetic night air, affording them a different kind of pleasure.

"Time to head back." No sooner had the thought surfaced than it drove sharp pains into her heart. Happy, sweet moments like this never lasted long. How she wished the moment would continue forever, but her parents were home, waiting for her. Their wrinkled faces, like the bark of trees, kept flashing before her eyes, each flicker cooling the blood in her veins.

"Let's go home," she said.

"Go home? Let's talk all night, what do you say?" The powerful temptation of his suggestion was nearly impossible to resist. All night—the whole night. Her heart pounded so hard she almost agreed to his request.

He put his arms around her waist, kissing her again and again, so eager and intense, nearly suffocating her. A violent, giant life force could breech any defense. She hated the thought of ending it now.

But she pushed away the hands groping her pants' cord and sighed. "I can't. I haven't stopped bleeding since my last miscarriage."

"You're lying."

"Why would I lie to you? I've tried lots of medicines, but nothing works."

He let go of his hands. Sensing his disappointment, she said:

"Please don't be like that. It's hard for us to see each other. Let's just talk."

He did not reply, so she continued, "At first I dreamed about talking to you, but later on I didn't even see you in my dreams. I had so much to say to you, but I can't recall any of it now that we're face to face."

"We don't have shit to say to each other. I should go home now. My woman didn't want me to come out, and I suspect she's looking all over for me."

"Would you be leaving now if I were well?" She wanted to ask, but suddenly she lost interest in talking to him, and began to regret agreeing to the tryst. Huaqiu was a different man, she realized.

Men are all the sense, she thought, as a strong sense of loss came over her.

3

Her mother sat up in bed, lost in thought, when Lanlan walked in. With a glance at her daughter, she sighed and said softly, "You should have worn a coat on such a cool night." Lanlan mumbled an acknowledgment. She spotted some sand on her lapels in the light of the lamp, a telltale sign of her whereabouts, so she flicked them off gently. She had an excuse ready in case her mother asked: she'd say she'd gone to Yue'er's house. But her mother did not ask; she sat deep in thought, after another sigh, as if she hadn't known that Lanlan had gone out, or maybe she knew all too clearly.

Lanlan did not have to explain, since her mother did not ask. That was fine with her, since she was always conscience-stricken when she had to lie. As she climbed onto the kang, she saw traces of sand on the edge; she'd forgotten to shake the sand out of her socks. She looked over at her mother, who was gazing elsewhere, giving Lanlan a chance to brush the sand off with her backside when she got down, pretending to get water.

"Want some water, Ma?" she asked.

"No." Another barely perceptible sigh escaped from between her mother's lips. Lanlan felt a load had been taken off her chest, for crying earlier had released her pent-up emotions, and her heart was now suffused with a rare sense of cool ease. As she poured a glass of water, she sneaked a look in the mirror. She looked normal; her face wasn't flushed, but was brimming with a youthful glow, making her much prettier than usual. "I'm still young," she murmured as she made a face at herself in the mirror.

Her father was fast asleep, snoring contentedly. His even, long, drawn-out rumbles posed a striking contrast to her mother's worry-laden face.

Lanlan got back onto the kang and set down the glass of water before leaning back against the wall. She wanted to talk to her mother, but could not find the words. Huaqiu was what she really wanted to talk about, but also what she most wanted to avoid. Her mother had so many lines on her face it looked like blackened tree bark. The sight pained Lanlan, who was reminded of all the worry she'd caused her mother. Her mood darkened when she imagined how a divorce would trouble her mother, if she did get one.

"What's on your mind, Ma?"

"People aren't worth a damned thing," her mother murmured, as if talking in her sleep.

She said that all the time, especially when someone in the village died. Lanlan was puzzled, however, why she'd say it now. What reminded her of that? Was her mother thinking about her late brother, Hantou, or something else? Lanlan had thought that her mother was worried about her, but obviously she wasn't. She was relieved and yet resentful. "She's not thinking about me."

"Let's go to sleep," her mother said with a sigh.

Her mother lay on her side, fully clothed, her usual bedtime manner. She always looked worn out, as if the day's labors had sapped her energy; she rolled into bed without taking off her clothes. Lanlan had talked to her about the need for the skin to breathe, and how bad it was for her health when foul air was kept in. But she wouldn't listen. Strangely, however, though she looked dead-tired every night, she was always first up in the morning. Being fully clothed when she slept did not seem to affect her rest, and she remained energetic and efficient, working from early morning to late at night, when she rolled into bed and slept like a lump of clay.

Mother wasn't moving, but Lanlan knew she was awake. It was possible she knew she'd gone out on a tryst, which embarrassed her slightly. Everyone in the village had known about her and Huaqiu back then, but she had not talked about it openly with her parents, who in turn had never asked. Once she'd overhead them talking. Her father's attitude was clear; he did not want his daughter to choose her own mate. From minute details like a frown whenever Huaqiu's name was mentioned, Lanlan knew her father did not like him. On the other hand, he had plenty of good things to say about Bai Fu, who was as strong as an ox and a hard worker; he liked a good time, and often gambled, which was not a problem in the villagers' eyes. Bai Fu did not steal, rob, or visit prostitutes. Playing a few hands of cards was nothing. To be sure, he'd taken these things too far, but everything would be fine once he turned over a new leaf. As for beating his wife, that wasn't a flaw at all. Every man in the village beat his wife, except for hen-pecked men who were ordered around by their wives until they had no standing among their peers. Laoshun himself had turned his wife's body into a woven mat with his whip. Which was why he tried to talk to his daughter about how men were ill-tempered during their youth, but would be better once they were older. Maybe. But to Lanlan, it would be torture to spend a lifetime under Bai Fu's fist and whip, and she had no intention of turning into her mother. Maybe Mother would understand how she felt, Lanlan thought. She'd been young once, had suffered beatings, and had tried to get a divorce. Now she was old, in body and spirit. So, she sighed along with her or shed a few tears when Lanlan was feeling down.

"Think it over and decide what to do. We can't be with you forever." Mother broke the silence, as if talking in her sleep. Lanlan made a noise to show she'd heard. This was the first time Mother had made her view known, however vaguely. Lanlan knew how hard that was for her. She could not encourage her daughter to get a divorce, but could not sit by and watch her abused either. She was caught in a bind. What she'd just said could be understood as, "Don't worry about us and do what you want," or "You should know better, because we can't worry about you forever." The former encouraged her to go ahead, while the later was intended to talk her out of it. Lanlan favored the former. It was true that they could not be with her forever, and it was up to her to decide whether to listen to them or not. She had to make up her mind and walk her own path.

Huaqiu had wept before her wedding, saying all he needed was a word from her and he'd take her to the ends of the earth. But she could not say yes. She could not cost her brother a wife, bring disgrace to her parents, and give neighbors fodder for gossip, all of which converged to become a mountain that kept her from eloping. Bai Fu had yet to show his true, abominable face at the time; all she'd heard was his fondness for gambling, which was not really a flaw. Plenty of the village men were into playing cards; when there was no work to do, they set up tables and played a few hands for enjoyment. Lanlan hadn't expected him to forsake human decency and reason. What a nightmare.

Now she had awakened, but was no longer the same woman. Tormented by life, she had lost her former self. Shedding her reserved nature, she did not shy away from a shouting match with her mother-in-law; forgoing her bashfulness, she went for Bai Fu's most vulnerable spot when he beat and kicked her; casting off subtlety, she became crude, and preferred blunt talk devoid of overtones, the same as other village women. Like a pair of scissors, life had shorn her of a young girl's nature, and only when it was quiet late at night did she remember she'd once been young, with aspirations and romance. She would then be struck by a profound sense of loss and guilt; this was not a life she was prepared to accept.

"How did I get to be like this?" she sometimes lamented, grudgingly.

But she knew how hard it was to shake off the nightmarish fate, just as it had been for her mother and for all the women of Shawan. Yellow sand, local customs, violent husbands, and grueling labor were a corrosive fluid that ate away a woman's feminine self. Without knowing it, they lost their best quality and turned into crones. Crones were not women, but were machines to cook, to reproduce, and to toil. A woman lost something innate; their interest in life vanished and their share of joy was stifled. They were unfeeling, shrewd, slow-witted, quarrelsome, disheveled, haggard, and gray, until they were finally reduced to a pile of bleached bones. Such was the trajectory of life that the women all shared.

Most horrifying was the common belief that it was their fate. Fate was a turning millstone, while the women were ants on the mill, expected to accept their destiny. Whoever tried to break the set order would pay the ultimate price, dying a cruel death.

"A cruel death it is, then," Lanlan thought. "I'll accept it."

When she thought of divorce, the only one she could not bear to face was Ying'er, her sister-in-law. No matter how Lanlan looked at it, they had married each other's brother so the men could each have a wife. Hantou, Lanlan's older brother, had died of an illness, but Ying'er remained with her in-laws; despite her tears and sighs, she entertained no thoughts of remarriage, determined to remain a widow and raise her child. Lanlan would not want Ying'er to be a widow forever, and yet she was loath to let someone else take such a good woman as a daughter-in-law.

"Hantou, my dear brother, how could you be so luckless?" Lanlan mused.

During her days at her parents' house, Lanlan had several heartfelt talks with Ying'er, talking about everything except the subject of divorce. She nearly blurted it out a few times, but swallowed the word in the end. Bai Fu was, after all, Ying'er's older brother. Lanlan could not bring up a topic that would put her in an awkward position. Nonetheless, she knew that Ying'er was the only one to whom she could open up, the one person who knew what went on in a woman's heart, who understood the pain inside her, and who, more than anyone else, could grasp the traumatic blow to her spirit brought on by the death of her daughter. They were fellow sufferers, so naturally they found affinity in sentiments.

"You don't have to say a word," Ying'er once said. "I understand."

Lanlan knew exactly what she meant.

The inborn resilience of Liangzhou women helped Lanlan survive the pain of losing a brother and a daughter. The same went for Ying'er. She remained as quiet and serene as before; except for being somewhat gaunt, for the barely noticeable lines under her eyes, and for the occasional far-away look when no one was watching, she did not look like a woman who had experienced the tragedy of losing her husband. Lanlan naturally was happy to see her like that, but a shred of annoyance constantly cropped up: how could she recover so fast after Hantou's death? Maybe she'd never cared that much for him.

Lanlan was quickly mollified, however. Her sky had collapsed when her daughter died, and she had wanted to kill herself. Pain sliced through her heart whenever she thought of her daughter, and yet it grew numb after countless occurrences of searing pain that were created by countless recollections. The pain was still there, but the severity gradually lessened. Time was indeed the best remedy. The winds of time blew day after day, raising grains of sand that could eventually fill the deepest gully.

When they were together, they sang folk tunes after pouring their hearts out and shedding tears. They shared a fondness for songs of separation and longing. Like a fine thread, the tunes tugged at their hearts and drew them out.

A wolf bayed three times in the ravine,

A tiger ran out of the forest.

I called your name three times,

My heart nearly leaped from my chest.

At Jiayu Pass, thunder clapped.

By the Yellow River, the rain fell.

I cried so much over you my eyes were swollen

When I saw a stranger, I thought it was you.

They wept when they sang tunes that echoed the sounds of nature; their emotions resonated with each other, even though their minds were on different tracks. Such was the power of their folk tunes, whose melodies could erase unfamiliarity, disparity, and gloom, turning strangers into friends, even with a gap in age and personality.

Lanlan began to understand what went on in Ying'er's heart through these tunes. When Ying'er sang while gazing tearfully, eyes half-closed, at the vast horizon or the surging ocean of sand, Lanlan sensed the agony in the depths of her soul. It was, however, a forbidden place neither of them wanted to enter. Knowing without revealing anything was a shared option they had each made on her own. The folk tunes, on the other hand, rekindled Lanlan's memory of the romantic affair in her youth, a farcical episode in the eyes of the villagers.

Lanlan and Huaqiu could be considered childhood sweethearts, though she had grown up holding both Lingguan and Huaqiu's hands. While playing children's games like rolling down sand hollows, fashioning mud figures, catching zhazhas, roasting yellow rats, and so on, Lanlan grew up, and so did Huaqiu, their hearts expanding as they grew taller and bigger, creating stirring ripples that eventually sent them into the date tree forests by the Dasha River.

It had been a long time.

The vicissitudes of life and the hardships of making a living covered that past in dust, as her heart grew numb and her feelings dulled. Whenever it surfaced, she could only call up dusky images, as in a grease-soaked oil painting after years of neglect in a moldy house. They came back alive because of the folk tunes. Now with the lively totems, Lanlan refused to go around and around in the set track.

Was that good or was it sad?

"The girl from Gulang was also born with a hard fate," she heard her mother mutter. "Her no-good husband is always stirring up trouble."

Lanlan knew her mother was talking about Huaqiu's wife. Her mouth dried up as she realized how terrible it was for her to forget about "her."

The heated blood in her veins turned cold.

4

Lanlan was dizzy when she got up the next morning, wracked by regret over the tryst. Huaqiu had come alive in her memory before the meeting, but later she realized that he was only interested in her body. Lanlan sighed. She had been the victim of Bai Fu's spousal rape after they were married, which went on so long that she had lost all bodily desire. So sad it actually made her stomach turn when she thought about it. As a mother, she'd suffered the pain of losing a daughter; as a wife, she was beaten into submission, just as dough must be well kneaded; as a woman, she had only memories of rape, deprived of a woman's heaven-ordained pleasure.

Life is pointless, she said to herself.

Apparently what Huaqiu valued was the little she could offer as a woman. Lanlan was disappointed. I wouldn't have minded if you'd lied and uttered a few sweet words, she thought. Even if you hadn't wanted to, we could have stayed in each other's arms and let the feeling warm us until we were dizzy. If not, it would still have been better if you'd just spewed some nonsense. I was insulted. Maybe you thought we could not talk if we could not do what you wanted.

Lanlan tried to convince herself otherwise. She searched deeply, yet she found only anemic reasons, and it was plain as day that he'd only wanted a woman's body, especially one that was not his wife's.

Odious man.

Suddenly Beizhu's eldest daughter walked in. "Auntie, the bride is asking for you."

"What bride?"

"Huaqiu's wife." The girl bounded off.

Lanlan's heart raced. Why does she want to see me? Recalling the tryst of the night before, Lanlan was apprehensive about her wanting to meet me. Could she have detected something? Or had Huaqiu said something to her? Maybe he'd brought up divorce. That thought made her heart pound, which, she realized, was a sign that she still loved him.

She walked out the gate and spotted the woman standing by the wall of Beizhu's house. She looked sickly, probably because she was nursing; unusually skinny, she wore a sad, gloomy look. Lanlan's heart ached at the sight. She suffers, just like me, Lanlan said to herself.

The woman turned and walked off when she saw Lanlan. Up ahead was the hill where the Vajravārāhī Cave was located. A thought flashed through Lanlan's mind, "Would she try to harm me?" She had to laugh, since she did not think she'd done anything to deserve that.

The woman turned to glance at Lanlan before heading up the hill, where stalks of desert rice were scattered after the harvest. Someone had cut down clumps of Artemisia, exposing the bark on the twisted branches, an ugly sight. Rats had made holes everywhere and, when she went down the hill, they scattered. Undaunted, she stood still to wait.

Now Lanlan knew she'd picked the spot because she sought privacy. What did she want to say? Had she gotten wind of what had gone on between her and Huaqiu? Lanlan was no longer bothered by the question. It had happened so long ago.

The woman slowly turned around, staring at her blankly. Her eyes were like dry wells or a patch of rocky desert, making Lanlan cringe. She wanted to say a few soothing words, but nothing appropriate came to her. She's faring better than I am, Lanlan thought. At least she has a baby and Huaqiu. What do I have? The thought plunged her into a mood of bitter sadness.

The woman fell to her knees in a hollow spot.

"What are you doing?" Lanlan panicked. "Say what you have in mind, but get up first. Get up, so we can talk." She tried to pull her up, but the woman refused to get up and looked at her with her empty dry-well eyes. Lanlan took a look around. What would people think if they saw us?

"I saw you, late last night," the woman said flatly.

Lanlan blushed as she realized that the woman had followed Huaqiu. Good thing they hadn't done anything, she said to herself with some trepidation, but mostly she felt ashamed. She'd had a tryst with someone else's husband, after all; they had held and touched each other. She had to blush no matter how she looked at it. Her mouth dry, she wanted to say something, but didn't know what.

"For the sake of the baby," the woman said.

Lanlan shook her head hard, trying to shake off the embarrassment. The sun had leaped into the middle of the sky, sending bright rays all around. This comic episode would be apparent to anyone who showed up at that moment. She had brought shame to her parents' door; how would she face the world if it was made public? She kept tugging at the woman's arm. "Get up, and we will talk."

"Not unless you promise me," she said flatly.

"Promise you what?" Lanlan frantically tried to defend herself. "We didn't do anything." After another glance, she was relieved to see that they were still alone.

"I know what went on with you two back then. But we have a baby now, and it will kill me if you keep it up," She said robotically.

"No, we won't do that. We didn't do anything; we just talked." Lanlan repeated her self-defense.

"How about in the future?"

"I won't even talk to him in the future. How's that?" Lanlan felt herself going limp.

"Do you know he raped me and got me pregnant. I had no way out but to marry him." She looked at Lanlan with a sad smile. "It's a complete loss of face, and I have no more face to lose. I live for the sake of the baby."

"Fine, fine. You have my word." Lanlan shuddered.

"You won't do anything?"

"Nothing."

"Swear an oath, to the Vajravārāhī." The woman's eyes brightened a bit.

"You have my word. Why do I need to swear an oath?"

"I know you're lying again." The woman turned to look into the distance and sighed deeply. "I spent the night thinking it over and talking myself into coming to see you. It's okay if you don't want to swear an oath. You can go home now and I won't get up, even if I die here."

What's wrong with this woman? She's like a burl on an elm tree, Lanlan said to herself. "All right. I swear I'll never be with Huaqiu again and will die a terrible death if I do. Will that work for you?"

"What kind of oath is that? I do that all the time." The woman said. "Women aren't afraid to die, whether it's a good death or a bad one. They don't care. If you're serious, then swear on your parents."

"How can I do that, it has nothing to do with them?" Lanlan said unhappily.

"You don't avoid watermelon if you don't have malaria. Nothing will happen to them if you don't do anything." She was banging her head on the ground now.

"All right, all right. I swear that my parents will die a terrible death if I do anything with Huaqiu."

"Actually, I don't care whether you swear or not." She gave her another sad smile. "I'll just hang myself at your gate if I see you two together again." She banged her head a few more times before getting up and drifting off like a sleepwalker.

Lanlan was drenched in sweat by then. She collapsed as she watched the woman walk into a hollow.

The bright sun was harsh on the eyes.

Chapter Four

A tiger comes down the hill, a forest dies
A village grows, the people decline

1

Gold prospecting pits were multiplying fast at White Tiger Pass. Shuangfu had opened dozens of them. Zhao San, Big Head, and anyone else who could get their hands on some money poured in; large numbers of out-of-towners had shown up after hearing the news. In a few days, the riverbed was littered with well frames. White Tiger Pass had once been a part of the Dasha River, but the riverbed had turned into a patch of black rocky places known as gobis at some point in time. No one knew when.

The well frames were made of three logs with red flags on top. The riverbank seemed planted everywhere as far as the eye could see with red flags that snapped noisily in strong winds. Wooden supports were built of wood from trees bought or stolen at Nanshan. Even red willows in the desert fell victim to pit owners, who sent their people with camel-carts to cut them down. Given the loose soil at the Pass, these supports were essential to prevent sand from burying the diggers alive. The first incident of a collapsing pit had occurred to an outsider who could not build a support because the villagers would not allow him to cut down red willows. The pit fell in on itself at six meters, burying three young diggers, called sand boys, alive. Upon hearing the news, their parents rushed over and threw themselves down on the riverbank, where they wailed without tears. They had hoped their sons would earn enough money to get a wife and give their parents a grandson. The last thing they expected was losing their sons altogether. In Mengzi's memory, it was the first time since the onset of the gold rush that he'd heard people crying on the riverbank; this accident led to Laoshun's refusal to let Mengzi join in.

The price for land around the Pass skyrocketed. A four-meter wide pit had cost a hundred at first, but soon rose to two hundred, with signs of going up even higher. With money breeding authority, Big Head was elevated from head of the village production team to village chief, and became its most arrogant and popular resident, treated to the finest foods and drink and spending the day bossing people around, his face red from the effects of alcohol.

"You're a village leader, Big Head. I don't object to your selling pits," Meng Baye said. "But don't let them cut down any more red willows or dig up our needle grass. Don't you see how the two deserts are pressing closer, and once they merge, not even a ghost could exist here?"

"We're talking about human lives here," Big Head said with a belch. "If you won't let them cut down trees, will you pay for the lives lost when the walls collapse? Those three died because you got people to stop them from cutting willows to make a support. Three young lives lost just like that. People curse you over that."

Meng stamped his foot, but Big Head cut him off before he could defend himself. "That's enough from you. Whoever's in charge does not debate his policies. The party will take charge of serious matters. Take it easy, you worry too much."

Meng had to swallow his reply.

Big Head has changed his tune now that he has a new title, Meng said to himself. Human decency decreases as official ranks grow higher. Meng spat before telling his grandson, Huaqiu, to lodge a complaint with the Forestry Bureau.

Huaqiu came to see Mengzi after lunch. "They've finished digging two new pits for Shuangfu. Mao Dan says they've struck gold. I went to see this morning. The diggers did a sloppy job of panning the sand in water. I grabbed a handful to look at it under the sun, and I saw gold specks."

Mengzi had once gone with some people to the gold mines at the foothills of Qilian Mountains to pan residue, sand that had been panned once. If they were lucky, they could make ten to twenty yuan a day, better than hiring out as laborers. So he found some wood to make a panning device.

They were easy to construct: throw a few boards together to make a trough in the shape of a winnowing pan, one end longer than the other, and turn the bottom into a scrubbing board. Panning residue requires no capital; all you need is a shovel, a gold pan, and a mug for gold specks.

"What if they won't let us do it?" Mengzi asked.

"Who'd dare say no? The sky belongs to us, so does the land. All they have is some extra stinking cash. If they say yes, we're in business. If not, we'll get people from the village to fill in their pits. Then no one will dig any more gold." Huaqiu added, "My grandpa scowls and sighs all day. He says the earth's veins will be destroyed if they dig up any real gold. I don't believe shit like that, but I know that no one in Shawan will enjoy peace and quiet once a real gold mine opens."

Mengzi agreed. He'd muddled along in the past, not giving much thought to such things. Later, he'd traveled with Meng Baye, met some people, heard some things, and his horizon was expanded. In his spare time, he'd leafed through some books and seen how so many good things had begun to deteriorate.

Laoshun saw the two men involved in something and spotted a gold pan. "Let me be clear. I don't have any money and I won't take out a loan. Everywhere I look I see blood-sucking mouths and I'm not about to give the bank any of my blood. I checked. We'd need twenty thousand or more to start a pit, pay the diggers, and get the place set up."

"Start a pit?" Huaqiu said with a smile. "Sure, we'd like to do that, but we can't afford it. We just want to pan the residue."

"Well, that's okay with me," Laoshun said.

With their pans and shovels, they left for White Tiger Pass, passing only women; their menfolk were out prospecting. Yue'er was among them, looking unhappy.

"Come on, Yue'er. Let's go pan some residue," Mengzi said.

"Why should I work up a sweat for that? I'll tell you how to make money, if that's what you're thinking. Open a diner. See what's happening here? It won't take long before it's overrun with people, and you can make a bundle with a diner."

"Why don't you open one?" Mengzi asked.

"I don't care for that kind of work."

"It's a good idea. But money for something like that is hard to come by," Huaqiu said.

The two young men chatted as they headed to White Tiger Pass.

The Pass changed daily, with more and more pit supports and more and more piles of rocky sand, not to mention the swarm of gold spectators. The sputter of diesel engines resonated around the riverbed, and the only people who were talking were the pit managers, who greeted each other and chatted about one thing or another. The diggers were as busy as ants.

Shuangfu hung around the area all day now that some of his pits had reached bottom. Normally, he spent most of his time taking care of affairs in the city. People said he had dozens of construction sites, building multi-story houses, repairing highways, and running a factory. To take his factory public, he'd put out a call for several thousand workers, each to put up five thousand yuan, which gave him a capital of hundreds of millions; that would enable him to raise billions if his factory went public. Money would probably overflow the Dasha River. But even that wasn't enough; the greedy man came to pan gold, hoping that the money would flow into his arms like water. It usually took a month to dig down to the gold deposit. The rocks and sand were carried up and out by sand boys, whose baskets could carry only several shovelfuls. They earned twenty yuan a day going up and down dozens of times. With so many of them taking turns, the pit quickly grew deeper. Meanwhile, Shuangfu went off to take care of city business until his manager called him back to be there when it was time to clear the bottom.

Clearing the bottom was critical, since that was payday for a month of hard work. Gold concentrated at a dozen or so meters, under which flagstone blocked the gold from seeping down. They panned the sand from the bottom, since there was no gold in the sand and rocks at higher levels.

Beizhu was sifting sand in a pan under running water. Shuangfu was sitting on a stool, smoking and chatting with Zhao San. According to veteran spectators, gold was magical, and fate alone determined who was entitled to have it. Only lucky ones owned productive pits, and everyone agreed that Shuangfu had the best luck of all. Beizhu said they filled a mug with gold flecks on a good day, impressing people who wanted to dig their own pits, but were stymied by the proverbial fact that you cannot kill a man without a knife. The God of Fortune is not kind to the poor.

Mengzi stopped in his tracks when he spotted Shuangfu. Tossing his pan at Huaqiu, he said, "This isn't for me. Damn it, just thinking about eating someone's leftovers makes me sick to my stomach."

Huaqiu knew his friend cared too much about face. "Don't pull out your pubic hair to enlarge your beard. You're poor because you were born to it and that's nothing to be ashamed of. If you don't pan the residue, someone else will. Forget everything else and just think about how much you'll need to get a wife. Your father can't squeeze out any more money for you, no matter how hard he tries."

That effectively shut up Mengzi, who squatted on his haunches.

"Since you can't bring yourself to ask, I'll do it. Just keep panning, okay?" Huaqiu walked over to Shuangfu.

"Hey there, God of Fortune," he said with feigned bravado. "Now that you've feasted on the meat, how about letting us have some of the broth? Okay if we pan your residue sand?"

"Can you get every last bit of the stuff?"

"You saw for yourself. Of course, we can. At most there'll be tiny bits left."

"Sure, go ahead." Shuangfu said, "Just carry the sand you're going to pan downstream."

"No problem." Huaqiu knew that Shuangfu was afraid he might steal newly dug sand. "We'll do that." He took a sack off his shoulder and filled it with sand, which he carried away.

Water was flowing in the riverbed again, with many pumps working at the same time. They'd heard there was an underground river in the area. The surface was so dry the ground cracked, but water was plentiful below. Dozens of thick hoses brought up enough water to form large pools before it flowed into the Dasha River. Huaqiu and Mengzi picked a flat spot to build a little stone dam with an opening to let clear water flow through. Then they hunkered down to sift sand.

Minutes into the work, Mengzi began to rue his decision, unhappy with the loss of dignity. He'd screwed Shuangfu's wife the year before, and the two men had gotten into a fight. Now Shuangfu was in charge, and he was panning residue sand from the man's pit, which mortified him; but he had to swallow his pride when he thought about his financial situation. Everyone needs self-respect. But that requires capital; when you're too poor to afford a pair of pants, you'll be walking around with your old dick hanging out and who do you think will respect you then?

Huaqiu poured some sand into his pan and swirled it in running water. When the sifted sand flowed off with the water, the bottom of the pan came into view to reveal tiny, shiny yellow specks.

"Gold!" Huaqiu shouted.

"Is that the best you can manage?" Mengzi said. "You call that gold?" Having panned residue sand before, he knew there'd be tiny flecks of gold in it. Sometimes pea-size gold nuggets hid in the sand and ended up in the hands of people who pan residue.

"Not enough for you?" Huaqiu laughed. "This is from one shovelful. Just think how much we could get from a pile?"

Zhao San heard Huaqiu's shout and walked over. He scrutinized the pan and chuckled loudly. "You can pan my residue sand when my pit hits bottom." Annoyed by the jarring laughter, Mengzi looked up to see the man's boozy red nose, so offending his eyes he felt like smashing it.

"Sure," Huaqiu replied with a smile, "sure." Zhao chortled again and walked back to whisper to Shuangfu, who laughed too, but in a well-mannered way, as if to humor the man.

Feeling blood rush to his head, Mengzi had to take several deep breaths to keep from flinging away his pan. Huaqiu did the same. "Damn you, Zhao San," he cursed. "What are you laughing about, you big ass? You're a damned butcher, a man who kills animals. You think you can act like that because you've got some stinking money, don't you? Remember what Lingguan said? Poverty is the most terrifying thing in the world."

Tears flowed from Mengzi's eyes when he heard the comment.

"Toss in more sand," he said hoarsely.

It took about an hour for Mengzi to finish going through the sand Huaqiu had brought over. Altogether the specks in his mug were about the size of a soy bean. He wondered if he should laugh when he spotted people crowding around Shuangfu.

2

The wind picked up after the sun went down, a dry, chilly wind that blew over from the heart of the desert to ravage their skin. Water turned bone-chilling cold. When his hand grew numb, Mengzi tossed away his pan and said that was enough for him. His stomach by then was an empty sack.

Huaqiu cast a shifty look all around and whispered, "We'll get some new sand after dinner. If we're lucky, that'll be better than panning residue dozens of times. I took a look earlier. They haven't worked on the new sand yet."

"We can't do that. They'll call us thieves if they catch us," Mengzi said.

"What are you scared of? Gold dust is a gift from Heaven. If they can have it, so can we. What gives them the right to have it all?"

Mengzi had to agree, as they divided up the gold specks they'd panned. He went home and handed his father the gold wrapped in paper. Laoshun's eyes grew wide when he opened it. He marveled over the contents, touching gold that felt heavy in his palm. His wife and Ying'er came up to look. "Watch out, don't drop any." Laoshun carefully wrapped it up after everyone had had a chance to touch it; his mood improved dramatically as he felt the yellow seep into his soul.

Huaqiu came for Mengzi after dinner. Each with a fiber sack in hand, they groped their way toward White Tiger Pass. It was pitch black out, but the riverbed was brightly lit. The pumps continued to putt-putt amid the faint sound of the sand boys talking.

"We're too early. They're still awake," Mengzi said.

"They work in shifts. These are the night workers," Huaqiu said.

They crawled toward Shuangfu's trough. The surface was smooth at first, but turned rocky from sand and pebbles brought out from the pit, with wet spots here and there. Mengzi shuddered as a chill crept up from his palms. "Huaqiu's right," he said to himself. "Gold is a gift from Heaven. He'll just use it for his own enjoyment, eating, drinking, gambling, and whoring away what he gets. Who knows how many good deeds I could do with it?"

As they got closer, the sound of the machinery was as loud as a mountain torrent. They shifted down to the riverbed, where the land slanted downward and they could follow the low ridge to the trough. There was water in the riverbed, and they were soon soaking wet, the chill boring deep into them. Mengzi carelessly fell into the river and was swallowed up by the icy water. Huaqiu shivered, probably because he too had slipped. Mengzi shuddered, though he was strangely keyed up by the excitement. Life had been insipid for too long; he'd eat, work, and sleep, over and over again, like a donkey turning a mill. It was so boring. Only when he slept with another man's wife did he feel refreshed, but after a few times of that it was back to the same old routine. On this night, he felt like a spy in a movie, enjoying a rare sense of doing something different. He was cold, but his heart raced happily.

Mengzi had matured a bit after what he'd gone through over the past few years, and had gotten smarter; he now often pondered matters that had formerly escaped his attention. At first, he'd been too lazy to use his head, but later life forced him to think, despite his reluctance, which, strangely, began to give him ideas. It was not a welcome development, for troubles sprouted once he began thinking on his own. Like a child's unstoppable growth, he had increasingly complex thoughts, and there was no turning back. He was a donkey that balked at going uphill, but the whip of life lashed him along; being tugged from the front and pushed from behind, he arrived at a place totally new to him, pursued by worries and troubles.

The water was getting colder now, its chill boring into their bones. Huaqiu was breathing hard. The gurgling sound of water drowned out the diesel pumps. A path that had looked short in the daytime seemed to have come under a spell to drag it all the way to the horizon. Weird.

Suddenly they heard talking. Mengzi held his breath and saw Shuangfu duck out of a tent with a young woman behind him. They were laughing as they walked toward a nearby makeshift room.

"That ass is gnawing on a young gourd again," Huaqiu sniggered. "Do you know many women crowd around him, hoping to be his next kept woman."

"The world's gone mad." Mengzi frowned with a sigh, as if all established order had been turned upside down overnight. Information from the outside world was forcing its way in through cracks, as TV, migrant workers from the Hui area, and young women working in the city brought with them things incomprehensible to the villagers. Before he knew it, the village had changed. They'd likely see more and more oddities. He could think until his head exploded, but he could not understand why some of these things were happening.

Shuangfu and the woman walked out of a lighted area and blended into the hazy night. Our two young men continued their crawl and reached the trough, where a moist, warm pile of sand and the water seemed to smile at them. Climbing up to look around, Mengzi saw moving shadows, but none was headed their way, so he murmured a signal to Huaqiu. They opened their sacks and began filling them with sand until they felt full. Mengzi strained to fling his sack over his shoulder, but it barely moved. Too heavy, he knew, so he poured some out. Pea-size gold nuggets could be pouring out with the sand, but there was nothing he could do about that.

Dragging sacks of sand along, they backtracked, but quickly realized that what had seemed easy in their mind was actually as hard as climbing into the sky. They could not transport the weighty sack while moving on all fours. Mengzi was already gasping for breath after a short distance, so was Huaqiu.

"We'll be in the dark if they look over from under the light, so let's get up and walk. It'll be okay." Mengzi saw the sand boys busy at work, and no one was looking their way, so he got up and flung the sack over his shoulder.

Walking erect was better, but they didn't dare move too fast in the dark, probing with their feet as they went along. Mengzi spotted a sand boy carrying a basket toward the trough; he sucked in cold air at the close call. They dropped to the ground, just as the sand boy turned on his flashlight and stomped over. He shone the light all around after dumping the contents of his basket on the sand pile.

"Oh no, he saw us," Huaqiu whispered.

"Don't worry. I think he's looking for gold." Mengzi was barely finished when the sand boy yelled out, "Someone's been stealing our sand!"

Mengzi was startled. "Why didn't we smooth it over?"

"Thieves, let's go get 'em," the sand boys shouted.

Mengzi and Huaqiu ran off with their sacks, chased by sand boys who bore down on them like maddened stone birds. Mengzi pinched his nose to shout in a funny voice, "I'll shoot if you don't stop." He picked up a rock and flung it at them; it missed but did the trick. The pursuers kept their distance.

"Oh no, my sack broke," Huaqiu shouted. Mengzi was wondering why his sack was getting lighter, so he felt it. There wasn't much sand left. Rocks had worn a hole in it as they crawled along.

"Fuck!" Huaqiu cursed. "Suffering all that cold for nothing."

They returned to pan residue sand the next morning and saw some sand boys checking the path. One of them said the thief had scattered stolen sand all over the path. Shuangfu sent someone to check and found a gold nugget the size of a walnut.

"Damn. Even the gold is against us." Mengzi gave his friend a dejected look.

The sun rose halfway in the sky, exposing the ugly riverbed. Shuangfu was building houses on a hill, where the workers were pouring concrete. It looked permanent. Sand boys hired by other managers were either digging pits or throwing up tents, creating all sorts of strange sights at White Tiger Pass. The world is really getting weird, Mengzi felt.

Huaqiu looked on listlessly. Obviously, he was still thinking about the nugget that had escaped from his sack. Mengzi also rued the loss, but he knew he wasn't meant to have it. His father had pounded that idea into his head for years.

3

After lunch, Mengzi's father told him to attend a matchmaking meeting with Shaman Qi. Laoshun had been occupied with the matter for days now, and Mengzi knew it had to do with what had happened at the bean stack. He'd thought he would be too ashamed to look his father in the eye but, to his surprise, his face toughened like cow hide after burning briefly. What could he say? With all the things he'd gone through, naturally, his skin had thickened.

"There's nothing bad about the girl. She has everything you want, nice hair and fair skin, needlework and cloth-making and housework and meal-cooking." Shaman Qi talked so spiritedly her spittle flew. "You can trust my eye. That girl and this boy are a perfect match. I don't think you'd need lots of betrothal gifts either. They don't look greedy to me."

"Hey, I trust you completely, *Qinjia*. Whether it works out or not, you needn't worry. We'll be sure to pay you for your effort." Mengzi's mother looked moved by the Shaman.

"I'm doing this for you only, *Qinjia*." Shaman Qi pursed her lips. "I swore to never take on another match-making after Huilanzi raised a stink at my house. I had the best of intentions, talking till my mouth was dry and my tongue was parched. I earned credit for hard work, even if it didn't amount to much, don't you think so? She still blames me after she's had a whole passel of kids. She really hurt my feelings. Don't you find it strange, *Qinjia*? If Big Head beats her, that's his problem. I didn't add a kick to her backside or stir up trouble, so why get mad at me? How brazen is that! Boy, that galled me. You have to agree I had every reason to be upset, *Qinjia*. So I didn't have anything nice to say to her. Instead, I chased her with the ghost-expelling vinegar stone. I tell you. It's not like I have trouble getting by. I have so many people coming for my help they've worn down my doorsill. Would I care about a pittance from matchmaking? I only agreed to thread this needle because we're neighbors. Does that sound right to you, *Qinjia*?"

"Sure, *Qinjia*. But that's their business, so forget about them. But you have to do this for us. Mengzi may be rash, but he's honest and simple. He won't let the girl down."

Mengzi was amused as he listened outside the door. The two women kept calling each other *Qinjia*, but they were in no way related, not by blood or marriage. Shaman Qi had way too many so-called in-laws, in his view. On the other hand, he was touched by his mother's characterization of him as honest and simple. He coughed loudly before walking in.

"Come in," his mother said. "Offer a cigarette to motherly Qi. She's found a girl for you, from the Bao family. You go with her to meet the girl after lunch. If you like her, we'll get things settled; if not, then—well, you have to like her. It has to work, as long as she's not missing an arm or a leg. There's more to life than good looks."

"What are you talking about?" Shaman Qi said. "That girl of theirs is a real beauty, with large, limpid eyes and a shiny black braid. Actually, she may think you're not a good match."

"How does she compare with Yue'er?" Mengzi asked.

"Hah!" Shaman Qi said in a drawn-out, nasal voice. "No comparison. She's much better looking. Yue'er is a crow, she's a phoenix; Yue'er is a noxious weed, she's a pretty rose; Yue'er is a red willow stump, she's a coral tree. But she'd be no match for Yue'er as a seductress. That girl is so restrained she doesn't even use face cream. Just think. What age is this, and she's still wearing pigtails? What's Yue'er but a foxy demon—this is just between us. Keep your lips sealed and don't let Yue'er's mother hear a word of this. But look at her bright red lips and puffy hair, the way she shimmies when she walks and pouts like a coquette when she talks. She acts like a loose woman, not a maiden from a good family. I hear she was kept by a businessman in the city when she went to work, and after using her like a new shoe, he kicked her out, like a worn one. She's not the type to be happy as a housewife; she's going to always look for something better. This hill is never as high as that one and that mountain is always better, with its longevity peaches. She was born to be a maid, but dreams about being queen of the realm. Of course, there's no comparison."

Mengzi was incensed by the Shaman's criticism of Yue'er, but he couldn't let his anger show. Besides, deep down he had to agree that Shaman Qi wasn't entirely off with her characterization of the young woman.

"Say, *Qinjia*. I'm getting to like her more and more. I want her, I want this girl to be my daughter-in-law. The boy's in luck if it works out, so I must trouble you to talk it up for us."

"You don't need to tell me that. Your business is my business. No matter what, we follow the same Buddhist teacher, and I must do my best for the sake of the Vajravārāhī."

After feasting on a chicken, Mengzi got on his bicycle, with the shaman, who was belching from the meal, on the backseat. He was dressed in new clothes from head to toe, which felt unnatural, but it was a convention he couldn't break. They'd laugh at him if he showed up at their door in rags. He was to meet their unmarried daughter, not a widow, which called for proper attire.

Local custom dictated that the man must bring gifts at each visit to the woman's family, and the first one had to be special. So, Mengzi bought four catties of rock candy, four bags of soy milk powder, and four canned goods, as well as four catties of "gift squares," which were actually just pork. He should have also bought Shaman Qi a new set of clothes, but his mother said they'd send it along later. Mengzi knew she didn't want to waste money in case he didn't like the girl.

Before they set out, Mengzi's mother shared some matchmaking secrets. "People buy piglets based on what they see in the sow, Son." She told him to pay attention to the girl's mother, her cooking skills, her hygienic habits, her temper, her interactions with them, and so on. As for the girl, he could only see the outside, not what she was really like inside. A nice, clean girl might actually have dirty habits. A mother might not care about her appearance, now that she's no longer young, and that could reveal how she's brought her daughter up.

Shaman Qi could not stop raving about the girl, making her out to be a rarity on earth, which was nothing new to Mengzi, actually. She did the same for all her matchmaking prospects, flapping her lips and wagging her tongue to turn a hideous looking girl into a fairy maiden. He let her prattle on, as he was reminded of Shuangfu's wife. After her husband had walked in on them, they'd made a semi-serious pledge to be together, but even now she was still tethered to Shuangfu by a piece of paper. Humans were not harnessed like farm animals, so they chained themselves with documents; no matter what they did, they were a pair of grasshoppers tied by a string. Under the circumstances, he did not think he'd broken his promise by going to a matchmaking meeting, even though he felt he was somehow disloyal.

Villagers were weeding in the field by the road, common work for women from spring to autumn. It was their most time-consuming task of the year. A woman spent her life weeding the field, as a girl living at home, as a housewife, even as an old grandma. It was the labor that dominated her life, as if she'd been born to weed fields. Her face withered, her hands became calloused and dark, as she gave up her youth and dreams amid pulling up weeds.

"Going to check out a girl, Mengzi?" Fengxiang, who was among the women, joked when she saw Mengzi. "Say, you're dressed all in new clothes."

"Jealous?" Mengzi got off the bicycle. "Ask the shaman to find you a man. Kick Beizhu out and get yourself a handsome, rich one, so you won't have to weed anymore."

"Never happen, I'm too old." Fengxiang smiled. "But keep your eyes open and make sure you don't get a radish that even pigs won't eat."

"In his eyes, she'd be a fairy maiden even if a pig turned her down." Beizhu said. "Mengzi isn't picky, he can feast on the young and the old. Isn't that right, Shaman Qi?"

"It's a real fairy maiden he's meeting today." Qi smiled. "She glows like a rose and has skin white as snow, not like Fengxiang, who'd disappear if you flung her into a pile of cow dung."

"What do you mean disappear?" Mengzi joined in. "She'd be darker and stink worse than the cow dung."

"What a rascal you are." Fengxiang threw a weedy dirt clod at

Mengzi, who dodged. It hit Qi instead.

"Hey, Shaman. Look at those weeds, they're ass-kissers too, cuddling up to the rich," Fengxiang jeered.

"Show some respect for your elder. These old bones of mine can't take hits like that," Qi said.

"Behave yourself at your mother-in-law's house, Mengzi." Fengxiang shouted from behind.

They arrived at the Bao home to find a smallish yard and a squat, rammed-earth house that looked quite crude. The walls were peeling, like a molting camel. Eying the appearance, Mengzi told himself that a girl from a house like this would be less than ideal.

"*Qinjia*, dear *Qinjia*." Shaman Qi shouted at the top of her voice. Everyone was her in-law.

"*Qinjia*'s here." The greeting was given by a spindly, shriveled, old woman. Shaman Qi took the gifts off the handlebars and handed them to the woman, who accepted them and said with a smile:

"Come inside, come on in."

Mengzi noticed the dirt on her hands, which had clearly accumulated over many years. People buy piglets based on what they see in the sow, he said to himself. Her daughter probably wasn't going to be all that clean.

They'd clearly made an effort to pick up the house though. A portrait of Chairman Mao hung in the middle of the main room, flanked by pictures of Guanyin Bodhisattva and movie stars. On the wall was also a piece of yellow cloth inscribed with "Longevity Like the Southern Mountain." Blankets were folded neatly atop a new, red-and-white checkered sheet, presenting a tidy look, but Mengzi couldn't put the dirt on the old woman's hands out of his mind.

"Bring some water, Ju'er," the woman called out.

Ju'er came in, with her eyes cast down, but Mengzi could see she had nice features. She wasn't as pretty as Qi had made her out to be, but not a radish that would make a pig turn up its nose either. To use his mother's words—average. She had an average look and an average figure, just the type to spend a life with, Mengzi thought. A wife like that was easy to train, putty in your hands.

"Please, have some tea," Ju'er offered him a cup of tea.

"No, thanks," Mengzi said.

"Don't worry, we won't charge you anything," she said as she set the cup on the table and smiled, her face brightening up. She'll do, Mengzi said to himself.

"That's right, look each other over, and make sure no one's missing a nose or an eye, or an arm or a leg." Qi was all smiles. "Ju'er, turn up the light."

"What's there to see?" The young woman smiled again. "Just seven openings, nothing more."

"Right. Just nine openings, nothing more," Mengzi said, adding two from elsewhere on the body. Qi covered her mouth and giggled while Ju'er blushed, but also smiled.

"A very interesting young man, I can tell." The old woman laughed.

"A normal guy never gets the girl." Qi said. "Where's the man of the house?"

"Out plastering a house." The old woman turned to her daughter. "Go get your father, Ju'er."

Ju'er walked out after a glance at Mengzi, who felt his heart stir. The girl's not bad. At first glance, she looked homely, at second, she was fine, and now, after the third, hey, she's actually quite pretty.

"Now, *Qinjia*, you have to agree that this is a match made in heaven. The boy and your daughter, they're like Golden Boy and Jade Girl, a unicorn and a phoenix, or a golden pestle and a jade mortar. A perfect pair no matter how you look at them. Why don't we get it settled now? It's okay if you want to go over and check out their family finances and okay too if you choose not to. There's really no need to. They're the best in Shawan, with everything you can think of. I keep saying to his father, 'What good karma you accumulated in your previous life, Laoshun! You get to eat and drink what you want and wear the best. You have everything. Take rabbit meat. They have enough to last them from autumn through spring. They eat meat at every meal. Some families get to see a scrap of meat only a few times a year, but at Laoshun's house, it's like a liquor lake and a meat forest. If they had three palaces and six chambers to install seventy-two consorts it would be an imperial palace. Your girl will be the empress when she marries into their family."

Mengzi had to snicker. Only the rabbit meat had a bit of validity in the Shaman's compelling narrative; not a shred of truth in everything else she said. He had to admire the woman's eloquence.

"I trust you, *Qinjia*. You take care of it," the old woman said.

Ju'er's father walked in while they were chatting. He was covered in mud, obviously having just gotten off at a construction site. The girl seemed unhappy with her father's appearance, as she brought over a basin of water and set it on the floor. The old man greeted Shaman Qi before washing up.

"It's time to sit back and enjoy life, *Qinjia*," Qi said.

"Enjoy you say?" The old man said as he wiped his face. "An old cow doesn't stop shitting till the day it dies. We were born to a tough life; I have to work hard so we won't end up eating the wind.

"Enough of that talk," Ju'er complained.

"Do you think I'm an embarrassment, girl? We're peasants, and we have to eat the five grains. There's nothing shameful about making a living with our hands. I earn fifteen yuan a day. That's good money for good work."

"No more of that," Ju'er said.

"Working in the field isn't enough anymore these days. You do what you can to make a little extra," Mengzi said. "At least you can get a little extra income."

Ju'er gave him a look while her father said, "You're right."

"This son-in-law of yours—" Qi spoke up, making Mengzi laugh silently. Nothing had been settled, and he was already their son-in-law. He stole a glance at the girl, who happened to be watching him. She blushed when their eyes met. "This son-in-law of yours is very talented. He has a head for business and is an old hand at training rabbit hawks. He's generous and he's loyal; whenever someone in trouble comes to him, he hands over fifty, even a hundred. They call him 'Timely Rain.'"

Ju'er chuckled.

Mengzi's face turned red, upset over the Shaman's inappropriate boasts. As for business, he and Baigou had traded in some agricultural by-products and lost money. And as for Timely Rain, that was pure fabrication. He rarely had a hundred yuan to keep for himself, let alone give it away.

Alerted by Ju'er's laugh, Qi reined in her tongue with a few bantering words before saying to the old man, "They're the richest in Shawan, with impressive property. His older brother is dead and his wife will remarry one day. His younger brother left home to find a job in the city. I hear he struck it rich and won't come back to the desert if his life depended on it. So he stands to inherit both of their shares too. Pool what's on three plates and you get a big bowlful. Your girl will be in charge when she's married, holding gold in her left hand and silver in the right, kicking away a scale with one foot and shutting the storage room with the other. The two of you will have more than enough to enjoy for the rest of your lives. When that happens, don't stuff yourself until you can't move; make sure you save some for me."

Ju'er glanced at Mengzi, smiling with her lips pressed together.

"I trust you, *Qinjia*. Whatever you say is fine with us. But I have to make my demand now. Our son has moved out to set up his own household, and we have only this girl left; we want enough wedding gifts for us to live out the rest of our lives."

"You're blunt," Shaman Qi said, "I like that, a man who says what he means and means what he says. I love dealing with people like you. You don't have to worry about the wedding gifts; all you have to do is ask. You name your figure and they'll make it happen. To them it's like plucking a hair off a cow. But you don't look like the type to make unreasonable demands. I've never met anyone with such a kind, decent look as the two of you. You can't see your way clear to demanding a big figure, can you?"

After exchanging a look with her husband, the woman replied:

"But we need to be taken care of."

"Listen to you." The shaman was smiling again. "You'll be taken care of, even if heaven and earth aren't. Let's focus on this fairy maiden of yours. She'd be worth several gold nuggets if you just cut her up and sold her in the market. But the girl has to live among them over there, and she'd have a bad reputation if you asked for too much. People would think you're selling your daughter to get by. I've been telling everyone I meet that the Bao family might be poor, but they're principled. They don't have much, but they have plenty of self-esteem, unlike some people, who have no scruples, dress in fine clothes, wear gold bracelets, and walk around with lots of money. The Bao family has little money, but lots of self-respect."

Mengzi was overcome with admiration for the shaman. He could never match her eloquence and cunning. Ju'er kept her head down, but she was smiling and stealing titillating glances at him.

"But we all have to eat." The woman finally found a chance to interrupt. Obviously, she was not taken in by all the fancy talk.

"Listen to you, *Qinjia*." Shaman Qi took a drink of water. "Do you think you'd suffer, with a talented son-in-law like him? His parents are the righteous type who'd go hungry just so others would have enough to eat. They'd never watch you suffer. Besides, there's me. I'm responsible for the match, and I'd never let anyone cheat you out of your fair share. Like I say, you can cheat heaven or earth, but you can't cheat your *Qinjia*. I refuse to think anyone would dare slap me in the face. If all the men in Shawan lent him their guts, he still wouldn't cheat you, not to mention the fact that your in-laws are righteous people."

Deep in thought, the old man sat silently for a while before finally asking:

"How much do you think is the right amount?"

"You decide, *Qinjia*; whatever works is fine." The shaman kicked the ball back to him. "You'll be two families if you don't get along, but one if you do. You need enough to be compensated, but not so much it would make your daughter look bad. You should ask just enough. A horse runs too fast and a cow plods along, but a donkey's pace is right down the middle. Somewhere in the middle will do."

Overwhelmed by her torrential output, the old couple exchanged looks, unable to come up with a middle-of-the-road figure. Ju'er was embarrassed by talk of her marriage prospects. She'd seen enough of such negotiations in the livestock market, so she left the room. Seeing that the old couple felt awkward coming up with a figure in front of their son-in-law-to-be, the shaman said to Mengzi, "Why don't you go out for a while and let us talk it over?"

Mengzi walked out and spotted Ju'er leaning against the gate gazing at a sow. He followed her gaze; the sow was standing next to a pile of manure and a stack of wheat stalks. A dozen squealing piglets were chasing each other. He wanted to talk to her, but didn't know what to say.

"How much schooling have you had?" she broke the ice.

"I finished middle school."

"Me too. I wanted to go to high school, but my parents wouldn't pay for it."

"My parents would have paid, but I didn't want to go on. It's a waste. After spending a fortune for college, you don't get a job assignment after graduation. What's the point?" Mengzi said.

"What do you mean, a waste?" She glanced at him. "It's better than living like an animal. Weren't you watching? It was like they were selling mules at the market."

"Then you shouldn't be asking for money," Mengzi said half in jest.

"You think I'm cheap, don't you? These days, people don't respect what comes free." She shot him a harsh look. "I didn't know that's what you were thinking."

"How would you know what I was thinking?" He smiled. "I'm not thinking about going to school, and I don't have time to think about anything else. Look at you. You're a tough customer. You say you're being treated like an animal when your parents ask for money, and you say you're being treated as cheap if no money's involved. You can't have it both ways."

"Raising me hasn't been easy. They deserve to ask for a mountain of gold."

"A mountain? How about an ocean of gold? I'd have to sell my parents to marry you, and the moment you moved in, you'd have to go begging for food."

"I actually envy those beggars who travel all over the place. They've been everywhere and seen everything. Us, we're nothing but two grasshoppers trapped under a bowl." She finished with a sigh.

"The *Qinjia* wants you to come inside," her mother walked up and said to Mengzi, who went in to hear Shaman Qi say to the old man:

"That's a good figure. There are no losers. Mengzi, it'll be ten thousand, including clothes and other necessities. Four thousand at the time of engagement, and the rest at the wedding. If you want to be a good son-in-law, buy them each a new set of clothes. If not, they won't let that bother them."

"Sure, I can do that." Mengzi quickly consented. He knew it was a middle-of-the-road figure. The Shaman herself had paid fifteen thousand for her daughter-in-law, and that didn't even include the other expenses, such as money for winter and summer clothes, spending money for New Year's and other holidays, and other crazy fees for opening trunks and unfolding bundles. These charges had long been an entrenched part of a marriage arrangement.

4

Shaman Qi came to confirm the agreement and select a date, so she could get back to the bride's family. Laoshun did not want to discuss marriage details with a young man whose skin was thicker than the city wall, so he told his wife talk to him. Mengzi had agreed to marry Shuangfu's wife once she was divorced. But she was still married, while he now had a marriage prospect, and it didn't feel right to him. So he thought he'd sound the woman out before taking the marriage discussion any further. Setting up a matchmaking meeting was simple and uncomplicated, and all it cost was a few gifts. Engagement, on the other hand, was different, for it required serious gifts. If the woman changed her mind, everything had to be returned to the man's family; if the man backed out, the woman got to keep the gifts as a way to save face. This was an iron-clad custom passed down over a thousand years. When his mother came for his answer, Mengzi hemmed and hawed, skirting the issue. Shaman Qi flew into a rage over the lack of a firm response.

"The mother-to-be is in no hurry, while the midwife can't wait."

All Mengzi wanted to know was what Shuangfu's wife had in mind.

After dinner, his mother did the dishes and then went in to practice Vajravārāhī meditation with Lanlan. Mengzi walked out and saw a crowd in conversation at the bridgehead. Nothing more than a pile of dirt, it was a convenient spot for people to gather, which was how it became a place for village gabfests. By standing atop the mound and looking east, you could see the desert, known as the Tengger Desert in books. It was a lively scene when men and women came together to share news after dinner.

After his younger brother left home, Mengzi had one less person to talk to, which left an empty spot inside. He and Lingguan were anything but confidants, and they'd bickered and bantered, but often ended up sharing a laugh. Now there was only his father when he looked up and his mother when he looked down, and they had a perverse interest in arguing, often fighting over trivial matters until they were red in the face. He felt stifled at home.

Worse yet, life was getting harder. When he worked in the field, he exhausted himself to the point where he was snoring the moment his head hit the pillow. The bad part was between farming seasons, when the fields lay fallow and life stagnated; the days were short, the nights long, and just getting by became a burden. He could not think of anything to do but join in the idle chat at the bridgehead. It felt like slogging through life, and when the sun went down each day, he'd managed to slog through two half days. The village supplied nothing to help while away time; he was simply bored.

That was bad enough, but there was also the sense of having nothing to look forward to. That had been his parents' lament, and at some point it had wormed its way into his heart, where it sat heavily, giving rise to feelings of hopelessness. More had awaited him in the past; he'd thought about food when he was hungry, clothes when he was cold, and women when aroused. Now he no longer needed to worry about being hungry or cold, and women were just that, women, useful to him for a few minutes only. Once it was over, he could take them or leave them. There ought to be something to look forward to, just as his parents had once hoped that his brother would get into college, that wheat would ripen every month, and that they'd enjoy a few good days. It sure is better to have hope, he thought.

His feet carried him to Shuangfu's door, a towering structure that had always seemed oppressive. He was intimidated by a soaring entrance that rose up, as if taunting him like a bully. The irritation would last until Shuangfu's wife was naked, at which time Mengzi could finally look superior to the man. So what if you have an impressive entrance? I can mount your wife any time I want. But he was deflated once she got dressed again, because her clothes, furniture and the appliances were as threatening as the gate.

Shuangfu and his wife had stayed married. Mengzi heard that one of the reasons was that Shuangfu was so busy. With growing wealth, he had put in bids for large-scale construction projects, which took time away from dealing with piss-ant matters like divorce. Another reason, a widespread one, was his hope for a Model Laborer Award, either on May or June First, though no one was sure which "first" it would be. They thought it had to be June, since the sixth month had greater appeal to country folk than the fifth. Shuangfu did not want the divorce to impact his image. To be sure, there was yet another reason: Shuangfu's property would have to be divided in two.

Mengzi felt dwarfed, physically and psychologically, as he stood in front of an awe-inspiring gate. In the end, he turned his feelings of inferiority into a long sigh.

The door opened and out walked Shuangfu's wife. She sneered when she saw him, as she flung away some water in a basin.

"Well, come in. Are you a toad praying to heaven? It's hard to deal with a guest who isn't sitting down," she complained.

Strange though it might sound, Mengzi's respect for her grew as he got to know her more, while his desire to marry her dwindled. What is a woman! Marrying a woman is like buying a donkey, one to beat, the other to ride. But with a proud, ambitious woman like this, Mengzi knew he could congratulate himself if she didn't ride him. He wasn't sure when he considered marrying her, as he knew his own limits. Like they say, a saltless meal is tasteless, a penniless man is like a ghost. He couldn't fill a plate with his hair if he plucked out every strand, and was a rooster unable to spread its wings in front of a hen. But one thing was sure—he was getting increasingly attached to her. In the past, he'd only thought of her when a fire burned in his gut. It was different now; her lovely face stole into his heart when it was empty. He was reminded of the term soul mate when he thought about her, someone who understands what goes on in your heart. Yet he knew he had little "soul" for her to take to heart. But that at least sounded more urbane than "heart-liver lover," "treasure," or "sweetheart." The times were changing, so were people. Mengzi was more cultured now.

Shuangfu had taken their daughter to school in the city, and the house was empty. To Mengzi it was like a fresh mantou on a plate—he could come take a "bite" any time he wanted. Everything she said impressed him, animating his mind and enlightening his brain. He'd heard that a good woman was like a book. Well, this woman was surely one of them, a tome that he'd never tire of reading and savoring, though he wished he could read it all the way through.

They no longer talked about getting married, since she was still officially Shuangfu's wife. A path opens up when the cart reaches the hill. Shuangfu was in no hurry to go through with the divorce, and neither was she. You cut firewood on the mountain you're on. She had Mengzi, so she got what she wanted, and there was no reason to hurry. It was the same with Mengzi. His father was the one in a hurry; too anxious to sit and wait, he kept going to see Shaman Qi, hoping to burn the proverbial wool on the sheep's head. To borrow Shaman Qi's phrase, "The mother-to-be is in no hurry, while the midwife can't wait." Mengzi smiled at the saying.

"What are you smiling about?" she fussed. "Got your eyes on someone now? You'd better turn up the light to see better, so you won't be a radish even a pig won't eat."

"She's a true fairy maiden, not like you, a mountain of flesh. I feel like a needle falling into the ocean when we do it."

"Didn't you learn a tune from your sister-in-law?" She chuckled. "How does it go again? 'My sweet little sister, don't complain about my small size/I can wrap it with cloth and wind a rope around it.'"

"That's all you think about." Mengzi laughed. "It's strange how folk tunes cover everything. There's one for every thought you can think of. It's odd, but I like it. There's a tune I'm reminded of whenever I can get away to come here."

"What is it?"

"'The date-red horse runs well/An embroidered ball is tied to its tail. I didn't bring you a gift/I stuttered like I had a soybean in my mouth.' Now doesn't that sound nice? Too bad I can't carry a tune. When I sing it, even rats can't control their bladders."

"I don't mind if you don't know what to do. But why do you have to hold a soybean in your mouth?" She couldn't stop laughing. "Actually, people are better than anything, living treasures. Don't you find it odd that in our short lifetime, some people don't give a damn for a loving marriage and instead choose to pursue other things, like money, fame, or some other gain? It never ends, and it's time to die when you finally get hold of whatever it is. Why can't two people just love each other? Why can't he find a way to add spice to their love, instead of chasing after hollow fame or short-term gains? I simply can't understand it."

Mengzi stared at her through half-closed eyes for a moment before finally saying, "Didn't you say a man is nothing more than a cock?"

"I did say that, but there's actually more to it. Feelings and affection are important. Women want something to hold on to. When they find it, they'll hand their life over, but if they don't, they can't even force themselves to smile. It's the same for everyone. Some look forward to love, some to children, some to a husband. The heart dies when there's nothing to look forward to, and then the only differences between us and domestic animals are our ability to talk and the lack of a tail."

"What about you? What do you want?"

"Me?" She frowned. "I need my pride. I want to keep my eyes wide open, so I can watch that the shallow bastard who changed the moment he had money gets what's coming to him. You know that Heaven has had a grand scheme since the day Pan Gu separated the sky from the earth. No one can escape it—the higher you fly, the harder you fall."

Mengzi felt a chill on his back.

5

Mengzi walked out the door, still shaken from what the woman had said. She was quite a woman. He sucked cold air in through his teeth when he thought about the prominent, arrogant Shuangfu alongside the lonely, sad woman. One swaggered like the mid-day sun, thanks to his wealth, the other was left behind, a straw widow. He smiled and shook his head at that thought. The contrast squeezed his heart.

Xiuxiu had married Shuangfu when he was penniless. What had he been like then? An obstinate loser, a nobody. And her? A real beauty. To quote the blind storyteller's lines, "Her teeth are white, her lips red; a face like a peach flower, she walks with grace, a willow branch swaying in a spring breeze." The matchmakers nearly broke down the door to her family's house. Her father said he'd rather die than let her marry Shuangfu, while she said she'd rather die than marry anyone else. Back and forth, a tug of war was waged between father and daughter, until finally he relented and she married Shuangfu, seemingly a happy ending. Then everything changed when the jackass Shuangfu struck it rich. Blinded by wealth, he no longer had an eye for her, like a man who wears a basket and thinks he has the sky over his head. Catching her in some minor fault, he demanded a divorce, obviously wanting to discard the old and bring in the new. He could have stuck his finger up his ass to see if he could still call himself a man.

Mengzi gnashed his teeth when he recalled her phrase, the higher you fly, the harder you fall. The point on a steelyard would return to zero and the man would know what he was worth when he was so poor he couldn't keep a thing, not even the snot in his nose.

Everyone pitches in to smooth out uneven road surfaces.

You think you're hot shit, don't you? You will fail!

Mengzi was deflated when he recalled the image of the swaggering Shuangfu, a prominent, arrogant giant among men. The thought of the man was like conjuring up an image of the heavens, since there was nothing Mengzi could sink his teeth into. If Shuangfu's money was stashed at a place guarded by ten thousand, Mengzi would like to find a way to turn into a mouse and douse himself in gasoline to sneak in and burn everything, leaving Shuangfu destitute. A popular storyline in Liangzhou drama was that floods and fires can render a rich man penniless overnight. But Shuangfu wasn't just a large pile of bills; he had businesses, high-rises, and construction material rumored to be worth millions; he also had plenty of cash. Beyond that, even if a flood washed away everything he owned, he could still get loans to start over and make it big again just on the strength of his name. Within a few years, he'd be the prominent, arrogant Shuangfu again.

Mengzi finally realized how powerful the man was, though, strangely, the woman was equally impressive. Her sneer rolled around in him like a rock, and he could not forget the grand concept: the higher you fly, the harder you fall.

He could see how Shuangfu flew high, but did not know how to make him fall. He could not swallow up the sky even if he were a tiger.

Unaware of where he was going, Mengzi had left the village and arrived at a sand dune. Sitting down on a rise covered with bunchgrass, he looked at the village, which seemed to cower in the folds of an ocean of sand, his heart as heavy as if it were filled with lead. The image of Xiuxiu kept flashing before his eyes. He knew she would get a divorce sooner or later, for, as his father liked to say, "sooner or later the hair on a sheep's head will burn." When that happened, Shuangfu would still be the prominent, arrogant Shuangfu, while she would remain in a small compound in the desert, laughing like a witch and keeping her eyes bright in the dark, a witch waiting for him to fall.

Night descended. A lonely white moon shone down on the desert, on the village, and on Mengzi, who had somehow managed to grow up, and somehow managed to learn how to ponder life's baffling issues. A wind blew over, carrying a mixture of smells—desert rice, Artemisia, and others—drifting softly toward him and massaging his heart until he seemed to melt in the breeze.

A long time later, a barking dog made him shudder and drove fear into him. Everything was blurred and mysterious in the moonlight, including the desert, home to desert foxes, desert rats, sand babies, sentimental little life forms, grave mounds, and drifting will-o'-the-wisps. And ghosts. On this night he was inclined to believe in the existence of gods and ghosts. Usually he was like his father, never fully believing in them. His father was a believer when necessary, like occasions to visit graves, burn spirit money, and make offerings to gods and ghosts.

At other times, such as during an argument with his mother, he would disregard his belief and hurl their incense burner, curse the Buddha, and spew sacrilegious outbursts.

There ought to be gods and ghosts on a dark night like this, Mengzi said to himself. The moon blurred the majestic outlines of an enormous yellow ridge nearby, where generations of Shawan forebears were buried. On the ridge were countless rings of bricks and stones, inside which were the graves of entire clans. The clans all had names—White Tiger Pass, Xiangdaoli, Jinyincheng—each denoting a major family. Swarms of their filial sons and grandsons came every year during Tomb Sweeping Day or National Day to burn spirit money for their ancestors, who, pleased, turned into little whirlwinds to enjoy the offering. They then left with the money so they could be wealthy ghosts for a few days.

It was a big, very high ridge, like a mountain, with a name, Yellow Dragon Mount, where there had once stood the Yellow Dragon Temple. Offerings had to be made on the first and the fifteenth of each lunar month, for, if not, the angry dragon would howl, the winds would scream, and the sands would wail. Mountains of sand would slither down, toppling houses, burying crops, and obliterating all signs of human existence. After the temple was destroyed during the "Smash Four Olds" campaign, the villagers did not feel like rebuilding it; since they had incurred the wrath of the god when their offerings lacked substance, they decided against offering anything more, so they could live in peace.

The Earth God's Temple remained, however, where a statue of a good-natured old man was installed. It did not matter whether they burned incense or not, for the Earth God never lost his temper and kept smiling. Above the temple was the Vajravārāhī Cave, supposedly a renowned historical site. But that was history, and Mengzi had no interest in learning more about it.

The yellow ridge had been around for ages. The dark-skinned Daoist priest said there had once existed a dragon's vein, meaning an emperor could rise out of the area. Mengzi did not envy the life of an emperor, except for his three palaces and six chambers, where seventy-two consorts and three thousand palace maids lived. Just holding early morning court was a huge headache, he'd heard. He agreed with his father's comment, "I don't believe the emperor enjoyed his delicacies from land and sea any more than I do with my wild rabbit."

According to the Daoist priest, the imperial court severed the dragon's vein in Shawan at the very moment that an emperor was about to emerge. He said the current emperor lacked self-confidence, so he set up a "Sky Observing Post," with an astronomer studying the sky every day so the emperor could sever dragon's veins whenever a dragon aura appeared somewhere. What did a dragon aura look like? No one had ever seen one. The priest said the aura was red inside and yellow outside, with three more colors in between, some resembling a dragon, some a phoenix, others a turtle, a large umbrella, even a giant who stood to the west of the sun, his hands at his sides. The aura would reach all the way into the celestial court. Afraid that the imperial court would discover the vein in Shawan, Heaven sent down a dark-cloud dog, mangy and scabby, to leave piles of droppings, totally obscuring the grave in order to shield the dragon aura. One day, when someone saw a dog shitting on their ancestral tomb, he clubbed the dog to death and cleared away the dog droppings. That was bad! The dragon aura shot up into the sky, pushing the North Star into the opening of the Big Dipper, which alerted the imperial court to send someone to sever the vein. Lore had it that the vein grew back every night, drawing crowds, and yet the surface remained unmarked after a month. One night, when someone came to retrieve a pickaxe that had been left behind, he heard people talking in the mountains: "He can't sever a damn thing unless he uses red grain chaff mixed in black dog's blood. The following day, the mixture was sprinkled while the attack was ongoing, and finally a reed shoot was dug up. Dark blood shot out of a well dozens of *li* away when a spade hit the shoot. In the last days of the Qing dynasty, one of the descendants from the well owner's family became an important official. Niu Jian was governor-general of three major provinces, which included Jiangsu. Mengzi had read about him in history books. Niu had run off with his tail between his legs the moment the foreign devils fired the first cannon shot, leaving behind the lore and the Niu Family Garden, a famous Liangzhou site.

According to lore, the reed shoot was the dragon's vein. According to lore, blood ran in every reed sprout. According to lore, the night the vein was cut, a baby girl was born to the thirty-second generation of a Shawan family. She was supposed to be the empress. On the same night, the family's mare gave birth to a golden pony. Both the future empress and the pony died when the vein was severed.

There was much more to the lore.

In the moonlight, the Yellow Dragon Mount looked inky black and, it seemed, much bigger. Nighttime and the moon were magical, embellishing ordinary objects and giving them an enigmatic appearance. See that? The majestic soaring dragon under the moon is nothing but an earthen ridge in the daytime, stark yellow and austere, with rocky soil. A gap was noticeable at the spot where the dragon's head was lopped off by the imperial court.

Suddenly Mengzi had an idea.

That's right, split the tomb.

Everyone in Shawan knew that Shuangfu made his fortune purely because his father's tomb was placed at an auspicious spot, low in the middle and high on all sides, surrounded by a ring of reed shoots that would sprout into reed leaves in the summer, like colorful banners that swayed noisily in the wind.

I'm going to dig up that damn jackass's ancestral tomb!

Chapter Five

Lying on my side, lying on my back
I cannot hear you herding camels back

1

Yue'er asked Ying'er to teach her some folk tunes, and Ying'er agreed. Yue'er had learned from a newspaper article that a teahouse in Lanzhou, the provincial seat, was hiring young women who could sing local folk tunes. She decided to learn a few, hoping the skill would one day take her out of the desert."

She had supported Lingguan's decision to leave. "In a tiny corner where even wolves won't shit," she said to Ying'er, "there are two options—you either suffocate, or you lead a happy life, like our parents, who don't even know they're suffocating. "

For Ying'er, Lingguan's return had become her most ardent wish, the one thing she could look forward to. He had not made any promises, and yet she was convinced he would be back one day. So were the villagers, who constantly asked Laoshun:

"Is Lingguan coming home soon?"

"Yes," Laoshun would answer cheerfully, "he is."

"Yes, he is," was music to Ying'er's ears.

During the process of teaching Yue'er the folk tunes, Ying'er had a chance to savor the past. Each affecting tune brought back indelible memories. The melodies had the power to tug at her heartstrings; they embodied tearful intimation, weepy laughter, detachment after enlightenment, and smiles from intense suffering. She could barely manage a few notes before tears welled up in her eyes, and Yue'er understood what she was feeling without any explanation. It was the power of the folk tune, which, like a magical hand, extracted the vigor of life from the heart and instilled it in the minds of the listeners, inducing resonance from deep in their souls.

You can tie me up with a rope,
You can make me kneel down at the base of a pole.
You can cut my head off with a sword,
I'll keep doing what I do if I don't die.

Osmanthus window, osmanthus door,
By the palatial lantern in the heavenly court.
The sword for killing, a basin to catch the blood,
There is no regret in little sister's heart.

Ying'er seemed to be the strongest person in the world when she sang tunes like this. Her dedication, strength, and willingness to die for love seemed to have emanated not from her delicate body, but from Heaven. Yue'er was deeply moved. In the many novels she'd read, she'd encountered a fair number of strong characters who made powerful speeches, but they had far less impact on her than these tunes.

"My body is bruised from head to toe, but I'll do the same thing over and over till the day I die. Lop off my head, and my bloody body would still lie next to you." It was no longer about love, but a belief, a kind of religion, the only consolation life had to offer. That was what the tunes were all about, songs unique to China's West, the poetry of the soul, and the bunchgrass of impoverished lives, resisting the sand and wind with its multiplying green. Listening to Ying'er's plaintive voice, Yue'er bit her lip, tears sparkling in her eyes, as she trembled from the enchanting melody.

While they sang, they were immersed in the special artistic ambience of the tunes. Their hearts now brimmed with the comfort of shedding a heavy burden, the exuberance of a good cry, the relief after a screaming, and the gratification of a quest.

After nursing her baby, Ying'er put him to bed and asked her mother-in-law to keep watch so she could leave with Yue'er, who wanted to have Lanlan along. But Ying'er, knowing her sister-in-law was meditating, held her finger to her lips.

They were singing when they reached a sand dune on the village outskirts. It was the spot where, in her imagination, she had stood to watch Lingguan recede into the distance. She'd created a tableau next to an Artemisia bush, a deeply touching scene. A path, like a thin gray line, extended into the distance and led to a larger world. There ought to be someone walking down the sandy path, growing smaller under her gaze, eventually blending into the horizon. She would sing "a tearful tune flooded my heart," her voice painting an intoxicating image of a world set off by sand.

Bunchgrass and other desert vegetation covered the dune, rat holes were everywhere. Rats were running amok, so frightening Yue'er that she shrieked and held onto Ying'er, who wore a faint smile. She had once been afraid of the rats, but, after her husband's death, nothing scared her anymore. That was true. Was there anything more horrifying than death? If there was, then it had to be her dead heart.

An inchworm on Yue'er's shoulder insolently arched its body as it moved. Immersed in the realm of the folk tune, the women were oblivious to the outside world, including caterpillars weaving spider-like webs under the trees. One had made it onto Yue'er's shoulder. Ying'er quietly flicked it off without alarming her friend, before discovering another one crawling boldly up her pant leg. She flicked that one off too.

Ying'er realized that she had become a different person, seeming to have understood a great many things, her spirit reaching a wide, open space. What had she finally understood? She wasn't sure, except that she felt a new understanding, and could let go of things that had once bothered her. Her heart had been elsewhere, led astray by some sentiment. For instance, caterpillars had once frightened her, their fuzzy green bodies raising goose bumps all over. Now she realized there was nothing to fear from caterpillars, which neither bit nor attacked people. Another example: she had been loath to part with Lingguan, the mere thought of which led her to despair, as illustrated by the line in one of the tunes, "After you left, melons are my sole companion/I hold a melon vine, my heart a gray pall." Now that she had experienced desolation, she knew her heart would be warm and resplendent again. None of her fears mattered much. Maybe she had made some progress. If so, what had caused it? She knew, of course—it was death.

Her husband was dead. Someone she'd spent every moment with, but had not loved, had suddenly disappeared from her life. Death was the best teacher. You can learn about life from it.

Ying'er sat down, squinting at the path that, in her imagination, Lingguan had taken to reach the outside world. She looked back at the village through the clumps of Artemisia; the houses seemed sparse, compared with the vast desert behind her. With the sand as a backdrop, the village appeared bleak. On a large plot of land close to the dune a farmer was plowing his field behind an ox. Chickens pecked for food around wheat mounds at the edge of the field. That was it: desert, village, people, ox, chickens, wheat mounds, and rats scampering at her feet made up the world of her existence.

Over the past few years, depending on her experience and emotions, that simple but crowded world was alternately ugly, pretty, romantic and sad, before eventually becoming insipid again. It was a manifestation of the lyric: "An ordinary life, that is reality."

"See that? That's our hometown." Yue'er stopped singing and sneered.

Ying'er frowned. There was a lot she liked about Yue'er, but one thing she disliked. Yue'er longed for the outside world, which was acceptable, but her longing was accompanied by a denunciation of Shawan, which bothered Ying'er. She found the village remote and backward, but could not abide criticism from Yue'er. Shawan might have been small, impoverished, and barren, but it was her hometown, Lingguan's hometown, the baby's too. Her heart skipped a beat at thoughts of her baby. This was the place that had produced Lingguan, who had gifted her with the most brilliant, most splendid period of her life. You shouldn't complain about the place, Yue'er, she said silently. The city might be great, but it doesn't belong to you. She frowned, but did not share her thoughts. Her breasts were full, so she opened her blouse and squeezed to relieve the tension, shooting milky white liquid at the Artemisia.

A red sunset painted the western sky, a cozy color that warmed the heart. There was no scene to compare with a sunset, so beautiful it made her want to cry. Its pretty red hue evenly infused the dune, the Artemisia, the village, and the thing called life. Can you feel the beauty, Yue'er? This is the song of nature; can you sense it? The silent tune can spread into your heart. Listen to the wondrous melody, will you? Or are you like a pole of pine, a bucket of willow, which can never carry you to enlightenment? If you feel none of this, you can be a folk tune singer only, and will never be a folk tune fairy. Do you know what that is? She is the outlet of the tune. She sings not with her own, but with nature's mouth, which opens to let flow its sound.

2

Now Ying'er understood how love had developed between her and Lingguan, and she was convinced that it could not have happened between him and Yue'er. Yue'er was virginal, pretty, and splendid, but she lacked whatever it was that caused a resonant linking of hearts. Oftentimes, when facing the desert, the starry night, or another phenomenon that touched her deeply, Lingguan would mention it the moment the wondrous feeling struck her. Take this moment, for instance. If he were here, he would have spoken emotionally about the sunset and the desert, perhaps glorious, perhaps bleak. What he said would be what she had in mind. Yue'er, on the other hand, disrupted nature's most beautiful melodies with the noise of "longing" and "aspirations."

Ying'er described to her friend types of local folk tune structures, such as "dantaozi" and "shuangtaozi," or single-set and double-set compositions, to which Yue'er paid close attention. Yet Ying'er could not help but feel that Yue'er learned the tunes for their practical value, while she sang them as expressions of love. That was a fundamental difference between them. One could only be a singer, while the other could become a fairy. To her, love was the ocean and the tunes were ocean spray; they flowed naturally when there was love—

> Fish in the river cannot live without water,
> How can they exist when there is none?
> The folk tunes are a treasured part of me,

How could I live if I could not sing them?

Soldiers arrived at the Yandongshan
Their swords took many lives.
They came after me with a club,
I would choose the folk tunes over my life.

You see? The folk tunes are more precious than life.

The feeling grew stronger as she explained and sang the tune, so Ying'er pretended she needed to relieve herself and walked off into a distant hollow. It was overgrown with weeds that had dried up after the frost and rustled in the wind. Rings of sand rippled outward until they became part of the sky. On the other end was Lingguan, who was on her mind and in her dreams all the time. Do you know that I'm thinking about you now? "I think about you so much I cannot blow out the candle/Melted wax fills the holder." Your name is the tune that fills my heart, Lingguan. My *yuanjia*, the lover I ought to hate. Even if you were to die the death of a thousand cuts, it still would not erase the bitterness in my heart. What are you doing now? Have you forgotten this sandy corner where even wolves won't shit? Do you still recall that there is Ying'er, whose limpid eyes have dried up from looking forward to seeing you again? It's getting cold. Don't forget to dress warmly. Do you know that what I cannot bear to hear is the tune "A Young Man Leaves Home": "A cold wind blows and snow falls, but who knows how a young man feels?" Do you know that these lines are like a dagger forever stabbing my heart?

Do you know that your son smiles now? His smiling face looks eerily like yours. Everyone looks at me funny when they see the baby. They can look all they want, I don't care. Except he will have to call you *shushu*, even though you are his father. Oh, "*shushu*" is what city folks use for "uncle." Here in Shawan we use "laolao." One day he'll address you as

"Laolao—Laolao—" like your mother calling the pigs. How funny.

Ying'er smiled at the thought. It was a real smile on her tear-streaked face.

3

Her breasts had dried up.

Ying'er realized she had no milk for her baby when she came home. Not a drop came out, no matter how hard she squeezed. "Did you spray your milk away? You mustn't do that," her mother-in-law said.

"No, I didn't. But earlier this afternoon, when I went out with Yue'er, my breasts were so full they hurt, so I squeezed some out onto a sand dune."

"That's it then, that's how your breasts dried up. You know it's there for the baby, and you can't spray it. That's how they dry up. You have to get it back. Take me there, and we'll get what we can. We're going out to catch hog badgers tonight. Shaman Qi keeps pushing for Mengzi's engagement, but we don't have enough money. We have to do what we can to get the money, even trapping hog badgers."

"Who buys hog badgers?" Ying'er asked.

"Not the hogs themselves, but the fat, a cure for indigestion. It's an effective remedy for domestic animals with stomach problems. Ten yuan for one liang, a hundred per cattie. A large one can give up seven or eight catties." She continued, "This is the time when they're fattest. They turn thin when winter comes, and we wouldn't get much fat even if we trapped one. They're funny animals. When they hibernate, they sleep in a circle, head to tail, and fat ones transfer their energy to thin ones. That's how they make it through the winter."

They talked as they headed toward the dune. Ying'er was amused at how her breasts had dried up after only a few squeezes. How odd.

But they had dried up; once swollen breasts were now shriveled and the abundant milk was gone. The baby bawled when he suckled and failed to get anything. How amusing.

Done with talking about hog badgers, her mother-in-law began nagging her about something else. She told Ying'er not to spend too much time with that woman, Yue'er. "Just look at her face and you'll know she's up to no good. She set her eyes higher than the sky and her fate is as flimsy as paper; always casting her flirting glances here and there, she does not act like a proper woman. You learn to be good when you're with someone upright, like beating the River God when you hang out with the Dragon King. She could change you, and not for the better, if you spend too much time with her." She moved on to something else, telling Ying'er not to talk and laugh too much out in public. "You're in a merry mood with Hantou barely gone. They'll think you have plans, that you can't stand being a widow any longer. There's nothing terrible they won't say."

Smiling faintly, Ying'er held her tongue. Her mother-in-law was always saying, "I can be kind to my daughter-in-law in my heart, but not in my actions." Kindness in the heart was enough for Ying'er, who knew that her mother-in-law did have a good heart, so she didn't talk back.

"Some places have ominous auras that people with weak demon-repelling qi should avoid, or they will be in trouble. People who starved to death in 1960 were buried by the sand dune; so many died that the corpses piled up high in the pit, which is now a well-known site for hungry ghosts. They must have stolen your milk. It used to be a threshing ground, but too many odd things happened there. The production team suffered repeated losses, even when they had a bumper crop. Team members on night guard saw thieves steal grain, but never succeeded in catching anyone. The stamp on the wheat sacks remained intact, untouched by anyone. Isn't that strange? One day, I spotted Meng Baye when I went to assume the night guard shift. I called out to him, but he kept walking with his head down, so I went after him; I couldn't catch up and then he just vanished. When I got back home, he was talking to my husband. He said he'd been there all along. Wasn't that strange? You were at a potter's field, so of course your breasts dried up."

Ying'er smiled, she'd heard all this before. She wondered how she'd forgotten about the potter's field when she went with Yue'er. Her husband's death seemed to have emboldened her. "Hantou died too young, his spirit won't be as peaceful as an old man's. Are you afraid?" Fengxiang had asked her in secret.

"Why should I be afraid?" Ying'er wondered what had happened to her fear.

"Strange how I lost my milk," she said with a smile.

"What's strange about it? You can lose water too, not just milk. That happened to us the year you married Hantou. A vat brimming with water suddenly went dry. Shaman Qi said we had to look for the water right away to keep from dying of thirst. We went looking for it, searched up and down and ran until our neck tendons snapped, before we found it in Niutiwo in the western slope. A single ladle of water, just that, but everything was fine when we got it back. Did you know that also happened to Mao Dan's family? They couldn't find it, and in the end everyone but him died. They ran a fever, saying they were thirsty, and their lips turned black from the heat. Isn't that strange? I haven't been around a very long time, but I've seen a lot, including all sorts of weird things."

They reached the sand dune. The sun had set, but it was still light out. Vegetation was slowly crossing into the night. A cold wind blew over, carrying an eeriness that made Mengzi's mother shiver. Talk of ghosts scared her, but when she looked at Ying'er, she laughed to see how calm the young woman was. I'm worse than a young woman, Mengzi's mother said to herself before clearing her throat, stamping her foot, and brushing her lapels. She looked as if she were about to utter something earth-shattering after that, but instead she got down on her knees, to Ying'er's surprise.

Ying'er smiled secretly.

She looked around. Everything in the distance had blended into the dark night, while nearby the sky was faintly gray, like the color of dawn, generally known as fish-belly white. An unusually large moon hung in midair, presenting a jarring sight, like an alien object barging into the evening sky. She hadn't seen a moon like that for quite some time, and this sighting tonight was stirring. What had happened over the past year felt like ancient history. One had died, another had been born; she'd experienced both love and separation. Her heart was at peace after seeing or personally experiencing birth, aging, illness, and death. It felt odd to her that events, no matter how major or calamitous, were just events once they were over, nothing but lines in the notebook of her life. Every event, big or small, got one; in the fullness of time, it was hard to say which were more serious than the others, or which lines were darker than the rest. In fact, major events oftentimes blurred in her memory, while what cropped up in her mind were usually insignificant incidents, such as the agonizing yawn on Lingguan's face when he first woke up.

Ying'er's mother-in-law remained on her knees as she tried to light incense. Her matches flickered briefly, but the desert wind blew them out each time. So, she spread her lapel to shelter a match, and it stayed lit. An unusual fragrance drifted over, a whiff of which calmed any disquiet one was feeling. It was a comforting wind to the souls of the dead, flitting and floating, driving away all troubles in the mind and softening the heart. Ying'er did not believe in the self-cultivation practiced by Lanlan, but she had no trouble accepting the fragrance. To her, the smell felt much like the things that Lingguan had used to say, not searing, passionate words of love, but occasional, random expressions that meant little, atmospheric words that seemed to wind around her until she entered a trance and felt nothing but the mesmerizing sensation.

She did not like him to expound on important matters, which, to her, were meaningless. Why must he stuff his head with these strange ideas? No one forced him to do so, he did it to himself, messing up his head and darkening her mood. In fact, he had no need to think too much. "God starts to laugh when human begin to think," he used to say, but why must he trouble his own head? Why?

She thought she'd understood everything, while he had not. Ying'er no longer felt guilty about their affair; she did not know at which moment it happened, but her guilty conscience became a thing of the past. It felt right to her. There had been nothing, neither love nor romance, between her and her husband, a couple in name only. There was nothing real about their relationship, while with Lingguan it was the opposite, for which the little Lingguan was the proof. The thought of the boy brought a smile to her face. Why should the real feel guilty for the nominal? In her view, a crime was committed when one party interfered violently with the other; nothing was wrong when both parties were willing.

A fire started, its flame flickering from the "petition" paper her mother-in-law was burning. She could never understand why Liangzhou people call the yellow spirit paper petition paper, just as she wondered why uncles were called laolao. Petition paper it was then, and *laolao* was fine with her too. She did not understand, but did not care to use her head, unlike Lingguan, who was always puzzling over something, stirring up the chicken coop in his head with his thinking cap. What was it to you whether the chickens in your head were sleeping or moving about? You'd worry needlessly if you did not let your brain rest, like the yellow hen that flapped its wings and fluttered about all the time, fanning up dust all over the yard. What did it accomplish by all that? It was still cackling in the yard. You could hop and fly all you wanted, and I'd watch until you panted like a hard-working bellows. I'd laugh at you secretly. You foolish *yuanjia*.

Her mother-in-law chattered as she burned the paper, "You're human when you're alive and a god when you die. The underworld and human world are separate realms, each with its own source of nourishment, so please return the baby's milk. He's bawling from hunger." She pleaded with the hungry ghosts before switching to the Earth God, "Dear Earth God and Earth Goddess, I'm here to fetch the milk." She muttered and banged her head on the ground while putting pinches of dirt in her bowl.

She stood up when she was done, and thumped the dirt off her knees, no longer clearing her throat with feigned confidence. It was dark now, and everything was hazy, even with the big moon overhead. She took Ying'er's hand, and they stumbled off the dune together. Recalling the scampering desert rats from earlier that day, Ying'er was worried they might flatten and destroy their nests. Then she had a change of heart: it would suit them right, she said to herself. Maybe the greedy rats stole the milk. She smiled at the thought.

When they got home, her mother-in-law poured water into the bowl and told Ying'er to drink it once the dirt settled to the bottom. By dinnertime, Ying'er could feel her breasts swelling again; she touched them and, strangely enough, they were full of milk again.

4

After dinner, Laoshun took a flashlight, lit a lantern, and picked up a club. Meng Baye came with a musket, a rope and a piece of canvas. Mengzi got himself a spade and pickaxe. They then headed toward the cliff where they'd found signs of hog badger tracks. This was not Laoshun's first time, so he knew they were in for some hard work. He asked Lanlan along to lend a hand. She then asked Ying'er to go with her.

A huge moon suspended in the sky softened the starlight. It had lost some of its earlier brilliance, and now had the same texture as the sky. Meng said something to Laoshun out of Ying'er's earshot, and the two men laughed conspiratorially. She wondered if it had something to do with her. An evening wind blew over; she felt refreshed inside, as if washed clean.

The lantern swung back and forth, shining on Laoshun's legs and casting two black pillars on the ground, where they crossed and moved past each other. It was his favorite lantern, with a glass cover and a round knob to control the flame. A turn clockwise brought on a bright light and a turn counterclockwise dimmed the flame to a flickering pea size, seemingly on the verge of going out, though it would stay lit all night. It was convenient and never wasted fuel. In Ying'er's mind, hawks, the lantern, camels, and a pipe were extensions of her father-in-law. He always had the lantern handy when he trained his hawks, fed livestock, irrigated a field, or transported salt from the salt lakes. Those two black pillars had been moving for more than half a lifetime already.

The village was still awake. They could hear sand boys at White Tiger Pass shouting as they played drinking games and, faintly, Yue'er singing folk tunes. "Listen, Yue'er is in a romantic mood, singing about lovers," Lanlan said.

"Girls her age are all the same," Ying'er replied. "I think it's wonderful they have these feelings."

"Once they're married and have spent a few years around a stove, and they have to slop the hogs, they'll stop singing about lovers," Lanlan said. "Their songs will be 'lao-lao-lao.' A romantic mood will turn into vapor in a steamer, which they won't be able to keep even if they wanted to."

"You know what's really odd?" Ying'er said. "Liangzhou people call their uncles *laolao* and their swine *laolao* pigs."

"Haven't you heard Father calling Ma a pig? When I was kid, he was always telling me to go fetch your pig."

"Same difference," said Meng. "You can be a mother, an uncle, or a pig, but you have one life and need to keep at it. We all get by the best we can."

"What do you mean, the same?" Laoshun objected. "How can we compare ourselves with pigs? The *laolao* pigs sleep after they eat and eat when they wake up. A life of ease."

"But they get the knife eventually," Lanlan said.

"No one can escape that," Laoshun said. "Forget tubal ligation and surgery, and just think about the final moment of your life. It's made by the knife in the hand of the old man upstairs. It cuts softly, and the rope is thin. It all goes slowly. You won't breathe your last until your eyes are sunken and dry, and your lips turn black and parched. For a pig, it's quick and neat, a sharp knife in the heart."

"It's not what you think," Meng Baye disagreed. "They are, after all, living slabs of meat. Humans are different. We all have the same organs, but we could not be any more different from one another. There are criminals and saints among us, do-gooders and evildoers, it all depends on how you live your life. We have different minds and so we live different lives; the bigger your heart, the bigger the person."

"Did you go through the initiation rite, Meng Baye?" Lanlan asked. "Those are things the Master said."

"What power do I need? My heart is my master."

By then they'd reached the Dasha River, whose banks were marked by hillocks. No one knew how long they'd been there. They heard it had once been flat land. But then snow melt from Qilian Mountains had carried the soil and sand away, creating caverns. Whenever rain fell for several days, mountain torrents roared down, with tongues of angry water licking at the cavern walls until they collapsed into themselves. The remaining sides were the hillocks to the locals.

They were long, extending as far as the river; and they were high, as high as the sinkhole depths. Villagers continued to call them hillocks even after the river dried up. Wild animals showed up and dug holes or made nests to breed, prolonging the history of their existence.

A few years earlier, when water still trickled in the Dasha River, a green dragon formed out of wild grass, clumps of willows, reeds, water plants, and bunchgrass. The dragon twisted its way into the desert, where it transformed itself into a verdant world called a *magang*. In those days, the reeds grew tall, as did the willows. People could hide in vegetation like crested wheatgrass. When she was little, Lanlan and her playmates hid inside to relieve themselves when they were out playing. After she started school, she had to laugh, secretly though, when the school children learned to read "The sky is broad, the wilderness vast, when a wind blows, grass flattens to reveal cows and sheep." What was revealed in the grass had been her peeing. There was also bunchgrass, and Chinese irises, with pretty blue flowers. She could weave the leaves into butterflies, grasshoppers, and animals, all life-like. The tall reeds, dense willow trees, crested wheat grass with teeth-like leaves sharp enough to cut fingers, birch, and blackthorn screened the Dasha River banks into a secluded world, where wild rabbits, tiaotiaos, foxes and wolves lived, each in its own style.

Lanlan liked playing in the Dasha River, where a spot called Heavenly Spring was her favorite. It was hidden in dense vegetation, which was why her mother tried to get her to stay away, claiming there were wolves there. She went at high noon, a time when ghosts were out and about, but wolves and foxes slept. She was afraid of ghosts at night, not wolves. The ghosts at noontime, invented by her mother, did not scare her. As a young girl, Heavenly Spring had been irresistible. She had heard that it was connected to the springs in heaven, whose water, when ingested, made her smart and pretty and lightened her complexion. Everyone believed in its power; it was not clear if her fair skin had come from the water she drank, though she'd had her fair share. Later, the crested wheatgrass was cut to make ropes, the willows became parts of houses, reeds were burned to ashes, the foxes left for the desert, and the wolves migrated to a *magang*, leaving the dry riverbed and the cliffs.

But the wonderful Heavenly Spring continued to ripple in her dreams. Fine sand ebbed and waned with the current, making beautiful patterns around the spring, like a kaleidoscope that shifted its image from wind to cloud. She felt herself turning into a fine sand pattern if she watched it too long. Then she would bend over and bury her face in the water, washing away the heat and irritation in her mind and body. It would be years before she learned that Heavenly Spring was the regular watering hole of a fox fairy. Every morning a white fox sauntered through morning dew to drink at the spring. One day Bai Fu and Hantou placed a trap called a head-snapper; it broke one of the fox fairy's legs. When it dragged the trap to see Bai Fu, he clubbed it to death. After that, she had a daughter, Yindi, whom Shaman Qi claimed to be the reincarnation of the fox coming for its life. Bai Fu led Yindi into the desert, where she froze to death. For Lanlan it was an unbearable nightmare.

She shuddered at the recollection.

5

The hog badger's burrow that Meng had found was one of hundreds, all alike. Some were occupied, others stood empty; some might be decoy dens, some were deep holes caused by water erosion, some were paths for underground waterways, and so on. It took an experienced eye to determine if one was an active burrow. Once, when Baigou got Mengzi to go digging for the animals, they were at it until midnight, but failed to find even a whiff of an animal.

Meng Baye was an old hand at recognizing animal tracks, so naturally he knew which burrow would produce a badger, about how many males and females there could be, and how deep they'd burrowed into the ground. But all his experience would accomplish was the certainty that they would see results, without helping to reduce the labor. It was hard work. First, they had to enlarge the den enough for one person to crawl in. Then the person in the burrow started digging, while the two above ground carried the dirt out on a sheet of canvas by tying a rope to both ends and hauling it up. At some point the alerted hog badger would use one of two strategies: one, seal off the den to make the digger think he'd reached a dead end when the opening disappeared. Two, dig deeper, as the human gave chase, waging a contest in stamina. Sometimes the exhausted digger would simply stop, pour water down to drown the badger or light wheat stalks to smoke it out and catch it that way.

Water was ineffective for a burrow on a hill that was rife with cracks and filled with openings called "drill holes." Water would simply flow off somewhere. In addition, the water source was too far, and carrying water was more strenuous than moving dirt. Smoke was not a good option either, since it would escape from the drill holes, no matter how much was piped in. Usually nothing would happen for a long time when smoke was used, until suddenly a screeching animal shot out of the hole, frightening the diggers, who would miss it once they recovered from the shock. Badgers ran like piglets; they were not aggressive, but fast and gifted with enviable stamina. To catch up, one had to find a way to first turn into a deer.

Mengzi loosened the dirt around the burrow and deposited it far off. Hard work was Mengzi's only worthy trait in his father's eyes. It did not take him long to enlarge the opening enough for him to crawl in. Meng Baye tossed down the canvas with a rope attached for Mengzi to tie one end to his pants cord before shoveling dirt into the make-shift transport. He would shout frequently for those above the ground to pull at the other end and haul the dirt up.

The lantern went in with Mengzi, leaving the others in the dark. All was quiet except for the sound of a shovel and the old men's heavy breathing. Night air surged around them, cold as ice water. Ying'er, who had left in too much of a hurry to take a coat along, was shivering, so Lanlan draped her jacket around her sister-in-law's shoulders.

"Go dig up some potatoes, build a kiln, and fire it up," Meng Baye said to the women.

"Good idea," agreed Laoshun. "It'll be a while before we get a badger out, so we need something to eat. Roasted potatoes sound good to me. The plot east of the hollow belongs to Big Head. He's always eating our food, so tonight we'll let out some of his blood."

"What do you mean, let his blood out?" Meng said with a laugh. "I'll talk to him tomorrow. I'll tell him I ate some of his potatoes when I came out to dig up badgers. It's not like we're yanking out his teeth."

Ying'er and Lanlan went over to a hollow. It wasn't far, but the ground was uneven, so it took a while to grope their way out of the riverbed in the moonlight. Knowing it wasn't late, Ying'er nonetheless felt they'd been out a long time. Being away from the sound of Mengzi digging, it seemed to her as if she were tumbling headlong into a lonely cavern, although the pumps at White Tiger Pass were faintly audible. She sensed Lanlan gripping her hand, out of fear, she knew, so she started singing softly. A few tunes later they were in Big Head's plot. It had once been a graveyard, so the soil was fertile and the potato vines gave off a rich oily sheen at night, seemingly dripping in green liquid. After fingering some of the thicker vines, they started to dig. After they'd dug up a dozen or more potatoes, they smoothed the dirt over. "My first time as a thief," Ying'er said with an embarrassed laugh. "My heart's pounding like a fawn."

"You call this stealing? Didn't you hear what Pa said? Big Head got his share of riches after gold was found at White Tiger Pass."

"Is that so? Well, Huilanzi has had her eye on my camel-hair coat, so I'll give it to her to make up for these potatoes."

"Don't be serious. It's just a few potatoes."

"If you take a needle without permission, that's stealing," Ying'er persisted.

Lanlan swallowed a response while reproaching herself: Aren't you doing something good? There are big hearts and small ones, but not big good deeds and small ones and not big vices and small ones. You've failed in your practice of self-cultivation.

"I remember once as a kid, someone came to sell buttons and thread to the production team. I managed to sneak off with one extra spool and I was so happy I was still smiling when I got home. My grandma grinned and said to me, 'Ying'er, is it possible to die of poverty?' I was so ashamed. Since then I've not taken anything from anyone, not even a needle, not till these potatoes. Well, Huilanzi, consider this a trade. I'll give you my camel hair coat, and you'll be happy." Ying'er smiled when she finished.

Lanlan made a sling out of her jacket for the potatoes and thought that maybe people are born with either a kind heart or an evil one. Ying'er was born into the same mundane world as she, but she was exquisite and spotless, as if nothing filthy could stick to her. She seemed to have been born that way. But after a moment of self-reflection, Lanlan changed her mind. In her unenlightened past, she was happy to come out ahead a little and upset if she lost out, even on something small. Now, she was on the path to doing good, wasn't she? She reminded herself that during her daily meditative lessons, she made vows to improve the lives of the masses. But, what could she say about what she was doing now? She wouldn't have considered taking the potatoes stealing if Ying'er hadn't said something. They were neighbors, so what was the big deal if they ate a few of their potatoes? Back when she was little, she and Huaqiu were always digging up the production team's soybean seeds to roast and eat. No one ever thought they were thieves.

With their jacket lapels filled with potatoes, they left the hollow, walked across the riverbank, and headed toward the flickering lantern light. Warmed by the exertion, Ying'er began to think about her baby, wondering if he was hungry. The thought of her mother-in-law's doting affection for the boy and the convenience of powdered milk put her mind at ease.

Mengzi worked hard and fast, and soon he was out of sight, accompanied by faint, eerie light. Laoshun was huffing and puffing, as if he were the one who had been strained by the heavy work. When the two old men dragged out another load of dirt, Ying'er detected an odor unique to a strange animal and her nose itched before she sneezed. Lanlan quickly handed her the coat Ying'er had returned earlier.

"Hurry," Laoshun said. "My empty stomach is crying for help."

"Now that you mention it, I'm hungry too," Lanlan said.

"A wind blows and you think it's going rain," Ying'er chided while taking the flashlight from her father-in-law. She built a pyramid with large dirt clods, leaving an opening at the bottom, and then picked up some twigs and branches, lit them, and stuck them through the opening. Snaking flames merrily leaped out through the cracks between clods. Soon the dirt turned red from the heat, a transparent redness in the dark night. Shawan had good soil, easy to light and burn. Lanlan lowered potatoes in through the top before smacking the pyramid flat with a shovel. What a shame. Ying'er was sorry to see the brilliant tower go. Pretty things are only good to look at; they are ruined once you put them to use. Everything was like that, though, as they say, cooking a crane and burning a lute.

"The animal—it's blocked the hole." Mengzi said, breathing hard.

"Smash it through. Dig in the soft spot. It just blocked it, so the dirt has to be soft." Meng said.

"I know, I know."

They were hauling the canvas out more slowly, a sign that Mengzi was finding the digging increasingly hard. Ying'er could almost see the hog badgers scurrying and frantically digging deeper, for their lives depended on it. Using their front paws as pickaxes and hind paws as shovels, they dug and moved dirt out of the way, their stumpy, powerful paws moving swiftly, kicking up masses of dirt to block the path behind them. The Angel of Death was pressing in. It had a sturdy pickaxe and a fast shovel, superior to their inbred instinct to flee and their dull paws. Could they outrun the Angel of Death? They could be strong, but their energy would run out at some point, and the relentless shovel behind would catch up to deal them a fatal blow. Poor hog badgers, Ying'er lamented, while her thoughts shifted to death. People were not that much different from these animals, for no matter how you schemed and strove, the Angel of Death continued to press ahead and descend on you like the dark night. You would understand, at the last moment of your life, that all your efforts were in vain; it was a hopeless race. Human endeavor seemed insignificant when confronted by the omnipotent law of nature.

Ying'er sighed, puzzled by her thoughts. Since Hantou's death, thoughts like that constantly flitted through her mind, like shadows.

Lanlan pushed the dirt apart with a stick to retrieve the potatoes, whose thick fragrance spread immediately. It was the unique burnt aroma that can only come from potatoes roasted in an earthen kiln. The skins were scorched yellow and gave off a hollow, crisp sound when you thumped them. It made you drool. Lanlan picked up a handful of grass to brush off the dirt before summoning everyone.

Meng tossed down the rope in his hand and shouted into the hole, "Time to eat!"

Mengzi came out with the lantern, drenched in sweat. "Those crafty buggers are really smart. I keep digging, so do they. But it won't take long now. I've reached their lair, and they won't last a few more feet, no matter how powerful they are."

They brushed dirt off their hands and started in on the potatoes, skin and all. It was thoroughly enjoyable. There are many ways to cook a potato, but roasting is better than all others, while roasting in a kiln raises it to an even higher level. The earthen kiln produces a unique flavor that no metal stove or oven, or any other method, can match. The "art" of eating a potato like this is to keep the skin on; just brush the dirt off with grass before biting into it. The crispy yellow skin has enough potato meat attached to make for a great taste. Meng was blowing hard, scalded by a hot potato, but his mouth never stopped moving, and he wolfed down several in no time.

Ying'er liked the taste of roasted potato, but not the way they ate it. She could not bring herself to swallow the dirt-speckled skin, so she peeled it under the lantern light. Before she'd finished peeling one, more than a dozen potatoes had disappeared into the stomachs of the others.

"That was one of the five grains." Meng clapped his hands and thumped his belly as he said, "I'll enjoy the sixth before we start again." He took out his pipe and was soon puffing contentedly.

6

"Get ready!" Mengzi shouted a while after he went back down. "I see them. Three of them."

Meng Baye told Lanlan to shine the flashlight into the hole. Laoshun waited with a raised club, while Meng got his musket ready. "Give them a few jabs with your shovel and hurry back out," Meng said to Mengzi, who grunted a response, accompanied by ear-piercing shrieks from the animals.

"Out of my way!" Mengzi yelled as he backed out.

A dark shadow flew out just as he cleared the opening. An experienced hawk flyer, Laoshun had sharp eyes and a good aim; he brought his club down and the shadow tumbled to the ground. Mengzi followed up with his shovel, hitting it so hard that the animal screamed in agony.

"There goes one," Lanlan shouted amid the commotion. "It's getting away." With a shout, Meng Baye took a few strides before firing into the dark night at a spot where the noise came from. "Got it. Don't worry about it now." Sure enough, they heard shrieks from below the cliff.

"What about the third one?" Meng panted heavily.

"It's long gone," Meng said. "The two that got out are big ones, the small one ran off."

Lanlan stuck her tongue out. No sooner had she noticed a dark shadow leaping out than it had disappeared before her eyes. How amazing that Meng Baye had seen it coming, and even more amazing was the shot that took it down. It had stopped shrieking now.

The one on the ground had also stopped moving. Ying'er went up to shine the lantern on it, her breath taken away by the horrific sight. The fangs were exposed, its lower and upper teeth intermeshed, a hideous look that showed its refusal to die. Mengzi took the flashlight down the cliff to pick up the hog badger that had rolled into the river. "You're a crack shoot, Baye. It took the buckshot in the chest."

Ying'er shuddered.

She was still feeling uneasy when they returned home. She'd been a chubby girl, and recalled how her grandma had liked to pat her on the bottom and call her a little badger. Now two real badgers were lying on the floor, stone-cold dead. The excitement over the new experience was gone, replaced by a heavy sense of compassion. How pitiful they'd been, trapped in their own burrow. Her heart ached when she imagined them frantically digging dirt to escape death.

Meng cut off a paw and handed it to Ying'er. "Dry this, make a hole in it with a heated rod, and string a rope through it for the baby to wear around his neck. It will bring him good luck and keep him healthy."

The paw looked like a baby's hand, a sight that unnerved Ying'er, but she accepted it once she heard of its protective power.

Laoshun started scraping the bristles. The innards were filled with dead worms and bugs, so he tossed them away. He scraped at the skin, with Meng holding it taut. Badgers stored their fat right on the skin, unlike other animals. As Laoshun scraped away, the basin slowly turned a ghostly white; his wife boiled the fat into a liquid, which she bottled. Meng Baye reminded her to avoid water, or the contents would be ruined. Pure badger fat will keep forever. Meng did a quick calculation based on market rate, and came up with several hundred. A few more times like this would give Mengzi a wife.

"This is tough. I'm not doing it again." Mengzi said.

His mother was all smiles as she chided him, "You won't do it? Then you'll be hauling donkey droppings for a living."

Laoshun was bent at the waist, puffing loudly, his forehead beaded in sweat. He scraped and wiped the knife blade against the rim of the pot each time, sending a bead rolling into the boiling liquid. "Keep the meat." He wiped off his sweat and said, "It smells like wet dirt, but tastes great cooked. A good cure for stomach chills."

"It does taste good, but I'm not eating it," Lanlan said, to which Ying'er agreed. "If I did, badger fat would show up on my belly."

"Besides, they eat bugs, the filthy things."

"They like bugs the way I like rabbit meat. What's filthy about that?"

Laoshun huffed. "All the more for me if you don't want any. My ribs are like a washboard, and I can't wait to see fat show up on my belly."

Chapter Six

Thunder crashes at Jiayu Pass
Rain falls on Yellow River banks

1

Lanlan went to Shaman Qi's house to learn how to "Slay the Red Dragon."

It was a useful thing to know. Once a woman mastered the technique, she would never again have to endure a menstrual period. Lanlan had heard that monthly menstruation was an impediment to self-cultivation; whatever spiritual progress she managed to accomplish would be lost when her period came, which was why a woman needed to slay the red dragon before starting on her spiritual practice. It was an easy enough method: maintain energy at the spot between the breasts, keep the mind in its place and the soul from wandering, and over time the qi will solidify and the red dragon can be slayed. She had not recovered completely from a miscarriage, partly because she was in an emotional funk and partly because she had to work in the field, so the spotting never stopped. She had tried a few medicinal potions, but they had done nothing to improve the situation, and she did not have money to try other cures. Then her mother told her that Fengxiang had suffered the same affliction and had been cured by the spiritual practice. Since it cost nothing, why not give it a try, Lanlan thought.

She enjoyed practicing every day and never tired of it. The Vajravārāhī was important to her, a support for her lonely, helpless heart.

The deaths of her daughter and brother were constant reminders of the fact that she too would die one day. She felt a colossal void every time she thought about death. Generations died, fading into the void and left no trace behind. She did not know if they had fallen into an unfathomable black hole on their own or if they had disintegrated and dissolved into the void. She shuddered when she thought she would disappear from the world like dissipating smoke until nothing was left of her.

Was it really true that death was like dousing a lamp? Would it be extinguished for all time?

An extinguished lamp was not necessarily a bad thing, because it could always be lit again. But who would restore the light for her long-suffering brother and her daughter? Who?

As tears coursed down her cheeks, Lanlan was choked with sobs. She asked herself the question over and over, and silence was her only response, after which she stubbornly followed up with more questions. The black hole called death terrified her. She wondered if it contained acid that would dissolve bones, flesh and everything else, eventually liquefying and returning her to the colossal black hole.

Millions of lives had entered the black hole, but it remained so capacious that no sound emerged. The bottomless cave in *Journey to the West* actually had a bottom, but death seemed like a true bottomless pit.

Lanlan had no answer, nor did anyone else. The Vajravārāhī smiled in the time and space of her fate, telling Lanlan that the black hole was not a bottomless pit, but a tube of cycles, one end called birth and the other death. The current of life flowed through the tube, sometimes dead and sometimes alive; life was death and death was life, as the water of life continued to flow on and on.

Your daughter, Yindi, still flowed in the tube, merging with countless water molecules, sometimes under this name and sometimes taking another, sometimes entering this vessel and sometimes going into that little pond. "Yindi" was a temporary name used when she flowed in your vessel.

Was that true?

Yes, and so was Hantou. One day, when their befuddled natural instincts were awakened, they would burst out of the tube. There was only one way to be reunited with one's natural instincts, and that was to practice asceticism.

Which was why Lanlan started her spiritual practice, meditating in the lotus position, calming her mind and regulating her breathing, sitting upright and letting her thoughts roam far, reining in her mind, envisioning the Buddha's image, and reciting the incantation.

Ying'er had to laugh.

She laughed several times, but then stopped when she realized that Lanlan was serious. When Lanlan sat down to meditate, she became the Vajravārāhī in a thangka painting, and Ying'er often found it difficult to see her so serene, so dispassionate. Lanlan practiced four times a day, during each session she sat silently envisioning herself as a deity. By contrast, Lanlan's mother was much less disciplined in her devotional practice, which consisted simply of burning incense, kowtowing, and making sacrificial offerings.

Ying'er did not understand how Lanlan had undergone such a significant transformation; she could not know that Lanlan was a different person after experiencing death several times. She was now on a unique quest after coming out of purgatory, where her soul was tested by fire.

2

One day Bai Fu came to take Lanlan back home with him. He started out with gentle cajoling before switching to harsh language, but she was swayed by neither.

"People make mistakes." Bai Fu said. "I was wrong, and more than once, but never again. Can't you forgive me one more time?"

With her eyes half-shut, Lanlan sat as motionless as a clay figurine and did not respond, so he pressed on.

"We're all just muddling through life, so there's no need to take things so seriously. I won't let anything stop me on this. I'll be okay if you do what I want; if not, whether it's with a knife or a gun, there's nothing I won't do. Worst case, I'll get my hands on some explosives and end it all."

Lanlan got up, stretched, and called in a drawn-out voice, "Ma— I'm going for my seven-day meditation." She headed out to Vajravārāhī Cave, leaving Bai Fu behind to gnash his teeth, "Go on, then. Let's see you go all the way up to the sky." He went into Ying'er's room and said to his sister, "Ma told me to tell you this: if that slut does what we want, you'll be okay. But if she's hard-hearted enough to put a black mark on our parents' family, then you need to pack up and come home with me. No matter what everyone thinks, this was a marriage swap, and I don't believe we can't rein her in."

"Go home and tell Ma not to involve me in your marriage problems," Ying'er said lightly. "Hantou's gone, but I have a baby. I'm part of the Chen family when I'm alive and I'll be a Chen ghost when I'm dead. But it's okay with me if you want to take my dead body back with you."

"Don't threaten me. You're Ma's daughter, she carried you for nine months. You didn't pop out of a rock or a hollow. How dare you ignore her wishes!"

"Go home and tell Ma I've died once already. Can't she let me live in peace?" Ying'er was getting emotional. "You take care of your problems and leave me out of it."

"Actually, I know you're suffering." Bai Fu relented when he saw her tears. "But, you're still young and you need to plan for your future. Don't be stubborn. What Ma says is for your own good."

"I know what's in my heart and I know how to live my life. All I'm asking is for all of you not to push me too hard. Let me live in peace." She dried her tears.

"I won't push you, but I can't say about Ma. She flies into a rage every time she mentions that slut; she'd tear her to pieces if she could. If she insists on going her own way, then you have to do what Ma wants."

"Go tell Ma if she really considers me her daughter, then she should leave me to live my life," Ying'er said after a prolonged silence. "Don't mix the two marriages again. All right?"

"What two marriages? It's only been one from the beginning. Would you be here if she hadn't come to our house? A swap marriage looks like two on the surface, but it's actually just one."

"So, does that mean I can't even be a widow?" Ying'er shed and dried more tears. "I've always done what Ma wanted, but this time I'll have to defy her wishes. Go tell her not to torment me and to let me live in peace."

"All right." Bai Fu choked up as he looked at his sister. "I'll go tell her—I'll become a bachelor again if it comes to that. It's no big deal, really." He rubbed his face and got a handful of tears.

Her mother-in-law heard some of the conversation. By getting down on her knees and pressing her eye up against the cat door between the two rooms, she got a pretty good sense of what was going on. Her face turned increasingly pale as she listened, and soon her eyes were moist over thoughts of her dead son.

"She's getting ideas," she whispered tearfully, surprising herself when the words were out. She had heard Ying'er firmly reject her mother's plan, so why did she feel that her daughter-in-law had different thoughts about her future? Maybe she too was thinking that she had to go home because Lanlan came back.

"What's wrong?" Laoshun asked.

"Bai Fu wants Ying'er to go home."

"Is she going?"

"She told him no, but it's not up to her, is it? Everyone knows this was a swap, and now Hantou is gone. But even if he were still around, they'd have to bring their daughter home when ours returned. That's how it works. Besides, Hantou—" She was sobbing so hard she couldn't finish.

"Stop acting like a little donkey scared by its own fart, will you?" Laoshun frowned. "She didn't say she'd go home, did she? You cut firewood on the mountain you're on."

"It's not easy dealing with his family. Lanlan's come home, and they can't take the loss of face." She dried her tears.

"Then tell Lanlan to go home with him."

"Go home? You old fool, you'd be pushing her straight into a fire pit. When she came back this time, there were bruises all over her body."

"Every couple fights," Laoshun said snidely. "When we were first married, I nearly kicked the life out of you. Have you forgotten? Everyone makes mistakes. It'll be all right once he changes."

"Changes? He'll beat your daughter to death if you keep giving him chances to change. You're a black-hearted man, there's nothing good in you. You didn't carry her for nine months, so you don't care if she lives or dies. Is that it?"

Laoshun spat in rage; it was all he could do to stop from slapping that sallow face.

"What's going on?" Ying'er came in when she heard the commotion. "Are you fighting again? Can't we have a little peace?"

"I know it's hard on you, Ying'er," Laoshun said. Everyone has parents, after all. I won't be upset if you want to go back."

"What are you saying?" She realized what they were fighting over. "They're them and I'm me? Besides, I have my baby."

"She's right," his wife fumed. "You black-hearted old devil. What do we live for? Isn't it to have a son to give us a grandson? You don't know how to make friends."

"All right, okay." Laoshun laughed. "I admit I'm no good at making friends." He turned to Ying'er. "She's afraid you'll leave, so she takes it out on me."

"Who's leaving. They can say what they want." Ying'er smirked before adding meaningfully. "Me, I'm staying even if you kick me out." She turned and walked out.

Laoshun's wife exhaled, as if reassured. After a while she said, "She's still in her twenties, too young to remain a widow. But what can I say? Big Head's mother was a widow in her twenties, and it looks like she made it through."

"Would you stay a widow?" Laoshun blurted out, having lost his temper. "You keep talking about being a widow. Would you stay a widow if I died?"

Rendered speechless, she blinked, but managed to spit out her words after a moment. "Who do you think you are? What makes you think I'd have any reason to remain your widow? I can't wait for you to die, actually. You haven't done enough good for me to remain your widow."

"Of course," he said with a grin. "So stop all this widow talk. It doesn't sound good. You sound like the King of Hell every time you mention it."

Now she knew what he was getting at. Wanting to snap back,

something else occurred to her and she grinned too. "I wonder what you're cooking up in that black heart of yours, since you don't want her to be a widow. I was hoping to trade in my donkey halter for a new head scarf."

"Donkey Halter" was a nickname given to Yue'er's mother. One night, after sending her daughter-in-law to cover her night shift guarding water, she slept in the young woman's room. Around midnight Yue'er's father sneaked into the bed, stuffed a new red head scarf into her hands, and had a good time with her. "Ah, my son has it so much better. My old lady's been an old donkey halter for some time." When he woke up in the morning and saw his wife in a red head scarf sweeping the yard, he asked, "Old hag, where did you get that scarf?" "I traded my donkey halter for it," she said loudly.

Laoshun frowned and shook his head. "Don't joke about something like that." But then he couldn't keep from laughing. "You have a dirty mind."

She felt so much better after joking with him. When Bai Fu left, she kneaded some dough and fried up several flatbreads for Ying'er.

But she spent the rest of the night thinking and getting increasingly restless, until she was wide awake. Experience told her that Ying'er's mother would not drop the subject so easily, that she would surely create an incident, and Ying'er would never be able to stand up to her. A broken bone sticks inward; she was after all the woman from whose belly she emerged. No matter how she looked at it, wanting a woman in her twenties to remain a widow forever was unreasonable. But she did not want Ying'er to leave. She tossed and turned, like flipping a flatbread in the pan, until she hit upon a solution. "As they say, never leave night soil in someone else's field." She nudged her husband. "I've thought about it all night. There aren't many girls like Ying'er, and the Bai family will raise a stink at some point. She can't be a widow forever, so can we—like some others have done—get the younger brother to marry his widowed sister-in-law?"

"Go to sleep." Laoshun said crossly. "Remember, you cut firewood on the mountain you're on. Why must you chatter away so late at night?'

She quieted down, but not for long. Soon she was poking him. "I think that's the only way to keep Ying'er around."

He was already snoring by then.

"Think about it." She poked him again. "Now that Lanlan is back home, they'll raise a fuss. Since it was a swap marriage, Ying'er will take the baby with her, leaving Hantou with nothing."

Finally, Laoshun woke up. He stared into the darkness. "Who? Lingguan?"

"No, he's too young. Mengzi."

"Nonsense. Shaman Qi has already made that match. The girl's family has agreed, and they're eager for them to be engaged. I'm an honest man, I can't go back on my word, or people would call me a liar."

Again, she went quiet for a while before saying, "No problem. They don't know everything Mengzi's done, so we can get someone to talk about him, and they'll change their mind."

"People would rather tear down ten temples than break up a marriage. Who would do such an immoral thing?"

"It's a long way from being a marriage yet. We'll find someone to tip them off. They'll be the ones to say no first, Shaman Qi won't be angry at us, and we turn down the proposal."

Laoshun mulled it over. He had to agree that what she said made sense; they could save themselves a big stack of money, if nothing else.

3

Laoshun went to White Tiger Pass early the next morning and brought Mao Dan back to ask him to spoil Mengzi's marriage prospect.

Mao Dan chuckled, baring his yellow teeth. "I'm the man for the job. I don't have to mention anything but his affair with Shuangfu's wife."

"Don't go that far." Laoshun frowned. "I don't want everyone to know about that. Can't you find something else?"

"Sure, all right. I don't want to ruin his reputation. He's still young and will never get a woman if he has a bad name. So I won't talk about him. I'll focus on the parents. I'll say, 'You're sending your daughter to hell. I focus on the father—he's not a sleeping dog, you know. He's been frisky with too many women, including his daughter-in-law and sister-in-law, a real womanizer. He's done everything you can think of. A real old donkey.' How's that?"

"How dare you ridicule me like that? That's no good." Laoshun gave him a rabbit chop and then pointed to his wife. "How about her?"

"Okay, she'll do too," Mao Dan said. "I'll tell them, 'If you want to marry your daughter into that family, you'd better send her to the Shaolin Temple first to learn some martial arts skills and turn her into a tiger-slaying hero like Wu Song. Why? The mother-in-law is a tigress, ill-tempered, a real mess. The filth on her clothes makes a noise when she bumps into the door and she won't even wring her rags dry. Their house is such a pig sty it could collapse under the mountain of filth and leftover food.' How's that?"

"I'm okay with that," Mengzi's mother replied with a chuckle. "You can make me sound as bad as you want, just kill the agreement."

Laoshun chortled with pleasure. "How did you know so much about her, Mao Dan? You're so good at sketching this old hag you could be a painter."

"That's right." His wife was smiling too. "I didn't expect you to know so much about us. You've seen the old thief's true colors, if nothing else. If I'd heard some of this when I was young, I'd have become a nun instead of marrying into the Chen family."

"Want me to put the donkey halter incident on him too?" Mao Dan said with a smug laugh.

"Absolutely." Laoshun's wife roared laughing." She turned to her husband, who stared wide-eyed, but was laughing despite himself. "Now you'll have to get me a red head scarf to make the story real."

"Mao Dan, you should lose your head." Laoshun managed to stop laughing. "Say all the bad things about her you want, but no nasty talk about me. A few years back, after Fengxiang ducked under my blanket while trying to escape the people from family planning, the story spread like wildfire. When people mention Mengzi, they say, 'Dragons beget dragons, phoenixes beget phoenixes, and rats' offspring are only good at making holes.' That's not me, but the rumor would spread like the wind if you made me look that bad."

"I forgot all about that one," Mao Dan said. "Can I use it? It's not slander, you know. There were people who saw everything. You did it right in front of everyone, bedding someone else's wife. Only Papa Shun could have done something like that."

Laoshun jumped down off the kang and pushed Mao Dan down to spank him with the sole of his shoe. "This is just to clear your memory, so you'll know what to say and what not. I'll pay you thirty yuan for your effort if it's done right; if not, I'll, I'll break your leg."

"I get it." Mao Dan stopped laughing. "It's like cracking open a door to let something in, saying enough to feed their imagination without spilling the details."

"Now you've got it," Laoshun said.

Mengzi's mother brought out a plate of flatbreads for Mao Dan.

After asking where to go, he gave them a wink and walked off.

4

Ying'er's heart sank when Bai Fu showed up. He reminded her of the swap marriage, a reality that had become blurred. She knew her mother well; a prideful woman, she had never admitted defeat verbally or mentally. Lanlan coming back to her parents' home would be such a loss of face to Ying'er's mother that revenge was a sure-fire reaction. She had one option, and that was to bring her daughter home, with the baby. That would be a hugely damaging rebuke to Ying'er's in-laws.

Everything in her life had renewed meaning whenever she looked at the baby. She knew that what she hoped for was more like wishful thinking, but it was still better than having nothing to look forward to. Living with her in-laws was stifling, except for the many reminders of the past, which always brought dizzying happiness. It was in this room where they'd spent their first night. An unforgettable night! She'd responded urgently but mechanically to his clumsy kisses. Every spot in this room was infused with a sense of exhilaration, the brief moment of rapture, the seamless understanding between their souls, and unspoken longings. This was the most beautiful corner of her soul, the paradise she would hate to leave. Every time the door latch stirred in the wind at night, she felt he was coming in. See him tiptoe up and look around; he holds his breath, his face is flushed, as he gently nudges the door open; he enters, carrying a chill like moonlight, and rubs the dirt off his feet; he comes up to the bed. My Lingguan. Ying'er moaned in agony and joy, followed by tears that streamed down her face.

The little room, her own little room.

Everything in the room was familiar and sweet, as scenes crystalized in front of her eyes, seemingly smiling at her; his naked body, their intertwined limbs, their whispered lovers' talk. When they talked, he would raise the blanket and duck under with his arms around her, murmuring in her ear, "Not so loud. They can hear everything through the cat door."

"I don't care," she said. But they kept their voices low, except for the few moments when they could not stop the moans escaping their lips. Later, when she thought back, Ying'er found the silence enchanting— smiling silently, moving silently, getting aroused silently, heart racing silently and wildly. That was the allure of a tryst. Once he murmured to her, "A concubine's better than a wife, and sleeping with someone else' wife is better than a concubine, but desiring someone else's wife and not having her is the best." She bit his ear viciously, "You rascal. You slept with someone's else's wife, but now that's not good enough."

All that had taken place in this room.

Now her mother wanted her to return to a home where they fought all day. Ying'er hated the idea.

Everything she loved was here—the little room and the backyard, where she'd given him the first hint of love, to which he'd reacted by fleeing. It amused her each time she thought about it. There was also Xihupo, an otherworldly realm of pleasure for her, every recollection of which made her want to sing a folk tune: "A white peony falls into the river/quickly scoop it up or it will flow away. You must have a good time in this world/quickly have some fun or you'll soon be old. My beloved, you must have a good time/don't act like a white peony that has fallen into the river. I quickly scoop it up, but I'm not fast enough, and you slip away. Then there's the magical world of the desert. Lingguan, do you recall the night we all went out to gather desert rice? Remember the desolate, lonely star? You held me to ward off the bone-chilling air, but it was useless. It was a cold night, but also the most fervent in my life. Do you know that, *Yuanjia*?

She would hate to leave all this behind.

Ying'er knew fully well that her mother did not want her to stay where she was. She would not give up a daughter-in-law she had traded with her own little treasure of a girl and let her son be a bachelor again. Mother, why won't you leave me alone for a while? I want to live out my life in peace and quiet, desiring nothing but the baby; we would live a quiet life, waiting for the hard-hearted man to return. I'll be all right whether he returns or not; there's something to look forward to in life, and that is better than nothing. Mother, you've been strong-willed all your life, but you have nothing to look forward to. Why won't you let me have something to look forward to? Mother.

Ying'er cried, then she was lost in thought, unaware of time passing, until it was early afternoon. Since her mother-in-law had fried some flatbreads, she did not have to make lunch, giving her a rare moment of rest.

She had barely started her lunch when Yue'er came. The girl had learned all the tunes, but had yet to convey the full flavor, though at least she got the melodies right. Ying'er forced herself to concentrate on the tunes and taught Yue'er a few more *hua'er ling* tunes—the "Stable" tune, the "Peony" tune, and "Pony" tune. Yue'er wrote down every one.

After a while, Ying'er was in no mood to continue. Yue'er could tell she had a lot on her mind, but did not ask, afraid she might evoke sad memories. She did not know what to do next, when Mengzi's mother called out to her, "Yue'er, come over here. I have a question for you."

The older woman whispered what she had discussed with her husband the night before, asking Yue'er to sound Ying'er out.

"Do you think she'll agree?" Yue'er was bemused.

Mengzi's mother curled her lip. "Why wouldn't she? Mengzi is still a virgin."

Yue'er strained not to laugh or expose Mengzi's false front of being a virgin. "Would he agree?"

"Why wouldn't he? Besides, it's not up to him. We have to come up with piles of money for him to get married. If he could find one, I'd give him a virgin for a wife."

Yue'er nodded and went back to Ying'er's room. She felt like laughing as she tried to sound Ying'er out, but for some reason she simply could not bring herself to start.

She failed to get a clue to Ying'er's reaction, before she left.

5

Mao Dan swaggered into the yard that afternoon, a sign to Laoshun that it was done.

Sure enough, before he even asked, Mao Dan's spittle was flying. "Ha, that old hag was scared witless. Her face turned pale before I finished. She was yelping and beads of sweat rolled down her forehead—"

"What did you tell her?" Laoshun cut him off.

Mao Dan merely raised an eyebrow and said, "What do you think, should I have run down your son?"

"Of course not." Mengzi's mother replied. "He's still young."

"You're right. I thought about making him look terrible, but was afraid no one would want to marry him, so I put most of the burden on you two."

"She deserved it. This old hag has gossiped about others all her life, now you've gossiped about her. It's payback time."

"That's what I thought." Mao Dan tucked in his neck and sucked in cold air. "But then I told myself that smearing Auntie's name wasn't fair. I'm like an upright judge who doesn't play favorites. I needed to be fair and slander you both, since you're sort of like the dirt on the heel that needs a few serious scrapings."

"Absolutely." Mengzi's mother laughed.

"What did you say? Tell me," Laoshun pressed.

Mao Dan picked at his nails, wrinkled his nose, and glared, putting on airs. "*Qinjia*, I said—that's what I called her—ha ha, you're sending your girl to a good family. The father-in-law is a good man who knows to treat people well; the mother-in-law is even better, and she's giving her son a wife."

"How could you say that?" Mengzi's mother was clearly unhappy.

"Shut up and let him talk." Laoshun glared at her.

"The old hag's brows were dancing when she heard me. She wanted to go ahead with the engagement immediately and send the girl over after New Year's. So, I said, 'Sure, the sooner the better. The old couple's funny. Once, when the old lady went to water the field, their daughter-in-law stayed home with a headache. Well, the old man saw the young woman alone at home, went out and bought a head scarf—'"

They laughed. "Shit. How could you put that on me?"

"So, I said, 'the old woman is very sharp, you know. A single glance could tell her what her husband had in mind, so she went home and told their daughter-in-law to water the field while she lay down on the kang. Soon the old man returned.' What are you laughing at? Stop laughing and listen. 'He got on the kang, gave her the scarf, and became a dirty old man. ' He said, 'My son has it so much better. My old lady has turned into a donkey's halter. ' The next morning the old woman put on her scarf to sweep the yard. Her old man asked, 'Hey, where did you get that scarf?' She said, 'I traded a donkey halter for it. ' Now don't you think that's a really decent father-in-law? See how well he treated his daughter-in-law. *Qinjia*, when your daughter is married to his son, she'll enjoy good food and drink, and she'll dress in red while her husband wears a green cuckold's hat. Isn't that wonderful?"

"What did she say?" The old couple was still laughing. But they managed to stop long enough to ask.

"What do you think? She was stunned. She said, 'With an old donkey like that, I won't marry my girl to that family if my head shrinks to the size of a clove of garlic.' She asked me what the old donkey was called, and I said he was called Chen Shun, Laoshun to everyone in the village."

"How could you do that to me, Mao Dan? I didn't do what you said."

"We sent him to ruin the prospect." His wife smiled. "What did she say?"

"She cursed Shaman Qi."

"Oh, no." Laoshun's wife stuck her tongue out. "You put the blame on her."

"That's easy." Laoshun said, "We'll give Shaman Qi all the gifts returned by the family. That should make up for it."

Laoshun took out thirty yuan and handed it to Mao Dan, who accepted the money and walked off with a grin.

The couple laughed happily now that they'd broken up the marriage without offending Shaman Qi.

They were still laughing when Ying'er walked in. "What did Yue'er say?"

"The girl's a chatterbox; one thought in her head comes out in ten phrases." Ying'er replied.

"What do you think?"

"Think about what?" She looked at her mother-in-law, not knowing what she was getting at. "It's better not to think too much or you'll get a headache."

"That's true. It's better to go with the flow," Mengzi's mother said.

"Right." Ying'er smiled as she took some flatbreads for Lanlan, who was still meditating.

She had no idea she herself had become a flatbread on a chopping board.

Chapter Seven

A donkey turns a flour mill in Jiulishan
A mouse is too weak to steal the millstone

1

Zhao San was talking loudly at the well, like a gruff butcher. He couldn't help it, because he was born and raised in a butcher's family, whose trade he himself had plied for over a decade. Newly found wealth did nothing to help shed his butcher's manners. It was clear he did not want to look like a butcher, and he did his best to act refined, but the essence of a butcher continued to ooze from his pores. There was nothing he could do about it; he was born to be a butcher, raised as a butcher, and acted like a butcher.

Shuangfu, on the other hand, was infused with cultured airs. Back in the old days, when he'd been so poor he couldn't afford a pair of pants, he was nothing but a country bumpkin. Later, he struck it rich and made it into the city, where he took on some urban airs. He gave a reserved nod while Zhao jabbered away. But no matter how reserved Shuangfu looked, Mengzi still found him repulsive. Having learned a bit of refinement, but only superficially, Shuangfu could not mask his disagreeable nature;

no matter how nicely he packaged his outward demeanor, he was rotten inside.

"Look how he swaggers." Huaqiu said. "He was just a pitted potato, but once he got some money he acted like he was a gold nugget. Have you heard how he panned more than enough gold recently to recover his original investment? From now on, if they find more gold it'll be pure profit. Let's buy a pit. What do you say?"

"How do we do that? You haven't got enough meat and bones on you to fill a platter. So where does the money come from?" That drew a sigh from his friend.

When they arrived at the water by the panning trough, Huaqiu went to bring over some of the leftover sand from Shuangfu's pits. Mengzi looked at the mountains through half-closed eyes; shrouded in gossamer fog, they seemed far away, but were near enough to reach within a few hours by camel or on foot. They were the Qilian Mountains, stretching over a thousand li, twisting and turning to create a narrow gorge. A path snaked along, flanked by mountains to the west and a desert to the east, the so-called Hexi Corridor. Mengzi did not care for the piss ant crap they were dealing with; all he wanted was to vent the noxious feeling building up inside. Wishing he could scream, he knew he'd be treated like a braying donkey if he did. Lacking the status required to scream, a poor man encroaches on others if he dares let out a few shouts.

"I won't stop you if you want to pan the leftover sand, Huaqiu, but don't you dare steal the newly dug sand," Mengzi heard Shuangfu say to his friend.

"I wish I could. I'd be lying if I told you I didn't want to." Huaqiu said. "I heard someone stole sand the other night and nearly made off with a few ounces of gold."

Zhao laughed, a true butcher's chortle, loud, coarse and obnoxious. "The thief was born to be poor. If he'd taken the sand, he'd have made a thousand, or at least eight hundred. But too bad for him. He wanted to be rich but that wasn't in the stars for him."

Mengzi could sense the insinuation in the man's words and wondered if they suspected him, since they were the only two who were panning leftover sand. To be sure, someone else could have done it, but not as easily as the two of them. His temper rose, for he hated having people say he was born to be poor. "From what you said, Zhao San, you were born to enjoy a good life." Mengzi just had to talk back. "If that's the case, then why do people say a butcher's son is just one more warm body?"

The grin on Zhao's face vanished, as he jerked his head up. He was not that close, but Mengzi could see the taut muscles on the man's face.

"What do you mean by that?" Zhao asked angrily.

"Nothing," Mengzi said listlessly.

Knowing he'd hit a sore spot, Mengzi chuckled silently, though it did not help him get over the butcher's hurtful words about his fate. It hadn't been a problem in the past, when he'd been too lazy to think, so long as he had had enough soupy millet to fill his stomach. But recently he'd wised up to the fact that poverty had become a dagger, pricking him now and then. Poverty was nothing when it only affected his chance for survival, for there was plenty of available food, like wild rabbit, pheasants, or desert rice. Once he ate his fill, he'd laze about, sunning himself without a care, oblivious to the weighty burden of being a man. He had to pay attention, however, when poverty impacted his dignity as a man. Granted, he'd only recently started to worry about dignity, but the thought took root the moment it entered his mind and reared its ugly head to jab him over and over.

Poverty didn't seem to bother his father, who was always saying, "I'm poor because I deserve to be." He'd been saying that all his life, and he said it with no qualms, seemingly happy to submit to the will of Heaven, content with his lot. He'd worry when confronted with hardships brought on by poverty, sucking in cold air, but he took the punishment calmly, rarely cursing his fate or blaming others. "I can take whatever Heaven doles out to me," was his mantra, and he used his calm acceptance as a weapon to challenge Heaven. Mengzi could sense his father's dignity when he accepted his lot, but he refused to follow his example. Unlike his father, he cursed Heaven when dealt with injustice, "Fuck you, Heaven!"

Mengzi did not believe in Zhao's idea about not being born to be rich. He refused to be taken in by the existence of Zhao Gongming, an ass-kisser to the rich, who tossed gold bars to every wealthy man he encountered. He wanted none of that. Staying at home didn't bring in any money, but he could always take a rabbit hawk out to catch rabbits and sell them in the city. He would have earned it, not received it from Old Man Zhao, the God of Wealth. Zhao San made his fortune by taking the lives of thousands of pigs, cows, and sheep. Mengzi did not believe that Heaven wanted Zhao San to take lives, but if he did, then that was more reason to curse Heaven.

Huaqiu carried over a sack of sand, panting as he laid it down. No longer interested in idle chat, Mengzi took out his pan, shoveled some sand in, and held it under the running water. The loose sand whirled in the pan before the water carried it off. Mengzi liked the feeling of stirring and rinsing sand, enjoying the fluid beauty of eddying sand that rippled outward, with no distinct pattern. The lines were washed off, replaced by new each time, never repeating itself. As it flowed away, the rocky remains knocked and banged against the pan. Mengzi picked up the rocks, wishing he could throw them at Zhao, but that was just a wish; he tossed them away. Poverty chills ambition and hair hangs long on a skinny horse. No one was to blame for his impoverished state, so he should not try to vent his anger on others.

A few specks of yellow were exposed. The yellow glint was what he'd been hoping to see, but for some strange reason, he was so disgusted that he flung the pan away; it arced in the air before dropping into the river.

"What's got into you?" Huaqiu asked unhappily.

Mengzi got out of the water lazily, lay down on the sand, and let out a long sigh as he closed his eyes. Huaqiu muttered away, but Mengzi ignored him. A long time passed before Mengzi got to his feet and barked at Huaqiu, "What's the point of eating someone's leftovers?"

"Go start your own pit if you can."

2

Once again, Mengzi agreed to go along with Huaqiu's scheme to steal sand. The idea was, they'd steal half a sack of newly dug sand and, if they managed to pan gold worth thousands, with that and some more they'd find a way to get their hands on, they could start their own pit.

Big Head set a new policy regarding the use of land. Anyone could start a pit as long as they coughed up five hundred yuan. It wasn't a lot, but it only allowed digging at White Tiger Pass, an area that had lain unspoiled for hundreds of years. Anyone who'd needed rich soil for hot peppers could have simply taken it. Now, under the new policy, it was no longer free. They'd heard that the city government wanted a piece of the action and that a new policy would be announced soon.

"The fee is only five hundred now, but who can say how much it'll be later?" Huaqiu said. "Five thousand? Fifty thousand? Hei—hei, whatever they say."

What right did Big Head have to do that? Mengzi thought. Just because he'd kissed the township head's ass enough to be the village chief?

But in all fairness, five hundred would be a bargain if they actually found gold. The problem was: five hundred only allowed you to dig a four-square-meter hole. You needed to hire diggers, who had to be fed and paid. The surface might look parched, but underground it was wet, like you get when you touch a loose woman; any minor disturbance to the soil sent water shooting out. For more than a thousand years, this had been the course for snow melt from the Qilian Mountains into the desert. When a reservoir was built upstream to dam the water, drying up the river above ground, water continued to flow below. It gurgled up if a pit was dug at the wrong spot, and a gold prospector would either be a drowned rat or would have to pump the water out. And smiling at the sales clerk in Liangzhou alone would not get you a pump. You cannot kill a man without a knife. Money talks.

Huaqiu's idea made sense.

That night Mengzi groped his way with a sack toward the Dasha River with Huaqiu. When they set out, the sky was studded with sparkling stars, as if laughing at them, but the stars were gone by the time they reached the river, where glaring electric lamps gave off haloes of light that seemed to bore into their heads. The pumps were drawing water, some sand boys were cursing each other, others were shouting drinking games, all of which created a buzz in their heads.

The world had gone mad.

To ward off thieves, a light had been hung on the highest spot, so bright it would blind a wasp, let alone a crawling man. Worse yet, a tent had sprung up nearby, big enough to sleep two or three people. Someone might be laying wait inside with a club.

Mengzi exhaled and nudged Huaqiu, who remained silent. Then they spotted several black spots leaping and hopping up to the tent. Mengzi saw they were dogs. When the sand boys had their meals, they were too lazy to wash their hands and left sand on the steamed rolls; they peeled off the sand-specked skin and tossed it away, attracting the dogs for free food.

"I've got an idea," Huaqiu said. "We'll dress up like dogs."

Before Mengzi understood what his friend meant, Huaqiu was gone and became part of the night, his departure amplifying the noises surrounding Mengzi. His head felt crammed with rumbling machinery. Somehow deflated, he felt himself under the control of a power that stopped him from accomplishing anything, even though he did not believe in fate.

A long time passed before Huaqiu rejoined him. They were hiding by a sand ridge that extended from one end of the desert into White Tiger Pass. It twisted and turned its way over, creating an unintended hiding place for a pair of thieves, though Mengzi did not feel as if this was stealing. It was odd. He felt guilty when sleeping with someone's wife or stealing objects, but his conscience was clear when he stole sand. In his view, the sand, like the sky and the earth, belonged to everyone. Shuangfu could dig up the sand because he had some lousy money, but he should not be allowed to keep it all for himself. What right did he have to monopolize? Because he's a fat-ass rich man?

"Put this on and we'll crawl over there. We'll look like dogs searching for food." Huaqiu handed him a dog skin. Mengzi burst out laughing, and yet he saw that no one paid the dogs any attention. "Your father is always calling you a natural born thief. He's right, obviously."

"So, you're not a thief? What do you call sleeping with someone's wife?" Huaqiu poked him. "We'll wait till after midnight, when most of them are asleep, before crawling over. Now they keep their eyes open and could easily spot us even if we're covered with the dog skins." When he finished, Huaqiu spread the skin over the ground and lay down. Mengzi followed suit and looked up at the sky, which, polluted by the electric lights, was not as clear and bright as usual.

"Life is really getting hard. Staying in the village is like being in prison, and getting a job in the city feels like being exiled to a corner of the world where everywhere you look is steel and cement and everything is cold, devoid of human contact. Tell me, how can we make something of our lives this way?"

"The world sure has changed. In the past, everyone got their share of hot soup, now some people die from eating too much, others starve to death. It's clear we can't go on like this. I just muddled through life, snoring as soon as my head touched the pillow. But that won't work anymore; the world refuses to let me live in ignorance, poking me here and pricking me there. It's not like being hit by a hammer, but the pinpricks aren't easy to take either. Sometimes I feel like jumping down a well when I think about how I'd lived my life so far." He jerked at the dog hair as he continued, "Look at our village. It remains in this tiny corner of the desert for who knows how long, doing nothing to provoke anyone. But that won't work anymore. It tries to stay out of trouble, but others won't let it be."

"I heard the city government is going to create small towns. Our county is going to work on it, so maybe we'll have city residency someday," Huaqiu said.

"Droves of people in the city are being laid off. What kind of shitty job would you get if you were a resident there?" Mengzi sneered before jumping to his feet and spitting out his words. "There's only one way to live like a decent human being, and that's to have money. A saltless meal is tasteless, a penniless man is like a ghost. Remember how Shuangfu was bullied when he was poor, and now that he's rich, even a stray dog wags its tail at him."

Huaqiu stood up, picked up his dog skin, and shook it. "That's right. I'm happy to be a dog if I can get a little money. Too bad I'm not a woman. If I was, I'd be long gone from here. Look at all those nice girls, pretty as a picture, they marry stupid men, who beat them like donkeys and spread them out like a blanket. They lose their looks within a few years, shrivel up like dry dog shit. So, what's the difference if they're being screwed by a stupid jerk or a rich guy? The lucky ones could make a bundle and swagger just like Shuangfu. Why stick around this shitty corner, like a bashful rose blooming in obscurity? It's pointless. It's not a beauty if no one admires it."

"People in the village would bitch if they heard what you just said." Mengzi said with a smile.

"They can curse all they want, but they'll be lapdogs once I have money."

"True. These days, people look down on the poor, but not prostitutes."

"Liangzhou residents laugh at both of them, but not at middle of the road people. A loafer like me is their preferred laughingstock."

The crowd on the riverbank thinned out as they bantered. Lights were out at some pits, the newly dug ones, while others were worked all night, with three shifts. Rocks from the pits were strewn everywhere, some piling up like hills, giving the riverbank an ugly, chaotic look.

The light over Shuangfu's sand pile was still on, but they'd be invisible by following the uneven terrain. With the dog skins over their backs and sacks in their hands, they made themselves smaller by crawling along lower spots.

A pungent, acrid odor hit Mengzi's nose as soon as he put the skin on. It was not completely tanned, he figured; there must have been some dried blood on it. He didn't let that bother him, though; you can't be picky if you're a dog. What Huaqiu had said sounded terrible, but it was the truth. In this day a man's just got to have money. If you can't afford a pair of pants, dignity is like the hair on your cock. He hoped something better would come his way this time, now that he was a dog. He'd have a few days to show off if he got some sand that yielded enough to start a pit.

Creeping like dogs, they headed for their destination. The once familiar terrain had been so badly disturbed that everything looked different, making their movements difficult. But they were in no hurry; they'd accomplish their goal if they got some sand before daybreak. It made no difference if they got there early or late, so long as they were not discovered. Mengzi had to agree that Huaqiu had a great idea. If no one looked carefully, from a distance, they were just like the other dogs. Once they got nearer, then the differences would be obvious. But the sand boys usually stayed clear of the dogs. A few days earlier, one of them had wanted some dog meat, but had been bitten instead and came down with rabies that landed him moaning in Liangzhou. The recollection had Mengzi worrying about sand boys throwing rocks at them. It was possible. He always threw rocks at dogs, stray or not, and it cheered him when he hit one. He had a feeling that a rock was flying at him, whizzing through the air, but when he looked up, he realized it was a just an illusion.

He hated the hanging bulb that swayed and sent out haloes of light. He would surely lose his mind at this rate. The noise was irritating, but tolerable. On the other hand, he was almost happy to have it around to mask the sound of his pounding heart, which must be filling up the desert. He couldn't help it. He had a bit of a history as a thief, but it was the same each time, just as his heart never stopped racing every time he slept with another man's wife. It was actually damned exciting. With all that had gone in recent years, his heart felt numb, well worn by worries, like the calloused soles of his feet. Only something unusual could excite him now. His father was always saying he was no different from a cow, except he could talk and had no tail. But it was hopeless; only novelty brought him excitement. Nothing had changed with the village, the desert, or the wind and sand, since the day he was born; he could not come up with anything new, and so, after working days on end, sleeping when he was tired and eating when he was hungry, he was like a donkey circling a millstone.

Around and around he went, but did not have the wherewithal to come up with something new. Stealing sand added excitement to his life. Mengzi shuddered, as a sense of vitality coursed through his mind.

He had no idea what time it was and didn't care. On second thought, it would spell trouble if there were watchful eyes on the sand pile, and now he wished it was at least midnight. His back was sore. He hadn't thought there was anything special about walking upright until now that he was a dog, walking on all fours. The ache was something he'd never experienced as a man. His back had been sore before, when he was on top of Shuangfu's wife, for instance, but that was accompanied by pleasure, while this was just soreness. No, there was also pain in other places. The rocky surface scraped his knees, which felt as if they were on fire, and must surely be bleeding. He heard Huaqiu panting hard amid the crisp rustle of their dog skins, expected since they weren't tanned. If not for the rumbling water pumps, the noise from the dog skins alone would have betrayed them. Mengzi felt like laughing. Would real dogs make that kind of noise when they searched for food?

They groped their way off the ridge and across a rock-strewn riverbank to be near the water. Dozens of working pumps introduced coolness to the formerly dry riverbank. They had to wade through the water to reach the sparkling sand, but this was no ordinary water. Mengzi reached out to touch it; its chill exploded inside him. Night air was cold to begin with, and they would likely get sick if they got into the icy water. But Huaqiu was already in, sucking in air like an old dog with a cold. Oh, fuck it. I'll freeze to death if I have to, Mengzi thought as he waded into the river. Every pore was shivering, contracting nonstop. Holding his breath, he found river rocks to steady himself, so he wouldn't slip and fall.

The fear of falling was compounded by the icy coldness rising from his soles, running crazily through his body and boring into his bone marrow, like a snake. It was unbearably cold. The noise of the pumps disappeared almost instantly, as the sound of running water filled the space around him, water demons laughing, fear crumpling his heart. Luckily, the river was not too wide, and he collapsed on the other bank when the terror spread from his heart to his legs. Huaqiu was cursing the water or somebody, he wasn't sure which.

After what felt like a very long time, Mengzi stuck his head out from under the dog skin to see if the area near the pits was devoid of onlookers, leaving only a few moving shadows. It must have been close to midnight by then. The sand boys on night guard shift were probably asleep, he thought, and he felt sleep sneaking up on him too. Mengzi yawned as he fought off the urge to turn the dog skin over and fall on it for a good night sleep.

They crawled, like two dogs, toward the pile of sand that seemed to smile at them. The rising pile cast enough shadows on one side that they were not exposed under the bright light. Mengzi's back felt as if it were about to break, which was, luckily, offset by the powerful allure of the sand pile. It did not feel as bad then.

Finally, they could smell the moist, newly dug sand. Look, there are even flickering gold specks. Huaqiu began shoveling sand into his bag, making a rustling noise like roaring floodwaters, amid the sound of Mengzi's racing heart. Strange. What happened to the rumble of the pumps? His heart was thumping so hard his chest hurt.

Mengzi opened his sack to shove in handfuls of sand. The wet sand scorched his hand like fire, a wonderful sensation, more titillating than screwing Shuangfu's wife the first time. He laughed merrily inside, feeling as if he'd fallen into an ocean of boundless happiness, where he swam freely, completely unaware of the shadows pressing up from behind. A net for snaring hawks silently came down, as impossible to fight off as the dark night.

3

Clubs rained down on him; dry and wet sounds erupted all around. It did not hurt, and he knew the dog skin blunted most of the hits. That was the advantage of an untanned dog skin, whose dried blood and stiff pelt worked in concert to form armor. Huaqiu, on the other hand, was screaming, hard to say if he was putting on an act or if the pain was truly unbearable. He sounded like a production team cow that had gone mad a few years back, as if the noise were flowing out from his chest, rather than his vocal cords, spewing in all directions. Mengzi wanted to stop him, afraid it would draw people from the village and, worst of all, his father, with his aging face. He hoped they'd let him go after the beating. Holding his breath to soften the pain from the blows, he reached up to check out the thing that had him caught. It was a net for snaring rabbit hawks, he could tell. He heard Beizhu's voice among the huffing and puffing club wielders. It could very well be the net that Beizhu had asked him to weave for him. He'd used it catch rabbit hawks many times, now it was being used on him. He found that funny.

"Beizhu! Are you planning to club me to death?" Mengzi heard Huaqiu yell.

The clubs went quiet. It had to be Beizhu. Mengzi stuck his head out from under the dog skin when Beizhu brought a light over to shine down on Huaqiu's bloody face. Mengzi was shocked by what he saw. "You'll have to pay with your life if you kill him, Beizhu."

Silence fell after that threat.

Several pairs of hands pulled and tugged to let the two of them out. Mengzi was grateful for his dog skin when he saw the damage to Huaqiu's face.

"Wow! We thought it was a human being," Mao Dan shrieked.

"I'm not a human being, I'm your Father," Huaqiu ranted.

"Don't be pigheaded and refuse to admit defeat, Huaqiu." Mao Dan spat at him. "Now that we have you, we might let you live, but you'll at least lose a layer of skin."

"You're an ass, Mao Dan." Mengzi said. "No, you're an ass-kisser. You lick the ass of anyone with money. Get out of my way. I'm going home. I'll start a tab on the beating I took and return it, with interest, one day when I have nothing to do."

"Don't even think about it," someone spoke up. "A thief has no rights."

Mengzi lost his sense of certainty when he saw it was someone he did not know. With Mao Dan and the others, he might be able to bluff his way out, but he didn't know what would work with a total stranger. I should just slip away, he thought, before flicking his hands behind him and kicking Mao Dan off him. He was far away by the time Mao Dan realized what had happened.

Huaqiu was yelling again, stopping Mengzi in his tracks, as he knew that running away was not what a friend did. "I'd die with him if that's what happened," he told himself before shouting, "I'll fight you to death if you don't stop beating him." He walked back to see Huaqiu slumped on the ground, where he kept kicking, knocking Mao Dan, who was holding his legs, from side to side. Obviously, he'd wanted to run too, but Mao Dan had caught him by the legs.

Several sand boys were running their way.

"What do we do with these two thieves, Mr. Chairman?" the stranger asked.

"What we always do." It was Shuangfu.

Enemies meeting on a narrow road, Mengzi thought. After what I did with his wife, now that he has me, he won't let me off easily.

Mao Dan and the others dragged and pushed Mengzi and Huaqiu up to the opening of a pit. A flashlight beam swept over them, blindingly harsh on the eyes. Mengzi figured it had to be Shuangfu, so he glowered at him. All was quiet around them. He could not see Shuangfu's face, but could sense the wounded anger in the man's eyes. He spat, and the flashlight went dark.

"They're dogs, they don't need to use those skins," an unfamiliar voice said, followed by an eruption of laughter. Mao Dan's laugh was loud and jarring. He and Mengzi got along well, so Mengzi was surprised to hear him laugh like that. He felt like slugging him. How could he be like that, Mengzi asked himself. Has he sold his conscience for money? His mood plunged when he remembered his circumstances; they were laughing at a pair of thieves.

Expecting Shuangfu to say something to embarrass him, Mengzi found it odd that he didn't say a word. Granted, the others had said what he'd want to say, and Mengzi could not shake the image of his glinting eyes. If Shuangfu had condemned him, Mengzi was prepared to return with the worst rebuke, including calling him a cuckold, to humiliate him. But Shuangfu was silent. A quiet Shuangfu was like the dark night spread over him; Shuangfu seemed to be everywhere, and Mengzi could not fight back, sort of a tiger trying to swallow the sky.

Mengzi was pushed up to the pit, still in the dark as to what Shuangfu meant by doing it the way they always did. A new way or an old one? His father had once told him that back when they panned gold in Qilian Mountains, any sand boy caught stealing gold would be buried alive. Mengzi was confident that Shuangfu would not be foolhardy enough to do that, though it was hard to say in a day and age when anything was possible. For those in the underworld, killing a man wasn't all that different from killing a chicken. He'd have begged for his life if it had been anyone else. A real man always adapts to circumstances; it was no big deal to admit a wrong. But this was Shuangfu, the almighty Shuangfu, whose grand house gate made Mengzi choke with resentment. In the past, whenever he screwed Shuangfu's wife, it was as if he were stabbing Shuangfu; admitting defeat would have to wait until their next lifetime.

Some sand boys tied the two of them up with practiced hands, which seemed to indicate that Shuangfu had set the rule.

"Are you really going to bury me alive, Shuangfu?" Huaqiu shouted. "If you do that, you'll have to keep my wife and raise my kids."

Shuangfu was quiet, while the sand boys laughed.

"How's this? I'll raise your kids if he doesn't want to." Mao Dan piped up. "I've been looking for someone to cook and do the dishes, but I must have your wife too."

Mengzi wished he could give that face a vicious kick. He fought to run at Mao Dan, but the sand boys held him back and threw him into the pit.

He fell into darkness, as a wind whizzed past his ears like a howling wolf. The protruding parts of the wooden framework sank their teeth into him; he felt like his body was on fire. I'm going to die. He had more thoughts to process before dying, but his head was crammed full of the darkness, the wind, and fear. Darkness rushed at him, pounding so hard his head hurt, a maw sucking in a fly. Shouts escaped from his throat. He did not want to scream, but his throat continued to release sounds that bounced against the bottom of the pit and came back up, pummeling his heart.

Something moved on his back, and everything went quiet. He realized that the rope had stopped him in mid fall, which told him that instead of burying him alive, they intended to play a game with him. He'd heard about the game, another way to deal with a sand boy who stole gold. He'd be suspended from a rope on a pulley and then dropped and raised over and over in the well. The motion would take the air out of you, not to mention the pain from bumping against the side.

Sure enough, the rope tightened on his back and he was yanked up.

The rope bit into his skin, while his insides rumbled. I'm going to die, he said with a shudder. The side of the pit nipped at him again, the willow and poplar branches, which had looked so harmless, now bared their fangs to bite him with a sinister grin. It was like a bad dream he'd often had; a bunch of children swarm up to pinch and bite him. He wants to beat them, but never succeeds. If he strangles one of them, the kid comes back alive and grins with teeth bared once he lets go of his hands. At this moment, many imps were lying in wait inside the dark pit, one tearing at him and another biting him, their laughter seemingly ringing in his ears.

Mengzi could hear Huaqiu sobbing. Though it was indistinct, Huaqiu must have been sobbing loudly enough to drown out the whipping sound of wind that roared like giant waves lapping at the shore. He got a sense that Huaqiu must be shouting and wailing as he pleaded for forgiveness. "Stop begging," he shouted. Yet deep down he also hoped they'd let him go.

His mind had been a blank when he was first dropped into the pit, but now fear surged; he was not sure what he was afraid of, except that he was terrified, the fear pickling his pores. The normal Mengzi would have shouted about power and grandeur, or hurled insults at Shuangfu that could be about anything, so long as it showed his intent to curse the man. But not this time, not when fear had crowded everything out of his head. He was not afraid of death, though, for dying was not so scary at this moment; yet he could not shake off his fear. It was hard to say what terrified him, which made the terror truly visceral. Strangely, however, his mind was unusually clear and empty, which merged with his fear, making them impossible to distinguish.

A ball of light fell on his head. He knew it was the pit opening, and they were up there laughing at him. He wanted to admit defeat, but his mouth refused to follow his brain's order and continued to make surprised shouts, as if it were not his mouth but another life form. Let it scream then. Suddenly he felt a breeze as he was yanked up. His legs betrayed him, turning to mush as he desperately tried to steady himself. Their laughter rolled his way, tearing at him like those kids in his dream.

"Why not admit defeat?" Beizhu came up and murmured to him before straightening up and saying, as if putting on a show, "The Chairman says he'll give you three choices. You have to choose. One, he'll call people from the village to take you back home to the clan shrine, where you'll be dealt with in accordance with clan rules. Two, we follow the rules around here and make you a sand boy for two weeks, with no pay. Three, you can admit wrong."

Mengzi shut his eyes and took a deep breath. He considered the offer for a moment before he finally understood what Beizhu meant. "I'll be a sand boy." He didn't feel like saying more, for the fright had sapped his energy, including the strength to take a deep breath.

He never imagined that this choice would nearly deliver him to the underworld.

Chapter Eight

A fawn's head is caught in a net
Tears stream from its eyes

1

Yue'er told Lanlan about Mengzi's mother's idea.

Lanlan's immediate reaction was positive. A daughter-in-law like Ying'er was hard to find, even if you searched with a lit lantern, as the proverbial saying has it. Moreover, it would save her parents a great deal of trouble and they would never have to lie awake worrying about Mengzi's marriage again. It had become an image etched on her mind, her father sighing as he tossed and turned, never enjoying a good night's sleep. Her parents had to think about Mengzi's marriage after Hantou's death. Then Mengzi had slept with Shuangfu's wife, incurring unbearable criticism from their neighbors and making it an urgent matter to get him a wife; they had to do something about it. So Lanlan was in total agreement when Yue'er revealed the plan. For a woman, life is nothing but getting married, having children and grandchildren, and spending time in the kitchen. Like a hen, laying eggs is its natural duty, and it can't hope to fly into the sky without the wings of a hawk. Once a woman sees through that, she knows it does not matter whom she marries. To be sure, this was what Lanlan would say to Ying'er, though she had a different view where she herself was concerned. That's how it was for everyone.

Lanlan asked Ying'er about her mother's idea.

"Don't be ridiculous," Ying'er said.

"I'm not being ridiculous. They've already done everything they can to annul the arranged marriage, all they're waiting for is your consent."

It finally became clear to Ying'er. No wonder her parents-in-law had been whispering conspiratorially. She was amused, which in turn made her realize how ridiculous the idea was. And yet she felt that she could no longer live in peace. She did not know why, but she was sure her life as a widow was not going to be easy, even if she was allowed to stay that way.

"What do you say?" Lanlan pressed her with a smile.

"Don't be ridiculous."

Ying'er truly had not given the matter a moment's thought. She had no feelings one way or another for Mengzi, whom she approached like the desert date tree by the gate. It belonged to Lingguan's family, so did he; that was all. Now confronted with the strange choice, she was completely caught by surprise while a strange fear rose inside. She did not want to talk about it, but Lanlan was relentless.

"Tell me, what are you doing here? Why aren't you at your husband's house?" Ying'er asked Lanlan, urgent to change the subject.

"You mean you don't know? Why are you asking me?"

"Answer me. Don't dodge the issue."

Lanlan was about to answer, but did not want to disparage Ying'er's family, and was confused by the question.

Then she knew why when she noticed a cunning glint in Ying'er eyes. "You're saying I want you to do what I myself don't want to do."

"Am I wrong?" Ying'er grinned.

2

"Have you done something about that matter Yue'er talked to you about?" Lanlan's mother asked when she finished her meditation that night. "Yue'er's worthless, ought to be tossed to the wolves. She turned my request over to you."

"I did ask her."

"What did she say?" Her mother followed up urgently, so amusing Lanlan that she decided to toy with her.

"What did you think she'd say?"

"What exactly did she say?"

"You're well aware of your son's reputation."

"Oh, no." Her mother blanched. "That's exactly what I was afraid of. What do we do now? Go talk to her again and make her come around. A sow knows the temperament of the piglets she raises. Despite what he's done, Mengzi is honest and reliable. And he's a virgin, too, better than someone who's been married twice."

"A snake doesn't know it's poisonous," Lanlan said after a cry of amazement. "You can't find anything wrong with him because he's your own flesh and blood. Forget you're his mother for a moment, and think about what a woman lives for. Is it for food? Clothes? No, it's a man, isn't it? What does the woman want in a man? His face, his looks, his physique? Yes and no. At the very least he has to be respectable, doesn't he? Put your hand over your heart and think, Ma. Is your son a respectable man?"

Her mother went quiet, her face ashen.

"Your warm butt's been greeted by a cold kang, you old hag," Laoshun cut in with a dark face. "You're okay with it, but she isn't, now that the marriage prospect has been annulled. I'm washing my hands of the whole thing. You take care of it."

"Why is it all on me?" His wife glared at him. "You want a share of anything good, but when there's a problem, it's all mine. Where were you when we were doing this?"

"Would it have happened if you hadn't been such a busybody and let me sleep?"

"If I told you to eat shit, would you do it?" She fumed. "What kind of man dumps everything bad on his wife? Are you some kind of limp dick?"

"Enough, that's enough." Lanlan laughed at her arguing parents. "She didn't say no."

"I thought so." Laoshun smiled. "I suspect she's more than willing. No matter how wide she opens her eyes, she can't find a better family than ours."

"You're right," his wife said. "And it's even harder to find a lecherous father-in-law like you. I bet she's waiting to wear a red head scarf."

It was a story Lanlan had heard before, so she felt like laughing, but did not think it appropriate for her mother to joke about that in front her, so she said:

"But she didn't say yes either."

The old couple was deflated.

"Will you just spit it out?" Laoshun grumbled.

"She didn't say yes and she didn't say no."

"It'll work out then." Her mother cheered up. "She's shy. Naturally, it's hard for her to give a straight answer."

"You think so?" Laoshun was dubious.

"How would I know?" Lanlan said.

"It will work. It will." Her mother was all smiles. "No matter what she thinks, Mengzi is a virgin, and this will be her second marriage."

"Would you stop with that?" Laoshun snapped. "What virgin? That spoiled son of yours is an old donkey now, so stop talking about his virginity. You'll be a laughingstock if you do."

"You're the old donkey," she fired back. "Everyone makes mistakes, don't they? Have you never made a mistake? What about groping your way into someone's bed?"

The muscles on his cheeks tightened, but he swallowed his anger after a look at his daughter. "That's enough with all your petty grievances. If you keep blabbing away like that, don't blame me if I break your teeth."

She wanted to fight back, but changed her tone when she saw that he looked about to explode. "Don't talk like that about your own son. You're his father and that will only make him look terrible."

He gave her a dark look before wordlessly walking out.

"You shouldn't be picking at his old scabs all the time," said Lanlan. "Like they say, you don't hit someone in the face and you never expose their shortcomings. I remember when I was a kid, you were always at each other's throats over this. He's a grandpa now, and there's no need to make him lose face."

"You have no idea how I feel." Her mother complained. "I've put up with this humiliation for decades. I told myself not to care, but I can't help it. I don't want much out of life, but is it too much to ask for an unsullied man?"

"He made a mistake once," Lanlan said with a frown. "You don't have to keep at him like a cat watching a mouse."

"I can never forget the humiliation." Her mother sighed.

"What do you expect Ying'er to think if you feel that way about your life? What he did turned the world upside down. Everyone knows about Mengzi now."

Her mother froze and stayed quiet for a moment. "You're right. I'm afraid she won't go along. Go try to make her see reason. That no-good boy, how could he have done something so shameless?"

3

Bai Fu came back for Lanlan again the next morning. She wanted nothing to do with him. When an emotional bond is broken, it's worse than broken furniture. At least you can still make do with broken furniture, but you cannot tolerate the notion of "make do" when the feelings are gone. Lanlan could not believe she had slept in the same bed with someone like him for all those years. She was so disgusted with herself she thought she'd need to soak in water for three days to wash it off.

He'd lost weight, looking rather pathetic now. His clothes hung on him, which she noticed the moment he walked in, but not out of concern over his well-being. She just thought he looked different, like a stranger, and very strange, disgustingly strange; it went beyond her ability to tolerate, especially his bow legs, which made him waddle when he walked. She could not believe she'd left Huaqiu to marry that man. Outside of the consequential trade—herself for a wife for her brother, had it been her fate?

Lanlan believed in fate, that everyone had a preset track in life, one destiny. And yet she refused to accept her lot in life. She'd once heard a fortuneteller talk about changing one's destiny the way time and one's luck can change. He said he'd told many people's fortunes, and that most of what he'd predicted had come true. A few had not, because those were people who practiced self-cultivation, one building a bridge, one repairing a road, one setting free captured animals, and one doing other good deeds. They had ended with a better fate than they started with. The heirless one got a son, while the one without an official position gained one. One of the books Lingguan left behind was called Liaofan's *Four Lessons on Life*, which talked about how to change one's destiny. It was easy for Lanlan to accept, for it dealt with the mind. The greater your ambition, the grander the accomplishments you'll achieve. Shuangfu was more ambitious than Mengzi, so Shuangfu enjoyed a more impressive career. With the way Bai Fu's mind worked, he would have destroyed their daughter sooner or later. Her mother was narrow-minded, her father was not; Lingguan had too much on his mind, Meng Baye had an expansive, generous mind. Their minds determined what they did. The difference between people is actually in their minds. Fate is just a person's mind. When the mind changes, one's destiny is no longer the same. By doing good and being morally upright, a small-minded man can become a gentleman with the destiny of a noble person. A small-minded man hurts others to benefit himself, while a gentleman sacrifices his own interests for the sake of others. No one likes a small-minded man; a gentleman earns everyone's respect. Everything is different when the mind changes.

So Lanlan believed in fate, but still refused to accept her destiny.

The truth was: she'd considered divorcing Bai Fu even before learning of her brother's terminal illness, which meant that the swap marriage was no longer a consequential matter to her, and she refused to be controlled by fate. After going through so much, a girl will grow up to be a woman and will eventually open her eyes to her destiny. She only lives once, and when it is over there is nothing left. She frequently questioned herself whether the man before her was worth throwing her life away. If he was, she would stay with him; if not, she must make a different choice. Otherwise, she'd have wasted her life; it happened to so many women, she knew, and she refused to join their ranks. She wanted to live for herself, if only for a few years, a few months, even less than that.

Bai Fu was still going on and on with her mother. She did not even want to hear his voice; she knew what he was saying without listening. He'd either plead by looking pathetic or threaten to do something rough. That was all he could do. She knew every little thing that went on inside his head; he was too simple-minded to scheme. For Lanlan, it was better to put everything out in the open, so he'd stop pestering her. She went into her parents' room and, with her eyes fixed on a large wardrobe, said:

"You know better than anyone what you've done. It'll be the next lifetime before I walk back into your house." That did not sound right to her. She wouldn't want to go back there even then. "Not for eighteen lifetimes." She added. "I'd rather evaporate than spend another day in your house."

Bai Fu stopped his rambling and fixed a vicious glare on her, his default expression. Lanlan sneered, too used to his expression to be frightened, like the tiger in the fable that, after the initial scare by a baying donkey of Qin, is no longer impressed.

"Whore." Bai Fu forced the word out through clenched teeth.

"You can eat whatever food you want, but you can't say whatever comes to mind, Bai Fu." Her mother objected. "How is my daughter a whore? Have you caught her in the act?"

"I'll trade my lamb's pelt for your old sheep skin." Bai Fu raised his voice, showing his intention to fight to the bitter end, using his young lamb's life to take her parents' old sheep's lives. Lanlan smiled at her husband's shifting threat, from killing her to scaring her parents. She was sure he was bluffing; a barking dog never bites and a biting dog never barks. Bai Fu did not have it in him to risk his life. She knew that was true; he'd lost both his energy and his spirit ever since taking their daughter out to freeze to death in the desert. He often screamed in his dream, haunted by the fear of a white fox coming to take his life; or he was racked by fear when he dreamed about police. Like a nearly deflated sheepskin raft, he retained only the outward appearance, but would sag and flatten out if touched. Lanlan was the opposite. Nothing frightened her any longer; at worse she'd die like her daughter. If death did not scare her, why would she be afraid of living?

"All right," her mother said. "Your father and I are tired of living. If you'll do us the favor and deliver us from suffering, I'll kowtow to you. The earlier we die, the sooner we're out of this ordeal. You can stop trying to frighten us."

That took the wind out of Bai Fu's sails.

"Tell me, what do I have to live for?" He was choking up. "I can't sleep, and I'll give up on life if you don't take pity on me. I don't have anything to look forward to, nothing." He began to sob.

Lanlan crinkled her nose in disgust; her heart had grown cold. Not even his blood, his death, would sway her, let alone his tears. That puzzled her; never hard-hearted, she had trouble watching someone cry or seeing an injured animal. Some of the things that were ordinary to others would move her, everything but Bai Fu. Love lingers forever between a couple who have been together for one night, as the saying goes. And the emotional attachment is deeper than the ocean for those who have been husband and wife for a hundred days. But not her. She only found him repellent, like a glob of mucus; she felt nothing but disgust. I'd have been better off if I'd hated him, since hate sometimes can be a different manifestation of love, but no. She found him revolting, clear indication that the karmic connection between them was severed. Both love and hate were part of the karmic connection, and repulsion meant it was severed. People got together because of a karmic bond and separated when the bond was severed. So, it was time for them to go their separate ways.

"Don't be so revolting, will you?" She crinkled her nose again.

Bai Fu stopped crying and sat, dispirited, a sorry sight. Looking at him now, one could not imagine how vicious, how violent he could be. The drastic change made him appear like two very different animals, a wild boar then and a sick deer now.

Her mother seemed to be relenting, glancing at Lanlan and then at Bai Fu. She wanted to say something, but changed her mind. Lanlan knew what her mother was thinking. If he hadn't been there, she'd have said, "A prodigal son who changes his ways is worth more than gold," and would have wanted her to reconsider. That was how her mother was; she was easily swayed by tears, with no sense of principle. Lanlan, on the other hand, had steeled her heart, which she believed was good for Bai Fu as well. He could start over and find a new wife to enjoy a good life together, since he was still young. If she dragged it out, she'd be holding him back.

A dispirited Bai Fu got to his feet and sort of sleepwalked his way into Ying'er's room. As Lanlan had expected, her mother whispered to her the moment he walked out, "You ought to think it over."

"Ma." Lanlan was unhappy. "Don't give him any false hope. Let him give up the idea altogether."

"I'm just afraid, afraid that Ying'er will take the baby with her. That, he's Hantou's heir, you know." Her mother sighed.

"It's her baby, you can't keep him here."

"Nonsense," her mother said stubbornly, "I won't let her take him even if I have to put my life on the line. I'll take good care of her if she stays a widow here. Of course, it'd be even better if she married Hantou's brother. She has to leave her baby here if she wants to go." Her mother softened her tone as her eyes turned watery. "How can the sky fall just like that? Our family is breaking up, one dead, the other gone away."

Lanlan knew that the tears would not stop once her mother mentioned Hantou, so she changed the subject, "Not so loud. Let's hear what they're saying."

Her mother stopped crying, cocked her ear, but could not hear anything. She went over to close the door before sprawling by the cat door to eavesdrop.

Lanlan was amused.

"Nothing important." Her mother got up after a while. "The bum didn't say anything, just bawled his eyes out. Ai, I have to say I feel sorry for him."

Lanlan felt herself giving in. She'd been disgusted by the way he cried in front of her, but was swayed by him sobbing in front of Ying'er, his own sister. A man must be in terrible shape if he has to go crying to his own sister. She almost had a change of heart, but that ended when she was reminded of thoughts hidden in the depths of her soul.

"Crocodile tears." She sneered.

"Don't say that, my girl." Her mother looked upset with her. "We're all humans and we all have worries. We shouldn't gloat over others' troubles."

"I'm not gloating." For some reason, Lanlan's heart ached, though that did nothing to alter her decision. You muddle through life if necessary, but once you see the light, no one would want to continue living in ignorance."

Ying'er came in, appearing to have cried along with her brother. "My mother wants me home for a while," she said with difficulty. "My brother says she's not well."

Lanlan's mother's face fell. "Sure, you can go." She managed to say, "I'll take care of the baby for a few days."

Ying'er blanched.

4

After lunch, Ying'er went into the yard to gather the dry diapers off the clothesline and fold them before handing them to her mother-in-law. Then she went to a shop to buy powdered milk and sugar and left with her brother after she'd made sure everything was in order.

Her tears flowed the moment they walked out, coming too fast for her to dry them. Some women on the road gave her funny looks. She hated herself, but self-loathing failed to stop her tears.

Her mother-in-law had begun to be wary of her.

It was a reality that she could not, but must accept. For some time now, she had been feeling a pair of eyes on her back. She'd blamed it on oversensitivity at first, but on this day her mother-in-law's message could not have been clearer—she no longer trusted Ying'er. She was afraid her daughter-in-law would not come back and the baby would be a sort of hostage. Put differently, Ying'er could stay with her parents if she wanted, but she could not take the baby with her. Either way, her mother-in-law's distrust felt like a knife plunged straight into her heart.

Her premonition had born out; she could not even be a widow in peace.

Sitting on the back of Bai Fu's bicycle, Ying'er seemed to be sleepwalking. A cool breeze raised dust on the road, a sign of impending bleakness. Her mind mired in similar desolation, she wanted throw herself into someone's arms and cry her heart out over her bitterness and resentment. But where was that person at this moment?

The sun cast pale rays. Trees were bare but for the hanging insects that swayed in the wind. She was no longer afraid, too busy to worry about them falling on her head or face. A heavy liquid sloshed inside her, making everything before her eyes dusty and blurry.

Her tears slowly stopped when they passed the village path and entered the potter's field on the riverbank. A familiar sensation smoothed things out like an iron and warmed up the heavy liquid. It was this pitted, ugly spot on the riverbank that had given her the most beautiful moment in her life. She and he had been frenzied and crazed, cried and laughed. He had been panting hard when he pushed her down behind the sand hill and infused her soul with dizzying happiness. It felt like a wonderful fantasy, not reality. It was true; sometimes she had trouble believing she had once had him, a real-life man. If he were to materialize before her, she would likely faint from immense happiness.

The hope, though just a hope, cheered her greatly. She did not know when the thought would become reality, but she was willing to spend her life waiting for it to happen.

With that hope, she was no longer a widow, but a woman in waiting; she would be happy if she could spend her life waiting.

But her heart tightened when she recalled the scene before her departure. Naturally she was not worried that her baby would suffer. Her mother-in-law had rich experience in raising children and, given her love for her deceased son, the baby was in good hands. What she found impossible to accept was the wariness from her mother-in-law. When Hantou was alive, Ying'er had been part of the family, and now that he was dead, she became an outsider, a widow waiting to be married off again. What frightened her most was, under their watchful eyes, when would her widowhood come to an end? Could she wait until the hope became a reality?

Impossible to know.

Moreover, once the "guard" was up, a series of corresponding actions would occur, a chilling thought. How could she keep living like that?

How could she not worry?

Dust thrown up by gusts of wind felt to her as if it was blown into her heart.

5

Ying'er's mother threw her arms around her daughter and wept. She had lost weight and there were more gray strands in her hair. Considered the shrewdest woman in the village, she could be as fierce as a lightning strike when she was on a tear and could rouse heaven and earth when she cried. She'd had a positive opinion of Hantou, over whose death she'd shed many tears, and she was forever using his good nature to highlight her negative view of Lanlan. She was always saying things like, A dragon breeds ten little ones and nine will be different from the other; or, Hantou and Lanlan were from the same mother, but he was so decent while she was like a demon in human skin. Even though she disagreed with the characterization, Ying'er understood why her mother felt that way, like all women who cannot get along with their daughters-in-law. A mother raised a tiny baby until he was tall as the top of a wall, and once he was married he forgot about her. Naturally, she would vent her anger and frustration on the daughter-in-law. To that was added the animosity caused by Lanlan's demand for a divorce; she was clearly much angrier than other mothers-in-law.

Her mother cried energetically, the same way she laughed, and it was over quickly. "What's the slut doing?"

Ying'er noted that her mother had not asked about her, the baby, or anyone else, only Lanlan. So that's who she had to talk about.

"She thinks she's going to become an immortal, doesn't she? She won't even be a decent ghost when she dies. She'll be a sorry-looking wronged ghost or a messy one covered in blood." Her mother spat out every word through clenched teeth.

"Don't curse her like that, Ma." Ying'er frowned.

"Curse?" With a savage look, her mother said, "I wish I could cut her up. She's done us great harm. After all these years, she suddenly wants a divorce. It's like dew wetting only half the hill. She shouldn't have gone through with it if she didn't think it would work. My girl is as pretty as a flower, and we wouldn't have had any trouble finding someone to swap with. Now when the rice is cooked and the girl has become a woman, she's making a fuss. I told her to be careful and not break an arm or a leg. She's like a sparrow standing on a grape trellis, using the false height to puff herself up, hoping to fly into the sky. My son had to be blind to fall for her. If it had been up to me, it would have been over at the first meeting. You want to be my daughter-in-law? You're a disgrace to her ancestors."

"Would you stop?" Ying'er frowned. "You haven't met a single good person in your whole life."

"What do you mean? My girl is a good person, one who can be found only in heaven, not on earth."

"You always favor your own flesh and blood." Ying'er said.

"You've put on weight." Her mother finally pulled her up and studied her. "You have to eat well, my little girl. Don't worry about your figure; you'll turn into a skinny monkey if you're afraid of overeating. What you eat will be in the milk for your baby. Oh, is he a good baby?"

"He's a very good boy. He sleeps after he's fed, never fusses."

"That's wonderful. They say that raising a child is like shedding a layer of skin. When I first had you, I never had enough to eat, so I didn't have any milk; you sucked the blood out of me. That was hard, really hard. You were so tiny, the size of a shoe sole, and I still managed to raise you to adulthood. Then you had to go marry into that family; just thinking about it angers me. Since Pan Gu separated heaven and earth, there's been no custom to keep a daughter at home. If there had been, I'd never have married you off." Her eyes were turning red again.

"There you go again." Ying'er said with a smile.

"A mother always feels closer to her girl, no matter how good the son is." Her mother smiled. "Look at your brother. He stuffs his face, but he has mush for brains, and he's forever arguing with me." Her mother lowered her voice, "Are they good to you? Your mother-in-law, I mean."

"Very good."

"I don't believe you. You're an outsider now that Hantou is gone. Come back home if life gets too hard over there. You can stay home forever, I'll take care of you." She watched her daughter's reaction carefully.

"How would that look?" Ying'er laughed. "Besides, I still have legal rights and my share of contracted farmland. I don't think they'd want to get rid of me."

"Of course, they wouldn't." Her mother sneered. "They have extra help for free. I'll be honest with you, my little girl. You can do whatever you want as long as the slut agrees to be with your brother. You can stay with your in-laws or you can come home. If she stirs up more trouble, you'll have to show some backbone for your mother."

Ying'er knew something was about to happen. Lanlan was stubborn, and her mind was made up about the divorce. When she went ahead with her plan, Ying'er would have no more peace. Why was life so hard? she wondered, swamped with bitterness.

"Actually, you ought to be more flexible," her mother said, as if she could read her mind. "You're still young, and there's a long road ahead of you. We're living in a new society now, and no one will erect a chastity arch for you if you remain a widow."

Her father walked in. Another one of his "big business deals" had gone nowhere. He'd heard that Li Zongren, the Republican President, had opened a safety deposit box in a Swiss bank, but left the key in the care of a certain individual in a certain village in a certain city and county and province in China. If he could come up with thirty thousand, he could buy the key from that person and, with the key, open the box to retrieve thousands of gold bars. So he went around borrowing money to join a pool, but one of the contacts took off with the money and vanished without a trace.

Indifference and numbness joined the wrinkles on her father's face. He did not greet his daughter. Her mother's face darkened as she scolded him. When he went out, her mother said, "See that, my little girl? That's your father, a man who is afflicted with a 'money craze.' I told him to forget about his big business deals and focus on working the field to get something to eat, or we'll starve to death. But he tricked me into handing over the money I got from selling the pigs, then he swindled me out of the soy bean money, even tricked all our relatives and neighbors to the point that no one will have anything to do with us. In the end, he lost everything."

"Enough. That's enough!" Her father walked back in. "Would you stop clawing me to pieces? Even the penniless official Zhu Maichen got rich in the end. Don't underestimate me. I have my eyes on an antique pearl that sparkles in the dark. If it goes through, my share will be eighty to a hundred thousand. We'll see how you react when that happens."

"Ugh!" Her mother turned her back on her husband and patted her rear end. "You're a disgrace to your ancestors. Go find a hollow, pee into it and look at yourself. With that pointy mouth and those monkey cheeks, you were born to be poor, and you can't hope to even sniff something nice. I must have had bad karma accumulated over eight lifetimes, to suffer the fate of marrying a mad donkey like you. You're like a horse racing the wind, dying of exhaustion at the end. You've squandered away over four thousand of mine, so where's the money you make? Hand it over. It'll make me feel better."

Her father's face reddened, the veins on his neck pulsing. He looked as if he would disappear into a hole in the ground if there'd been one.

"That's enough, Ma," Ying'er said unhappily.

"Let her talk, girl. She jinxes everything and won't shed a tear until she sees the coffin. She's just like the wives of Zhu Maichen or Jiang Ziya, carping over their poverty. We'll see when the time comes!"

"When the times comes?" Her mother snickered. "When the time comes, you can copy those husbands and splash a basin of water on the ground for me to pick it up. Wish all you want, it's not in the stars for you."

"You old hag. You can know what's gold and what's silver, but you can't know what's in a person's heart," her father argued lamely.

"I can see right through you, from one end to the other, including every twist and turn. You think about money until your head shrinks, but no none of it comes your way."

"That's enough, Ma. I don't get many chances to come home, and this is what I come back to, listening to you argue." Ying'er stamped her foot.

Her mother gave her father an ugly look and shut up.

Her father was sweating profusely.

6

Later that afternoon, Pockmark Xu, a professional matchmaker, showed up. A repulsive man, he had a pitted face and a nose like a clove of garlic. Seriously nearsighted, he could squint and press his face up against someone's nose, and still fail to see if he was talking to a man or a woman. A bachelor who loved alcohol, he was often seen dropping in on people with a bottle of liquor, working a match to earn thank-you money to support himself. He differed from the shaman in that she worked both as a midwife and a matchmaker. He had one job, matchmaking. His daily activity consisted of visiting neighbors to gather information on a family's daughter who's reached marrying age or a woman who had just lost her husband. When he got what he needed, he'd visit a bachelor's house to make the match. Once it was done, he'd be rewarded with two or three hundred; if not, he'd still be given money for liquor and cigarettes for his effort.

Ying'er did not like Pockmark Xu. For one thing, he was always supplying tips for her father's business deals. He enjoyed talking up a deal without taking part, and his tongue had pushed her father into a pit of debt. Secondly, Xu loved liquor and women. After he had a few sips or whenever he saw a woman, the marks on his face glowed until they were shamelessly red. The sight of him nauseated her.

Though in the same trade, Pockmark Xu and Shaman Qi did not fight over prospects, and in fact often worked in concert and shared information. They were the ones who had made the swap match for Ying'er and Lanlan.

Ying'er knew the purpose of the man's visit the moment he walked in. Hantou was barely dead, and they were already trying to find her a husband. She had to laugh.

Ying'er's mother was hostile to Xu, because he never stopped giving her husband false leads. Her father, on the other hand, believed that Xu had good intentions, even if he'd gotten into debt over the man's faulty information. He said to his wife when Xu walked in:

"Go buy a pack of cigarettes."

"Where's the money?" She showed him her hand.

"And buy a bottle of liquor on credit," Ying'er's father said, unperturbed.

"I need money." Her mother's hand was out again.

"Didn't I just say to get it on credit?" Her father glanced at Xu.

"Can't do it. Do you have any idea how much we owe them already? You have the nerve to ask for more credit when they call you a donkey behind your back. You'll have to go if you want more credit from them. I have too much pride." She looked somewhat shrewish.

"Forget it, I've got cigarettes." Xu smiled as he took out a pack and tossed it on the table.

"I can't smoke yours again. I'm like a bedbug feasting on a guest." Her father was apologetic.

"See, he's got cigarettes." Her mother softened her expression. "*Qinjia* Xu is a competent man."

"Not really. I just pick up what I need to feed myself."

"Enough steamed rolls can fill a pot." Her mother glared at her father before continuing sarcastically, "Not like a toad that received the essence of thunder with nothing real to show for it."

"There you go again." Her father smiled awkwardly. "Please, no more."

"That's enough." Xu said. "Don't argue. As the saying goes, a young couple will eventually grow into life-long companions, as long as they hold your tongues. I've got something important to say. Don't be upset with me when I tell you, all right?"

"Now you're acting like a stranger, *Qinjia*. Don't beat around the bush." Her mother guessed the purpose of the man's visit.

"I watched her grow up." Xu said after a prolonged, squinting study of Ying'er. "When she was young, she was like a beauty walking off a painting, with rosy cheeks on snowy white skin. She still looks the same after having a child. I heard—this, um—I wonder what she's thinking."

Ying'er was amused, yet suddenly felt she'd gone through way too much in life. Not so long ago the same pockmarked man had made a match for her and Hantou. Several years later, he was dead and she was a widow. Now the man was back to make another match for her with someone else. So much had changed already, who knew how things would be in another few years?

"What could she be thinking?" her mother replied confidently. "We're no longer living in the old society, where a chastity arch would have been erected for her. Even if we were, it was inhumane to ask women to remain widows. I heard they tossed coins in the room after nightfall and turned off the light to grope around looking for them in the dark to pass the lonely nights. I wouldn't want my little girl to suffer like that. Come on, *Qinjia*, tell us what you have in mind."

"Ma," Ying'er said. "He's not been gone that long. Aren't you afraid that what you've just said would make people laugh at us?"

"Let them laugh. It was a natural disaster, my little girl. You didn't poison your husband. He's dead, and no one asked you to die with him. Please, *Qinjia*, tell us what you have in mind."

"That's right." Xu smiled. "It's perfectly natural that Heaven sends down rain and widows get remarried. You don't have to be shy about it. Do you know Zhao San, the butcher? He has a gold panning pit at White Tiger Pass. Right, that's the one. He was married to a woman from Lintao, but she ran off, so he's looking for another one. He's had his eye on your girl for a long time; he fell for her before she was married and nearly lost his mind thinking about her. He was disappointed to lose out to Hantou. He came to me a few days ago and asked me to sound you out. If you agree to the match, you can ask for any betrothal gifts you want."

Ying'er's heart sank. She hadn't known she'd devalued so much until that moment. Zhao San was a well-known drunk who was always up to no good. He'd poached trees along the highway the year he built his house; he was caught and paraded down the street with a sign around his neck after he stripped the bark of the wood and put it on the unfinished house. A scum bag like that dared have his eyes on her, proof that she was a different person. Even if Lingguan were to return, she'd probably not be a good match for him any longer.

Tears flowed.

"I hear Zhao San has a bad temper." Her mother did not notice her reaction. "He loves to drink and he beat the woman from Lintao. That's why she ran off."

"People can say what they want. Even your teeth fight with your tongue sometimes." Xu smiled. "Every couple fights. Beating a wife is like kneading dough. He may have hit his wife, but he was still a good husband. The rain from the sky flows on the ground, and couples fight, but bearing a grudge is not sound. A husband and wife never carry an argument into the next day. You've been there yourself."

"That's true." Her mother smiled. "You're right about that."

"The gifts are no problem. He's said that whatever you want, just ask. These days, the rich are like grandfathers, lording it over the poor grandsons. You're lucky he's picked her. Other women wanted to marry him, but he didn't think they were good enough. I even heard that a few of them were still virgins."

Ying'er quietly dried her tears and stopped herself from crying out loud. Knowing she might do that if she stayed any longer, she left the room and walked out the gate.

7

It had begun to drizzle. Fine rain like the hair on a cow draped the village with a hazy gauze. Everything looked unreal; the mountains, trees and the villages turned dream-like.

The topography of her parents' home differed from Shawan. Although similarly close to the desert, her parents' village had bald mountains to the south that gave off the feel of poverty and bleakness. When it rained, however, the mountains turned lively and gained a charm from the hazy desolation. She let the rain wash her tears away; tears and rain sparkled on her face, impossible to tell one from the other.

She was made aware of her situation by Pockmark's proposal. Her worth had kept dropping over the past few years, from "Folk Tune Fairy" to "Hantou's wife," then to the rank of "widow." According to Xu's design, it would not stop there, and she would fall farther to become a "Butcher's Wife." She recalled the saying that a woman was a lady when she married a scholar and had to clean pig's guts after she became a butcher's wife. Ying'er knew she did not have the good fortune to be a lady—in her eyes Lingguan was a true scholar—but she hated the idea of cleaning bloody guts. People in her village scorned butchers because they were filthy, having to deal with blood and pig shit, and because they took lives. Villagers showed them little respect, as they considered their sons the heirs to support their families, while the butchers' sons were just to make up numbers. "Making up numbers" meant they were dispensable. If they had a son, they added a warm body to the population, but it didn't matter if they did not, since he would grow up only to be another butcher. One butcher was the same as a hundred others, the only difference being the change in numbers. And now a butcher had sent someone to propose marriage. She felt wretched.

She recalled something Lingguan had once said about women of Liangzhou going through the six reincarnations: as a maiden, she was an immortal fairy born into the fantastic heavenly kingdom, where she lived happily and worry-free. When she got married, she came down to the human world, where she fretted over daily necessities, like oil, salt, soy sauce and vinegar. When she had a fight with her husband, she was an Asura, a malevolent spirit filled with anger and resentment. She was a beast of burden as she took up household chores, toiling away year after year, with no rest in sight. Emotionally she was a hungry ghost, who searched high and low, pleading and beseeching fruitlessly, wailing all night long. If she married a terrible husband, then her body and soul were in hell, where the nights were dark and long, with no sign of light; she was engulfed in noxious flames, under cruel torture, crying pitifully forever, with no deliverance in sight.

That was the story of her life.

She'd had hopes of marrying Lingguan, but she knew he deserved a different kind of life. If he married her, he would be tied to the land, like a kite that's grounded no matter how high it can fly. He needed to soar like a hawk, the thought making her heart ache, yet she'd hoped he'd fly down a broad, open path.

What she wanted was to quietly finish her life's journey. Following her current trajectory, she'd live with her baby and have something to look forward to, suppressing romantic notions and facing reality as she carried out her destiny. She wanted to say to the world, "Please don't bother me, let me live in peace."

That was all.

But it seemed that even that modest wish had become a luxury. "What have I done to anyone?" she wanted to ask.

Bai Fu was digging up the stump of a tree he'd cut down days before. It was a big tree with large, deep roots. Steam rose above his head. Her heart grew heavy at the sight of her brother. She knew that her fate was tightly bound up with his. Ahead was a path she was afraid to even imagine.

The drizzle fell on her and seeped into her heart. A damp sensation rose up; she felt like crying, but no tears came. The feeling grew stronger, until it was so heavy it turned into a folk tune—

Dark, dark, it's truly dark.

Tree shade overlays the road.

Watching you walk into the distance,

I feel like a piece has been cut out of my heart.

I cry morning and night.

My tears fall and an ocean forms.

The road ahead is a steel knife,

That takes my life.

8

The sky darkened as Ying'er cried and sang, while the rain turned from a rustling drizzle to the pitter-patter of a light rainfall. When she came through the gate like a sleepwalker, she heard Pockmark Xu and her father playing a drinking game. Xu was shouting at the top of his lungs, "Sixty-sixty, everything velvety! Three stars shining high above. Five brightest men!" She knew her mother was happy to hear what the man had said, and had even bought some liquor on credit.

As the drinking game went on, Xu bragged about himself. "Don't you worry, *Qinjia*. I've plied this trade for half my life, whether I do well or not, and I know how to read people. Zhao may look uncultured, but he'll provide well for your daughter."

Ying'er frowned and went into the kitchen. Chicken blood had pooled on the floor where her mother was plucking a chicken. Obviously, she meant business by killing a chicken to thank the man.

She sneered.

"The man is ugly, with his pitted face, and he's nearly blind." Her mother pattered on as she pulled off handfuls of chicken feathers. "But he's got talent enough to eat well and drink enough. I heard he was involved with several women. He ran a fever and threw up one time. The Shaman told him he shouldn't have had sex with a woman during her period. He was jinxed. He owned up to what he'd done. Just think, he's got a face like sandy ground after a rainfall, a pomegranate peel dried inside out, or a naked butt sitting in winnowing pan, but he's sharp as a tack."

Ying'er was in no mood to reply. The tell-tale stench of dead chicken rose with the steam from the basin and made her slightly nauseous, so she moved off to sit and stare blankly at the red stove opening.

Xu's peculiar voice rose again, as he sang a common drinking game song, "A Funny Old Man." It was a folk tune that men sometimes sang to spice up their game. She was not a fan of the tune, because of its vulgar content, but a perfect choice for a man like Pockmark Xu. It would be an insult to a tune if he sang about love.

She laughed.

Her mother, who had noticed her glum look, was about to cheer up when she heard her laugh. "Actually, it's all to fill the belly, whether he's a butcher or not," she said, mistaking Ying'er's laugh as a positive response to the proposal. "In fact, I wish your father had been a butcher; at least we'd have had meat at every meal. I don't have any preference except for spicy fried innards. The words alone make me drool. But nothing doing. I married a bum so poor he has no hair to pluck and no blood to suck. It's my accumulated eight lifetimes of bad karma. I can't even smell a pig fart let alone taste some spicy fried innards. You have to consider yourself lucky. The spot where the first one slept isn't even cold and the second one is coming to take over."

"No more talk like that, Ma," Ying'er said unhappily. Hantou had been her son-in-law, how could she be so heartless, her feelings thinner than paper?

"All right, I'll shut up." Her mother had plucked the chicken clean and now lit some wheat stalks to scald it. Then she put the bird on a chopping board, picked up a cleaver, and began hacking into it.

Ying'er was depressed as she looked at the fire in the stove. "People are worse than animals," she said to herself. "When a gazelle dies, the survivor would rather be killed than leave its dead mate behind. But people, hell, listen to what she just said. Was that something that should have come out of a mother's mouth?"

More vulgar, coarse shouts came from the study. Bai Fu, with the gruff voice of an unhappy ox, sounded like he was arguing, not playing a game. He truly loved his liquor. He'd beat Lanlan whenever he had a bit too much, leaving bruises all over. Ying'er had to admit it had been hard on her sister-in-law. Why do women have such a hard life? Was it that whoever determined destiny picked on the weak and yielded to the strong, assigning a terrible fate to women for fear of antagonizing brutish men?

Her mother dumped the boiled water from the pot, wiped it dry and poured in cooking oil. When the oil bubbles disappeared, she lowered the chopped pieces into the pot and quickly fried them up. It was fare for honored guests, which showed how serious her mother was.

Grating laughter came from the study; Bai Fu was the loudest. The heartless man. Ying'er dried her tears as she continued to stare at the fire through misty eyes. How odd that her heart felt as gray as ashes when she was in front of a burning stove.

"I know people say a mother has no control over children's lives once they grow up, but they'll always be suckling babies in her eyes, no matter how old they are. I won't stop worrying about you as long as there's breath in me. I've been around longer, and my nose has taken in more smoke than you; I've gone through plenty and seen enough. Listen to me and you won't suffer. There isn't a mother anywhere who doesn't want the best for her children." She chattered away as she fried the chicken, unconcerned whether Ying'er was listening or not.

They ran out of firewood, so Ying'er went into the yard for more. It was quiet out there, despite the din from the men's drinking game. A drizzling rain was falling again. Perfect weather for lying in bed. Imagine sitting on a heated kang and leaning up against a bed roll to knit a sweater and watch the sleeping baby smack his lips. On the stove an earthenware pot slowly cooking soupy rice—stewing mutton would be even better. Next to her the "scholar" is leafing through a book. How wonderful that would be, but it was a luxury she could not afford to even fantasize.

She could lower her standard, she thought. Take away the noise from the game, the sizzling pot, and her mother's prattling, and replace it with the rain, the quiet, peace, and her daydreams. This could not have become a luxury too, could it have?

The roots that Bai Fu had dug up were piled in a shed by the gate, where they emitted a damp smell. She picked up some of the broken pieces. Damp roots did not easily catch fire, but once lit they burned for a long time, sort of like her, whose feelings did not catch fire easily but were long-lasting. It was the opposite of dry kindling, which crackled and sent flames high into the air, but quickly turned to ashes. As a young girl, Ying'er had been different from other village girls, who kept changing their secret love interests; she'd had only one, existing in her heart and not in reality, her private totem. Later she was married, and after that her imaginary love interest and Lingguan became one. Like the damp firewood that finally caught fire, her emotions remained aflame.

She sighed.

Despite the rain, it was still light out, white with a hint of green. A perfect night for the lovelorn. If there'd been no men playing games and none of her mother's chatter, she'd put the baby to bed and push open the window to let in the moist but refreshing night air, the seemingly non-existing and unreal raindrops, and lovesickness that drifted like gossamer. She'd imprison the longing in her heart to ferment into a heady feeling until it was tipsy. A night like that would shine bright with Lingguan's eyes, which would quietly gaze at her, imbued with purity, longing, cleverness, and kindness. She would let him look, as she complained silently about his lack of concern for her. Wouldn't that be wonderful! Admittedly, it was exacting to be missing someone, and yet it was a beautiful feeling, the lack of which could turn her into wood or stone. But it had to be fine and soft, like the drizzle, wafting over, nearly invisible and almost unreal. It would never be a downpour, for then the longing could wash her under, which had been the case during the month after Lingguan's departure. She'd felt like a drifting vine in floodwaters, forever at risk of being carried away in the torrents of lovesickness, where she swam and swam until she would slow down and regain the control of her wandering life.

She sighed again as she carried kindling into the kitchen. The moment she walked in, she was besieged by the sizzling and crackling chicken frying in the pot and the acrid cooking smoke, which dashed her romantic mood from the night rain and landed her in the real world. Reality was real, impossible to hide from, no matter how hard she tried. Sometimes she thought she'd managed to escape, but that was an illusion. The bubble burst when it collided with reality, no matter how alluring or how lovely. It was a hopeless situation. She inserted the damp wood into the fire chamber and pumped the bellows to make it sizzle and bubble. Looking at the bubbles, she dimly felt she'd become one herself, crackling in a fire, only to soon vanish without a trace. She'd have liked to become a bubble that would be nothing after brief suffering. Was "nothing" the nirvana that Lingguan often talked about? Was it life or was it death when the bubble vanished?

Ying'er was dizzy. The damp wood caught fire and water bubbles sputtered, seemingly in pain. A warm fire spread soothingly, unlike the scorching heat from dry kindling, and baked her face. Her mother was still chattering, while her heart was aflame. Ying'er knew what her mother was saying without listening, for she said the same things over and over. And did the same things over and over. People said that a father knows his son best; well, so too a mother and daughter. Ying'er knew all too well what her mother was all about.

After quick-frying the chicken, her mother put the dark red pieces on a plate and picked out the drumsticks and thighs to place in a bowl, before heading into the study. Pockmark Xu's dramatic voice immediately sounded:

"Why go through all this trouble? How does that make me feel?"

"It's just a chicken, something born to be food for us. Why do you think I raised it if not for you to have it?"

Ying'er was amused. Her mother had always been disdainful of Pockmark Xu and, when his name came up, would either mock him by saying his face was rain-splattered sandy land or a bare ass sitting on winnowing pan, or berating him for being a terrible man who'd insist on having sex with a woman during her period. But on this day, she made an about-face, even killing their best laying hen. Listening to her, you'd think that only Pockmark Xu was good enough to enjoy the chicken.

Her amusement was short-lived, replaced by sadness. Why hadn't her mother asked her opinion? Could she have agreed that Ying'er was a match only for a butcher. Years ago, she'd said her daughter could only be found in heaven, not on earth, and only a prince was worthy of her. Later she demoted Ying'er by turning her into an object to be swapped. Now she was toadying up to Xu just so she could marry a butcher. I'm human too, Ma. If you'd asked me just once, that would be treating me like a human being.

She picked up a scoop to cover the embers with ashes from the stove. As she gently tamped them down, she recalled what her mother-in-law had said; her heart raced and tears fell unchecked. Heartless man, she cursed, as Lingguan's face flickered before her teary eyes. You're a true rascal, *Qinjia*. Ying'er stared at his eyes in her imagination. I'm not lucky enough to be your wife, so I'll be your brother's wife instead. One's dead, but there's another one.

She began to cry, despite the urge to laugh.

Ying'er had a good cry amid the merry laughter from Xu and her mother.

Chapter Nine

Not enough to eat, too much work,
The muscles weaken, health suffers

1

Being a sand boy had not seemed so hard to Mengzi until he became one. Now he realized how tough a job it was. He nearly fell apart after half a day, his every joint and pore screaming in agony. Yet he did not regret his choice. No matter how exhausting the work, it was still better than the humiliation he'd have suffered at the clan shrine, where the code of conduct dictated that a thief, man or woman, would face all the members as the crime was read out before the miscreant was spat on. Mengzi would rather die than that. He knew that Shuangfu was capable of doing that as a way to vent his suppressed anger, but he never expected the work he chose to be so grueling.

When he was going down into the pit, the earth squeaked and squawked as it pressed violently against the wooden wall support. The earth had greeted the digging of the first pit without the safety framework with sinister laughter, and then when it shook, sand boys lost their lives.

After that, they built wooden supports with crisscrossed logs woven with willow and birch branches. But the earth did not give up easily, refusing to let holes be opened up on its body. So, it pushed and pressed, sending creaks to Mengzi's ears, who steeled himself to keep going, following a rope ladder that trembled under his feet, swaying dizzily. It did not bother the other sand boys, who ignored the screeching earth and quaking rope. His manhood at stake, he followed them down.

His nose was immediately struck by a humid mildew odor; signs of moisture were everywhere, but no water was oozing out yet. It was a newly dug pit, still a long way from the bottom; this was the hardest part of the process, where there was scant hope to see gold. All he could do was work like a demon, filling his basket with sand and rocks before climbing up the quivering rope ladder to empty the contents onto a man-made hillock.

As space down in the pit was limited, four men worked as a shift, two to carry up the sand and rocks that a third man shoveled into their baskets, and the fourth doing the digging. At Mengzi's pit, Baldy Wang was the digger, who swung his spade like a madman, littering the scarred earth. Mengzi shuddered when he saw the look of loathing in Baldy's eyes. He thought the work must be hurting the Earth God. The long spade cut into the earth, making a noise that set Mengzi's teeth on edge and made his gums hurt. Ordinarily, he'd cover his ears, but on this day, he wanted to see how much he could take. Damn you, ears, you can take it if I can! Recalling the glint in Shuangfu's eyes, brimming with mockery, Mengzi sneered and spat before picking up the full basket and getting onto the rope ladder.

His basket had been overfilled, probably because the man wanted to get in Shuangfu's good graces. Mengzi had noticed that, but was unfazed. In his eyes, the man might as well be Shuangfu. Go ahead, fill it as much as you can, and I'll carry it up, Mengzi fumed. But the rope cut painfully into his shoulder, so he adjusted it before continuing up the ladder. Made of thick coir ropes and stakes for rungs, the ladder jerked perilously, sending the basket thudding hard into his body; his back began to ache after he'd taken only a few steps up. Rippling like waves, the ache quickly spread throughout his body, but he said to himself spitefully, I'm going to hurt you, hurt you badly, you damned worthless back!

He looked up and saw they were watching him, probably having assumed that the shovel-man had played a trick on him and that he was suffering. So, Mengzi stomped on the rungs, his energy nearly spent, sending him to the brink of total collapse. He was thirsty, his temples were pulsing, and the rope on his shoulder pressed hard down. I could fall! He dared not look down; bedeviled by acrophobia since childhood, he was terrified of losing his grip.

He held his breath and tried to swallow, but his mouth was dry. To hell with you, Shuangfu, you ass! But I don't give a damn. The thought of Shuangfu gave him a strange new supply of energy. Mengzi climbed a few more rungs before leaning against one of the steps to catch his breath. He sensed the danger he faced; if he lost control of his hands and feet, he would plummet to the bottom and wind up as a pile of broken flesh, like an old cow rolling down a hollow.

Oddly, he was reminded of what his father said, "I can take whatever Heaven doles out to me." His father had directed his retort at Heaven, but for Mengzi, that would be Shuangfu. He disliked the comparison, but there was nothing he could do about that; he had no control over Shuangfu's intent to take the place of Heaven. Which was why Mengzi protested silently: Yes, I can take whatever you dole out to me.

"Come on up," Huaqiu shouted from above, after carrying one load. "The first load is always the hardest."

Mengzi struggled to climb up, cursing as if it were a contest. Strangely, each curse seemed to invest his feet with greater strength, which then got him closer to the bright spot step by step. Suddenly he felt as if hands were pulling him away from the ladder. Terror rose. Is this it, am I going to die? He was reminded of Harelip, who had fallen to his death, and Harelip's wife, whom he had bedded at Pig's Belly Well. His scalp went numb at the thought, and he nearly let go, before straining to turn his head and spit behind him, his mother's trick to drive away a ghost. "Stop your foul spit. Hurry up," he heard the shovel man yell up at him. Mengzi smiled and spat a few times.

Mustering his strength, he reached the top of the pit. Huaqiu came over, took the basket, and pulled him up. "Dai! You filled the basket with too much sand. Are you trying to kill him? You'll pay with your life if you do."

A cool breeze blew and the blue sky seemed to pour its color into Mengzi's body, refreshing and soothing him inside and out. His pores seemed to cheer: "Wonderful! It feels just wonderful." A puffy white cloud floated over a distant hill, so white it dazzled the eyes. It's good to be alive, Mengzi thought.

"Shuangfu said you can go home if you don't want to work here." Beizhu walked up. "So long as you own up to wrongdoing—in front of all the sand boys."

Huaqiu glanced at Mengzi.

"It's just fifteen days, isn't it?" Mengzi spat. "I'll do it. I have nothing to own up to."

2

Mengzi apparently had a curious inner barometer that made it possible to foretell a disaster. He later recalled how, before the wall support collapsed, his muscles twitched violently. He was outside the pit, taking in huge lungfuls of air blowing his way from the desert. Refreshed by those few breaths, his insides cleared, though he suddenly experienced a severe thigh muscle spasm—thump, thump—as if kicked by a rabbit.

The support isn't going to collapse, is it?

He went down all the same, because Shuangfu was having such a great time chatting with other owners. Mengzi sensed that Shuangfu was watching him out of the corner of his eye. Mengzi spat on the ground and went down in the pit.

He was greeted by mocking eyes from the shovel-man when he reached the bottom. Being the leader of the shift, the shovel-man could overfill a basket if he wanted to punish the carrier, who would pant like an injured donkey. He'd show mercy if he wanted to be nice. He was the one most likely to spot gold, which was why he was usually the owner's most trusted employee. The digger, called "bashi," was second only to the shovel-man, and might also find gold when clearing the bottom of the pit. The sand carriers had the toughest job; their bodies nearly fell apart after a shift.

Mengzi hated the shovel-man, the sort who would be a corrupt official. His face betrayed his cunning, and he was always looking for an excuse to scream at the men. He was ten times as overbearing as a provincial party secretary. Mengzi had to restrain himself from slugging him.

That was when the wall support collapsed, he recalled.

The creaking noise from the supporting frame intensified. At first, Mengzi thought he was imagining it, for by then he'd gotten used to the trembling rope ladder, and his sweat seemed to have washed away his aches and pains. He knew, however, that the pain was just biding its time in his bone marrow, where it would brew and stew until it was released, and would devour him. He had no time for the pain, for he wanted to focus on what he was doing and do it well, now that he'd chosen to take on the work. At this moment, doing his job was the only way to maintain his dignity, and he did not intend to slack off, though, in fact, he couldn't even if he wanted to. The shovel-man started digging the moment Mengzi reached the bottom. Something terrible was virtually assured if he once again over-filled the basket, so he filled it this time with only slightly over three shovelfuls. When he stepped on the ladder, Mengzi mustered the strength to climb up in one go. He discovered that the faster he stepped on the ladder, the easier it was to go up; if he went too slowly, even his body picked on him. With a total weight of well over a hundred pounds, he had to be quick at grabbing and stepping. He did not feel like dawdling, wanting to test himself to see if he was cut out to be a sand boy. He had worked in the fields, but that was light work, while carrying sand used up all his strength. Time to see if he'd improved over his former self, muddling through life. Now he wanted to put his experience to work toward a decent life. Knowing how hard it was hard to stay alive, he might as well start with the tough life of a sand boy.

He was surprised that the wall support was making such a noise. The creaks were getting louder by the time he reached the bottom, screeching like a pack of squealing giant rats. It was terrifying. Then sand began to fall. Huaqiu, who was relieving himself in a corner of the pit, screamed:

"Oh no, the support is collapsing!"

"Shut up!" Baldy Wang yelled.

Mengzi was complaining about Huaqiu and his unlucky words when the creaks grew even louder; sand rained down as a tremor spread down from above. I'm going to be buried alive. Mengzi panicked. He wanted to look up, but sand and dirt poured down like water, a loud bang went off in his head, and everything turned blank. As fright gripped him, he heard the shovel-man scream and Baldy Wang growl. Huaqiu was wailing. He could have made it out; he should have gone up when Mengzi got down. But no, he had to piss in the pit; the wall support would not wait for him to finish. The earth shoved and pressed, pushing the support's limit to the extreme, until it snapped.

A din filled his ears, but Mengzi could not tell what it was, except that it pounded on his head; darkness crowded in on him, so real he could reach out and touch it. With his eyes shut, he felt its viscosity, mixed with dirt, dust, despair, and terror. Everything around and below him was shaking, like an earthquake; he had experienced one of those as a child, when the ground shuddered like a sow shaking off lice. He and Lingguan had grabbed hold of each other, trembling, their minds wiped clean. Death had always felt distant, until that time, when it was right there near them, but the fear subsided after a while. Once death was no longer a threat, Mengzi returned to his old self. Death surprised him by tailing him stealthily, baring its teeth when he was not paying attention. He might die this time, he thought. Oddly, though fear was there in him, the idea of death was what really bothered him. It was a jumbled emotion, not a clearly defined thought. He just felt that dying now would be a waste.

More severe quaking followed. Rocks fell on his arms, which he'd wrapped around his head. That's it, he thought. His mind went blank. Dust motes flew, and he heard someone cough, then scream in pain, and then sob. It was Huaqiu, Mengzi could tell.

"Ma!" Huaqiu bawled.

Finally, sand and rocks stopped falling, but the support was still creaking. Mengzi was not courageous enough to look up, though he had the feeling that the palm-sized sky was gone. Cautiously, he opened his eyes, but could not see anything. He was horrified by a void large enough to overtake many things—the sky, the earth, and the heart. Terror crowded out everything, leaving only an overwhelming void.

Little by little, when his heart crystalized in the void, he realized that the leaden blackness was crushing his head. A cymbal was banging in his ears: Kuang! Kuang! Kuang! Holding his head, he sat on his haunches as he thought, Do what you must, old man in heaven!

Someone rushed up and wrapped his arms around Mengzi, followed by another one. He was happy despite the fact that he could not tell who they were. There was no need to know who, so long as it was somebody. When a calamitous misfortune strikes, the greatest comfort is having someone to hold on to. That notion is most precious at the moment of death.

All noise ceased as the darkness deepened, but Huaqiu had stopped crying. No one made a sound, obviously because they were stunned into silence by the disaster that had come too suddenly for them to think rationally. Mengzi could tell, however, that the pit was sealed, though it had yet to collapse completely; the willow logs had stopped most of the sand and rocks, and what was falling was fine grains of sand sifting through the gaps. His mood brightened by the new discovery, he squeezed someone's hand and asked:

"Is everyone all right?"

"What do you mean, all right?" Baldy Wang grumbled, "We're buried alive."

"Thank goodness for the wooden supports," Huaqiu said.

Mengzi was relieved in spite of the stuffiness in his chest, which was likely caused by the swirling dust in the darkness. Feeling a load off his chest, he said to himself, Luckily, the pit wasn't too deep; we'd be drowned rats if we'd reached the water table.

"It's all right, they'll dig us out," Huaqiu said.

"With the little air in here, we'll be corpses by then," Baldy Wang said.

Mengzi felt himself going numb. Baldy was right. Why hadn't it occurred to him? With everyone breathing, what little air remained would soon be gone. It was hard to say if they would be dug out, but even if they were, they'd be corpses. Huaqiu was sobbing again, a depressing sound in the viscous night.

"What are you crying about?" Mengzi reproached him. "A real man is never afraid to die."

"My wife just had a baby—" Huaqiu said between sobs.

"Don't be afraid they'll starve to death." Baldy Wang said coldly, "You see, there are more bachelors than widows in the world."

That effectively shut Huaqiu up.

A somewhat soft hand reached over, which Mengzi could tell belonged to Huaqiu, so he gave it a squeeze. Huaqiu slumped to the ground and, leaning against Mengzi, began to pant.

"Go ahead and die." Baldy mumbled. "All of you."

Mengzi sensed something warm and moist in his feet; he reached down and his hand came up sticky. An acrid stench assaulted his nose, and he thought it might have been from Huaqiu peeing. "Baldy, get a light on." He called out several times before light followed a loud click to show Baldy's mud-spattered face and Huaqiu staring wide-eyed in terror.

Under the light Mengzi saw his sticky hand was stained red. "Blood!" Huaqiu yelled out. Mengzi had spotted the shovel-man, lying in a heap. Baldy had seen it too. The light went out and the thick darkness pressed up again.

"Get the light on. Get it back on." Mengzi called out.

The light came on. Mengzi got close enough to see that half of the shovel-man's head was missing, and there was a pool of red and white around it. The light flickered before going out again.

A numbness spread from the top of Mengzi's head to his limbs. He shivered and rubbed his hand on the sand to clean it, while his stomach churned.

"Mengzi." Huaqiu called out to him and reached over. Mengzi took the hand and squeezed hard a few times.

"Is he dead?" Huaqiu asked in a quaking voice.

"Half of his head is gone." Baldy said. "He couldn't live even if he wanted to."

Mengzi couldn't stand the repugnant man, who talked about the shovel-man like a dog or cat. "Get the light on again." Mengzi flared up.

"I don't have much lighter fluid," Wang said.

"I said light it." Mengzi snarled.

Light filled the pit again, following Baldy's unhappy complaints.

The top of the pit was still pitch black, making it impossible to see the degree of damage. But it seemed that the wall had collapsed not far from the opening, for he could vaguely make out the jumble of logs, which must have been holding up the fallen rock and sand.

He nudged the shovel-man's body; it was limp. The man had to be dead by now, unless a man can survive on half a brain. A blank look showed on what remained of his face, one that had worn a mean expression only moments before. Now, half the face was gone, taking his spite along and leaving his body with half a head in a pool of his own blood. Death had become their shadows, Mengzi realized, and made a presence when opportunity allowed.

Huaqiu crawled away from the dead man when the light was on. He had been right next to the shovel-man and would have been a goner had the rock shifted direction just a little. But he was clearly oblivious to the possibility; it was the corpse that frightened him. His fear spread from his quaking body out into the small space, where it fermented.

Mengzi shifted his body and squatted back down as he extinguished the lighter, while the other two moved closer to him. Darkness blotted out the sight of the corpse, but the gray brain matter and red blood were lodged in his head, where they seemed whirl. He felt nauseous. Strangely, he was no longer afraid. Where would I be now if the rock had hit me?

An unusual sensation came upon him, flashing by each time he encountered death. His head would be empty except for the feeling, which changed everything under the sun. Money, wealth, reputation, and women all faded out, and what had weighed heavily on his mind became light and insignificant. Normally, he would have been gripped by fear, but now with the sensation fermenting in his mind, he was unaffected by the corpse, the brain matter, or the blood. All he could think of was, Where would I be now if the rock had hit me?

Someone grabbed his hand again. From the new callouses, it was easy to tell the hand belonged to Huaqiu. Mengzi knew his friend was scared to death, just as he had been. His hair had stood on end when he'd seen a skeleton once at a hospital. Later, when he'd seen enough dead bodies, he realized he also had a skeleton that went everywhere with him. There was nothing to fear. Terror was gone, replaced by another reaction at some point; he hated the thought of dying like this.

If he died, then people would say he deserved it, after stealing sand. Mengzi did not want to die as a thief. If he'd known he would die here and now, he would have used a knife in the fight with the poachers. Now it became clear that a man's death mattered more than his life. He would be a thief who deserved death if he died now, while back then he would have been a martyr. He would be the same man but his true worth would differ based on how he lost his life. As he continued the train of thought, Mengzi rued the lack of careful thinking that had led him here with Huaqiu. To be sure, he hadn't considered himself a thief at first. In his view the sand did not belong to the Zhang or Li family, but to anyone who could get his hands on it, but he would not be able to stop foul-mouthed people from calling him a thief. His parents had raised him for twenty-some years, and he would have wasted his life if he were to die as a thief.

His mother would cry, he was sure. She'd weep for him whether he died a thief or a martyr. But not his father; he would curse Mengzi for not making a name for himself, but maybe shed a tear or two. Mengzi could care less for his father's tears, while he could not rid his mind of the sound and image of his mother weeping. Touched by the thought of her crying for him, a stabbing pain touched his heart.

How would she go on living?

It was quiet at the bottom of the pit, now that darkness had overwhelmed everything. The sounds of heartbeats and breathing filled the cramped space. Mengzi could not see the other two men, whose despair and terror were palpable. At a moment like this, death was a near certainty. Once the frame holding back the debris wore out, tons of sand and rocks would come crashing down to bury him; or, a few sneaky rocks would slip through the barrier and whiz down to pose a serious threat to his head. Or, the sand and rocks were so densely packed that no air could get through, and what little air they had would last them only a few hours. A sand boy had died of suffocation in another pit several days before.

He heard a faint din that came from outside. He wondered what it was like out there. Were the villagers alerted to the disaster? They had to be. Mao Dan would surely be talking up a streak, not to mention those sand boys, who loved to gossip. Gawkers would fill the riverbank and spread the news to the village. How his mother must be wailing over him.

"Dai!" Huaqiu shouted hoarsely at the opening.

"Don't shout, they can't hear you." Baldy said in a chilly voice. "They're frantic and frenzied out there now."

He's right, Mengzi thought.

3

It had quieted down outside, followed by a deafening buzz that echoed his heartbeat, though it could have been just his imagination. Mengzi exhaled deeply. He hated it that death was imminent, though he had claimed he was not afraid of dying. He reflected upon what he'd done so far: he'd screwed Shuangfu's wife, endured Hantou's death, traveled to Pig's Belly Well with Meng Baye, and bedded Harelip's woman. That was all there was; in less than three decades, this was the sum total of his achievements. Was this really his life's worth, that which Lingguan had talked about?

"What are you thinking about, Mengzi?" Huaqiu asked.

"I'm thinking I've wasted my life. I realize I should have done more—good deeds, of course. It's too late now, even if I wanted to. So, I'll just have to let it go. I don't have long to live, and crying is useless. Tell me, what's the first thing you want to do if we get out alive?"

"I want to leave the village and see what the outside world is like. What about you, Papa Wang?"

"I'd take a bag of explosives to blow up all the corrupt officials who have cheated and hurt people." Baldy Wang gnashed his teeth. "I have to die, so I'd want them to die with me." Wang had lived a life of degradation owing to poverty, was respected by no one; cadres from the county office kept confiscating his grain because he'd had more children than family planning allowed.

"I've wanted to do that, too." Mengzi laughed. "But a lot more would take the place of the ones you killed and continue cheating you."

"The old Daoist priest once said they're entitled to cheat people. Do you know who they were in their previous lives? They were local bullies and evil gentry who had been cast out. You took their land and split their property, so they were reborn to get it back in this life."

The banter died out, for no one was in a talking mood. Slumping against the wall, Mengzi told himself that everything would just be a dream if he were to die there. His past, present, and future would be a dream, so death must be the same, but what happened after death? Was there really another lifetime, or did everything end here? It would be nice to have another chance to go through life. He was loath to disappear from the world like a burst bubble. His mother had given birth to him after carrying him to term; how would it be different from not being born at all if he died without accomplishing a thing? Mengzi rued his lack of diligence at school. He had always believed that education was useless. Later on, as a middle school graduate, he'd worked in the field with Lingguan, a high school student, and still failed to see the advantage of more education. But then Lingguan had escaped, leaving Shawan for an unknown world, while he remained to turn the soil. Life circled around and around on the same path, like a millstone; nothing had changed except for his boyish face, which had aged. Now he was stuck at the bottom of a pit, like a rat. If he had known this would happen, he'd have left home to see the outside world, the kaleidoscopic world that had lured his younger brother away. Now he was no different than a toad caught under a little bowl, a palm-sized space where life and death were determined. How could he willingly accept that outcome?

Breathing deeply, he shook his head and drove his mother's sad face out of his mind. He did not want to think about anything unhappy, since he was about to die, and yet her face kept finding its way into his head. His older brother was dead, he continued his train of thoughts, and his younger brother had not been heard from, so it would be the end of her if something terrible happened to him. Tears flowed as he choked up, but he struggled to hold back his sobs and swallow his tears. He could hear Huaqiu doing the same.

"We're going to die, but I'm not even thirty years old, and I've yet to make something of myself," Huaqiu sobbed.

He's right, Mengzi thought. If they died now, they'd have lived a muddled life, with nothing to show for it. What he could recall were brief moments, not all that different from not having lived at all. He should have done more, if only he'd known he would perish so young; or he should have studied more. He'd have been a better student if he'd known his life would end prematurely. For someone born to live off the land, education did not mean much, since all the material would eventually be buried in the dirt. Yet, death would swiftly come when his mind was still a jumble of thoughts; he might have understood more if he'd studied more. He did not want to die yet.

Mengzi wished he'd known the secret of life and death. What was death? His father was always saying that death was like blowing out a lamp. When the light was out, was that the end? The flame of life that had been burning bright went out in the wind. Where did it go? Did everything really just disappear? A lively person could be gone all of a sudden, like a burst bubble. He found that depressing. Now he'd prefer to believe in a next life, even if he had to suffer the lethal flames in hell, for it was better than bursting like a bubble. In folk stories there were eighteen levels of hell, where denizens were cut by knives, cleaved by saws, burned in fires, stoned by rocks, and so on. He would take them all, anything, so as long there was something more. No pain was too great if there would be something else.

The three men fell silent. Mengzi stared at the darkness, willing a dot of light to appear, but it didn't work. It was the darkness of nothingness— not even darkness but just a sense of its existence. He could feel the texture of the wall behind him and the people nearby, which was proof that he was not dead yet. Proof—he had stolen the concept from Lingguan. If he died this time, his tomb would be the proof that he had lived. No, he wouldn't even have a tomb. Based on local custom, those who had no children were not qualified to be entombed in a coffin. He would simply be taken to a distant sand hollow, where a stack of wheat stalks would be set up to cremate him, and whatever was left would be fed into the bellies of dogs or wolves. The villagers called anyone dying under this condition a "Big Dead Baby."

Mengzi could not stand it when he was hit by the possibility that he would end up as a "Big Dead Baby." After those in his generation died

out, no one would know Mengzi had lived. No one. Even now, the proof
of his existence was sleeping with Shuangfu's wife, stealing sand, and
being buried in the pit. That was all. These events of no significance were
the proof that he'd been here.

He'd have left more behind had he known he'd die so young. To
be sure, it would have to be something positive, like repairing a bridge,
or paving a road, helping people, or doing deeds his mother considered
good. If possible, he'd do his best to help lonely old people. Lingguan had
been right when he'd said a man's worth is manifested in his actions. One
chose to be an immortal, a saint, a demon or an evil spirit. Sadly, he'd
come to his senses too late. Lingguan had also said that death was the
best teacher, he recalled; when one understood what it meant to be alive
is when one knows about death. These thoughts, which he'd normally
considered nonsensical, would not have occurred to him if he hadn't been
buried and was about to die.

The stickiness under his feet did not lessen. It must be the shovel-
man's blood or brain matter. He was not interested in figuring it out,
for the thought of the man still conjured up his cunning face and mean-
spirited look, plus the gray matter and red blood. That was all. Perhaps
those were the shovel-man's proof that he had lived. He would likely
wear a smile to leave a better image behind if he'd known a rock would
take away half of his head.

Death was the best motion-stopper, freezing everything in eternity.

4

There was no day or night in the darkness, so he had no idea how
much time had passed. He was famished, a hunger different from all
the others, the kind that rose when his heart was suspended in the air to
be roasted. Talking no longer interested him; whatever he'd wanted to

say died inside him, now that he was at death's door. When one died, whatever one said was pointless, like a fart vanishing as soon as it emerges; it was the same as saying nothing at all.

Huaqiu, on the other hand, expressed quite a bit of regret that came from hindsight, incurring a rebuke from Baldy Wang, which shut him up. Baldy was right to chastise him. At a time like this, it was better to keep quiet, since nothing he said was of any use, except to make himself feel worse; he should just steep his heart in the darkness and reveal nothing, until the large net called death came down on him. He should not worry needlessly, since he was certain of the final outcome; instead, he should pass his remaining time as best he could. Everyone dies in the end.

Mengzi knew no one lived forever, but the realization did not lift him out of the funk. He was surrounded by darkness, but his heart was an ashen gray; it felt as if he were all alone in a vast wilderness, where everything looked bleak. The air was stilled in the pit, but a chill wind blew past his heart. Now he thought he could understand Hantou, who must have felt the same before he died. At such moments, no one can help you, you are detached from everyone, including lovers, friends, parents, and children. You must face the inevitable alone.

So he ought to put his mind at ease and stop giving himself a hard time.

Why don't people make it easy on themselves when they're alive, since no one can avoid the final outcome? he asked himself. All the fights, possession by force or trickery, and worries were meaningless. Mengzi was gripped by profound regret over his disputes with others.

He had been utterly foolish, he thought. Consumed by only what was in front of him, there was nothing he wouldn't fight over, even if it cost him his life. The little gain and pathetic gratification were long gone, while his ferocious look, like the mean expression on the shovel-man's face, stayed behind, frozen by death.

Mengzi let out a long sigh.

"I'm dying before I know what life is all about." Huaqiu sighed. "Do you think there's really an old man up there?"

"Forget him. It doesn't matter if there's one or not," Mengzi said. "I used to believe there was," Baldy Wang said. "How would we live if there wasn't one? Everyone picks on you and you have no place to lodge a complaint. Only the thought of him made me feel better. I could tell myself not to be intimidated because the old man had eyes to see. But not anymore. I've long since given up on him."

"Why is that?" Huaqiu asked.

"I've kept my eyes open for decades now; I look and I watch, but he refuses to see what's happening. See how those who cheat, hurt, deceive, and bully people all occupy the highest positions and get to eat and drink the best. Then look at me. Do you know I've never even killed a chicken or argued with anyone, but what good has that done me? I'm so poor I can barely afford a pair of pants. Why else would I become a sand boy?"

"I hope there is an old man up there," Huaqiu whimpered. "Please help me, old man up there. I'm still young."

"Shut up." Mengzi snapped. "You're pissing me off."

"He's right." Wang said. "Why don't you get some rest? Talking requires energy too, you know."

"I'm starving," Huaqiu complained with a sigh.

The hunger pangs were raging with a vengeance. It had been a long time since they'd had their last meal. It was hand-cut noodles. His mouth watered at the thought of the noodles in heavy sauce. He kicked himself for not eating more. It was torture to think about it, for his insides seemed to be churning, impossible to bear. Mengzi found himself envying the shovel-man. See what a clean death he had. Half his head was taken off when he least expected it, so he likely felt no pain. The hunger, the darkness, and the feeling of waiting to die were beyond his ability to endure. What was most frightening was not death itself, but the lucid knowledge of irreversible death and the unavoidable wait that gave rise to helplessness, terror, and anxiety.

That was the deadliest.

Mengzi heard Baldy gulp mouthfuls of air. "That's odd," Baldy mumbled. He flicked his lighter to fill the space with light and Mengzi's field of vision with the disgusting dead body.

"Turn it off," a disgruntled Mengzi said. They'd been in the dark too long, and the light hurt their eyes, while the dead man was a painful sight. Ignoring him, Baldy shone his lighter all around before stopping on something. He shook it gently. Mengzi saw it was a small water pump, a necessity once they reached ten meters, in case they could not get the water out fast enough.

"See this? It gives us some air to survive on." Wang tipped the lighter toward the pump head and the flame dipped to the side.

"We're saved!" Huaqiu shouted. Mengzi perked up too. He stood up to touch the rubber hose, which to him was more captivating than any woman in the world. A hint of a breeze escaped through the gap, sending a coolness deep into his heart.

"Don't shake it too much. We'll be doomed if the top falls shut." Wang said.

With the help of the lighter, Mengzi could see the top, where the logs were buckled, and broken willow branches hung down. He knew they were holding back the lethal sand and rocks. Most frightening was a boulder the size of a small cow that was held back by the logs, but looked as if it could crash down if he breathed on it. He sucked in cold air; the exhilaration over the pump vanished.

Wang put the hose into his mouth and shouted like a wild animal. Mengzi figured the sound would likely travel up along the hose. Huaqiu added a shout.

When they stopped after a few shouts, a voice slipped down, "You're not dead yet."

"You're the one who's dead," Huaqiu yelled out. Then they heard noise.

"Don't be afraid. We'll get you out."

"Don't worry about that now. Get us something to eat, we're starving," Wang said. "Send something watery down that won't stop up the hose."

"That bald head of his has some good ideas," Mengzi laughed. "How about something soupy?" he said. "Not too sticky," he added before looking up cautiously.

The light was out. The boulder was rocking in his heart.

Chapter Ten

Dark clouds gather at Nanshan like a knotted rope
Thunder roars, lightning strikes, comes a rainstorm

1

Six days went by before Mengzi and the others saw daylight again, he was told later. Fortunately, the hose had supplied them with oxygen and liquid food. In the meantime, Shuangfu worked with his sand boys to dig a tunnel diagonally, skirting the wall supports to reach the bottom of the pit and bring up three live men and a dead one.

They were carried back to the village, with their eyes shielded. After a prolonged stay in the dark, anyone would go blind when a sudden bright light shone on them. Covered in several layers of black cloth, Mengzi could still feel the sunlight stream through and prick his eyes; it was a dazzling red light that seemed to blanket heaven and earth. He felt his body burning; his ears detected a cacophony of wind and human sounds that included his mother's urgent, incessant questions. He wanted to get down and walk on his own, but the burly man's back held him in place as its owner stomped heavily on the ground.

He knew the village must have been turned upside down over those days. Sand boys died all the time, but having four buried at one time meant funerals at four families, something that had never before happened in the village. Mengzi did not want to think about it; he'd be dead and gone and that was that. But he survived, so he did not need to dredge up unpleasant thoughts or ponder pointless matters. But he found, to his surprise, that the commotion over their accident and rescue was quickly overshadowed by what was going on at White Tiger Pass. The machines continued to roar, and the sand boys kept busy; the life and death of the four was no longer the most arresting event. The people's eyes were once again focused on the cold gold in the burning hot sand.

He lay down when he got home. The familiar odor of manure heating the kang instantly wrapped him in the warmth of home. Stretching his arms and legs, he savored the luxury of his new-found freedom, so comforting that he felt his soul melting. His mother kept asking what he wanted to eat, while his father coughed constantly. The acrid smell of tobacco spread over, rekindling a long-lost feeling.

After some noodle soup, he removed the cloth from his eyes, but did not feel blinded by any bright light. Then he saw his mother had closed the door and pulled down the curtains. There were people in the room, but none of them said anything.

"Ai! Wealth is determined by your fate and your life is your wealth," one of them said after a long silence.

"We'll live poorly when we're poor," his mother said. "Don't go back to the site. Over the past few days, I've shed enough tears to fill a basin, if not a bucket."

Mengzi felt terrible; he wanted to say something, but did not know what.

Mengzi did not get out of bed for several days. His legs were wobbly, his temples pounded, and his head hurt. Knowing he wanted to use the toilet, his mother handed him a wash basin, but he pushed her hand away and found his way to his shoes. He thought his eyes should be used to light after several transitory days, but the bright rays created sharp pains the moment he opened the door. He quickly covered his eyes.

"What's wrong? What's the matter now?" His mother rushed toward him.

"Nothing." He squinted as he followed the walkway out the gate. As soon as he was out in the light, countless golden needles rained down on him. Afraid he might still go blind, he quickly found a spot to relieve himself.

Mengzi could hear the faint noise of machines roaring at White Tiger Pass. A strange queasiness rose, his heart was palpitating. He moved to the wheat stack by the wall, where he squatted down. A warm sunlight enveloped him snugly, licking at his heart again and again.

"Mengzi!"

It was Baigou's voice. Mengzi mumbled a reply.

"I want to dig a pit too," Baigou said.

Mengzi detested the topic. His stomach churned the moment he thought about the pit. For days he had subsisted on a liquid diet; the watery food, along with the sand and filth in the hose and its rubbery smell, had etched itself into his soul. Just thinking about it made him sick.

"In this day and age, a coward starves to death," Baigou continued. "Look at Shuangfu. He bought this and sold that, and became somebody after a few risky ventures."

Mengzi frowned. He was exhausted, wanting only to be alone for some peace and quiet. The sun licked at his eyelids, creating a red brilliance, but his heart seemed mired in the darkness of the pit. Everything else was a dream.

"Leave him alone, Baigou." Mengzi heard his mother say. "We were born to make a living off the land, so that's what we'll do. You want to be a phoenix or a dragon, you go ahead, but don't go dragging him into this."

"I'm giving you a gold bar, but you're tossing it away like a brick."
Baigou smiled. "You don't know what's good for you, Aunty."

"You can soar into the sky or sink to the ground, and I have no say.
But I want you to stop egging him on. Huaqiu put him up to this and it
nearly cost him his life."

"Huaqiu's mother blames Mengzi." Baigou laughed. "And you blame
Huaqiu."

Mengzi had to laugh. It was impossible to tell who egged who on.

"Give it some thought, all right?" Baigou patted himself on the back.
"Did you know that the city government plans to set up a municipality in
Shawan? Put everything aside, White Tiger Pass alone is a gold nugget.
When that happens, the land will be more valuable than gold and you can
rue all you want, but it will be too late."

"Go on. Get out of here." Mengzi's mother said in jest. "My head
hurts when you breeze in."

Baigou yawned and walked off.

Mengzi leaned against a stack of wheat stalks to soak up the sun until
every bone in his body went soft. Emptying his mind, he let himself melt
in the warm sun.

After a long rest, he went over to Huaqiu's house, where he learned
that his friend had had a speedy recovery, and had left for the city to make
some money. Reminded of Baldy Wang, Mengzi decided to check on
him. They'd had little to do with one another before the disaster, but it
had changed everything. No matter how he looked at it, Wang and he had
come out alive together.

He had barely rounded the wall when he saw a crowd outside Wang's
house. Someone told him that Wang had failed to pay the water fee and
a fine for breaking the family planning law, so the county government
sent people down to confiscate his grain and some rickety furniture.

The peasants no longer had to pay agriculture taxes, but the water fee had gone up several times more than the taxes. Baldy Wang had started working as a sand boy precisely because he could not pay the fee. Later Mengzi would wonder if the seed for the shocking bloodshed had been sown on this day.

2

After the county cadre left, Baldy Wang's wife continued to wail, her dry howls drowning out the machines at the Pass. Meng Baye tried to console her, but failed to stop her from crying, so he told some villagers to keep an eye on her in case she decided to take the easy way out. He went home for some flour to tide the Wang family over, before heading to Laoshun's house; he wanted to ask Mengzi's mother to go talk to Baldy's wife. She had honed her eloquence after arguing with his father all their married life; she might not be much help in a crisis, but she was very good at talking people around. Whenever villagers got into an argument, she was able to resolve the issues for them.

Meng Baye walked in to see the old couple beaming. When he asked, he was told by Mengzi's mother that Ying'er had returned from her parents' house with an agreement to marry Mengzi. Laoshun then told Meng about Mao Dan breaking up the marriage proposal, so amusing Meng that he laughed till he cried.

"What about Lanlan?"

"The girl has made up her mind. She'd rather die at our house than go back there," Mengzi's mother replied.

"But that could spell trouble. It was a swap marriage, so they'll raise hell if she stays here." Meng said with concern.

"Where marriage is concerned, if both people are willing, not even a knife can sever the tie," Mengzi's mother said.

"It's not a bad idea and it makes things easy for her to marry the younger brother," Meng said after mulling it over. "You'd save a large sum of money while Mengzi gets a son without doing a thing. That daughter-in-law of yours is one of the best girls around, with a pretty face and a good heart. But the Bai family is tough, especially the tigress; a simple breath from her could turn the weather bad. Do you think she'd take it lying down if Lanlan refused to go back?"

The smiles disappeared from the couple's faces.

"Bring her out and I'll get a straight answer from her," Meng said.

Ying'er was teaching Yue'er a few common tunes, such as "Sister Yellow Flower," "Big Eyes," and "Sweetheart." A fast learner, Yue'er could sing them pretty well. She could also improvise with the lyrics and make them sound natural and pleasing, which surprised Ying'er. What she found wanting were the lyrics, which were too literary and lacked the rustic flair of a folk tune. Ying'er got up when her mother-in-law called for her.

The serious look on Meng Baye's face told her what he had in mind. She'd rather not talk about the matter, but liked even less what Pockmark Xu had in mind. At least Mengzi was related to Lingguan.

"Are you really willing?" Meng asked, not saying what he was asking about.

Ying'er nodded.

"What if your family objects? You have to think it over carefully; they are, after all, your family."

She nodded again after a momentary hesitation.

"Once the arrow leaves the bow, it can never return. You must stay strong, not in like a tiger and out like a lamb."

A muscle on her face twitched before she gave another nod.

"If it works out, it'll be fine. If not, don't ruin his good name. He's still a virgin, and his value will plummet. People will say, Mengzi's been spurned by a widow, and that would just about kill him."

His last phrase was harsh, but Ying'er knew it was the truth, so she nodded again before walking out.

"That's good." Meng breathed a sigh of relief. "The girl is pretty and even- tempered, not the flighty type." Meng continued, "Any word from Lingguan?"

"No, but I figure it's about time." Laoshun said while his wife sighed softly.

Meng then told Laoshun's wife to talk to Baldy Wang's wife. She agreed, but grumbled that they had their own urgent matter to deal with, and she was in no mood to help someone else. In the end, she went to the Wangs' house, taking along half of sack of flour and spewing half of cart load of talk.

She could not hide a premonition that the Bai Family would not give up so easily. Sure enough, Ying'er's mother arrived right after lunch. After a string of seemingly cordial "*Qinjia*" she came to the point and wanted her daughter home for a visit.

Laoshun frowned but did not respond, while Mengzi's mother said:

"She was just there, and now you want her go back again?"

"By going home for a visit, I mean stay for a while. She didn't have her baby with her when she came home last time, *Qinjia*. Her heart was in one place and her body in another, so she didn't get to really enjoy the visit. This time I want her to bring the baby along so she can stay longer, have a good time."

Laoshun jumped to his feet and went out without a word.

"That's not a good idea." Mengzi's mother smiled. "A married woman shouldn't be back at her parents' all the time."

"So, you know that too, do you?" Ying'er's mother said, her face grim.

Knowing the woman was referring to Lanlan, Mengzi's mother

changed the subject, "The baby is comfortable only here at home. Didn't he have some stomach trouble the last he went to your place?"

"That was nothing. Every child has stomach troubles." The sincere smile she'd worn at first vanished, replaced by a mocking look. "Every girl comes from a mother's belly. Some people can keep their married daughter at home year around, so why should mine stay behind to toil like a donkey?"

That did not sit well with Mengzi's mother. "Who toils like a donkey? Call her in and ask her. We treat her like royalty. If she's cold, we make her warm, and if she's hungry, we take food to her. Not even the Empress has it better."

"Like the Empress, that's fine." Ying'er's mother softened her tone. "I didn't come here to fight. It's clear, if your daughter comes, mine goes. If your daughter won't go to her in-law's house, mine will come back to her house. That's how a marriage swap works. I don't know about you, but I don't want to lose face."

Mengzi's mother's face fell, and blanched. She began to sob, "It's all Hantou's fault, karmic retribution."

At the mention of Hantou, the look on Ying'er's mother's face softened. She too was about to cry until Mengzi's mother glanced at her, which she took as a sign that the sobs were a ruse, so her face turned grim again.

Lanlan, who had just finished her daily meditation, walked in and said coolly, "What are you howling for, Ma? You're not going to cry him back to life, you know." She did not look at or greet her mother-in-law.

Ying'er's mother's face turned bright red, as if burned, when she saw Lanlan, but not a word escaped from her mouth. Instead, she went to Ying'er's room, picked up the baby, and dragged her daughter toward the door. The old couple stood guard, ready to fight.

"Put the baby down," Mengzi's mother demanded. "She's your

daughter, but he's my grandson."

The new development sent Ying'er's mother back inside, where she laid the baby on the kang. She might have been a bit heavy-handed, for the baby began to cry, along with Ying'er.

"What are you crying for, you worthless girl? Their daughter came from her mother's belly, do you think you burst from a rock?" Ying'er's mother shouted.

Laoshun squatted on the steps outside, with his head down. Tears streaked his wife's face, while Lanlan went to her room with a blank expression.

Ying'er's mother reached out to her, but she shook her mother's hand off. "Why won't you let me have a few days of peace, Ma?"

"How about me? Tell me, why won't anyone let me live a good life? Their daughter knows how to make her parents' happy, why can't you?"

Ying'er started crying again. The baby was bawling his eyes out by then, so Mengzi's mother went in to pick him up. She patted him while tears wetted her face.

"What's the point in living?" Laoshun mumbled as he swayed to his feet and walked out the gate.

Baby in arms, his wife caught up with him and whispered:

"Where do you think you're going? What will I do if she wants to take the baby with her?"

"She can't do that, there are laws."

"She's the baby's mother. The law is on their side," she said, stopping him in his tracks. He followed her back and sat down on the step.

"They think they have reason on their side." They heard Ying'er's mother talking. "Their daughter has the right to stay home with them for however long she wants, but mine can't even go out."

"Let her go. Let her go home," Laoshun roared as he jumped to his feet.

"I won't do it!" his wife shrieked. "I still have some say about my daughter-in-law."

"So I don't have any say about mine?"

Mengzi's mother had nothing to say to that, while her husband pointed at her and said, "Let her go if she wants. Don't be a troublemaker. You can't tie her up."

His wife turned her head without a word.

"You go on home, Ma," Ying'er said tearfully. "I'll come see you in a few days, all right? Please, do me this favor, won't you?"

"Not on your life!" Her mother responded shrilly. "They're killing me slowly, so why should I be nice to them? You have two options; you come back with me or I stay put. You like the Chen's house so much, I should stay too."

"Sure. You're welcome to stay." Mengzi's mother cradled the baby in her arms and clapped.

"So he can have a wife and a concubine?" Ying'er's mother was not finished.

"Stop the nonsense!" Laoshun yelled at her. He didn't understand what the woman meant? There was his wife, but who was the concubine? Herself or Ying'er? Was the woman implying he wanted to keep Ying'er for himself? Either way, he'd be a laughingstock if anyone heard that. "Go on, go home. Tell them to go, old hag. Why do you want to keep her here? The frost hasn't killed off all the women yet."

"Let her talk," Mengzi's mother raised her voice, "Sure, go ahead. You're welcome to be whatever you want, a wife or a concubine. A mother even. I can take whatever you say."

"Bullshit, total bullshit!" Laoshun roared.

"Remember, you said it." Ying'er's mother came out of the bedroom, grabbed Laoshun by the wrist, and dragged him over to the next room, where she began unbuttoning her blouse. "So, that's it. I'll be the concubine if you're up to it."

"Let go of me! Let go!" Laoshun yelled.

The commotion sent Meng Baye rushing into the room, where he was greeted by the sight of Laoshun tangled up with the woman, who held his wrist to keep him from running off, while he clutched her other hand to prevent her from unbuttoning her blouse.

"You're putting on such a great show you should be on TV for the New Year's gala." Meng burst out laughing at the scene, and they dropped their hands.

Laoshun was tired from grappling with the woman, a big woman who was too much for a skinny man like him. Who could tell what embarrassing development might have ensued if Meng hadn't arrived in time. The other men, including Yue'er's father, came in to talk her around, calling her "qinjia."

Meng could not stop laughing. A glance at Laoshun and then at Ying'er's mother sent him into another laughing fit. Laoshun shook his head and laughed too, but his qinjia wore a steely look.

"One qinjia and another qinjia, like a hammer handle stuck between cheeks so tight you can't pull them apart," Meng jested.

"I want you to decide which side is right." Ying'er's mother fumed. "I'm here to take my daughter back to spend some time at home, but they refuse to let her go. Even a prisoner is let out for exercise. Tell me, do I have the right to ask my daughter to go with me?"

"Of course, you do," Meng said with a laugh.

"Do you have to ask?" Mengzi's mother came in with the baby. "You're like Liu Bei borrowing Jingzhou, with no intention of giving it back."

"Listen to her. Listen to what she's saying." Ying'er's mother sneered.

"What am I saying? I didn't say anything wrong," Mengzi's mother spat. "Don't think I don't know what goes on in the narrow mind of yours. Hantou is gone, but it was a legal and formal marriage, and you can't just come here to take your daughter back. You think everyone in the Chen family is dead, is that it?"

"My daughter was legally married to your son. What about your daughter? We didn't snatch her," Ying'er's mother jeered, and Laoshun's wife had nothing to say in return.

"Be nice to each other." Meng tried to smooth things over. "You're all getting on in years, so don't act like a couple of frightened little donkeys. You're both right. I think you're right to come get your daughter and you're right to want her to stay. You're her mother, so you want her back home for a few days where you can talk to your heart's content. Mother and daughter can spend time together and pour out their grievances."

"What grievance could she have?" Mengzi's mother said with visible displeasure. "I wait on her like an empress."

"Shut up," Laoshun barked. "Let him talk."

"You're right to ask her to go back." Meng smiled. "But you're also right to want to keep her around. Why? If your daughter had been acting like a bitch, they'd have shoved her out long ago. They wouldn't want to keep her. But they got along so well, she doesn't want her to leave. She misses her daughter-in-law even if she's gone only a few days. I know Ying'er is a good girl who's happy to call her mother-in-law Mama. And her mother-in-law treats her like one of her own, so she can't live without her, even for a few days. So that makes her right, too."

"Are you saying it's right for their daughter to come home and refuse to return, like a hawk leaving the nest?" Ying'er's mother glared at him.

Meng had nothing to say to that. He realized the woman was not to be taken lightly; every word she said was on target. Besides, no matter what they said, the Chen family had little justification; their daughter could come home to stay indefinitely while the other family could not even have theirs back for a visit. So, he said, "Where's Lanlan? Tell her to go back."

"Go—back?" Mengzi's mother drew her words out. "If she's back there, I'm afraid we won't even see a corpse later. She was an inch from death, and that has happened many times. She'll not step through the Bai family's door, even if her life depends on it."

"Listen, just listen to her." Ying'er's mother sneered. "As if only their daughter were raised by her mother."

"Why don't you talk about that spoiled son of yours? He's a bum," Mengzi's mother retorted.

"What about your son? He's dead, so go find my daughter another husband."

Laoshun's face darkened before she even finished; he stared daggers at her, as if ready to chew her up. Laoshun's wife blanched and fell silent, before she began to weep for Hantou.

"Now you're in the wrong." Meng Baye gave Ying'er's mother a disgusted look. "You never hit people in the face and you don't expose their shortcomings. How could you say something like that?" The other men echoed their sentiment. Knowing she had said the wrong thing, Ying'er's mother felt chastened.

But Meng knew Ying'er's mother had told the truth. Bai Fu was a living man despite his abusive tendency, while Hantou was gone. Separated by death, he was clearly no longer a real husband for Ying'er. Recalling what the couple had in mind, he realized it was the perfect opportunity to bring it up, like leading a donkey down the slope. "But I have to agree that what the Bai qinjia said makes sense." He decided to bring it out in the open. "Hantou is gone and Ying'er is still young. You can't ask her to be a widow forever. Laoshun, you and your wife have no justification to keep her. You could end up laughingstocks. What the Bai qinjia said might sound cruel, but its meaning is sound. You ought to find her a mate, no matter what. Lingguan is too young, so why not Mengzi. You don't have to spend any money for either one, and it saves lots of trouble."

"That's not what I had in mind." Ying'er's mother lost her calm.

"You didn't, but now you do. How's that? You've made it crystal clear and we're in agreement. I'll take it upon myself to talk these two around."

Even Meng Baye was impressed by what he'd just said. From the way he presented it, you'd think the idea had come from Ying'er's mother, and they needed to work on Laoshun and his wife. This way, Laoshun would not lose face. When it worked out, it would look as if Meng had talked them into it; if not, it was due to Laoshun and his wife's objection. They would not look bad in front of anyone.

"No, no way." Ying'er's mother was adamant.

"Why not?" Meng smiled again. "Don't be embarrassed, there's nothing to be embarrassed about, *Qinjia*. I think it'll work. Laoshun can object, that makes no difference. Why wouldn't it work? It'd bring everyone closer, and you all know what everyone is like, so your girl won't suffer. Ai. It's easy to raise a daughter, but hard to find her a good husband. You can know what's gold and what's silver, but you can't know what's in a person's heart. Some people may look pleasant, but deep down can be awful. If a girl marries someone like that, her life will be hard, but that's not the worst; she might end up dead. It happens all the time. Some parents are lured by money, and marry their daughters to bad seeds, ending up by sending their girls to the underworld. But with your ideas, we don't have to worry about that. It's perfect. You know what they're like, so you won't ever have to worry about your girl's well-being."

Hitting the mark by a fluke, Meng had managed to get Ying'er's mother thinking in a different direction. She had also heard that Zhao San, the match made by Pockmark Xu, did have money, but was into whoring and gambling. He was no good. She'd had her designs on the betrothal gifts, which she'd use to get her son another wife if Lanlan went through with her threat of divorce, but she'd been worried that Ying'er might suffer if she married Zhao. A mother is always closer to her daughter, who in turn understands her mother. Bai Fu, with his bad temper, often erupted and made her unhappy. As time went by, she got used to his temper, but her affection for him also waned. She would always worry if Ying'er suffered in a bad marriage. Mengzi had been coming to her house to help Lanlan out in the field, taking the hard work like a bull, and he had a good heart. Ying'er would not suffer with him. She pondered the matter,

"Hmm, this is—"

"No this or that." Meng sounded more resolute when he could see Ying'er's mother starting to come around. "Let's go ahead with it."

"This may sound terrible, but I have to say it now," Ying'er's mother said. "My daughter-in-law has to come back to us."

"That's no problem." Meng's vague reply sounded like a promise, but in fact he had not given any guarantee. I said all right for now. I'll try to talk Lanlan around later, Meng said to himself, before calling out to Mengzi's mother, "Why are you still standing there, woman? Go kill a chicken."

Mengzi's mother, who had been lost in thought, handed the baby to Laoshun and happily went out to catch a chicken.

"Make sure to choose the right time and place when you want an intimate moment," Meng teased Laoshun and Ying'er's mother, who blushed and smiled sheepishly.

3

Mengzi's mother promptly brought out some quick-fried chicken and wild rabbit. It was against their belief to eat meat right after a temper outburst, for people in Liangzhou thought that anger caused cancer. But a meatless meal in a light broth would not demonstrate affection toward each other. In order to prevent cancer from growing, Meng Baye asked Mengzi's mother to warm up some liquor to go with the meat; meat and alcohol worked together to stave off health hazards.

Ying'er came in with the baby, looking visibly pleased with the unexpected outcome. Lanlan, however, would not relent and stayed in her room to continue her meditation. Meng knew that she and her mother-in-law would spoil the mood for everyone if they were forced to be in the same room, so he let Lanlan stay where she was. Laoshun and his wife, Meng Baye, and Ying'er and her mother sat around a table, eating and drinking in high spirits.

It had been too long since Laoshun and his wife had been so happy, for they had been consumed by worry that Ying'er would leave and take her baby with her. They had mourned the death of their son and fretted over the possibility of her departure, constantly on tenterhooks. Meng's glib tongue had removed their fears. Demonstrably happy, they kept putting tender pieces into Ying'er's mother's bowl, no sign of the earlier spat on their beaming faces.

A few cups of liquor elevated Meng's mood even higher. A well-mannered drinker, he laughed heartily, his reddened cheeks making him look younger. The alcohol drew Ying'er's mother out of her reticence.

Intending to heighten the good mood, Meng downed three cups in a row to start a drinking game. Custom required anyone who wanted to start a new game to do that before they began. When he finished the third cup, he explained the game and the rules.

It was called "Two little bees." He gestured as he taught them the lyrics to a ditty. Two players raise their thumbs and sing "Flitting among the flowers" while uncurling their fists to imitate bee flight. "Flitting and flying," is followed by extending two fingers, showing a fist or an open palm to represent rock, paper, scissors. A pair of scissors cuts the paper that covers the stone that smashes the scissors, every object having its mortal foe. The winner raises a hand to slap the loser, who jerks his head and moans to mimic being hit. Whoever errs in the gestures is forced to drink.

Ying'er's mother easily mastered the simple steps.

What made everyone laugh was the moment when the same gesture was made by both players, which was called "west chamber" and required the couple to pucker up and air-kiss audibly.

Meng's act was so real that Ying'er's mother blushed from his air kisses; she could not bring herself to act it out and was penalized too much to want to continue.

Ying'er doubled over laughing, as did her mother-in-law. Laoshun tried to hold back, but could not keep from chuckling.

The game had dramatically enlivened the atmosphere.

Their mood reached its height after a few more rounds. Meng Baye no longer urged them to drink up; instead he wanted to stop them. When Liangzhou people invite friends to drink, if the guests do not throw up, the host is amiss in his task. A host should never stop the guests from drinking, for that would spoil the fun. Meng was never a fan of people throwing up, and always found a way to stop the drinking before that moment arrived. But this time, that introduced even more merrymaking.

Meng had a voice and singing style to match his character. His finest performance was a Liangzhou doggerel with a vast repertoire, including the likes of "Ten Li Pavilion," "Flying a Kite," and "Brother Wang Grazes Sheep," which touched upon every aspect of the residents' life. On this day he picked "Fifth Watch Disturbance" about the bride's first night.

In a surprisingly good voice, he began—

When the girl reaches twenty-one, she is delivered to her in-law's house;

Her figure, like a nice green onion, makes you marvel the more you look.

At the first watch, under a bright light in comes someone to make the bed.
Walnuts and dates clatter and roll around on the kang.

Ying'er smiled at the familiar scene. On her wedding night, once the jokesters had left, Huilanzi, who had accompanied the groom on his way over, tossed walnuts and dates all over the kang when she came in to make the bed and offer auspicious words. Walnuts representing a boy and dates a girl, all meant to wish the new bride a pair of children.

At the second watch, they blow out the lamp and kiss;
They want pillow talk, but are wary of others listening.

Let him listen and let him hear, the little woman does not care.
The eavesdroppers are those Pan Gu left behind.

Ying'er had missed the second watch experience. Hantou had lain stiffly facing the wall and remained there the whole night, too timid to touch her. It was not until the fourth night that he felt his way over, but it ended before it barely began. Later she learned that he was impotent. Beizhou and his friends, crouching outside the window, listened several nights in a row, but did not hear any stirring. Her mood darkened at the recollection, as Hantou's face floated into her mind. What a sad life he'd had, she thought.

At the third watch the moon rises, little brother stamps his foot.

Don't stamp your foot, little brother, I understand how you feel.

Unbuttoning the undergarment exposes the fair skin on the belly.
Arms tightly around each other, lips touch lips ever so sweetly.

Everyone laughed, all but Ying'er. That scene would not occur for her until one night several years after the wedding, and the little brother was Lingguan, not her husband. On that night, Lingguan floated under the moonlight toward her, splashing ripples of happiness in the harbor of her life. At that moment, a profound sense of longing swelled inside; as she looked at the baby's face, she was besieged by a bitter pain that flowed into her eyes and rolled down her face. Bending down to kiss the baby's face, she used the opportunity to wipe her face on his sleeve.

At the fourth watch, chickens cluck on the perch,
I curse the feathery creatures for calling so early.

A faint smile appeared on Ying'er's face. She had indeed cursed the chickens that night. Afraid that dawn would arrive if she shut her eyes, she had stayed awake all night, her arms wound tightly around Lingguan, nibbling him softly. It was not to waken him; she just simply could not stop herself, wishing she could swallow him whole. But, "The crescent moon travels west before daybreak/The chicks chirp in their coop. Wake up, sleeping elder brother/It's time for you to leave." Lingguan quietly dressed, quietly climbed down off the kang, and quietly turned back to bite her gently before quietly blending into the waning moonlight.

At the fifth watch, the moon sets; happily, I fall asleep.
My chin presses up against little brother's nape.

The groom's brother comes to "tread the threshold" and calls out, but no reply.

He pokes through the window with his stick, finally wakening the bride.

That brought another smile to Ying'er's face. It was a tender scene, though it had taken place not on her wedding night but several years later, and the little brother was not her husband. During the woefully few times they could spend the whole night together, Lingguan always turned his back when he slept, so she'd held him from behind and pressed her chin against his nape, rubbing it over and over like grinding an ink stone until he woke up aroused. Whoever made up the lyrics was quite something. How could he know all those details?

She recalled Lingguan coming to "tread the threshold" on the quiet, dull morning after the wedding. Custom required a groom's younger brother to tread the threshold, after which the newlyweds could leave the room. Ying'er woke up early, so did Hantou, who quickly dressed and sat on the bed, head down. When Lingguan knocked on the door, she let him in. He was still a middle school student, a typical schoolboy. Naturally, it had not occurred to her that one day the schoolboy would enter her life to fill the colossal void before leaving an even greater emptiness.

Lingguan walked in. He seemed shy, as he looked down at the floor, a plate of "oven buttons" in his hands. Wordlessly, he turned his back to her and emptied the plate of food items over his head into the wide lapel she'd held up for that purpose. That was the rite of treading the threshold.

She still recalled how she had placed the food on a table and taken out a red packet containing twenty yuan, a reward for the groom's younger brother for performing the rite. He'd taken it and walked out. Who knew he would later tread not only the door, but the bride herself? The thought brought another smile to her face.

Meng Baye's voice was getting increasingly spirited, evoking even louder laughter—

The little sister-in-law goes to tread the threshold, smiling with pursed lips.
The new bride sneers and says, don't laugh, little girl.
When you get married, you'll know how it feels.

This scene had not occurred. Her "little sister-in-law," Lanlan, was married on the same day. Ying'er married Lanlan's brother, while Lanlan married Ying'er's, thus bringing their longing for love and romance to an end.

Her in-laws and mother were so amused they could not stop laughing, but Ying'er felt tears well up inside and soon they were brimming in her eyes. She turned to quietly wipe them off.

Her sense of joy disappeared when the doggerel was over. Once stirred up, her emotions surged, causing her to ache for Lingguan. Suddenly reminded of the talk about Mengzi and her, her heart skipped a beat.

Will he come to tread the threshold when that happens? Resentment toward him rose, but she was not sure if she resented his departure or something else. But she smiled smugly when she contemplated the injury he would suffer if he had to perform the same rite again.

4

The festive air continued into the following day, when the in-laws laid their cards on the table, including the marriage prospects for Ying'er and Mengzi. Hantou had been dead for more than a hundred days, which made it acceptable for such a discussion. Once double-seven, the important forty-ninth day, passed after someone died, the hundredth-day mark was the next milestone. Human when alive, the dead are now deities; Hantou was done with everything in this world and became a deity.

Laoshun and his wife were delighted, killing two birds with one stone and untying the knot in their hearts. Ying'er's mother was pleased too. She and Lanlan argued all the time, but deep down she had to admit that Lanlan was all right and that she might not find anyone as good as her for her son. Moreover, Ying'er would have someone for the rest of her life. In her eyes, Mengzi was sharper than Hantou, and his being a virgin meant the Bai family would not lose face. She left in high spirits, with two wild rabbits from Laoshun.

Ying'er was conflicted, relieved to be free of Pockmark Xu's pestering and yet stressed over the impending marriage to Mengzi. Rationally, she knew it was an ideal situation, but marrying Lingguan was out of the question, and she could not remain a widow. She would rather be Mengzi's wife so she could continue to be Lingguan's sister-in-law than marry someone else and leave the Chen family. But her mood was clouded by the inability to control her own fate, like duckweed carried by the currents. Once her mother went home, she no longer had to put up a happy front, and gloom returned to her face.

Yue'er came to keep her company.

Yue'er had learned nearly every ballad Ying'er knew, but had not mastered them and could not match the indispensable simplicity. It was only with an unadorned mindset that the authentic, true quality of the folk tunes came through; affectation would ruin the tunes, which could then be called "songs," or anything but Liangzhou ballads.

What are Liangzhou ballads? "They are the thoughts in my heart and I cannot control them when I start. If you cut off my head, I'd still sing the same way forever." That says it all. To be true to the tunes, a singer must have a special understanding of life; if not, what comes out of the mouth will be dry and uninteresting notes, not folk tunes spiked with tears and blood. In folk tunes there is joy with tearful smiles, and tears with joyful smiles. There was only understating from the heart, with no need for interpretation through language, for they would no longer be folk tunes if colored by rationality.

Yue'er had yet to understand this.

So Ying'er began to sing; her profound longing flowing naturally as soon as she opened her mouth.

A pair of doves flies up,
Drinking water at the base of the cliff,
Clear-headed, I've turned foolish,
I thought I saw you with my own eyes.

The cow drinks from the big river,
I see rain coming from the mountains everywhere.
In my sleep I dream of you,
Talking and laughing, and I wake up.

She sang emotionally in a plaintive voice, but with no tears, despite her tendency to cry, for she had turned her tears into a tune. Yue'er cried, however, seemingly understanding what Liangzhou folk tunes were all about. This tune was not into yelling and screaming about life and death; instead it expressed restrained, subtle longings, faint as a mist or hazy smoke. It recounted clear-minded foolishness, absent-minded wakefulness, as well as a happy surprise in the dream, obscuring the pain and sense of loss from lovesickness. No love or hate, yet not a single world masterpiece could so vividly describe the longing in her heart.

Yue'er remained under the spell of the melody for a long while, seemingly able to read Ying'er's mind. She felt like asking, but Ying'er, her eyes half-shut, had lost herself in another tune. Now came the tears as she sang with a fierce and despairing voice:

On a sheet of white paper was written a word in black.
On a sheet of yellow paper was the rubbing of a print.
With money came a smiling face,
With no money came a bolt of cloth.

If you care about me, come back to see me.
If you don't care, come home to end it.
If you're alive, send me a letter,
If you're dead, show up in my dream.

Unable to continue, Ying'er threw herself down on the bed and began to weep. Yue'er wanted to comfort her keening friend, but teared up instead, so she leaned against Ying'er and started crying herself.

After crying her heart out, Ying'er had a strange, instinctive premonition that more complications would arise.

Chapter Eleven

A white grasshopper on an indigo hill
Kicks its legs, fighting against all odds

1

Lanlan was practicing the Seven-Day meditation, keeping body and mind clear for seven days; putting aside every life entanglement, focused on reciting the Vajravārāhī incantation. In the thang-ka illustration, the Vajravārāhī stands with her feet atop the sun and moon on a lotus flower, holding sacred objects in her hands. These images all have symbolic references, lotus for quiet and purity, the moon for compassion, and the sun for wisdom. But every symbol, no matter how numberless, points to being good and kind. Since the notion of kindness entered Lanlan's mind, the image of Huaqiu dimmed, for her contact with him did not meet the principle of kindness. All her vivid recollections of the past now lost their luster and dimmed.

The Vajravārāhī Cave, being small, could only accommodate seven or eight practitioners for each seven-day meditation. During the period, no one was allowed out (except to relieve oneself), or in (except those delivering food), or to talk (except the one enlightening the disciples), or to loaf. In any case, there were taboos against many things.

Meditating alongside her were Yue'er's mother, Baldy Wang, Huilanzi, Fengxiang, Huaqiu, and Dark Skin, the old Daoist priest. Huaqiu had not wanted to make the effort, but decided to take his mother's place when he learned of Lanlan's participation. Dark Face, who was there to lead the sutra chants, had a deep, full voice that resonated so nicely that no one could object to his role.

The practice required four sequences of meditation every day, with two hours for each sequence, during which time they had to remain motionless. Once the sequence was over, they could walk around, reciting the incantation as they moved about, but speaking was strictly forbidden. They took turns to eat and sleep for no more than four hours a day.

Over the seven days, they must never stop reciting the incantation.

The villagers had laid out bedding on the floor of the cave, and some stools. Those who could sit with their legs crossed took the floor, those who could not claimed the stools. Except when they ate or slept, the practitioners were free to keep their eyes open or shut as they recited the incantation over and over either in a loud or a low voice for seven days, like stringing beads.

That was what they did.

2

Lanlan was enveloped in a wondrous aura, bathed in a holy light. As she continued to chant, the seemingly common incantation seeped into her heart, where it spread in ripples to cleanse her, like warm ocean water washing over rocks. Everything in the past dissolved, her worries, pain, and aspirations melted away, leaving no trace behind. What also dissolved were her mind, her body, and a concept called Lanlan. Often there was only spiritual clarity, and even it sometimes vanished.

Dark Skin was adept at leading the incantation, his soft, rich voice ringing out with the cadence of the wooden fish. They chanted the incantation, comprised of a dozen words; accompanied by the wooden fish and inverted bell, by sandalwood incense, as well as by a solemn look and heartfelt devotion, the words morphed into a pool of warm sweet dew that billowed and dissolved the body and the mind, melting the weighty "self" in the wondrous rhythm.

Lanlan needed the rhythm for her life. When her heart was filled with suffering and tears that drowned out hope, it would resound in her soul. It did not matter to her whether it was a Buddha or an Immortal, for she treated it as the notion of "kindness," which encompassed all, be it Allah, God, Brahma, or Buddha.

All the bitterness and hatred in her heart was washed away by the notion of "kindness," while a unique emotion slowly rose; like evening glow at sunset, the emotion would change the face of the world once it showed on everything. There would be a measure of tranquility, a measure of transcendence, a measure of compassion, and a measure of open-mindedness. These measures combined could lead to enlightenment, which was the goal of meditation.

A transformation of quality induced by these changes in quantity was the ultimate aim of this religious self-cultivation; one could pursue wisdom through tranquility, reach the Pure Land via piety, roam the mundane world freely by rising above it all, aid all living creatures with compassion, or attain nirvana from enlightenment. This was the proper practice.

If something looked the same on the surface, but with different aims, achieving private gains by pretending to serve the masses, would be heterodox.

The mind determined what was orthodox and what was heterodox.

3

It did not take long for the participants to show their true colors soon after the meditation started.

Fengxiang and some others, who were in it for the excitement, or, to use a common Liangzhou expression, selling sow meat at a lively spot, were disappointed that it wasn't very much fun at all. Once the novelty wore off, they were bored and tired; they could not stop yawning and dozing off into a dreamland. Huilanzi, who looked devout, had her mind set on self-cultivation, but with little control over her body. Normally, she could sleep as much as she wanted, but here she was allowed only four hours. Her mind was willing, but her body was not, so she seemed unhappy and irritated, yawning constantly, followed by a few loud chants. She had meant to rouse herself, but it ended up sounding like quarreling.

Huaqiu was disappointed too. He had come purely for Lanlan, for he had imagined something interesting transpiring among a group of men and women over a seven-day period. He did not want anything to develop between Lanlan and any man, unless he happened to be that man. It came as a surprise to him that being shut in to mediate would turn out to be so grueling. Besides sleepiness, his legs and back ached, and his painful joints felt out of whack. Most disappointing was Lanlan, who was devoutly focused on meditation, like a saint, with her eyes fixed on her nose and her nose focused on her heart, not giving him even a single glance. It would not have been a problem had they been alone, for he knew ways to animate her. But it was not to be; several pairs of eyes were always open, and they had to take turns sleeping. In order to keep the recitation going at all times, at least three people had to stay awake and chant during bedtime, which denied him the chance to make eyes at her.

Baldy Wang chanted the whole time, yet cast glances all around suspiciously, constantly checking this one and that one, as if he'd come to watch these depraved men and women, not to practice self-cultivation.

Sitting posed no problem for him. Except for eating and sleeping, he sat in a corner in the lotus position, sometimes looking glum, sometimes wearing a sinister or pensive smile, and sometimes appearing to have had a sudden realization of something, unnerving the others.

Lanlan threw herself wholeheartedly into her incantations, the same way she worked in the field. Losing her voice after a day, she continued to recite in a hushed, hoarse voice, but with the same piety. She treated everything she did as farm work, always diligent and conscientious.

Dark Skin was experienced in meditating. He always presented himself as an accomplished practitioner, making sacrifices to deities, presiding over funerals, and exorcising demons; naturally, he maintained the proper appearance as he sat in front of his fellow villagers, chanting somberly.

He had converted because he truly believed in the Tantra Master, whose magical powers he had personally witnessed. His conversion stemmed from a desire to acquire some of the occult skills.

4

On the second day, Dark Skin asked Yue'er's mother to lead the incantation.

She perked up. A proud person all her life, she had yet to have anything to show for it. When she was young, she was as lovely as a flower, which had her hoping to marry a high official or a rich man, at least a handsome youth from the city. To her disappointment, she married Yue'er's father, a genteel man who looked respectable, except when he was with another woman. He had incredibly good luck with them, actually. She had hoped her sons would study hard and make something of themselves, but none of them were into anything good; they looked foolish when they opened a book, but were sharp and smart when carrying out wicked acts, thus dashing her hopes. Fortunately, Yue'er not only grew up to be a beauty, but also enjoyed school; she did not get into a college, but her mother held out hope for her, since a girl's future was determined by her marriage, though she was less confident when reminded of her own life. Nothing was certain; anything could happen, as is seen in a song by the blind storyteller, "Hopeful of becoming a lady now that her husband is an official, imagine her surprise when she ends up in a brothel." So, her mother suffered self-doubt. After a life of frustrated aspirations with mounting bitterness, she turned to competing with her daughters-in-law once her sons were married, constantly disparaging them. Later, after they divided up the property, the sons and their wives set up separated households and lived their own lives, thus depriving her of an excuse to find fault with them, which served to increase her resentment and frustration.

Leading the incantation did not amount to much, but she was, after all, the temporary leader of the group, so she raised her voice and put real effort into the job. Yet, her heart was not really in the sutra, so she ended up deviating from the Daoist's standard recitation.

That made Baldy Wang laugh.

The Daoist corrected her a few times, and she tried to mimic his standard chant, but her mouth had a mind of its own, and she veered off again. Finally, he had no choice but to appoint Lanlan to take over, bringing a disgruntled look to Yue'er's mother's face as she smiled sheepishly.

Chanting incantations was a voice from the heart. With a tranquil mind, Lanlan produced a standard, accurate recitation. She was blessed with a good voice that carried a metallic echo, produced a crisp, resonating effect. Dark Skin joined in with his rich baritone, and soon their voices merged into a single melody that rippled, driving away impure thoughts, sleep, and anything superfluous in the meditation room.

Little by little, Lanlan felt herself melt into a state of supreme serenity while the incantation seemed noisy to her. Her tranquil mind guided her mouth to lower her voice until she was chanting silently, until even her heart vanished. There was only nothingness.

For a long time.

They were surprised to find the brief tranquility had lasted two hours, when the bell sounded for the end of the session.

5

Baldy Wang left without saying good-bye on the third morning.

He could no longer abide what he considered pure nonsense. In his view, the whole experience was outlandish, including the priest pretending to be learned and profound, Lanlan performing with such devotion, and Yue'er's mother's jealous gaze at Lanlan. Everything, in a word, confounded him.

The only reason he'd joined the group was the protective blessing Shaman Qi had given his baby. His next life was too far off to ponder, and he had enough to worry about in the present—medicine for his sick wife, pants for his children, and the unpaid fines for exceeding birth limits that the county office had tried dozens of times to collect. The prospects of the world coming to an end or the onset of a plague did not concern him. If all the people in the world were taken by the plague, he wouldn't mind going with them. No reason for him to stick around to suffer. Besides, he was not convinced that the off-key recitation by Yue'er's mother would deliver him to the Land of Buddha, just as he rejected the belief that anyone could live in the shimmering sky with its cottony white clouds. He would not have even stepped inside if not for the Shaman's sake. Now see what happened? He got an eyeful and was surprised to notice how his neighbors had shown their true colors after knowing them for years.

From where he sat in a corner, Wang had observed the goings-on coolly for two days, seeing and hearing every possible grotesque look, expression, voice, and situation. He did not think any of the others could come up with something new. Besides, his legs hurt and he could barely keep his eyes open, so he entertained the idea of sneaking home to wrap his arms around his sick wife and get some good sleep. An ailing wife was still a wife, and being with her was better than sticking around to witness strange behavior and endure hardships. So, he left. He wanted to inform the shaman ahead of time, but he quietly walked out instead, afraid the old witch might raise a stink.

"What are you—" She happened to be walking in and exclaimed in surprise when she saw him leaving.

"My wife doesn't feel well." He cleared out before she could react.

That sparked a major disaster.

A form of religious seclusion, meditation dictated that a practitioner would die inside before backing out halfway through. The seven-day rite was meant to eradicate bad karma. In the bitter sea of the six realms of transmigration, a man could be Zhang Three one moment and Li Four the next, a tiger then and a poisonous snake now. Over these many lifetimes a man might commit many evil deeds, which accumulated in his body and mind like poison, and there would be a reckoning when the day came. The good would be rewarded, the evil punished, just retribution that no one could escape, even if equipped with wings. Which was why the first step in religious cultivation was to eliminate bad karma, and that meant enduring hardship. The seven-day meditation was an ideal rite for reaching that goal, as aching legs and back, fatigue, and torpor all worked to eliminate karmic sins. And so, the biggest taboo during the period was to back out before it was over. Whoever did that would transfer all his bad karma and sins onto others. Baldy Wang obviously was not aware of that, or he would have laughed himself silly.

What made it worse were the incantation strips pasted over the entrance. It was acceptable for a practitioner to use the toilet, since he would still be chanting to contain his mind. But when someone dropped out, holes would appear in the protective net woven by the talismans, and the demons waiting outside would steal in, creating serious trouble for those meditating inside. They might be gaining illumination, but the demons brought with them temptations and, if they were not careful, they could veer into harmful hallucinations.

Dark Skin wore a tense look, as if ready to fight, making signs of magical power with his left and right hand; enraged and ready to exorcise the demons and evil spirits, he muttered a demon-subduing incantation, as he hurled black beans that clattered to the floor. It was the magical act of "creating soldiers out of sprinkled beans." In the eyes of a living Dark Skin, those were merely rolling beans, but to the demons and evil spirits, they were soldiers from heaven and celestial generals. Then, ignoring the taboo, he followed the act with the explanation of "leaving bad karma behind when someone leaves" to warn the remaining practitioners. He exhorted them to stay so as not to do harm to others. Yue'er's mother spoke up before he finished:

"So, we're to pay for his sins, is that what you're saying?"

"She's right," Fengxiang echoed. "He got off easy."

"Let's drag him back," Huaqiu said.

"I'm going out and leaving my bad karma here," Huilanzi said, making her the fifth person to break the oath of silence.

"Stop complaining," Dark Skin said with an unhappy look. "He left his bad karma, but do you know what he took with him?"

"What?" the women asked.

"You'll know soon enough." He wore an enigmatic smile.

His response took away their concerns. Everyone was aware of his abilities, as he presided over sacrifices to the deities and offered appropriate Daoist services at funerals. When he sprawled over the offering table to communicate with the other world, his sallow face made you think he was dead, and everyone said that his core spirit had left to report to the celestial palace, leaving behind the empty shell of a body. Once he completed his task, the core spirit returned to the body and the sallow skinned dead figure turned back to be Dark Skin, the Daoist priest. That was what everyone said. Rumor had it that his core spirit had once reached Vajravārāhī's stupa, where a Buddhist relic was stored, and received a mark on his chest when the Guardian deity slapped him. The indigo green mark was well known. His ability to travel outside his body became a legend in Liangzhou, despite his defeat at the hands of the Guardian deity. When he stayed mum about the calamity Baldy Wang caused for dropping out, the practitioners all knew that the smile meant "Heavenly secrets should not be easily divulged."

6

It would appear that Wang's early departure had invited demons in.

The practitioners were all affected. First came the sleep demon, stopping the flow of their thoughts and gluing their eyelids together. Their eyes shut whenever they lost their concentration. Huaqiu sprawled across his blanket and snored, Fengxiang nodded off, like a pecking hen, and stopped chanting, though she fought against the desire to lie down. Yue'er's mother leaned against the wall, a trickle of saliva hanging from the corner of her mouth, quivering like a sparkling string. Huilanzi paced the floor, stopping constantly, seemingly awake when she moved along and clearly asleep when she paused. She enjoyed the special talent of sleeping while standing.

Lanlan was sleepy too, but she employed methods to stay awake. One, she sat in the double lotus position, creating such searing pain that she remained alert. Two, she knelt on the floor. Once her body turned numb after sitting in that pose, she unfolded her legs, which felt as if they were broken, and in turn woke up. She alternated between standing, kneeling, and walking, chanting loudly with her eyes open. Despite being hoarse, she raised her voice. The worst that could happen, she said to herself, was to die in the meditation cave, that's all. She'd rather die for enlightenment than live like a pig.

Every time a new session began, Dark Skin made the gestures with both hands, his eyes glaring ferociously as he tried to quell the demon, which remained recalcitrant.

Another sign of demonic presence was discontent among the practitioners.

Yue'er's mother was jealous of Lanlan for having taken her place. Drawing out her old-man's gruff voice, she insistently maintained her off-key recitation. Soon the others were following her, blurring the original, authentic chanting style. As she chanted, she stared at Lanlan in a strange way, and Lanlan knew she was competing with her.

Lanlan was most concerned about Huilanzi, however, for she was too sensitive and displayed a blind sense of piety; she was a likely candidate to become a shaman. Immersed completely in her own realm, Huilanzi chanted with an expression of devotion, so deeply emotional that tears streaked her face. She seemed to have lost control of her feelings, as if the Vajravārāhī were her dead mother and she was a filial daughter crying at the funeral. Time and again she stood up and got down on her knees to bang her head on the floor until she shook, a rosy glow of happiness spreading across her face until she abruptly burst into wails.

At first, she frightened the others, who stopped chanting to help her by pinching the spot above her upper lip. The Daoist dismissed it with a wave of his hand, "Don't worry, it is the spontaneous effect of recitations." They had not heard that before, and it spurred Yue'er's mother into another round of contention. She stood up with a look of devotion, but no tears came; she did, however, manage to quake, but no rosy glow of happiness showed on her face. Instead, she panted like a laboring cow, as she moaned and collapsed onto the kang before giving up.

Besides shaking and wailing, Huilanzi shrieked frequently, so annoying Lanlan that she snapped, "Please show some respect. This is a meditation cave, not a livestock trading post."

Huilanzi blushed as she stood blankly for a while, but with no more "effects."

7

The demons eventually went into action.

Lanlan was wide awake on the night Yue'er's mother replaced her; she was dead tired, but not sleepy. The chant came to an abrupt stop, followed by peculiar laughter from Yue'er's mother and joined in by Huilanzi. Lanlan opened her eyes a crack to see the two women whispering, while Fengxiang, who always went along with them, was sound asleep.

"I don't believe I can't handle a young woman." Yue'er's mother was saying. "Never, in my whole life has a girl humiliated me. You think you're doing a good job leading the chant? Well, we'll see about that."

"She looked so mean when she railed at me, like a tigress," Huilanzi replied. "I've never seen anyone look so vicious. I always thought she was gentle and quiet."

"What do you mean, gentle and quiet?" Yue'er's mother said. "More like the so-called chaste Wang Baochuan, who carried on with many men.

She was a tramp when she was little and had something going on with Huaqiu. Obviously, nothing changed after she got married, and I heard she was involved with a young man in the production team, so her in-laws kicked her out. In any case, I'm fed up with this meditation, but I won't go quietly. The insult is too much for me to take."

Lanlan felt her scalp tingle. She was surprised to find that a sacred practice in her eyes was simply a game to them. The chanting should be continuous, but they had obviously stopped for a quite a while already. More surprising was the degree of loathing Yue'er's mother felt for her. If that was the case, she wondered why they had chosen to suffer here rather than sleep in their beds back home.

"I'll tell Huaqiu to sleep next to her tomorrow," Yue'er's mother continued. "When they start to get frisky, we'll beat them and chase them out. I want her to lose face and see if she dares strut again."

"How do you know they'd do that?" Huilanzi asked.

"Why wouldn't they? Cotton burns when it touches fire."

"Well, with his shifty eyes, he'd want to even if she didn't."

"I don't care if she wants to nor not," Yue'er's mother said. "When I say they did it, then they did it. Who'd try to figure out if they really did or not?"

"Isn't that a bit too, you know— She's staying with her parents, after all."

"She's too vicious for me to care about that. I'll remember that glare she gave me till the day I die."

Lanlan broke out in a cold sweat. She was in the same group as Dark Skin and Huaqiu. When their shift was over, they lay down and began to snore, no matter where they slept. She would never be able to clear her name if her reputation was sullied. It puzzled her why she deserved their reaction after leading the chant only once. Granted, she had snapped at Huilanzi, but that was to help everyone continue. Why would they hate her so much? If the practitioners behaved that way, then average people would be even worse, she lamented.

She was marveling over her realization as the women continued whispering. Soon it was time for Lanlan's group to take over. Yue'er's mother came up and gave Lanlan's face several gentle slaps. "Time to get up, you wolf meat." The older woman roused her sweetly. "You sleep so deeply you don't have a pulse in your rear end. How can you go on with your practice?"

Amazed by her sudden change of attitude, Lanlan managed to yawn loudly and mumble, "I was so sleepy."

8

On the following night, Lanlan was so exhausted she was in a dreamland the moment the session was over. Suspended in the air, she could soar into the sky and swoop down to the ground at will, free and unfettered, nothing like she experienced while awake. Suddenly a hand reached out and pulled her down to the ground, and she was startled awake. A pair of hands were working on her chest, soft, tender, long fingers moving gently. It was Huaqiu, she could tell. He'd done that every time they'd met before she was married. A familiar sensation rushed at her, as her body heated up. She was about to respond when she was reminded of her meditation. She shuddered and pushed the hands away. "What are you doing?" she hissed. "We're meditating."

"Don't worry," Huaqiu was breathing hard. "They're all asleep."

She realized that the chanting had stopped. Indeed, the sacred practice in her eyes was a mere game to the others. Why didn't they go home and sleep in their own beds? What were they doing here? She wondered as she lost heart.

The hands did not stop, so she jerked them off. If they'd been alone, she'd have yelled at him. This was terrible! Where did he think he was, the Dasha River? She marveled. Wasn't he afraid he'd be punished by the Guardian Deity?

Suddenly she felt several people pressing down and pushing her and Huaqiu together. "Tie them up." It was Yue'er's mother. "A dirty couple up to no good in a meditation cave."

Lanlan broke out in a cold sweat when she recalled what she'd overhead the night before. She wanted to explain herself, but did not know what to say.

"Tell them to get dressed," Yue'er's mother said again.

I didn't get undressed, Lanlan thought.

"They're dressed now," Huilanzi said.

Now Lanlan knew they were pretending. Huaqiu squirmed as he complained, "I didn't do anything. What are you doing to me? Get off."

A light went on. Lanlan saw two pairs of eyes staring at her.

"You're shaming your ancestors," she spat. "I heard everything you said last night."

Huilanzi blushed and looked away.

"What did you hear?" Yue'er's mother said. "What did I say? When the road is bumpy, everyone joins in to smooth it out. You came here to carry on with your rotten things, so why couldn't I say something?"

"Old tramp. What are you jabbering about?" Huaqiu snapped. "What did we do?"

"You know what you did," Yue'er's mother said. "Let's beat them and kick them out."

Lanlan looked over at Huilanzi, who lowered her head, while Yue'er's mother, contrite now, quieted down after a few melodramatic shouts.

"I can't believe you people are here for self-cultivation," Huaqiu sneered.

"So, you think you're better than us, do you?" Yue'er's mother sneered back. "Why were you doing something indecent in a meditation room?"

His face darkening, Huaqiu went up and gave her an unexpected slap; she howled like a wolf and bawled.

"My God! This is a meditation room." Dark Skin stamped his foot.

"They were doing something indecent in here, and he slapped me when I criticized him. This is the end of me, I can't go on. Never in my life has anyone laid a finger on me. I have a son who's as tall as the wall too. He's not the only one with hands." She wailed and blew her nose as she walked out.

Dark Skin frowned and again stamped his foot, but did not try to stop her.

Fengxiang paled. She nudged Huaqiu, "Quick, get out of here. Baigou is a thug, and he'll raise hell when he gets here."

"I'm a man too." Huaqiu stiffened his neck. "I'll wrap my head in a hemp rope if he breaks it. I'm not afraid of him." Courageous though he sounded, he walked out.

Lanlan knew the fiasco would stain her reputation and spread far, but remained unmoved. After going through so much over the past few years, she did not care about her reputation any longer, as if a callous had formed on her heart. Yet she was overwhelmed by sadness when she realized that the seven-day meditation had not been completed, and that ruined her chances for a better karma. How bad could her life be? She asked herself. Why couldn't she even finish a seven-day rite? Discomfited and disappointed, she insisted on making a sacrifice before going home.

The moment Lanlan walked in the door, her mother told her the village was in upheaval and that everyone was talking about the indecent business between her and Huaqiu. She explained to her mother, who was outraged. "I'm going to see that old witch. How could she do something so vile?"

"Don't." Lanlan smiled weakly. "She has a mouth, so she can say what she wants." Lanlan was worried about Huaqiu, though, since Baigou was such a bastard he would not let Huaqiu get away easily, not after that slap.

Just as she was fretting, Huaqiu's wife appeared. Her hair disheveled around a bloodied face, she wailed as she reached the gate and dropped her pants to pee, not caring if anyone was home. There was no greater insult to Liangzhou people. Laoshun was livid; a family's gate was the doorway to wealth, and a woman's filth comprised a serious taboo. He was fuming, when the woman climbed up the date tree with a rope, formed a knot, and tied one end to the tree before looping the other end around her neck. She jumped. Her eyes rolled back. Thrown into a panic, Laoshun lifted her up and cut her down. Once her breathing normalized, she took a screwdriver out from under her jacket and, to everyone's surprise, plunged it into her own throat and twisted it. It was plain she did want to live. Laoshun and his family sent her to a hospital, where she stayed for a few days and came out alive, but with a crooked neck.

Lanlan felt an eerie chill every time she saw the woman with the crooked neck gazing at her parents' gate with a spooky look.

What did she have to live for, now that she had brought shame to her parents? She wondered.

Chapter Twelve

Yellow silk threads woven into a fishing net
Cast into the water, it fails to catch sprays of foam

1

Meng Baye settled Huaqiu's wife down before walking into Laoshun's house with a plan to talk Lanlan around. He'd made a promise to Ying'er's mother, and now it was time to fulfill it. Laoshun, too, hoped his daughter would go back; he had lost both money and face from the uproar over Huaqiu's wife, which had exhausted him mentally and physically. If Lanlan stayed, who could say if something else might happen? He was a firm believer in first marriages. As the saying goes, a divorced man will starve, but it's worse for a divorced woman, who cannot pick and choose. Their ancestors also passed down an adage, "Pick over melons and you're left with only bitter ones." So, he said to Meng, "Do your best to talk her around. Your glib tongue can talk a dead man alive. Why is she making such a fuss, anyway? Grit your teeth and put up with things, and you'll get through a lifetime."

With a blank look on her face, Lanlan seemed ready for something terrible to happen to her; Meng Baye was deflated.

Mengzi's mother understood what was going on in her daughter's head. As someone who'd had a similar experience, she knew Lanlan all too well. She never would have asked her to marry Bai Fu if not for Hantou's sake. Similarly, if not for Mengzi, she'd have done all she could to talk Lanlan into divorcing. But now, it was up to the girl.

With an aloofness typical of a religious practitioner, Lanlan was first to speak:

"I know Bai Fu works hard in the field; I know gambling and wife-beating aren't serious flaws; I know a first marriage is like newly milled flour; I know one day lived means passing two half days and that a lifetime is over in a blink of an eye." She turned to Meng Baye. "Do you have anything new to say to me?"

Caught off guard, Meng opened his mouth but nothing came out.

Lanlan glanced at her mother. "Couldn't you have found a way to marry off your son without trading your daughter?" she asked coldly before walking out without another word.

"That's it, then." Meng looked at Laoshun, who was finally convinced of Lanlan's unshakable determination to stay. A few words from her had ruined what they'd been working on for days, frustrating Mengzi's mother into sobbing again.

"What she said makes sense," Meng said after a prolonged silence. "Mengzi won't have any trouble finding a wife. She's traded for her older brother, and now you want her to swap for her younger one. It doesn't seem right when you think about it. You shouldn't have trouble scraping together enough money."

"It's not about money," Mengzi's mother said amid sobs.

"She doesn't want to lose her daughter-in-law." Laoshun sighed.

"She doesn't want to leave either. Where's she going to find a good family like ours?" She dried her tears. "But, how should I put it? If both people are willing, not even a knife can sever the tie."

Meng knew what she was saying: Lanlan could do what she wanted, stay or return, and Ying'er's mother could do nothing so long as Mengzi and Ying'er agreed. It made sense. Not even a high official can stop his daughter from marrying a penniless man, which has long been fodder for folk tales about money-grubbing parents who object to an impoverished man while their daughter secretly agrees to marry him. The problem was: in the story the couple is in love. Mengzi was such a blockhead, how would he know how to win a girl's heart? On the other hand, no one can tell about matters like this, just as you can know what's gold and silver, but you cannot know what's in a person's heart. It wouldn't be the first time a blockhead conquered the heart of a smart, sensitive girl. "You're right."

Laoshun glanced at his wife and then at Meng. "How about this?" she said. "We get them to consummate the marriage; once the rice is cooked, what else can anyone do?" Finally realizing what his wife was up, Laoshun barked at her:

"That's a shitty idea. She's a widow. Are you hoping to see her dead? I thought something better might have come out of your foul mouth." He wrinkled his nose and looked at her as if she were a pile of dog shit.

Her face reddening, she shrieked, "Is there a better idea in that dumb-ass head of yours? If so, let's hear it."

Meng Baye laughed and tried to intervene. "I'm afraid her idea is best," he said to Laoshun, who replied:

"What's so good about it? It sounds immoral to me."

"Not if you don't force her. It'd be ideal if they're both willing. You can't touch or get hold of feelings, but nothing can be done without them. If you force her, then it's rape and a crime; worst case, your son gets shot, and you lose an heir. If there are feelings between them, it could turn out wonderful, no matter how badly it starts. A disgraceful act would become the subject of romantic stories, and people would say the couple was lucky in love. It's hard to define, and only feelings make the difference. If Mengzi and your daughter-in-law have feelings for each other, the old woman couldn't separate them if she used a hay cutter. If she insisted, we could file a complaint against her interfering with the freedom of marriage. Lanlan has no feelings for Bai Fu, so you'd be breaking the law by forcing them together. So, that's that. We can give it a try. Love lingers forever between a couple who have been together for one night, as the saying goes. And the emotional attachment is deeper than the ocean for those who have been husband and wife for a hundred days. Whether they have feelings for each other or not, it would not take long for them to develop enough attachment that you couldn't pull them apart."

Laoshun said nothing, though he experienced pangs of conscience when he thought about Ying'er's mother. Everyone's heart is made of flesh, and he felt guilty as he tried to imagine how she would feel.

2

Mengzi's mother found an opportunity to tell him about Ying'er's willingness to marry him. He responded with an indifferent look, treating his personal matter as if it were someone else's. Strange.

"Everyone agrees," his mother said gleefully. "Ying'er's mother didn't object, so it's all settled now."

He finally took his mother's words seriously. Frankly, he'd always treated Ying'er as a sister-in-law, and she held much less attraction than Shuangfu's wife. He preferred someone who was sort of tempestuous, sort of direct, and sort of voluptuous, a woman with few inhibitions, and none of this described Ying'er. Delicate and pretty, she appeared frail, not overtly sensual, like Shuangfu's wife; naturally reserved, she was not lively, lacking a wanton provocative nature that could arouse him. Ying'er was translucent and ethereal, as if she were above the material attractions of the world; she appeared distant, posing no concrete or powerful lure for him. He preferred a woman with folds of flesh that jiggled alluringly when she laughed and rolled seductively when she was in his arms. What suited him best was when she put up a half-hearted resistance and moaned licentiously when he conquered her. That's it; that's the kind of woman he preferred.

Ying'er possessed none of that.

But it did not take him long to change his mind. He knew that a woman to sleep with—whom the city folk called a lover—should be sultry, but as a respectable woman—a wife, to be more precise—Ying'er was more suitable. He also knew better than to explain himself, so he said, "What's the hurry? I'm still young."

His mother laughed, but did not respond, though he felt she'd said a lot in that laugh. A few years back, after Shuangfu had caught him in bed with his wife, he had shut his father up after he beat him by saying, "Get me a wife if you can; if not, don't beat your son." Now his parents had found him a wife, and yet he said he was too young. Even he had to laugh, so he rubbed his head and smiled.

"It's settled then. Now don't cause me any trouble by changing your mind," his mother said with a smile before walking out.

Mengzi wanted to see Ying'er now that his mother had put everything out in the open; he'd like to see if there was anything different about his future wife. But she was holed up in her room, not showing her face; he could only hear her cooing the baby from time to time. Her voice was melodious, almost fluid, so loving it bred a tender reaction from him, despite his obtuse insensitivity. His body heated up at that moment, so he walked out and went into Lanlan's room.

Lanlan had changed the room into a sutra hall by draping a yellow cloth over the window and hanging a red one on a wall to install the image of Buddha. On a long narrow table were offerings of dates, colorfully wrapped candy, and pears. Incense was burning, a sesame-oil lamp was lit. She was sitting on a rush mat at the table, fingering her prayer beads, her lips moving each time a bead was moved. Amused by the sight, he jested, "I see you've become an immortal." Lanlan did not respond or pay him any heed, so he backed out utterly miffed.

He walked out the gate and let his feet take him wherever they wanted to go. When he heard someone singing a tune, he following the sound and found Yue'er practicing atop a sand hill. She was concentrated on practicing a trill over and over, and he was quickly bored. "Enough already," he said with a laugh. "You're scaring the sheep. They thought it was a wolf." Yue'er's face livened up when she saw him. He liked her smile, so dazzling and open, like the clear sky after a rain, a radiant smile unique to young girls. None of the women he'd been with smiled like that. Suddenly, he found himself a little bit in love with Yue'er, which reminded him of his pending marriage to Ying'er. Young women are better, he told himself.

"Did your mother talk to you about something?" she asked him.

"What?" He feigned ignorance, aware that she knew all about it.

"Something fantastic." She laughed and squinted into the distance for a while before heaving a sigh. "What a shame."

"How's that?" His heart skipped a beat. She frowned with a distant look.

"Why do women all seem born to suffer?"

She looked at him with a nearly imperceptible smile before gazing off again. The blank look in her eyes slowly turned moist, as tears formed, and she began to sing—

Dark, dark, it's truly dark,

Tree shade overlays the road;

Watching you walk into the distance,

I feel like a piece has been cut out of my heart.

Flatbreads bake in a pot blackened by smoke,
Cooking smoke enshrouds the village;
The cuckoo bird cries until it spews blood.
Calling out over and over until it dies.

I don't believe I cannot pluck a star,
I don't believe I cannot grab the moon;
I don't believe I cannot call back a spring breeze,
I don't believe I will not cry until I bleed.

Her face was soon tear-streaked as she sang, turning the tune into a sad protest.

Mengzi was puzzled by the girl he was watching, who seemed almost deranged, laughing one minute and crying the next.

"I like Ying'er better," he said to himself.

3

In Ying'er's ears, Mengzi sounded no different than a chicken, bringing her neither joy nor sorrow; it was just a voice. Her indifference surprised even her. She had agreed to marry him, so that was what she would do. A woman was born to be married, and it was a marriage no matter who she married. She would count herself lucky if she married someone who was relatively good. Everyone thought she ought to marry him, so she'd go through with it; obviously she'd look peculiar to others if she continued on as a widow. In the old days, she'd have been considered abnormal if she'd remarried, but now widowhood was an anomaly. Evidently, a woman appeared eccentric all too easily if she was not careful, so she needed to strive for a plain, simple life. She had something to look forward to, which was better than nothing.

And now there was one more hopeful prospect in life. The sight of her baby gave rise to a wondrous feeling, a reaction similar to the sensation she had when being with Lingguan. She was shocked by the discovery; it was hard to tell whether she had transferred her love for him onto the baby or she had treated him as a child back then. Or maybe a woman's love for a man had always been rather maternal. She could not tell. Her inability to tell the difference did not dilute the feeling; on the contrary, it spread out like warm water through her body and filled her heart.

At dinner, she noticed that Mengzi was looking at her in a strange way, to her consternation. She wished he'd behave as before, treating her the same way he treated Lanlan. Now the odd gaze made her uncomfortable.

She did the dishes and fed the pigs after the meal. Uninterested in the soap opera on TV, she went back to her little room and locked the door from the inside. She played with the baby, wool-gathered for a while, prepared material for another lesson with Yue'er, and considered possible tunes to share, before undressing and getting into bed. Cradling the baby in her arms, she felt a tenderness unique to a mother from his soft skin, and soon she felt asleep.

Some time passed when she felt something poke her and was startled awake. She reached out to touch it; it was a wooden stick. The smooth texture on one end told her it was a hammer handle. The glass pane on her window had been broken and replaced with craft paper, and now the hammer handle poked through the paper and rumpled her blanket.

Fortunately, the baby was sleeping right by the window, or the handle would surely have bruised his face.

"Who's there?"

The handle froze. She realized it was Mengzi. No one else would stoop to this.

"It's me," he murmured. It was indeed Mengzi.

Ying'er tensed up. She was apprehensive; it would be so embarrassing if anyone else knew about it. He deserved to die a thousand deaths! How could he do something like this?

"What's the matter?" she mustered enough courage to ask, but it took him a moment to whisper back,

"Something's up. It's urgent."

She knew what he meant, and yet strangely she was no longer worried. Grabbing the handle, she slowly pushed it outward. "Whatever it is; it can wait till tomorrow." She'd have scolded him severely if not for fear of embarrassing him.

"I could climb in through the window, or though the fanlight." His voice quaked, he sounded different.

The fanlight was not barred, and would be easy for a grown man to get through. Her heart was pounding and she was frightened, but then she had an eerie sensation of her mother-in-law watching in the dark. The thought calmed her. "I'll scream if you do."

"Don't. That deal, you agreed to it, didn't you?"

She frowned, suddenly disgusted with that deal, which had been settled for what he now had mind. Repulsed, she hissed and spat her out words slowly, "At—the—moment—I am—still—Hantou's woman— you—are—a—beast—harassing—a—widow."

The handle stopped moving and then slowly retreated. Everything went quiet for a while.

Ying'er could "see" Mengzi's mortified expression, and her heart softened. "The steamed buns stay on a plate if you don't eat them." She meant: I'll be your wife sooner or later, so what's your hurry?

Rustling sounds on the outside faded as he went into another room.

She was astounded. The blockhead slept in the same room as his parents, and yet he'd had the nerve to come to her room.

4

A shame-faced Mengzi groped his way back onto the kang. Rejected by a woman for the first time, he wanted to crawl into a hole, and the thought of his brother made him so ashamed he could kill himself.

The image of Hantou faded, so did his sense of shameful guilt, but he was still wondering why she'd called his visit harassment. Based on his dalliance with Shuangfu's wife, he knew that a woman also longed for a man. He did not believe there could be a woman who would reject a man.

He couldn't figure it out.

He had thought that poking the handle through her window would bring him a surprised but happy response; her door would be flung open and he would be greeted with two soft lumps of flesh. It came as a shock that his proverbial hot rear end would fall onto a cold bed, and she had given him a measured lecture.

How mortifying.

Holding his breath, Mengzi pricked up his ears for any movements in the room. His father was snoring, as he'd done all his life, and would not stop even if he were engulfed in a fire. His mother was quiet. Mengzi recalled hearing noise from her when he got down off the kang and sneaked out of the room, barely able to contain his thumping heart. It was a soft, faint, wheezing sound, which, along with his father's snore, had emboldened him to walk barefoot over to the little room. He'd pushed at the door, and, when it did not budge, had gone for the hammer.

Now there was no more wheezing. Was she awake? His face burned at the thought of his mother awakening. He wished he could plunge headlong into a boiling cauldron in Hell. How truly mortifying.

Maybe she'd been awake the whole time. Earlier that evening, a TV program had shown a mother objecting to her daughter's marriage to a factory worker. She'd said, "The young man is such a fool. Why not go ahead and sleep with her? Once the rice is cooked, what could the old witch say?" His father had snapped at her, "We all have children. How would you feel if that happened to your own daughter?" Mengzi remembered getting a funny look from his mother.

However, he'd sneaked out and picked up the hammer, not because of the possibility of "cooked rice," but because of his sudden recollection of a scene. During the lying-in month after childbirth, Ying'er had not gone to the outhouse so as not to fall ill in the wind, so a straw mat had put up in the yard around a pile of ashes for her to relieve herself. There was a hole in the mat. One morning Mengzi happened to see fair buttocks through the hole. That night, those buttocks floated strangely into his mind when he lay down; they did not belong to Shuangfu's wife or Harelip's woman, but were attached to Ying'er's delicate face. He was immediately aroused.

How could he face her now? They lived in the same house, too close for him to avoid her. After the embarrassment of the night, he did not know to how to act in the daytime. Then there was his mother. What if she'd been awake and watched him sneaked out? What if she'd heard the conversation and then seen him slink back? That would be mortifying.

Gnashing his teeth, Mengzi reproached himself until his gums hurt.

5

Everything was normal the next day, however. Ying'er carried on with household chores, as usual, and his mother busied herself with work inside and outside, as usual. His father went out, as usual, to his three hawks, whose training had him running around frantically. He would leave the red hawk in order to pick up the yellow one, while the black hawk waited; he worked so hard his shoulders ached, and that put him in such a bad mood that he screamed at everyone in sight. That was how he'd always been. Everyone deserved a harangue when he was working. He'd beat his daughter, curse his sons, or find fault with "the old scourge" and carry on an intense argument. He'd been like that all his life.

But something wasn't quite right with Mengzi's mother and Lanlan. After breakfast his mother went into Lanlan's room, where a whispered conversation ensued. At some point, his sister complained in a loud voice:

"I won't do it. It makes me blush just thinking about it. How could you, as a mother, bring it up?"

"Fine if you don't want to do it. No need to get all worked up." When she came out, his mother looked uneasy when her eyes met his.

He realized that she knew about what had happened the night before and had asked Lanlan to talk to him about "being a good boy." With his face burning, he scurried over to touch the hawk on the perch and got a vicious peck in return. "What a lousy bird," he cursed unhappily.

The hawk's reaction reminded him of Ying'er's rejection. When even a winged creature picked on him, what had the world come to? As his mood soured, he went into the kitchen to cut a piece of turnip before putting on his leather glove to grab the hawk. The bird shrieked, flapping its wings and pecking at him. With his hand protected by the glove, he let it have a few pecks before cramming the turnip into its mouth and forcing it down its gullet. It would soon make the hawk feel uncomfortable enough that it would coo pitifully. Suits you right! You shouldn't have picked on me, Mengzi said to the hawk silently. You're not a turtle that grows bigger in a larger pond. He can yell and scream, because he's the father, but you, who do you think you are? The hair on someone's dick. He felt better after the silent tirade.

The hawk punished, he walked out the gate to see Huaqiu come looking for him. "Hei—getting married is like being trapped in a jar," he said softly, "and having a baby is being shackled. It really makes me mad. After that farce of hers, my woman doesn't have enough milk for the baby. So, my grandpa told me to get her a rabbit to see if she can make more milk. Let's go catch one."

"Go ask my father first. I don't want to get ripped apart again."

"I did already. He told me to take the yellow hawk, since it's caught rabbits before."

Mengzi went back inside, only to come face to face with Ying'er, who was walking out with a bucket of slop for the pigs. Ignoring him, she went straight to the sty; his face burned again.

"Go on then. But be fast on your feet," Laoshun said from inside.

"I know," Mengzi snapped. "I can handle a hawk. No need for you to badger me." He said this to cover up his awkwardness, and stole a glance at his sister-in-law, who was scrutinizing the pigs as they gobbled up the slop. He cringed out of embarrassment.

Wondering what was going on with them, Huaqiu said in a loud voice:

"Mengzi's sneaking a look at you, Ying'er. Watch out, or he might try to get into your bed at night."

She did not react, to his disappointment, so he nudged Mengzi, and they went inside to get the hawk. They picked up a rabbit head and went out into the desert.

With the hawk perched on his wrist, Mengzi kicked bushes along the way, sending dust swirling around them, but not flushing out any animals.

"No rabbit would hide around here. Too many people come this way and scare them off," Huaqiu said.

"Says who? Rabbits are everywhere. I once found one hiding in the needle grass by our back wall. It was young and inexperienced. I was coming out to feed the hawks when it ran out. Hei, that was perfect. I sent the hawk off and it landed on the rabbit. They're sneaky. Sometimes you step on them and they don't make a sound. Go break off a branch and see what we can scare up."

Huaqiu broke off a branch and began to beat the bushes. A gray dot shot out from under a clump of grass and reached a distant sand hill in the blink of an eye.

"Hei, a rabbit." Huaqiu yelled out.

Mengzi flicked his wrist to send the hawk flying, its wings slicing through the air noisily. In no time, the two creatures were in a tangle on a sand ridge, the rabbit's shrill, child-like cries echoing in the sand hollow. "Hei—hei." Mengzi ran up.

The hawk sank one of its talons into the rabbit's back and the other into its head, while pecking repeatedly to send rabbit hair flying. Mengzi brought out the rabbit head and handed it to the hawk; as the hawk pecked at the head, Mengzi retrieved the live rabbit from under the talons and put it in a canvas bag. "Hei, this one's good with its talons, hitting all the vital spots," he said as he tossed the bag on a sandy hillside.

Their mood buoyed by the good beginning, Huaqiu continued to beat at the bushes, and soon roused another rabbit.

This was clearly a smart one. As it ran for its life, it did more than just flee; it constantly checked the hawk that pressed closer, like an arrow in flight. At the instant before it plunged its talons into its back, the rabbit spun around and the hawk overshot his target. By the time it turned around, the rabbit was so far off, it was just a gray dot.

"Hei! Hei!" Mengzi yelled out.

The hawk flew off and closed in on the rabbit again.

But it missed a second time when the rabbit leaped into the air, and the bird had to fly up.

"Lousy damned bird," Mengzi griped.

"Amazing, I've never seen a rabbit leap that high." Huaqiu said breathlessly.

Enraged now, the hawk circled the air a few times before it dove down. This time it bounced up like a ball, rolled down the hill, and, flapping its wings, cried out pitifully, while the rabbit slid off the slope and disappeared.

"Oh, no!" Mengzi shouted.

The hawk was cowering and shrieking when he got close, its majestic airs gone. "It got kicked. It's done for," Mengzi said with an ashen face. "My father's going to kill me." He reached out to touch the hawk's craw, and his hand came away with blood.

"It'll be okay after a few days' rest," Huaqiu tried to comfort him.

"Sure, it'll recover from the injury, but it's all over for this one. It'll never try to catch another rabbit and will actually be scared shitless by even a dead one. That was some strong rabbit. It ran up the slope like a flash, and one kick caused serious damage. It hit the hawk's craw, its most vulnerable spot." Mengzi picked up the hawk and smoothed its feathers, bringing out more blood and a few dreadful shrieks.

"Rabbit!" Huaqiu yelled.

The first rabbit was writhing on the slope, after escaping from the canvas bag. Its back broken, it dragged its body along, trailed by a bloody stain.

Mengzi ran over with the hawk and flicked his wrist to send the hawk for the rabbit. With a shriek, the bird dodged to the side as if fleeing from danger.

"See that? It's over. It'll never land on a rabbit again." Mengzi said unhappily.

He picked up the rabbit and smacked it on the ground repeatedly. "Hei, you damn near survived, didn't you?"

6

Sure enough, Laoshun flew into a rage before Mengzi even finished. "What were you doing, you shithead? Why didn't you chase the rabbit?"

"I did," Mengzi mumbled.

"And did you shout?"

"I did."

"Bullshit. I've been flying hawks for decades, how many times have I seen a rabbit kick a hawk? You're a born shithead. Training a hawk takes a lot of work. This was a great one, a loyal and skillful hunter. "

Not daring to talk back, Mengzi looked down as his father continued to rant.

"It was a sneaky rabbit," Huaqiu said, "Hei, it leaped into the air. I've never seen anything jump that high." Laoshun glared at him to shut him up.

"It's all right." Laoshun's wife said. "He didn't mean to do it. He didn't kick it, a rabbit did."

"What were they doing?" Laoshun roared. "If they'd chased it hard, the rabbit wouldn't have had time to do anything but run."

"It was so fast," Huaqiu said. "It shot into the distance like a flash. I didn't think a train could travel that fast. We ran after it until we were out of breath, but still couldn't catch up."

"You could have shouted. It wouldn't have had time to kick if it was scared."

"We did," Huaqiu said. "I lost my voice. Listen, I'm still hoarse."

"It was an old rabbit," Mengzi murmured in self-defense.

"Old rabbit?" Laoshun pointed at Mengzi, his lips quivering from anger. "Old rabbit? I've caught plenty of old rabbits. Do you think they're any different?"

"The one that kicked your hawk last time, it was an old rabbit too."

Mengzi kept his voice low.

That earned him a loud jeer from his father. "You've got the nerve to argue with me? You think you're right after you ruined a hawk, don't you? What was that rabbit last time? It was a king rabbit."

"Well, we ran into a king rabbit, too," Huaqiu said. "It was so long and so big, and it could jump like crazy."

"The one I saw was the real king rabbit; otherwise how could it have kicked the hawk?" Laoshun said, unaware that his tone had shifted to argue about which one was the true king rabbit.

"They were both king rabbits, all right? It was just a furry creature, so what are you arguing about? It's pointless," his wife said with a little laugh.

Knowing his father's anger was pretty much spent, Mengzi took a section of gauze and went out to bandage the hawk's wound. Crying out pitifully, it shrank into itself and suddenly looked so much smaller, and listless, sort of like a frightened sparrow. Mengzi smoothed its feathers, to which the hawk responded with soft calls, as if to vent its grievances.

Lanlan came out when he was finishing up. Huaqiu's eyes lit up when he saw her. Mengzi knew about their past, so he tried to find a pretext to leave, but Lanlan turned to him. "I need to talk to you." Huaqiu, who had thought Lanlan had come out to see him, was crestfallen when she greeted him with indifference, as if he were a passerby. She might as well be telling him to leave, so that's what he did. Mengzi ran inside to pick up a rabbit, ran after Huaqiu, and tossed it to him.

Mengzi figured his mother must have said something to Lanlan, and he was upset when he thought about what had transpired the night before. How shameful. He shook his head, dreading the conversation, for she might scowl and lecture him. But he couldn't avoid her forever, nor could he delay the talk, so he went with her.

It was an open space, broad enough to see the undulating desert extending into the distance. Clouds massed above the desert, shifting into strange shapes. He let his eyes roam while waiting for the ugly words he was sure to come from her. Surprisingly, nothing broke the silence. He saw her looking around through half-shut eyes. Some time passed before he heard a soft sigh.

Lanlan had definitely changed, a look of transcendence showed on a face that was now devoid of both exuberance and dejection. She said flatly, almost robotically, "Ma wants you to get the rice cooked; she doesn't want the Old Coquette to stir up any trouble." The term, Old Coquette, like Old Witch, referred to an old woman who wore a flower to look coquettish as she paraded her unseemly appearance around town. She meant Ying'er's mother.

"What rice?" Mengzi asked and immediately realized what she meant. "The rice is cooked and a young girl becomes a woman," went one of the villagers' favorite phrases. He'd wanted to do just that the night before, but Ying'er had said, "The steamed rolls stay on a plate if you don't eat them."

"It's immoral. You can't do that or you'll be some kind of animal," Lanlan added. Mengzi's face burned, convinced that she too knew about his night-time adventure. Wishing he could find a hole and crawl into it, he was sure he'd never try again, even if someone were to embolden him, like the hawk, forever shying away from a rabbit after a single kick.

"I want to be frank with you. My mind's made up. I'll leave if I can't stay here, even if it means I'll end up dead somewhere. I'd rather die than walk through the Bai family's door again."

"No one wants you to leave," Mengzi said as he noticed the steely look on his sister's face. Shuangfu's wife often had a similar expression. Women can change just like that. They can be as meek as a kitten, but once they're riled, they can be harder to deal with than a wild boar, he muttered to himself.

"You can't force it," Lanlan said, her eyes still half-closed. "A melon isn't sweet if it's picked before its time. Don't listen to Ma. In any case, my mind's made up. I don't even want my dead body to go back to them. So, look out for yourself. Dew wets only half the hill." She spun around and went back inside.

Mengzi stood blankly before he understood what she meant. In plain and simple terms, she meant she was determined to stay, but the Bai family would not give up, so they'd come to take Ying'er back with them. Once they did that, even if they were married, he'd be a bachelor again, like dew that wets only half the hill.

That would be a big problem, Mengzi thought.

He swallowed dryly.

Chapter Thirteen

A gale turns the millstone around and around
Black dragons bellow, white tigers roar

1

Ying'er's mother obviously knew that Lanlan was no one to take lightly. She returned a few days later with the simple aim of getting a definitive answer: what's on the girl's mind? The heightened hospitality from her qinjia was a kind of a heart-warming lubricant, which, when applied repeatedly, had confused her formerly clear mind. When she was back home and "enlightened" by a meddler, she realized she'd forgotten the one thing she should have remembered: finding out what Lanlan planned to do. Once she knew, then she'd repay kindness with kindness, but would retaliate if treated unfairly. She'd do what the other side did. So now she was making a second visit with a clear goal in mind: either Lanlan returned to her husband's family or Ying'er came home with her.

She'd told Bai Fu to come along. They'd use force if gentle persuasion failed.

The sight of Ying'er's mother walking through her gate put Mengzi's mother on edge. The Old Coquette has not come with good intentions, she said to herself, but outwardly was even more welcoming than the previous time.

"I've just about worn down your doorsill. I hope I'm not being a pest, *Qinjia*." Ying'er's mother put on a brilliant smile though she felt anything but cheery.

"That's nonsense, *Qinjia*. When people are at odds, they're like strangers, but when all is well between them, they're like family. My house is your house. You must stay longer this time, so we'll have more time to chat."

Family or not depends on that brat of yours, Ying'er's mother complained silently, while saying, "I can't. An old cow doesn't stop shitting till the day it dies. It's all up to me to take care of the pigs and feed the dog. Father and son sit by like the true masters of the house; they have a belly for food but no mind for anything that requires thought. I'm their old maidservant, and, as long I'm alive, I have to work, unlike you, *Qinjia*. You live a life of leisure."

"Leisure? I'm like an old milk cow with nine calves who must do everything for them. We're the same. I'm just like you."

Laoshun frowned. He was sick and tired of that kind of exchange. The two women had hearts as prickly as porcupines, but they were honey-tongued when they talked to each other. The woman's return visit worried him. It was never good news when she entered their house, like a bad-luck owl. He was almost afraid of her, a typical tigress. He lost every verbal engagement with her, since there was nothing she wouldn't say. Obscenities that would make an average person blush slithered out of her mouth like elm-leaf slurry, which was so slippery you could practically inhale a bowlful in one breath. Large chunks of dirty words oozed out as soon as she opened her mouth, and no one stood a fighting chance. Physical combat would bring even worse consequences. If hit lightly, she'd unbutton your clothes while untying her own pants and corner you onto the kang. If hit hard, she'd turn shameless, dropping her pants to expose a pale rear end, pee on the stovetop, stomp on the blanket as if it were an area rug, and turn your house upside down. He'd heard this was her killer strategy, and that no one in Bai Fu's production brigade was a match for her.

"A fat pig grunts, so does a skinny one. How could you say that when you have such a wonderful husband? Aren't you afraid of hurting his feelings?" Ying'er's mother said as she cast a glance at Laoshun.

He knew it was her way of a greeting. It was awkward to even think about their previous argument, so he mumbled a reply before putting on his leather glove, picking up his hawk, and calling Mengzi over to tell his son to stay home. Then he walked out, but hadn't gotten far when Beizhu's oldest daughter caught up with him, "Grandpa Shun, something terrible has happened. A big fight."

"Where?"

"At your house. My mom says you have to go home to break it up."

Laoshun was flabbergasted.

2

The battle was over by the time he walked in the door.

Bai Fu's nose was bleeding, and Mengzi had bloody scratches on his face—caused by Ying'er's mother, Laoshun later learned. The two women also had bloody streaks on their faces, the work of long fingernails. It didn't look like a fierce battle to him, for no major damage was visible in the room.

His wife later told him that Bai Fu was oblivious to what was going on. His caustic words had so enraged Mengzi that he'd grabbed Bai Fu and hit him like lashing a donkey. Ying'er's mother had impulsively pounced on Mengzi, leaving bloody scratches on his face. That had so enraged Mengzi's mother that she'd left bloody streaks on Ying'er's mother's face and received a few in return when the other woman retaliated.

That was it.

Ying'er was crying, her hands covering her face, Lanlan wore an indifferent look. Bai Fu was furious, looking darkly at Mengzi, who stared with a defiant pout.

"You want it your way, don't you?" Ying'er's mother was practically shouting. "Your daughter spends days and weeks at home, but mine can't even come home for a visit."

Laoshun had to agree that she had a point, so he stared daggers at Mengzi. But his son refused to meet his gaze.

Some village children had gathered outside the gate to enjoy the show. "What a loss of face," Laoshun said to himself before walking out to shoo the children away and closing the gate. "A good dog never bites a visiting guest. People will talk until their tongues are tired when they hear about this. Losing face is as easy as drinking cold water." He came back in to say to Ying'er's mother, "Please keep your voice down, *Qinjia*, so we won't lose face."

Instead the woman raised her voice even louder: "What do you mean, lose face? The skin on your faces is thicker than the city wall, so what are you afraid of? For better or for worse, we're kin. When we come to visit, we deserve some nice words, even if you don't think nicely of me, or at least a pleasant face if you can't find anything nice to say. But we get a beating instead. Come over here, Bai Fu, so he can hit you again. I want to see if he'll swallow you and shit you out."

Bai Fu was quiet, still staring darkly at Mengzi before he walked out, pushing his bicycle along. Laoshun did not try to stop him, since the two young masters were always primed for a fight, verbally or otherwise, when they met.

Ying'er's mother turned her firepower on her own daughter, who was still weeping. "What are you crying about? You're worthless the way you make us lose face. Look at their daughter. She's always on their side, but not you, you and your retribution. You never make me proud."

"Don't stir things up, *Qinjia*," Laoshun said. "We grown-ups should be the rock on top of a pickle vat, keeping things down whenever possible."

"What?" Ying'er's mother asked shrilly. "That's easy for you to say. Let me ask you. How did you keep it down? If you did, why is that young mistress of yours still acting up like that?" That shut Laoshun up. Like a fish out of water, he opened and shut his mouth, unable to say a thing, so he just gave Lanlan an ugly look.

"You call that keeping things down?" Lanlan sneered. "If it hadn't been for his father, your young master would have been in prison or executed long ago. Don't be a Kitchen God who doesn't know his face is blackened. You know perfectly well what he's done. Even a rabbit will bite if it's cornered, you know."

Unnerved, Ying'er's mother looked around, turning red, and then purple, and then red again. That went on for a while until she began to wail.

It was a drawn-out, despairing wail. All her life she'd wanted to outshine others, but did not have what it took to succeed. Her husband was a well-known failure who refused to behave according to his meager talents, so he was frequently swindled. Debts kept piling up. And yet he obstinately stuck to the wrong course, never bored with it, scampering around like a mangy dog that had gotten a whiff of meat. Her son turned out to be no better. His gambling addiction was bad enough, but he was a dimwit to boot, constantly causing trouble. People came to her every time he had a fight with someone over something minor, but she could never fight back. Then there was Ying'er, who defiantly refused to go home with her. Her ambition degenerated into full-blown resentment that had now erupted. Sitting on the floor and covered in dirt, she bawled at the top of her lungs, hurling accusations amid her wails while snot and tears fell and flew. Following the rhythmic pounding of her hand on the floor, columns of dust rushed at the open door into the inner room. Ying'er dried her tears and went to pull her mother up, who rewarded her with a vicious screech.

Laoshun was at his wit's end when he saw the normally proud qinjia lose control so uncharacteristically. He poked at his wife to get her to calm the woman, but received an angry glare instead. Obviously, she was still upset over the scratches she'd received, bloody streaks from just below her eye all the way down to her chin—nearly gouging out an eye—plus a sideways scratch on her cheek, clearly from her thumb. With bloody marks on a face whose muscles twitched from the angry glare, Laoshun's wife looked riotously comical, and it was all Laoshun could do not to laugh.

Things were truly getting out of hand. The woman was pounding the dirt floor, sending dust flying, and her wail was loud enough to reach the sky. Most people in the village must have heard and were probably whispering and winking among themselves by now. Those who did not like the Chen family would surely be saying ugly things about them. Mengzi's face was twisted, Ying'er was sobbing, and Lanlan wore the look of a hanged ghost.

Ying'er's mother was gaining momentum in her wailing, her voice soaring into the clouds before drifting downward, as she complained constantly amid her tears. That went on and on, over and over. Finally having a chance to let it all out, she wanted to cry to her heart's content. If no one tried to stop her, it would be over once she'd cried enough. But now she redoubled her effort to improve the effect; by raising the volume, she increased the frequency of nose-blowing. From time to time, she slapped the ground and blew her nose; her face was quickly smeared in mud, and, with the bloody scratches bestowed by Mengzi's mother, she was turned into what Liangzhou people called a "streaky face."

Slowly but noticeably, her wails took on a different tone, as she banged her head on the ground, weeping and whimpering like a funeral mourner, like a filial daughter at a parent's bier: mouth agape to let out long howls that were drawn-out as much as possible, as sad as possible, bawling and recounting all the good memories of her parent and her own sorrows. She stopped just long enough to talk, turning her bawling into a kind of accompaniment to her plaintive recounting. This had been Mengzi's mother's specialty, a wailing style that usually won praise at someone's bier, but was inauspicious on other occasions. No one had died, so why was she crying like that?

It finally dawned on Mengzi's mother that her in-law wasn't just venting, but was using her wails as a weapon, the sort that she herself had wielded before. When bullied but unable to fight back with words or physical strength, she would howl all the way to the other party's house. If something more powerful was needed, she could always roll on the ground before getting onto a kang, where she'd spread out the blanket to cry on it. If even this weren't enough, she could then go cry at the stove and urinate on it. With that her bawling would offend the Kitchen God, since a woman's urine was inauspicious, and the family would surely suffer a decline.

The villagers called it the "ruination wail."

It seemed that Ying'er's mother meant to ruin their family fortune. It would spell trouble if she'd made up her mind to do just that. They could not defeat her in verbal combat, and could not afford to beat her physically. If they dared touch her, she'd make a move to cut her own throat or hang herself, with no regard for her life. Death meant nothing to a woman who was set upon ruining your family.

That was Liangzhou women's lethal weapon.

Laoshun knew it would be a tremendous headache if the tigress adopted that strategy. As he was stressing over the possibility, he heard Big Head's voice:

"What's this? The in-laws are putting on quite a show." He walked in and tried to smooth things over, "Enough, that's enough already. You're family, so talk things over if there's a problem." His voice filled the yard.

"You came at the right time. Hear me out and see who's right." Ying'er's mother was still wailing as she continued, "Their daughter—wah-wah—can come back and spend time at home—my daughter—wah-wah—isn't even allowed to walk out the door."

"We didn't lock her in." Mengzi roared, "We never tried to stop her."

"Shut your trap," Mengzi's mother yelled at him. "The baby is still nursing. Once he's old enough, she can spend as much time as she wants back home."

In Laoshun's ears, something was off in what they said. Mengzi's outburst sounded as if he was trying to get rid of Ying'er, while his wife seemed to imply that Ying'er could be remarried if she wanted, once the baby was older. He rushed in. "Let's talk it over. We can talk it over."

"Stop it. Get away from me. I'll kill myself if you keep at it," Ying'er's mother barked at Ying'er, who was trying to get her to stop making a scene.

Mengzi let out an angry snort, stamped his foot, and stormed out.

3

Mengzi knew something had happened when he got home that night. His father was smoking, his brows knitted, his mother was drying her tears, the baby cradled in her arms, and Lanlan was leaning against the door, wearing a wooden expression.

Ying'er had been snatched away by her family. Bai Fu had stormed in with some of his friends and, without so much as a word, grabbed Ying'er and left.

It was a drama common among families who exchanged daughters to marry their sons. To the locals, it seemed perfectly justified; if you were unkind, then I'll be unjust. If you won't come, I won't go. If you do this for me, I'll do that for you, and no one can raise a stink.

His mother managed to keep the baby with her. Bai Fu and his lackeys had not used brute force, as that could have led to homicide. Laoshun had a chopper in his hand and stood in the doorway with an angry look,

"You want his mother, we can't argue against it, but the baby stays. Force the issue, and I'll lop off those bloody gourds on your shoulders, or I'm nothing."

"Sure, the baby can stay," one of his friends said. "Bai Fu, don't try to grab the boy. It's fair that they want to continue the family line, but it's also fair that the boy should be with his mother. So, we have to leave it to the court to decide which one is more justified."

Mengzi walked in with a heavy heart, but oddly, it seemed strangely light at the same time. He'd been feeling awkward since the night Ying'er had shamed him out of her room. Now that she was gone, he felt an odd sense of relief, though he wasn't sure why. After that night, the last person he could bring himself to think of was his oldest brother, Hantou. Her words had been so pointed they'd pierced his heart. She was right; she was still a widow, his brother's widow. He felt so ashamed. The mere thought made him want to run headfirst into a cliff.

Ying'er had rarely looked him in the eye since that night, so he couldn't tell what was on her mind. He had mistakenly thought that every woman liked to do "it." Beizhu was always saying, "A woman has a dog's mind, you do it with her and she stays by your side." Which was why he'd been so eager to mess with her. He was greatly disappointed, like a warm cheek meeting up with a cold rear end. It was so embarrassing he'd have jumped down a well if he could. With resentment filling his heart the year before, he had felt neither shame nor fear when Shuangfu had walked in on him and his wife. Instead, he'd even acted heroic, for he was dealing with Shuangfu, a rich man whose wealth gave him the confidence to speak louder than others. The more his belligerence, the more Mengzi was shown to be a man to be reckoned with. But that other night he was—according to Ying'er—harassing a widow. Their ancestors had long proclaimed four actions as unforgivably immoral: trapping a white wolf, ambushing someone, storming a widow's door, and digging up a grave. They said that retribution was imminent on anyone committing one of them.

She had been kidnapped, but, as the younger brother-in-law, Mengzi was in no position to say anything. He could not take friends to snatch his sister-in-law back, for that he'd be a laughingstock. Nor could he talk his sister, Lanlan, into returning to her in-laws so Ying'er could come back to be his wife. All he could do was fume over Bai Fu's strong-arm actions, like putting maggots in his eyes. Mengzi could not find an acceptable reason to attack him either, since it was clear they were in the right. Someone in his family had breached the agreement and refused to go back to them, so for them to come and take her home was seen as fair and proper by villagers.

Mengzi thought his father would explode, so he was surprised that Laoshun didn't so much as glance at him. His mother was still drying her eyes, but went off to get a bottle ready when the baby started crying. Lanlan's blank look offended the eye; she was like an unblinking marionette.

Bai Fu had gone too far, Mengzi reflected. No matter what, he had a body and a brain, and how could he show his face if he let Bai Fu get away with it? His nostrils flared. Picking up a shovel, he made for the gate. His mother ran after him and grabbed him around the waist as he was opening it the gate. He tried to shrug her off, shaking her like a children's rattle, but she hung on obstinately.

"Let go! Ma. I'm going to kill that bastard."

"Don't cause your mother any more trouble, dear boy. Let me have a few peaceful days." She was choking on her tears.

"Let him go so he can kill his mother and father first." Laoshun walked out. "You could be a dragon or tiger after that. You've got mush for brains, and are no good for anything serious, but always ready for a fight. Put your hand on your heart and think carefully. How good are you? A good dog doesn't bite a guest."

Mengzi slunk back inside.

Laoshun cast a dark look at his daughter. Obviously, he was blaming her for what had happened. If she'd gone back as they wished, nothing would have happened. He'd opposed her rebellious act. One muddled through life, the less trouble the better, he'd said.

So now he was looking especially glum. Unhappiness surged along with the smoke in his mouth. His Adam's apple moved up and down, but in the end, he could not swallow the words rising inside.

"Let me be clear, young lady. It's fine if you don't want to go back, and I don't care what happens to you from now on. I don't expect you to go through with another swap marriage. Huaqiu is no good, though. Now the whole village is talking; you should hear what they're saying. All kind of things, as ugly as they come. You can't imagine how awful. I know what I'm going to say isn't nice, but I have to say it. You can marry anyone you want as long as it's a solid, reliable man who works the land. I'd never allow you to marry a crook. Now get rid of all the Vajra stuff in your room tomorrow, or I'll do it for you."

Still looking indifferent, Lanlan paused before saying coldly:

"Out with it, Pa. You want me to do another swap and give you a daughter-in-law. Why bring up something so far-fetched? You never said a word before about my cultivation practice. You waited until they took her away. I know you're unhappy with me, but there's no need to be angry with the Vajravārāhī. What puzzles me is, there are men in this house, but they're acting like they have no balls and pin all their hopes on a woman. Would the family line stop without me? Why couldn't you put your thoughts and efforts into improving the family fortune instead? How much would you get if you sold every ounce of my flesh and my bones?"

"That's bullshit!" Laoshun blew his top. "What are you talking about? I've managed to survive for several decades without you. You can plant peppers without dog shit, you know."

"I've done it once, like a beast of burden," Lanlan said in the same cold tone. "And you want me to do it again? Well, I won't do it. You raise a son and you have to find a way to get him a wife. You can't expect your daughter to do that for you."

"Shut your trap," her mother yelled before bursting into tears. What Lanlan said had touched their sore spot. Laoshun's face darkened as he opened his mouth, a dry, black hole. Mengzi's face reddened. She was right. How shameful that a grown man can't find a wife on his own and must rely on his older sister for an exchange.

Laoshun screamed as he charged into her room, where he shoved everything off the altar, Vajravārāhī thangka, offerings, and incense, and threw them all into the yard. He then stomped on them as he yelled, "I—I—your father—would never trade you in a marriage exchange for money—I—I—can't stand crap like this. I—I—your father—" He couldn't say another word but "your father." But it was clear that he was so outraged he was out of his mind. He'd have taken a club to Lanlan if she'd been a man, but she wasn't, and he couldn't. So, he vented his anger and frustration on the things she valued most; destroying them felt

264 Chapter Thirteen

so much better than beating her.

Sure enough, Lanlan blanched and the light went out of her eyes. She was quiet for a long time after staring at him. Finally, she said in measured tones, "You can destroy all this, but—can—you—destroy—this?" She pointed to her heart.

As if in a dream, she got up, walked over and knelt to kowtow to him. "Pa."

She turned to kowtow to her mother. "Ma."

Then she got to her feet slowly and dream-walked to the gate.

"Where are you going?" Laoshun cried out in fright.

Without a word, she drifted out the gate, followed by Laoshun's wolf-like wail.

Lanlan went back to the Vajravārāhī Cave.

Chapter Fourteen

Dark clouds blot out stars in the sky
Rain falls, wind blows, again and again

1

Ying'er was hoarse from crying. She missed her baby.

Her parents' house was mired in agitation. Bai Fu spent his days with his unsavory friends. Father had his eyes on antiques, again, running off to see tomb raiders all the time.

Mother was forever whispering with Pockmark Xu, Zhao San the Butcher their eternal topic. Xu had once brought Zhao over. A fat, greasy man with a head like a pig's, when Zhao had a bit to drink, his nose turned red, a bulbous garlic. He looked a bit like Big Head, but lacked the other man's expansive nature and was actually quite stupid. Just the sight of him made her stomach turn. She knew her mother praised him to the skies because he had money. After being a butcher for more than a decade, he'd slaughtered enough pigs and cows to wear the four-inch thick knife down to a willow leaf, so naturally he had considerable wealth. Now he'd started a gold panning site at White Tiger Pass, and people said he'd struck it rich. He'd let it known that he'd spare nothing for Ying'er's sake, and his offer would double if she brought her baby along. Gaining a son and growing a beard were hard. His first wife had run off after he beat her for not giving him a child. He felt unsettled without a son, and wary of the chance he'd ever have one. Now he could have one without doing a thing, he'd gain a sense of certainty, and he could sneeze as loud as a thunderclap, so naturally he was happy to double his offer.

"What are you afraid of?" Ying'er's mother countered. "My girl already had one, and should be good for a dozen more."

She knew she was justified in bringing her daughter back for a visit; no one would dare raise an objection, especially if she was forceful about it. The baby was a different matter; he was Hantou's son, and they would never give him up, even at the cost of their lives. She'd seen with her own two eyes the fearless way Ying'er's mother-in-law had snapped up the baby, an unnerving sight that shattered her confidence. Besides, she could never be hard-hearted enough to grab their baby for money.

"Everyone knows the baby is your daughter's," Pockmark Xu argued. "Go ask a judge who should have him now that his father's dead, his grandparents or his mother? It's clear, it's the law. It's your right."

"Really?" Ying'er's mother was dubious. She could not believe that the law would sanction snatching other people's family line.

"If I lied to you, my ancestors are donkeys," Xu swore.

She was beginning to believe him, but still wasn't sure if she should pry that baby out of the woman's arms. No, she wasn't just not sure; she felt it would harder than flying up into the sky.

"The witch would fight with her life," she said. "The baby means more to her than her own life. She wouldn't let my daughter bring the baby home. Let's forget that. You can think until your head hurts, and you'll never have that boy. He's worth more than gold; you want him, but they want him more. Besides I couldn't bring myself to do it. They've just lost a son. How would it look if I snatched another from them?"

"He's your daughter's. That wouldn't be snatching," Zhao had promised Xu two thousand yuan if he could bring the baby along. That was several times more than the fee of a regular match-making job, so naturally he had to do his best to make it happen. "It's only fair that the baby goes with the mother. It's immoral to pull a baby off his mother's breast."

Ying'er's mother felt her resistance softening. Ying'er had been sobbing for days now, saying she wanted to go nurse her baby. Her breasts were full, swelling so much it brought tears to her eyes. Her mother had steeled her resolve and kept her at home, but she felt sorry for her daughter. Her heart ached when she saw how her face had turned sallow and sort of shriveled.

"Why don't you look into it? If that's what the law says, then we've got a just cause."

"I already did," Xu said with a smile. "Someone has to help out if the miller doesn't know how to turn the stone. I asked a lawyer who said if he took your case, he guaranteed you'd get the baby back."

"But wouldn't that cost a lot?"

"You wouldn't have to spend a cent. Zhao San would pay for it, whatever it cost. Besides, he often treats people at court to food and drink, so he's tight with them. They told him there'd be no issue. Once you agree, he'll ask someone to write it up and send it to the court. They'll take care of everything."

"All right, I agree," Ying'er's mother replied happily. It was like a gold ingot dropping from sky. She'd thought the baby belonged to his in-laws and never expected the law to be on her side. What a wonderful surprise. She felt bad when she recalled how Hantou's mother had cried her heart out over his death; yet her heart turned to stone when she reminded herself of the shrew's red, angry face when they argued. So it went: her heart softened one moment and turned stone cold the next. The advantage to her family won out in the end after several changes of heart. She also considered how difficult it had been for Bai Fu to get a son, and was worried that Ying'er would suffer at her new husband's home if she could not give him a boy.

"I'm so glad I have you in my corner," she said to Xu. "Do what you have to do. You'll be rewarded if it works out and we won't fault you if it doesn't. I hadn't hoped to have the boy back, and would still be in the dark if you hadn't mentioned it."

"The lamp turns bright only after you raise the wick." Xu smiled. "We have everything we need. What worries me is that girl of yours. She must be firm and stand her ground when we're in court."

"Don't you worry about that. She'll be fine. The girl has just about lost her mind thinking about her baby."

2

Ying'er did feel she was going crazy.

She could hear her baby crying and calling out to her, which broke her heart.

At the sight of Pockmark Xu, she walked out the gate and down a small village path, ignoring the dirt, not caring if it got on her shoes, her socks, her pants' legs, even her heart.

Her heart did feel covered in dirt, a dusty pall. She couldn't think straight, her mind a confused blur, as if she were living in a dream. Her aspiration as a girl was a dream, so was the burden of being a young wife, and the sorrows of being a widow. And then there was the blissful happiness—a happiness of overpowering joy; that was also a dream. Everything in dreams was gossamer, drifting in clouds and fog, impossible to catch. Even the pain, the pain of being away from her own flesh and blood, felt dulled, shallow, shrouding her heart like flimsy smoke, hazy and turning her reality into a gray pall.

The trees along the path had gone bald, all the leaves blown off, their branches pointing into the sky to present a jarring sight. After the wheat harvest, the field lay in disarray, a mirror image of her feelings. People in the distance were blurry, as were those nearby. She could only mumble a response when someone greeted her. She was no longer the Ying'er of the past. She was a widow, a kite adrift in the wind whose thread had been cut by reality. But she was still a mother, a thought that tugged at her heart. Her breasts hurt from too much milk, while her son was crying out in hunger somewhere else. Was the word mother mocking her?

It had been a long time since she'd last been on this path.

She'd often walked down the path as a student memorizing her texts, and dreamed about her future, a bygone future filled with colors. Sometimes she would herd the sheep over and lean up against a tree to read books that made her young heart quicken. The future was beautiful; she'd longed for it, even called out to it.

To be sure, she had not imagined that in that future she would be married as an exchange, to be Hantou's wife, and later a widow, as a mother without her child, to be sold like a farm animal and devoid of hope. From this side of her life she could see all the way to the other end. Her mother's present was her future; she would suffer more than her mother, however, because she had been to school and had sketched out a future.

A wind blew over, a cold, cheerless wind. Autumn winds can sweep away leaves, dust, and loose grass, but can it lift the gray pall in my heart, or the pent-up feeling that dogs me even in my dreams? Why can't it take me away to the end of the earth, make me disappear completely or pulverize me to disperse in the desert? Can you hear me, autumn wind? You're so heartless you can only roar by in desolation.

She cried soundlessly. Fate had been good to her, for it left a space between heaven and earth for her to cry in abandonment.

After sobbing against a tree trunk, she squinted into the overcast sky. She envied Lin Daiyu, the female protagonist of Dream of the Red Chamber. Lin had her own residence, the Xianxiang Hall, a loyal maid, Zijuan, and Baoyu, who was always worrying about her. Daiyu was the luckiest girl in the novel, who saw it all and enjoyed it the most, but left way before the mansion collapsed. She departed this world at the most beautiful moment of her life; she had been born with a pure nature and had departed with her purity intact. How lucky! Ying'er had heard of another woman by West Lake, Su Xiaoxiao, who had also died in her prime, and had earned laments in history for more than a thousand years. They were fortunate. Why had fate bestowed upon them such luxury?

The great desert was not far off, a place that contained many memories she savored. If she headed north she'd reach a spot, the bridal chamber in her heart. A massive bridal chamber with ripples of yellow sand, it had gifted her with the most memorable, dizzying pleasure of her life. Lingguan, why are you so heartless? Have you forgotten the great desert, and the person who supported you with her life, who now drifts in loneliness? She had changed, her rosy cheeks replaced by lines of life's many tribulations. When they met again, she would not look the same. Do you know that, my love?

The desert spread ripples of sand, higher and higher until they turned into a mountain. She'd heard about foxes praying to the moon deep in the sand mountain. They had prayed with sincerity and persistence for hundreds of years in order to shed their animal skins and turn into humans. But what is so good about being human? The government protects the foxes, but who's here to protect me?

Would praying to the moon help me shed my female form? If so, I'd pray to it until the world ended and I became a free fox. Can I do that? Answer me, autumn wind.

The adorable Yindi had perished in the chilly corner of the sand mountain. Ying'er's heart ached over the thought of her little niece. Lingguan had once said that Yindi had been born with a trying fate. Women in a similar situation, he had added, managed to survive, but not Yindi, who had been deprived of that right. That is pure nonsense, my love, Ying'er chided silently. It was clear that the outcome would be the same, so better to leave this world as early as possible. No matter what a woman does, she can never overcome her fate, so it is best to be released from suffering at the earliest possible moment. What was so good about growing up, or getting married? What was there to enjoy in life?

Sometimes she thought it would have been better if she hadn't been born, but that had not been up to her. By the time she understood that, she was all grown up, accompanied by endless worries. Lanlan had told her that belief in Vajravārāhī would take her to the land of Buddha, away from this mundane world with its five impurities. Was that true? Ying'er wanted to believe her, but could not shed her doubts. Like a wakeful person who is unable to comprehend what goes on with a sleepwalker, Ying'er had trouble understanding her sister-in-law.

Maybe she should just leave. Let her feet lead her away, no matter where it went.

3

Ying'er paused by an Artemisia shrub. The autumn had spared no vegetation, including the Artemisia, which had dried up. Some distance away, women were picking the seeds, talking and laughing loudly as they worked. Ying'er had to envy them. Their life was clearly hard, but they were undoubtedly happy. Maybe that was what life was made of, a combination of suffering and happiness. She recalled the books on Buddhism she'd read, all the many kinds of suffering—suffering from birth, from death, from separation from the beloved, and from being stuck with someone you hate. So much suffering. Back then she'd been too dizzily happy to feel any pain, and it was only later that she slowly began to suffer. Putting aside all the other kinds, the pain of separation from her beloved alone was more than she could bear. She felt herself pickling in the bitter juice of suffering day and night. When the baby was born, she was cheered by his smile. The dimple on the tiny face was the on-and-off switch of her happiness, which flowed endlessly once it was turned on. Now that she was away from her baby, the pain and suffering returned. She could hear the baby crying all the time; her heart aching, she was constantly distracted. Her mother said she should put up with it as best she could, and that she would feel better in a few days. But a few days seemed endless. One day truly felt like a year. She could bear it as long as something good came from it, but that was not to be. Separation from the one she loved was like being parted by death, a heart-rending severance. Even the sun had turned into a black ball.

She began to sob soundlessly again.

Since her beloved left, the baby was her everything, looking at him always reminded her of bliss, despite the sense of loss that followed. The process of recollection was filled with excitement and delirium; her heart swelled at the surging waves of happiness, creating a thrill as her reminiscence continued. To be sure, emptiness was impossible to endure once she left the memories behind and returned to reality. How she wished she could put her arms around that living body and let the engulfing pleasure endure. Do you remember the line in the tune? "You've come to this world, so hurry and savor the pleasure, for if not, you will soon be old." Getting old, you know that? I'll be an old hag when you return. How terrible that thought made her. Something was stuck in her throat, but she could not bring it up. How wonderful it would be to retch and expel her heart? It was better not to have a heart, like the women working nearby, who talked and laughed so freely.

Was life about suffering or happiness? It did not seem to be about happiness, but was not entirely about suffering either. Longing brought pain, but she would be happy beyond words if he were to fly up and wrap his arms around her. Ying'er smiled privately at the thought. Her mood always brightened when she thought about him. "Elder brother is a powerful elixir, Little sister is the one needing medicine." How true. The tune was a prefect description of the human heart.

"Come here, Ying'er," one of the women called out to her.

It was Xiangxiang, an old friend from before she was married. She went over to her. The women all stopped to look.

"You've lost weight," Xiangxiang said. "You were like a true fairy, with rosy cheeks on fair skin that would ooze water if I pinched you."

"I'm getting old," Ying'er said lightly.

"What do you mean, old? You're still a young pup." The women laughed.

"Don't take everything so seriously," Xiangxiang said after giving her a look of concern. "You move ahead when you need to."

"Moving on" was the villagers' euphuism for a widow getting remarried. People had asked her a while ago, "Are you moving on?"

"I haven't even thought about that."

"You have to move ahead when the time comes," they'd said to her.

In the eyes of Liangzhou residents, life was like walking down a path. When you're a girl, you move along with your parents, when you're married, you travel with your husband, and after the death of your husband, you go forward to find another partner.

"I hear Pockmark Xu is trying to make a match for you and Zhao San. He's very rich, you know. I hear he has a gold site at White Tiger Pass and that he's been doing very well there," a red-faced woman said.

"That would be a waste. Forget him," Xiangxiang said with a laugh.

"Marry a scholar and become a lady, but marry a butcher, and you clean pig's guts. Zhao San is unworthy of a fairy."

"Being a woman, you always deserve better than you get. Sometimes you see a pretty girl treated like a mattress. But Zhao San has people working for him. You won't have to clean pig's guts when you marry him. You'd be the boss lady the moment you moved in." the red-faced woman continued.

"I hear he's a drinker, that he shouts and yells when he's drunk, and that he beat his wife. That's why she ran off."

"I heard it was because she couldn't give him a baby," another woman joined in. "He was devastated, that's why he drank. He didn't use to, though he is a gambler. During the first month of each year, he takes a bag of money to gambling dens all over the area. But he knows when to call it quits. He stops when he wins a bagful and never loses more than what's in the bag."

"Hear that? Listen to you." Xiangxiang laughed again. "A butcher, a drunk, and a gambler. He doesn't deserve a fairy like you. Is it settled? If so, you have to break it off. A frost hasn't killed off all the men in the world. You can find males everywhere. But find a good one if you want to move forward. One with a good temper, good looks, a prosperous family, and a few years of education, to top it off. Only a man like that deserves Ying'er."

"Watch your tongue." The red-faced woman glared at Xiangxiang. "As the saying goes, you can tear down ten temples, but never ruin a single marriage."

"Is it settled?" Xiangxiang asked. She stuck out her tongue in embarrassment.

"Of course not." Ying'er smiled. Xiangxiang was a guileless, simple woman who always said what was on her mind. Back when they were in school, they'd often shared a bed and shared whispered secrets. Later on, she'd carelessly been made pregnant by a no-account young man, and had no choice but to marry him.

"Then drop it. You're still young, wait till a good man comes along."

"Good man?" the red-faced woman demanded. "Men are all the same. Be practical, so you won't end up like us, having to make a living in the field and in the desert. A single hair from Zhao is thicker than our waist. I hear girls are breaking down his door to marry him. It'll be a practical marriage, no matter what."

"That would be so mortifying," Ying'er said. "His looks alone make me sick. Just listening to you turns my stomach."

The women went quiet as they continued to pluck at the shrubs and toss the seeds into their sacks. An aroma unique to Artemisia permeated the air.

"Could it be that you have someone else in mind?" Xiangxiang persisted. "If you do, of course your stomach turns when you look at him."

"Don't be silly," Ying'er said with a laugh, but silently: You're right. He's a scholar.

"I'm going back, I'll leave you to your work," she said.

Her mood had lightened after the bantering, but, afraid they'd go on about Zhao, she walked off and cut across a corner of the desert. There was an abundance of Artemisia on the sand hills that were also home to many rats' nests. The sand lost its serene pattern when she stepped on a slope; a close look revealed scurrying rats. Ignoring them, she squinted at a towering sand ridge extending into the distance. The sun was mild, and she felt cool when a breeze blew over. Walking across a sandy slope crisscrossed with rats' nests, she reached the top of a sand hill, a clean spot with little vegetation and no rats' nest. She sat down and let her thoughts wander with her eyes half shut.

Puffy clouds were a bright white against a clear blue sky. Typical autumn weather, when the air was fresh. It was the sort of fine weather that put people in a good mood; being glum was wrong. So, she tried to cheer herself up as she looked at the sky, the desert, and at the women at work.

The familiar surroundings evoked familiar feelings. It would do justice to such great weather only if Lingguan were here to talk and laugh with her, or to pick Artemisia seeds together. If she could have that, all those so-called ideals and aspirations could go to hell, and so could "future." The present moment would be wonderful; a turning gaze or a dancing smile would speak volumes, for their tacit understanding would blur the differences between them and all existence.

Do you know, Lingguan, that the most beautiful thing in the world is not great mansions or great power, but mutual understanding, sweetness, and serenity. Your knowledge and pursuit have done you a disservice. You gave up what you should have treasured and instead chased after the illusory, the unreal, and the transitory. Was it worth it, Lingguan? Wouldn't it have been better to embrace a real body with a beating heart as you spend the rest of your life lying on the sand to gaze up at the stars and the moon? Or, on a snowy day when a pot of mutton is bubbling on the stove, you read with a blanket around you while I lean against you to knit a sweater, and our clever son plays with building blocks on the kang? Wouldn't that have been wonderful? Why did you have to leave home?

Look, the sky is so wide, the earth so vast. Why couldn't it contain your restless soul? What will you do after you pursue great prospects and reach the future you long for? Will you have love as pure as this? Will you appreciate the beauty of tranquility, or the pure, natural beauty of a happy family life? If you can, then there would have been no need to leave for the world outside, since it was something you could have grabbed hold of by just reaching out. If you will not, then there was no point in running for it. Lingguan, studying has ruined you, and it has ruined me. Just look how happy those illiterate women are? They laugh as they pick handfuls of seeds; they are happy. I wish I hadn't gone to school. What was the use? Was it really to rid me of ignorance? What has happened now that I'm no longer ignorant? I actually suffer more now. It would have been better if I'd remained ignorant to muddle through and live a happy life.

Everything would have been so much better if I'd closed my eyes and kept my mind in the dark. Why did we have to have our eyes opened? Once they were opened, they could not be closed again.

Ying'er let her thoughts run untethered. She'd said all she wanted to say, but it only brought more tears. She choked up. She knew she should be cheerful on such a bright, clear autumn day, but she could do nothing about her choked-up heart.

So, she told herself to let go and cry.

And she did.

4

Her mother told her what Pockmark Xu said when she walked in the door. "I'll leave if you're thinking I'm eating too much of your food, Ma. I don't believe I can't get myself a bowl of food out in the wide world."

"How can you say that?" Her mother replied. "You're our flesh and blood. Who else would worry about you if I didn't?"

"Why don't you save yourself the trouble this time? I'm old enough to know what to do. Can't you let me take care of my own business just this once?"

"What do you know about taking care of your business? You'd be in the dark when someone abandoned you. It's clear what the Chen family has in mind. They want to sell their daughter again, but they want my girl for free, like picking up the sole of an old shoe. They can think about it till their heads hurt, but they're not going to have it their way. They had their girl after a nine-month pregnancy, so what makes them think mine came after ten days or two weeks?"

"Would you stop that, Ma?" Ying'er frowned. "All I hear when I walk in is you complaining about this or cursing that."

Her mother's lips moved as if to get more air, while tears welled up in her eyes. "You too? The old man said it, the young one did too, and now even you join in to tear me apart. Every day, I get up before dawn and work till midnight. Who do I do it for? For you two, of course. Now you won't even let me say what's on my mind. Very well then. You're grown up now, like a bird with dry feathers and sturdy wings. When a pond grows bigger, so does a turtle. You don't like to hear your mother nag, then show me the way out; a knife or a rope would do. I'll stick out my neck and kick out my feet one last time. There's nothing more to worry about, and you can do what you want. I have an idea. Why not deal with your father and feed Bai Fu some rat poison? That way you can take the family possessions and go live with that blockhead Mengzi."

Tears were coursing down Ying'er's face, but she had no response, so she ran into her room and cried until she could hardly breathe.

"Don't worry, I'm not long for this world." Her mother's voice came from outside. "The lump in my belly is still growing, probably the same problem as the one that got your dead husband. Who knows if Heaven will let me worry about you? So, you don't have to be in such a hurry."

"Enough, already." Ying'er's father bellowed. "Would you shut up? Look at the state she's in. How can you prattle on like that?"

"What state are you talking about? That's not a turnip between my shoulders. I don't want to be blown off by the wind either. Since you want to be the good one, you can deliver the girl to the Chen's door, but you'll have to find your son another wife."

"Sure, sure. When the antique—"

"Ptui!" She spat in his face before he finished. "A disgrace to your ancestors is more like it. You've been going on about big business deals and small sales all these years, like there's a screw loose in your head. I haven't seen a single coin from you, while you've squandered everything I got from selling pigs, soy beans, and vegetable seeds. You have the nerve to bring up that antique nonsense of yours. All day long, antique this and antique that, so pathetic. Why don't you plunk your hot buns down on the cold ground and ask the Earth God to plug up the hole down there for you, so you'll stop spewing nonsense."

The old man's face reddened, his mouth was half open. He pointed a finger at her, but was completely deflated.

"You're a witch. You've mocked me all my life. You'd better stop bullying me. You can know what's gold and what's silver, but you can't know what's in a person's heart. If I make it big, I'd—"

"You'd swallow me whole and shit me out, is that right?" She spat again. "I can see through you. I agree you're a master of big talk and empty words, but you're not worth a single toe on my foot when it comes to doing anything serious."

"Well—well—" He shrank back and scowled, acting like a man who refused to fight with a petty woman.

Instead of thrashing him like hitting a drowning dog, she glanced at him and snorted before looking toward Ying'er's room and saying to her:

"Pockmark Xu came with good intentions. It's your baby, so you have to go get him. Who's going to raise him at their house? The parents are half dead already, and who knows when they'll breathe their last? Mengzi is a blockhead. He can't even take care of himself. He's always in trouble. One of these days, he'll get into such serious trouble that he'll be arrested or shot. And Lingguan, who the hell knows where he is or if he's even alive? No one's seen him or his corpse. Not even his parents can expect to him to support them, so what can your baby hope for from him? And that little vermin of theirs will be married again sooner or later. Who else will raise your baby if you don't? Even if Mengzi and his family want to do it on account of his dead brother, would his wife agree? She wouldn't be someone who brought a child, born or unborn, into a marriage or get pregnant before the wedding, so why would she want to be a mother when she's still at her parents' house? As the saying goes, it's better to grow an elm tree than raise someone else's son. How can you expect them to raise the child for you? If a father remarries, you can no longer count on him. Besides, the baby isn't his, and I don't believe Mengzi or Lingguan would fight with their wife for the baby's sake."

Ying'er listened with a blank face. At first, she found her mother's words distasteful, but slowly she was swayed, for she had to admit that what her mother said made sense. In their village, a stepchild was called an "Extra Lump," and many of them suffered badly. People often said the sun in the clouds and a stepmother's hands were the vilest of things.

She'd heard a Liangzhou tune called "A Brother Talks to His Kid Sister," in which the sister had suffered so much at the hands of her mother-in-law that she wanted to kill herself. Her brother talked her out of it. One phrase that had stuck with Ying'er was, "If Heaven sends down a dust devil, the motherless child will be in for a hard time." A dust devil in winter can blow so hard you can't find shelter anywhere. If you aren't dressed warmly, you must wrap your arms around yourself and cower at the base of a wall. Ying'er shuddered at the image.

"Short-term pain for long-term gain." Her mother was talking again. "Just clench your teeth and everything will soon be over. The law is clear that it's right and proper for a mother to keep her baby. If you fear a wolf and are afraid of tigers, the baby will suffer most. Besides, there will be many things to occupy your mind, you can't be worrying about them all at the same time, or you'll make yourself sick. The way I see it, it's easy. If you agree, we'll ask for a judgment; the baby will belong to whoever the court sides with."

It occurred to Ying'er that she'd been sidetracked by her mother, who had said so many different things she'd lost focus; now it seemed as if she'd accepted her mother's plan, and the only remaining issue was the baby.

It took Ying'er some effort to extract herself from the scenario her mother had created. Why had she been thinking about leaving the baby? A woman can remain a widow if she wants. She was a married daughter, like spilled water, and to the villagers remaining a widow was perfectly acceptable. But her mother would not let her go if Lanlan did not come back to Bai Fu. That was how exchange marriages worked, a string tethering two creatures, neither able to move independently. But Lanlan was Lanlan and she, Ying'er, was Ying'er, and that was that. Worst case, she went back to her in-law's and set up her own household. She would work herself to death, sell herself, if necessary, to make enough money to find Bai Fu another wife and buy her own freedom. But what a childish idea. A family working the field for a year can barely make enough to get by. It made her dizzy just thinking about the amount needed for a man to have a wife. It seemed to her that she'd become a kite in her mother's hand, money being the kite string.

But she really couldn't blame her mother. Clearly, Bai Fu had to find another wife if Lanlan refused to return, and that would be a great expense. This being his second marriage, the prospective bride's family would demand more, which was the same as her mother's plan to have her marry Zhao San.

With her mother prattling on and on, Ying'er couldn't think straight. Mother hadn't stopped talking since she came home, her lips seemingly flapping even in Ying'er's head. She often felt her mind dulled, with everything turning into a blur. What remained clear were her swelling breasts, a pulsing that reminded her of her baby—crying louder and louder and making her cry.

She sighed and dried her tears. It felt like a rope was being wrapped around her heart, leaving her no peaceful moment. But an idea was coming into sharper focus by the minute: she did not want to give up being "Lingguan's sister-in-law" to become "a butcher's wife." A bird returns to its nest eventually, so she'd wait.

Why not marry Mengzi? Everything would work out if Lanlan returned, but if not, she'd ask her in-laws to put up some money for Bai Fu's second wife. It would be a loan from her in-laws, and she'd do whatever it took to pay them back. She hoped Mengzi would agree once she explained it to him.

But first she had to convince her mother. If Mother opposed the idea, she would stage a hunger strike and die a slow death.

5

The wind began to howl in the afternoon, sending clusters of sand flying. She'd heard that the desert would eventually spread to the Pacific Ocean and, sooner or later, fill it in. She'd also heard that the United Nations was worried enough to offer China money to deal with the sand. She'd heard many other things, but none merited her attention. What the wind did was remind her of the whirlwind in the tune "The Dust Devil," as well as the image of her baby shivering in the wind, his eyes big, his neck thin, like the little revolutionary boy in the documentary. How odd. Her baby hadn't learned to walk yet, so why would he be teetering in the wind? His legs were as spindly as sesame stalks, his body swaying and his feet leaving a row of uneven footprints in the sand. Ying'er's vision blurred. She recalled a picture of two-year-old Lingguan, who was sucking on his fingers, his little pecker showing. A feeling like warm water rippled inside her, which was all too brief.

Stop thinking about him, Ying'er told herself.

But she couldn't help it. Scenes of carnal pleasure flashed past her mind's eye, as she lay in bed facing the wall, feeling sweet giddiness at one moment and bleak sorrow the next, smiling one moment and gritting her teeth the next.

She found an opportunity to share her plan with her mother, who reacted angrily, pulling a long face and spewing a torrent of verbal insults, none of them pleasant. At a moment like this, Ying'er wondered if she herself might have been an "extra lump," not her mother's own flesh and blood, for what she was saying was not fit for a daughter's ears. Her mother was convinced that she had been "with" Mengzi, even going so far to accuse her of wanting to "take a bite of the old and the young." Ying'er managed to hold her outrage in check and not talk back. She was, after all, her mother, and parents can do no wrong. They could curse or hit you any time they felt like it, since they were the parents. But her eyes betrayed her and sent cowardly tears down her face; her mouth, on the other hand, held up well and swallowed the sobs rising up inside. Ying'er cried with a blank look, choking up every once a while, but never breaking out with wails.

After that, she lay facing the wall with a blanket over her head and refused to eat. It was not a strategy she used often. Once when she was young, her mother wanted her to quit school, saying, "A girl was born to be someone else's dog, so it would be a waste of money." Ying'er had remained steadfast until her mother relented. This time she made up her mind to starve to death if her mother would not give in to her. Death is a relief when life becomes unbearable.

The wind howled outside, billowing the plastic covering over the window. There had been glass panes at one time, but during a fight with her father, her mother had smashed them along with the mirror on the chest of drawers. Without the glass, the window looked all right covered with plastic, except when there was wind. The sheet puffed madly and flapped noisily, though sometimes it helped dampen the sound of the wind.

Mother walked in; she was not alone. Ying'er could tell it was Xu from the wheezing sound of him clearing his throat. She loathed the man, the way his shifty eyes were always ogling her. He had even touched her hand once, when she offered him water, as if, the way he saw it, widows were all women who were too hungry to be choosy. In all fairness, Ying'er longed for it too, especially late at night when she recalled what she had done with Lingguan; she wished she could do it again with him, just him, not anyone else. Women were odd like that; when she had someone on her mind, there was no room for anyone else. But now fate had forced Mengzi upon her, and she had to accept it. That was what being a woman meant.

A hand was on her forehead. She could tell from the skin texture that it belonged to Xu. Mother had rough hands, almost like the teeth of a saw. Xu's hand was spongy, the typical hands of an idler who never engaged in manual labor. Ying'er was so disgusted she wished she could spit on the floor and say, "Where does this wandering ghost come from?" If only she could bring herself to do that. Instead, she fended him off with a thrust of her arm to show her unhappiness.

"She's not running a fever," Xu said awkwardly.

To be fair, Pockmark Xu was an important person, without whom the villagers would experience a host of inconveniences. For example, if your grown daughter has her eyes on Zhang Five's son, you cannot go to him yourself. It would be fine if you asked and everything worked out, but if not, it would be a slap in the face and your daughter would lose her value, since people could say, "They didn't want her when she offered herself to them." Young men in the village would say, "You mean someone like her? Why would I want her when she wasn't good enough for even Zhang Five's son?" With Xu around, he would spread the word and try to make a match by sounding people out, either by praising the girl or finding a way to make Zhang Five ask for his help. It would look as if Zhang Five were the one asking for the girl's hand. Then Xu would say, "Sure. I'll go on your behalf, and if it works, it'll be your son's good fortune." What made him a nuisance was his tendency to think that everyone was just like him. He liked Zhao San, so he believed that Ying'er would too; he believed that widows had trouble staying unattached, so he was convinced that Ying'er wanted a man. He would do anything to make a match if it looked good to him.

"What do you mean, no fever? She turns down the cushy position of a boss lady and insists upon crawling into a shit hole. What's so good about the blockhead, Mengzi? Everyone know he had something going with Shuangfu's wife when he was young, and he didn't even try to hide it. What good will come of it if you marry him?"

Mother had hit her sore spot. That was exactly what Ying'er could not stand about Mengzi. When she hadn't been involved, she'd treated his dalliance as a joke; but now the thought of marrying him was repellent. She'd always been someone who would give up on something if it was flawed. Was Zhao San perfect? How about herself? Wasn't she imperfect in others' eyes? "A cracked gong has a broken mallet," as her mother said all the time. Well, I'll be the broken mallet then.

"That's no problem," Xu was saying. "A real man samples a hundred flowers. The question is, will Lanlan come back? If she does, then you can go, and no one can say a thing about it. But if she doesn't, there's a rule to follow. Your brother can't be a bachelor the rest of his life. You can't just think about yourself, you know. Lanlan has sent word that she'd rather feed her body to a wolf than walk through the Bai door." Xu's words had hit all the right notes.

"I—won't—have—her—back." Ying'er mother spat out her words.

So, do all men without a sister have to remain single? Ying'er wanted to say. "A grown man can't find a wife on his own and must rely on his sister for an exchange? How shameless." She swallowed the words. Whatever she said would make no difference, so she might as well keep her mouth shut. "It's no use having children." Her mother continued. "Family planning is a good idea. The more children you have, the more worried you are and the harder you have to work. You toil like a donkey, but no one appreciates you. Everyone has to eat, but no one wants to share my burden. I do all the work, and you'll all starve to death the day I die."

"Not every orphan dies of hunger. Why don't you save yourself some trouble and let your daughter live her life for once?" Ying'er swallowed this comeback too, because it was equally useless.

"You can't let your daughter have her way with some things. Parents all want the best for their children. They have, after all, lived longer than you; they've seen what they've gone through themselves, heard what they've not seen, and considered what they haven't heard. They have more experience."

Sure, you have more experience. Ying'er sneered. So why is life getting harder and harder? Why can't you even find your son a wife and must exchange your daughter again and again? She sighed, telling herself to keep the thoughts to herself. It was the truth, but her mother would take it wrong and get all worked up over it.

"You're right." Mother sounded smug. "Just as I said. The way I see it, the world is going to pot and life is getting hard. Why? Because people are turning evil. You see, when people turn bad, Heaven does too. Now we're getting these sand storms, with sand and pebbles flying everywhere. I hear even the wolves are causing trouble. They got to Shawan's pigs and sucked their sheep dry of blood. Mark my word, it will only get worse."

What about you? Are you good or evil? You say people turn evil and so does Heaven. Then why don't you do some good? On second thought, she found it hard to say whether her mother was good or evil. Her ideas and actions seemed to benefit her son. To be fair to her mother, Ying'er knew how hard it had been for a woman who had to marry off her daughter and save her son from a life of bachelorhood. But their family was just too poor. The little they got from the land was barely enough to fill their bellies. Mother was simply trying to survive. When she read Rickshaw Boy at school, Ying'er had loathed Xiao Fuzi's father, who was always railing at her for not using her body to provide for her family. Now Ying'er understood him better. She was convinced they would not be so hard on her if her parents had a better solution. As a little girl, she had been her mother's favorite, her father's too, and they'd always made sure she was well treated.

Her father had been out a lot lately, returning with exciting news that was elusive at the same time. She knew he was trying to make her feel better. What he did not say was, "Wait until I make a killing reselling antiques and then you can do whatever you want. Zhao San will be nothing by then." Father had lost so much weight his face was as gaunt as a monkey's pointed face. He'd done a calculation ten years earlier and come up with a conclusion: "Fieldwork is fruitless, hard labor for nothing, the most you can get is to eat your fill." Since then, he'd stopped pinning a hope to change his destiny on fieldwork. A big business deal was his dream, without which he had nothing to live for. So, he never tired of being scammed, and continued to happily sketch out a future that was better than the "Land of Ultimate Bliss."

Tears fell from her eyes.

She had long wanted to cry for her father's sake.

6

Back and forth, Pockmark Xu and her mother took turns trying to talk her around, but it was useless, like swatting cold water. They left.

The room turned quiet.

She was feeling hunger pangs after having skipped a few meals, but she had to keep at it once she started. It was the last trick in her bag, like the fictional donkey of Qin, and, if it failed, her mother could do anything she wanted. Ying'er did her best to boost her own morale.

It was funny. She'd felt like laughing when she first heard about pairing her with Mengzi; it was insulting. But in her current state it was a luxury, something that only threatening with a hunger strike could make happen. It was funny when she thought about it, the ultimate proof that the affairs of the human world are fickle.

She knew the future was unsettled, but she was willing to put up with any hardship to ensure the purity of her heart and wait for his return. But if that happened, then what? She did not want to think about that; she just wanted to go where things took her. That, not results, was most important in a person's life. Life is a process, as are romantic relationships. Everything is a process, for there is only one outcome, death. Everything is transient, only death is eternal. I'll stay with the process and wait for the constant.

Tears again filled her eyes. She did not try to hold back. It was sign of good fortune. Soon, she was afraid, she might not even feel like crying. Living would be no different from being dead when that happened. So, cry while you still have tears.

After sobbing awhile, feeling the need to relieve herself, she got up, slightly dizzy. Running her fingers through her disheveled hair, she picked up a mirror and saw a pair of red eyes on a sallow, bloodless face. She carefully wiped her face with a towel, unwilling to let village women see her sad. She'd once been a "folk tune fairy," now she was a featherless phoenix, looking worse than a chicken. Everyone knew about it, and yet she still did her best to freshen up. Whatever she did was not going to cover up the pallid look, but she couldn't care about that; better to look refreshed.

She got down off the kang, put on shoes and a jacket, and walked out of her room. Scraps of paper flittered in the yard. The sky was a dusty yellow, trees swayed madly in the wind. Ying'er felt weak, so she shuffled out using the wall as support.

A strange noise popped into her ears when she rounded a corner. It sounded like Pockmark Xu panting. Mother was speaking softly, but still audibly.

"Don't worry. They're not home. Those two no-good men won't return until it's dark out."

"How come it's dry?" Xu was breathing hard.

"You have to work at it." Mother laughed. "I haven't done it in many years. I lost interest just looking at him."

The door creaked noisily from the pressure.

Ying'er was so repulsed her knees buckled and she slumped in front of the door. Her hand banged against the door, and everything turned quiet inside. A buzz went off in her head as she struggled to her feet and walked out the gate before thumping off the dirt.

The wind was strong; gusty gales blurred her eyes and took her breath away. Standing with her back to the wind, she tried to catch her breath. How could she do that? Hatred of her mother rose up when she recalled her pitiful looking father.

After relieving herself, Ying'er stood in the wind to regain her calm. The gale in her heart overpowered the wind around her, tree branches seemed to sway into her heart and jumble her thoughts. Yellow clouds churned in the sky, a sign that the wind would not stop any time soon. Pitiable sand, blown by the wind, drifted with no discernible pattern. The wind will die down at some point and the sand will stop flying, but when will her body and soul have a moment's peace?

Finally, her face stopped burning. She wasn't sure she could face her mother, who had always bragged about being righteous. Today she was clearly working on Xu, so he'd do his best to bring the happy matter to a conclusion. Knowing her mother, Ying'er was sure she'd find Xu's disgusting face repellent, and yet— Ying'er felt nausea for her mother's sake. Her earlier stumble must have alerted them, so how would she face her?

Nausea assailed her despite her effort to ignore it; she retched a few times, dry heaves.

"Ying'er."

She turned to see Father walking toward her with his arms crossed. Sand whipped at his back and dwarfed his figure. Racked by the wind, his thin yellow beard stood up and seemed to swagger on his face; a drop of water hung from the tip of his nose. With a rope around his waist, he looked like a beggar.

Ying'er felt like weeping.

But he was smiling. "That business of mine, it's almost a done deal, my little girl. Once it's finished, I'll give the old witch ten thousand and tell her to leave you alone. Ying'er, my little girl, you're like the beauty in the painting, and you've never been treated so badly before. You won't have to marry anyone. I'll keep you here and take care of you once the deal is sealed."

Tears welled up in her eyes; she turned to blink. The tears drifted on the wind to places unknown.

Her father had been talking about "almost done deals" all his life. She knew how he felt, and knew he sympathized with her. Her nose ached, and she nearly blurted out her agreement to marry Zhao San. She'd sell herself for her father, who had stumbled along his whole life, to let him enjoy a life of ease for a while.

"Come on, let's go home. The wind's so harsh it could crease your face if it's wet." He reached out to dry the fresh tears on her face.

Ying'er was reminded of what had happened and how terrible it would have been if he'd been there. Poor Pa, poor Ma, and poor her. She sighed softly.

"Why so sad, my little girl?" her father asked comfortingly. "No one dies from not peeing. Heaven always rewards hard-work. I don't believe I can't pick up a little here and a little there while others are cinching big deals. All we need is one kernel of the wheat, just one kernel. Hei, it'd be enough to set you up for life. Come on. Let's go inside."

Ying'er walked back inside only after she heard her mother's signature loud voice. She was banging the pots and bowls in the kitchen, talking at the top of her voice about nothing in particular. Ying'er knew what she was implying: "I didn't do anything; I've been cooking." She glanced at her father, his face bluish from the cold wind, and felt an ache in her nose.

She went to her room, got on the kang, and lay down as before. Father was talking about a nearly-done deal in his unique, bragging tone.

"Hei, it's cat's eye and it looks right at you no matter how you turn it. Hei, it even glows in the dark. I heard it was gift to a personal maid from a wealthy man before he fled to Taiwan years ago. She's managed to keep it all these decades. Can you guess how she did it? You'll never guess. She hid it in the stovetop and it was there the whole time she worked in the kitchen. She wants four hundred thousand for it, not too much. I found a buyer for her, and they've agreed to give us thirty thousand each as a thank-you. When I get the sixty thousand this time, little girl, you can have whatever you want to eat and drink, and wear anything you desire. I'll give the old witch ten thousand to shut her up so she'll stop bothering you like a wandering ghost. We can give her twenty thousand if you like. I'll take twenty to open a gold panning site at White Tiger Pass and, who knows, I might dig up a big gold nugget. You can have the last twenty thousand and spend it any way you want. You can live on your own if you don't want to move ahead. No one would dare bully you. You can eat when you want and go to bed when you desire, and raise the baby of yours to be a scholar. You might even be an official's mother and get to wear a jeweled head dress and fancy robes. You'll look impressive."

Ying'er smiled to herself. She didn't want to think too far ahead; all she wanted was for her lover to come. One look at him would be enough. Her mood darkened when she recalled the noise she'd just heard; she felt sorry for her Pa.

"What's the big business deal this time?" It was Pockmark's voice.

Nausea overtook Ying'er, who pinched her throat. It was that disgusting face that had— she fought to suppress the thought when she heard her father's cheerful greeting. "Is that you, Xu? What wind blew you here?"

"A northwest wind. It was a wind from the northwest." Xu replied breezily.

Ying'er wondered if Xu was secretly laughing at Pa. The low-life was acting as if nothing had happened, utterly without shame. She'd like to see if the pockmarks on his face were emitting shameless, despicable lights, if not for a fear that she couldn't hold back her disgust.

Ma didn't think he was disgusting.

Father was gleefully talking about the cat's eye, to which Xu responded with an equal measure of high spirits. It didn't take much flattery for Father to lose his head, and he was getting boastful. That was how he got the nickname, "Big Talk."

Mother brought food she'd just made to Ying'er. She refused to eat, as usual. Hunger pangs gnawed at her, but she ignored them with gritted teeth. She knew that a little bit of self-respect was all she had, and she wouldn't be able to speak her mind if she lost it.

Father continued to comfort her with his big business deal, his passion unflagging despite the pointed mockery from Mother. Ying'er could not stop shedding tears.

7

They drank at night. A typical sot, Xu would trade his life for something to drink.

Ying'er felt a fire burning in her belly. That was odd; it was empty, so how could that be? She tried to ignore it and the hunger pangs, for they had little effect on her. The sound of the men playing a drinking game, on the other hand, grated on her ears, especially Pockmark Xu's phlegmy, slurred voice, which made her want to throw up. His pockmarks must be glowing, shiny red by now. Things went on as always: Father bragged about his big business deal, Bai Fu mumbled something irrelevant. Naturally he vastly preferred Zhao San, who got meat to eat, liquor to drink, and money to spend, over Mengzi.

Mother was sewing a shoe sole with a pensive look; she was quiet, which was unusual, and could only mean that she realized that Ying'er knew about the terrible thing she'd done. She avoided Ying'er eyes, and Ying'er ignored her. When the noise rose to an unbearable level, she struggled down off the kang and went to Lanlan's former room.

Her legs felt rubbery, steps unsteady. Exhausted from the mental torment and hunger strike, she got onto the kang with difficulty; she was having difficulty catching her breath when she dragged the blanket over and lay down. She stared into a dark night ripped apart by lightning, followed by heart-stopping thunderclaps and splashing water. The sloshing seemed to fill up the space between heaven and earth, as well as her heart, which she surrendered to the noise so no other emotions could sneak in. The wind grew stronger, howling like a baying wolf. Ying'er emptied her mind as the wind howled outside.

Where is he now? Is he drenched? The thought jumped into her mind. She could not do anything about it. Like a leather ball in the water; she could force him down, but he shot up whenever she wasn't paying attention. Pop up if you want, then. And I'll think about you, your face, and the time we spent together. But you're playing hide-and-seek in my mind. What happens to your face, your charm, and your liveliness? Where are they hiding? Why is my mind a blank, even though I strain to recollect? The buzzing in my head grows louder. Don't hide from me. Are you too stingy to give me that little bit of luxury? If so, go away from me and let my heart die on its own. Why won't you die, heart of a dog?

The room brightened as lightning crackled, making the paper dust cover snap. Her mind was leaden. Crack all you want, Ying'er thought. Why not blow up my body, my mind, and the world? She'd seen lightning split open the sky, giving off a sulfuric odor, and scorching everything it touched. During the year the Vajravārāhī Temple was built, the villagers donated grain and money, some of which Big Head embezzled. One night the lightning went looking for him; it stormed his house and whirled around, charring the paper dust cover on the ceiling. He panicked, managing to save his life only by wearing his wife' s blood-stained underpants. Ying'er had not taken ill-gotten money, but had coveted something more valuable than life. So, go ahead and blow me up, she said silently. Annihilate my body along with my heart, and obliterate this woman called Ying'er, blending her into the great void, or melting into the darkness. Better yet, just let her vanish without a trace.

The drinking game grew more boisterous next door, where they seemed to be shouting at the top of their lungs. Father was as high-spirited as ever; Xu was getting thick-tongued, his usual, wretched reaction when he drank too much. Mother had joined the conversation in good spirits, as if nothing had happened. Go ahead, laugh, while I wait for lightning to blow me up. Come on, come blow me up. Why don't you?

The sounds of splashing water grew louder as the howling wind picked up. The ground must be flooded, and the boundary between heaven and earth is gone, underwater. Water is wonderful, submerging everything in its path. Isn't there a line in the local tune, "Tear submerges my heart?" Wouldn't it be wonderful if it was indeed submerged? But it isn't; it's merely soaked in tears. Her heart felt briny, stuffy, and stopped up; she would rather it was completely submerged.

She heard her mother's crisp laughter, loud enough to drown out the wind and rain. Ying'er frowned; she was choking up when she thought of Father's face, leathery as the bark on a desert date tree. What has he worked for all his life? He's been cheated so many times, and yet he never regrets it. Maybe that's the right attitude; it's better to have a dream. Unlike Mother, who is always complaining about the heavens and blames others, forever in a bad mood, because she has no more dreams. Without them, life is hard. Ying'er felt she was more like her father, willing to be swindled, even with full knowledge that what she hoped for was only a sham. Far better to have a dream than to have none. But now even reality was trifling with her pathetic dream, making it impossible for her to continue. Once the dream is torn to pieces, the heart will be broken.

Darkness pressed down on her, and the black rain came down in force. Sparks of brightness had once shone through the darkness of her heart, but now they were gone, perhaps blackened by the heart itself.

She was parched. It would be wonderful to have a drink of water, but the hunger strike meant she shouldn't drink water either. Ying'er did not want to cheat; life wouldn't be worth living if she did that. She must be principled and honest with her strike and refuse even water. The worst was death, which was nothing to fear; in contrast, what her future held made her shudder when she thought about it.

You got up and vanished, leaving a vast emptiness behind, forsaking me to deal with the colossal emptiness on my own. Life has been bleak for me. I know you felt pent up and stifled, but since your departure, the same feeling occupies me. And it has grown much more powerful and willful in the heart of a woman so weak she cannot even bring herself to sing the flower tune. Do you remember the song? "The carrying pole has broken, and fresh water splashes all over the ground, turning my body black as you travel down a wide-open road." I changed the word carefree to wide-open, changed it to wish you well. I believe the road before you will grow wider as you travel, while I have come to a dead end. The water splashing on the ground has turned my body black and darkened my heart. Listen. The sound of rain is fresh water splashing on the ground. It makes even the sky dark. You blind Heavens, you strike out with lightning, but in the end, you're shrouded in darkness. My lover and I are forever star-crossed, in our previous life, in this life, and in a future life.

Lighting struck less frequently and lost its intensity, but the wind continued to howl. The night felt strangely heavy, overwhelming the game and the laughter in the next room, and pressing down on her eyelids.

She fell into the deep, heavy darkness.

8

The darkness felt heavier, twisting and tearing at her. Ying'er awoke to a groping hand; the smell of liquor assailed her nose. The heavy, wheezing breaths were the sound of chronic bronchitis. It was Pockmark Xu.

"Ma—" she cried out.

"Shhh—be quiet." Xu whispered. "They're asleep. Here, take the money and buy yourself a head scarf."

Ying'er felt paper thrust into her hand. It disgusted her. She flung it to the floor.

"Get out!" she yelled.

She wanted to sit up and slap him, but the man's audacity so outraged her she went limp, powerless despite her wish.

"Get out, you bastard!" She'd never in her life cursed anyone like that.

"Be quiet. Don't fight. Just a little while, it only takes a little while." Xu was breathing hard. "Cotton burns when it touches fire." He threw himself on her and tried tearing off her clothes.

"Pa—" She shrieked her plea, choking up. She heard voices next door, a man's and then a woman's, but soon they went quiet.

"Elder Brother—" She screamed, her voice rising over the sound of the storm outside but failing to penetrate the silence next door.

"They, um, know. Don't be afraid. Pluck a turnip and the hole remains. You're no virgin. I'll buy you a new pair of pants tomorrow, all right? Something made of fine material. I'm a man of my word. If I lie to you, I'll grow a canker sore on my back." He pinned her hands under her while unbuttoning her blouse.

"Ptui!" She spat and cried. One of his hands was on her breast, while her hands were pressed under her. She was powerless to fight him off, as his other hand went for the pants cord.

"Wah—" She wailed, a sound that did not sound human, surprising even the hands to a momentary pause. She sent all her strength to her vocal cords, her only way to fight back at the moment.

"Be a good girl and don't cry." Unnerved, Xu covered her mouth, giving her a chance to free one of her hands to scratch his face. It obviously hurt, but he pinned the hand back. The stink of alcohol pressed closer as her face felt something scratchy, followed by a powerful stench.

"Ma—" She cried out again, a voice that rent the night, but failed to rouse her mother. Why? she wondered. Have they told him it was okay? Are they really so afraid of upsetting Pockmark Xu, afraid to ruin the family's great prospects? She despaired, her will to fight fading. I'll just die. It's better to die. She sobbed helplessly.

The stench followed her sob and found her, making her stomach turn. Suddenly a light went on in her head and she took a big bite.

An animal-like howl erupted.

She was calm now. After all her pleas for help had failed, she actually regained her composure. "Get out!" She ordered in muffled voice.

The man muffled a reply.

She let go of her teeth. A lightning strike gave her enough light to see a twisted face, accompanied by groans and heavy breathing.

"Get out!" She screamed.

The muffled groan began to recede.

Ying'er felt like throwing up, but nothing came, only tears. She wept as she put on her shoes and walked into the yard, where she wept in the pouring rain.

Every pore of her body was sickened, and her heart seemed to overflow with something sticky. Her body was indeed tainted black now. Rain came down, like someone splashing water on her. Keep pouring and cleansing, wash away the filth. Still crying, she opened her mouth to take in the rain. She was quickly soaked, and her clothes stuck to her. She wished she could strip naked for the rain to wash her clean, inside and outside. I'm soiled now, my lover. I'm filthier than a toilet. I can't let you touch me ever again. She whimpered before bawling frighteningly.

The rain was absolute, blotting out everything between heaven and earth. Gone were the lightning and thunder, leaving only the rain, like an understanding friend, pouring down to cleanse everything.

9

She walked into the room and turned on the light. Xu was shamelessly snoring away, but her parents were awake. Bai Fu was also snoring without a care in the world.

"I'm going back to the Chen's house," Ying'er said to no one in particular, her face a blank.

Her father just sighed, but her mother said sternly, after a moment's hesitation, "No, you're not."

Ying'er responded with a shrug and a sneer, "I want to go back there, but not to do what you suggested, gnawing both the young and the old." She raised her chin to point at Xu. "He's the one who wants that."

Her mother was deflated.

Ying'er walked out the gate to pitch darkness all around. The rain had let up, but the wind was chilly and harsh, seemingly blowing straight into her heart. She shivered, and an itchy nose told her a cold might be coming. That was nothing, now that she'd shed a heavy load inside. She'd not expected to leave her parents' house so easily, and had thought only the threat of death would release her. The nausea, on the other hand, seemed to have taken root deep inside her soul, and she felt like throwing up when she thought about it.

The narrow path, vaguely visible in the rain, was muddy and slushy, which did not deter her; she didn't mind tripping and falling now and then. One was meant to stumble through life, all but those who are paralyzed or dead. What worried her was not falling down, but the possibility that the disgust would never leave her. It was so gross, and it wasn't going away, even after she'd washed her mouth countless times. I'm not good enough for you any more, *Yuanjia*. She choked up at the thought, and tears spurted from her eyes.

A wind blew over, splashing rain on her face. She slipped and fell. One side of her was covered in mud, though she wasn't cold. Her body was numb, but not the disgust, which was spiritedly writhing inside.

She wondered what time it was. Midnight, or early morning? That wasn't important. For Liangzhou residents, night belonged to ghosts.

She didn't mind that it was a spectral world, which the former Ying'er would have feared. Now she had nothing to be afraid of. Would a ghost devour her, tear her clothes, or carry out evil deeds, like those people? Of course not. So, what was there to fear? What she feared most was people, those who were humans in appearance only. Ying'er was now feeling apprehensive about her parents. What role had they played in the night's show? She wasn't sure; It was better not to know; if she did, she would lose them. I'll just pretend you were asleep, like dead pigs. Will that work?

She wept again.

It had been a while since she'd last seen a lightning strike, and that was fine with her. The light was bright and lit up the road ahead, the world, and her heart; there would be nothing but dark night once it went out. Let it be dark then, let the dark solidify to blot out heaven and earth, as well as her heart.

Lightning to her was very much like schooling, a flash of bright light lit up for her to see a prospect, a future, and happiness in life, but that went out under the weight of reality, and everything was shrouded in darkness. It would have been better if it had been dark all along. You cannot suffer if you do not seek happiness; you cannot find darkness unacceptable if you do not long for bright light; you cannot complain about the present if you do not construct a future. It truly felt like the figure Chaos in the Chinese fable: it had lived a carefree life in an amorphous state, but a meddling wise man decided to create seven orifices and caused it to die in agony. She was convinced that she'd have been better off without going to school; she'd live a muddled life and would die ignorant.

And you, *Yuanjia*, you're also like the lightning; you shone brightly in my life and brought me dazzling beauty, only to quickly go out. The darkness after the light was terrifying. If I'd known, I'd rather not have met you. Back then, I'd already surrendered to my fate as Hantou's wife, and I'd have submitted to the life of a widow or move ahead, and be shredded by reality. Maybe I'd have simply grown numb and not felt any pain. Xiangxiang and her friends have no trouble enjoying life, do they? *Yuanjia*, you've made me suffer so much.

Ying'er choked up, as tears blurred her vision. She ignored it, since she did not really need to see clearly. The dark night had obscured everything, but the road went on in her mind, so she would not deviate, even if her eyes were shut.

The muddy surface improved once she turned onto the main road. Sandy soil had its advantage, for, after being drenched by rain, it wasn't slushy when she walked on it. A desert date tree on the roadside was inky black, like a phantom. This spot was rife with ghost stories. She'd heard that a female ghost dressed in red was seen sometimes at noon. Several women in red garments on their wedding day had hanged themselves on this tree, which was the cause of ghostly appearances. She wasn't afraid. You're just a ghost, nothing more. Even as a ghost, you're still a woman, nothing to be feared. Nevertheless, she was apprehensive enough to move to the middle of the road. Her mother had said that the middle of the road was guarded by a demonic spirit that ghosts feared. Heaven had placed it there for night travelers. I'll walk in the middle; it's better there. Her father often said, "A horse is too fast and a cow too slow; I'd rather ride a donkey down the middle of the road."

She walked on, following the road. It seemed to brighten up a bit. There were few roadside trees. In recent years, people had been cutting down more and more trees, turning the lush green canopy into houses and furniture. They could do what they wanted, she didn't care. With fewer trees, the area looked less gloomy, less eerie. Everything was blurred— sand hills, sand troughs, and vegetation—as it all blended into the dark night. She was fine with that, for it would also conceal the ghosts. Who knows if they weren't laughing at her for living such a sad, fearful life. What's so funny? You aren't that different from me now. You forget the pain once the wound has healed and you laugh at me. That's not right. They looked sheepish at her stricture, which made her smile. Go on now. I'm glad you know you misbehaved. You're free now, relieved from suffering, and that's your good fortune. Don't laugh at others. I'm the you of yesterday and you're the me of tomorrow. What's there to crow about?

The rain continued to lessen, from a storm to a downpour, then to a shower. Morning light in the East grew brighter, like a drop of ink spreading on rice paper, small at first then larger, its hue turning darker, as it licked at the curtain of the night. Shades of the night dissolved slowly. Go ahead, dissolve, or not. She didn't care if it gelled into a block. To her it was all the same, except, if this were daylight, with her as wet as a chicken in the soup, she'd draw questioning gazes. It was actually embarrassing, when she thought about it, for she had been a "folk tune fairy," at one point. Now she was a wandering ghost on a night journey. So what if she was a wandering ghost? You cut firewood on the mountain you're on. They could laugh till their teeth fell out for all she cared.

She was reminded of her father. When she was little, he'd have a turmoil of activity if she cried, wishing he could pluck a star from the sky to make her happy. Now he'd changed. The man's voice from the night before was his, but Mother had shushed him. Pa, poor Pa. How could you watch your daughter be abused like that? Pockmark Xu was a mere matchmaker, but so brazen he could put maggots in your eyes. There are people more bullish than him, how could you survive if you acted cowardly before them? Pa, my long-suffering Pa. I know it's been hard on you, and you feel bad, don't you? A saltless meal is tasteless, a penniless man is like a ghost. Poverty chills ambition, and hair hangs long on a skinny horse. You'd swallow your tooth if you bit through it. Isn't that so? I know poverty has softened your backbone, right, Pa? She broke out in tears again.

What about Ma? She's always wanted to outdo others. She was the proverbial strongman, whose arms were powerful enough to support a galloping horse and a fist sturdy enough for someone to stand on. What happened to her? You were poor, Ma, but you had your dignity. You were always saying, "I'm poor because I was born into poverty." You sounded as if you could take down the sky. Now you've lost that, along with your dignity and self-respect. You have nothing left. How could a powerful force collapse so easily?

Ying'er dried her tears, ruing what she'd said to her mother before walking out. Her heart ached over her thoughtless act. Ma had it tough already, she thought, and had to go along with the disgusting Pockmark— and yet Ying'er had taken a stab at her like that. She was worse than human. Ying'er bit down hard on her lip. Worried that it might already be a mess of broken skin, she spat viciously—at herself. She wished she could turn back and kneel before her mother and bang her head on the ground until it bled, until she forgave her. Ying'er almost turned around, but she forced herself to stay the course. She knew that leaving this time might bring a change to her life. She did it for her *yuanjia*, for whom she had hurt her mother.

Like a she-wolf, Ying'er howled several times as she dropped to the ground and, facing the direction of her parents' house, kowtowed repeatedly.

When she got to her feet, she realized she'd sat down in water. No matter. The mud and water dirtied only her clothes; everything would be clean again when she washed them. It was nothing to worry about. But what she'd said to her mother had stripped her of the qualification of a mother. Please forgive me, Ma.

Ying'er sobbed as she stumbled along. The road had turned uneven, filled with potholes, and she'd trip and fall if she walked too fast. It didn't matter. She would get up if she fell, the bruise would disappear and a wound would heal if she hurt herself. It would best if she died from a fall. But the pain she felt continued. She had been blinded by outrage against her parents, but now her mind cleared, and she keenly felt their hardship. If given a second chance in life, she vowed to strike out on her own, to start a venture and make enough money so she could watch them smile and enjoy life. But it was too late for her. All she could do now was watch helplessly as her father and mother snapped at each other, like two spiders in a jar, tormenting each other as mortal enemies.

And it was all caused by poverty.

Finally, she understood why Lingguan had left. He'd done what she wished she could do.

It was getting light out, but she could not see what awaited her ahead.

Chapter Fifteen

A magenta banner tied to a wooden pole
When a wind blows it falls on its own

1

Lanlan continued her Buddhist cultivation in the Vajravārāhī Cave.

With her eyes shut, she sat in quiet meditation and entered a free and natural state, where her mind and body were detached from anything tethering her to the mundane world, as a spiritual light flickered before her. Silently, she chanted the Incantation.

She felt she had a deity in her life now.

What is a deity? A deity is just that, a deity, an omniscient and omnipotent being that prevents disasters, expunges transgressions, eases suffering, and cures illnesses. It is a savior, with compassion and kindness, that helps the needy and relieves the distressed. The poor can ask the deity for fortune, the weak for protection, the barren for children, the bedridden for a panacea, and the unfortunate for rescue. Those who gain fame and fortune thank the deity for its benevolence. Her parched soul was nourished by the willow branch in the deity's vase, while her hope-filled heart was sheltered under mounds of incense ashes.

The deity is also a judge, who, with a mirror hanging high, can see the minutest detail. The good will be rewarded and the evil punished; retribution is certain, it's just a matter of when. Rewards and punishments will be exacted sooner or later—on one's progeny if later or on oneself if sooner. Those who do good will affect the deity enough to bestow blessings on you—even if that happens after your death—and those who do evil will never escape censure, which could happen as late as two hundred generations in the future. There is no need to fight against evil, for the deity is there, ten feet above one's head, seeing everything and taking care of all.

So Lanlan felt her body infused with a force that billowed, roared, and crashed, but her heart became light and then empty, a state that required hard work. It now felt as if she had no heart, no will. She was a clear sky with no clouds, still water with no ripples. She had reached transcendent tranquility and achieved an awareness after seeing through falsity.

The sense of emptiness slowly spread out. Her body was gone, so was her mind, as well as everything before her eyes, all of which fell into a colossal, tranquil quietude. It was an emptiness, where no "I" or anything else existed, a quiet that was devoid of waves and ripples. But at the same time, the light of wisdom flickered to keep her mindfully alert. It was trance-like, undulated, far-reaching. There was no language, no content, no dregs, not a bit of filth, no greed or want, only revelation, a baring of the soul as she poured her heart out.

Lanlan's silent soul seemed to flow. Go ahead and flow away. It wasn't hers anyway, for she had reached a state of supreme emptiness. Her body felt unusually light and vacant, so did her heart; there were no distracting thoughts, no yearnings, no self, no nothingness. Whether there was a deity or an immortal was something well beyond her concern. A flight without wings and a sketch without lines; freedom with no boundaries, revelation without complaint or anger, a display without bitterness or grievance. Now she understood what it meant to achieve a state of supreme emptiness.

Immersed in tranquil contentment, Lanlan's heart came to a standstill. Little by little, she felt happiness, but that slowly dissipated, leaving only emptiness. It was a sensation that eliminated suffering, removed worry, ended sorrow, and stopped pain, turning the corrupted world into a heaven on earth. Could this be Vajravārāhī's mandala? This was an unrivaled site, with its natural grace, nothingness, serene void, and spirituality.

A wondrous fragrance seeped into her bones. It smelled like the flowers on a desert date tree on the Dasha River shore. Waves of aroma, as well as bouquets of fruit, liquor, and other sacrificial offerings surged and rushed toward her, intoxicating her. Could this be what it meant to receive an offering? The old Daoist Master once said that the offering a deity receives has no shape, no texture, no color, and no taste; it is the essence of the offering. The essence was like a human soul. At that moment, Lanlan thought she understood it all. Slowly, her senses began to dissolve into the spiritual void, where only a spot of her spirituality flickered.

What a thoroughly satisfying sensation, which she could still savor even after reaching the zenith of emptiness. It was true; the sensation was real only when she experienced the great void. She felt like singing, like jumping, like flying into the void. Her body could no longer accommodate a revelation from the merriment of the great void, which was likely the case for the sky as well.

If it could no longer accommodate the merriment, then so be it. Emptiness was never easily accommodated. On the contrary, it accommodated everything in the universe. Only when all was supremely quiet would the emptiness manifest itself and the spiritual flicker appear. Could the flicker be wisdom? Don't people say that a focused mind breeds wisdom?

She'd felt a similar sense of tranquility in the past when she was practicing the seven-day meditation. Sometimes she would gesture uncontrollably when it was all quiet, something incomprehensive to ordinary people. The Daoist Master called it jue. Lanlan did not understand what he meant by jue, so he asked her:

"You know about antennas, don't you? Without an antenna, there will be nothing but static on a radio. Jue is like an antenna; once you put it up, you will be able to reach the deity."

So now she knew.

Lanlan had practiced the seven-day meditation with the Master a few times and grown to be fond of him. With a solemn appearance, he was competent and knowledgeable. He was impressive as he walked like a fast wind and sat like a bell. He commanded respect from everyone who met him. Lanlan held him in high esteem even though he had only recently undergone the rite of passage.

She felt more settled since she'd become a devotee of Vajravārāhī. Before then, she had just been an empty shell of human form, without a heart, which was why she was constantly distracted by the outside world. Her body was no better than a walking corpse. The Daoist Master once said that his ancestors knew how to walk the dead, using black magic to make them get up and walk for long distances. Seen this way, her former self was nothing but a corpse her heart made to walk. Now that she had subdued the heart, her body and soul had come together, and she felt that her life was more settled.

She knew that in her father's eyes religious practice was impractical. Fieldwork to fill one's belly was the only reliable way to go through life; everything else was pure nonsense. To him nothing but crops, the land, and the farmwork carried out by the ancestors were real. Her mother did believe in the Vajravārāhī, but from a utilitarian angle, for she hoped that her belief would produce good, such as averting disasters, making her rich, or bringing her good luck. At least, she hoped, she could be reborn into a decent family and live a good life. Lanlan had higher aspirations. She had too many questions with no answers, even after going to school and asking questions, so religious practice was her solution. Once she found her true mind and discovered her true nature, reaching the great awakening, nothing would ever bother her again.

Her mind was clear and her desire lessened after she installed Vajravārāhī in her heart, and nothing seemed serious to her any more. In her eyes, everything was like a blown-up pig's bladder, which, carried on the wind in her mind, lured her to chase after it. After pursuing it all her life and wearing herself out, once it popped, she would wind up with nothing but a stink. Now she would stop chasing it. Let whoever wanted go chase after it. She had seen through the illusion.

Most of what pained her dulled after she saw through the illusion, including the pain of her daughter's death, which had been heart-rending, but was much reduced now. She knew now that one headed toward death the moment one was born. It was death, whether one died at the age of ten or a hundred. A magical deer could live for a thousand years, but in the end, it had to die. Death was the eternal outcome of life and living was temporary and accidental. There was nothing to pine over when one could conceive of the world in such a detached manner. Yet she did not know if that meant she was numb or that she had risen above it all.

Only one question lay behind her, which was finding a place for her body. Her mind had a place, but her body was still like a soap bubble. Neither the Vajravārāhī nor her religious practice could solve the issue for her.

Bai Fu had long been pushed out of her mind. She'd rather spend the rest of her life with a pig than lie down beside him again. Huaqiu had said he wanted to see her several times, but she'd refused, because his wife was carrying his baby. Lanlan would be immoral if she continued a relationship with him. Before her rite of passage, she'd hoped they could remain lovers, but the idea vanished. Her self-cultivation, she said to herself, would start with giving someone back her husband. That woman had a tough life too.

2

Yue'er came to say good-bye to Ying'er after breakfast, after an old schoolmate had found her a job in a Lanzhou teahouse that offered folk song performances. She'd learned all the popular tunes, now all she needed was to capture the essence. Ying'er sincerely hoped that Yue'er would make something of herself after leaving home. Her mindset was different now, after what had happened recently; if given a second chance, she would live another way. But it was too late for Ying'er; she felt like the camel that had been tethered to a little wood stump when it was young. It never thought of breaking free, even when given the chance after it grew bigger. She felt the same. Now it finally became clear to her why her husband, who'd had little schooling, had wanted to visit the Confucius temple shortly before his death. It brought tears to her eyes when she recalled this heart-breaking scene. Maybe he had only realized this when he was about to set off for the underworld.

What a pity it was too late.

She knew it was too late for her too. Like a yellow leaf rising and falling on cresting waves, she had no control over her body and had to go with the flow, letting the water of destiny carry her here and there until she reached a shore where there was a pier. But she agreed with Yue'er's decision to leave.

After saying good-bye to Ying'er, Yue'er went to the Vajravārāhī Cave to see Lanlan. Lanlan did not see eye to eye with Yue'er, but kept her disapproval to herself. She did not think that Yue'er would find happiness by leaving home. What was happiness? It was an emotional state. You could have a full stomach, drink your fill, wear satin and silk, ride a steed, and still feel so unhappy you wanted to slit your throat. By contrast, a couple of beggars could be as happy as immortals when they looked into each other's eyes with an understanding smile, after getting the other person to eat a slice of bread someone had given them. Based on Lanlan's explanation of happiness, the more you see and know, the less happy you'll be. Greed brings worries, and desires speed up the wrinkling of your forehead. What a bliss it would be if you could, like her, empty your heart, eliminate the utilitarian mind, and let tranquility move in.

Lanlan did not voice her objection to Yue'er's departure, however. A chicken scratches the ground backward, a pig roots what's in front, and everyone has a different way of living. Happiness is a dish with a hundred flavors, it all depends on what you feel like eating. Go then if you want to go and return when you feel like coming back, but just be aware that you'll be a different person when you return. With higher aspirations, you're destined to have a hard life, and with too many desires you're less likely to feel contentment. In the end, it will be just as the Daoist Master said, "A piece of five-foot long white cloth covers a rotting corpse/A handful of yellow dirt sprinkles over dry bones." An earthen mound ends it all. If you think about it carefully, what's the point of rushing about and searching for something?

It takes only three or four generations for people to forget their ancestors, Lanlan said to herself. Hence, three or four generations from now, we'll disappear from the memories of our descendants. A group of people is born and a group of people dies, and each group leaves behind nothing but its own emptiness; all the emptiness forms a massive void. Who can explain to her the purpose of life?

Go on then, Yue'er, Lanlan said silently. Maybe our life has no purpose, thus it has no meaning, only process. To go through the process is to experience life. The value of clusters of clouds lies in the fact that they slant across the void and display patterns before vanishing without a trace. When a bird flies across the void with a swoosh, can its flapping wings leave a mark? It will continue to fly even if it leaves nothing behind, for what is important is the process.

It was probably the same with those Buddhist practitioners. They are as shriveled as dry wood, their face as sallow as ashes, and their minds stilled after being rid of knowledge, as they embark on a strenuous pursuit. But how many of them can actually become immortal and rise into the sky? Where are they now? Perhaps success merely means to see through the great void.

Go on, Yue'er. Go see through the void, experience the process, and pursue the serenity of your soul.

3

Laoshun was troubled.

Gossip about Lanlan and Huaqiu continued to swirl, each tidbit uglier than the previous and difficult to bear. Some even maligned her by insinuating something between her and the Daoist Master. It got so bad that Laoshun was beginning to feel the futility of life. A person cannot live without face, just as a tree will die without bark. She had brought the family such disgrace that even their ancestors were blushing, like Master Guan in folklore.

She must have been possessed.

Lanlan had been a considerate, filial, and caring daughter, so why had she ignored everyone in the family once she began to practice self-cultivation and sought to do perform good deeds? Could she be like Daji of Su State in Investiture of the Gods, who became a demon despite her human form?

Laoshun vented his frustration on Meng Baye, but did not feel the heavy load in his heart lessened as a result.

"You just have to wait and see what happens," Meng said. "You can't worm into her heart and snatch her thoughts. A human heart is the hardest thing to change. Even Shakyamuni and Confucius, all they wanted to do was educate and persuade the people, but the human heart has only gotten more evil after thousands of years of their teaching." He continued, "Your little girl, Lanlan, has nothing to live for, so anything, even a straw, is like a lifeboat to her."

"When you think about it, the girl has had a tough life," Laoshun said with a sigh. "Nothing has gone her way since she was little. She wanted to go to school, but I had so little that the boys wouldn't have been able to go if I'd let her. When she was older, she was forced into an exchange marriage. No problem if it'd been someone nice, but Bai Fu turned out to be a horrible husband. Then, at least she had Yindi to comfort her, but the little girl died. What's there to live for?"

"We do need something to live for. We can endure poverty if we have something; if not, we're no different from cows or horses. Lanlan was looking for something. She happened upon Vajravārāhī, and that's what has worked for her. And that's okay. What matters in life? Our feelings. Happiness is a feeling and so is pain. When you feel happy, you're happy. When your heart's in pain, you're in pain, and nothing else matters. Millionaires will jump off the roofs of tall buildings, while a poor man can happily sing opera the day long. A rich man will lose sleep on a soft bed in his mansion over his troubles, while outside his window a poor man snores away in sweet dreams on the hard ground. Everything depends on the heart. At least Lanlan now has something to live for, and her empty heart has been filled. Don't you agree?"

"So, it's a good thing she believes in Vajravārāhī?" Laoshun asked.

"It has nothing to do how alluring it sounds when you try to tell legitimate doctrines from illegitimate ones. Legitimate ones benefit all living creatures, illegitimate ones do them harm. The distinction lies in the heart. I've heard that Vajravārāhī is a true doctrine of Tibetan Buddhism, there's a note from the city government in the Cave to classify it as a legal religious site. So, it's all right."

<h1 style="text-align:center">4</h1>

Another group of villagers would finish their meditation and leave the Cave the next day. Once they were out, Mengzi's mother would prepare to start her seven-day meditation. One can start only after all the birds have returned to their roost. Though called a seven-day mediation, it lasted nine days. One entered in the evening of the first day and left in the morning of the last day, making it seven full days in the Cave, hence the name.

Since the first initiation rite, the Vajravārāhī Cave had never been empty, with one group coming and another leaving, and no break in between. It was said that no one can be a true practitioner without the seven-day meditation; when the Angel of Death comes, one loses control of one's consciousness, but it will be led by one's karmic accumulations, and might easily slip back into samsara, the karmic cycle. The more meditation one practices, the more focused one becomes, which then enables one to reach Buddha's land after death. Mengzi's mother, who had yet to experience her first meditation, suffered from nightmares in which she saw turbulent mud turn into flames to engulf her.

"You need a seven-day meditation," Grannie Shaman told her.

"I want to. I wouldn't be a true believer if I didn't. But I can't leave or she may come and snatch the baby."

"Don't worry. The Guardian Deity will protect you once you're in meditation. She wouldn't succeed even if she tried."

Reassured, Mengzi's mother whispered instructions to her husband and son one more time that evening before entering the Cave, along with Huilanzi, Yue'er's father, and Lanlan.

Laoshun had had enough of it. To him his wife, the old hag, had too much free time. He'd been averse to their religious practice ever since Lanlan became a different person, someone who cared nothing about her family. He hated everything his wife did at home, including burning a candle before the portrait of Vajravārāhī every morning and evening, offering incense, kowtowing, yawning, and mumbling prayers. He tolerated everything but burning a candle, for that was a waste of money. A candle cost two *mao*, and if she burned one every three days, it would amount to the price of as much as five *jin* of wheat a month. Add the incense and other offerings, and she would waste more than ten *jin* of wheat. And there was more: every first and fifteen day of the month, she offered whatever she thought of. Who knew how much whatever she thought of would cost him? They did not have money for much, but at least there were packs of cigarettes and bottles of liquor. He would like to be the recipient of the offerings to enjoy himself instead of seeing her engaged in something like that. But she complained about his appetite for liquor every time he had a cup or two. Your Vajravārāhī has more of my liquor than I do. Liquor had the essence of five grains and helped him put meat on bones that were stronger. What was so good about a candle, which burned down to nothing? He was outraged. Once, when she decided to set up a so-called "Lamp offering," he exploded:

"What the fuck are you lighting?"

That scared her. How could he use such language for a candle for the Vajravārāhī?

"Don't say that. You'll be punished," she managed to say.

"What kind of fucking punishment?"

She kept her mouth shut, for fear that he might bring up more "fucks."

It did not take long for the other practitioners to learn that Laoshun had called a candle for the Vajravārāhī something vile. They all tried to talk sense into him, including Yue'er's mother, whom Laoshun held in low esteem.

"In the future you should say, keep the light on a bit longer to accumulate more good karma," she counseled Laoshun.

"I haven't seen you accumulate anything."

"What do you mean? My girl Yue'er has gone to Lanzhou, hasn't she? The tea house doesn't hire just anyone who wants to sing. It's comfortable work and very presentable. Many girls wanted the job, but they were all turned away. Some had gone to school, but no one would hire them. If the parents don't accumulate good karma, they can't blame their children for not accomplishing anything."

"What did you say? Are you saying I hadn't accumulated enough good karma for Lingguan to get to college?" Laoshun was outraged.

"I didn't say that." But behind his back, she said to others, "It's hard to say with matters like this. We all agree that Lingguan is smart and that he learns fast, so why didn't he go to college?" Laoshun was to blame, she was implying.

His wife had planned the meditation this time to accumulate good karma for later generations. She'd barely revealed her intention when Laoshun flew into a rage:

"You blame the heavens when you're blown over in a wind. He wasn't good enough to get into college. Don't blame his parents."

If this gets out of hand, Laoshun said to himself, some people might attribute his eldest son's death to his blasphemy. It could happen. His mood darkened by these thoughts, he went to check out his field. That was his habit whenever he was unhappy. The sight of the lush, fertile land was uplifting, as if something had washed away the gloom in his heart.

He reached Xihupo, where Meng Baye was digging soil. "With all your sons and grandsons, they should be the ones out here digging."

"A cow doesn't stop shitting till the day it dies," Meng replied with a sigh. "Look at this land. It's so fertile it would sprout a calf if you stuck a cow's tail in it. Why don't they want it? Did you know that Huaqiu wants the land to lie fallow, saying no gold will come from it? See how his head got turned by gold? Heaven will punish you if you let such wonderful soil lie fallow."

"Mengzi is the same. He's been saying farming is worthless. They have no brains. How can they turn away from the land? I said to him, wait until you're so hungry a stink comes out of your mouth, and you'll know that the land is our treasure." Laoshun sighed.

"Big Head said the developer who has his eyes on Xihupo has been working on the people in the city government. I told him Xihupo has the most fertile land in Shawan, and we can't sell it, no matter what," Meng said.

"You're right. What'll we eat if the land is sold, the wind? It's all because of White Tiger Pass."

They both sighed despondently.

5

Pockmark Xu, whom they hadn't seen for a couple of years, came by that afternoon. They'd heard he'd found a match for Ying'er, which, if true, meant he'd come to sound them out. Laoshun gave him a cool reception, as he held the man in low esteem. Neither a true nor a serious farmer, Xu had given up on the land. Yet he'd worked with Grannie Shaman on the exchange marriage, so Laoshun could not act the way he wanted, for that would make things awkward for everyone.

"Hey, you old fart, I haven't seen you in years. You're looking younger." Xu was given to uttering such words whenever they met. Laoshun knew it was pure nonsense. Younger? Laoshun replied silently. My face looked nice and smooth a few years ago, but now it's turned into the bark on an old desert date tree. Still, it pleased him to hear Xu's compliment, which sounded better than reminding him of death.

"What do you mean young? I'm getting old, halfway in the ground already. Unlike you, you get to drink and eat meat every day, so you're as strong as a donkey. Now what wind has blown you over?" Laoshun said, in a sort of mocking tone.

"A black wind." Xu looked around with eyes that remained a slit no matter how wide he tried to open them. "Where's the missus?"

"Off doing her seven-day meditation." Laoshun felt sheepish the moment the words were out, as if meditation was no different from thievery or robbery. He had to curse his wife.

"Ah, her too." Xu looked around again. "Where's your daughter-in-law?"

"She's around." Laoshun called out, "Bring some water, Ying'er."

He heard movement in the kitchen, followed by Ying'er's voice, "I'm taking food to Ma, Pa."

The noise went out the gate.

Laoshun was left to get a cup himself and pour Xu some water. After sizing the pockmarked man up, he was surprised to see that Xu actually did look younger. Every spot on his face glowed, and Laoshun detected the smell of liquor, which cascaded toward him like waves. He craved a bit himself, he knew. Say, what a coincidence. My wife is away, so why can't I? Too bad Xu isn't the best company for enjoying some liquor. As the saying goes, a thousand cups of liquor aren't enough when drinking with someone you like, and one word is too many with someone you don't. It was a waste of money to drink with a man like Pockmark.

As he mulled this over, Xu took a bottle from his pocket.

"We have liquor here," Laoshun said. "You should have said you wanted a drink. You're no stranger in my house."

"It's all the same. Makes no difference. What's mine is yours." Xu reached into another pocket to retrieve a wrapped item. Laoshun detected the familiar smell of meat and, hei, it opened to show pig's knuckles.

Now Laoshun felt terrible. He'd been cool when the man walked in, showing him nothing but mockery. Now look at him, he brought liquor and meat. Laoshun recalled the saying that you should never hit someone who's smiling, and regretted the cold reception he'd given the man. If it'd been Ying'er's mother, her glib tongue would have spewed torrents of warm expressions. He wasn't good with words and couldn't bring himself to do that, so he said instead:

"I'm like a bedbug feasting on a guest."

"That's what a woman would say." Xu laughed. "You and I go back a long way, so why worry about what's yours and what's mine?"

The reply made Laoshun forget his negative thoughts about the man, who now became an old friend. He smiled. The ancestors were right about being deferential to those who bring gifts, he reminded himself.

Taking a pig's knuckle from Xu, Laoshun was about to sink his teeth into it when he realized he was drooling. To avoid embarrassment, he sucked his saliva back in. His favorite pastimes were sipping liquor, eating meat, taming his rabbit hawks, and smoking. Pig's knuckles were his preferred meat dish, the thought of which made his mouth water. But unlike rabbit meat, which he could enjoy by taming a hawk, pig's knuckles had to be bought, and cost five or six yuan. So he could only swallow whenever he thought about it. On this day, however, he was like a sleepy man given a pillow. What a friend Xu is!

"Go ahead, try it. It's cooked all the way through. I told them to simmer them an hour longer. My teeth are bad. They might be too mushy for you."

"It's just right. Not mushy at all." Laoshun mumbled as he chewed. The taste and texture were just right. What a wonderful sensation! A while back, when Meng Baye bought a few pig's knuckles, Laoshun had his craving satisfied, and he hadn't seen one since, not even in dreams, except for those still on his pigs. This was like New Year's. Someone has brought me pig's knuckles the moment my wife left to meditate, Laoshun said to himself. Instant results! He'd tell her to go meditate whenever he felt like having a pig's knuckle. He smiled at the thought.

A few bites and the first one disappeared into his belly. Laoshun wiped his lips, regretting having eaten too fast. He wished he'd chewed a bit longer, but once the meat was in his mouth, an invisible hand reached up from his stomach to drag it down, completely beyond his control. Still savoring the taste, he smacked his lips, but shook his head firmly when Xu pointed to another one.

"I'm full. You go ahead. I'm like a bedbug feasting on a guest," he repeated.

"I already had two at the shop. These are for you."

Laoshun wanted to take the second one and gobble it up, but instead he swallowed and said, "I'm full. I really am. You take it."

"You can save it for your daughter-in-law. Pig's knuckles help milk production. A nursing mother will have plenty of milk after eating one."

Laoshun kept quiet, for that was not a proper topic for a father-in-law.

After a few rounds, they'd finished Xu's bottle. Laoshun insisted on bringing out half a bottle left from earlier. He'd barely uncapped it when Xu started to cry.

"Are you drunk?" Laoshun asked.

Xu didn't reply, just kept crying and wiping his face.

Laoshun hated to hear people cry. Not a seriously superstitious man, he nonetheless found the sound upsetting, believing it brought bad luck.

He frowned.

"I've been miserable for several years now," Xu sobbed. "When I think about it, I feel like there are knives slicing through my heart. I've not done well by you."

"What do you mean?" Laoshun was startled.

"I did something terrible to you, though I did it out of good intentions."

"What did you do?"

Xu did not say what he did. He kept crying, his face twisted out of shape.

How can a grown man cry like that? Laoshun frowned again. He suddenly found Xu detestable, despite the pig's knuckle he'd enjoyed.

"I've done something terrible to you, Hantou." Xu changed to grieve over Laoshun's dead son, which quickly diluted Laoshun's distaste for the man. As a warm sensation rose up inside, Laoshun also felt like crying when he heard Xu say between sobs:

"I had no idea the Bai family could be so devious."

Laoshun was confused, for, within a very short time, Xu had wept over three things. He was about to inquire further, Xu stopped, dried his tears and said, "Drink up."

Putting his questions aside, Laoshun had a few cups with the man before asking, "What's the matter with the Bai family?" He wondered if Xu was apologizing for making the rumored match for Ying'er. "It's all right. Many families want a good girl for a daughter-in-law, and this is how you make a living."

His comment seemed to make Xu feel worse, for he started sobbing again.

"Drink up. Have another cup," Laoshun offered, fearing the man's face might get twisted out of shape from his crying.

"I can't swallow another drop. I wish I was dead whenever I think about how I sent your wonderful son to his death."

Laoshun was confused again. His son, Hantou, had died of a liver disease, how had Xu managed to send him to his death? He was about to ask when Xu said:

"Did you know the Bai family kept a big secret from me? Their girl is a white tiger with a sting."

"What are you saying?"

"So terrible." Xu ignored his question. "It was so powerful it killed Hantou."

Laoshun was beginning to see what this was all about. From what Xu had just said, Ying'er was apparently a white tiger who brought bad luck and killed Hantou. Like everyone else in the village, Laoshun knew that white tigers were women with no pubic hair. Rumor had it that these were the unluckiest of women, and that a man would suffer great misfortune if he met, let alone touched, someone like that. Any man who married a white tiger would die prematurely. Laoshun did not know what a sting was, but decided to let it pass. Luckily, they were alone; people would laugh their heads off if they knew that he, a father-in-law, was discussing such an intimate matter with someone else. Why would he care about pubic hair? they'd wonder.

"The sting means there's single strand of pubic hair, the absolute worst. Any man who touches a woman like that will not live long," Xu explained.

Laoshun wrinkled his nose while casting the man a disdainful glance. He might be tipsy, but Laoshun hadn't forgotten who he was. An outsider, let alone a father-in-law, would find such a comment hurtful. "Drink up. Have some more."

"It's all my fault." Xu continued with a sigh. "They were already married when someone who knew told me. If I'd known earlier, I'd never have helped arrange the marriage, even if my life had been on the line. I caused Hantou to die young."

"Let's keep drinking and talk about something else. People would laugh their heads off if they heard," Laoshun said. He'd always been suspicious of fantastic esoterica, unlike his wife, who believed everything and got herself all worked up. Besides, even if it were true, his son was dead, while his widow had to continue to live. How would she face the world if people knew?

Xu continued to sputter, spewing more and more indecent details. Laoshun lost his temper and slapped the table, "Do you want to drink or not? If not, I'll put it away. But you stop the bullshit now."

"Bullshit?" Xu was obviously getting tipsy. "Is that my reward for good intentions? I'm doing this for your own good. At first, I was thinking the girl has a good nature, and I wanted to talk you into marrying her to Mengzi. Here he had a ready-made wife, who did not have to return to her parents' home. I didn't know what was what until I asked around."

Now it was clear to Laoshun. Xu had come with a mission to break up a marriage by driving a wedge on one end and working on a deal on the other. Laoshun had once sent Mao Dan to do something similar.

"I appreciate your good intentions," Laoshun said. "I'm an old hand at this myself." He stuck his finger down his throat to make himself throw up; he retched a few times, but nothing came up. "I shouldn't have eaten your filthy food." He tried to catch his breath. "Get out of here. I'm through with you. You're lucky my wife is in meditation, or she'd cover your face with spit."

Seeing Laoshun discard the need to be cordial, Xu did the same. "Why spit on me? I don't push girls into men's arms or tell women to dally among men. Why spit on me? You should know the Daoist priest wants to gnaw at the young and the old. Get the wax out of your ears and ask around. Everyone knows but you. The trick of meditation may deceive others, but not me. Men and women spend days and nights together.

Cotton burns when it touches fire, that's for sure. And yet here you are, complaining about me."

He snatched up the pack of cigarettes and the half-eaten pig's knuckle and stormed off.

6

Laoshun was shaking with rage. He knew he shouldn't be angry after eating meat, for that could cause cancer, but he couldn't help it. He was clearheaded enough to know that liquor was the antidote when you lose your temper after eating meat. So he sat, intent on drinking and fuming alone.

Mengzi walked in and saw that his father's face was red.

"Did Pockmark Xu say something to make you angry? I saw the old beast cursing and jabbering as he walked out the gate. Looks like he was drunk too."

Laoshun's tongue limbered up and he said to his son:

"Go out there and break Pockmark's legs. Smash his bones until they're mush. Go on now. You're not my son if you don't."

"You've had too much, Pa." Mengzi laughed. "Drunken words are farts in dreams. Just ignore him."

"Are you going or not?" Laoshun looked at him sideways. "You're not my son if you don't."

Mengzi picked up the bottle and put the cap on. "A little liquor and you're acting like this. 'Has anyone taken food to Ma?'"

The question felt like a pebble skittering across his heart, as he recalled what his wife had said about keeping a close eye on the baby. It dawned on him that he hadn't seen Ying'er for a long time. He cried out:

"Oh no. The baby, they've taken the baby away."

"Not so loud." Mengzi cautioned with a laugh. "She's by the gate.

Not so loud, or she'll hear you."

Laoshun stumbled out through door unsteadily, his head buzzing as if hammered. The pig's knuckles had dampened the effects of liquor, so he remained clearheaded. When he saw Xu gesturing and clamoring down the way, he yelled:

"Dai! Pockmark. Come fart right in front of me if you dare."

Pockmark shuffled off when he saw Laoshun lumbering toward him.

"White tiger with a sting? What bullshit!" Laoshun said to himself, before his temper flared again, as he thought about how his daughter, Lanlan, had forsaken her parents and caused the family such a great loss of face. He wished he could grab her and slap her, something he'd never done, not since the day she was born. But at this moment he really wanted to slap her—not just want to, but, if she had been in front of him at the moment, do it until her face was swollen. Shameless girl. Didn't you hear what Pockmark said? Your father has to suffer over what you did. Listen, listen to what they're saying. Men and women together? Cotton burns when it touches fire.

Then he recalled how Lanlan had changed after she started meditating. Before then, she had been meek and gentle, and now she ignored everyone in the family. So, had something really happened during meditation? She had in fact spent time with the Daoist priest. The wild jackass! Anger rose again when he thought about the priest. If he were to see him now, Laoshun would bite down on his throat, and suck out all the warm blood, like a wolf drinking sheep's blood. Even that would not be enough to quell his anger.

Then his thoughts turned to his wife. The old hag was also in meditation. Meditation? It didn't sound right, not after what Pockmark said. Laoshun racked his brain to recall the others joining his wife: Huilanzi, a slut, and who else? He didn't know. But maybe Yue'er's father too. What kind of man was he? He was well known for his unsavory actions, trading in a donkey halter for a new head scarf, a certifiably indecent man. Why did he join them? Maybe Xu was right about cotton burning when it touches fire. Yue'er's father's aging face flashed before his eyes, beaming with a disgusting lewdness, his eyes on Laoshun's wife.

Disgusting. Flames of anger flared up and roared inside him.

Laoshun fumed loudly, wanting to throw a rock at the disgusting face. He searched the ground, only to see people staring at him.

"Are you drunk, Papa Shun?" one of them asked.

"He's practicing drunken boxing," another one said.

Bullshit, Laoshun responded silently. How could I be drunk? The cymbals were still banging away in his head, though, and now there was a drum beating on his ears. The rage was billowing its way through his limbs; he was not steady on his feet, but took forceful steps.

He picked up a rock and stumbled forward. "I'm going to kill you," he shouted as he walked.

The others laughed.

"Has Papa Shun lost it after too much to drink?" someone jested.

"You're the one who lost it." Laoshun retorted as he found his tongue getting thick. He held up the rock, scaring the man enough to back away. Laoshun thought he looked familiar, but his brain failed him, and he couldn't recall his name.

"Let's go, hey hey hey, up till the ninth month, ninth day," a youngster was singing.

Following the tune and rhythm of the child's singing, Laoshun walked up to the Vajravārāhī Cave.

"I'll kill you," Laoshun yelled.

No one came out, nor was there a guard at the opening. On the door a piece of paper with strange inscriptions fluttered in the wind. He went up, tore it off, and stomped on it before kicking the door open. A harmonious stream of chanting greeted him.

"I'll kill you!" He yelled again. A quick look showed him where his wife and the others were. Their chanting came to an abrupt stop, while they stared at him with wide-eyed surprise.

"What are you doing here?" his exasperated wife shouted. "Get out. Get out of here."

Get out? Laoshun thought, she's telling me to get out? "Hell no," he said. "Cotton burns when it touches fire." With the rock raised high, he twirled and said, "Men and women staying in the same cave doesn't look right." Though filled with anger, he felt his tongue failing him, his voice soft like that of a drunk.

"He's drunk. A drunk. Get out. Kick him out," Huilanzi cried out.

Laoshun threatened to throw the rock, effectively shutting her up. I'm not going to hit you with this, he said silently. Your head would split like melon. That's no good. He strained to look around him: it was an ordinary cave with several common looking bed rolls, an average looking thangka of the Buddha, simple lamps, and familiar fruits as offering. That's it? This is what enthralls his daughter? What a joke. Sleepiness sneaked up on him and he yawned.

"Get out! Get out of here!" his wife demanded shrilly, sounding more like screaming at their son.

You can't make me! Laoshun struggled to figure what he should do now that he was inside. He raised his hand and looked at the rock as another yawn occurred. He wanted to sleep, but he also wanted to find a place for the rock before he dozed off. People were walking toward him, which flustered him enough to fling the rock at the offering table. It rolled and bumped into all the things on the table before snapping the Vajravārāhī's tablet into two.

Two men came up and grabbed his arms while he drifted into dreamland.

He even heard himself snoring.

Chapter Sixteen

A yellow hawk and a black hawk fight
The yellow hawk's wings are broken

1

Lanlan woke up early. Strangely, she'd dreamed about her father, who was looking at her tearfully from a distance. The image was so clear it made her heart ache, so she woke up. It was still dark out, but the usual dank smell was gone from the cave. She learned that people were easily deceived; they cannot detect smells, good or bad, after being in one place for long. When she first arrived, she found the damp odor powerful, but could not smell it after a few hours. That was fine with her. But her father's face flickered before her eyes and made her choke up. Her feelings were complex when it came to her father. She had always been close to him, and he had loved her more than the boys. She had agreed to the marriage exchange partly because she didn't want her brother to remain a bachelor, but also because she couldn't bear to see the worried look on her father's face. He had sighed over those days, sneaking glances at her, but he did not want to force her into the marriage.

I'll give up this lifetime for Pa's sake, she told herself and gave her consent.

Later, tutored by life, she realized he wasn't the brilliant man she'd once thought. He was actually quite foolish, often engaged in foolish behavior, sputtering foolish things. Some of things he said did not sit well with her, and she started to rebel, internally. She couldn't help it; she didn't want to oppose him, but her mind would not let her stop. Such as when he told her to make do with life with Bai Fu. She thought she could do it, but her mind refused to make it happen. Or when he told her not to believe in the Vajravārāhī. All right, I won't do it, Lanlan had said to herself, since religious belief could not provide her with food or drink. But her heart objected: What will you believe in if not her? Life would be meaningless if she had nothing to believe in. Besides, it was addictive. At first, she didn't believe a word, then she was dubious, and finally she was a believer, until she was almost obsessed over her beliefs, in her father's words. He was surprised to see the change in her, incredulous, in fact, as if she'd become a different person. There was actually nothing strange about that. People's minds matured as they grew up. When animals hibernate in the winter, they emerge at the time of Insects Waking; when seeds are sown, they will sprout. One's heart changes constantly, and when that happens, one becomes a different person.

But Lanlan could not eliminate him from her heart. His image had been etched on her mind for more than two decades, and it would not be realistic to simply erase it. When the image appeared, a sadness seeped into her heart, and she could not shake the guilty feeling that he had raised her for nothing. She was an unworthy daughter, as she had failed to give him even a few days of peace. Then again, how many worthy daughters are there in the world? She lived like a naked woman running after a wolf. Survival was an issue; the wheels of life chased after her and put her in such a tight spot that she lived in fear. It was only after she learned of the Vajravārāhī that she finally could live for herself. If nothing else, her mind calmed and her heart was fuller, no longer empty as before, or with no one to lean on when she looked helplessly all around. Why are you crying, Pa?

Tears flowed, but she quietly wiped them off before forcing back the choking sensation rising up in her throat. She had not felt this way in recent days. She knew she must appear to be someone who had disowned her family. The prerequisite for being part of a family was to do what her parents wanted, which would make her less her own person and turn her into the person her family wanted her to be. Lanlan had turned countless times around life's millstone with its preset track. Back then, she had done everything they wanted, but life had not displayed its brilliance to reward her submission. Now she no longer sought beauty in life; all she wanted was tranquility, a quiet so absolute her mind would be blank. After undergoing raging storms, she wanted to find a peaceful harbor to gain rest. Why are you weeping, Pa?

The emotion brought on by the dream of her father subsided, and Lanlan regained her peace of mind. She'd heard that in life's endless transmigrations, any of the masses in the six great divisions on the wheel of karma could have been her parents in previous lives. Once one reached enlightenment, one could rescue all these parents and deliver them from samsara. For the sake of the parents from past lives, she had to ask the ones in the present life to suffer a bit. Many preeminent masters of Buddhist learning had renounced their families.

Lanlan continued to silently recite the incantation, during which she walked down a long winding path without traveling, experienced a great deal without doing anything, heard lots of voices without listening, and said something without uttering a word. She liked it this way. Many things receded into the background once she started chanting. Whatever she'd experienced turned into a colorful brush painting of the sky; the brush strokes never stopped, but left no traces.

She liked silently reciting the incantation, for, after a while, her heart took off to an island brimming with peach blossoms. Her body traveled over gently rippling ocean waves, while a warm, fresh breeze brushed past her ears. Her body and mind dissolved in the water and the wind, and her "self" blended in with a vast sky and boundless water.

The site of her existence changed instantly; gone were the dampness, the disorder, and the agitation, replaced by peace, serenity, transcendence, and coolness. How had a Zen master put it? "One does not need a scenic site for meditation/Coolness rises on its own when the heart's fire is doused." It was a sensation called the "joy of Zen."

If Lanlan had started her religious practice purely out of desperation over reality and wanted to find an anchor in the illusory world, now she did it all for the "joy of Zen." It was beyond words, it could not be experienced by someone with worldly desire, and it could not be bought with money or extorted through power. When one reached that state, one felt only happiness and no suffering. She'd heard someone compare religion with opium, true words from those who knew. Indeed, the joy of Zen was fleeting, hazy, sweetly dizzying, but with the added sensation of coolness and tranquility.

Some had made such religious practice symbolic and blatantly applied their own analysis, forgetting that these practitioners were first and foremost human beings. Humans have consciousness, and everyone has a spiritual world of her own. There are no two leaves that look exactly alike, and no two persons completely identical. All analysis pales when facing a real, living being. A whole variety of medicines is required to cure an affliction of the mind, as the saying goes. She kept these ideas to herself, however. The best defense for one's innocence is no defense, for you can have many tricks while I have my own understanding of the spiritual world.

She shut her eyes. Eyelids are the most encompassing item in the universe, for once shut, they block out the whole world. It is better that way, since what one sees is mostly the source of worries. Everything one hears, smells, tastes, and touches brings forth worries. They are the six highwaymen the Monkey King vanquished in Journey to the West. Isn't there a line in the Heart Sutra that says, "The five compositional elements of our existence are all void?" "Form is empty and emptiness is form." "Our feelings and perceptions are the same." What one's eyes see, one's ears hear, one's nose smells, one tongue tastes, and one's body touches all lead to greed. One suffers when one wants something, when one desires nothing, one is strong. Lanlan wanted nothing now. Love was beyond her reach, so she would not desire it; fame and riches were nowhere in sight, so she would not think about them; her ideals were in vain, so she forgot about them. She would give up petty love for something grander, choose minor desires over major wants, devote herself to the Vajravārāhī, to the lives in the six realms of transmigration, covet the Buddhist land of Dakini and the eternal happiness of Nirvana.

A heavy wave of sadness came at her, followed by a warm current rising inside and out of her eyes; she felt a coolness on her face, a sensation that often surged and inundated her heart, when everything was at its quietest. She heard that it had to do with the effects of feeling great compassion. The Guanyin Bodhissatva had often shed tears over the suffering of the masses, and her countless tears turned into many meditation deities known as Tārā. Princess Wencheng of the Tang dynasty was the reincarnation of a green Tārā. She also heard that many accomplished practitioners wept bitter tears when they thought of all the suffering lives. Based on that theory, Lanan had clearly made progress, but the compassion often created angst. She knew that her compassion was minor, not the grand kind, and that it came from an emotional response deep inside. Her mind was thrown into chaos when her emotional reaction brought forth the image of her father, like an aging tree.

She understood now that she was not yet free from human desires and passions.

2

Gossip proliferated in the village after Laoshun disrupted the meditation. Some wondered how the Vajravārāhī could protect the villagers if she couldn't even stop Laoshun's rock from snapping her own tablet in two. Others questioned how the guardian deities could block fiery winds or fierce beasts when the end of world came if they could not even watch over the cave. Big Head had made several visits to the cave to intervene with the believers, trying to talk them out of superstitious practices and into doing hard work to enrich themselves. Many were lured away to White Tiger Pass, where the gold shone brightly, visibly reducing the number of meditators. Only Lanlan was in the cave most of the time, with her a few women who usually spent their time chatting.

Lanlan was chanting one day when Fengxiang came in. "Your father wants you home," she whispered.

Lanlan did not react. She had not wanted to see anyone from her family after leaving home; she thought of them often, but was afraid to see them. Once an arrow leaves the bow it cannot turn back. She would rather die outside and feed her corpse to the dogs than go back for more disapproval. A married daughter is like spilled water. Besides, she had returned in defeat and left the same way. The images of her parents flashed past her mind's eyes often, but she shook them off each time; only when she wasn't paying attention could the images sneak up and drag the sadness out of her.

"Your father's outside," Fengxiang repeated.

"Take a message for me. Tell him to consider me dead," Lanlan said.

"He's here just to see you. Come on. Come out to see him."

"Tell him to consider me dead."

"I've never seen a daughter like you." Fengxiang sneered. "What kind of religious practice is this? How can an unfilial daughter be practicing religious cultivation?"

Lanlan shuddered as she slowly got to her feet. When she was outside, from a distance she could hear her father's voice coming from the Earth God's temple. A strange emotion stirred inside. She felt like crying when she heard her father say:

"I raised her, but I can't control her mind. I'll have to consider raising her to be a waste of time."

His outburst snuffed out the warm, sadness rising inside her.

She lowered her gaze so as not to look at him. But she felt his burning stare trained on her and heard the familiar wheeze when he breathed.

"Come home, my little girl," he was saying, "I've gotten your room ready for you."

Her face a blank, she wanted very much to look at him, to see if he'd lost more weight, something that had been bothering her all along. But she reminded herself. Be strong. One look, and your resolve will soften, and once that happens, you'll have to do what he wants you to do. You'd rather die than go back to the Bai house. She began to recite the incantation as she stood there woodenly. The sutra erased her father's presence; he was gone, though he was still standing in front of her. She could hear him breathing hard, the heavy sound piercing her ears. Normally it was a sign that someone in the family would suffer, usually her mother. She was afraid of him; she chanted silently, the words sweeping back and forth like a brush to push out all information about him, but the fear remained. She would likely tear up if she were to look at his face. So, she steeled her resolve, turned around, and said, "I'm going back inside."

"You can go in there to die for all I care," her father bellowed.

Laoshun was outraged.

He'd spent a lot of time getting ready for this visit, emotionally for the most part. His wife had tried several times to talk him around. "Put your hand over your heart and think carefully. You're her father, what have you done to your daughter?"

Laoshun "put his hand over his heart" and thought about that until he slowly realized what he'd done wrong. For one thing, he'd never had a heart-to-heart talk with her. When she cried before the exchange marriage, he'd said to her:

"Why are you crying? Women have to get married. When a girl is born, she is destined to be someone's wife."

When Bai Fu beat her and she cried, Laoshun had said:

"Why are you crying? It's only natural that a man hits his wife. Your mother nearly died from one of my kicks."

When Lanlan's daughter died and she cried, he'd said to her:

"Maybe that was the girl's fate. There's a reason for that, I'm sure."

When Lanlan wanted a divorce, Laoshun had said to her unhappily:

"A good man likes many women and a good woman belongs to one man. The best flour is freshly made. You put up with it, and soon you spend a life together. What's the point of a divorce?"

He had scolded her each time and never once asked, "What do you think?" Now he had to agree with his wife—she's right. What's on Lanlan's mind? Mental worries need a cure for the heart, he thought, which was why he came to the cave full of hope for a heart-to-heart talk with his daughter. He hadn't expected an outright rejection, like warm buttocks landing on a cold kang.

What outraged him most was her cold indifference. They were father and daughter after all, like bones connected by tendons even when broken. Besides, they hadn't seen each other for quite some time. He'd only seen her three times, all in his dreams, since she'd stomped out of the house and entered the cave. Once he saw her profile and twice he saw her from behind. It would be an overstatement to say he missed her even in his dreams, but he did think about her from time to time. Too stubborn to express his feelings verbally, he would rather hide them than have them move his feet. Now he came with a lot to say, even if it meant "toppling a gold hill or tippling a jade pillar": I came to see you without regard for face, even slapped my own face, so you ought to take two steps forward to meet me halfway. You should do likewise when I kneel or when I put my self-esteem aside. But look at you. You didn't even look up. This was simply too much for Laoshun.

"What are you shouting for?" Yue'er's mother said with a laugh. "You'd cry until your nose is crooked if she were really dead."

"I wouldn't." Laoshun yelled. "She's an ingrate who won't even acknowledge her own father. She should never have been born."

Laoshun tossed a bundle from Ying'er into the cave, turned around, and walked down the hill. A wind blew over, swirling yellow leaves and scraps of paper, carrying dusk and an indescribable stench. He took it all in and his mood turned foul, seemingly worse than when he'd heard about his eldest son's cancer. Back then, he'd only felt excruciating pain, while now there was a jumble of emotions. The sky was in turmoil and so was his mood.

"If I'd known, I'd have sat on her when she was born and fed her to the dogs," he said to himself. "Family planning is better. The more children you have, the more worries you get."

He was drained, so he leaned against a small tree to look at the sky, where a mass of clouds rolled. The single shout at his daughter had taken all his energy and released most of his bitter resentment against Lanlan.

She's lost weight.

He spat when realizing that he'd been worried about the ingrate. *I'm useless. Why worry about her after she's disavowed you?*

He shook his head angrily, but could not shake off the thoughts on his mind. So he tottered off. *I should go home and stop worrying about her,* he said to himself. *You're no longer a father to her, so stop thinking about her. What an ingrate.*

Beizhu was coming his way, his oldest daughter hanging on his arm. She looked up at Beizhu and said something with a smile.

Envy rose inside at the sight of the pair. *Look at them. See how he raised his daughter. Did he have better karma?* The thought of karma reminded him of all the things that had happened in his family. He realized that they had come in a line, one after another, before the previous one was even over. But on second thought, he found that no one in the village was spared troubles, some faring even worse.

Compared to those ahead, they weren't doing so well, but better than those behind, he was thinking.

The comparison eased the heavy feeling in his heart.

3

He felt a twitch all night long. Experience told him that twitching was a bad omen. He was worried that his daughter would take to heart his outburst that she could die for all he cared. Early the next morning, Big Head told him to go and talk Lanlan into coming home. He was concerned that something bad might happen, with too many people congregating in the cave. So Laoshun and his wife went.

Her mother was the first one Lanlan saw. Mother had aged, her temple graying, eyes sunken, cheekbones more prominent, her face covered in wrinkles, her nose dripping with clear snivel. She had been a neat, clean woman who cared about her appearance, and the snivel looked terrible on her.

Father sat on a chair with his head down, not looking at her. She sensed that he was still bearing a grudge. Yet she knew him, a simple man, and he'd love her even when he wished she could have been better. The angrier he was with her, the more he loved her.

Lanlan wished she could throw herself into her mother's arms and cry, a scene that appeared in her head when she least expected it. But at this moment her heart had grown dull, like a sand hollow devoid of Artemisia. She did not even feel like crying anymore, so she looked down and waited for her mother to speak.

And she did. "You've lost weight. Do you have enough to eat?"

"I do." Lanlan replied.

"How about sleep? Is it crowded here?"

"No, it's not."

"We've thought it through. You can get a divorce if you want. It's not like a frost has killed off all the men in the world. You can get remarried if you want. If not, you can stay home and we'll take care of you. We always have enough for an extra mouth."

"I've thought it through too," Laoshun said, his eyes fixed on the tip of his shoes. "I'm staying out of your life. I can't be with you forever. I know it now."

It didn't feel right to Lanlan. They were talking about her life, and yet she felt it had nothing to do with her. What her father had just said showed his new liberal attitude toward her divorce; it was a compromise on his part, and yet oddly, her heart was still, like stagnant water without a ripple.

"See, my little girl. We've thought it through. Let's go home. You can start over and be on the road to a good life. Do whatever you want, I won't interfere."

"That's right." Mother cheered up. "The Vajravārāhī is always there in your heart. No need to stick to some ritual."

Laoshun turned quiet; only the wrinkles moved on his face.

"You go on back and let me think about it," Lanlan said.

She turned and reentered the cave, a sudden wave of sorrow rushing at her. I can't figure it out. I want to do good and practice my belief. What harm does it do to others? Tears ran down her face at the thought.

4

The good cry helped relieve her pent-up emotions and emptied her mind. Once worries arose, the serenity vanished. Detachment was required for her kind of practice; when interfered with by other sentiments, the awareness turned to frost under the sun. The mind would not be quieted no matter how hard she tried

Help me, Vajravārāhī.

Tranquility left her after her father's visit, no more spiritual emptiness, nor the mysterious aura surrounding her heart. Only worries, which sneaked up on her.

Grannie Shaman also went with her parents to talk her around. After Big Head, representing the government, got involved, the Shaman's fervor slowly died down. Maybe she realized that no one would believe in her again when they became true believers of the Vajravārāhī. Her business slowed. Her tongue seemed to have been fitted with ball bearings and spewed whatever she needed to say. Grannie may be a shaman, but she doesn't appear to believe in deities, Lanlan said to herself. Obviously, it's just a job to her.

Peace and quiet were gone from the Vajravārāhī Cave. Put three women together and there will be drama, plus lots of disputes. They argued over the most trivial things every day. A deserted stone cave was transformed into a rumor mill, the source of the gossip about Lanlan and the Daoist Priest.

Little by little, the halo born from their religious beliefs disappeared, and everyone showed her true colors. The practitioners had already splintered into cliques that fought over unsignificant gains and constantly stirred up trouble. Meditation was halted, only one perfunctory meditation session was performed once a day. They spent most of their time engaged in idle chatter.

People are really strange, Lanlan told herself. They act holier-than-thou when they feel it's necessary and more despicable than ever when they fall. It was only a while ago when the women paraded themselves as righteous and chaste, all wearing somber looks and displaying their piety, as if they could rip out their hearts to show the Vajravārāhī their devotion. They were more odious than ever when the noble façade collapsed.

Once the novelty passed, trouble began to brew. Yue'er's mother, the first to consider leaving, exerted influence on the others to go along. It was like sprinkling sand on food she did not want to eat. Perhaps she believed that retribution could not be applied to the masses even if it existed.

With doubts sprouting, the others behaved differently in their subsequent practice, and their chanting of sutras no longer had the same effects.

"The feeling is gone," Fengxiang whispered. "I suppose the Vajravārāhī must be mad at me and will take back the spiritual energy."

"I don't think the Vajravārāhī cares," Yue'er's mother replied. "After reaching Buddhahood, if she cared, she'd be no different from us."

Lanlan snickered silently, knowing that the older woman was laying the groundwork for a future decision.

"Of course, the Vajravārāhī would not stoop to your level, but it's hard to say when it comes to the Guardian Deities," Lanlan wanted to say. "Your whole life would be over if you acted with ill will."

She had heard similar notions from Grannie Shaman, who, to her surprise, said instead, "It depends on how you look at it. Studying Buddhist teaching depends on the circumstances. I haven't seen anyone punished for not believing."

Lanlan knew that the shaman was planning to leave too. Grannie Shaman had been initiated not purely for her beliefs, but mainly to profit from the practice. Vajravārāhī, look at your disciples, Lanlan said silently. How could they act like that? A wave of sadness rose up.

Religious beliefs can be harder than steel when they are strong, but when they are weak, a wind can easily bring them down, Lanlan believed. When she examined herself, she had to admit that she too had been shaken by Big Head's threat. She let out a long sigh. Everything in the cave jarred the eye now. A bramble nest had been a land of purity when Vajravārāhī filled her mind, but now the people around her seemed irritating, as did the place. A moldy odor wafted over and the air was damp, sticky with a musty smell. How many times had the air swirled in the lungs of the other women before it was exhaled? The thought turned her stomach. Obviously, instead of the Vajravārāhī redeeming the people, the people actually needed the Vajravārāhī. With her in mind, people felt a certainty in their heart, and without her they were empty inside. She was a towering tree in the heart, with a canopy of shade; worries had no place to hide when the Vajravārāhī was there.

But now everything had changed.

"You have magical eyes, so tell us, is there really a Vajravārāhī?" Yue'er's mother asked Grannie Shaman, a blasphemy in the past for sure.

"It depends on how you look at it. She's there if you believe in her and she doesn't exist if you don't. How do you explain the fact that people have been worshipping her for a thousand years if she doesn't exist? Then again, no one has actually seen her."

"No one has seen her?" Yue'er's mother perked up.

"Some have." The shaman licked her lips. "During meditation or in dreams. Chanting the sutra with devotion did bring magical, beneficial results to some. The sick recovered their health and people had their wishes fulfilled. But there have been just as many incidences with no result at all. I have my doubts too."

Lanlan was discouraged. In recent days, the Vajravārāhī had become a pillar in her life; she would suffer or rejoice, depending on what the Vajravārāhī brought her, and lived or died because of Her. It was the Vajravārāhī who bestowed tranquility and transcendence on her, and added color to her pallid life. She was grateful to Grannie Shaman, who served as a mentor; she had not expected these comments from the shaman. What would others think if even the shaman herself was puzzled?

5

Laoshun sent Mengzi to bring Lanlan home. Like a sleepwalker, she walked out the cave on unsteady feet, her heart empty.

"It would be hopeless if the Vajravārāhī did not exist," she thought, as she rued the way she'd treated her father during his last visit. He must have been furious with her. She shouldn't have done that, she realized. As much as she wanted to see him, she was afraid to face him now, for she did not know what to say. After hurting his feeling so many times, she could only feel guilty, but the more guilt-ridden, the more tightly she closed herself off. It had now become a vicious cycle.

The impossibly blue sky leaped into view the moment she walked out.

Mengzi looked at her wordlessly. She saw he had lost weight and was severely tanned, a moustache showing above his lip. He looked even more like their father now, a discovery that pained her immensely. She wondered if he would suffer the way their father had.

The village looked different too. The fervor of White Tiger Pass was infectious. Noise assaulted her eardrums. There had always been noise, of course, but with the Vajravārāhī enthroned internally, the sacred, pure light cuddled her heart and softened the world in her eyes. Now everything was bleak and gray. The world around her was splendid, but it belonged to others. The air, however, smelled fresh, the only refreshing element to her.

In a daze, she set off on the road home, greeted along the way by familiar sensations, which had been the first to warm her heart when she came home after the abuse she'd suffered at her in-laws'. It was her hometown whose unique flavor had seeped into her blood long ago.

Meng Baye and Huaqiu, as well as his sickly wife, were repairing the irrigation ditch, but she pretended not to have seen them.

"Your father has been to see you several times, Lanlan," Meng shouted from a distance. "The old whelp is all tough talk, but he's soft inside. When he sees you coming home, I bet he'll be leaping happily like a mule."

Lanlan hurried past them with her head down.

Chapter Seventeen

Lightning in the underworld, thunder in the human world
Frighten off cuckoo birds calling people out to the fields

1

Ying'er and Lanlan left the village, each leading a camel.

Ying'er wanted to earn enough money to redeem her freedom. She told Lanlan that her parents were also in a tough spot, but they would stop forcing her once she earned the money to get her brother another wife. Lanlan replied, "I'm partly responsible for the redeeming cost, so if the sky falls, we'll hold it up together." Ying'er planned to trap badgers, but Lanlan thought they were no match for badgers fleeing for their lives and besides, whatever money they got would go to their mothers if they asked for help from their father and Mengzi.

"How about picking Artemisia seeds?" Ying'er suggested.

"My skin broke out from the fuzz on wheat stalks during the month-long lying-in. Shrubs still makes me itch terribly and they cause hives," Lanlan said.

Each brainstorm came up against the need for capital. A woman's body was capital, but they didn't want to go that route.

"Let's not even dream about scooping up a lump of gold with a ladle either," Lanlan said. "How about bringing salt back from the lakes? In the countryside people love cheap salt, and one bowl of it will get us a bowl of wheat. Do it long enough and we can get what we need, like collecting bits of fried bread to fill a pot."

Huaqiu's wife, with her crooked neck, roamed the village, and Lanlan wanted a job that would take her away so she could be "out of sight, out of mind."

"Sure," Ying'er said. "We'll go at it one day at a time."

Their idea did not sit well with Laoshun, who said there would be bad people in the desert.

"How about taking Mengzi along?" he suggested.

"Forget that," Lanlan said. "You feed your belly with the food you make, and you become enlightened through your own cultivation. We're the cause of the problem, and we'll be the solution."

Lanlan knew that once Mengzi joined them, whatever money they made would belong to the family. "Don't you worry." She added, "If we lose the camels, we'll pay for them ourselves. I don't believe we won't make enough to pay for an animal, even if we have to cut off our flesh and sell our bones."

Her comment had him appear to be choking on a potato; he opened his mouth, but couldn't find anything else to say.

Their "home" was carried on camels. They'd be carrying salt back, so their "home" was simple—kitchen tools, bedrolls, water, and food. In order to carry as much as possible, Ying'er got the family camel, while Lanlan borrowed one. She wanted to borrow more than one, but Laoshun said one would be enough for their first, exploratory trip.

"When we went to carry salt in the past," Laoshun added, "we only had to offer some rabbits to the warden for him to load up the camel. It's hard to say now though, so take some money along."

They went into the city and sold badger fat for capital. This would be money borrowed from Hantou's mother, Ying'er said to herself. I'll pay her back once I sell the salt.

They had reached the belly of the desert after traveling east for several days. The salt lakes were lakes cradled in the arms of the desert, which had very likely been an ocean years ago. With the change in the earth's crust, some of the water went elsewhere, and some was sucked dry by the sun, leaving salt crystals in the lakes—this was Lanlan's hypothesis, though she wasn't sure if she was right. To her, it wasn't important whether she got it right or not; what was more important was the fact that she'd thought about it. Many things in life turn out just the way you think about them. Take the Buddha Land for example. No one has seen it, so you can imagine it in any way you like. What you have in mind could be the way it is. Buddha had said that all the Buddhist teaching comes from the heart.

Lanlan had traveled to the salt lakes as a little girl. She still recalled how the sand hills rose and fell once she was set up on their camel's hump, where she felt dazed, as if in a dream. After a while she fell asleep. Sometimes in withered, yellow dreams, she would hear the sound of a three-string instrument that produced a forlorn sound, as if weighed down by so much hardship and tears and blood it made her heart ache. The sound carried suffering, brimming with tears and blood, and yet nurtured hope for a better future. It was a future that, though hidden behind the faint mist rising from the sand, unreal as a mirage, had moved her with its forward-looking prospects.

They got onto the camels after walking for some time. Traveling on the sand atop a camel was slow but steady, and the ripples of the sand became even more visible. Camel hair was toasty warm, like the arms of their mothers, spreading a sense of security through their hearts. Camels are wonderful, Ying'er thought, better than her mother, her mother-in-law, and anyone else in her life. They gave her a sense of security in a world filled with uncertainty.

This must be how Lanlan feels when she thinks about the Vajravārāhī, Ying'er said to herself.

You are thrust into a strange life filled with loneliness the moment you're born, and everyone needs a sense of security. She herself was waiting for a similar kind of protection.

Ying'er had been feeding the camel, so an emotional bond had developed between them. It was a docile animal that touched her hand with its lips each time she fed it. Its clear eyes were filled with understanding and tender kindness, with a sad gaze when it looked at her. She knew the animal understood her. Sometimes, when she was distracted, she treated it as her absent lover, her *yuanjia*, and looked at it; its deep, ocean-like eyes seemed to take her in, and she wished she could enter them.

Camels are wonderful, so is the desert. The yellow ripples that reached out on the vast land felt like a gentle breeze caressing the souls. She was constantly thinking about the soul after the brief affair with her *yuanjia*. She knew that suffering was a constant companion when one begins to think about the soul. Before she was married, she seemed to live in a haze, and her dreams were unclear. She had no idea what a soul was, so her soul slumbered alone. Naturally, she could not have imagined that one day it would wake up and trouble her so much she would not know what to do.

The sand ridge twisted toward an unknown future, like a long night troubled by nightmares. Bells on the camels' necks traveled into the distance in threads like silk shredded by the wind. What she heard more clearly was the sound of the camels' feet, a rustling noise as muted and indistinct as a dream. Lanlan scolded her camel frequently, for the animal kept shaking its head in an effort to free itself. It was no match for the ring made of softened elm, which looped through its nose and was tethered to her reins. A single tug could send sharp pain into the camel's head, enough to make it weep.

But none of them could imagine that jackals, with their fangs bared, were hiding in a strange corner of their fate, watching them with sinister eyes.

2

A so-called camel's trail was in fact a path connecting oases; it could be etched on road traveled by carts and horse, or in a desert where no human traces are found. Camel's trails in the desert are mostly shaded hollows. Wind blows loose sand into sunny hollows, while shaded ones hold years of accumulated sand, and feel solid under the feet. When she spotted a wider, shaded hollow, Lanlan directed her camel to walk alongside Ying'er. Sweat formed on the tip of her nose. Around the corners of her eyes were soft creases. Lanlan had once been pretty, which was why Ying'er's mother had agreed to the exchange marriage. The two girls were about the same, so neither family could claim it came out second best. But Lanlan was no longer pretty, with eyes ringed by crow's feet. I must look the same, Ying'er thought, which brought on a wistful sentiment. We're getting old before living our lives fully.

Lanlan dried the sweat with her scarf and squinted into the distance.

"Don't worry," she said softly. "Even the foolish old man moved the mountain. We'll make enough money as long as we have our two hands."

Ying'er merely joined her in squinting into the distance.

"See there," Lanlan said as she tilted her head, "where the sand mountain connects to the sky? When we cross that mountain, we're past the first gully, and the salt lakes will appear after we pass a few more."

Ying'er knew that reaching the gully, which sounded so easy the way Lanlan said it, would be like walking to the end of the sky. She had collected desert rice before, but that was more like skirting the edge of the desert; she had yet to cross a single gully. The thought of going to a strange place all the way to the horizon made her fearful.

Lanlan could tell what was on her mind, so she patted the musket and Tibetan dagger hanging down the side of the camel.

To be ready in case they ran into wolves, Lanlan had brought the musket along, a weapon she knew how to use. When she'd craved something to eat as a young woman, she'd take it secretly and hide under wheat stacks by the village pond to wait for thirsty sand grouses to come for the water. She would let out a soft cry and pull the trigger. The hammer would strike the flint, which in turn would ignite the gunpowder and send buckshot into the flesh of the sand grouse in flight. Usually fat and tasty, they produced a heavy aroma when they were roasted on a skewer.

"Don't be afraid," Lanlan said. "I have a musket, two gourds filled with gunpowder and over a kilo of buckshot, plus more than a dozen ball bearings. If we run into a wolf, I'll feed it some steel."

The mention of a wolf sent panic through Ying'er, who feared even dogs. But on second thought, why should she be afraid? Suffering like this in life was worse than becoming food for wolves. There was nothing to fear when she saw through it. Life had been monotonous, but hadn't appeared that way before she met Lingguan; she'd been lonely, but didn't know it. She'd been born to steep in massive monotony and loneliness, and had managed to live into her twenties without being aware of it. But after meeting him, monotony and loneliness sprouted teeth to gnaw at her. If a wolf shows up, I won't mind being delivered from suffering, she said to herself.

One night they reached the first gully, a spot overgrown with weeds, also called a *magang*. There was water for the camels to drink all night and enough grass to sustain them through the next day. Lanlan could tell that the green *magang* had shrunk. She'd heard that water from the snow mass on Qilian Mountains was a relative constant, its average amount stable, even though the amount could change due to weather. It was relatively constant how much rain and snow were required to keep an oasis viable; when there were more green spots upstream from the snow melt, there would be fewer downstream. Developments over thousands of years meant merely shifting locations of oases, until now, when the amount of green in a *magang* grew smaller because large plots of land were being farmed upstream.

They unloaded the camels and put up a tent, which was pieces of cloth sewn together, good enough to block the wind, but not to keep out the rain. Luckily rain wasn't a common occurrence in the desert, so no one worried about waterproofing. After crisscrossing several wooden stakes, Lanlan threw up the cloth, tucked the edges into the sand, and spread out their bedding in the middle, while Ying'er tethered the camels to a spot dense with vegetation. Normally they would wind the reins around the camels' neck so they could graze at will, but they did not want their animals to roam too far and delay their travel the next day. So, they decided they'd keep moving them to different spots to graze. It was always better to be cautious when away from home.

After gathering dry kindling, they lit a fire and drank some water by the fire. Ying'er was tired and wanted to just have some steamed buns for dinner.

"That won't do," Lanlan objected. "We have to eat well on the road. If we skip a good meal here and a good meal there, soon our health will suffer. The piles of bones we'll see are from people who skipped meals and failed to make it out of the desert." She told Ying'er to lie by the fire to rest and add kindling while she retrieved a wash basin, scooped out some flour, and cooked a meal of hand-pinched noodles.

Darkness had taken over by the time they finished eating. Moonlit nights were Ying'er's favorite time, but obviously, Heaven couldn't bring out the moon any time just because she liked it. Lanlan lit the lantern; it cast a circle of light, small but bright enough. It's fine as long as there's light, Ying'er was thinking. What she was hoping for was also a light in life, wasn't it? Even if it were small, life would be in the dark without it. She recalled a movie she'd once seen about Jews living under the Nazi regime, constantly threatened with death. Unable to see a shred of hope, some committed suicide. To give the people hope, the protagonist in the movie made up lies, including telling them he had a radio, fabricating hopeful tales every day, so some of them managed to keep on living. It was a fantastic story to Ying'er. No matter how one looked at it, life always ends with death, the unalterable, hopeless outcome. So, everyone should find something to hope for in life.

"Could religions be compassionate lies made up by sages who had reached enlightenment?" she wondered. It didn't matter to her whether or not there was really a land of Buddha; what was important was the belief that the other shore of life was an eternal, beautiful world. It was the same with her. There are many things in the world that no one can explain well.

Darkness pressed down, seemingly making the light from the lantern cower. It was a weak light. The darkness also quieted Lanlan. Ying'er was convinced that Lanlan was pondering similarly serious subjects, for she knew the other woman suffered just like her. She knew that Lanlan had never had a day without hardship since her marriage. By comparison, Ying'er felt herself lucky, for her mind was mostly taken up by longing that was a mixture of happiness and pain, unlike Lanlan, whose life was shattered by reality.

Ying'er reached out to touch Lanlan's face, and was surprised by the wetness on her hand. Lanlan was sobbing.

"What are you thinking?" Ying'er asked.

"Pa must have been heartbroken after what I said to him that day," Lanlan said after a long silence. "I'm a terrible daughter."

"Don't think like that." Ying'er felt a warm current in her heart. "I'm sure Pa has put it out of his mind already."

"He may have forgotten, but I still feel guilty. When you think about it, you have to agree that Pa has never enjoyed a restful day. I really should have been a better daughter to him."

"That's what life is all about," Ying'er replied. "Isn't he always saying he can take whatever Heaven doles out to him? It's true. Who doesn't suffer in life? Heaven gives because it's within its power; you can take it and it's a tribute to your dignity if you do."

"If I can make a lot from the salt, I'd like to take Ma and Pa into the city for some restaurant food. Ma loves noodles with fried bean sauce so much that the mere thought makes her drool," Lanlan said after drying her tears.

That reminded Ying'er of her own mother, which tugged on the most fragile string in her heart. Her mother preferred spicy fried pig's intestines, and drooled at the mere mention of it. She made up her mind to buy some pig's intestines and peppers for her mother after the trip. She began to miss her mother terribly; as she recalled all the good things about her, she regretted what she'd said even more.

She picked up the lantern and walked out of the tent to move the camels after lengthening the tethering rope. They would now have a larger area to graze. Above her were brilliant stars. Perhaps because the desert air was pure and clean, the stars appeared larger and lower than those she'd seen back home, as if she could reach out and pluck one out of the sky.

She went back inside the tent to lie down. Lanlan was sighing. Afraid to make Lanlan even sadder, Ying'er refrained from asking more questions and said instead:

"Let's go to sleep now. We'll have to get on the road early tomorrow."

3

Ying'er stuck a flashlight under her pillow before blowing out the lantern. She reminded herself not to sleep too soundly so she could get up and move the camels to a different grazing spot. When traveling in the desert, one had to make sure the camels had a full stomach. To be sure, they stored fat in their humps, but that was like an emergency reserve that should not be easily squandered.

To avoid losing sleep, she tried not to think about anything that would make her thoughts run wild. Luckily, fatigue lent a hand, and it took little effort to fall asleep. In her dream, she was also spending a night in the desert, with her lover, who was staring at her coldly. Does he think I'm dirty? she asked herself. That made her feel terrible. Then she noticed Pockmark Xu leering at her and touching her calf with his icy paw. She cried out and woke herself up to actually feel something touching her calf. After nudging Lanlan, she turned on the flashlight.

Lanlan sat up quickly.

"Something got into my pants," Ying'er said.

Lanlan snatched away the flashlight, while Ying'er felt the thing writhing.

"Oh no!" Ying'er cried out.

"Don't move; don't move," Lanlan said, "Good. I got it."

Lanlan screamed when she took the thing out, and smacked it on the wood frame of the tent, making it wobble. She kept slapping at it, the best way to deal with it in a tent.

"Smack it on the ground," Ying'er cautioned, afraid that the tent would fall apart.

"Light the lantern." Lanlan panted, her voice quivering.

Ying'er groped and found the matches. It took several tries to finally light the match, after which she saw Lanlan collapse on their bed.

The lantern lit up the thing in her hand. A snake, as thick as a tea cup. Ying'er feared snakes more than anything. Her legs gave out as she screamed:

"Throw it out. Throw it out."

"It's dead," Lanlan said, breathing heavily.

Sure enough, the snake's head was smashed. Its blood covered the frame and had splashed onto their blanket also.

"Were you bitten?" Ying'er asked. "Did it bite you?"

"I don't know," Lanlan replied with a sigh. Her hand was covered in blood but it was hard to tell whose it was.

She wiped her hand on the blanket. When Ying'er shone the flashlight on Lanlan's arm, she noticed a tiny opening on the wrist. It was bleeding, but she wasn't sure if it was from a snake bite.

"It's all right," Ying'er said, "it wasn't poisonous."

Ying'er had heard that to tell whether a snake was poisonous or not, you must check the head. If it has a triangular head, it's poisonous, one with a rounded head won't be. She swept the light over the snake, but its head was smashed out of shape. This'll be terrible if it was poisonous, she said to herself, terrified that Lanlan might die. If she did, how was Ying'er going to survive in the desert alone? That was a selfish thought, Ying'er realized. How could I be thinking only about myself?

As if finally waking up, Lanlan tossed the snake out of the tent:

"I'm going to die."

"No, you won't. I won't let you." Ying'er said, as she took Lanlan's arm and sucked on the wound as if her life depended on it. When the sticky, putrid venom entered her mouth, Ying'er recalled her cold sores. Some were already festering. She'd be poisoned if the snake was toxic.

So what? I'll take care of the venom first.

After a while, she figured if the venom was toxic, by now she must have sucked all of it out. She stopped. Then she thought she ought to look around the tent to make sure there were no more snakes inside. Tossing the blankets out, she did a thorough search without finding anything but zhazhas fleeing in panic.

The search put her mind at east at last, but Ying'er was still concerned about the venom. She asked Lanlan if she felt a tingling sensation on her arm. Lanlan said it felt numb, but not tingling. Ying'er, on the other hand, thought her tongue tingled.

"It was my fault." Lanlan said, "Pa gave me a pile of used tobacco when we were leaving. I put it in a plastic bag but forgot to take it out when we got here."

Now she took out the tobacco to surround them with its special odor. Her father had told her that a snake can detect the odor and will slither off. Still, they were worried, so they went out together and moved the camels to a grassy spot. When they returned, they remade the bed but neither felt sleepy. They fell asleep only after the light from the Eastern sky shone in.

4

Ying'er woke up when the sun shone into the tent. She had a slight headache, but everything felt the same in her mouth. Lanlan's arm, lying outside the blanket, was slightly puffy, but the skin hadn't turned black. She felt better now.

She walked out of the tent and saw the dead snake, whose substantial size almost made her heart stop. A good thing she'd woken up. She'd heard that a snake had once slithered into a woman's private parts when she was out collecting desert rice. The thought made her shudder even now. The long body stretched out on the ground, its dark blood having seeped into the sand. She was in awe of Lanlan. If it had been her, she didn't think she'd have been so bold; she'd have gone to pieces even if she'd had the courage to grab the thing.

The camels were lying in a sand trough chewing their cud; there was still some grass left around them, which meant they'd had enough to eat. Burrow openings were scattered all over the trough, but it was hard to say if they were rats' nests or snakes. It had been completely dark out when they'd bedded down the night before. We have to pick a better place in the future, she said to herself, to be as far away from nests like these as possible.

Lanlan woke up and rubbed her arm.

"Does it tingle?" Ying'er asked.

"Don't worry. The poison wasn't strong. My mind is clear. If it were serious, it would have affected my thinking."

"You're right," Ying'er said. Still, she sucked in cold air at an arm that was so swollen the skin had a sheen.

"It might be weak, but it wasn't entirely harmless. There may be some venom, but it's all right." Lanlan added, unnerving Ying'er.

Lanlan gathered dry kindling to start a fire before choosing a branch to pierce the snake and roasted it over the fire. Ying'er had known she'd eat the snake, and the thought turned her stomach.

"You go ahead, I don't want any," she said.

"This is a delicacy from the Yellow Dragon King." Lanlan responded with a smile. "He'd be upset if you didn't have some."

Lanlan added that she'd had eaten many wild animals, such as porcupines, ground squirrels, and sparrows. Porcupines were the best, with tasty meat that was easy to pull apart.

She added more kindling to make the flame screech happily over the snake, which sizzled. Ying'er smelled the fragrance, but could not stop shuddering when she recalled how the fragrant creature had actually crawled into her pants.

"Snake is tasty, but it smells awful if it isn't cooked right," Lanlan said. "The key is to avoid contact with metal objects. A bamboo knife is best if you must cut into it. But roasting produces the most delicious meat."

"Well, it bit you and now it serves as a tonic," Ying'er said as she looked at Lanlan's shiny, puffy arm.

"Here's an offering to the Yellow Dragon King." Lanlan stripped the charred skin and tossed it into the fire. She tore off a piece of the snake and handed it to Ying'er.

"I don't want any."

"You'll regret it." Lanlan laughed as she sprinkled on salt, tilted her head back, opened her mouth wide, and lowered it in. From her expression, Ying'er was sure it must taste wonderful.

"You should have some. When you think about it carefully, many of our habits are actually problems. Take your need to be clean, for example. You're just punishing yourself, no matter how clean you want to be." When Ying'er didn't respond, Lanlan continued, "We can't change the world, but at least we can change ourselves."

That made Ying'er waver in her resolve. She was right, Ying'er told herself. Hadn't she already gone through changes in recent days? Some she'd brought upon herself and some were brought upon her by life. Whether she wanted them or not, changes had been occurring without her noticing them.

"Give me a small piece, then," she said, and got a large piece instead.

Ying'er took a bite. It tasted different from any meat she'd ever had, but not so different she wanted to spit it out. After eating a few more pieces, she actually began to enjoy the unusual flavor. They ate the meat with their steamed buns until they were both belching.

They got on the camels and set off. Riding a camel is not as easy as one might think. An experienced rider will not be able to avoid bumping her tailbone against the camel's backbone, so instead, she'll shift to the side. Being inexperienced, by noon Ying'er's tailbone felt as if it were on fire. Lanlan took down a blanket from her camel, placed it under Ying'er, and gave her some important tips.

"It's okay. Everyone's the same when they first ride a camel. It'll get better in a few days," Lanlan comforted her. "You'd better enjoy the ride now though. If you want to ride a camel after we load the salt, you'll have to wait and see if it has enough strength to carry you."

She's right. I have to toughen myself, Ying'er said to herself. She alternated between riding and walking, but though her tailbone felt better, now pain knifed through her calves.

5

Around noon that day, they ran into two old shepherds herding a flock of sheep that were enervated by the sun's warm rays.

"Ai, are you fox fairies?" one of them asked.

"Are there really fox fairies?" Lanlan replied with a smile.

"Yes, there are. We saw a woman dressed in red combing her hair at the base of a wall. We flicked our whips and she screamed. We heard her first scream at the wall, but the second scream came from ten *li* away. What was that if not a fox fairy?"

"I wish we were, but they won't let us be, so we'll settle to be musketeers." Lanlan laughed and patted her knife and musket.

"If everyone who carried a fire stick and called himself a musketeer, then the desert would become a den of them." The old man laughed too. "Do be careful. This is the year of jackals. One of the *magangs* is filled with them, like sesame seeds. They'll go for your camel's guts."

Ying'er had never seen a jackal, but what the old man said made her tremble. In her mind, it was a sinister animal, worse than wolves. She shuddered to think about how it felt to have your guts pulled out by jackals.

"Jackals are living creatures too, so what's there to be afraid of?" Lanlan patted her musket.

"It's good you have that," the old man said with some embarrassment.

"What you need to fear is not jackals," the other one joined in. "With such a pretty face, you have to watch out for bad characters. Some of the herders are worse than their animals. It never hurts to be careful."

"He's right. They're out here the year round without ever seeing a female, so it's hard to say if they'll get ideas."

"Even if their minds don't get ideas, their bodies might," the second one followed up. "Those who get shot realize they did something to deserve it only after they've done it."

Ying'er's heart beat violently when she realized they were telling the truth.

"I'm not afraid. I've sparred with petty thieves before. It only took than a few rounds to put out their lights." Lanlan had used the patois for blinding someone, an expression often used by Meng Baye and his friends. Ying'er felt like laughing when she heard it come from Lanlan's mouth, yet she couldn't help but feel apprehensive.

"Since you obviously know how to defend yourself, we won't waste our breath," one of them said with a laugh.

"They must know," the other whispered. "They wouldn't dare come out into the dessert alone if they didn't." They muttered something as they walked off.

"What they said made sense," Ying'er said.

"Who'd come out here if there were a way to avoid it?" Lanlan sighed. "At least we're living in peacetime, and I like to think people are law-abiding."

Despite what she said, they stopped and smeared their faces with ashes. From Lanlan's face, Ying'er could tell how ugly she looked. She had to laugh, but a wave of sadness stole into her heart. You heartless man, see what you've turned me into?

They hadn't brought any nice clothes precisely out of that concern. Instead, they'd picked out dark, durable pieces. They'd also brought straw hats and wore head scarves to block out the sun. Those were in the same drab colors as their clothes, so from a distance no one could tell they were women.

"We'll stay clear if we see any men, so they won't be able to tell who we are," Lanlan said.

"Those men at the salt lakes aren't blind, you know." Ying'er replied.

"Those places are crowded with people. There's safety in numbers. We'll be fine there."

Misgivings dogged them in spite of what Lanlan said; neither felt like talking as they walked on.

To settle their nerves, Lanlan stopped to fill her musket with gunpowder, but kept the flint off to prevent misfiring. She then slung the weapon over her back while Ying'er held on to the Tibetan dagger. Now they felt better.

They entered the second gully after crossing a dune that rose halfway into the sky. The began to see more desert vegetation. Along the way they spotted quite a few camel carcasses, the sight of which made their own camels toss their heads. Obviously, they feared death, just like humans. Ying'er was scared. Some of the blanched bones had turned gray; who knew how long they had been there. Others were clearly newly killed camels, shreds of flesh still connected to the bones. She'd heard that wolves had created mayhem in the desert in recent years. Ying'er was terrified of wolves, and jackals too; she shuddered just thinking about them. There was a good reason why jackals came in first in the four fearful animals—jackals, wolves, tigers, and leopards. She sometimes wondered how painful it would be if she were a camel and her guts were dragged out of her by a jackal. Worst of all, she could not shake the horrifying image; she could almost feel her guts convulse.

She felt like turning back when she was reminded of the terror of jackals.

"We're not carrying salt so much as probing our way. There are many roads in the world, some we don't want to take and some don't fit us. We must find one that works best for us," said Lanlan.

They got down off their camels and took the animals to some grass to sneak a few bites while they rested. They fetched their water jugs and ate steamed buns. In the heat, moldy spots had begun to show on the buns. To prevent them from going completely bad, Lanlan divided them into two piles and wrapped them in gauzy scarves for the desert breeze to pass through freely and carry away the dampness.

The sun was still high enough for them to travel a bit farther, so they set off again. Based on the commonly traveled route, they would spend the night in the next *magang* along the way. Ying'er, still reeling from the snakebite the night before, had a different idea. *Magangs* were usually swampy, breeding ground for snakes. She wanted to find a relatively dry sand trough, where they could bed down as long as there were stalks from desert plants. They could drink less water and give the camels more to make up for the moisture they'd miss from not eating grass.

"Normally you look after the camels first when you're in the desert, because they mean everything," Lanlan said. "Without one, you could cry out for heaven and earth and you'd get no response."

On the other hand, Lanlan understood how Ying'er felt. Anyone who'd had a snake slither into her pants would do the same.

"Okay, we'll stop wherever we are. All we need is the stalks. We don't have to pay to spend a night in the desert, so it's all right if we're a day behind."

6

The two old shepherds were telling the truth about the year of jackals. They were barely one li out of a *magang* when they saw a dead camel on a sand ridge. Ying'er had heard about wild camels in the desert, but couldn't tell if this one was wild or tamed. Wild camels were under government protection, and there were none in the Tengger Desert, she'd heard. Some camels ran loose in the desert, but they were normally escapees, not truly wild.

This had been a skinny one, its humps sagging on the sand like an old woman's breasts. With no wood ring in its nose and no sign of a harness, it had clearly roamed the desert for years, even if it wasn't a true wild camel.

Obviously killed recently, the camel looked like its guts had indeed been dragged out, the sand around it still a scary, bloody sight. The sad scene frightened Ying'er more than a snake slithering under her blanket; she gripped the dagger tightly. Lanlan got down off the camel and cried out, "Dear God of Fortune, you've sent us money." She followed up with an explanation when she noticed Ying'er's questioning look,

"Do you know how much a camel pelt sells for?" She answered her own question without waiting for a reply. "We got over three hundred yuan for the cowhide last time, and that was just a calf. See this? This camel is dead, but its pelt remains intact."

"It doesn't belong to you no matter how much it's worth," Ying'er said.

"It doesn't have a master," Lanlan continued, "Pa once said that quite a few camels escaped from a camel farm years ago. They bred and reproduced in the desert and went wild long ago. Meng Baye roped one. He did his best to tame it, but nothing worked. It bit and kicked, so in the end he let it go."

"If this had been a domestic camel," Lanlan said as she pointed at the dead camel's nose, "this spot would be hairless."

"That makes sense," Ying'er said.

"This one was sick and couldn't run fast enough, so its guts got dragged out. But you see how the pelt was largely undamaged? If we don't skin it, it wouldn't take a night for the wild animals to come to ruin it." Lanlan added, "Heaven has given us a camel pelt, but it's okay if you don't want it. It has to be worth more than a cowhide."

Lanlan tethered her camel to a desert rice plant.

"Let our camels graze while I skin this one. If they want it at the salt lakes, we'll sell it there. If not, we'll take it back and sell it to the cobbler." She asked Ying'er for her Tibetan knife. Ying'er knew it was too long for skinning a camel, so she took out a smaller knife from her bundle. It was a dagger Hantou had bought for protection. It was very sharp.

Maybe Heaven has taken pity on us. When we sell the pelt, it'll fetch as much as selling salt, Ying'er thought. This isn't bad. We'll get the money we need faster if we have many sources. You'll have to stop forcing me then, Ma. See how I'm trying to get money for you. Her eyes welled up when she thought about her mother, so she raised her head for the tears to flow back in.

Ying'er knew how hard it was to skin a camel. Usually it would take several strapping men to take care of one. The difficulty lay not in the actual skinning but in turning the camel over.

"Don't worry," Lanlan said. "We don't care for the meat, so we'll have our camels turn it over. I don't believe two live camels can't handle a dead one."

"Listen to you. You sound like a professional butcher." Ying'er laughed, but a frown crept onto her forehead when she was reminded of Zhao San, the butcher her mother wanted to force her to marry.

Lanlan rolled up her sleeves and chased away the flies. There weren't many on the dead camel, but they were big, the size of bees. Most unnerving was that their heads emitted an eerie emerald light like fireflies. Ying'er detected a stench, and her stomach churned, but she told herself to bear it.

You have to pay a price to live with dignity, she said silently. Cleanliness had been so important to her that she'd had trouble dealing with her husband's sweat odor. Now she had to put up with the stench of a dead camel. Living is the best doctor, it can cure all your afflictions. See, without knowing it, she had started treating her earlier need to be clean as an affliction. That was the power of living.

Wrinkling her forehead, Lanlan searched for the best angle to start, a sight that moved Ying'er. How lucky to have a sister to weather the storm with her under such dreadful circumstances.

"Let's start on the belly," Lanlan said as she poked at soft spots. Ying'er covered her nose as a precaution, for fear that something foul would spurt out from a knife cut. Luckily only a few air bubbles appeared. Disgusted nonetheless, she felt like looking up at the sky, but that seemed disrespectful of Lanlan. Her brow tightly knitted, Lanlan slid the knife across. It was a great knife, creating an opening on the dead camel's belly like a skiff skimming the surface of water.

Suddenly they heard a shrill cry. Before Ying'er could react, a black ball shot out of the opening. Lanlan tried to dodge but tripped over the camel's hind leg and fell down on the sand. The black ball spun around in midair before pouncing down on Lanlan. Stab it, Ying'er cried out. Lanlan screamed as she stabbed at the thing while Ying'er ran to pick up the musket, but failed to act. She didn't know how to fire the weapon, but even if she did, she'd hit Lanlan. The thing was not big, about the size of a leopard cat, but it was unusually nimble. Lanlan repeatedly stabbed at it, but never managed to connect, though she was able to protect her vital parts.

Hit it with the butt! Lanlan yelled.

Ying'er was terrified, but Lanlan was in grave danger, so she had to put her fear aside. She swung the musket, and brought it down. The thing leaped into the air with shrill yelps; when it landed, it scrunched up its body and bared its teeth, but was no longer courageous enough to charge. That gave Lanlan the opportunity to roll over, grab the musket from Ying'er, and put the flint on, but before she fired, the thing ran off, trailed by its shrill yelps. The old man had warned them. It made the first yelp nearby, but the second one when it had reached a distant sand trough.

"A jackal," Lanlan said as she crumpled to the ground.

A few more black balls shot out before she finished and darted off to distant sand hills.

Ying'er stared wide-eyed, her mind a blank. They would be dead for sure if they'd all attacked at once.

"Good thing we brought a musket," Lanlan blanched and said, breathing hard. "They smelled gunpowder. I never imagined they'd crawl inside the camel from the rear to eat its organs."

Lanlan sat up and aimed the musket at the opening on the belly. She yelled a few times but nothing happened.

"Let's forget about skinning the camel," Ying'er said. "What if there are more inside?"

"Go get a club and poke at it. I'll fire if more come out." She laid her finger on the trigger, girding for action. Ying'er took a club from one of the camels' loads and stuck it into the dead camel's belly. She threw up after a few pokes.

"They're gone," Lanlan said. Her ashen face was bathed in sweat, her energy drained from the fright. But she smiled when she saw the worried look on Ying'er's face.

"I should at least fire once at the belly for safety's sake, but the cobbler may turn it down if there are holes on the pelt."

"You're still going to skin it?" Ying'er asked in shock. "What will you do if there are more jackals?"

"We were caught by surprise, but now I'm prepared to stab it if one comes out," Lanlan replied with a smile, fear betraying the feigned calm look on her face.

She'd be long dead if a jackal had sunk its teeth in her throat, Ying'er thought. "Let's forget the pelt," she said. She spotted blood on Lanlan's shoulder and rushed over.

"It's all right. Just a scratch from the jackal's paw. Good thing I fell down. Otherwise I'd be on the road to the Underworld by now."

The wound was shallow and Lanlan wasn't bleeding much, so Ying'er burned some camel hair to sprinkle over it. The after-attack fright had her crying.

"Don't cry," Lanlan said. "Tears won't buy you freedom." She drank some water and slowly got to her feet. "Come on, let's keep at it. We can't suffer the fright for nothing. Don't be afraid. Jackals are vile, but they're no bigger than a leopard cat. If there are more in there, I'll stab them the moment they come out."

Lanlan raised the musket to aim at the hole, while telling Ying'er to poke around and drag out the intestine with the club. Ying'er did what she was told, but soon felt nauseous again. Lanlan handed her the musket and told her to aim at the opening, "Pull the trigger if a black ball comes out."

She stuck the club inside the camel. She wanted to drag out the intestines so any jackal still inside would have no place to hide, but Ying'er could not stop dry-heaving, so she tossed the club aside and, keeping a watchful eye on the opening, began skinning the camel.

A camel pelt is much thicker than a cowhide, so it was tough going. But the knife was sharp and Lanlan could keep at it since she wasn't worried about getting a clean pelt with no meat attached. Nothing happened inside, so Ying'er, finally reassured, forced back her disgust and came up to help. Tugging as they went, they then tied a rope to the camel's legs and attached it to the load on their own camels; they turned the dead camel over without much difficulty. After two hours of hard work, they had a camel pelt.

Dusk was descending, and the sun, suspended above the sand hill to the west, seemed to shower them with praise. Lanlan wiped her forehead; she was soaked in sweat, even her back. Ying'er hadn't worked as hard, but sweated from trepidation. As she wiped Lanlan's face dry, she realized that she didn't really understand her sister-in-law, but at this moment she admired her. There was something extraordinary about Lanlan, she discovered. What a shame her brother was not fortunate enough to keep someone like her.

The pelt was so heavy Ying'er could not lift it using all her strength. After taking a break to catch her breath, Lanlan came up. They wanted to hoist the pelt onto the load, but failed after a few attempts.

"We've worn ourselves out today," Lanlan said. "Let's stop here, find a clean spot, and spend the night."

After locating a trough with desert rice, Lanlan took the camels over and unloaded the rack for them to graze the desert stalks. After many stops and starts, they women finally managed to drag the pelt into the trough.

"We're tired, so let's not cook tonight. We'll just have some steamed buns," Lanlan suggested.

"You get some rest. I'll make noodles," Ying'er said.

With the trough filled with kindling, she quickly gathered a pile.

She was cooking when they heard shrill cries from somewhere

nearby.

"Jackals!" Lanlan cried out.

Chapter Eighteen

A wolf bays three times in the valley
A tiger streaks into the forest

1

Mengzi and Beizhu left their village to defile Shuangfu's family grave.

The night was a dusty gray. The moon craned its neck over the mountains, stealthy and sinister as a male warlock watching a widow relieve herself at night.

In the moonlight, the site looked more than ever like a graveyard, half brightly lit and half shrouded in darkness, a true confluence of yin and yang. An eerie gloom emanated from the dark. Looking at a barren tree that had been snapped in two by lightning, Mengzi was reminded of a hemorrhaging female ghost that was said to live under trees like this. Feeling his mouth dry out and his heart race, he coughed loudly to drive away the fear.

Beizhu looked like an apparition in the misty night, disappearing into the dark one moment and emerging into the gray light the next. If not for the sounds of his footsteps to prove he was real, he would be a spirit born of the illusory ether.

"Beizhu—" Mengzi called out in a voice that sounded sheepish.

Beizhu stopped walking.

"It's here. I remember the spot," Mengzi said.

"Are you sure?"

"I'm sure. I was there when his father was buried, to the east of that dead tree. There was another tree behind the grave, but it was taken down. I don't know if the stump is still there."

"Here's a stump. Was it a date tree?"

"Maybe. Look at the ridge. Shuangfu said it meant good fengshui. He laid into me when I dug up a few spadefuls of dirt two years ago while reinforcing the grave."

Mengzi glanced at the ridge, which was small but imposing in the nocturnal air. Was it really this ridge that helped Shuangfu strike it rich? Mengzi wondered. He'd been dubious at first, but had to believe it since everyone said so.

That asshole got rich overnight.

"Did you know, Mengzi, that he donated over a hundred thousand yuan for the village school to renovate their classrooms?" Beizhu said. "Just thinking about the amount makes my scalp tingle. Ai, is the grave really as good as everyone says?"

"Who knows? That's what everyone says. The spot is like a golden fishbowl."

"In any case, it's weird. Ever since his father was buried here, he's made so much money it's freaky. Everyone knows who he is. He was so poor he couldn't hold a fart between his legs, but now, hei, he's filthy rich, chairman of the board, real hot shit. Wherever he goes, even commissioners and mayors tag along behind him."

"That's true. In this day and age, anyone with money is the big shot. Officials are no big deal. Without money, you're nothing but turtle spawn," Mengzi echoed.

"Damn. Just think. Who was he anyway? A hothead who played up to my Pa during the commune days. And now? Ptui." Beizhu spat. "He treats my Pa like a beggar, won't look him in the eye. Sure, my Pa struggled against you, but what could he do? Why did you have to steal corn? Besides, he wasn't alone. Who could avoid struggling against someone if they were old enough? That asshole was damned stubborn. They told him to lower his head but he refused, even when they thumped his neck until was a bloody mess. No one had seen a thief like that."

"He's a man worthy of the name, like a—ah, that's enough about him. Let's get to work."

Mengzi looked up at the sky, where the moon was an eerie sight. The mountains were an inky black mass, enclosing the gravesite like a screen. The spot did feel like a "bowl," and he wondered why no one else had made a fortune, since Shuangfu's father wasn't the only one buried in this bowl.

"Will digging up the grave really change his fortune?"

"Everyone says so," Beizhu said. "Meng Baye once said that the Bao family's ancestors were high officials, but they started to die off after their ancestral tomb was raided."

"Let's do it then. I can't stand his swagger," Mengzi said.

"Me either. I'm doing this for all of Shawan. When one man removes the spring, the others can only smash the lock to get some money. We can't let him remove our spring. We all need to survive. Did you know that Zhu Hongwu, the first emperor of the Ming Dynasty, removed the spring from Fengyang? There's even a doggerel about it. 'I'll tell you about Fengyang, so lend me your ears/Fengyang was a great place, with no peers/When one became Emperor Zhu, they suffered a famine nine out of ten years.' He sucked up all the essence of the place so it would be a wonder if they hadn't had a famine."

"Stop chattering. Let's get to work," Mengzi said.

Beizhu had more to say, but he drove his spade into the grave. It met with soft, damp soil, no sand or rocks. So, he dug deep and tossed the dirt to the side with great force, creating a muffled boom in the sand trough.

"Easy does it. Don't let anyone hear us," Mengzi cautioned.

The village was asleep. From the sandhill, the houses looked like dirt clods strewn across the ground. Lights were out, no dogs were barking. But they could hear the distant clamor at White Tiger Pass. For now, after Mengzi and others had nearly been buried alive, the men from the village had stopped working as sand boys, saying the money was good, but life was precious. No one would trade their lives for money. Most of current group of sand boys were from out of town, an unending onrush of voluntary workers, despite the possibility of being buried alive.

How will the people react when they hear about what's happened tonight? Mengzi wondered. They'll certainly curse the act; it would be weird if they didn't, because they'd be able to prove their innocence by joining in to condemn the perpetrators. But what will they feel deep down? They'll be laughing, Mengzi told himself. It'd be even stranger if they didn't. No one can stand seeing a beggar using a fine china bowl. Why should Shuangfu be the only one striking it rich? Who is he anyway? A hothead who stole the village's autumn harvest and got struggled against to the point where he could barely stand, the son of a red-eyed old man who'd been so poor he couldn't hold a fart between his legs. Why did he deserve to be rich? That was too much for the villagers. If Mengzi didn't do it, at some point someone else would.

"Back to work," Beizhu said, breathing hard.

"I'm taking a break."

Beizhu stopped and straightened up to wipe his sweaty forehead. A wind blew over, cool and strangely refreshing. Somewhat unnerved, he needed to say something to drive away the eerie apprehension he was feeling.

"Did you get some of the money Shuangfu was handing out over New Year's?"

"No. Did you?"

"Of course, I did." Beizhu replied. "Only a fool would pass up money. A brand new, stiff hundred-yuan bill. Why didn't you?"

"How could you take his money? Didn't you see how he doled it out, like dismissing a beggar? Disgusting. He was snickering silently despite the look on his face. The most disgusting were those who had done the worst to him during the struggle session. They were so happy to give away their souls for his money they couldn't tell heads from tails. You call that money? It was dog shit he was smearing on your face."

"Who cares. It might be dog shit or it might be something else. I'd take it if he wanted me to have it, but it didn't mean I should be grateful. I'll stay angry at him if I ought to and curse him if necessary. But why not take his money? The rich aren't righteous and the righteous never get rich. What do you prove by not taking it?"

"Hei, it's like there's an epidemic in the village, with people seeing only money. They might as well have called Shuangfu Daddy or wished him a long life. What did they lose when they took his money? Dignity."

"Hei, don't get so worked up. Mengzi, don't be an ant in a harness pretending you're a farm animal. When you're poor, you're poor. What's dignity when you're so poor you can't even afford a pair of pants? It's your bare ass. You didn't take it. Well, you can do what you want. You think people will praise you for not taking his money? They'll say you plucked pubic hair to paste on your face as a beard; you wanted to look good, so you put up with the pain. A hundred-yuan bill. Why didn't you want it? Why? I was born to be poor, all right? He wanted to give away his money, so I took it. Ai, Mengzi, it cost him a lot that day. Everyone he met got a hundred, even little babies. He must've given out ten thousand."

"Ten thousand, twenty thousand, I don't care. To him it was a single hair, but you all got down on your knees. You know that? You got down on your knees. You might have been standing straight, but in fact you were kneeling in front of him. Fuck! He saw what was in your heads and in your brains. He might as well have spat on the bill and asked you to lick it off. And you were all smiling broadly, grinning happily. Ptui! Remember why he left the village? He was forced out by people like you, neighbors and friends. He was driven out, so he had to learn a skill, and then he became a labor contractor and struck it rich. Now you welcome him back like a god, ready to call him grandpa. It was just a hundred yuan. You can spend it in the blink of an eye, but you can never wash off the humiliation."

"Don't overthink this," Beizhu continued, "I did take his money, but I still hate him. I'm not the only one cursing him behind his back. Look at me, I'm digging up his father's grave, aren't I? Don't for a minute think I'd be overwhelmed with gratitude just because he gave me money or renovated a school. The newspaper called him an entrepreneur who loves his hometown. Ptui! Not to me."

"That's why he's smarter than us; he spent his money on the school, where people could see it." Mengzi sighed and shook his head. "No matter what you say, he might be an entrepreneur, but deep down he's just a businessman. Haven't you heard about unscrupulous businessman? Every businessman is unscrupulous, you can't be a businessman if you're not. The papers say he remembered his hometown after he got rich and didn't forget his school when he made a name for himself. Hei, what a crock of shit. He's a shrewd accountant who's got plenty more where that came from. You can fill a donkey pen with someone like him in Liangzhou, someone with a little bit of money. But he's smart. He helped renovate the school so he could make it into the papers and onto TV, getting famous in the process. See how he's making big money again?"

"The asshole's clever, all right." Beizhu sneered. "I hear he's put up a couple of hundred thousand to set up some kind of scholarship to help with the education of children from poor families. Naturally, the scholarship has his name on it. He wants to be remembered after he's had enough to eat and drink, had his fair share of whoring and traveling around. He wants to leave a good name that will live forever. Hei, hei. But the truth is, we'd have to put up the money if he didn't help renovate the school. All of us are so poor we can't keep a fart between our legs, so where would we get the money? In other villages, they collected nearly a hundred each from everyone . . . In any case, he's done some good for our village, no matter how you look at it."

Mengzi snickered, as he was reminded of a complaint Xiuxiu, Shuangfu's wife, had once uttered. Now her words came out of his mouth:

"What do you know? You think he renovated the school to help lessen your burden? You think he was filled with gratitude to the villagers? Actually, he wished he could take a bite out of every one of you. Have you forgotten how his father died? He died from struggle sessions staged by hungry vultures like you people. Why did he leave the village? He was driven out by mad dogs like you. You think he was grateful to you, don't you? What have you done for him? What favor have you done for him that he should be grateful, be overwhelmed with gratitude? You think he loves his hometown, don't you? What's his hometown but a corner in the desert with barren soil and a dry stream where even wolves won't shit, the home of impoverished bullies who'd wanted to skin him alive. Why should he love this place? Tell me, why? Because you people pounded his father's head so much it was bloody gourd? Stick your finger up your ass and think about it. This is a conquest, you understand? Do you think he was showering you with his love when he threw money at you? Or was he feeling sorry for you? No. He was beating you up. Hei. He offered you buckets of swill with a few pieces of fat pork swimming on top and you gobbled it up. Hei. It's disgusting." This had all come from Xiuxiu, but it felt like words from the bottom of his heart when he repeated them.

"You sound just like Shuangfu's wife." Beizhu could tell. "She was always saying things like that. Hei. People who have gone to school, like you, bore me. The more you study, the more maggots you produce. Conquest? What kind of stupid idea is that? Sour grapes! Actually, he just wanted to show off his wealth. Even if he did have what you say in mind, wouldn't it be just the odorless fart of a new mother if we didn't know about it? In any case, we took his money and spent it, but we didn't feel any silly humiliation, so we're not humiliated. On the other hand, I'm going to dig up the grave no matter what. Hei, hei."

"Let's get to work then," Mengzi replied with a sigh.

They got back to work, and soon their spades were making hollow sounds.

"We'll see the coffin lid soon. Should we open it?"

"You decide. It's a bit gross for my taste," Mengzi replied.

"What's gross about it? It's a pile of white bones. The flesh is long gone. But it does feel creepy to me too."

After mulling it over, Mengzi tossed down his spade, squatted on the pile of dirt like a desert money, lit a cigarette, and took a deep drag. He'd lost interest, and the urge to show his outrage over the injustice done to Xiuxiu vanished. What he'd been doing suddenly felt meaningless, and a sense of self-loathing rose up.

Beizhu stared at the flickering tip of the cigarette and said:

"Let's hurry if we want to do it. You know how it'll look after dawn, when people see us here. They won't look favorably on us digging up an ancestral grave."

Mengzi heaved a sigh, and the tip of his cigarette sparkled brightly. "We've done enough, let's just quit. We dug enough for him to know what's happened. With all his swagger and arrogance, he should know he can't act like he does just because he renovated a school. I can't stand his cocky attitude. I'm poor, but I have backbone. I get to smear some dog shit on his face, and that's enough for me."

"So that's it?" Beizhu asked.

Mengzi mumbled his answer.

"No way!" Beizhu shouted. "I brought everything. Here's chaff from red millet mixed with the blood of a black dog. We're here and we have to carry it through. I'll do it if you won't." He swept away the remaining dirt on the coffin lit, threw down his spade, and picked up a crow bar to pry open the lid, making the noise of rotten wood crumbling by force. "Why should he be the only rich one? Why?"

"Do you really think he got rich because of his father's grave?"

"Of course. Everything is carried in the ancestral tombs; if it's not in there, then you can pray all you want, but you still won't have it. Didn't Chiang Kai-shek try to topple Chairman Mao by raiding his family tomb? Lucky for us he didn't succeed. The Daoist Master said Chairman Mao's ancestral tomb is a site with good fengshui. It remains dry no matter how much it rains. You don't believe me?"

"Forget it." Mengzi waved. "Let's talk about something else. I don't want to hear another word, all right? I don't care if he's rich. I just can't stand his swagger, and I want to shame him."

"What's good does that do? What the fuck good will that do? With money he'll always look better than us. What the fuck can you do? We have to get to the root of the problem. A featherless phoenix looks worse than a chicken, and a rich man is like a ghost when he's broke. We have to destroy his good fortune, don't you know? He's rich now, but once the fengshui is ruined, his fortune will suffer a fast decline, like water running through a sieve. He won't know which hole to plug up first. Hei, he couldn't plug them all up if he tried. You can be a rich man overnight and lose it just as fast. What makes it all happen? Luck. And where do we find luck? In the ancestral grave. Sure, he looks impressive now, but once his luck is going the other way, he'll lose it so fast he won't be able to even keep his snot in. Hei-hei."

"What are you so happy about?" Mengzi wrinkled his nose. "What's it got to do with you whether he's prospering or not? Actually, you might benefit when he's doing well, but if he's on the skids, then you won't get anything, not even a fart."

"Hei-hei. I won't get a fart but it'll make me feel good. I took his money, but deep down I felt terrible, though I was smiling. Why can't he give away handfuls of money while I, I can't even afford a decent pair of pants. The motherfucker. Why? Why? Because he knows how to brag, scam, cheat? Ptui! What do I care!"

"You talk big. You say you don't care, but you wished you could grab ten of those hundred-dollar bills when he gave you only one."

"Hei-hei. That's a totally different thing. He thinks he's a big shot in Shawan after giving me money and rebuilding the school? Ptui. He's like a single strand of hair, no, not even that. But he's showing us how wealthy he is. Hell, he brags about his wealth and shows me up. I had a good life before he came back. I ate all the steamed buns I wanted. I had potato slurry. I could eat whatever I wanted. It was so much better than a few years back. It was only after his return that I realized how terrible my life has been. Fuck him. Damn, that makes me feel shitty."

"He works hard for his money. But you, you lie on your kang and sleep your life away, so naturally you're poor. He never stops working and thinks it's a crime to take even one day off. Not us, we can spend a whole day sipping two liang of liquor. I heard he has no time to drink even though he has the money."

"Hell! He's barely left this corner of the desert, and now he's criticizing us, saying 'you people this' 'you people that.' I said to him the last time, Pigs root the ground in front and chickens scratch the area behind; everyone has his own way of living. They're happy working hard for money while we like a life of ease, and neither is wrong. Guess what he said? He said I was just trying to make myself feel better. Hell, did he really think I'm jealous of his stinking money? You only live so long, and you can't take it with you when you die. I refuse to believe that he enjoys more from rare delicacies than I do from eating potato slurry. Hei, I didn't argue with him though. I took his money and turned my back to curse him when I felt like it and did what I wanted. I can pick up his bowl to eat and curse his mother when I lay down your chopsticks. Why are you acting like you're better than everybody? Look at me, I spent his money, and now I'm digging up his father's grave."

Mengzi was quiet for a while before heaving a long sigh. "This is pointless, really pointless. I mean it. He's still an entrepreneur no matter how I shame him, and I still have to work the field to fill my belly. He walks around with a swagger? Of course, he does. He's rich. But you, what do you have to swagger about? No, it's pointless, really pointless."

"Hei, what are you mumbling about?" Beizhu ignored his pensive friend and went to a stump behind the grave to retrieve the millet chaff that had been mixed with a black dog's blood. He sprinkled it over the grave, making a rustling noise that made Mengzi's shudder.

The moon hung over the hills to the west. The area was suffused with a deepening sense of dreariness. When a night wind blew over and bored into Mengzi's sweat-soaked body, he felt cold inside and out. Gone was the indignation before they started digging, only a dullness remained. Beizhu, who was hexing the upturned grave with filth, looked comical from behind, and he couldn't suppress a rising disgust over his friend's seeming addiction to the act.

"Can you take a piss?" Beizhu asked.

"Why?"

"You can piss into the grave. That's the worst you can do to a place like this."

"No, I can't!"

Beizhu failed to recognize the discord in Mengzi's tone, as he hummed a tune and brought his tool out to piss noisily into the gaping dark hole. Then he walked over, still humming in a smug way, and came up to Mengzi, huffing and puffing to show how hard he'd worked. He smacked his lips and chortled repeatedly.

"Great. It's ruined. It's done."

"Let's go." Mengzi said coldly.

The moon set as they were leaving the graveyard. Mengzi heard a rooster crow.

What will the villagers say about this? He wondered.

2

With the late-night activity, Mengzi decided to sleep in. He got up around noon time. After washing up, he walked out the gate, where neighbors were talking about what had happened. He heard Shuangfu had simply laughed it off and sent a few of his sand boys to fill up the hole.

He didn't say a word.

Everyone in the village cursed the tomb-raider for the immoral act, which, to them, was in the category of trapping a white wolf, ambushing someone, or bullying a widow.

Of course they would curse.

Mengzi was feeling down. Maybe the woman will curse me too.

Sure enough. Later that night, Shuangfu's wife gave him a long, cold stare.

"You did it, didn't you?"

"Did what?" Mengzi felt his heart race.

"You want to ruin him?"

"What are you talking about?"

"Or to show how you feel sorry for me?"

"What do you mean?"

Feeling sheepish, Mengzi detected a new tone in her voice. This woman's demonic. He could probe, like using a pair of chopsticks, but could never reach the bottom of her mind.

With her eyes half shut, she was quiet for a while before heaving a sigh. "Whether it was you or someone else, what's done is done. I'd have spat on whoever did it. How shameful. He has money because he works hard; he's rich because he deserves it. What does that have to do with his family tomb? Besides, I don't believe you can dig up his good fortune. Everyone digs his own fortune and no one can do it for him. What others do would be like digging up their own graves, wouldn't it? Whoever did it will end up digging something out of his heart. I refuse to believe that someone who could do this will amount to anything."

Mengzi felt his scalp turn numb. Her words were like a switch lashing his face until it was red hot. If I didn't, Baigou would, he replied silently. If Baigou didn't, then someone else would. As long as Shuangfu continues to enjoy good fortune, there will always be someone to dig up his family tomb. That's a fact. The problem is, Shuangfu didn't do anything to anyone, so why do people treat him like a mortal enemy? Ruining him won't do anyone else any good. The common saying is, hurting others to benefit yourself; it makes no sense to harm others for personal gain, and no one profits from digging up a grave.

"Remember what I said last time? Heaven has drawn a line to determine how well or how badly a person will fare, and no one will be spared." She sneered. "Shuangfu dug his own grave, and whoever did this gained nothing but useless sweat. It was pointless." She continued, "I don't care if it was you or not. If it was, your good intentions mean nothing to me. If you're good enough, have it out with him to prove you're a real man. Don't sneak around, like kicking someone from behind a door, or trapping a white wolf, ambushing someone, kicking in a widow's door, or digging someone's grave to cut off his family life. Shuangfu's family line is pretty much finished. I couldn't give him a son, and I don't think any of the women he's slept with have given him anything worth looking forward to either. Naturally, it'd be great if it wasn't you. I'd like to stay clear of disgusting things like this. Actually, both you and I know he's a man of substance, an upright man who touches the heavens when he stands and covers the earth when he lies down. You can't blacken him like a crow just because he hasn't been treating me well."

Mengzi left her house in total dejection.

An evening wind blew over, rousing a sense of self-loathing in him, so he spat at himself viciously.

This was not the first time he'd slunk out of her house, feeling worthless. He had been the domineering type, but now he was strangely afraid of her.

You call yourself Xiuxiu? Is this how you "show" me up? Mengzi shook his head, feeling a sense of injustice.

Chapter Nineteen

A dragon rides above black clouds
A python emerges in the sky

1

Ying'er saw blurry black dots on the sand dunes, some racing toward the dead camel, while others remained where they were. She realized they were jackals, though she didn't know when they'd showed up. The sight so shocked her that her tongue went dry as she looked at Lanlan with beseeching eyes. Musket at the ready, Lanlan studied the scene for a while.

"It's all right. They came for the food. The skinned camel is big enough to feast on, and they won't attack us without regard for their own safety."

Ying'er knew Lanlan meant to calm her nerves. Maybe we're the food in their eyes, she felt like saying, but a tingling sensation coursed through her body and her legs went soft.

With their eyes on the distant sand dunes, ready to fight, the camels grunted and made loud chuffing noises. They were trying to intimidate the jackals, Ying'er realized. She knew that wolves are intimidated by camel spittle, but had not heard that jackals were too, though she was moved by the camels' reaction. At least they were helping out. This alone was something. Most people were ready to pelt you with rocks when you were trapped in a well, put personal gain before righteousness, or stand by and watch you suffer; rarely would they help you out. Sometimes even a single comforting word could be the much-needed aid to someone on the brink of despair.

After chuffing a while, her camel turned to look at her as if to say, "Don't be scared. You can count on me."

She was touched by the gaze. Everything is all right. Even if I die in the maws of these jackals, I won't be a lonely ghost, she told herself. The thought drove away some of her fears.

"Don't be afraid," she said to Lanlan. "Even if they come after us, it's no big deal. The most they can do is kill us."

"You're right." Lanlan smiled as she lowered her musket. "When you think about it, there's really nothing to fear. Living isn't what it's cracked up to be. I just can't stand the idea of being swallowed by the jackals."

"When you see through everything, it doesn't matter who swallows you. To us the jackals are savage, but their cubs love them. Let's not worry about it. If we have to die, we'll go with a full stomach." She set up a pot, poured in water, lit the fire, and started making noodle dough.

Lanlan pulled herself together to cut down nearby shrubs. A commotion broke out among the jackals when they heard the sound of a knife hitting the wood. Obviously, they aren't fearless, Ying'er thought.

After eating, Lanlan started a fire. She had collected enough firewood to last them all night. Instead of putting up their tent, they spread their bedding by the fire. Fearing that the jackals would attack their camels, Lanlan did not let them out to graze in the shrubs, but had them lie by the fire facing out. The jackals would have to get near the fire if they had designs on their camels. Knowing what the humans had in mind, the camels lay down docilely by the fire, while Ying'er brought over some tender branches for them gnaw on.

Lanlan spread the newly skinned camel pelt on the ground, furry side up so the sand would soak up some of its moisture overnight, reducing its weight. Once they reached the salt lakes, they'd sprinkle salt on it to keep worms from ruining it.

Shortly after nightfall, they heard the sounds of biting and tearing around the dead camel. The jackals' deep, angry voices rippled in the evening sky and echoed back, a grating sound. Their camels twitched their ears and made chuffing sounds. One of the calmest of animals, they do not hastily twitch their ears, which could mean they too were afraid. Despite her bravado about not being afraid to die, Ying'er shuddered when she recalled how the jackals looked.

The sounds of biting and tearing grew intense, meaning the jackals' fight over food was getting fierce, and the camel might no longer be enough for them. Ying'er was terrified. If the dead camel could sate the jackals' greedy appetite, she and Lanlan would be relatively safe; if there were more jackals than meat, then the beasts would remember them once they finished off the camel. Suddenly she flashed back to the village and her mother, a scene that at that moment seemed impossibly distant and hazy, as if it were a lifetime away; her mother wore a loving smile. If she'd known what would happen now, she wouldn't have fought with her. And yet, she could not swallow the idea of marrying her to the butcher. *Yuanjia*, I'm waiting for you, she said silently. A bird will always return to its nest. I'll wait for you. Once she made enough money for her brother to marry again, her mother would stop pressuring her.

Lanlan brought out her gunpowder pouch and the buckshot, and lay them down a little distance away from the fire. Ying'er tossed wood onto the fire, but not too much. She'd heard that wolves feared fire, and she wondered if it was the same with jackals. If not, they had little hope of surviving the night. It was clear that even a machine gun would be no match for the jackals should they attack all at once.

The sound of jackals tearing into the camel were getting increasingly violent; that led to fights that produced pitiful yelps and angry roars as they threatened each other and barked. The myriad of sounds, with intermittent howls, came at Ying'er all at once; she wondered if there might be a wolf among the beasts. Her scalp tingled.

"If jackals are fighting wolves over the feeding ground, there are enough of them to kill the wolves," Lanlan said.

The pandemonium grew louder and spread like an explosion, even cowering the stars into disappearing. The noise seemed to form a giant whirlwind raging in the sand trough, rushing this way and that. Then, suddenly, throaty sounds of tearing teeth ripped through the howls that broke off now and then until they were slowly overwhelmed by the biting teeth. A lone howl broke through and fled into the distance. Ying'er thought she saw it being chased by animals with bared fangs and sinister grins.

Lanlan squeezed Ying'er's hand, and Ying'er squeezed it back with a smile. Their palms were sweaty.

"What do we do now?" Ying'er whispered. "Should we take off?"

"It's too late. You can't outrun a jackal, no matter how fast you move. Let's gather more firewood and make it through the night first." Lanlan asked Ying'er to hold the flashlight while she cut down all the branches in the sand trough, dry or not. She gave wet ones to the camels and tossed some of the others onto the fire, producing a noisy sizzle.

With the jackals in the sand dunes fighting over the food, the camels calmed down, though the sounds of tearing and biting were getting louder. Jackals don't have a regular feeding ground; they go wherever there are dead animals. Put differently, wherever they find an animal, that is their feeding ground. They do not have dens either. Pregnant females spend a few months in one spot during birthing seasons. Once the cubs are big enough, they turn into desert whirlwinds, racing to wherever food is available. Jackals have no sense of territory, unlike wolves or leopards, which mark their territory with urine. The jackals have no need to do that, for they never fight over territory; roaming the world, they are everywhere. They appear wherever there are living creatures, and bite and tear into whatever they want. They are, in a word, a desert nightmare.

Lanlan was tending the fire with great care, so it would neither die out nor flare up. Like the musket beside her, it was one thing they could count on. Before they left, Laoshun had added two lighters, one with gas, the other with lighter fluid, to go along with their matches. When there's fire, there's hope in the desert. He had put the items in different bags. Now Lanlan understood why; he was afraid they might lose one or use it up. She recalled how she'd laughed at his "foolish" act.

She put the camel litter by the fire, moving everything except the gunpowder close to her. Once in while the wind carried over the stink from the pelt spread out on the sand.

We'd have been far away, if not for skinning the camel, she said to herself. You can't be sure about so many things. No one knows if an easy gain will be followed by a loss. Why think about it? I did it, and there's no need for regret. Good fortune will remain the same and bad luck can't be avoided. Who knows if we might have run into a pack of wolves if we'd traveled farther along?

She moved the musket safely away from the fire.

"They're too busy to bother us now, so you can get some sleep. You won't be able to do that if they don't get enough to eat and turn on us," Lanlan said.

"You get some rest. You must be dead tired from skinning the camel."

"Sounds good to me. Take care not to let the fire die out, but don't use too much firewood. I've armed the musket, so be careful.

She leaned against the litter and soon was snoring lightly.

She really is unflappable, Ying'er was thinking. She can actually sleep under these circumstances. Then again, what's there to keep her awake? The worst is death, so what's point of being afraid? There was indeed nothing to fear, but still she couldn't abide the thought of dying in the maws of jackals.

Ying'er added more wood and the fire grew brighter. She felt as if she'd been through a great deal, as if she'd already lived hundreds of years. It wouldn't be a premature death if she were to die on this night; at least that was how it seemed to her. Sometimes, when she thought about it, she realized that everyone was born to suffer, so it would amount to not living at all if one died without experiencing something. That's that, then, she thought with a bitter smile.

The sounds of jackals fighting died down a bit, but not completely, which meant there was still food left, and she had time to think about herself. But she didn't feel like it, since it served no purpose. One cannot change one's fate simply by wanting to, and sometimes thoughts bring only exasperation.

On the other hand, thinking was important. Like when she thought about seducing Lingguan—she smiled contentedly at the word seduction, and a certain part of her body turned warm right away. If she hadn't thought about seducing him, she wouldn't have acted upon it, and without the act, nothing would have happened, which would in turn have taken her life onto a different path. Apparently "thought" is how one's destiny changes. Some of the widows in the village moved ahead not long after their husbands' deaths and laughed happily at the side of another man. They must have had certain ideas that resulted in their action, which then helped form their future.

Don't think about that anymore. Ying'er poked at the fire and blew on it to ignite the wet branches. She liked the sizzling sounds damp branches made, like bird calls, the prettiest music in nature. If the jackals weren't threatening her life, she thought, wouldn't the sounds of their fights also be a kind of music? Listening carefully, she detected gentle notes beneath the externalized ferocity. Could that be the sound of a mother jackal feeding her cubs? She was reminded of Panpan, whose lovely face appeared before her and stoked wave-like emotions; she wished she could fly back home and nuzzle her baby.

The sound of fighting was all but gone now.

An immense silence rolled over. Ying'er could even feel the texture of the oppressive quiet and thought she saw green eyes in the dark. She hadn't had a chance to study jackals' eyes, but she'd seen the eyes of rabid dogs in the village, which must be how a jackal looked at humans. Rabid dogs have blood-shot eyes, though, while those on a jackal were green. Red or green, they were tinged with avarice and ferocity. She could imagine what hungry eyes looked like, like the gaze Pockmark Xu cast on her. The thought made her gag, and she gave her head a fierce shake. But she couldn't conjure up an image of ferocity. She recalled her mother's "ferocious" stare when she wished Ying'er could have done better, but she wasn't sure if that was the proper word to describe her mother's gaze. She racked her brain but still couldn't find a real-life illustration of the word. All she saw in the darkness around her was a combination of the expression in Pockmark Xu's and rabid dogs' eyes and those of the jackals.

She dry-heaved a few times from the nauseating thought. She'd rather be surrounded by the eyes of rabid dogs than be around Xu again.

Suddenly the camels were spitting violently, which frightened her, for that could only mean they sensed pressing danger. After nudging Lanlan, she turned on the flashlight and hurled its bright beam toward the distant sand dunes, which were now blanketed with green lights. Those lights presented a powerful reality as they roamed like will-o'-the-wisps, drifting here and there. Ying'er shuddered as she added a handful of dry wood and blew on the fire to make the flames shoot up.

"Don't worry, they're afraid of fire," Lanlan whispered, as she picked up the musket and pointed the muzzle into the sky.

"How about firing a shot to scare them?" Ying'er said.

"Not yet. We won't provoke them if they stay where they are. Right now, it's like attacking a wolf with a hemp stalk; we humans and the beasts are afraid of each other. We'd be doomed if they got used to the sound of a gun." She brought over the lantern and lit it.

To prevent a sneak attack, they pointed the bed rolls and camel litter in a different direction; instead of facing the camels, they now had their backs to the animals. Camels can see in the dark, so the change added two more pairs of eyes to watch the jackals' movements. Their backs clear, they could focus on what was in front of them.

Lanlan wished she'd cut more firewood, though she had no experience to know the size of the fire to hold back the jackals. If the firelight failed to curb them, and they kept pressing forward, then they'd need a bigger fire, she thought. The little wood they had would not likely last them till dawn.

Ying'er felt terror seep into her heart.

2

The jackals were deadly quiet, not making a sound. Clearly, they were watching their enemy. Now that their bellies were full, they weren't in any hurry. The camels had stopped chewing, but they weren't spitting either. All was quiet except for the noise of a roaring fire. To Ying'er, the silence had turned into two walls, and she was shut in between them. It was a strange sensation. She had always preferred quiet and loathed noise, never expecting that silence could lash out at her heart and make it thump so violently against her chest. The sand dunes seemed to be filled with other racing heartbeats. Slowly she heard many of them, from Lanlan, the camels, and the jackals. Lanlan's sounded like a club pounding something, the camels' were millstones rolling slowly, and the jackals' were pebbles stirring in a broken wok. They set her teeth on edge. Steadily, the grating noise grew louder, and she felt many blades sawing at her nerves. She clenched her teeth, shook her head, and held her breath, as if it had been taken away by pain, but the noise continued. The jackals must be grinding their teeth. She'd heard Laoshun talk of seeing thousands of rats grinding their teeth, a noise that could cause a mental breakdown. The sound of jackals grinding their teeth wasn't any better, she thought. Oddly, though, her heart was beating so loud she was afraid it could not hold out long.

Lanlan added more dry wood and the fire grew, but only big enough to light up a dozen meters all around, limiting their vision. In fact, the distant sand dunes turned hazy under the bright light. If the jackals stole up and pounced, Ying'er thought, they'd never react in time. She turned on the flashlight and sent its powerful beam straight to the sand dunes, where the black dots broke out in commotion; they might have mistaken the flashlight as a lightning strike. She'd heard that animals were afraid of lightning, which killed them in the desert. And it wasn't just average animals, even rare creatures that had acquired uncanny abilities were afraid. They could practice self-cultivation for a thousand years, either by praying to the moon, lapping at virgin blood, or sucking up a virgin boy's essence, but would turn to ashes at a lightning strike. Surely, they would be afraid of a column of light that resembled lightning.

The sight of restless jackals put her mind somewhat at ease. We'll be fine as long as we have something you fear, she thought. So, besides the fire and the musket, we have another weapon that keeps them at bay. There were four batteries in the flashlight, and they had eight more, so it would last them several hours if they kept the light on the whole time.

She doused the light and they turned blind again, barely able to see the blurred outlines of the sand dunes. The green lamps in the distant darkness were only visible when the fire died down, which presented a dilemma. If they kept the fire low, the jackals might attack, but they were blinded if they burned it brighter. It felt as if the jackals were watching a show played by humans and camels; the audience trained their eyes on the two of them, who could see nothing but a blur. It was dangerous.

Lanlan came up with an idea. She told Ying'er to tend to the fire, while she went to lie a bit away from the fire, with her musket, gunpowder, and the flashlight. The firelight would not affect her eyesight, and if the jackals sneaked up on them, she would greet them with her musket.

Once she was away from the fire, Lanlan saw many more green lamps around them. The lamps drifted, meaning the greedy animals were pushing forward. Picking up a spot with dense green lamps, she aimed and pulled the trigger, spewing flames like a broom. Yelps erupted and the green lamps retreated.

"If I don't show you what I'm made of, you'll think I'm holding only fire tongs, won't you?" Lanlan said with a laugh.

The crack from the musket, like a muffled thunder clap, had an immediate effect, as the spots covered by the column of flashlight were much smaller now. They looked to be about a hundred meters away. The barrel could accommodate a considerable amount of buckshot, but it could only reach twenty or thirty meters. She had hit some jackals, resulting in superficial wounds. So she picked out a ball bearing, which could reach a great distance and could take down a gazelle. She would be surprised if it didn't kill a jackal.

"We'll have some peace if I kill one of them. We'll show them what we can do while they fight over the dead one. That will buy us some time. Things will be easier after daybreak. Maybe jackals are like foxes, which are used to nighttime activities; their heads hurt when they're under a hot sun."

The human heart, it seems, is a strange thing; in time it can grow numb, no matter how terrifying the situation. They weren't as nervous now, even though they were still surrounded by a menacing enemy, and their lives hung by a thread. To see their enemy more clearly, Lanlan went over to dim the fire, leaving only embers, immediately bringing the oppressive darkness down on them.

"Shepherds in the desert usually travel with their muskets, so the jackals must be wary," Lanlan said.

"But maybe this is their first encounter with one," Ying'er said. "They wouldn't have run so far off if they had been used to it."

Lanlan agreed. She swept the beam of the flashlight around and saw that the jackals were mostly gathered to the east, with no black dots visible on the dunes to the west. Following an age-old custom when pitching their tent, they had selected a dry spot with the wind at their backs. They faced the relatively open sand trough, against the sand dunes to the west.

"This is no good," Lanlan said. "If they go onto the sand dunes, they could just roll their way into our midst and I wouldn't have time to pull the trigger. We have to move into the sand trough. They'd have to run quite a distance no matter where they came from, and that would give us time to prepare."

While the jackals had yet to recover from the musket fire, Lanlan lit a torch and found a wider spot in the sand trough to start a big fire, before the two of them, like mice moving to a new nest, took their litter, bedding, firewood, and camels over. Half an hour later, sure enough, black dots like sesame seeds covered the sand dunes to the west. Yet, Ying'er thought they might not have been bold enough to go up onto the dunes, which was within range of her musket, if they hadn't moved their camp site. Now the move meant they faced attacks from the front and the back.

The cold desert wind felt significantly stronger once they were away from the shelter of the dunes. Ying'er felt a chill on her back, so she opened one of the bags and took out two coats; she draped one over Lanlan and put the other on herself. The camels at their backs were agitated, for they'd obviously spotted the jackals on the dunes.

"We shouldn't have moved," Ying'er said.

"There's an upside to moving and an upside to staying put. I was afraid of a sneak attack if we stayed put. I had the feeling that they'd simply roll down the dunes. Now we're out in the open and so are they. We're within sight of each other. We can fight with everything we've got and the worst case is we end up in their bellies." Lanlan continued, "I've thought it through. In this life of ours, the earlier we die, the sooner we'll be released from suffering. We all have to die sometime. So, you can cower and die, or you can fight bravely and die. After meditating, I feel I now understand what life is about. Of course, I'm a long way from meeting the Master's demands. Shakyamuni Buddha could let a tiger have his body and cut a piece of himself to feed a vulture. If I were to pursue the same standard, I should strip naked and lie down to feed the jackals. But I don't want to do that. I wouldn't mind if they were as docile as lambs, but what are they? They're vicious beasts that prey on others, drinking their blood and ripping out their guts."

What Lanlan said reminded Ying'er how she'd overlooked their enemy's vicious nature, after the prolonged stand-off. If they'd attacked all at the same time, the two of them would be reduced to skeletons in the blink of an eye. The thought terrified her.

"Don't be afraid," Lanlan said with a laugh. "If you really have to die, you will whether you're afraid or not. Just like life itself, you can live in laughter or in tears, so why not be happy and enjoy life? Don't you agree? I really have seen through it. Mood is what matters most in life.

What we call happiness and suffering are just moods. We're happy when we're in a good mood. If we live a life in good moods, then we have a happy life. We can't change the world, but we can alter our moods, don't you think?"

Ying'er felt a new admiration for her sister-in-law. Lanlan had gone through a lot recently. What she'd just said could not have occurred to Ying'er. When she thought about it more carefully, she realized it was her mood that elated and tormented her. And then again, the mood was what made life worth living, wasn't it? If she could actually attain the ultimate state of quiet mind, like still water, she might miss a lot of what made her human.

Lanlan shushed her as she swept the beam of the flashlight across the dunes, stirring up the black dots. She then told Ying'er to shine the light on a spot while she lay down, aimed at the area, and fired. A plume of fire leaped out. They did not hear any yelps, but a commotion broke out among the dots.

"Hei. I missed," Lanlan said. "A single bullet can reach a great distance, but with less accuracy. Buckshot is better."

"Maybe you shouldn't be firing randomly like that," Ying'er said. "They may be frightened if you don't, but if you keep firing, they won't be afraid for long."

"I just want to show them what we've got," Lanlan said while refilling the barrel with gunpowder. "I didn't expect to miss after taking such careful aim."

Ying'er was right. The local saying had it that when you confront a wolf with a hemp stalk, it thinks you're holding a club and will stay away. But if you hit it even once, it will realize you're bluffing. The jackals were disturbed after the shot, but they quickly recovered and advanced, edging closer than before. Moreover, they'd gotten used to the flashlight and no longer stirred no matter how much Ying'er swept the beam over them.

Once they're used to the musket and the fire, it will be feeding time. Will my *yuanjia* ever imagine I met with such an end? What will he think if he learns that I ended up in a jackal's belly? Will he cry for me? Maybe, but who knows for how long?

She'd seen many loving couples, one of whom would cry for a while after the other died, but would soon be laughing again. That thought flung her into total despair. Life is pointless, maybe filling a jackal's belly is actually better. She recalled how her mother had often called her "Wolf's Meat," as a girl. It sounded endearing at first, but now she had to wonder if her mother's words were in fact prophetic. She would not be eaten by a wolf, but jackals and wolves are both ferocious beasts, despite their different appearances.

So what if that's the end of me? I'd rather be jackal's meat than stay alive to think about that heartless man.

"Hurry. Get to the fire. Light it," Lanlan called out urgently, rousing Ying'er, who saw that the embers had shrunk to a dark red dot. She flicked a lighter on some small branches, but they were wet and only sizzled. Lanlan handed her a bunch of dry wood to get a fire going.

"You have to separate the dry ones from the wet ones," Lanlan said. "Looks like they're ready to attack. Surround us with firewood, and then light it when they attack; they'll be burned if they charge." She shone the light around them, and Ying'er nearly gasped when she saw the startling density of them. She could see the outlines of closest ones.

"You take care of the fire. Make sure not to let it die out. I'm going to fire a few shots. If I don't show them, they'll climb all over us."

At that moment, the silent jackals suddenly let out cries that were deafeningly loud, like the yelps of rats falling into boiling water.

Lanlan fired a shot but failed to overcome the sound.

3

Lanlan turned up the lantern to pack in gunpowder and fire the musket. The jackals howled or yelped; they did not charge, but neither did they disperse. They had gotten used to the sound of musket fire, it was no longer a threat. Just think—a jackal is about the size of a leopard cat, but it will fight a wolf over food and usually wins, proof that they are as vicious and cunning as a wolf. Lanlan kept firing, repeatedly sending buckshot whizzing into them, but it was losing its menacing power. Terror crept into Ying'er's heart again, and Lanlan looked rattled.

"Don't use up all the gunpowder," Ying'er said.

"We're okay. I brought a lot, and we'll have no trouble making it through daybreak."

"What will you do if they stick around after that?" Ying'er asked silently.

It took a few minutes to reload, and each time a few jackals would leap forward during the pause. They were probing. They appeared to be afraid of the fire. They'd have pounced long ago if we didn't have a fire, Ying'er thought.

Lanlan got smarter after seeing the jackals on a probing mission. She'd refill the musket and take careful aim, but not fire right away. Instead, she waited for bold ones to draw closer, until they were no more than a dozen meters from the fire. Some shrieked and fell, making hair-raising yelps that seemed to be more from anger than pain. Apparently, they hadn't thought much of the two women until, to their surprise, they suffered at their hands.

One of the jackals limped off, while the others gradually quieted down after a racket of yelps and howls. The buckshot was obviously on target, which elated Lanlan, who said while she reloaded:

"Buckshot is better. It has a short range, but can reach a wide area."

But the camels were spitting again. Several jackals had appeared to their west, where they playfully jumped around, like a provocation or an attempt to dodge buckshot. It was the way they always showed up. They rarely attacked, like tigers, except when they were confidently dragging out a cow's guts. Usually they jumped around, playfully, it appeared. Not one of the most powerful animals, they used their short teeth and pointed fangs to their greatest advantage, with the aid of explosive leaps.

After refilling her musket, Lanlan held her breath and aimed at the bounding black dots. In fact, there was no need to aim, since the buckshot, which sent only a small flame the size of a wine cup rim, would spread the fire to the size of a wagon wheel after it went beyond several meters. It was a scary sight in the dark night.

She pulled the trigger when the jackals sprang closer, but they heard only the firing pin. Turned out she had been too eager to remember the flint. One of the jackals charged, maybe understanding what the sound meant. Ying'er shook in fear, but she managed to shine the flashlight on the animal, which, when it got closer, scrunched up its body and bared its teeth. It huffed like a bitch protecting her pups, and would have pounced on her if not for the roaring fire. If it had enough courage to attack, it wouldn't take long for it to tear something off her. Ying'er had seen how they ran on the sand, like streaked lightning. She wanted to pick up her Tibetan dagger, but would have to put down her flashlight and would then give the jackal the opportunity to come at her. It snarled, its teeth ghostly white, and its eyes, no longer green, had a shifty, vicious glare, almost showing off. Jackals had fox-like pointed mouths and sculpted cheeks. Ying'er loved foxes for their mythical aura; she even envied their magical airiness. Jackals, with their murderous look, were actually nothing like foxes. Finally, she understood what savagery meant; it was spurting from the bared fangs, the snarls, and the puffed fur.

The jackal growled and pressed forward. Ying'er found that the fire had lost its power to intimidate. Just as there were wise ones among humans, there must also be smart jackals that might realize that fire was a paper tiger. It had to be. Her father-in-law, Laoshun, had met up with a wolf unafraid of fire. It had been following him, so he'd lit a fire as a last resort, but, to his amazement, the wolf had leaped across the fire repeatedly, as if to provoke him. He would not have survived and sired Lingguan and his brothers if Meng Baye hadn't fired his musket.

It would have been better not to love the heartless man, Ying'er said to herself. I couldn't keep him around no matter how well I treated him. The complaint drove away her fear of the jackal.

"Get away from us! Your heartless creature."

The musket fired.

A handful of buckshot spewed out of the barrel. It was a swarm of burning mosquitoes; screeching and banging into each other, they were bees after a rain surging excitedly toward flowers or hungry flies converging eagerly on blood, young stallions in mating season leaping cheerfully over a fence, sperm raging up a womb, or tadpoles trapped in drought-starved mud happily welcoming fresh water. They shredded the thick night into pieces, and appeared in the jackals' field of vision before entering their bodies. The jackals had tiny hearts, but their eyes were as big as the world, which did not escape the buckshot that flew at them.

Ying'er had the feeling that the buckshot turned to look at her, tails flapping as it shot forward.

"How could I bear the parting glance she gave me?" She recalled her *yuanjia*'s favorite line.

The jackal's eyes opened wide at the instant the buckshot pierced its body; apparently, it realized that the merrily flying red tadpoles were coming for its life. It was right. It only had time to twist a few times before its legs kicked out and its eyes stared blindly at the sky.

"Get your dagger ready. Looks like some aren't afraid of fire,"

Lanlan said as she wiped sweat from her face. Feeling a chill on her back, Ying'er quickly turned the flashlight toward the east, where she could see black dots closing in.

It was a good shot, but not enough to hold the jackals back.

Lanlan did not have time to take a breather. She kept refilling and firing, infusing the air with the smell of gunpowder. Not caring if she hit her targets, she refilled and fired into the east and then the west. The jackals backed off when the fire dragon leaped in their direction, but only slightly. When the firing stopped, they immediately inched forward. Ying'er brought out kerosene for the lantern, ready to pour it on the branches around them if the jackals charged. If they managed to break through the ring of fire, she'd set all the kindling on fire, jump in and let that be the end of it. Oddly enough, that thought took away some of her fear. No matter how deep-seated one's fear is, it will gradually diminish if given enough time. Her fear of death was no longer at the front of her mind; now her biggest regret was dying in the maws of a pack of abominable beasts. She was discomfited by the thought that her fine body would turn into food for the fang-baring, yelping monsters. What disgusted her the most was the drool from their mouths; she had the dry heaves when she imagined them drooling all over her pristine body. She had nothing to throw up, since they hadn't had much to eat the night before, and she was hungry. Her chest felt tight from the smell of gunpowder. Through the smoke, she saw how the sound was losing its effect. A jackal would fall to the ground with a shriek, but the others did not seem to care; they'd pause only at the instant Lanlan's muzzle pointed at them. They were merely dodging, not backing off, let alone running away. There was a good reason why the jackals, given their small size, were so feared. When they were fighting over food, they did not shy away from surging forward even as wolves tore their own kind into pieces, not to mention the fact that their current food source would be two tender, tasty women and two large camels.

She had heard people say that human flesh, with its high fat content, was a treat for carnivores. The Earth God had put down rules for His guardian dog—the wolf—but once it tasted human flesh it could not resist the temptation of delectable meat, and violated the rules again and again. And, humans enacted laws that a wild animal, no matter what category of governmental protection it fell under, would be killed once it had eaten a human. If it killed one, it would kill a hundred.

Could this pack of jackals have their eyes on human flesh?

The musket shots grew sparse. It was not an easy weapon to reload, requiring the tamping of gunpowder down the barrel with a ramrod before adding buckshot and more gunpowder. During the pause between shots, jackals would bound over and back off only when another shot was fired.

The range of their retreat was growing smaller. Ying'er made the fire bigger. Now, in the firelight, she could see their bared teeth. They were getting closer and closer. None had started leaping over the fire yet, but it was foreseeable that, if nothing changed, they would be doing that sooner or later. She recalled how, as a child, the villagers would start pyres when the winter solstice arrived, and the children were made to jump over them, called singeing the illness. The fire would cure whatever health problems a child might have. She had not been courageous enough to do that. As much as she envied her friends for bounding like leopard cats, the sight of the flames made her dizzy, so her mother held her to jump together. Ying'er had her eyes shut and screamed when they did it the first time, but on the second time she could keep her eyes open, and actually did it on her own on the third. Maybe it was the same with the jackals, she said to herself. They were afraid of the fire, but once they got used to it, they wouldn't be deterred by the flames and would attack en masse.

Then what? She shuddered at the thought.

Chapter Twenty

Clipping nettles on the mountain top
Lopping off the tail of a white snake

1

Mengzi slunk into the darkness to be a night prowler.

He hadn't wanted to, but Baigou insisted.

"Are you a man with balls or aren't you? Big Head is picking on us common people, peeing and shitting on our heads."

Mengzi was a man with balls, so he had to go along.

Yet he was, after all, stealing, so he felt eyes on him everywhere, from the sky and the ground, the stars, the trees, and houses, a sensation he'd had many times before. He remembered the first time, when he slept with Shuangfu's wife. Would that count as a theft? he wondered. It probably should. According to the villagers, he was the unlawful husband of Shuangfu's wife. Conversely, she was his unlawful wife. So, he must be considered a thief, which, in this sense, was something he'd done countless times. Nonetheless, it felt new to him. Sleeping with someone's wife, no matter how many times he did it, was just an affair; a real man should pluck a hundred flowers, for the more he did it, the more capable he would appear to others. Real theft, on the other hand, would be spat on, and he'd be called a "thieving lump." You see, he wouldn't be a man any longer, but a "lump." No wonder his heart was racing.

Big Head was the village chief, but he had only the second highest gate—the highest belonged to Shuangfu. As Liangzhou's famed entrepreneur, Shuangfu had enough wealth to speak louder than others. As people said, a strand of his hair was thicker than other people's waists. He had to have the highest gate, so Big Head's came in second. After serving as the leader of a production brigade, Big Head had become their village chief. A dead camel is still bigger than a living horse. He deserved to have a high gate. Next in line was Grannie Shaman, who, like a toad that received the essence of thunder, brought up deities—mouth open and mouth shut—and money settled into her hands like falling leaves. Her gate had to be high too.

Once the gold panning business at White Tiger Pass took off, Big Head acted like a donkey on suoyang, getting cockier by the day. Everyone sensed he might be corrupt, and some wanted to have him replaced. It wouldn't be hard to do; they'd hold a meeting, put up a new person, everyone would raise their hands to set the tone, and Big Head would no longer be the big head. The problem was, the county government would not affirm such a meeting and would only talk to Big Head. Without the county's support, whoever they elected could not get anything done and would have no say, like a ghost on the edge of the whirlwind by Jiayu Pass, whether it was at the water management station, the county office, the gold management station, or the land board. After all, after being in his position for years, Big Head had formed a net, which, though invisible, would catch you the moment you touched it.

Baigou could not abide Big Head's behavior. The village chief must have raked in a bundle just by granting permissions to pan gold. He acted with the eagerness of an aroused donkey when expropriating the land; a slice here and a slice there, and he never made the details public. Baigou gnashed his teeth in private.

"That asshole Big Head is getting out of hand," he said to Mengzi. "You put a bamboo basket over his head and he think it's the sky. He gets plenty as village chief, and now he's going overboard picking on us. He needs to suffer."

"Let's do it." Mengzi replied.

It was time to make Big Head suffer.

Shrouded in darkness, the high wall around Big Head's house stirred up a reaction similar to when Mengzi saw Shuangfu's wall. Mengzi joined Baigou because he could not abide Big Head's bullish behavior. He was overbearing, worse than the county head or the mayor, whose rank gave them the right to be arrogant. What right did Big Head have? Back when he was a little boy, still wearing open-crotch pants, he had stolen fruit from the production brigade and received a painful beating from Mao Dan's father. Was that what gave him the right to be a bully? And there was more. He never showed any respect when he saw Laoshun, treating him like a generational equal, though he was junior to Mengzi's father. To be sure, Mengzi could care less about that, and wouldn't have minded if Big Head treated his father as someone from his grandson's generation; he could call Laoshun anything he wanted. But now he treated the villagers like dirt, lorded it over them all the time, like a hungry louse sucking blood from the corpse of a starvation victim. If they didn't do something, Shawan would look like a place with no real men. There was something else too. Big Head was always leering at Ying'er, a scene that made Mengzi so angry he could hardly breathe. They had to deal with the asshole; it was the only way Mengzi could vent his anger.

Of course, they had to make him suffer.

Carrying a ladder over their shoulders, they tip-toed to Big Head's house, treading along a route as familiar as touching their noses. Baigou hadn't wanted to take the ladder.

"Instead of climbing over on a ladder, I'd rather smash a hole in his wall with a hoe and carry off the soy beans in his back yard," Baigou said.

"That won't do, too much noise," Mengzi said.

"So what if there's noise? I tried once to see what would happen and got him drunk as a pig. When he was drunk you could toss him into a fire and he wouldn't wake up."

"His woman won't be drunk."

"I'm not afraid of his woman. I'll step on her if she comes out."

"She could cry for help. Besides, they have a dog. You'd wake up the whole village if she cried out and the dog barked." Baigou shut up. He didn't care what they used, a ladder or a hoe, so long as they could fix Big Head.

They'd long wanted to do that, and had spent days on reconnaissance. At first, they decided to steal his three-wheeler, but it was too bulky, too visible, and hard to deal with. The same went for his TV set. After surveying the house, they decided on the soy beans in his backyard. They could take the crop to the county purchasing station, where it would be weighed and exchanged for money. Quick and easy.

Mengzi had to muster all his resolve, but it leaked out at every step he took. He recalled that during his older brother's hospitalization, Big Head had chipped in with a hundred yuan to defray the cost, which was a favor he could never forget. Each time it was brought up in the family, Father would comment that Big Head was a good man. He helped your family out, and now you're going to steal from him, a true case of repaying kindness with enmity. Besides, anything could happen, and he'd be called a thief forever if the theft was found out. He'd tried to steal sand at the gold panning site, but Shuangfu deserved that because he monopolized White Tiger Pass, which was public land. He'd also "stolen" someone's wife, but that was an act to boast about. This time was different, because staples like soy beans are paid for with sweat, which was why the villagers loathed a food thief. Once the foul moniker was attached, he'd never be able to live it down. Father was always talking about the two most loathsome deeds—thievery for men and prostitution for women. According to him, "it would bring such shame to the family that the ancestors would jump off the altar."

He stopped.

"What's wrong? Getting cold feet?" Baigou jeered. "Your father was right when he said you talk a lot, but get cold feet when it's time to act."

"Big Head is wicked, but can't we think of something else? Like lodge a complaint or hold a meeting to fire him."

"No way. You can lodge your shitty complaints all you want, but he has connections everywhere and nothing will come of it. You might even end up in jail yourself. Someone in Jiudun County in the north once lodged a complaint and fell into a trap that turned him into a rapist. He was ruined. You can't fire Big Head either, since the county office will deal only with him. Besides, what if you fire a sated wolf and his replacement turns out to be a hungry one? It would be worse. Come on, let's go. There's this law and that law, but we have to come up with a pay-back law. We'll be righting wrongs based on Heaven's decree."

Reminded of all the negatives things about Big Head, Mengzi's anger rose.

Night deepened, adding a sharp edge to the wind. Baigou had picked a windy day on purpose, for the wind stirred up enough sand to cover their footprints, thus ensuring the secrecy of their act.

Mengzi was sweating from the effort. The plastic bag rustling in his hand held a piece of pork, a bribe for Big Head's dog. As the saying goes, when you receive a gift, food or otherwise, you have to be generous to the gift-giver. Even the head of the customs office can be bought off, let alone a dog. They had, additionally, a hemp sack and rope to take care of the dog if it refused to be bribed. For Mengzi, who had once killed a wolf, dealing with a dog was nothing. If it pounced on them, he'd grab it by its scalp, loop the rope around its neck, and pull tight, and that would do it. Yet Mengzi couldn't shake off how his father would look if he was found out. His father nearly killed him last time, when he happened upon Mengzi with another man's wife; another incident would be like smearing his face with dog shit if the theft came to light. But this was not an ordinary theft; it was following Heaven's decree to right wrongs. In other words, Heaven wanted him to do it because of Big Head's offenses against Heaven. He recalled that Shuangfu's wife had said that Heaven was the people.

When they reached Big Head's rear wall, they raised the ladder. The noise wouldn't have been loud, but it sounded like a thunderclap to Mengzi, the sheepish reaction of a thief. Baigou adjusted the ladder before climbing up to look around. Mengzi felt his heart thump against his chest, so he told himself, Don't be afraid. I'm following Heaven's decree to right wrongs.

As Baigou came back down, Mengzi heard his muffled laughter.

"What are you laughing at?"

"You were talking about lodging a complaint. It's not going to work no matter who does it now. He didn't just offer money, he even gave away his woman. Go up and take a look for yourself, but be quiet."

Mengzi went up. The ladder swayed under his feet and made his heart flutter. An old hand at climbing, he had never been intimidated by tall trees. A chilled night breeze blew over his body, which was sweaty from the effort of carrying the ladder.

He looked into the backyard when he was atop the wall. He saw only a blur, but the faint glow from the crescent moon gave him a general outline. Suddenly he heard an unusual sound coming from under the trellis. He listened carefully and realized that it was Huilanzi moaning, while his eyes detected dark shadowy figures moving about. A fire erupted inside Mengzi, who now understood the reason behind Baigou's laughter.

"Hurry, Chief, hurry. Do it and let me just die." Huilanzi raised her voice, her breathing loud and labored.

Still laughing silently, Baigou stealthily climbed up alongside Mengzi as they heard Huilanzi cry out again:

"Dear Brother! I'll embroider a flower on your shoe tomorrow." She continued to moan, like a leopard cat in heat.

Mengzi laughed quietly about embroidering a flower on shoes, which was a joke. Fengxiang had said the same thing the time when Mengzi was fooling around with her. He swallowed and whispered, "I can't believe she isn't afraid of getting caught by her husband."

"Big Head is drunk as a lord." Baigou swallowed and murmured his reply. "I thought this guy went back to the county office. He's a lecher, always into something like this. He can really drink. He gets the man drunk so he can have his wife."

"How does it feel?" The man was breathing hard.

"It feels so good I wouldn't even dare tell my parents." The woman giggled.

"Now what? Should we head back?" Mengzi asked.

"Let's wait. They'll sleep like dead pigs when they go back inside."

Sure enough, they soon heard the couple kissing as they headed back inside and shut the door.

"Where's the dog?" Mengzi asked.

"Maybe she got the dog inside so it wouldn't spoil her fun. See how they get along? You were thinking about a complaint. If you did, you'd get an earful. A man will die before complaining about poverty and will never file a complaint against an official, even it means a wrongful death. Besides, the county office would be the one dealing with your complaint if you tried to go up to the central government."

Mengzi was thinking about something else altogether. "Huilanzi always acts so prim and proper, but she's as wild as Shuangfu's wife when she lets go." He continued smugly when he recalled how Big Head looked at Ying'er. "No use looking at other people's wives when your own woman is being screwed by another man."

They went up onto the wall, pulled the ladder up, and set it down on the inside. Baigou stayed on top to let down a rope for later, when they would drag the grain over the side, while Mengzi got down with the piece of pork for the dog. He had wanted Baigou to go down, but he had to do it when Baigou gave him the irrefutable reason, "You're the dog expert."

It felt as if the dog was everywhere; a pair of green eyes seemed to be hidden under the trellis, in the dark, and all the spots he couldn't see clearly. Dogs' eyes don't glow in the dark, but to Mengzi they were like a wolf's eyes at this moment, which made him anxious. I don't care if you leap out at me, Mengzi said silently. Just don't bark. He'd have to take off if it did. A survey of his surroundings led to the discovery of a shed for baking buns. If he got on the top of the shed, he could reach the wall with one leap, much easier than using the ladder. Finding a way out put his mind at ease.

Mengzi walked to the shed and counted the fiber sacks. There were ten of them, standing in a row. The couple had been having fun here just a moment ago. It looked to him that she had stood against the sacks as the man leaned into her. The villagers called the position "punching the sack." The image made Mengzi's mouth dry. He was surprised that an ordinary, plain looking, fat Huilanzi could ignite a fire in him. So Beizhu had been on target when he mocked Mengzi. What had he said? Ah, yes, "If he goes without a woman for three days, even a sow looks better than beautiful Diaochan."

Mengzi cocked his ear and heard someone snoring. No, not just someone, all three of them snoring, with Big Head the loudest. No wonder. The villagers had heard that the central government, with its plan to develop the West, had dispersed money for the villagers to obtain new electrical wires for free. But the county office pocketed the expense, claiming that the electricians, workers on public projects, and cadres had to eat too and couldn't go hungry. There was more money than needed for the work, which made it possible for Big Head and the like to snore.

Mengzi mustered enough strength to pick up a sack. His hands told him it contained soy beans. It didn't actually matter what it was, so long as he could drain some of Big Head's blood. The man had had too much of it, and it was time to leach some out. Sack in hand, Mengzi headed to the rope hanging from the wall, his footsteps deafeningly loud in his ears. Sneaky dogs were the scariest type, for they'd sink their teeth in when you weren't paying attention. If the dog followed him over stealthily, it could tear a chunk out of his calf. A barking dog never bites and a biting dog never barks. He looked around, but the dog was nowhere in sight. Had Huilanzi locked it up?

He hooked the sack up with the rope and tied it with a slip knot before Baigou hoisted it up to the top and over the wall. With a slight tug he released the knot and whispered, "Step a little more quietly."

"You try carrying a hundred *jin* and you'll see how to be quiet," Mengzi whispered back.

All the sacks made it out after a few trips, though they had a bit of trouble with the last one. In midair, it fell when the knot loosened. Mengzi tried to catch it, and instead was knocked to the ground, though he lessened the sound of the sack falling.

"You okay?" Baigou asked softly.

Mengzi was seeing stars, but he got to his feet and moved his arms and legs to find they all working just fine. He retied the knot for Baigou to pull the sack up before climbing over the wall himself.

"You go down first. I'll clean up the area," Baigou said as he took off a shoe, turned it over, and scraped it against the top of the wall. "That takes care of the foot prints." He was huffing.

"Oh, no. My prints are all over the backyard." Mengzi cried out at the realization.

"What kind of shoes are you wearing?"

"Cloth."

"With rubber soles?"

"No, cloth."

"Then you have nothing to worry about. "Everybody wears has cloth soles. Listen carefully tomorrow morning, and run over when you hear Huilanzi wailing; shout and act surprised, rousing as many people as possible. When they're here and they've trampled the ground, the prints will be gone." It was a pretty good solution, but failed to ease Mengzi's concerns.

"Do we leave these at your house?" Baigou asked as he pointed at the sacks.

"No way. My father would break my legs if he found out."

"Let's bury them in the desert, far from here," Baigou said after mulling it over with a frown. "It's the safest spot. It'll be hard to find, but even if they find the sacks, they won't know who stole them."

They took the ladder back home before returning for the sacks. The wind had picked up, lashing their faces with sand and scary howls. "Just what we need. The wind will cover everything up," Baigou said, but his words were carried off by the sandy wind.

Mengzi slung a sack of soy beans over his shoulder. It wasn't too heavy, but he had to strain against the wind, which billowed up his clothes and nearly succeeded in toppling him. Sand rushed at his head and pitted his face. The best thing to do on a day like this was sleep, lie on a hot kang and doze off amid the howling wind, one of life's great pleasures.

Being a thief was hard.

2

Mengzi would have still been asleep if not for the clamor the next morning. It was one of the things he was good at, sleeping through earth-shattering events. He was nibbling at Huilanzi in his dream when his mother nudged him awake.

"Get up," his mother said. "Big happenings at Big Head's."

Mengzi jumped to his feet when he was reminded of what he'd done the night before. He threw on some clothes and walked out the door. He didn't need to look surprised, since throngs of people were swarming toward Big Head's house, as if going to see an opera.

The sound of Huilanzi crying drifted in the morning wind, a long, drawn-out, shrill noise that grew suddenly louder and rose into the air before slowly gliding down like gossamer. She was considered by the villagers to be the number two funeral crier, second only to Yue'er's mother. Her wailing had an enduring quality as she cried and lamented at a funeral, her voice choking up and her demeanor displaying pain and sorrow, plaintive and affecting, her notes lingering in the air long after it was over. Apparently, she was now employing her funereal wailing skill, a riotous scene the villagers were loathe to miss.

Big Head's place was packed. Baigou was already there, expressing his surprise and cheering everyone on. A few women were supporting Huilanzi, who was crying her heart out, like a funeral crier. Heartbroken, she knelt on the spot where she'd had a titillating tryst the night before, repeatedly banging her head on the ground and smearing her face with mud. It was impossible to imagine her heavenly moans. When he took a glance around, Mengzi saw the county chief looking stern as he gave orders to the village cadres. Big Head hung his head, his eyes slightly puffy, the effect of too much to drink the previous night. "Someone has screwed your woman, Big Head," Mengzi said silently.

Big Head's son was drying his tears as he jerked at his mother's sleeves, trying to yank away her sobs. Meng Baye did his best to comfort her:

"Let it go. Stop thinking about it. You can't cry the dead back alive and the lost can't be found. What good does crying do?"

"What do you mean, no good?" She wanted to pick a fight, "It may go down easy, but it'll cause indigestion, trust me. Whoever stole my beans will have his family line cut off."

"Right. Cut off his family line completely," some villagers echoed, an attempt to prove their innocence. "I didn't do it."

"Whoever stole my beans will have a son with no asshole."

"Right. No asshole." More people echoed this time, in unison and very loud. Huilanzi blew her nose and wailed a few times before yelling, "He'll be flattened on the road."

"Flattened on the road." Now everyone shouted.

"His ancestors in the graveyard are jackasses."

"Jackasses." They bellowed thunderously, more spirited than shouting slogans during the Cultural Revolution.

Meng Baye had to laugh, and when he did, the villagers, sensing how ridiculous they were, also laughed so hard the yard seemed about to burst. Even the scowling county chief laughed. A funeral scene was turned into a skit.

Big Head got to his feet and yelled at his wife, "Get up. Don't make me lose face."

"What face? Whose face am I losing?" She bared her teeth and hissed. "I didn't cheat on you or sell my body. What's wrong if I cry over the loss?"

What do you mean, you didn't cheat on him? Mengzi said silently. You were going to embroider the man's leather shoe last night. The thought made him laugh as he turned to look at the county chief's shoes.

Leather, with no embroidery. An empty promise.

"Bitch," Big Head cursed her. "So what if we lost some sacks of beans? Just consider them gifts to our grandson as money for the medicine he'll need."

"Of course, it doesn't bother you." Huilanzi roared like a bitch. "You walk around, swinging your old dick, all day long. I'm the one who works her ass off to have that much. You don't care, but it feels a knife slicing through my heart. I'm going to curse the thief for seven times seven, forty-nine days. If it was a man, he'll get boils on his back, and if it was a woman, she'll have the unspeakable disease."

No one echoed her this time.

Mengzi shuddered. He'd heard about boils on the back, but he'd yet to see one. It could get so bad, they said, that you can see through the back of the afflicted, a pitiful sight. He'd heard of the unspeakable disease too. When a woman was affected, she could have maggots as thick as a finger crawling out of her private parts. Huilanzi's curse sent chills up his spine. Please don't let me get boils on my back, he prayed silently. What I did was right a wrong for Heaven. He even prayed to the Vajravārāhī, though he was not a believer.

"What a disgrace. Bitch," Big Head groused bitterly, but said nothing worse. He was a cadre, after all, and must behave accordingly.

Huilanzi hissed at him again. "Who's the disgrace? You've got shit for brains. You want your share of food and clothes, but never share a bit of worry. Who would dare come steal from us if you didn't drink so much? You can get drunk all you want, but you puke all over the place and get the dog drunk too. Big Head, you're a useless old fool, you eat and drink, whore around. You've got mush for brains, and you never do a decent thing."

Finally, it was clear to Mengzi that the dog hadn't barked because it had gotten drunk after eating Big Head's puke. That was funny. If he wasn't drunk, how could you be embroider the county chief's leather shoes?

Her jibe hit Big Head's sore spot. With little education, his greatest fear was that people would doubt his intelligence. The woman clearly wanted to get under his skin. She said his head was buried in a bowl of pigs' guts. What were guts? They came from the bellies of pigs, goats, and cows. She was obviously calling him a farm animal. That was too much for him. Before the others could react, he jerked her over and slapped her, sending blood shooting out of her nose.

"What do you think you're doing, Big Head?" Meng Baye yelled.

The county chief asserted his authority by strolling over and wordlessly pointing at Big Head, who quickly let go of his woman. She wailed and cursed at the top of her lungs, but her target was no longer the thief, but her husband.

3

The police station sent over men, who put on an act of checking around. They found nothing and soon left.

Big Head got the villagers together for a meeting under the big tree outside the clan shrine. He told them he hadn't wanted to hold a meeting, but the thief had picked his house, as if to challenge him. If everyone followed suit, how would he survive?

Built in the Daoguang Year of the Qing Dynasty, the shrine served as a place for the clan to offer sacrifices to the ancestors. Times had changed, and no one cared about doing that any longer. Except for laying down a few commemorative scripts on the ancestral graves during holidays, they rarely mentioned them. The building was old now, but retained its former grandeur, with four beams and eight pillars, as well as carved windows and soaring eaves, all made of high-grade wood. In the sixteenth year of the Republican Era, or 1927, a major earthquake hit Liangzhou and knocked down the Luoshi Pagoda, but the shrine remained intact. Later, it was turned into a storeroom by the local production brigade, after which it sat empty, except over New Year's holidays, when Huaqiu and his friends brought over a cassette player. With dance music playing, they men paired up and, arms around each other, shook their rear ends and swayed their hips, mimicking urban boys and girls, while the villagers whooped and shouted over their performance.

In front of the shrine stood a towering white poplar at least six feet around. After all these years, its branches were cracked and gnarled, its twisted shape brimming with a peculiar and quaint feel. White poplar trees have a short life span, and will hollow out if left standing after they are fully grown. But there was nothing the villagers could do about a tree planted by their ancestors. All the descendants, hundreds of them, had a claim over the tree, so no one would dare cut it down. A few years earlier, an oil mill owner offered to buy the timber for his press, but no one was in a position to accept, so it stayed. Now hollow, it was still a big tree that towered over other trees; the family shrine enhanced its imposing look, which was why Big Head picked that spot for a meeting.

The agenda for the meeting was: what to do about the theft of his soy beans.

"What a lousy thief, stealing crops," Goubao said. "I'm afraid our days of peace are over."

"He's right," Yue'er's father said. "Even bundled wheat isn't safe anymore. When we catch a thief like that, we have to cut his tendons so he won't steal again."

"That's right," several villagers echoed. "That's what we'll do."

I'd rather be a horse groom for a real man than the ancestor of a coward, Mengzi said to himself. We were fighting for you. How can you say that? He saw that the villagers agreeing with Big Head were the ones who complained the most in private. Now he realized that they concurred purely to assert their innocence. No wonder corrupt officials in Liangzhou can do what they want, Mengzi thought. With people like this, how could the officials not be corrupt?

"What do we do now?" an old man asked Big Head.

"The beans must still be in the village. So, what do we do?"

"Search!" Baigou said.

"What if we can't find them?" Meng Baye asked.

"Are you saying we shouldn't search for them?" Big Head asked Meng.

"I didn't say that. I just want to know what we do if we can't find them."

Now there were two questions, which expanded the agenda.

Crows on the tree cawed, raining down white droppings. The villagers usually avoided bird droppings, which, according to Shaman Qi, would bring a year of bad luck to whoever's head it landed on. But at that moment, they couldn't worry about bad luck, since their minds were all on what do to next.

"There's nothing more to talk about. Let's search," Baigou offered.

"Of course, we search. If we don't, we'll be letting the evil-doer off," Huilanzi shrieked in a voice unaffected by her crying. Her eyes, however, were puffy.

"What if we can't find them?" Laoshun had to ask, for a family was under suspicion when their house was searched. If nothing was found, then the family would not let that go. Besides, everyone had tablets for deities and their ancestors in their main room, where the searchers would have to enter; when they ransacked a house, like scared ghosts, that would bring bad luck.

"You fear nothing with a clear conscience," Big Head said.

"Don't say that, Big Head." Meng added, "We didn't tell you not to search. We just want to know what to do if nothing turns up."

"What do you say we do?" Big Head asked him.

"What do you all think?" Meng asked the old village men, who lowered their heads.

"No need to say any more. Let's start searching. If we don't, then people will think everyone in Shawan is a thief," Baigou said.

"That's easy for you to say. But just think, everyone has soy beans in their house. How will you know whose they are?" Laoshun asked.

"My soy beans are different. They're a new strain that looks like golden peas, without a black dot. If they're mixed with other beans, I'll spot them," Huilanzi said.

"Then forget the search," Big Head shouted. "You can't retrieve anything in a thief's den. A snake knows its pit. You fear nothing with a clear conscience." That sounded like a concession, but in fact was a veiled threat; whoever was against the search would not have a clear conscience.

"If you want to fart, make sure it doesn't stink, Big Head." Meng raged. "I'll be the first to open my house for you to search."

"I'll be second," Baigou shouted also.

"Go ahead with your search then. The asshole is pressuring us."

So, they did.

Following directions worked out by the Shaman, they searched one house after another, an uncommon sight in recent years, almost as lively as a mopping-up operation conducted by the Japanese army. To their surprise, they didn't have to search many families before turning up a bushel of "golden peas" at Baldy Wang's house. His face a bright red, Wang admitted that he had pinched some of Big Head's soy bean pods. He'd been infuriated by the outrageous water bill from Big Head, so he filched some of the pods, but he hadn't touched anything else.

"Do you admit your guilt?" Big Head asked. "If not, I'll call the police."

Wang refused, so Big Head went to the police station.

4

A police car parked at a corner. Policemen walked up, Baldy Wang in tow.

Wang's wife was wailing, so were their daughters. Their wails rose up and down along with the wind.

"I knew it was him," Huilanzi was heard complaining. "A cross-eyed man is up to no good. He's worse than a donkey. No wonder he has no son to continue his family line. It would be a wonder if Heaven doesn't cut it off."

"Don't use this as an excuse for something else, Huilanzi." Meng Baye cut in. "Don't go off half-cocked."

Huilanzi's outburst angered grim-faced Wang, who had been quiet up till then. He stopped and turned to glare at her, hissing through clenched teeth,

"Don't count the boy your son until he reaches the height of a wall. If I don't die in jail, I'll come out and trade this lamb's pelt for your old sheep skin."

Big Head, who had also been silent, couldn't hold back after Wang's curse. "Baldy ass, who are you trying to scare? You deal with me if you have an issue, but don't threaten my woman and children. I didn't put those beans in your house. You did it yourself, so don't blame me."

"Heaven knows what I did and what I didn't do," Wang sneered.

"You didn't do it?" Huilanzi shrieked. "Then how did the beans show up in your house?"

Wang gave her a sinister glare, but didn't say another word

"Let's go!" The policemen said. Wang started off robotically.

"It's unreasonable to arrest him over that little bit of evidence,"

Baigou said. "You did the search and you have to agree that several hundred kilos of beans can't be stashed in rats' nests. When catching adulterers, you have to find them together, and when catching a thief, you have to find the loot."

"We have the loot," Huilanzi replied. "The beans are from a strain developed by the Academy of Agricultural Science. Not many people in Liangzhou have it, let alone Shawan."

"Didn't he already confess that he pinched your pods?" Mengzi asked.

"That's an easy thing to own up to," Huilanzi said.

Baigou continued to speak up for Wang's innocence, and Mengzi knew why. They'd carried out the theft to punish Big Head, and now their conscience was bothered over Baldy Wang being blamed. They couldn't let him be falsely accused, even if it meant the case remained open.

"You need evidence to arrest him," Mengzi said to the policeman. "He admitted he'd stolen some pods, but is that cause enough for you to arrest him? I've pinched and roasted people's pods when I was out grazing the livestock."

"He's just a suspect," the policemen explained. "We didn't say he's guilty. We'll let him go once he's cleared."

"Go ahead with your investigation," Wang roared. "If you can't find anything against me, you'll have to support me for the rest of my life. Don't think you can get off easy and just let me go, not after you smear me with this shit. That won't do. I'd refuse to leave even if you want to let me go."

"All right. You can stay for a few years, even make it your permanent residence, if you want," the policeman said with a smile, while his partner went up with a raised fist. "Are you threatening us?"

"Drop it, will you?" the first policeman said to his colleague.

"Don't you dare beat him," Baigou said. "You beat me once and knocked the food right out of my stomach."

"He's right." Mengzi joined in. "If they beat you, Baldy Wang, remember their faces and sue them when you're out."

"Who are you anyway?" A third policeman walked up. "His accomplice?"

"Accomplice?" Baigou said with a laugh. "We're the culprits. So, why not arrest me?"

Mengzi sucked in cold air, but laughed and said, "He's right. We've committed a whole bunch of shocking crimes. Who cares about a few soy beans?"

"Shove off," one of the policemen said. "Don't interfere with police work."

Wang's tearful wife ran up, tripped and fell, but got to her feet and raced over; she was covered in dirt, her face tear-streaked. Her children were wailing too, but they didn't dare run after their father.

"He's innocent!" she howled.

One of the policemen went up to block her way. "What are you howling about? Don't worry. We never jail an innocent man or let a guilty one go free. We'll be lenient if he comes clean and strict if he resists."

"Hasn't he come clean already?" she sobbed. "He admitted pinching bean pods. But that was because of Big Head; he shouldn't have collected so much money for water."

"You see," Baigou said as he nudged Mengzi. "She shares our concerns."

"Shut your trap," Mengzi said with a wink.

"I've already explained that he's just a suspect," the older policeman said. "We'll investigate and gather evidence."

"You can't beat him." She stopped crying. "If you cripple him, I'll ram my head into your station door and die in front of you."

Its siren blaring, the police car drove off, raising dust, like dragging a gray dragon. Baigou poked at Mengzi to get him away from the crowd.

"Now what? He's taking the fall, we're like turtles tucking our necks in. That's not right."

"Don't worry yet. Let them look into it first. They have to let him go when they find no evidence." Mengzi added, "Don't outsmart yourself by going forward. Think about all the unsolved cases out there."

Baigou frowned but said no more. They listened as Baldy Wang's wife said:

"I told you not to put your hat—on the vat, but you wouldn't listen—see—I said you'd carry the vat on your head and be blamed for someone's fault—now it's come true—you're the scapegoat—the damn thief, we'll be blamed."

"Why are you cursing like that?" Baigou said to her. "It could have been a heroic man robbing the rich to aid the poor."

"If a thief becomes a hero, what would I be then? An evil official like Gao Qiu or Cai Jing?" Big Head was outraged. "Did I send my son to take your woman?"

"You could do that, but I don't have a woman," Baigou said with a smile. "Heaven knows what you are."

"Let it go," Mengzi said. "When dogs fight, they get nothing but mouthfuls of fur."

"Come on, get up." Meng Baye walked up to Baldy Wang's wife to help her up. "Don't cry. Who's going to take care of your kids if you get sick from all that crying? He didn't do it, so they can't lay the blame on him. Don't worry. You have to let them look into it; if not, he could carry the blame for the rest of his life. His innocence will be restored when they get the results of their investigation."

"Don't you think the thief is vile?" The woman was still sobbing. "He got what he wanted, and we're the scapegoats."

"There you go again," Baigou said. "The thief didn't arrest your man.

You should be cursing the police. They've got shit for brains, and can't solve a case like this, so they arrest a good man."

"Damn thief!" She ignored him.

"I've never seen anyone so confused." Baigou gave Mengzi an unhappy smile.

"I feel terrible that they're blaming Baldy," Mengzi said when they were away from the crying woman. "Shouldn't we find a way to make it up to him? He'll definitely be beaten in the police station. He shouldn't take a beating for us."

"You're right," Baigou continued. "We'll give his woman some money for now. Two hundred. To help her out. Later when we sell the beans, we'll give them a share. We'll divide the profit into three shares and consider him a partner. We can't let him take a beating for nothing."

"Sounds good to me. We'll each put up a hundred for now."

But news came from the police station that night: Baldy Wang had confessed. He said he'd sold the beans to a man passing through on a three-wheeler and he had no idea where the man was from.

"Now he's going to get a hefty sentence," said everyone who heard the news.

5

Baigou came for Mengzi early the next morning. Mengzi was shocked to see his friend in a cold sweat. "Are you sick?"

"You could say that," Baigou said a sad smile. "No, it's worse than death. Did you know Baldy's wife cried all night, howling like a wolf that had lost her cub. It was terrible."

"Why did Baldy confess?" Mengzi asked.

"It's not up to him when he's in there. They can get whatever confession they want. He's not made of steel." Baigou sighed. "I've thought it through. A real man has to take responsibility for what he's done. I'm turning myself in. I'm a bachelor, with nothing to tie me down. If Baldy gets sentenced, his whole family would die along with him. His wife has had hepatitis for years, and I hear it's turned into cirrhosis."

Mengzi's tongue turned numb when Baigou brought up turning himself in.

"My brother died, and the world just about ended for my Ma and Pa," Mengzi stammered. "If I—how would they keep on living?"

"You don't." Baigou smiled. "I'll take the blame. They can do what they want to do with me, even kill me. You'll sell the soy beans if a fine is required. It'll be great if we break even, but if not, you'll have to put up a bit of money."

"Sure, no problem." Relieved, Mengzi thumped his chest. "We'll split the cost, even if it means carving out our flesh and selling it."

"I'll focus on Big Head's corruption once I'm in there. You keep your mouth shut if I get something going; if not, you raise enough hell outside to get Big Head to drop the charges. The one who started the trouble should end it. Now only he can get me out of this," Baigou said.

"No problem. If nothing happens in a month, I'll start on my end."

"Rest assured I'll never give you up, even if they beat me to death. Don't worry and don't be afraid. Steel your mind to go after him. You get a bowl-size scar if you lose your head, so you have to fight till the bitter end. We won't let him go free if I have to serve out my sentence. The account won't be hard to check. You can't cram a big rock into the hole of a millstone. He can't get off easily, I'm sure." Baigou added, "I took out half of bushel of the soy beans and buried them under a dirt mound outside my door. The rest is still out there. Sell the beans when you get a chance and give the money to my father for bail. Remember to file a complaint if I'm still in there after a month. Make sure to get others to go with you and, if they ignore you, go into town and stage a sit-in outside the municipal office. Raise some hell."

Mengzi mumbled a reply as a warm current rose up inside. "You're a real man, Baigou. You and I will be friends for the rest of our lives."

"Real man?" Baigou laughed. "I don't want to be beaten either, but I'm such a softie. They say all great men are ruthless, but not me. I'm no great man."

Baigou went to turn himself in. The police didn't believe him, so he led them back to dig out the loot from the dirt mound. There was only half of a sack, but they were real "golden peas." His mother looked as if sky had fallen on her.

"Damn you. We have enough to get by, so why do such a shameless thing? I think we have plenty of wheat at home. You could have just told me what you wanted. I'd have suffocated you and fed you to the wolves if I'd known you'd grow up to be a thief and cause such a loss of face. Losing face is as easy as drinking cold water. The understanding type would know a mother can't do anything about her grown son, but those who aren't would think I'm a thief myself."

"No one said you stole the beans, so what are you grumbling about?" Goubao said, only to give the impression that she chattered away precisely because she had a guilty conscience.

Baigou's father squatted by the gate, with his head hung, obscuring the expression on his face.

"I admit I'm the thief, but I'm righting a wrong on Heaven's decree," Baigou shouted. "Big Head has sucked too much of our blood. Do you have any idea how much of the water fees he pockets each year? Where's all the money from selling the gold-panning sites? And then there's the kickback from land sales. Are you trying to cover all that up?"

Big Head looked outraged as he gave Baigou several slaps. "You bastard. You think you were justified to steal, don't you?"

Baigou's nose began to bleed, but, glaring at Big Head, he spat and shouted,

"If you dare touch me again, Big Head, I'll kill those sons of yours. Don't think I won't. Even if I have to go to prison, I'll do it after I come out. You asshole. Don't ever touch me again."

Big Head was about to pounce again when his wife stopped him. Baigou roared laughing.

The villagers were quiet as the laughter faded into the dusty distance. What Baigou had said felt like rocks hitting their hearts. They exchanged looks.

"No matter how you look at it, Baigou has backbone and a good head. He's a real man," Mengzi said, but got no reaction from others.

"Backbone?" Goubao shrieked. "He's got thieving bones, that's all. He's been caught, so he'll say anything. You think there's no thief just because you haven't caught one. When the brigade lost trees, were they stolen by someone out for payback or to vent anger?"

"He's right," some of the villagers echoed.

Goubao always toadied up to the village chief, no matter who it was, which disgusted Laoshun, who said:

"You're wrong there. Baigou was just a kid when the trees were stolen."

"Who knows? The little one didn't, but maybe the older one did."

Baigou's father jumped to his feet, walked up, and pointed at Goubao. "You donkey ass. Go ahead, keep yelping. He's my son, but he does what he pleases. You leave me out of this or I'll knock your teeth out."

"I wasn't talking about you." Goubao panicked. "I wasn't."

With a dark face, Baigou's father spat out his reply:

"Don't laugh at me. No one can guarantee his wife's virtue or his son's filial piety. If you want to chat, come with me and let's have a nice long one on the kang at my place. If not, go back to your house and stop humiliating people at their door."

Chastised, the others walked off sheepishly.

What if Baigou can't take the beating? Mengzi was worried. Will he give me up?

Chapter Twenty-One

The good old sun sets in Jiulongkou
A fierce lion holds a colored ball in its mouth

1

The musket no longer scared the circling jackals. Ying'er realized that Lanlan had blundered by moving their tent site, and now they faced the enemy on all sides. The musket fire had to cover all four corners to cause even a slight movement among those beasts, which were squeezing low snarls out through their fangs.

The camels continued to spit and chuff, for they were terrified by the frightful attackers. But the jackals were unfazed, no longer bothered even by the sound of the musket. The camels shook their heads violently in an attempt to break free of their tethers, but their tender nostrils were strung with softened willow. They tugged and rocked the branches they were tethered to, until they realized how futile that was. Their fragile nostrils, they discovered, were no match for the willow tether; they could break their nose and get loose, but they might not escape the maws of the jackals. If they tried to flee, they would become the first targets of jackals that had laid siege to the humans and their camels. They quieted down, no longer tugging at the tether, though they never stopped snorting. Ying'er knew they were trying to frighten the jackals. They won't be afraid of your spittle if they don't even fear the musket.

The situation was dire. First, they were short on firewood, which had looked to be enough when piled high. Sitting around idly, one could consume a mountain, let alone a fire that was kept burning the whole time. It felt like several hours had passed, but she wasn't sure, since feelings are not always reliable. Sometimes a hundred days pass by in an instant, while at other times a day is like a whole year. Ying'er wasn't sure about the time. She'd brought along a watch, but it was in a little purse with her money. The thought of a watch reminded her of the money, money for buying salt, which she should keep on her person. So, she took the flashlight from Lanlan, walked over to pick up her purse, and draped it around her neck. She touched the purse and felt the stiffness of the bills, as a sense of self-loathing rose up. I could die, so why am I worrying about money? How miserly can I get? she chided herself, but still she kept the purse on her. I'd be done for if the jackals got me, but if I manage to escape, then I'll need money. She took out her watch and saw it was almost four in the morning. "A little over an hour till daybreak," she said to Lanlan.

Ying'er wished they'd gathered more firewood at nightfall. Now the jackals had taken all the spots with vegetation and the net was tightening. She'd have to deal with the beasts before she could get any more wood. Ying'er pulled all the wood together; it made a pile as small as a grave mound. It struck her as unlucky to be thinking about such things. Maybe I'll really die here, she thought. Yet she didn't feel as nervous as before. Death didn't seem so terrifying. She'd often thought of death before, and it seemed as normal as eating or putting on clothes. But she'd hate to be torn to pieces by jackals. The beasts preferred animal entrails, and it made her stomach turn thinking about how they'd poke a hole in her belly, stick their pointed heads into her chest cavity, and bite and tug at her liver and lungs. She'd have preferred to die on that rainy night, had she known about this. On second thought, it felt good to leave no corpse behind, sparing her parents the sad sight of their dead daughter. When she disappeared, she'd leave no trace behind. That sounded just fine to her. Yet, she couldn't help shuddering at the possibility that the jackals would gnaw and make a mess of her face after devouring her internal organs. Since my beauty failed to keep you around, *Yuanjia*, I'll feed it to the jackals, the thought of which sent tears down her face, despite the ugly sense of pleasure she felt.

"Why is the fire dying?" Lanlan demanded angrily.

Drying her tears, Ying'er tossed several small branches onto the fire, blew on it, and got the fire going again. A few of the jackals were almost at the fireside now. Lanlan reloaded and, with a shot, took down two of them. Instead of fleeing, the remaining two bared their fangs at her; they did not back off until Ying'er threw in some wood to make the fire roar. Obviously, that was what they feared most, but unfortunately there wasn't much wood left. Once the fire died out, the sound of the musket would not deter them. Ying'er gave the sky a longing look. Maybe this would be her last glance at the sky. The stars were hazy, flickering in the fire light, like the hope in her heart. Would he look for her after she vanished from the earth like vapor? she wondered. Maybe he'd get on a camel and follow the crisscrossing gullies, calling out her name along the way and crying his heart out. You're late, she chided silently. Why didn't you cherish what you had? You turned down so many fine things in the world when someone offered them to you, but there will be none when you wanted them. He would not find her, even if he were to turn over every grain of sand. Ying'er had a feeling that she was playing hide-and-seek with him. She was resentful of his tardy return, but the possibility of his searching for her touched her. As she tossed more wood onto the fire,

tears ran down her face. She had always been like that—moved by her own fanciful fabrications.

The firewood was gone.

The jackals' circle tightened as the ring of fire grew smaller. Naturally, they'd noticed the disappearance of firewood. Humans could see their ferocity and they could detect human weaknesses. They shrieked in unison, their sound shrill and terrifying. Lanlan remained calm as she fired, but she wasn't reloading as fast anymore; she must be unsettled. Ying'er was unruffled, however. She thought she could see her beloved gazing at her. I can't lose my composure. I can't change my fate, but I must retain self-control. She knew no amount of crying or screaming would chase away the jackals, so she wouldn't cry. Then she noticed how the flames were shrinking. The flame was light, the light of life, the light of hope, the warmest object in the dark. But it was shrinking. She heard the jackals cheering. Food was no longer the focus of their contest; it had now transcended the material level, because they had stopped feasting on their dead companions. They had enough to fill their bellies, but the fire light and musket shots had obviously awakened a different instinct in them.

The fire went out. Darkness pressed down on them and highlighted a circle of green lights. Just as a cup of water cannot douse a burning mountain, their flashlight and musket shots were ineffective in intimidating jackals that were seeing a dawning victory. Lanlan slowed down even more as she reloaded, as if wondering whether she would continue the pointless resistance. They were in no hurry to pounce; instead they kept shrieking, as if frightened; maybe they were playing a game of cat and mouse. Anyone who has heard their sound knows how terrifying they are when hundreds shriek at the same time. It was the audio combination of rabid dogs barking, hungry wolves howling, shrews ranting, and butchers cursing, seemingly squeezed out between teeth, not from the throat, and accompanied by salivating and sinister laughs. Ying'er felt she was in a nightmare. The jackals slowly crept up, the green lights shimmering like water to shine on their drool, dripping as they moved.

Ying'er's only hope was for them to bite through her throat first before going after her intestines. What frightened her most was seeing her body fouled before she breathed her last; she abhorred the sight of her ugly self. She was reminded of the dead camel they'd found in the sand trough; it would break her heart if she were to die like that, and would prefer hanging or jumping down a well. She would hate for her flesh and her blood to be mixed with excrement, or swarms of green bottle flies buzzing around her, or, worse yet, for her body to nourish and sustain rows of their wriggling eggs. To her, the best way to end her life was to swallow a lump of opium, a reviled drug that can give rise to wonderful visions. They would be hallucinations, but delightful nonetheless. Life is an illusion, when she thought about it; everything before her was flowing east like a torrent, beyond anyone's grasp. That cherished thing called life was nothing but a sensation. Opium can end a life one no longer wants or can no longer possess, while creating a fantastic sensation, which naturally makes it the ideal solution. Ying'er wished she'd brought along the small cake of opium intended to ease Hantou's pain. Afraid he might use it to end his life, she'd hidden it in the rafters, pasted over with dust-paper. Then it occurred to her that the jackals would still tear her to pieces, even if she could kill herself with the opium. The flies would not shy away from depositing wriggling maggots on her remains. She felt like retching at the thought of maggots, so she prayed instead for the jackals to devour her completely and leave nothing behind. It occurred to her that, during sky burials in the Tibetan area, the lamas recited sutras to pray for the sacred vultures to finish off the dead completely. She had heard that it was unlucky if there was anything left, implying that the dead could not be reborn. It amused her to realize how fate had played strange tricks on her by changing her mind. Like the proposal for her to marry Mengzi. At first, she'd felt debased by the suggestion, but gradually she came to accept it until it eventually transpired into something she wanted but could not succeed in. And now this; she had been afraid of the jackals devouring her, but now she was actually praying for them to finish her off completely. Wasn't that amusing? There seemed to be no rhyme or reason in life.

The green glows were getting close enough for her to hear them panting. She waited for them to attack. After witnessing their jumps, she knew they could launch themselves into the air and, in a split second sink their teeth into her throat. Everything would be over at that moment, including her longing for him, her suffering, and her struggle. Maybe she'd sink into darkness; she wondered if she'd feel anything. Of course, she hoped she would; her heart tightened when she imagined herself turning into a senseless blob of darkness. Then she told herself not to overthink. She'd worry about that when the time came. Maybe lovely scenery awaited her at the end of her life—it was hard to tell, to be sure. The way she saw it, he had to be included in that scenery, which would lose all significance if he weren't.

With her eyes on the circling jackals, she stuck her neck out and said silently, "Come get me."

What are you waiting for?

She sensed a gust of wind rush toward her.

2

To her surprise, the blast of wind was followed by flames shooting into the air. Her nose detected the pungent odor of gunpowder. The fire leaped into the night sky, singeing her hair in the process. The jackals shrieked and stepped backward. Before she recovered from her shock, she saw Lanlan raise her hand, and the flames shot up again. Now she knew that Lanlan was sprinkling gunpowder onto the fire. It had a far more powerful effect than burning branches, so no wonder the jackals were scared.

"Don't just stand there waiting to die," Lanlan said. "Tear up the blanket and pour kerosene on it."

Ying'er got the idea; they had more things to burn.

With her dagger, Ying'er shredded their tent and a blanket. One blanket first, she said to herself. She'd cut up the other one later. They'd need a blanket if they made it out alive. She poured kerosene and camel hair on the pieces. They'd brought the kerosene for the lantern, without which they would not be able to travel at night. But they had to survive first. After pouring on the kerosene, she set the pieces on fire. She'd planned to put the burning blanket on the dead fire, but changed her mind after the fire began to roar; instead, she tossed the fire ball at the jackals. The bright, glowing ring of fire glided slowly eastward, landed on a jackal, and set its fur on fire. Terrified, it shrieked and, its back burning, dashed around, panicking the cluster of jackals to the east. They ran off. Jackals weren't particularly flammable, however, so once the kerosene burned off and the hair was gone, the fire went out. The jackal was still alive, though it howled from the pain, like a baying wolf.

Lanlan cheered. Putting down her gunpowder pouch, she lit balls of camel hair doused in kerosene and flung them at the jackals on the other side. It did the trick. The beasts ran off in all directions, but not too far; they refused to be sent off like that. After retreating some twenty meters away, they stopped and their green eyes stared back blankly.

"We can't wait any longer," Lanlan said. "We have to find a way to escape."

"All right," Ying'er replied, as she doused more blanket shreds and clumps of fur with kerosene, making sure not to pour on too much, just enough to set them on fire. She emptied two large plastic bags for the doused pieces, their homemade grenades, which she hoped would break open the siege. They loaded up the camels and secured the litter before gathering up their belongings. Lanlan held her musket and hung the gunpowder pouch around her neck. Each with a lighter and balls of camel hair, they got on the camels. Ying'er tucked away her dagger. I'm not going to stick my neck out for you to devour me, she thought, even if I'm doomed.

Riding in front, Lanlan had her flashlight on to cleave open the dark night ahead. The jackals just stared silently, as they had yet to recover from the shock, and hurried off to the side when they saw Lanlan coming. She had wanted to open fire to make way, so she was pleased when they moved off on their own.

"Let's take it slow and don't run. If we do, they'll think we're afraid." Lanlan told Ying'er, who had the fur balls ready to light and toss. Ying'er had been worried that the wind created by a running camel would make it hard to light the fur ball, so she said, "Sure. It's better to be slow. We can't outrun them anyway, and we'd just look afraid."

They wanted to go slow, but not their camels. Fearful of the teeth lying in wait, the camels snorted and let out long, monotonous cries. Lanlan had to jerk hard at the nose rings to keep them from dashing off.

Now that the jackals were quiet, Lanlan knew better than to provoke them. As they passed through the gap in the surrounding jackals, Ying'er flicked on her lighter, with a ball of camel hair at the ready. She would light the ball and toss it as soon as the beasts made a move. The jackals took a few steps back, as if they knew what she was thinking.

The flashlight beam shone on the undulating desert, where a faint, morning glow appeared in the eastern sky. It was the light of hope. Ying'er breathed a sigh of relief, as exhaustion crept up on her. She hadn't sensed fatigue under the intense pressure, but now her bones seemed hollowed out and her eyelids kept closing on her. For a moment, she even felt a loss of consciousness and wondered if she'd simply fallen asleep. She wished she could go to sleep, just close her eyes and sleep, even if a jackal were right at her heels.

Lanlan turned the flashlight to shine behind them. Under the beam, they saw the line of black dots had changed back to a circle and froze in the sand trough. The embers of their fire continued to send out a dim, yellow glow. A cool desert wind seemed to have risen from the camels' chiming bells; it blew over them like water and sent a chill into their hearts, a welcoming breeze to Ying'er. She was thirsty, from too much sweating, obviously. Putting the ball of fur back in the bag, she unhooked the jug from the camel litter and took a few drinks before handing it to Lanlan, who hung the musket around her neck, took the jug, and drank her fill. She had been careful with water, but the harrowing experience justified a reward.

The black circle grew smaller in the beam. Ying'er was relieved, though puzzled over how such fierce animals would be so frightened by ignited gunpowder and flying balls of fire. Maybe they were simply caught by surprise.

Dawn was deepening in the east. The wind turned cold and brisk, a wind the villagers called a downhill breeze, for it swirled down from Qilian Mountains. Just about every morning saw a wind like this. When the autumn harvest was over, the village old timers would rely on the wind to winnow the wheat. Ying'er felt it had taken some of her fatigue away. The camels snorted loudly, as if to celebrate the narrow escape, and began to speed up; Lanlan stopped jerking the reins. The farther they got away from those scary beasts the better, naturally, but Ying'er was afraid a faster pace would alert them. Lanlan shone the flashlight behind them, and they saw no black dots, for a sand hill had risen up between them and their foes. Feeling reassured, Lanlan let loose the reins, tightened her legs, and sent the camels flying.

Camel humps look sturdy, but do not provide as comfortable a ride as horses. When a horse takes off, its back rises and falls gently, while a running camel bucks its rider. Ying'er secured the plastic bag of fur to the rack so she could hold on to the hump with both hands. The last thing she wanted was to frighten the camel, for she would then lose control of her mount.

Sensing what might happen, Lanlan began to pace themselves. Her musket swayed violently across her chest, so she held onto it with one hand while tugging at the reins with the other. The camel was obedient enough to slow down. Ying'er's camel, following from behind, did the same.

But then they heard the jackals shrieking. Ying'er quickly retrieved a ball of fur. She flicked the lighter repeatedly, but each time it went out in the wind. After several tries, she finally lit the ball of fur and tossed it behind her, but it failed to stop the pursuing jackals, as they merely swerved to one side. The camels panicked and started running. When Lanlan raised her musket and fired behind her, she only heard a soft pop. The gunpowder must have spilled out during their bucking ride.

Ying'er clicked the lighter over and over, and yet the wind blew the light out each time. She knew they could no longer stop the jackals even if she set a whole bag of fur on fire. The desert was vast, with many paths, and they could avoid the fireball she'd struggled to light by simply making a slight detour. She put the lighter away and stuffed the fur back into the bag. With one hand on the camel's hump, she held the dagger in the other hand. So, this was it, the final struggle. Lanlan tried loading the musket several times, but the gunpowder spilled out each time, so she had to give up. The camel was running like mad, with no prompting from her legs. Their only hope for survival hinged on the camels' ability to run, though they both knew that jackals are one of the fastest creatures in the desert, and running alone would not spare them the beasts' sharp teeth.

Ying'er was not new to camelback riding, but they were mostly docile animals that moved at an even pace. It was her first time galloping like this, so she was nervous when her camel took off. Sprawling over the litter, she felt a constant pain in her tailbone from bumping against the hump, despite the blanket padding. It must be hard on Lanlan, she thought. After they shredded Lanlan's blanket, all she had were a few fur sacks. Seeing that fireballs could no longer stop the jackals, Ying'er unhooked her plastic bag of fur, nudged the camel forward to catch up, and handed Lanlan the bag to put under her buttocks.

It had gotten light out before they noticed it. Ying'er saw the pursuing jackals hang back a little, apparently still wary of any secret weapons they might have. That was good. The shrieks were now overpowered by the wind whipping past their ears and the clanking cooking utensils.

"Don't be afraid now." Lanlan shouted. "They should run off once the sun is up. Be careful and don't fall."

Her well intentioned reminder made Ying'er nervous. If I fell, she thought, I'd be immediately reduced to bones. What she feared most was the camel losing control over its front feet. With the desert filled with rats' nests, the camel would pitch forward if its stumbled into one of them and break a leg from the momentum. Rats' nests were mostly in the shady dunes, and that was where Lanlan headed, because the sunlit ones were covered in loose sand over which the jackals could run smoothly, while the camels could easily roll off.

Clearly the jackals were not ready to let a meal escape so easily. They continued their pursuit and grew bolder when they saw no more new tricks from their human targets. Speeding up as if engaged in a game, they got closer and closer, so unnerving the camels that their rhythmic pace faltered. If we keep running like this, Ying'er said to herself, it won't be long before the camel's legs give out. It was a terrifying thought, but the weariness in her heart overwhelmed her fear, so she gave the animal its lead. She could now hear the jackals' panting. Everything will be over, she thought, if they decide to outflank us after we go on like this for a while.

Out of the blue, Lanlan flung something into the air. Ying'er saw it was the plastic bag of camel hair. The jackals stopped momentarily but quickly sensed what it was, and swarmed up to tear the plastic to pieces. It was a hint to Ying'er. Lanlan hadn't stopped the beasts completely, but at least slowed down the inevitable. Grabbing the hump with one hand, Ying'er removed the sack of pots and pans with the other. She tried but couldn't untie it, and meanwhile a jackal was running alongside her camel, shrieking and threatening her. She sliced her dagger through the sack and, with a rip, its contents, pots, bowls, and chopsticks banged against each other as they fell to the ground with a crash. The jackals were stunned into standing still, probably mistaking the thundering objects as lethal weapons.

"That's right," Lanlan said. "Toss everything we can to save ourselves."

That was the break they needed to make some progress in their escape.

"Take out our spare clothing and leave only water and the steamed buns," Lanlan shouted. "Throw one item at them when they get closer. We'll worry about the rest later."

Ying'er groped around in the sack to retrieve the bundle of clothing when the shrieks again came upon her from behind.

Half the sun appeared in the sky, but the white disc emerging from the horizon made little difference to the jackals. The chase had turned into a farce for the animals, who displayed more interest in the women's colorful clothing. They ran up in great excitement when a piece drifted down; they tugged and pulled and tore, until shreds littered the ground like butterflies. One after another piece was flung off, piquing their interest again and again. Obviously sensing their opponents had run out of options, they took their time to enjoy the game of shredding clothes. Every time they finished off one item, they leaped and bounded happily. Fully aware that the pieces of clothing had slowed the arrival of death, Ying'er was nevertheless sorry to see them go. The last piece was a sky-blue blouse, a gift from Lingguan, testimony of his love for her. I won't throw this one away no matter what. I'll die with it. On a whim, she put on the blouse.

Lanlan had thrown away quite a bit on her end, which should have done whatever it was supposed to do. By then the sun had risen half as high as a white poplar. The sky was clear, with no red glow, meaning a hot day to come. But the pursuing jackals didn't look to be suffering from head pains. Lanlan said she got turned around running like this, but they would keep going east and would ask for directions if they met a shepherd later. The problem was, they couldn't shake the jackals, after exhausting their enthusiasm of tearing colorful clothes to pieces. The beasts were no longer interested in anything else they tossed after that. Worse yet, they seemed to be incensed by the women hurling objects at them, for they were shrieking loudly, menacingly. It sounded as if they'd seen through the women and knew they had no more tricks.

They'd start their final assault.

The sand trough was filled with their shrieks.

3

Jackals swept up like a whirlwind.

Ying'er stopped tossing stuff away now that the jackals had lost interest. Death was imminent, she knew, but she refused to accept it. A gloom rose inside, a common mood when she felt despair. The world was shrouded in a gray pall. The jackals' shrieks felt dream-like, so did the bumpy sand dunes and Lanlan, who kept turning to reassure her from the back of her hurtling camel. Ying'er could not believe she'd end up like this. A bleakness flared up from deep in her soul and felt like the sad notes from a village folk artist. She recalled how Lingguan had loved those stories and the weighty air, which she considered vulgar. What a surprise that she would recall those notes at the likely end of her life. The sorrowful strains felt like filaments of faint smoke hovering over the sand, deepening the illusion of dreaminess. She cast a dazed backward glance, and saw the jackals leaping like fleas on a hot skillet. They were coming for her life. Oddly, she felt only exhaustion, which rendered everything unreal, and she was transformed into a shadow.

The camel was bucking violently as it ran up and down sand troughs, nearly throwing Ying'er off. So what if I fall? She thought. I'll die sooner or later anyway. And yet, she lay down low and pressed tightly against the camel's hump. Lingguan once told her that your body is a castle of the gods. She had no time to pray to those gods inside her. Do what you will, she said to them. Go ahead if you want to fill the jackals' bellies. She was puzzled by her own thoughts, for it felt as if the jackals were chasing someone else.

The sounds disappeared behind her. She wasn't sure if they were truly gone or if it just felt that way. Either way they were just gone. The camel had stopped panting and the wind no longer whizzed by her ears. Everything seemed to freeze in a colossal piece of crystal. She could still feel the bumping sensation under her, though it, too, seemed faint. The bleak notes of a folk song lingered in her heart, where someone was plucking a zither, giving her a taste of spiritual struggle. This is real music, the notes condensed from souls over thousands of years.

She was so tired she wanted to go to sleep on the camel's back;

she wouldn't care even if the jackals were to chew her up. Despite the exhaustion, her mind retained a figment of wakefulness. Maybe the dim sensation of dreaminess was true wakefulness. She recalled how he was always saying that life was only a dream, which she'd refused to believe. With her arms around his young, vibrant body, she naturally hadn't accepted that life could be a dream. But now she was convinced; everything was indeed a dream, including her parents faraway at home, the jackals menacingly pressing close, the bumping camel hump, and her life, which hung by a thread. The musical strain of life was surely a dream as well.

Was this what people called "seeing through the mundane world?" She wondered, when one abandoned all hope, and everything felt unreal? A sense of regret drifted back and forth in her heart.

Lanlan slowed down, jerking her reins to maintain the right distance between her and Ying'er. But her camel had a different idea. It probably knew it could at least pass another camel, even if it couldn't outrun the jackals. Ying'er was grateful for Lanlan's action. It was only at times like this when you could tell if someone was a friend worth dying for. She thanked her fate for giving her a sister-in-law who was willing to die with her.

Lanlan was screaming, either to frighten the jackals or to draw them over to her. Ying'er laughed sadly. Would they fear her scream when they weren't afraid of her musket?

"Don't worry about me, Lanlan." She called out. "Run. At least one of us can make it out alive."

"What nonsense." Lanlan glared at her. "Don't worry. Their heads will start hurting once the sun rises higher.

Ying'er knew that Lanlan was trying to comfort her. She'd only heard of foxes getting a headache in the sun, not jackals.

She turned to look and saw them leaping and bounding, inching closer and closer. The closest ones were no more than fifteen feet from her camel. She could even see the greed in their eyes and the bared fangs, as well as the yellow sand they kicked up. The glance brought back the terror that had been lessened by her earlier sensation of illusion. It would be worse than death to be being bitten by those filthy mouths. Loathing for the jackals rose up inside, which made her tighten her grip on the dagger, despite her previous inclination to let Heaven take control of her life. Don't think you can sink your teeth in me so easily, she said silently.

"Walk carefully and don't roll off," she said to her ride, patting the camel's back. "I'll give the jackals a taste of my dagger."

The camel made a noise as if to tell her she could count on it.

Clenching her teeth, Ying'er struggled out of the fog of unreality, a dangerous condition, she knew. Jackals didn't care what state she was in, since she was clearly a meal to them. And death was clear too. No matter how she looked at it, she would let her parents down if she let the jackals shred the nice body they had given her without a fight. Tears flowed again when she thought about her mother. I shouldn't have said those things about you, Ma. If I make it out of here, I'll let you enjoy spicy fried intestines every day. She'd sell blood if she had to, but she knew it wouldn't be too hard to come by.

"Use your dagger!" Lanlan shouted. Ying'er turned her head to see a black dot leaping into her teary field of vision. Reflexively she plunged the dagger down and, it barely touched something, when she heard a shriek followed the black dot down a sand trough.

"Great! One down." Lanlan cheered.

Surprised, Ying'er looked at her dagger and sure enough there was blood. She was amazed at how easy it had been. On second thought, it made sense; a jackal was about the size of a leopard cat, and stabbing one was no different from knifing the other. Emboldened, she raised her dagger when she saw a jackal leap up as it went for her camel. Another surprise for her when several of her attempts came up empty, not even grazing the beast's hair.

Lanlan steadied herself to reload her musket. It took some effort to slip the ramrod into the barrel, but finally she saw progress, though she'd filled some gunpowder and spilled some. As she filled and tamped, she shouted at the jackals, like yelling at vicious dogs she'd run into back in the village.

Several of the jackals caught up with them. Like a cavalry soldier in the movies, Ying'er, much more courageous now, swung her dagger and sliced at them; she missed, but they were frightened enough to stay back. They shrieked and bounded, obviously trying to snap their opponents' nerves. She was afraid, but never let up stabbing. Her camel was the first to panic, as it began to twist and turn. She had to jerk the reins to keep it from running off; it was hard maintaining her place alongside Lanlan.

A jackal took the opportunity to pounce. It seemed focused on catching her dagger-wielding hand, but miscalculated and landed on the camel's tail instead. She raised her dagger and brought it down on the camel's backside. Blood spewed from a large gash and the camel panicked.

The smell of blood roused the wild nature of the jackals, which leaped up front, with the clear intention of blocking the camel. Her camel fell for their trick and swerved. "Grab its neck. Hold on tight!" Lanlan yelled. Before she understood what was happening, Ying'er was thrown off by a great force. She flew into the air and thought she even tumbled a few times when she felt sand pelting her. Keeping her eyes shut, she rolled over, as waves of sand lashed at her face. That's it, she thought. I'm in their maws now. Ma! She cried out. No matter how angry she'd been at her mother, it was she to whom she called out at this moment.

4

Hurry! Hurry!

Ying'er heard Lanlan's urgent shouts when she stopped rolling. She opened her eyes to see two thick camel legs, then Lanlan's hand reaching down for her. Ying'er got to her feet by holding the hand.

Come up! Lanlan yelled out again.

With difficulty, Ying'er climbed onto the camel's back by grabbing Lanlan's hand and stepping on her foot. Then she saw the fallen camel struggling on the ground, crying in pain, but it was already covered by jackals like fleas.

"It's hopeless," Lanlan said. "Its leg is broken. It probably stepped in a rats' hole."

Jackals continued to pounce on the bleating camel. One of them tried to get near the women, but Lanlan gnashed her teeth and put it down with one shot. She wasn't in a great hurry to leave, for she knew their fallen camel would provide enough food for the jackals for a while. She took her time reloading the musket.

Ying'er felt a buzz in her head, as if the sky had fallen. The camel had been Laoshun's favorite animal, which he'd refused to sell even when offered four thousand yuan. She'd have rather fed herself to the jackals. Staring blankly at the camel crying pitifully under the jackals' teeth, she wept.

"I wish I could take its place," she said.

"Don't say that." Lanlan comforted her despite her own sadness. "You can have everything when you're alive. With the two of us together, I don't believe we can't ever pay for that camel."

Ying'er finally felt the effect of the desert wind, blowing through her clothes and into her heart. She felt cold inside and out. The frenzied feeding of the jackals no longer disgusted her as much; the camel, quiet now, lay splayed on the sandy slope, only its feet showing, the rest of its body covered in jackals. The beasts left the two women alone and focused on the dead camel; they competed for food and began to bite and snipe at each other. Ying'er felt the sense of a dreamy illusion again when she thought about how a camel that had carried her running off just a moment ago was now reduced to jackal food.

"Let's go." Lanlan said with a sigh, after loading her musket.

She let loose the reins, and the camel, without prompting from her, turned and ran off. It must have been affected by its companion's fate, for it kept at a fast pace, even when sweat soaked its body. To be sure, the threat from jackals' teeth was a frightening whip.

Ying'er dried her tears. Crying is a waste of time, she said to herself.

"I can do without everything else, but I hate to lose that water," Lanlan said with a sigh. "But that's all right. We still have some left; we'll just have to pace ourselves."

The mention of water seemed to have turned on a switch of thirst and hunger, which came at them with a vengeance. They drank some water and had part of a steamed bun as they rode along.

"Lucky for us Pa was experienced and told us to divide up our provisions. If not, we'd die of thirst even if we managed to escape the jackals," Lanlan said.

"That just means we haven't suffered enough," Ying'er said with a sad smile.

"Don't worry. We have some gunpowder left. I'll get a couple of unlucky rabbits when we see them. I bet you've never tasted roasted rabbit. It's great, much better than roasted potatoes." Lanlan added, "Good fortune awaits those who survive a major calamity." She made a face.

Who knows if we'll survive? Ying'er thought. Maybe the jackals will come after us again after they finish off the camel.

Sleepiness spread like a large net when their nerves settled. They started to doze off, swaying back and forth on the camel's back. Lanlan tried to stay awake to make sure the camel kept to their route. They were lost in a place she'd never been before, but she knew they'd be fine so long as they kept going east. They would eventually reach Mongolia, where there were people, and that would be their salvation. With the two of them sharing one person's ration of food and water, they would not last long, and would become mummies if they just circled.

The camel was breathing harder. It had run a great distance, carrying two people, and it was using up the energy converted from the feed it had consumed the night before. It would not have any strength left if not for the hump supplying a source of nutrients. Lanlan knew they had to find a grassy area for the animal. They could rest too. She was exhausted, feeling as if she'd been hit by a tractor. Ying'er was sprawled against her, fast asleep. Lanlan feared that, without stopping to rest, they'd fall off the camel's hump, and it would be too much for the camel.

They rounded a sand ridge and saw some desert plants, which looked old but were still edible for a camel. Camels had a broad food source and ate most of the vegetation in the desert. Lanlan shook Ying'er awake, and they got down off the camel. Lanlan tied it to a shrub without removing the litter, and the two of them slumped onto the dry sand. They were in dreamland before they even lay down flat.

A long time passed when the scorching sun roused Lanlan. Her face was bathed in sweat and her throat was on fire. It was almost noon, and there wasn't a hint of breeze in the sand trough.

Their camel was gone.

Lanlan was stunned. She nudged Ying'er awake.

"The camel's run off," Lanlan said. A woman who did not like to show weakness, Lanlan was nonetheless choking up. Ying'er, who had been fighting jackals in her dream, felt her tongue turn numb when she heard. We're done for, she thought. The camel had our water and food.

This is the end for us.

They followed the camel's prints to search for their ride. They were lucky it hadn't been windy, so the camel's prints were clearly visible on the sand. Long rows of prints, some shallower than others, extended to the horizon. If the camel set its mind on fleeing, they would never catch it, Lanlan despaired silently. A running fox takes a human three days to catch. The same goes for camels, and it would take a very long time to reach it if the animal kept running. Theoretically speaking, camels understand humans and rarely run off at night. They know it is morally wrong to run away in a vast desert, no matter the reason. Besides, this one had been carrying their food and water. Lanlan had borrowed her ride from a neighbor, and it didn't have the same emotional bond as a family camel, which would never run away like that. Lanlan was overwhelmed by her feelings for the family camel; it had been the best in the village, and was called the King of Camels, after it had swung two wolves to their death when they hung on to its hump. It had done well when it went with Mengzi to Pig's Belly Well. Who could imagine that it would end up as jackal food?

Their breathing became labored after a while, for they hadn't completely recovered from their exhaustion. Lanlan wondered if the camel had left in search of grass and water, or if it had simply taken off. If the latter, then it was pointless for them to keep up the pursuit. They slumped to the ground and gasped.

"Let's keep looking for it. At least we should give it a try," Ying'er said.

They stumbled along the row of prints that swerved up a slope and down to a trough until they found a steamed bun that had rolled into an indention made by a two-toed foot. The camel was nowhere in sight.

"A camel like that deserved to be fed to the jackals," Lanlan said as she wiped off her sweat. "The one that should die lives and the one that should've survived died."

"Let's keep looking. The sack for the buns was obviously broken, so we'll at least catch some food even if we can't catch the camel."

Lanlan agreed, so they set off again. They came upon some buns and, after that, nothing but camel prints.

"Maybe the damned camel ate the rest of the buns," Lanlan said.

Sure enough, they found bits of steamed buns on a sandy spot.

"That's it," Lanlan said. "Let's turn back."

Chapter Twenty-Two

Puffy white clouds bring large raindrops
Dark clouds encircle the mountaintop

1

Baldy Wang was released as soon as Baigou turned himself in. The police let him out at noon, but he spent the rest of the day at the nearby lake and didn't slink through his gate until midnight, when all was quiet. He stayed inside after that, which made sense, since it had been a loss of face; to the villagers, being arrested was a disgrace. Their ancestors had said, "One would rather die in poverty than complain and would rather die a wrongful death than file an official complaint."

Several unusual incidents occurred over the following days. First, hens crowed, but badly, since they did not have the voice for it; still, they kept trying. Someone said the first to crow was Baldy Wang's spotted hen; it made eerie crows like weeping ghosts. With a butcher's knife Wang sent its head to the ground with a single swipe. But the hen refused to die; instead it flapped its wings and flew off at an angle, leaving a trail of blood outside his gate. Wiping the blood off his cloth shoes, Wang reacted with a blank look.

"What's a hen doing crowing like that?"

That surprised everyone. The next day hens crowed everywhere.

Next came howling dogs. One night the villagers heard eerie sounds coming from the desert. At first, they thought it was a woman venting her unhappiness after being beaten by her husband. Later they realized that the sound came from the ancient throat of an old dog. Then, as if joining a chorus, all the village dogs started to howl, sad and creepy. It was tolerable during the day, but the wails permeated the village after midnight, frightening anyone who heard it. "Maybe the end of world is here," they all said.

According to their ancestors, crowing hens and howling dogs presage a major disaster, one of which occurred in 1960, when the desert was strewn with the bodies of famine victims. The villagers panicked, everyone taking to burning piles of spirit money outside their doors to bribe gods—to beg for their protection—sprinkling their yard with lime powder—to keep out evil spirits—and hanging strips of red cloth on their gate—to ward off demons. From early morning to late night, the "protection chant," instructed by the Daoist priest, was heard everywhere: Heaven protect me, Earth protect me, Eight Guardian Deities protect me; protect my front and back, protect my nose and eyes, protect my soles and palms, so wind won't go through my ears and my body will be as strong as steel. Today the sky is clear, and the Grand Supreme Elderly Lord sent me here with his orders." When they walked out their gates, they beat the ground with peach branches while muttering, "The peach is of boundless origin, growing in the garden of the Queen Mother. First it defeats spirits from inside and outside the family, then it vanquishes demons and unscrupulous deities, and so on." For days, the villagers seemed to be wearing tattered clothing, for the wind passed right through. Their hair stood straight up. Sometimes even the sight of their own shadows made their scalps tingle and sent them screeching in fear, soon echoed by many others.

One night, when some villagers held a séance, a fox fairy appeared with the message that ten souls would be taken from the village as a warning to the world. The departure of the ten would be followed by the end of the world, when flood waters would reach the sky, the earth would be overrun by ferocious beasts, the ground littered with white bones, and the dead would have no place for burial. When the time came, there would be no sun, and the moon would be dim. Everyone would live in the dark. Rain storms that blotted out the sky would last ten months, gusty winds that uprooted trees would continue for eight months, with rampant plague, causing cannibalism. Evil-doers would have no place for a grave, immoral ones would suffer from painful boils that oozed bloody pus; they could not ascend to Heaven nor descend to Hell, and they could neither continue to live nor die. It would be the final testimony to karmic retribution. As a result, some bought packs of candles for the day when the sun and moon would not rise; some bought bushels of fried flour to stave off hunger when beasts overran the land. As soon as night fell, loud noises rose in the village, and if anyone cared to check them out, they would see sweaty men practicing martial arts and shouting something as they staggered around. They stretched their arms and kicked out their legs, thrust their necks and stuck their heads out, shouting as they practiced their martial art moves—iron palms, steel legs, metal shirt, golden shield, a deadly saber as powerful as five charging tigers, and a thunderclap sword. They wanted to master these moves to fight off the beasts when the time came. Some tied iron tiles to their feet and wore sand-filled vests, running down main roads day and night, popping neck tendons, in order to learn to fly and flee disaster. One out of every ten villagers had a dustpan under his arm and rode a small bench, following behind Grannie Shaman as she recited incantations, working hard on the skill of skipping along eaves, walking on walls, and flying into the sky.

2

Laoshun could not stop fretting. "Why is that dog howling like that?" It was contagious; all the dogs would start up once one of them howled, their baying sounds swirling and whirling, quickly permeating all of Shawan and nearly drowning out bustling White Tiger Pass.

One night, when the dogs started again, Laoshun went to get Meng Baye to see where the noise was coming from and whose dogs they were. Those that had howled at first had been killed by their owners and turned into pots of mouth-watering meat, which was then reduced to piles of stinky shit. They killed any dog that howled, greatly lessening the canine population, but the howling never stopped. Shortly after nightfall, the howls would start, spreading into the sky and all around the village, straight into the people's hearts.

A different sound was heard amid dog howls, soft and indistinct, either protection incantations or sutras to release the suffering souls of ancestors. Ever since hens started crowing and dogs howled there had increasing talk about the end of the world. The village had seen a sudden increase of filial offspring, who squeezed out enough money for the Daoist priest to perform rites to release the suffering souls of their ancestors, so they would be redeemed and become immortals or deities to protect their offspring. Hence, the sound of the rites, accompanied by the howling dogs, made such a din it was impossible to tell one from the other.

"Listen to that," Laoshun said. "Such chaos."

"It does feel like the end of the world's coming," Meng said with a sneer. "By the looks of it, the people will self-destruct, no need for gales, fire, or water. They're scared witless and they can no longer control their minds; they're like walking dead."

"They're out of their minds," Laoshun said. "That old hag of mine is into meditation again, saying I interrupted the previous round and this time she's going to finish the cycle."

"Let her go. She won't be happy till you do," Meng said. "I don't believe reciting a few words like that can help anyone avoid the great conflagration at the end of the world. When I see the priest one of these days, I'm going to burn him with my lighter and see if it leaves no mark."

They could hear the faint sound of howling dogs. On a moonless night like this, that sound brought sinister gusts of wind whirling out of the desert, into the village, and straight into the people's hearts. If there was a moon, it shrank and recoiled far back into the sky the moment a dog bayed, as if frightened by the sound, and emitted a ghostly white glow.

"This is getting weird," Laoshun said.

"What's weird about it? Every creature cries." Meng added, "Remember that year when the sky was overcast and it rained? We didn't see the sun for over two weeks. The foxes lined up and bayed at the sky, pleading with Heaven. Rain is bad for them, makes their cubs sick. A different explanation is, when rain floods the rats' nests and drowns them, the foxes will starve."

"But why is the dog howling like that?" Laoshun looked up at the lonely white moon, and then over at the village and the desert obscured by it. The sound of a howling dog continued to circle throughout the night.

"Every creature cries." Meng sighed. "And they have their reasons. When wolves bay, it's more terrifying than dogs. They line up, aim their mouths at the sky, and make this long, drawn-out howl. They're trying to chase off the gods of plague. Wolves fear plague too. It kills sheep, and wolves have nothing to eat, so they howl. I think the same goes for the dogs. In any case, there's always a reason."

"Like what?" Laoshun asked.

"How would I know? I'm not a dog."

Meng may not have known, but other villagers did. They were saying that the end of the world was near, and there's no more powerful reason than that.

As they walked along aimlessly, they could hear the dog howling, sometimes in front, sometimes behind, impossible to pinpoint. It could have just been echoes.

They found no howling dog after a long desert search.

"Let's go check on Baldy Wang, you old fart," Meng suggested. "I hear he's half paralyzed after the torture."

That sounded like a good idea to Laoshun. He'd never been close to Wang, but Baldy had once found one of his hawks and returned it to him without demanding compensation for the spotted rooster the hawk had killed. Laoshun remembered the kindness, so it seemed logical to go see Wang after what he'd been through. "Good idea. I was just thinking about going to see him," he said.

Meng bought two packs of soy milk powder along the way.

Wang was a different man, gaunt and dispirited. He didn't greet them when they arrived; instead he sharpened his knife, making a creepy sound. Laoshun could tell it was the butcher's knife Wang's father had used for decades. The blade, which had been two inches wide, was now only one. Impossible to say how many pigs he'd used the knife on. Wang's wife, on the other hand, was cordial. They could not afford medicine for her liver problem, so Meng brought back medicinal plants after each of his desert trips. The plant would then be cut into pieces and boiled to make a tonic, which had kept her illness at bay all these years.

"It's no big deal." Meng said to Wang, "Being blamed for someone's crime isn't uncommon. Don't let it get to you."

Wang ignored him and kept sharpening the knife.

"Remember how someone suspected me that year when the brigade trees were stolen?" Laoshun said. "I told them, I stand upright and walk a straight line; I wasn't afraid."

Wang tested the blade with his thumb without responding. His children looked at him with apprehension, then at their mother before glancing at the guests. They all seemed to be holding their breath.

"Don't be afraid when something happens and don't look for trouble when there is none," Meng counseled. "It's all in the past. They didn't do it on purpose."

"Of course, they did," Wang's wife retorted. "Poverty chills ambition, and hair hangs long on a skinny horse. No one dares make a noise about open graft and corruption. But we pinched a few pods and got such abuse. He was beaten and humiliated. If Baigou hadn't turned himself in, he'd have been blamed for sure."

"Hard to say," Laoshun said. "I never believed you did it."

"Maybe you didn't, but I didn't hear a word from you."

Laoshun's face burned. He had been convinced of Wang's innocence and had suspected Beizhou or Baigou, but he hadn't been courageous enough to speak up for Wang. Later, when he heard from the police that Wang had confessed, he'd believed them. "They said he confessed," he said.

"What else could he do?" She raised her voice as she walked over and pulled up Wang's shirt to show them the scars. Meng and Laoshun gasped as she continued, "They broke one of his ribs too. Where do we go for justice?"

Wang shoved his wife off coldly and shook his body to let the shirt fall before going back to sharpening the knife. The sound made Laoshun's teeth hurt, as if he'd been chewing on sand.

Silence fell in the room; neither Laoshun nor Meng knew what to say.

"Don't do anything stupid," Meng said to Wang hoarsely.

"He's right," Laoshun echoed. "When we run into a boulder, we walk around it. Decades go by quickly if you bear up, for your children's sake, if not for yourself."

Wang's wife sighed and glanced at him, but kept her mouth shut.

It felt awkward and uncomfortable. Wang had worn a hat for so many years that it had completely faded and the heavy paper around the rim had crumpled long ago. But he could not bring himself to throw it away. He wasn't the only bald man in the village, but, when he was around, no one dared to use words like "bald," "shiny bright," or "monk," for he would gaze darkly at you. He would not say anything offensive, but the stare was enough to send chills down your spine. Sometimes he'd suddenly say something disagreeable enough to stay with you a long time, though no one bothered to spend the time or mental energy to deal with it. Just the thought of his image was frightening, giving the feeling that the hat concealed not only his head, but also his inner world.

After sharpening for a while, he tested the blade again. Then he moved over to an old spring bed he'd found somewhere and busied himself with it. Laoshun wiped his sweaty forehead, the atmosphere getting too oppressive for him.

Wang's wife was obviously feeling that too, for she glanced at Meng with a pleading look on her sallow, bony face. Meng looked at Laoshun with a smile before saying in a loud voice:

"Dai. What are you doing, you old fart?"

Finally, Wang responded, "I'm going to kill someone."

3

Meng Baye and Laoshun walked out with a long sigh of relief after trying to talk some sense into Wang. Without knowing it, they'd both been holding their breath. A desert wind dispersed some of the pent-up feeling in their chests.

"For Baldy Wang, this is like hitting a bad leg with a club, with too many kids, a sick wife, and no son. How's he supposed to feel good after the recent abuse?" Meng said with a sigh.

"Do you think he'll really kill someone?"

"Hard to say." Meng heaved another sigh. "Everything will be all right if he can put it behind him. If not and he thinks he's at a dead end, he could do anything."

"He listens to you, so try to talk him around."

"I will, of course, but we have to be ready for anything. Go see Big Head and tell him to show Baldy some respect. Give him some compensation or at least say a few nice words. Baldy really hates Big Head, I think."

"Big Head has a big mouth and can't keep a secret, which would only make it worse."

"It's still better for him to go talk to Wang and show some good will. We should be on guard for any trouble. Wang has a different temperament than people who blow up like fried wheat, but quickly calm down. He's been holding things in for decades. He's like a powder keg, and it won't take much for him to explode."

They went to Big Head's house and told him about Baldy Wang sharpening his knife. They said he should find an opportunity to go see the man and mollify him.

They were unprepared for Big Head to fly into a rage.

"I might have given him a way out if he wasn't sharpening his knife, but he's gone too far this time. Does he think he can scare me? It was the police, not me, who arrested him. I didn't lay a finger on him." He wasn't done yet. "Don't take me wrong. It's just that I can't tolerate something like this. If I did, everyone in the village would be coming at me with a knife for trivial matters. I'm a man who won't wet himself just because someone threatens him."

"Don't worry," he added. "I figure Baldy Wang has the thought but not the guts to carry it through. Like they say, a barking dog never bites and a biting dog never barks. He wouldn't have told you if he planned to do it."

"Don't dismiss it so easily." Meng was still worried. "Say something nice to him if you can. It's not like pulling teeth. If you decide not to talk to him, don't tell anyone we came to you."

"Sure." Big Head was nonchalant. "Don't worry. You can lend him some courage, and he still won't have it in him to do it. Even if he does, he's not strong enough. Who is he going to kill when he's so frail he falls to the ground when the wind blows? Come in and have a drink." When the two older men shook their heads, he said, "Fine with me. I've got things to do." He went back inside, where they heard him say:

"Ah-ha, someone's trying to kill me."

"See that? He's turned your good intentions upside down," Laoshun chided Meng. "I bet he's going to find an opportunity to get back at Wang."

"Better a horse groom for a real man than an advisor to a simpleminded master. That's it then. We've done our best, he can do what he wants." Meng sighed and shook his head.

4

They made another round under the moonlight, but failed to locate a dog that started to howl in the distance once they were back at Laoshun's house.

"Damned weird. This dog is playing hide-and-seek with us."

"Forget it. It can howl all it wants. I don't believe it can turn our sky upside down," Meng said.

"You're right. We shouldn't be like a donkey afraid of its own farts."

"I'm going to start my seven-day meditation tomorrow, no matter what," Laoshun's wife said. "I've had chest pains ever since you interrupted my session last time. I've toiled all my life for others, so for seven days I'm going to live just for me."

"What's the point? There'd be no one left in the world if everyone became a Buddha after seven day's meditation," Laoshun said.

"Pa's right," Mengzi said. "Yue'er's mother did the whole seven days, but her head swelled up like a pig's when she left the cave."

"That's because she lacked piety," His mother said. "Grannie Shaman said she started causing trouble the moment she went in. She was punished by the Guardian Deities."

"Why didn't the Guardian Deities punish the Shaman? Think about our girl. Before she went in, she was reasonable and cared about you and me. But after she started, we're like total strangers to her," Laoshun complained.

"Pa's right. I'm like a pig in her eyes now," Mengzi said.

"Lanlan has suffered enough," Meng Baye said.

"I'm going to do it, no matter what you say. Everybody else is, so I have to. I heard just one session of meditation can bring peace and quiet to the family. I've been having bad dreams lately, and I've got a twitch. I'm worried something bad will happen. Ever since Hantou died, I feel my heart is in my throat all the time. One meditation will put my mind at ease."

"I wouldn't be so sure," Laoshun sneered. "When is your mind ever at ease? In the past, you were always running off to see the Shaman or burning spirit paper, kowtowing or offering incense. You said that was the only way to put your mind at ease. After going around and around like that all your life, is your mind at ease yet? Good fortune is never bad, but bad luck can't be avoided. I don't believe any calamity can be avoided if you mumble for seven days like a cracked pot bubbling with shit. Didn't Baldy Wang finish seven days of meditation? Then how come he was blamed for someone's crime and sent to jail?"

"You see!" she cried out. "He left after three days, which is why disaster found him. Have you heard of anyone leaving halfway through a meditation session? You have to stay even it means you die in there. How could he stop? I heard the Shaman say he'd meet with terrible retribution."

"What kind of believer is she? She's always hoping to see others suffer. The Shaman never means what she says," Meng said.

"That's right," said Laoshun. "When I see that old witch, I feel my breath catch in my throat."

"You're terrible." His wife retorted. "When you need her help, you call her qinjia this and qinjia that, your voice dripping with honey, almost wish you could kiss her ass. When you don't need her, you curse her. Why didn't you give her hell that time when she tried to find a wife for Mengzi?"

"Is Mengzi's marriage settled?" Meng asked, tilting his chin toward Ying'er's room.

"Forget it. The people in the Bai Family are terrible," Mengzi's mother said. "They sent her back, maybe to snatch the baby?"

"Quiet!" Laoshun spat. "It didn't look like that to me. She's a widow, so we let her stay if she wants. If not, we should be clear and let her go. Why must you spew all that bullshit?"

"Then you talk to her when she returns from the salt lakes, if you know what to do. Tell her you don't want her to stay, and ask her to find another husband."

"That's not the way to go about it. This is her home. She went through the proper rituals to marry into your family. Where can she go?"

Meng Baye offered.

"It's not that easy," Mengzi's mother said with a sigh. "No one ever thinks about my feelings. I'm worried sick about the baby being taken away. It's happened before. When they take the baby, where will you go to complain." She lowered her voice, "I have a feeling her family has sent her back. Otherwise, that mother of hers would have made several trips here and raised hell already. Why are they so quiet? Think about it. What kind of woman is she? A shrew, a tigress. Why isn't she raising a stink?"

"You're mad at her when she comes to raise hell, and now you're unhappy when she doesn't." Meng Baye laughed. "Mengzi, go to the Bai Family and ask them to come raise hell tomorrow. Tell them your mother craves action."

"You horrible wretch. Your skin itches for a good beating if you're left alone for three days," Laoshun said.

"It's not that I want them to raise hell, it's just . . . why aren't they? For a while she was here every day, carrying on. And now, isn't it strange that she's so quiet?"

"The Bai Family can do what they want, but you shouldn't doubt Ying'er. She has a good heart, not at all what you think," Meng said. "She's been in your family for several years now, so you should know her well."

"Everyone changes," she said. "No matter how you look at it, Bai blood flows in her veins. A broken bone bends inward. She has to be partial to her own family."

"Maybe not. If she wanted to remarry, she'd have stayed with them."

"Stayed with them?" Mengzi's mother said. "If she'd stayed there, she wouldn't be able to keep the baby with her."

"It's her baby, she can do what she likes. Let her take the baby with her, if that's what she wants."

"Right." Mengzi echoed. "I don't believe she'd do a worse job than you raising the baby."

"But he's Hantou's son. He'd have to take their name if he lived with them. Besides, who knows if Mengzi will give us a grandson one of these days. I feel much better with a healthy boy with us now. Otherwise, if you have one girl after another, you'll be weighed down by fines."

"You don't have to worry about me," Mengzi replied with a smile. "I'm pretty open about this. It'd be great to have a son to care for me in my old age. If not, I'm prepared to be fed to the wolves. In Nanshan even the most beautiful girl has a sky burial. Vultures probably wouldn't care for a dolt like me, but wolves won't mind."

"Stop saying things like that," his mother chided. "You can eat whatever you want, but be careful what you say."

"Then stop nagging. There's no need to think so far into the future. Aren't they all saying the end of the world is near? You can think as far into the future as you want, but once the world ends, you turn into ashes."

"End of the world this and end of the world that." A smile finally appeared on her face. "While we're alive, we just worry about today. In any case, I'm going through with the meditation."

Meng laughed. He was about to tease her when he saw a scheming look on her face as she said softly:

"Be careful over these seven days. Ying'er is in the desert, but her family isn't asleep. Make sure they don't come and take the baby."

Meng laughed. He'd expected something more important than that.

"I thought something good might come out of your mouth," Laoshun said unhappily. "You keep bringing up the same thing. Don't you have anything else to say?"

Mengzi shook his head and laughed.

Ignoring her husband's attitude, she explained, "I'd have gone in long ago if not for my concern for the baby. But I've asked Grannie Shaman for her prediction. During those seven days, Ying'er can't take the baby away, because the Guardian Deities will be protecting her. But still, you need to be careful."

5

Later that night, Mengzi's mother sat on the kang in the study to go through her bundle. It counted as her safe, and no one was allowed to touch it. Back when she and Laoshun were engaged, he had followed the custom of buying a length of fabric for her to sew into a bundle and tie with red string on which hung a coin. After decades of use, the red had faded; the coin was rubbed shiny, with an aging yellow sheen, bright and smooth. She loved to dig through the bundle, whether she was in a good mood or not. When in high spirits, it was a pleasure to look at its contents, and at other times, it helped ease her concerns. Whenever divorce was mentioned, she tucked it under her arm and walked out of the house. It was the only thing that was truly hers; the rest belonged to her husband's family. She had the right to take it with her, even if they did not go through with the divorce. Other than the bundle, she could not take a thing, nothing at all.

The custom had been in practice for hundreds of years.

What was in the bundle? Everything. She stuffed whatever she liked in there. There were her sons' baby clothes; Hantou had worn them first, then Mengzi, then Lanlan and Lingguan. She had wanted to give them to Panpan, but Ying'er thought the fabric was too coarse for the baby's skin. There was also a pair of insoles. She had made quite a few of them before her marriage; most had been given away as wedding gifts, and now she had only one pair left. The embroidery work was too fine to use, so she kept them as evidence she'd once been young and unmarried. There were also clothes, old and new, and fabric, filling it up and turning it into a true bundle.

She felt like her own mistress only when she rummaged through the bundle. She could give any item away and do what she wanted with the others. Anything else she would have to talk over with Laoshun. "Talking it over" was really just an expression, because when they agreed, they followed her idea and when they didn't, he took charge. It was a Liangzhou custom that men were the head of the household. Laoshun even taught his sons, "You have to use the tip of your tongue to call me Pa, but with your Ma, you only need the lips." Which was proof that father was closer to the children, and had more authority.

People said Liangzhou residents' ancestors mostly originated from the Qiang Tribe, who were portrayed as power-worshippers in ancient texts. Laoshun could never be an official, but his desire to be one never faded. He had hoped his sons would go to college, to win honors for the family, and become officials. But in vain he chased his dream of making his ancestors proud, like a dog chasing a pig's bladder. He fulfilled his wish to be an official at home. He beat his wife when they were younger, and now that he was older, he hadn't done it so often, but he refused to compromise whenever he felt his authority was threatened. Back when his children were in school, he never missed a parent-teacher meeting, because he was the master of the house. A master, no matter what.

When he saw his wife fiddling with the bundle again, he said to her in a tone unique to the "master of the household":

"You're playing with that bundle of rags again? What for?"

His question was an encroachment on one of the few rights she had as a woman, so she looked up and snapped at him:

"It's my bundle. I can do what I want with it. It's none of your stinking business."

"All right, all right." Laoshun had to concede. "Go ahead and fiddle all you want. We'll see if all that fiddling can produce a gold bar."

"You couldn't have it even if it did."

"I don't want it. I wouldn't want it," Laoshun said as he glanced at the bundle and saw something unusual. It was a piece of fabric. He knew his wife's bundle had nothing but old, shabby stuff, but this piece was brand new. The material looked to be quite good too, so he flicked it open. It was indeed heavy, high-quality material. "Where's this from?"

His wife snatched it away from him, folded it and put it back in. "Where do you think it's from? We can use it again next time there's an engagement."

Now Laoshun remembered; it had been the fabric for Ying'er when she and Hantou got engaged. "Did she give it to you?"

"Give it to me? It's from us; it's ours. Look, with the old witch in the Bai Family acting like a rabid dog, we're not going to get it done our way, and sooner or later she'll have to leave. She can go but she's not taking a single thing with her."

It finally became clear to Laoshun that his wife had taken it. "How could you do something like this?" he raged. "This is like trying to get rid of her. You said no one can touch your bundle, so how could you rummage through hers?"

"Everything in there is from us," his wife said. "It was intended for a daughter-in-law, not an outsider. But now she's had a change of heart, so I won't let her take anything, not even a needle."

"How can you say that? She ran back in the middle of night and said she'd rather die here. She never once said she'd remarry."

"Of course, she wouldn't say that. She knew what she wanted, and this was a smoke screen. She may be honest and upright, but there's a devious person working behind her. How can you guarantee she's not harboring wicked thoughts?"

"Wicked thoughts? You're the one with wicked thoughts. She's fine with spending the rest of her life here. What you did is unworthy of her."

"Oh, no," His wife cried out. "You see the surface, but never what goes on inside a person. Mao Dan's sister-in-law looked fine, but she ran off with their baby and everything."

Laoshun sucked in cold air. What had happened in Mao Dan's family was similar to his own: the oldest son had died and the second son, Mao Dan, wanted to marry his brother's wife. She had agreed, but ran off with baby and her money when no one was paying attention. Mao Dan's father wanted to take her to court, but it was her money and her baby; she could thump her chest and declare her rights under heaven, for she had the law on her side. Regret had festered in Mao Dan's father's heart for years until he got cancer; he screamed in pain like a cow for months and then died. For Mao Dan, it was like dew wetting only half the hill. It was bad to begin with, but he did nothing to make his life better, and that was how he became what he was.

"Every word that woman said was like music, but she ran off, even after sleeping with Mao Dan, when the rice was cooked, as they say. A couple can sleep in the same bed, but their thoughts are hidden from each other. You can draw the look of a tiger but not its bones, and you know a person's appearance, but not his heart. If we don't watch out, when something bad happens it'll be too late."

She nearly convinced him when he realized that she had changed the subject and grossly exaggerated the significance of the fabric. "You can watch out, but why did you take her fabric?"

"It's not hers. It's ours." His wife lowered her voice and continued, "Be careful over the next few days. It won't be a big deal if she takes off with our stuff, but we have to make sure the baby stays."

What she'd said turned Laoshun's attention away from the fabric to the baby.

He'd never let her leave with the baby, that was certain. For one thing, the boy was Hantou's son, but more importantly, Mengzi might not give them a grandson later. Lanlan had tried everything to have a baby boy, but nothing worked. There were quite a few in their village, like

Beizhu and Baldy Wang, who wanted a son so much their heads hurt, in order to have someone to continue their family lines. With Hantou's boy around, Laoshun would have no worries; even if Mengzi did not come through, he'd just adopt Hantou's son. That made things easier. Laoshun's scalp tingled just thinking about the fine for having too many children. No one could take the boy away.

"I've thought it through," his wife whispered. "Just being careful isn't going to be enough. You can't be careful all the time. Even a tiger dozes off now and then. If she finds a chance to take off with the boy, there's nothing we can say about it. I've asked around, and everyone says that she's the mother and it's her right to take the baby with her. She has the law on her side."

"Not necessarily," Laoshun said. "The people at the court have a heart too. I'd pit my life against anyone who ordered me to give up my grandson, after my son had died."

"Who do you think you can scare? You're a small arm up against a big leg. The court represents the law. They could drown you with her spit. We have to think of something."

"What do you have in mind?"

"I think we have to find a way to send her off without the boy. If the court orders us to give him up, I'll fight with my life. and I don't believe the court can do anything about it."

"This is her home. People would laugh at us if we sent her away."

"We'll use trickery," his wife said. "She's scared of many things, isn't she? When she returns from the salt lakes area, I'll get Mengzi to pretend he's a ground-pounding ghost. He'll raise a din or make scary noises. She'll leave after a few nights."

Laoshun was incensed. He stared at her with slitted eyes for a moment. "How in the world did you come up with something like that? Who is she? She was Hantou's wife and your daughter-in-law. You want to frighten her after she lost her man? You're worse than an animal." Her face reddened as she realized that her idea was too vile, so she kept her mouth shut and got into bed. Her eyes were barely closed when a spot on her leg started twitching. Experience told her that a twitch augured no good news. It put her mind on tenterhooks. Would something terrible happen while she was in meditation? she wondered.

6

Baldy Wang moved into the open to sharpen his knives. Now everyone could see what he was doing, as he worked on the knife he used on cows, then the one for pigs, and finally an old chopper. "I'm going to kill someone!" he shouted from time to time. Everyone said he might go through with it if her remained quiet, but no one believed him when he yelled. "Something's wrong with his head," they said.

He fashioned a suit of armor out of the wire from an old spring mattress after finishing with the knives. When people asked what he was up to, he shouted, "I'm going to kill someone!" They'd laugh, "Cutting off your old dick is more like it."

He put on the suit every night at the bridgehead to practice moves. Leaping forward and jumping back, he looked fierce, but staggered on unsteady legs. He was slaying someone in his imagination. Laoshun tried several times to talk him out of it, but Wang kept quiet as he dashed about madly before tripping and falling to the ground, where he stretched out his limbs and panted like an exhausted cow.

"I'm going to kill someone." he shouted, breathing hard. "I'm going to do it."

The villagers laughed. No one believed he'd actually kill someone. Like they say, a barking dog never bites and a biting dog never barks. He wouldn't make his intention public if he really meant to do it.

One night after taking food to Baldy's wife, Laoshun stopped to rest at the Earth God Temple by the Vajravārāhī Cave, when he heard panicky shouts:

"Baldy Wang has killed someone. He did it."

Laoshun thought it was a prank, but the racket got closer, and he saw a crowd. He put down the cup he was holding as Fengxiang ran out of a house near the cave and turned on the porch light before a figure with a head as big as a cow's swooped up.

"Is that really you, Baldy?" Laoshun called out.

"Get out of my way!" It was indeed Wang. "Get away from me." Wearing his suit of armor and a motorcycle helmet, he wielded a chopper in one hand and a long knife in the other as he screamed, "I'll kill anyone who stands in my way. I'm after Big Head's wife and no one else." He stormed into the meditation cave, where a commotion erupted and practitioners fled. Huilanzi shrieked and followed them out.

Wang gave chase.

"Hurry, somebody," Fengxiang shouted, "Get a weapon."

Laoshun picked up a shovel handle, but before he made a move, Wang shouted, "I'll kill anyone who gets in my way. Every injustice has its perpetrator and every debt has its debtor. I'm here to collect my debt, and the rest of you better stay away. My knife can't tell you apart."

Laoshun hesitated, while the Daoist Priest ran out, grabbed the shovel handle from him, and ran after Wang. By then Wang had caught up with Huilanzi and brought his knife down on her thigh. She screamed and fell to the ground. In the meantime, the priest's handle landed on Wang's helmet with a muffled thud. Wang staggered but remained standing, never letting up his attack on Huilanzi.

Several other men picked up weapons and ran up to beat down on Wang, but his armor blunted most of the attack. "Dai. You have to pay with your life if you kill someone," Laoshun yelled at Wang, who replied, "I don't want to live any more. Stop hitting me, or my knife will take you too." His voice sounded really scary.

"Help me!" Huilanzi cried out repeatedly in the pool of her own blood. An anxious Laoshun picked up a hammer, and, aware of Wang's protective armor and helmet, aimed at his leg. Wang fell to the ground, got up, and, with a hideous look, yelled at the crowd, "Don't hit me again, or I'll kill you all." He limped off.

Huilanzi was writhing in the bloody pool, her face a mess, though it was hard to say if she was seriously injured. Mengzi's mother was shaking uncontrollably, but her mind was clear enough to say, "Get her to a doctor." The Shaman laid a blanket out on a hand cart, they laid the injured woman on it, then dashed off.

Before they caught their breath, Beizhu ran up a hill, where he shouted, "Hurry up. Baldy Wang is going to kill Huilanzi."

"He's done that already," one of the villagers replied.

"Big Head's kids are dead. Lucky for him, he's not home." Beizhu added, "Baldy was asking about Huilanzi, so Meng Baye sent me here to alert you."

"Aren't the two kids all right?" Mengzi's mother asked.

"Dead. They're both dead," Beizhu said. "We wouldn't have known if Baldy hadn't asked about Huilanzi. Big Head sure picked a night to go out. If he'd been home, the kids would've been fine."

"Big Head would have been dead too," Laoshun said. "He's wearing armor, hitting him with a club feels like scratching an itch."

"Where is he?" Beizhu asked.

"He ran off," said Laoshun. "He actually went ahead and killed someone. I thought he was just trying to scare us."

"I didn't believe him either," others echoed.

7

There was blood everywhere in Big Head's study. The two kids were a bloody mess, their faces beyond recognition. The plaster wall was blood-spattered, the blanket on the kang was largely soaked through. Everyone who came in gasped.

Shuddering, Laoshun felt like this was a dream. The overhead light swirled, emitting rings of light to create a hazy atmosphere. Fellow villagers' surprised cries sounded unreal, while a hammer in his head banged away at his temple.

"Big Head doesn't know yet," Beizhu said. "That ass is probably having a good time somewhere."

"The kids were innocent. Why did Baldy have to kill them?" Mengzi's mother shivered, unable to say more.

"Who knew he'd actually do it?" someone said, to which several villagers added: "That's true."

"Baldy is so quiet, like a sealed-gourd, but once he decided to act he carried out something shocking."

"Someone like him is the scariest. The talkative ones say what's on their minds. But him, a sealed-gourd, he keeps everything in and stews over it."

"Where is he now?" Meng asked.

"No one knows." Laoshun replied.

"Quick, let's go find him," Meng said. "Beizhu, you call the police. The rest of you, get a rope or a club, and let's go find him. Killing one is no different from killing many. He could be in a murderous rage, and may want to deal with everyone who'd gotten on his case."

"You're right. Remember the guy from Nanxiang? He murdered over a dozen people in one night," Laoshun said, and sent fear to everyone's heart. They were worried Wang might go slay their children during their absence from home.

"Let's go to my house and see," a villager said, and several more began to clamor. Meng told them to get ropes and clubs ready before checking everyone's house with flashlights. Luckily for them, Wang did not take the opportunity to attack more houses.

With his heart in his throat, Laoshun picked up the hammer handle. Wang and he had no past grudges, but he had used the handle on him a while ago. He wondered if Wang had seen his face; if he had, then Wang would surely want to seek revenge. He sent his wife home and told Mengzi to lock the gate and be ready.

Meng wanted the other meditating women to go home and lock their doors, just in case the unthinkable happened. "The best is for several families to stay at the closest neighbor's house. With enough people around, you can watch out for each other. Men, take your weapons and go find Baldy Wang."

"He has his armor on, so you can't hurt him unless you hit him on his calf or foot," Laoshun said.

"Get two men to trip him with a rope and hold him when he's on the ground. He won't be able to fight."

Suddenly they heard shrill calls for help. Meng could tell it was coming from the direction of Wang's house, so he raced over with the group of men. Laoshun was light-headed, but didn't want to lag behind, so he stumbled after them, barely able to keep up.

After rounding a corner, they were stunned to hear the shouts coming from Wang's house. It was his wife, shouting at the top of her lungs, "Help." Her daughters were wailing amid the thuds of someone breaking down a door. "Open up, damn you! I did kill people. We agreed, didn't we?"

Meng shushed and everyone stopped to listen. It was Baldy Wang.

"Spare us. The girls are so young. They didn't do anything." The woman was sobbing.

"It'll hurt, but it'll be over quickly." Wang shouted. "When I'm gone, they'd harass you and the girls until you died too. Didn't you promise to die with me?"

"I did, but the girls didn't," she said. "They're still young."

"Are you going to open the door or not, damn you?" Wang yelled. "I'll break it down if you don't."

Then came the pounding of a foot on a door, accompanied by the frightened wails of the woman and her girls. The door did not give, so Wang screamed, "I'm going to split it open." He attacked the door with his knife.

"Quick. He's lost his mind," Meng shouted and ran up, but the others were afraid to follow him. Meng yelled out, "Baldy Wang, the police are here. Put down your knife." He shone his flashlight in Wang's direction and saw the monster turn to look at him. Wang kicked the door again before running into the desert behind his house.

"That was close," Laoshun said. "Who knows how many more lives he'll take if he carries out a murderous spree during the dark night."

Now that Wang had fled, the villagers were finally courageous enough to go up to knock on the gate. The woman and her daughters were crying inside, but they were afraid to open it for them.

"People say even a ferocious tiger won't harm its cubs. I can't believe Baldy Wang would want to kill his own family."

"Didn't you hear him? They'd agreed to die together, but she had a change of heart," Laoshun replied. "Now what?"

"We have to find him. If not, he may kill more before the night is over," Meng said. "Don't be afraid. He's not very strong."

"I know he's not," Yue'er's father said. "But I'm still afraid. He's a demon."

"Afraid or not, we have to catch him. He's like a rabid dog now, he'll kill anyone in sight. He's very dangerous," Meng said, while shining his flashlight on Wang's footprints that led the way into the desert.

8

The villagers slowed down in the desert, their clubs held in readiness. They were out in the open, while Wang was somewhere unknown. Blood would flow if he launched a sneak attack. They could only take comfort in the rows of footprints that showed the direction of his flight. He could not put his feet on his shoulders to lie in wait, which lessened their fear.

The early morning downhill wind was like ice water on their hands and faces. Roosters were crowing, not ignoring their jobs just because there had been murders the night before. Suddenly hungry, Laoshun found going tough.

The sand hills rose higher as they made inroads into the desert. Wang had traveled in the dark, and, too panicky to see where he was going, left many prints on shifting sand off the usual paths. The villagers' feet sank into sand causing them to pant loudly from the effort.

At last, they saw bits of his armor next to a large patch of chaotic footprints. Possibly, he'd been so worn out when he reached this spot that he'd stopped to rest and shed half of the spring mattress before taking off again. Meng told everyone to be prepared, for he did not think Wang could be far away.

The prints pointed in the direction of Wolf's Tongue Bend, a remote and quiet cove frequented by wolves, rarely by humans. When they had trouble with wolves, they could hear them howling from there. What was Baldy Wang going to do?

Their presence was exposed by flashlights beams, so they didn't have to keep quiet.

"When you think about it, Baldy has suffered a lot. I haven't seen him smile most of his life," Meng said.

"That's true. He has no son and his wife is always sick." Laoshun added, "And no money to send his girls to school."

"The old hag of mine told me he left halfway through the mediation practice. Later he was blamed for someone else's crime," Yue'er's father said. "And now this. Could it be retribution?"

"Retribution? I don't believe a word of it. I smashed the Vajravārāhī's tablet. How come I didn't suffer any retribution from her? This is all because Baldy lost all hope," Laoshun replied.

"You're right. Others suffer too, but they still have the Vajravārāhī. Not him. He has nothing. He's worked hard all his life, but has never managed to lift himself out of the pit of poverty. He has nothing to live for and feels bullied by everyone. Life means nothing to him."

"That's true," the others echoed. "It's so true."

An expert hawk trainer, Laoshun had keen vision. He searched like a hawk while taking part in the conversation. He followed the footprints with his flashlight and spotted something hanging on an Artemisia bush. On closer examination, he saw it was Wang's motorcycle helmet. "Enough talking now. Be careful. Don't let him sneak up and stab you," he said to the others. That's odd, he was thinking. Why does Baldy keep leaving things behind, like markers? What does it mean?

The villagers swept the area with their flashlights and discovered something else hanging on a clump of desert plants. It looked to be clothing, but no one was courageous enough to walk up and see. Beside the footprints in the sand, Laoshun also noticed a dark line; he touched it with his fingers. It was blood, still fresh.

"He's over there." Meng shouted. Sure enough. A dark lump surfaced in the beam of his flashlight, and the drops of blood leading up to it.

Meng got two men to hold the end of a rope each to trip Wang if he pounced. Then he told the others to keep their clubs ready. "Baldy," he shouted, "things blow over sooner or later. Why did you do something like that? The kids were innocent."

The dark lump was quiet.

With a club in one hand and a flashlight in the other, Meng inched cautiously over. Afraid that something could happen to his old friend, Laoshun followed, his flashlight gliding ahead. He was wary that the dark lump might be a decoy and that Wang was hiding in the dark, waiting for a chance to attack. Then he noticed something like a rope hanging on another shrub. He went up to check and saw it was a section of intestine. Stupefied, he cried out, "Guts!" Meanwhile, Meng had discovered another organ, so did the others. Some had started throwing up.

Several beams were trained on the dark figure to show it was really human. No one could say for sure if it was Wang, but it was no doubt a man. The abdomen was bared and a bloody mess, with a gaping hole, from which the organs had been dragged out. His face was marked by cuts, too disfigured to be recognizable, like Big Head's kids.

"It's him. I recognize his shoes," Meng said.

Laoshun did too. The shoes were called cow-licks, homemade, of rawhide; they looked clunky and ugly, but were sturdy enough to last many years. Wang was the only person in Shawan who wore those shoes.

"Is he still alive?" Laoshun asked. Meng went up to check and sucked in cold air. "No. He's long dead."

Dark blood had seeped into the sand, which was churned up, a clear sign that Wang had waged a frenzied battle before he died, but the opponent was himself.

"He'd obviously made up his mind to die," Meng said with a sigh. "Look at his insides. He cut them up so much not even an immortal could have saved him."

Everyone shuddered. The icy wind swirled around them, seemingly cutting into their hearts.

The flashlights were trained on Wang. On his mutilated, bloodied face were wide-open eyes, glaring at the inky dark sky.

9

The police came two hours later, followed by a crowd from the village and some sand boys. The sun stuck its head out from behind a sand hill to gaze down on the police, the villagers, and Wang's bloody corpse. It was as gloomy as ever; even the wounds could not cover up his perpetual look of glum, which had actually intensified because of the fading of life.

The section of intestine swayed from the shrub in the morning wind, like a showy, but hideous banner. It was the most extravagant act of Wang's life.

Big Head was absent; he had taken his wife to the city. Pockmark Wang, the village doctor, had gone along, trying his best to staunch the blood on the road; otherwise, she'd have bled to death before they reached the hospital. The villagers learned that she might live and might not. With no time for the dead children, Big Head told someone to ask Meng to take care of the matter. He likely could not bring himself to face the scene.

The police took pictures of Big Head's house and collected evidence before heading out to Wolf's Tongue Bend for more photos. It was an open-and-shut case, clear as fleas on a bald man's head, but they puzzled people by asking useless questions. What surprised the villagers was a new discovery they'd made: Baldy Wang's wife admitted she'd known of her husband's planned murder. Which meant she'd failed to inform the police and was an accomplice, more or less. She argued that she had told quite a few people about his plan, but that no one had believed her. She'd told Big Head too, but guess what the man said in response? "I didn't grow up being scared all the time."

Laoshun believed her, so did Meng Baye and everyone else. She was pretty much absolved, but the police took her in anyway, leaving her daughters behind to cry.

Meng told Mao Dan to wrap Big Head's sons in the bloody sheet and carry them over to Wolf's Tongue Bend. For the locals, dead children might be small, but they were imps, and could cause trouble, so they must be cremated. It usually fell to Mao Dan to carry out this task, and usually at Wolf's Tongue Bend. It would be best if the corpse was burned completely; if not, the wolves and foxes or wild dogs would take care of the rest. Baldy Wang had come here probably wishing to fill the wolves' bellies. They didn't use wood coffins, but cremation was still better than tossing the bodies out in the wild to bake in the sun.

With glassy eyes, the villagers held their breath as they looked at Wang and the two boys. Following Meng's instructions, they gathered a large pile of firewood. Shuangfu sent one of his sand boys over with a jug of kerosene. Mao Dan placed the bodies on the wood, collected the organs, poured on kerosene, and lit the fire to send the bodies dancing in the flames.

The murderer and his victims were engulfed in the fire, no longer clear who was strong and who was weak, except that the boys seemed jerkier. After the sheet was burned, their fair bodies turned black from the smoke and twisted madly, as if in unbearable pain or unbelievable joy. Wang was relatively calm until he saw the boys' violent moves and sat up in the fire with a scary look on his face. The women screeched from the frightful sight.

"Don't be afraid. It's just the tendons on his feet," Mao Dan said as he nudged Wang back down into the fire with his club.

As the wood slowly burned, the bodies provided the fuel. Grease oozed out of the boys' plumper bodies, while Wang, gaunt with little fat, looked like a piece of ebony wood. That marked the only difference between the sons of a rich chief and a poor villager. Mao Dan leaned Wang's body against the boys so their fat could help burn the gaunt corpse. It was a significant move, an "evening out of the disparity in wealth."

The onlookers sighed, but no tears were shed.

Only a pile of charred bones was left in the bend as the pyre died down, all but a few clumps that could be internal organs yet to be consumed by the fire. From the shapes of the skulls, they could tell which belonged to whom; the bones, however, were a jumble. The murderer and his victims were in a warm embrace.

Would Baldy Wang have killed the boys if he'd known their bones would end up hugging each other? Laoshun wondered.

Chapter Twenty-Three

Heavy snows crush peonies in Yangshan
Reeds are blown off the trellis

1

The sisters-in-law felt as if struck by thunder upon the discovery of the flight of the camel, which had taken along their steamed buns and water. Losing the food was tolerable, since there were desert rice plants to stave off starvation. But no water was a death sentence. It would not take long for the blood to congeal and stop flowing, with the sun's pulsating rays licking at the skin. Prolonged exposure will dry a person up completely. You can only exist through your soul, for your body will no longer follow your commands. Ying'er was reminded of drying mung beans. There were always insects that would bore a hole in the beans and worm their way in. She usually spread the beans out to dry in the yard. The insects feigned death and appeared as grass seeds. Ying'er never bothered to sort them, for be they insects or grass seeds, the sun would squeeze out the moisture indiscriminately. So now they will be like the insects. She wondered if this was retribution; the person who dried the insects was in turn baked to death. It was clear to her that she was dehydrated; she had sweated so much her blood must be fairly sticky. No wonder, she said to herself, even the camel was frightened. Every creature cherishes life. She was afraid of the jackals, and so was the camel. No one knew how much more danger lay ahead of them, so naturally the animal was frightened.

They sat on the sand as the sun beat down on them. Neither felt like talking. The fleeing camel had taken all chances of survival from them, and they could not travel far. Each step would deplete their bodily fluids, not to mention the sun, which would want its share. It was hopeless. Calamities never come one at a time.

They had been able to bear the thirst before the flight of the camel and just wet their lips to help relieve the craving. Now that the camel was gone, it felt as if their bodies were tormented by thirst, each cell crying out for water. Ying'er thought she could hear the popping sounds of her cells bursting from a lack of moisture, which sounded very much like walking barefoot over wheat stalks. Her throat itched, as if scratched by the paws of frenzied jackals, or, as if a swarm of maggots were squirming in a milky mass, sticky and disgusting. Disgusted with herself, she forced herself not to think about it. Fighting the jackals had been perilous, but she could at least see her enemy and deal an occasional blow. Now there was no enemy. Perhaps the glaring white sun could count as one, but nothing good could come out of going to war with the sun. Maybe, on second thought, fate was her enemy now. But what was fate? It was like a miasma that engulfed her, impossible to shake off whether she moved forward or backed off. She could not find a spot to strike when fighting against fate. Her body was the only opponent she could see and touch. As her thoughts continued, it appeared that her struggle had all been for the sake of her body, and that she'd worked hard to feed and clothe it. Wasn't it her troubling body that plunged her into the depths of torment from longing, even if she were to forget about the issue of her soul. She would not have to suffer from wanting him if not for the enthralling kisses and intertwining of bodies. Her body was torturing her again.

She lay down on the sand and looked helplessly into the sky. Her face was exposed to the rays, absent the protective measures she'd taken to avoid direct sun, for melanin accumulated from too much sun and formed spots on the face. Now, if she were to die of thirst, it didn't matter what she looked like. She could be mummified or mutilated by wild animals. Go ahead, roast me, she said to the sun. Dry me up quickly, so I won't suffer any longer. She could even become a museum exhibit if her parched body was buried in the sand and dug up a thousand years later. Lingguan had seen a thousand-year old mummy in Liangzhou's museum and said it was ugly. No one knew if she had loved, or what her life's trajectory had been, neither of which she revealed. Her life had become an enormous secret. Ying'er had heard that scholars had wanted to examine her life, but did not know where to start, like the proverbial tiger trying to swallow the sky. If her body was unearthed a thousand years later, Ying'er thought, it would be another colossal riddle; no one would know that she had loved or that she had had a heady romance with a boy called Lingguan. No research will unveil that secret, she said to herself, as she was delighted by the sensation of playing a prank. She smiled secretly. Go ahead, look into it. You'll be exhausted without fathoming my thoughts or my love for him. I'm sure you won't. Losers. She could almost see the embarrassed looks on their sweaty faces, and smiled happily.

But then again, if they could not find evidence of her love, would that mean it had never existed? A flower, no matter how pretty, is nothing if it blossoms in a remote valley where no one can see it. She panicked at the thought. She had tried to hide her romance from everyone, but, no matter what, someone ought to be able to discover the existence of her moving love story. Otherwise, wouldn't she be like a flower blooming where no one can see it? She had to find a way for later generations to know of the love she'd experienced.

Ying'er thought hard, but could not come up with a solution. If she had a rock, she would carve her story in it with her knife; she already knew what she would carve. But no rock materialized after her careful survey of her surroundings. All she could see was sand. What is sand, if not the least reliable thing in the world? You can give it your heart, but a breeze can erase it. A rock was something you wished fate would provide, but would not appear just because you wanted it to. She finally hit upon an idea. Two years earlier, a substantial number of ancient relics of the West had been excavated in the Vajravārāhī Cave; most of the objects were silk and satin of such high quality and fine patterns that the experts were amazed. Some had writing by dharma masters on them. If silk and satin could last thousands of years and survive till now, then perhaps her clothes would too. In humid areas, clothing, no matter how high the quality, decomposes, but here in the desert garments can keep for a long time, hundreds, if not thousands, of years. It could work; a thousand years or a hundred mean the same to the dead. It made no difference.

She decided to write on her clothes in her own blood. Putting an index finger into her mouth, she bit down hard, but, unable to bear the pain, she stopped. If a gentle bite was too hard to take, she said to herself, how horrible it must have been for the camel to be eaten alive by jackals. She shuddered, feeling bad for letting it down. If she'd been paying attention like Lanlan, maybe the camel would not have broken its leg. But her remorse quickly vanished, because what she wanted to do called out to her. Aware that her resolve would founder if she bit down slowly, she took out her dagger and ran her index finger over the blade.

Blood seeped out from the cut, slowly. Ying'er took off her shirt and started writing on it. She didn't expect the blood to stop flowing after a single stroke; it was too thick. In the past, she'd always been wary of bleeding, for once it started it was hard to stop. A doctor had said she was anemic and told her to eat more peanut skins. Blood always seemed to be the cause of her troubles. She'd bled and couldn't stop when she'd wanted to, and now, when she wanted more to finish her writing, it would not flow. She sucked hard on her finger until she had enough to write a line. The words were ugly, because she seldom wrote, but they were readable:

Ying'er loved Lingguan.

Hundreds, or even thousands of years from now, when her body was found, they would know her name was Ying'er and that she had loved someone called Lingguan. Her dessicated body would be different from the one in the museum. Maybe a curious writer would even create a touching story, with a male protagonist called Lingguan and a female counterpart named Ying'er. She could almost see people watching a TV drama hundreds of years later, moved to tears by her story. She was on the verge of tears. Her throat was so dry it was smoking, but oddly she had plenty of tears to shed.

She wept silently for a while before drying her tears. She was happy with what she'd done, no matter what.

Someone who was easily moved, she often shed real tears over fabricated stories. Her thirst, strangely, no longer bothered her. Maybe, she thought, it was the function of art.

Then another thought bowled her over: her writing would be gone if wild animals tore up her clothes and body.

2

Despair reclaimed her. It turned out that she could not last forever just because she wanted to. She often saw, along the river bend in the villages, shreds of garment rent by animals, as well as bones gnawed clean. If she were to die here, she said to herself, she'd end up just like that. Besides the jackals, there were wolves, rats, and many other animals with pointed teeth, and they would tear into pieces the eternity she longed for. What a shame. There were so many sharp teeth in the world. It was hopeless. Humans were born to suffer, so naturally pain had many origins.

Her heart ached over the possibility that her romance would be buried in the sand along with her body. It felt worse than death itself.

All of sudden, the thought of "buried in the sand" was traced by another drifting idea. Ying'er tried hard to catch it. Right, she thought, I'll bury myself in the sand, out of sight of the beasts.

Her mood buoyed.

A wonderful solution. Many excavated relics were preserved for thousands of years precisely because they'd been buried in the sand. That was true. She looked around and located a soaring sandy slope. I'll have to die anyway, so burying myself is better than dying of thirst. I wouldn't have to suffer long if I buried myself, while dying of thirst would be so much more painful.

I won't rush into it. I'll wait till all hope is gone and I have to die. But I might not have to strength to dig a hole when it comes to that. I should get it dug while I'm able. All I have to do at the last minute is kick out for the sand to fall and bury me.

She got to her feet and headed toward the slope, a towering one. After her eyes located a steep spot, she began digging. Lanlan's eyes were shut, her thoughts elsewhere; she opened her eyes to glance at Ying'er without saying a word. Maybe, she thought, Ying'er was digging a place for a nap.

Ying'er kept digging, carefully. Digging a hole on a slope was not tiring, but it had its challenges: she needed to create a large enough space, while keeping loose sand around the edges in such a way that a kick would bring everything down just before she died. It wasn't easy work, but she was getting it done. Yet she began to lose hope as she continued, for she noticed a dampness in the sand; even if she managed to bury herself in it, it would not take long for the humidity to destroy the inscribed shirt.

It was instantly deflating.

She felt terrible. I have such terrible luck I can't even find a dry spot to bury myself.

Lanlan came up from behind. "Reed roots, " she shouted.

3

"Do you know what they are?" Lanlan asked. "Sure, you know they're the roots of reed plants, but you probably don't know about the Daoist masters of ancient times who tracked a dragon's vein. They found the roots when they located the vein. These are the beards of the dragon's vein."

Her enthusiasm lifted Ying'er's mood a bit, for she knew that her sister-in-law was not the type to get excited over nothing. She recalled Meng Baye once saying that the so-called dragon's vein was a waterway, so she understood Lanlan's elation. The presence of reed roots meant they could find water. Of course, they should be happy, she thought. What else could be more exhilarating than finding water when stranded in the desert?

Seeing some of the gloom lifting off Ying'er's face, Lanlan said no more about the dragon's vein. Everyone in Liangzhou knew it meant a waterway, though it carried much more significance than that; for instance, a place with a dragon's vein produces important people, and so on. But Lanlan could care less about that at the moment. To her, reed roots mean only food, water, and life. She bent over to pull up a section of the root and, tucking it under her arm, scraped off the sand before breaking it in two. She gave the longer section to Ying'er.

"Chew on it. It has lots of moisture. Don't spit out the pulp. Just keep chewing and then swallow everything."

Ying'er took a bite and felt a coolness spread in her mouth. What a wonderful sensation. It was her first taste of a reed root, which to her looked woody; she never expected it to have so much juice. It was like the most delicious food she'd ever had.

Putting her piece in her mouth, Lanlan jumped into Ying'er's pit, where, following the complex root system, she slowly dug farther, tossing out roots as she went.

"Save some for later; they will be our life-savers," she said to Ying'er.

The roots were enticing, snowy white, plump, and watery. Ying'er wished she could swallow them all, as she felt hands reaching out from her throat for the roots. She took a plastic bag from her pocket, removed the tissue paper inside, and put the roots in; she did not want the dry desert wind to suck out the roots' moisture too quickly. Well then, she said to herself. We've found new hope. It's true, as people say, that Heaven never seals off all the exits. There's always a turning point when you think you've reached the end.

The roots were piling up beside the sand pit. Reed roots, like licorice roots, grow in clumps, and once a root is spotted, you can pull out more by following the root system. Folklore had it that the reed roots under the imperial tombs could spread thousands of li and that an emperor will be born to anyone whose ancestral tomb comes into contact with the dragon's aura. There had once been a dragon's vein in Shawan, but it had been severed by an emperor. So Shawan residents considered reed roots to be lucky, and a celebration was called for anyone who had a root growing in their ancestral grave.

Lanlan's labored breathing could be heard from the pit, for she had to toss out sand one handful at a time, as the pile of roots grew in the bag.

"Take a rest," Ying'er said. "I'll take over."

"I'm fine. I'm not tired." Lanlan smiled as she wiped her sweaty forehead. "How did you think of digging in the sand?"

Ying'er could not tell Lanlan she'd wanted to be known down through the ages, so she smiled but did not respond. Lanlan didn't care if she got an answer. It was obvious that she was happy. What a pleasant surprise, Ying'er said to herself. It would be nice to have a sand shovel. The thought led immediately to self-mockery: People are so greedy. I want a shovel now that we've found reed roots, then I'd want a tent and maybe even a car. That's how problems arise in life. She should have been contented. It was the greatest blessing from Heavens to have roots to fend off thirst and hunger when they were at their wit's end.

The bag filled now, she looked for something else for the new ones when Lanlan tossed out her head scarf. They had each worn one to prevent sunburn. Ying'er recalled the gauzy kerchief she'd put in her camel's litter. She told herself to forget it. Once lost, it was no longer hers.

Ying'er was about to change places with Lanlan when she saw sand slipping down the wall. That looked bad.

"Get out of there, Lanlan, hurry. The pit's about to collapse."

Lanlan got to her feet but before she could climb out, the sand rose to her chest without a sign of stopping.

Utterly terrified, Ying'er reached out to drag Lanlan up by her arm, but, to her dismay, the more she pulled, the faster the sand fell. Soon it reached Lanlan's shoulders, forcing her to open her mouth and gasp for air. Ying'er did not dare pull again, and Lanlan stopped struggling. Finally, the sand stopped flowing.

Ying'er did not know what to do. The situation was dire, and if the sand tumbled down again, it would bury her, and she'd be as good as dead. It would slip into her ears, nose and mouth, any opening it could find. Even if the buried person could be dug out in time, the sand in the body would still pose a danger to survival.

Afraid that struggling would only increase the sandslide, Ying'er told Lanlan not to move. The desert's yellow dragon had so much sand it would envelop her at the slightest provocation. The villagers of Shawan all believed in the yellow dragon, which was in charge of sand, with water in the domain of the green dragon. Those who drowned would enter the green dragon's palace, while those buried in sand became relatives of the yellow dragon. In earlier times, there was a temple of the Yellow Dragon, where the villagers offered sacrifices on the first and fifteenth of each month. If they missed even once, they drew the ire of the Yellow Dragon. Times were different now, and everything had gone downhill. The earliest sacrifices required virgin boys and girls, who were later replaced by cows and goats, until the temple was destroyed by the Red Guards. The elders said sand began to inch toward their village after that, covering a large area of land. Ying'er did not believe in deities, but at this moment, she'd believe in anything, even dogs. She pleaded with the Yellow Dragon not to take Lanlan, who in turn prayed to the Vajravārāhī, silently, and looked calm on the surface. The sand had pressed against her so much she had trouble breathing, but she strained to keep her composure, for she knew that panic would not help her.

The sand might start falling again, Lanlan thought. She should take the opportunity to settle things for Ying'er's sake. She was loath to die with regrets.

Ying'er came up with an idea. While still praying to the Yellow Dragon, she started digging another pit to the north of Lanlan, who might then be able to extract herself slowly, with another pit on the side.

Lanlan gave Ying'er a sad smile, but didn't stop her; she knew it was the only possible solution, not whether it would work or not.

"There are some things I want to say to you, Ying'er," Lanlan said.

4

"I feel bad about two people in my life; one is you. I know I caused you lots of trouble by leaving your family. I know, Ying'er. I know the harm I've done to you. I'm a woman too. Actually, you know that only a woman can understand what goes on in another woman's mind. I did all this, Ying'er, for one reason only—I couldn't take any more of your brother's beatings. It's true. I didn't ask for love or money, not to mention ideals. I just wanted to live like an animal. I mean it, like an animal. I envy pigs. Though a butcher's knife awaits them, it's the same for us humans. Forget about tubal ligation and surgery and look at the last knife cut from Heaven. No one can avoid that one. That's why I envy pigs. You know the kind of life someone leads when she envies a pig. I envy cows too; they have to work hard, but the hardship in my life isn't less than theirs. Did you know that I had to get up at the crack of dawn to sweep the yard, clean the house, cook, and work in the field till dark? It went on like that every day of the year. Weeding the field, digging and harvesting. I did it all. A cow works hard, but there's always a slack period for them, but not for me. Look at me. No one who sees me believes I'm only in my twenties. But I didn't mind these. I was born to a peasant's family, to a life of hardship, and I accepted my fate.

"But I just could not take the beatings. I couldn't. He slapped me, hit me with his fist and his elbow, and kicked me, but these were actually not too bad. What I feared most was the whip. You know how a single lashing will make an old cow's legs buckle? He went at it for an hour. An hour, sixty minutes, three thousand and six hundred seconds. When he was done each time, the whip had turned my body into a mat with bloody welts. And what did he do next? He sprinkled salt on the wounds, saying to prevent infection, because that would cost him money. It hurt so much, a hundred times worse than the lashing. I remember how I couldn't get away from the whip even when I was asleep; I'd be startled awake when I dreamed about it. Once, that time when you picked thorns off me, well, you know he'd gambled and lost. I said something, so he went and got thorny branches, and ripped my clothes off. I knew he'd learned that from tales by the folk singer. Remember? That's how those young men who had fallen on hard time were beaten in the stories. Why couldn't he learn from the good guys in the stories? They were so virtuous and filial, why couldn't he follow their example? Why did he only copy the bad ones?

"You happened to visit your parents the day after he'd lashed me with the branches. Didn't you pick out a handful of thorns? You didn't count them, but I did. There were four hundred and fifty-one of them. I vowed at the time that in our next life, I'd spear him the same number of times or shoot four hundred and fifty-one arrows into him. It's true. Don't be mad at me. It's what I was thinking at the time.

"Don't cry. Please don't. I'll stop if you do. I've been keeping this inside all these years and it's festering. I didn't dare tell anyone, because you know, some people, instead of showing sympathy, will actually laugh at you. I remember there was a woman in the village. Every time she railed at her daughter-in-law, she'd say, 'Don't you dare talk back to me, or you'll end up like Lanlan.' To me, that was a slap in the face. But how could I tell people? I had to do what the proverb says, swallow my teeth when they came loose after a beating. I suffered so much silently. Ma and Pa knew he beat me, but they had no idea how badly. Ma would be heartbroken if she knew. They've had a hard life, and I couldn't pour salt on their wounds, you know.

"I'd better stop. My heart aches when I hear you cry. See, I made you sad. All right, let's not talk about this. I just want you to know I asked for a divorce because I can't stand the beating any longer. If I hadn't, I'd have taken the easy way out, by knife or by rope, or maybe by poison. I remember once I tied a rope to the rafter but your father stopped me when

I'd barely stuck my neck through the noose. I also considered ingesting pesticide, the kind that rots your guts. I hear the pain is unbearable, but that was just short-term pain, while there was no end to my life of suffering.

"Then my brother died, and I knew I had to live. Ma and Pa nearly cried their eyes out when he died, and if I died too, that would be the end for them. I had to ask for a divorce. Don't cry. I don't want you to feel bad; I just want you to know I had to get a divorce because I couldn't live like that any longer. If I could have, I'd have gritted my teeth and suffered through it. It's only one lifetime, isn't it? We all have to die. I realized that I'd die whether I fought back or put up with it. Finally, I understood why some people killed themselves after they were beaten during the Cultural Revolution. That's right. We aren't born to be beaten. No matter how noble and great you are, you're still flesh and bones.

"Actually, I'm not an ambitious woman, nor do I care to be. I never had high aspirations and felt no need to rise above anyone else. I just want to live a stable, safe life, quietly muddle through. Humans were born to muddle through life, so that's what I want.

"Of course, I was heartbroken over the death of my little girl. I felt my world had fallen apart during those days, and I could understand the pain Ma and Pa felt over the death of their son. I couldn't bring myself to even think about it, but you know, pain dulls at some point. No matter how great the pain, you turn numb after a while, and I got over it. They thought that was why I wanted a divorce, and it's what I told them, but actually I just didn't want to be hit anymore. That's all. You've probably never been beaten. It's simply too much to take. So, the ones I admire most aren't Buddha or Bodhisattva, but martyrs under torture. To be honest with you, if it was me, I'd betray people after being beaten, no matter how great my belief was.

"Don't cry.

"After my little girl died, I cried my eyes out and raised hell with Bai Fu, but I can't cry her back alive. She's dead, and there's nothing I can do about it, it was her fate. But the thought of beating made me shudder and that's why I vowed never to hit anyone in my life. I'd once slapped her, and that became my eternal regret. It feels like a knife slicing through my heart every time I think about it. I vowed never to hit anyone. I suffered when I was hit, and it would be the same if I hit someone. We are not born to be beaten.

"All right, don't cry. I'll stop.

"I'm glad you know. For the longest time what I feared most was being awake, because I'd be thinking about all sorts of things. But I was afraid to sleep, too, because I wouldn't know when the whip would snap, which happened all the time, sometimes in real life and sometimes in my dream. For the longest time I couldn't tell the difference, since I'd be beaten whether I was awake or not. I was surprised when instead using the whip, he boxed my ears or hit me with his fist, for that amounted to a great kindness. You know, it hurt when he hit me with his fist, but it was dull, while the whip brought sharp, unbearable pain, a hundred times worse than being cut by a knife. Remember the black-and-white cow? It collapsed from one lash from him. One lash and it went down, shedding tears as big as soy beans. But me, I took much more. He took his stance and clenched his teeth before sending the whip whirling at me. One lash, and I crumpled in the yard.

"Those beatings put fear in my soul.

"Don't laugh at me. There was nothing I could do, because I'm a woman and I'm weak. I'm glad you understand, though.

"Don't dig too fast. Take your time. Be careful not to skin your fingers. Use both hands to cup the sand, right, like that. Don't use your fingertips. The skin there is too thin. Use your palms, right. Just like that."

Lanlan felt much better now.

5

"You can guess the other person I feel bad about. I don't have to tell you. Yes, it's Huaqiu's wife. Nothing happened between him and me, seriously, nothing. It's like the lines in the tune, 'Peel a big red fruit/ everyone's talking about me and you/but nothing happened, and that's true/upright people have their good names smeared.' The lines are so right. How did the songwriter know what was on my mind? That's so weird.

"I just never expected that she'd try to kill herself. I really didn't. So much hoopla has been created over Huaqiu and me, but nothing bad happened. Before I was married, we were like two kids playing house, and I was no longer in the mood after I got married. All the beatings took away my feelings as a woman. You know I was having some health issues for a while. But I have to admit that we kissed and he touched me. I don't have to hide that from you now. That's all we did, seriously. I'm not like you and Lingguan. You two were truly in love. Don't glare at me. Nothing happened between him and me, nothing.

"That time when I went in for the seven-day meditation, we did spend day and night together. Yes, that's true. We were together for seven days and eight nights, but you know we were meditating, in Vajravārāhī's mandala. How could I have done anything seedy? Besides, I was spotting off and on at the time, and I couldn't do it anyway. Besides, Fengxiang and other women were there, in addition to Yue'er's trouble-making mother. Think about it. I'm not a donkey, how could I have carried it out without regard for the occasion, even if I'd wanted to?

"How could she be so foolish? She heard a rumor and believed it. She thought Huaqiu and I had done it, so she carried out her own foolish act. It was his fault, if you ask me. Some women like to nag. He should have let her complain and pretend he didn't understand her. He could

496 <i>Chapter Twenty-Three</i>

have left the house when he couldn't tolerate it any longer. Why did he have to hit her? She was already fuming before that, and once he hit her, she naturally felt she had nothing to live for. Don't you think? If it had been me, I'd have used a knife on my neck too.

"But she had no idea that what she did turned groundless gossip into fact. It's nothing you can explain to people, because the more you say, the more they think you're guilty. That's how it works with human affairs. What could I do?

"You know, I felt like using a knife on my neck during the first few days after she tried to take her own life. I kept seeing her bloody neck and the air bubbles rising out of the cut. They kept popping before my eyes, a nightmare I couldn't escape. I took up a knife several times, but then I thought of Ma and Pa, and I couldn't let them lose a daughter after losing their son. If I died, Pa would be heart-broken, crying just like her father had with his arms around her. I couldn't let that happen. I really couldn't.

"Of course, I was also afraid of the pain, how the cut would hurt. I have to admire her. How could she have managed to do that to herself?

"Go slow. Don't be in too much a hurry to scoop out the sand. It feels like it's loosening up. That's right, scoop away the sand on my chest first. Right, there.

"I was surprised she lived. It surely was better that she didn't die, but, you know, everyone takes pity on her when they see her roaming the village with a crooked neck. They're also condemning me by showing sympathy. People would have stopped talking after a few years if she'd died, but now she walks around with a crooked neck. You've seen her. She looks weird, like a freak. I didn't want to leave my house, because whenever I walked out, I saw her sunning herself at a south-facing sheltered spot. She wouldn't say anything when she saw me, just cock her head and stare at me through sinister eyes. Those were scary eyes, more relentless than your brother's whip. I felt like her eyes were jabbing at my back. I mean it. Sometimes I'd even feel that her eyes were everywhere, in the sky and on the ground, emitting rays like spider-threads that turned me into a fly in the web. It was worse when others were around. They'd look at her and then at me. I knew what they were thinking.

"Sometimes I really did feel that there was nothing to live for.

"It's true. A whip awaited me at my husband's house and the eerie stare from a woman with a crooked neck at my parents' house, much worse than a whip. So tell me, what do I have to live for?

"Seriously, why don't you stop scooping? Go up to the slope and kick the sand down to bury me.

"I won't talk about it. I want to live, but thinking about all this takes the desire away. The sooner I die, the faster I'm free from suffering.

"Why is my life so hard? Do you know? Could it be that I committed heinous crimes in my previous life?

"You can stop now. Let's forget it. See, your fingers are bleeding. It's useless. You can scoop thousands of times, but it's no match for the shifting Yellow Dragon.

"I just want to ask one favor of you: if the Yellow Dragon takes me away and you make it out alive, would you help her out if you can? Her neck is crooked, but I've heard it can be taken care of in a hospital in Lanzhou. Simple surgery will straighten it. Of course, it depends on your ability. Forget it if you can't manage, but if you can, help her out. You know, her crooked neck is a mark of my shame. The villagers will denounce me for as long as it exists. Besides, Huaqiu is fickle, and a woman with a crooked neck isn't going to keep him around. Sooner or later he'll stray. She's suffered, so you help her out if you can.

"If you can't, at least take a message to Mengzi, and tell him his sister asks him to fulfill her last wish. He'll do it, I know. If the two of you are together, naturally I won't need to ask. Life would be better with the two of you working together. If it doesn't work out—you know your mother, she's too crafty—you move ahead and marry a rich man and you'll be able to help her. Listen to me, I'm putting pressure on you. You're not upset with me, are you? I have to say these things, I can't help it. If I don't, I'll feel much worse. Now that I've told you, it's up to you whether you do it or not, and that makes me feel better.

"Sometimes when I think about it, I really do feel I have nothing to show for my life. But what can I do? I believe in fate, but I don't think my troubles are entirely due to fate. Look at the women in the village. Every one of them has a tough life. I wonder if women are like ants on a millstone. Once we're on it, inertia makes us turn along with it. But I wonder if there's something else beyond fate. Just think of all the people who suffered during the Cultural Revolution. I don't believe that's all because of fate; there has to be something more. I keep wondering why, but I can't figure it out, so I have to give up. Actually, I think Pa's line is the best: I can take whatever Heaven doles out to me. Don't you agree? You can think until your head hurts, but you still have to put up with whatever you have to take. It's better to accept it calmly from the start, don't you think?"

6

"Don't cry if I'm buried alive. Tears are water too. You'll live longer if you conserve. You don't know the area, so just keep going east and don't stray. Forget about the salt lakes for now and make sure you survive first. The desert here is narrow east to west and wide north to south and you'll never make it out if you take the wrong route. Just keep going east. And don't walk when the sun is blistering hot, or you'll turn into a mummy before long. Best to travel at night. Follow the Big Dipper, make sure it's to your left, and keep going. Don't use the flashlight too often, and keep the musket with you. The gunpowder has to stay dry, but you can dry it in the sun if the rain gets to it. It's not that hard to fire a musket. Take a handful of gunpowder—not too much so it'll last—drop it into the barrel and tamp it with the rod, but not too tight. A dozen or so times should do it. If it's packed too tight, it will explode. After that you add buckshot. There's not much left, so you can add some sand pebbles, not too big, just about the size of buckshot. Then add a pinch of gunpowder and tamp it down again, to keep the buckshot in. Use the metal tongs to pick up the flint and fit it on the firing pin. Sometimes a doomed rabbit will run right into your muzzle. But don't fire at a gazelle. You need the steel balls for that, but they were in the sack around the camel's neck. Using buckshot on gazelles is a waste of gunpowder. You can injure it if you can get close, but you can't catch it even if it's seriously wounded. It will be wasted effort. You must conserve your energy. You'll die of exhaustion if you run after a wounded gazelle for an hour. Rabbits are your best bet. If you're lucky, one shot will get you a rabbit. Remember not to get too close. The best distance is within a dozen meters.

"Stop scooping now. See that? The sand is falling faster than you can scoop.

"When you get a rabbit, drink the blood first. You may think it's disgusting, but don't be put off by it, because you have to live. That's all that counts. You have to put up with the stench of blood; it's overpowering, but it has the most nutrients and moisture. You can get out of the desert and reach Mongolia so long as you can get some rabbits and don't get lost. Once you're there, find a house and ask for food and water—don't eat too much at first. They'll help you out.

"Don't forget to travel only at night. Mornings are okay. Just not at noon, when the sun is the harshest. When the sun is high up, find a shady spot and dig a hole, not too deep but deep enough to reach dampness. Don't dig too much when you see reed roots; don't be greedy like me. Make sure the pit has a gentle slope, so you won't be buried in falling sand. When you sense dampness, lie down to breathe in the moist air, one deep breath at a time. Remind yourself that you're drawing the moisture and subterranean essence deep into your heart. You'll feel better after an hour like that, no matter how thirsty you are. But don't get out yet, even if you're feeling better; you stay down there for the rest of the day. You'll be out of the sun while taking in moisture, and that will help you make it through the sweltering day. You can get on the road again when it's dark and there's dew on the ground. Make sure to pick some desert rice when you see the plants. They're prickly, but you have to take the pain to stay alive. Don't underestimate the tiny rice kernels, even though they're the size of a sparrow's eye. When you're in a damp pit, you can crack and eat them like melon seeds. They're small, but size doesn't matter when it comes to food.

"Remember not to let fear get the better of you, no matter what. You know what fear is? It's a knife to kill you. Once you sense it's there, it will get worse. You may start out slightly afraid, but little by little it will take root, sprout, bloom, and produce fruit. In the end, fear turns into a fog that blots out the sky and blankets you, or rising water to drown you. When that happens, you'll accept your doom. You won't want to walk and you'll stop fighting. You'll say to yourself, time to give up, it must be my fate. Then you're dead, because your heart has died. Once the heart dies, you die.

"Whatever you do to stay alive, remember to keep to one direction. Just walk, keep walking and don't stop, and you'll definitely reach your destination. When you aim right, you'll get yourself a rabbit, but don't ever try to follow it, because that will use up your energy. Don't give gazelles a single thought. You should know that any thought of them is mere greed if you don't have gunpowder and ball bearings. Don't ever, ever be deluded by pretty mirages either. Never forget that the desert is harsh and cruel, like life itself, so don't hope for any miracles. All you can do is keep going in the direction you choose. Keep walking and never stop, with the firm belief that you will definitely get there, and you will.

"At moments like this, your greatest enemy isn't the desert, but yourself. You're your own worst enemy, because you'll tell yourself to give up and accept your fate. You'll say, I can't get out of here. You'll mistakenly move a goal that could be inches away to the unreachable distant horizon. Ideas contrary to your need to get moving will sprout and mess with your determination. Don't look at me like that. This is what I learned from my Master Teacher. Do you know him? He's the Living Buddha that taught the Vajravārāhī doctrine.

"I don't think there's any better guidance in the world.

"Yes, I should struggle with myself too. Now stop scooping the sand around my chest and help me get my arms out first. Look at me. I was so busy telling you not to lose confidence that I almost succumbed to my own fate. I'll give it a try. I may cause more sand to fall, but I think I'll just pretend I'm already buried. The worst outcome is I will be buried deeper, isn't that so?

"Right. Like that. Let's try to get my arms out first."

7

Ying'er's fingers were bleeding, but she kept at it. I have to save Lanlan, even if my hands are scraped raw. She was shocked and heartbroken by what Lanlan had told her. People were the strangest animals. They'd been close for years, but she hadn't really known Lanlan until this day. But no need to talk about that now, for she had to get her out first. If Lanlan were buried alive there, Ying'er vowed, she'd do the same to keep Lanlan company. She would not leave her sister-in-law behind in the desert.

Ying'er's efforts finally saw results; a deep trough had been opened to the north of Lanlan. Loose sand continued to flow down, but her chest was freed. That was good news. Ying'er would keep going until she scooped out the sand pressing down on Lanlan's upper body, so they could then work together to free her legs.

After getting her arms out, Lanlan began pushing the sand away from her. She had limited movement of her hands because sand was still sliding slowly behind her. Luckily, it was damp and stuck to her body enough to uphold the sand wall around her. Even luckier, they were in a shaded hollow with packed sand, unlike the sunny hollows with loose sand that would have taken her life long before.

A dizzy spell came over Ying'er. She had sweated profusely from the hard work, which worsened her dehydration; now her eyes were blurry, and there seemed to be a porcupine lying in her throat. But she was upbeat, for she'd finally seen the hope of saving Lanlan, even though they were a long way from leaving the desert alive. At least they were about to storm through one of fate's iron doors, something one had to face a few times in a lifetime. Each successful charge brought a level of maturity, and, like the legendary Tang monk going to India for sutras, one had to weather eighty-one travails before attaining enlightenment.

Her fingertips were the first to bleed. She had just clipped her nails before entering the desert, so the sand scraped against the soft skin at the ends. She had no regard for them when she started digging, and wouldn't have cared if all ten were ruined. She worked hard digging, and soon the tips started bleeding again. Lanlan told her to scoop with her hands. It slowed her down, but the trough she was creating got deeper as she went.

Ying'er felt she was saving herself, not Lanlan. She'd been plunged into a dire situation similar to a sand pit, and was also trying to liberate herself. Oftentimes saving others is the same as freeing oneself.

The sun was moving westward; they had been trapped for over two hours. Hunger and thirst surrounded them like a spider web, and Ying'er felt she was about to pass out. They had nearly used up all their energy fighting the jackals all night long, and were overspent. All she wanted was sleep. Her hands continued to scoop, but her consciousness was about to enter a dormant state. How she wished she could sleep. She was unaware that many people who are dangerously thirsty die in their sleep. The sun extracts every drop of fluid from the body when they sleep. Those who die of thirst set off for the underworld after falling into a dormant state.

"That's enough now," Lanlan said and Ying'er stopped scooping robotically. Lanlan told her to move back a bit. They could see there was less sand constricting her chest and that she could struggle her way out if not for the fear of a sand slide. After Ying'er had moved back, Lanlan took her hands; she had to jump up swiftly because the effort would touch off the sand along the wall of the pit. She must act decisively after gathering her strength to vault out of the pit before the sand wall crumbled around her. Otherwise, she'd be buried anew in the cascading sand; not only would their effort have been in vain, but even more sand would fall, and the end would come when it reached the top of her head.

The two women prayed to their individual gods, Lanlan pleading with the Vajravārāhī and Ying'er the Yellow Dragon. Then Lanlan told Ying'er to steady herself before she called out, "One, two, three." Sand began to fall aggressively as they worked together pulling Lanlan up. Fortunately, she was able to extract her legs with one surge. They'd used all their strength to pull hard and ended up rolling together into the sand trough. Sand poured down and, in the blink of an eye, filled the pit where Lanlan had been standing.

Stunned, they stared wide-eyed at the spot for a while before wrapping their arms around each other and crying.

They cried with abandonment, to which the sand trough responded by echoing the sounds that bounced back and forth until they filled the space between heaven and earth.

8

They ate half the roots in the bag, the food for which they'd traded sweat and nearly a life; it was wonderful. If you chewed on the roots when you were parched, after baking a day in the desert, you were guaranteed a heavenly sensation. A gentle bite sends a unique sweet succulence and fragrance into your soul. The juice alone will make your soul tremble. If you are Buddhist, you'll feel it is sweet dew from the land of Buddha, and a single drop on your tongue washes away life's hardships.

All Ying'er's consciousness had been focused on Lanlan's safety, her mind had no room for hunger or thirst. The sensation awoke after the roots entered her stomach, which churned inside and felt kneaded by a spectral hand. She had to curse the fleeing camel again. She had appreciated its meekness when she borrowed it from a villager, never imagining the docile animal to have such a terrible disposition and take off when it needed to share hardships with its human riders.

The one that should have died lived and the one that should have lived died.

But she realized she couldn't blame the camel. Anyone would lose the nerve after an attack by a pack of jackals. Hadn't she been the same? She'd had no time for fear back then, but now the sense of fright had awakened and was intertwined with her hunger. She could hardly believe she'd experienced such a harrowing battle; everything felt like a dream, a sensation she'd had over the past few days. Now as thirst and hunger grated on her every nerve, her consciousness seemed stuck in a sense of the unreal.

The sun's fiery rays were relentless. And there was no wind.

"Let's dig a hole in a shaded hollow and wait till nightfall," Lanlan said.

Though feeling lingering fears over digging a hole, Ying'er

nevertheless knew they'd get heat stroke if they stayed under the blistering sun. The little bit of bodily fluid was no match for the sun's ferocious tongue. She followed Lanlan to pick out a spot. Experience taught them to dig a wider, shallower pit. They crawled in when damp sand came into view. Sleeping on wet sand can be unhealthy, but neither of them cared about that. Ying'er felt an unusual fatigue and dreamy sensation growing denser as they enveloped her, and she fell asleep.

The sun was hanging above a sand hill to the West when she awoke. Fiery red clouds decorated the western sky, portending another hot day. She wished it would rain, naturally. She felt sticky and filthy, hungry and thirsty. If she could strip and let rain wash over her, that would easily outdo chewing reed roots.

Lanlan was still asleep. The sight of the musket and gunpowder sack outside the pit gave Ying'er a sense of security. She was in no mood to worry about anything else; they weren't out of danger yet, but she didn't want to think about that, for she knew it was pointless to think too much at a time like this. They had no food, and thinking wouldn't bring them any; the same went for water. Best not to spend any mental energy to spare herself excessive worry, which would only result in a loss of confidence. We'll just have to go slow and see what happens, she thought. It would, of course, be wonderful to leave the desert alive, but there was nothing they could do if that was not possible. With what energy remained, they were no match for Heaven or their fate. She tried to do what she had to, which was not lose her sense of dignity. Except for the happy tears shed after freeing Lanlan, she hadn't cried much. In the past, she'd shed and dried tears constantly, like Lin Daiyu in *Dream of the Red Chamber*. Now she rarely cried, because she knew it was pointless, and that felt like progress. It's true, she said to herself, life does not believe in tears; life is just life. It is sand dunes encroaching upon oases, floods submerging innocence, a reality she must take seriously. There was nothing she could do about it; when confronted with life, you had to grow up, even if you didn't want to.

Suddenly something stirred under a shrub close by. It looked very much like a jackal, and her heart nearly stopped. She wanted to wake up Lanlan, but wasn't sure if her eyes were playing tricks. Slowly she reached for the musket and breathed only when her fingers wrapped around it. But the moving dot disappeared under the shrub. She laughed at her jumpy nerves; it was like a fear of buzzing for ten years after being stung by a bee. A careful survey of their surroundings turned up no jackals. As she breathed a sigh of relief, the thing moved again and she tensed up. She recalled that the musket was loaded, so she took out a flint and placed it on the firing pin. It was nothing to fear, even if it was a jackal, and she assumed it was a dust devil; but no, another look told her it was a mud-yellow rabbit.

She was elated. Heaven had sent them tasty food. Slowly she aimed the musket at the shrub. Lanlan had told her that the buckshot, if fired several feet away, would spread as wide as a wagon wheel; she thought she could hit her target. Recalling that Lanlan had said the key to aiming was to line up three points, she was about to pull the trigger, but her heart was thumping. This was, after all, her first time firing a shot.

Forget it, she thought. I should wake Lanlan up and ask her to shoot. But a thought grew ever more powerful in her head: she wanted Lanlan to open her eyes to the happy surprise of seeing a rabbit. The idea started to overwhelm her fear of firing her first shot. Then she saw how, every time she inhaled and exhaled, the yellow dot leaped around the sight, so she held her breath and worked hard at the trigger. Now her heart was thumping uncontrollably. After struggling to pull the trigger, she realized she'd actually been pulling against the trigger guard, so of course nothing happened. She laughed at herself. She ought to give up and ask Lanlan to do it, she thought.

Lanlan cut an inelegant figure lying in the pit with her sandy face. Ying'er nudged her several times, but failed to interrupt her snoring. She was absolutely exhausted, Ying'er thought, hating herself for trying to wake her up. I'm worthless; I don't even have the guts to fire a shot, she chided herself, which bolstered her courage. Holding her breath, she aimed at the moving yellow dot and pulled the trigger. The butt recoiled violently and smacked into her shoulder, while her eardrums rang from the deafening noise. She didn't see flames, but she knew the musket had fired.

Lanlan jumped to her feet.

"What was that? Jackals?"

"I shot a rabbit." Ying'er said, as she laid down the musket, climbed out of the pit, and ran toward the shrub. But before she reached the spot, a yellow dot sprang out and bounded away up a sand hill.

Lanlan caught up.

"Look at you." She felt like laughing despite the situation. "You were too close. That's a musket, not a rifle."

Sitting down in dejection, Ying'er was crestfallen, for she'd forgotten the distance. She felt like kicking herself for not getting Lanlan to shoot. It would have been satisfying to have roasted rabbit. But she'd missed and it ran off.

"Don't feel bad," Lanlan said, despite her wish for a different outcome. "Rabbits don't wait nicely for you to shoot them. It's not your fault. It ran off because you weren't supposed to get it."

She was right, Ying'er told herself when she got over her self-reproach. There was no point in being upset over it, now that it was gone. No matter what, she'd fired the weapon, and she learned that it wasn't all that hard.

"Watch me reload," Ying'er said. She followed Lanlan's instruction and asked Lanlan to teach her how to aim. Finally, she asked about firing distance and so on.

9

The desert cooled at dusk. They finished off the rest of the roots, having no desire to touch the steamed buns they'd picked up from the fleeing camel. Without water, they couldn't possibly swallow buns that had been dried by the desert wind.

Lanlan decided that they should travel at night, heading east. The salt lakes were located to the north, but now they needed to get to someplace with human habitation, where they could find ways to survive. They would see what they could do to reach the lakes, where, they'd heard, there were plenty of job opportunities. After losing her family's camel, Lanlan would be ashamed to face her parents. Even if she were to reach the lakes with nothing, she said to herself, she'd find ways to make money, at least earning enough to buy two camels before she could walk in the door. The change in plans sent them both into a funk. They had hoped for a way out when they entered the desert, never thinking that human plans are no match for heaven's design. They hadn't made any money, and had actually lost two camels. It worried Ying'er a great deal, because, with the current market value of a camel, at the very least it would be a loss of five to six thousand yuan, more than enough to pay for Bai Fu's new wife. Lanlan lamented their situation until she noticed the downcast look on Ying'er's face.

"Don't think about it now," she tried to comfort Ying'er. "One's dead and the other ran off, but it might go home on its own. Then we've only lost one camel."

What Lanlan said made sense, but that was only a possibility. The escaped camel knew the way and might make it back, but it might also run into jackals again, or wolves, or a herder who would keep it for himself.

"If the camel went back on its own, they'd worry about us," she said.

A scene appeared before Ying'er's eyes: her mother-in-law is crying out of anguish, while Laoshun wears a dark look as he squats on the kang, puffing on his pipe. The villagers are there, trying to make them feel better. It was a scene from the time her husband died. If I die, they won't feel the same degree of sadness as when their son passed away, Ying'er thought, as a sense of self-pity rose.

"Let's not think about that now. So many things aren't worth worrying about," Lanlan said. "The important thing is to get on our way. We'll stay in damp sand pits during the day and travel at night. We'll consider it the end of our lives if we run into jackals again. If we make it to the salt lakes, we'll think of something."

"That's a good idea," Ying'er said.

But she was dog tired; she'd like more sleep or at least a few days' rest. But it was only a thought. They could do what they wanted if they still had their camels, along with water and food. Now they'd die in the desert if they stayed.

When the sun sank behind the hills to the west, they set off, Lanlan carrying the musket and Ying'er holding a flashlight. The reed roots had long been eaten and digested; there seemed to be little birds chirping away in their stomachs, a problem caused by the roots. They remained thickly wrapped in the web of hunger and thirst. Thirst, in particular, came at them in waves. Lanlan's lips were purple, alarmingly swollen, and thickly scabbed. She'd licked her lips too often. Ying'er recalled Laoshun's caution against licking lips when in the desert, no matter how thirsty you are. Saliva is toxic and makes lips swell if you lick them. Ying'er had been careful and had reminded Lanlan, but Lanlan paid her no heed. Now her lips were an inch thick. Moreover, her cheeks were sunken on a face with large, dull eyes as if glazed over. Ying'er could guess what she looked like from Lanlan's face, and knew it wasn't pretty. Her lips weren't swollen, but they must be black and covered in a brown film. She reached up to touch her face; it felt dry and slack, obviously caused by a lack of water.

Water. The thought brought first coolness heart, then a wave of thirst.

Rubbing her back, Ying'er strained to look ahead. There were no stars out yet, and a red glow bled into the hills to the west, which gave the inky black hills a lovely outline. A breeze had started up, warm but with a slight chill. It would have been a wonderful trip if they'd come with a full stomach and plenty of water. To Ying'er and Lanlan, who were fighting for their lives, the scenery meant nothing. Ying'er glanced at the hills woodenly and swallowed with great difficulty. If he were here, she thought, he might be in a mood to write poetry. Oddly, though, her mind felt dull when she thought about him; gone was the stirring sensation she'd once had. He had been . . . love is just a feeling. The lack of water alone had diluted the feeling.

They walked slowly, for their feet had lost their spring. Ying'er even detected a dry, rustling noise from her moving legs; she knew that came from her joints, as she could feel the pain of bone on bone. She recalled what her mother had: standing is worse than walking slowly. Every step took them closer, she reminded herself. She wondered if Lanlan shared her thoughts, as she swayed violently, her body now with a mind of its own. It took them a surprisingly long time to get onto a gentle slope, and it frightened Ying'er to look at the soaring sand ridges in the distance.

Lanlan plopped down on the sand when they reached the top of the slope, while Ying'er lay down face up. It was dark, and the wind was cool, the air growing damp around them. It was the best time for night travel, but Ying'er knew that while their minds were willing, their bodies no longer obeyed them. They could have strong bodies, but like automobiles that needed gasoline, that was not enough. Lying in a damp pit during the day and traveling at night sounded good, but Ying'er knew that required a strong body, as well as plenty of food and water. The little bit of reed roots had provided them with a pathetic amount of nutrients, barely enough to ensure that they would live for a short while. It would be impossible to cross the towering sand hills and traverse the vast desert.

Ying'er slumped next to Lanlan. The wind was much cooler now.

"We have to keep going," Lanlan said.

"Yes, we do," Ying'er echoed.

"We can't be stuck here."

"You're right."

"Let's go," Lanlan said.

"Yes, let's go."

They kept talking about going, but neither made a move. Ying'er let out a long sigh as she pillowed her head on Lanlan's abdomen.

She wished she could just go to sleep; her body felt like it was stripped of both marrow and blood.

"We have to go even if it means crawling. Heading east, the desert is only eighty li wide, and I think we've traveled more than half that. Once we're on the other side, we'll see herders."

"Yes, even if we have to crawl," Ying'er said.

They stood, arms out to help each other up, and walked along a ridge.

Thirst at first obscured the pain in her legs, but after a while, Ying'er felt a knife was slicing into them. Not a frequent desert traveler, she'd only come to gather desert rice occasionally, so she was not good at walking in the desert. Lanlan was the same, but she had done heavy work at her in-law's often enough that she had more stamina. On the other hand, the musket on her shoulder used up a lot of her energy; it wasn't particularly heavy, but it turned into an energy sapping tiger when they had to travel a great distance. Even the flashlight in Ying'er's hand felt as if it weighed a ton.

It was pitch black, but they were fine. With the Big Dipper shining brightly above, they wouldn't walk in circles, as if trapped by walls erected by evil spirits. Like the musket, the Big Dipper felt reassuring. It was just that their thirst was getting worse; they could neither see nor think straight. Their eyeballs were moving noticeably slower, even making a grating noise; the sounds of joints creaking as they walked grew louder, crackling in the dark night. All these were new to them.

Their legs ached, but each eastward step took them one step closer to hope. In a momentary daze, Ying'er thought she was heading closer to Lingguan; she even saw him wave at her in the dark night, and was energized. That was odd; an illusory sensation had brought her real strength. She tried to clarify the dazed moment. It was no accident that fate had given her a hint at that moment. Maybe he really was a herder in a pasture off to the east. It was possible. She recalled how he'd often said he loved horseback riding, and the image of him on horseback appeared before her eyes. She'd never seen him ride, and the image had him bucking as if on a camel. If only you were here, you could ride anything, even a goat. The thought renewed her energy. She wanted to share her formula when she noticed Lanlan's difficulty in walking; she knew that Huaqiu could not be in the pastureland. Besides, from the way Lanlan talked about him, Ying'er sensed that he did not mean much to her anymore. Her formula would not help relieve Lanlan's fatigue.

Strangely, though, the momentary daze had lightened her steps; her legs still hurt, and thirst shrieked from every cell in her body, but it was more bearable once she gave "meaning" to their night travel.

She was amused.

10

The "meaning" had limited power, however. Shortly after midnight, Ying'er could not take another step, and climbing required help from Lanlan. She was barely conscious. Lanlan had turned the musket into a cane and used the stock to help her along on sand. She wanted Ying'er to use it, but Ying'er didn't even have the strength to hold it. They walked by holding on to each other, with Ying'er supported by Lanlan, who was helped by her musket. They were able to travel some more like that, but collapsed after crossing a gentle slope, their will and determination destroyed by the brutal feelings of thirst and hunger.

"I don't care if I die. I've done my best," Ying'er rasped, barely audibly, but Lanlan understood her. She did not respond, for she knew that death was closing in, unstoppable as a coffin carrying them out the gate. Even if they were spared the blistering sun the next day, the approaching thirst would end their lives. They'd gone without water for a very long time, subsisting exclusively on the miniscule amount of water from the reed roots. She remembered how excited she'd been when she first dug them up. She'd hoped they'd sustain them enough to leave the desert. To her disappointment, the roots she'd nearly paid for with her life were inadequate to combat raging hunger and thirst. She didn't dare imagine what fate awaited them the next day, when the punishing sun reached above their heads.

Ying'er thought she was dying. Her life was like a candle in the wind, flickering, always on the brink of going out. Her heart beat weakly, as if it would stop at any moment. Finally, she understood what people meant when they said life existed between breathing in and out. Once her feeble, silk-thread-like breaths ceased, the desert would gain another lonely ghost. The old Daoist Priest had once said that the King of Hell refused entry to those who died away from home, the wandering ghosts.

They had to stay near their drying bones and cry, and their souls could finally rest in peace only when the bones became part of the soil. The many rumors about death circulating in her village now came rushing back to her. She wondered what she would become after she died. It didn't matter what, as long as it wasn't to be another human, for that was exhausting. She preferred being a bird, the best being a lark that sang all day in the trees. Or a fox. Like Lanlan, Ying'er liked the clever creature with the air of a fairy, an immortal. It truly was a sprite, coming and going like the wind, leaving only plum-flower footprints as evidence of its existence. Ying'er would like most to be reborn as a fox praying to the moon; she would pray day in and day out until she became a fox fairy through self-cultivation, and would try to seduce a bookworm. By then Lingguan would be old, but he'd still be Lingguan and never too old for her. If he needed it, she'd spit out a pill of elixir that she'd worked hard to obtain, and he would swallow it to regain his youth. When that happened, people would leave them alone. She could come and go without a trace, and her mother would not force her to remarry or carry out an exchange; there would definitely be no disgusting men like Pockmark Xu to bother her. If necessary, she could give birth to a den of little fox fairies and call them Lingguan, but adding a number, such as Lingguan No. 1, Lingguan No. 2, Lingguan No. 3, Lingguan No. 4, and so on. She laughed when she imagined a den of Lingguans with their pointed mouths and monkey chins. Yes, a den of them would be a comical sight. They would frolic in the desert, sing, raise a racket, pray to the moon, and travel like the wind. Their springy steps would kick up mist-like dust and sprinkle the dunes with their plum-flower footprints. Even the best painter of the human world could not possibly recreate those prints, for their free and easy poise was a gift from heaven and earth.

Thirst reminded her of the imminent passing of her life, and she sensed she would not see another sunrise. Death was no big deal. It had seemed earth-shattering when she'd thought about it in the past, but now it was just like dozing off. As long as she'd done what she needed to do, it was perfectly fine to close her eyes and "doze off." Her thoughts turned to Panpan, who, oddly, had not been on her mind in recent days. Obviously, she had full confidence in her mother-in-law; the baby would never suffer, even if he were to become motherless. Of that she was certain. She felt herself to be an undeserving mother, for she had not felt the kind of deep and everlasting longing for the baby that she had for her beloved. She was helpless about that however, since everything positive was overshadowed by him and became, for instance, just "Lingguan's family," "Lingguan's baby," "Lingguan's hometown," or "Lingguan's parents." Hopeless; she knew it was unfair, but could do nothing about it. She hadn't meant for it to happen like that; it just felt it had always been that way.

Her mind was a blur, turning the baby into a blur. She had been taking shallow breaths and her heart was beating even more weakly. I don't mind dying, she thought. Even a sacred deer can't escape death after living a thousand years. But she didn't want to die of thirst. Back in the village, the ghosts of those dying of thirst often showed up to jinx people, and those affected would be thirsty all the time, even after gulping three basins of water. At a time like this, the villagers would send for a sorcerer, who would cut the afflicted on the forehead until the face turned bloody and sinister before lashing it with a whip made of hemp rope. The thirst had left such an indelible impression on the victims' consciousness that it stayed in the depths of their souls even after they died. They wailed through the night, searching for water, which would turn into a charcoal fire and bloody pus, however infrequently they were successful—they'd never be relieved of the thirst. Ying'er did not want to be that kind of ghost. She'd come into this world pure and clean and wanted to leave the same way, with an uncorrupted body. Her heart had no blemish, even though the sun had covered her lips with scabs. Yes. Please, Heaven, let me be reborn as a fox.

She strained to roll her eyes to gaze at the evening sky. They felt dry as axles that hadn't been oiled for years. The stars sparkled noisily, as if having an argument; they creaked, like leg joints rubbing against each other, like stir-frying soy beans in a suspended wok. She hadn't expected stars to make such a din. That was odd.

The darkness around them seemed to fade after the long, nighttime trek, and the shapes of the dunes were dimly visible, their blurred outline an enigma. To Ying'er, the enigma felt as thick as blood, as the exhaustion leading to death enveloped her again. The stickiness of her blood turned into a noose, while her heart, depleted of nutrients, could not withstand its weighty burden, no longer able to stir blood that was as thick as slurry. If she fell asleep now, she'd wake up to find herself turned into a wisp of gentle mist, her soul drifting above the desert like a wind.

She recalled her mother-in-law's stories about the wuchang, a demon sent by the King of Hell to seize people's souls. Hantou hadn't been able to breath his last when he was dying, all because of Lingguan's presence. The wuchang demon had to stay away and thus failed to take Hantou's soul. Her mother also said a virgin boy like Lingguan carried too much evil spirit and, in the eyes of a wuchang, was fire that made the approach impossible. Hantou died as soon as Lingguan left the room. What her mother said sounded eerie, otherworldly, sending chills down her spine. Now Ying'er wondered if a wuchang was waiting nearby to take her life. Lanlan was snoring. Ying'er was frightened. It was strange, though; she wasn't afraid to die, but she feared ghosts. She'd be a ghost herself when she died, but she was still afraid of them. She didn't dare turn to look, afraid she'd see a wuchang. The demon on an opera stage had a ghastly pale face, was tall and lanky, and wore a hat with a pointy tip. If she saw a figure like that, she would be frightened to death, not die of thirst.

Fear took away the fatigue enveloping her, and she heard footfalls behind her. Real footfalls. It could only be ghosts making a noise like that in this remote, forsaken spot. Her heart beat frantically. What a strange organ; it had been about to stop, but now it was acting like a ground-pounding ghost. Could it be the same ghost that was making the noise behind her? One of them resided in an old mill back in the village, and it would start pounding the ground after nightfall until the roosters crowed. Ying'er even forgot her thirst as her scalp tightened. The sound was getting closer, and she could hear it breathing, heavy and laborious, as if the ghost were carrying a colossal iron chain and hook. She would have cried out if she hadn't been afraid of scaring herself.

The huffing noise was right behind her now. She thought it was reaching out to get at her neck. Her mother had told her when she was little that ghosts pinch people. She was always saying that headaches, fevers, bellyaches, constipation, and chest pains were caused by a pinching ghost. Puffs of hot air were actually blowing down her neck. What do I have to fear? She thought, out of desperation. The worst that can happen is death, isn't it? I want to see what the ghost looks like if I have to die now. She groped around to find her flashlight and spun around.

An immense dark, oddly shaped figure appeared in front of her.

She turned on the flashlight and screamed.

Chapter Twenty-Four

A bird breaks out of a cage, soars into the sky
A rabbit escapes a trap, flees into the mountains

1

Yue'er came home. Her father had opened a dancehall at White Tiger Pass and needed help, so he told her to come back, which she did.

The villagers didn't think she should have, saying she'd been born to live in a city. But she returned. She looked about the same, though she had lost some weight, her skin was paler, and there was weariness in her eyes. People had placed much hope in her, too much perhaps, and they were surprised to see her back home, though their reaction quickly passed. Each year many "Yue'er"s left their village and many "Yue'er"s returned, their leavings and homecomings a common sight, like swallows returning to their nests. Their departures took nothing away from the village and their returns adding nothing. They brought back trickles of information about the outside world, but it was just that, information. In the end, they realized that Yue'er, who had left and then returned, was just a female worker from the countryside who could not be expected to change much of their convention.

But on a depressing evening, Yue'er was sad to see that the village had changed.

Some peculiar, ugly, multi-story structures had risen in a creased corner of the desert. They were ugly to her because she had no good feelings about steel and cement. She had developed an aversion to cities, after what she'd gone through out there, which had made her miss the small village terribly. When she thought about it, she felt something like warm water swirling in her heart. It was her hometown. To her, "hometown" was like an iron that would smooth out the scars on her soul. But now, the cold monstrosities had stalked her into her hometown.

More than that, a hell-raising racket had followed her into her hometown: machines rumbled, dust flew, and people clamored; along the banks of the Dasha River rows of buildings gave it the look of a real street. And there were young women in bright clothes and make-up, whom she had encountered in the city. All simple girls from rural areas, they were turned into urban ornaments that decorated the city with their youth. Virgins when they went to the city, they were scarred and bruised when they left. Now they showed up in her hometown. In the dancehall at White Tiger Pass, a mere ten yuan would allow a man to put his arms around her and dance, and he could touch her however and wherever he pleased. The sand boys swarmed into the hall like crazed ants every night.

She recalled how eagerly and urgently she'd wanted to flee home, but she found herself rootless after she left. The city she'd yearned for was arrogant and cold. She'd wanted to run back home after she'd been hurt several times, to hide in a secluded, quiet corner and lick her wounds like a fawn. When she thought about her hometown, a warm current coursed through her heart; believing that the village was her spiritual homeland and, moreover, a clean, uncontaminated spot, she realized that her home was gone the moment she stepped foot in it.

The village path in her memory had been widened, and the carts that had traveled down it had been replaced by whizzing monster vehicles. White Tiger Pass had become a menacing ringworm lapping at areas around it.

Her village had become cramped.

In addition to erecting rows of tall buildings, the sand boys dug troughs in the riverbed, built walls, laid out birch branches, covered the ground with shrubs they'd cut down in the desert, and spread out their bedding, making it their home.

Trouble began to mount once the population grew. She heard about a man who went out to water his field one night. A sand boy sneaked into his house. His wife was too sleepy to tell the difference, and they carried on until the man got back. He hit the sand boy with his shovel, crippling him with a shattered pelvic bone. The incident alerted the village men. Some had rented empty rooms to sand boys, but not after that. An additional hundred yuan each month was enticing, but not enough to assuage their fear of being cuckolded, bringing shame to their ancestors, and being laughed at behind their back. They raised the proverbial broom and swept the sand boys out the door.

She had also heard that, within a few months, three tycoons emerged among the gold mine owners, for whom the Liangzhou residents created a doggerel: Zhao San's old dick, Kong Da's tunnel, and Shuangfu's never-ending law suits. Zhao San was a whoremonger. Kong Da, who had invented a diagonal tunnel system, found lots of gold and took up more land. Law suits piled up for Shuanghfu, mostly for two reasons. One, his factory had hired thousands of workers, who each put up many thousands, but were never called in to work. Two, he was always giving out promissory notes to peasants who sold him corn, rumored to be in the amount of a billion yuan. So, they came to White Tiger Pass to demand their money, cursing his mother, and in turn were beaten by his security guards till they cried and railed at him, drawing police attention.

2

Two days after Yue'er's return, Baigou was bailed out of jail, thanks to Big Head, but people had different versions about why he bailed him out. Some said Big Head was worried about Baigou's relentless charges of corruption, plus Baldy Wang's murderous assaults; he was afraid Baigou might do the same to him. Besides, they lived in the same village and would bump into each other all the time, so it wouldn't do to be on bad terms. Another version had Meng Baye telling Big Head to post the bail. They said Meng had exploded when he learned of Baigou's theft. "Rabbits don't eat the grass around their warren. How could you do such a terrible thing? You deserved to lose your head." But then when he heard that Baigou was just carrying out justice on Heaven's behalf, he noisily puffed on his pipe for a long time before sending Baigou's father to Big Head's house, promising to make up the loss and offering the village chief a promissory note. Big Head then went to the police station with Baigou's father and sweet-talked the police before paying a fine to bail Baigou out.

Baigou had been beaten black and blue, but that was just what people could see; what they could not see was the "stomach punching." He said they had hit him until he threw up everything they'd fed him, but with no visible marks.

"Ai, it really was more than I could take. Try it sometime if you don't believe me," he told the villagers. But he kept his vow, saying he did it alone, refusing to name an accomplice. He claimed to have fought against injustice, on account of Big Head's corruption.

"I have nothing to lose. Worst case, I die. My lamb's pelt for Big Head's old sheep skin. But I'll let him know that Shawan has a hero, a real man, so he'd better check his head before he does anything against his conscience."

That same night Baigou and Mengzi sneaked out and dug up the soy beans they'd buried in the desert. They sold them for enough for Baigou's father to retrieve the note from Big Head. A rough calculation showed that their "righteous act on Heaven's behalf" had failed to affect Big Head at all and had landed them a fine of a thousand; all Baigou got was a series of beatings.

Mengzi was moved by Baigou's personal loyalty.

"You're a true friend, Baigou," he said. "You'll be my friend until the day I die."

"Stop blowing hot air. If you really believe in me, how about joining up to open a panning site? What do you say? Poverty chills ambition and hair hangs long on a skinny horse. These days, you can't stand up straight if you don't have money in your pocket."

Mengzi was tempted.

The fright over having nearly been buried alive had slowly dissipated after swirling around in his head for over a month. In the beginning, his legs turned rubbery any time he heard the sound of the machine, but a callous began to grow on his timid heart. He managed to stay away from the river for a while. He saw how the scale of gold-panning kept growing and that something peculiar had popped up in the area. After asking around, he learned that they were tents belonging to the gold management station, a newly created municipal office. He also heard that a national survey team had concluded that the area did not have a large enough gold reserve for the government to open a mine. That was a good outcome for everyone involved, since they'd have to eat the wind if the government took over.

The villagers had been scared witless when Mengzi was nearly buried alive and dozens of sand boys had died a horrible death. Only Mao Dan wanted to be a sand boy. But no one was against making money. Besides, Mao Dan was unharmed after traveling up and down a rope ladder for months. Then they heard that a certain sand boy had picked up a gold nugget and gotten rich overnight. Or another sand boy had washed up a golden egg while he was relieving himself. Little by little, the village men returned to be sand boys again. It was hard work, but it had visible material benefits, compared to working at construction sites like beasts of burden for a year and still not seeing a cent. More village men joined in. Those with means and connections got enough money to open a site, and two or three out of ten struck it rich. With models like these, the "money-crazed" among Liangzhou residents, eyes aglow, poured into White Tiger Pass; some made it rich, others lost everything. Most people ignored the latter, while the former made their heads turn. In addition to the gold miners, shop and restaurant owners also came and settled with their families.

More and more myths about gold were created. They heard that a golden arm had been unearthed in Shuangfu's pit; people from the management station rushed over, only to end up with nothing, like a fly chasing after a fart. Rumors like this abounded, and every one of them tantalized Mengzi, a feather tickling his heart.

A fair number of so-called barber shops popped up near the steel and concrete jungle. An entrepreneur opened a shop to try it out. She hadn't expected sand boys to swarm to her place the moment she opened for business. For ten yuan, they were massaged by women who could have stepped out of a painting, and could find an opportunity to touch their breasts, pinch their faces, even manage a kiss or two. The women didn't seem to mind, only half resisting, chiding coyly or laughing.

More barbershops followed after the first enjoyed a land-office business. With rocks everywhere in the Dasha River, all anyone needed to do was truck over some cement and bricks and throw up a building in a few days. By the time Mengzi had been there only a few days, redbrick houses dotted both river banks, crazier than a mirage. They say girls blossom into womanhood at eighteen. But the number and speed of their changes could never match that of White Tiger Pass.

Mengzi gaped at the structures that had sprouted during his absence, as if in a dream. He noticed the young women lining outside the brick houses, in numbers the likes of which he'd only seen on TV. Now a casual glance brought into view many pretty, smiling faces. His mouth went dry. He could see that many funny things went on in those barbershops, and that they did not come cheap. But when he learned it only cost ten yuan, he checked his pocket, looked around, and went in.

The crude walls were brightened by pictures, and Mengzi thought he was dreaming when he saw all those pretty faces looking at him. His head reeled as he pointed to one of them. She smiled and directed his attention to a stool. He sat down, still puzzled when a warm stream poured over his head, and he realized that she was going to wash his hair. Never in his adult life had a woman done that. The hands rubbing his scalp were soft and gentle, while something supple swayed and brushed against his ears. A heat rose inside him when he sensed what it was.

Lying on a narrow bed in the room, he felt good all over as the woman kneaded his body. After enjoying it with his eyes closed, he opened them to see her dark eyes on him; she looked familiar, but he couldn't place her right away. She giggled as he was about to ask. It was Ju'er, whom he had met for match-making.

"You, what are you doing here?" Mengzi sputtered.

"You're here too, aren't you?" She said with a pout. "if you can be here, why can't I?"

Their meeting had not led to an engagement, but still it made Mengzi feel that her current profession was a bit of a slap in the face.

"Aren't you afraid people will laugh at you?"

"For what?" she said off-handedly. "Who cares about being laughed at when you're too poor to afford pants? Besides, I work hard for my money. I don't steal or rob, so why should I feel ashamed?"

Mengzi wondered if she was referring to his theft of sand when he heard the word steal, but one look at her put him at ease. Her eyes were on him, and her hands never stopped spreading the pleasurable sensation throughout his body.

"Are you the owner?"

"I work for her."

"How much do you make?"

"Seventy-thirty split, she gets seventy."

"That much?"

"I won't get rich, but I won't starve to death either," she raised her voice. "It's better than my father's hard labor. Sometimes he toils away for a measly ten yuan. I make the same amount giving massages for half an hour. I can't let him wear out his old bones, can I?"

She was right, Mengzi said to himself. He sighed when he recalled the old man with the aged, walnut-shaped face. She was a filial daughter. But he sighed again when he considered the criticism she might suffer.

"What will you do in the future?"

"I'll think about that when the time comes. I don't know what future is. I just don't want my parents to work like beasts of burden again, and I want my kid brother to go to school. I haven't thought about my future. But, I'll be okay if no one wants me and I turn into a spinster."

"That'll never happen." Mengzi smiled, feeling sorry for her as he looked into her pretty little face.

"What would happen if I didn't do this and became a woman with a proper job instead? I'd find a husband and marry a country bumpkin, giving him a son who would bring him a grandson. I'd raise pigs and feed the dogs, turning from a girl into an old hag. Then I'd end up in the ground. That's how it looks to me. It'd be okay if I married a nice guy; if not, I'd be worked like a donkey, until I lost my youth and got old. And not a thing I could do about it."

"You're right," Mengzi said with a smile. "Do you like what you do?"

"I don't know." She sighed. "It's better than staying home, where I'd quietly grow old. Over here, at least I have people who admire my looks, who accept my labor. I make them feel good while supporting myself. As for the future, I haven't given it any thought. Actually, what is the future? Death. That's everyone's future."

She paused and continued, "The future is death, so why not have a few happy years before worrying about it?"

While they were talking, one of the young women came in with a sand boy, who pulled her close and started kissing her as soon they were in the room. Ju'er must have been kissed by those sand boys, Mengzi's mood darkened at the thought.

He took out a stack of crumpled bills after the massage; he wanted to give her all the money, but he realized that it wouldn't add much to her income. Instead he picked out a few crisp ones and handed them to her.

After walking out, he turned to see Ju'er smiling at him. He'd hoped to see tears in her eyes, but no such luck. She was smiling, looking quite radiant actually.

3

A major transformation had occurred at the riverbed. Hills of sand and rocks rose up next to the well frames, tents, and ramshackle huts. Like ants moving to new nests, the sand boys carried loads of sand and rock up from the bottom of the pits to the top of the hills. Shuangfu had begun using a hoist to greatly increase the rate. His sand boys no longer had to work themselves to death transporting a few shovels of dirt; now, with the roar of machinery, baskets filled with dripping wet sand and rocks popped out of his pits.

But most sand boys still had to carry sand. In the main, their bosses were locals who were too cheap to invest much; afraid of not making a profit quickly enough, they made do with human labor, unaware that Shuangfu's machine created ten pits in the time they dug one. He used a detector as the digging went on, and his panning trough produced jugs of placer gold.

Villagers who could find a way to get loans had opened pits; those who failed either worked as sand boys or poached. More and more were doing the latter now. Unorganized and disorderly, they piled sand anywhere they wanted and blocked up the river; pathways for the underground water they pumped were often dammed up. Once the water even flowed into a pit that wasn't finished; luckily, the sand boys escaped to avoid drowning. As a result, pit owners demanded that the gold management station ban random digging like this, but the villagers continued a kind of guerrilla warfare, retreating when inspectors appeared and moving back in when they left.

See there. Baigou is standing in mid-stream with a pan. A man from the management station takes off his shoes and socks and shivers the moment his toes touch the water. Another man calls out:

"Come on up. We promise not to give you a hard time."

"Go try that on a ghost," Baigou said. "Confess and you'll be treated with leniency, but you end your days in prison; resist and you'll be punished, but you're home by New Year's. I don't believe a word you say."

One of the policemen raises his gun, ready to shoot. Baigou thumps his chest.

"Aim right here, you bunch of pussies. The rich get to screw up the riverbed, while I poach a little because I'm poor. Why pick on me like a rabid dog?"

The other policeman is outraged; he flings away his shoes and socks and wades into the water. Rocks fly at him as soon he's in, creating small geysers all around. His partner says:

"Let him be. Can't you see he's desperate?"

"You're the desperate ones," says Baigou. "You value money more than your lives."

The policemen curse as they walk off.

"I see you're afraid too, Uncle Policemen," Mengzi said in jest.

"We're not afraid," one of them turned to reply. "We just don't want to be bitten by a rabid dog. It's not worth it."

Baigou shouted back, "You're the rabid dogs."

He got out of the water when the policemen were far enough away. "The cold has bored into my bones. I couldn't have held out any longer if they'd decided to stay." He was shivering as he put down his pan, inside which gold sparkled. Just specks, but the glittering bits elicited a vocal response from Mengzi.

"Look at this, after Shuangfu's people have panned it," Baigou said. "Gold is pussies, running to whoever has money."

"He's got a metal detector," Mengzi said.

"He struck it rich before he got the detector. At this rate, White Tiger Pass will be turned upside down within a year. I'm trying to find a way to get a loan so I can open a pit. People far and near have turned into hungry mayflies and mad fleas, swarming over here to suck our blood. Drag your feet and the stink will blow right past you. Haven't you heard? The city's getting envious and will soon take total control. Once that happens, even Big Head will have to stay out of it. I'm going to get a pit and take a chance while he still has some say. I'll either get rich or become a beggar."

Mengzi was tempted again. He wanted to talk his father into sticking his neck out. He didn't pin his hopes on a loan; for a poor man that would be like waiting for food to rain from the sky. He hoped he could get his father to sell the goats, trees, and the extra grain to give it a try. It was up to fate whether they succeeded or not.

"You need more than ten thousand to open a pit. I can't shoulder the whole amount," Baigou said. "How's this? You, me, Huaqiu, and my brother get together. We split the profits if we make it and share the costs if we don't."

"Then you'll have to convince my father. His brain's like a burl on an elm tree, one you can't open with eight axes. But if you can open it a crack, I'll be able to carve it wider."

They picked up their pans and went to Mengzi's house. At the first mention of the idea, Laoshun dumped cold water on the idea, and with reason, "Can't you see that no more than three out of ten actually make it? Why give up the old life and go through all the trouble just to end up without a pair of pants to put on?"

The two young men walked out dejected.

"You have a ready-made God of Wealth. Why don't you go see her?" Baigou said, "A strand of Shuangfu's wife's hair is thicker than our waists. She can have a share and join in on the profits if we make it."

So, Mengzi went to see Shuangfu's wife, who agreed to lend him five thousand after he talked himself hoarse. It was a loan, and she'd have nothing to do with the pit, whether it paid off or not.

"Sure," Mengzi offered. "I'll make you a golden carrot if we find gold, so you can sleep well at night. If we fail, you can have me as the repayment."

Within days, Baigou, Huaqiu, and Beizhu each put up five thousand, and the four of them went to see Big Head to purchase panning rights.

4

They had to offer sacrifice to the Earth God before they started digging. It was their convention, treating the deity before opening holes on his body. If not, he could quake and you'd be buried alive, no matter how good you are.

The sacrifice consisted of killing an animal. The Daoist Master told them that the Earth God loved blood, so a blood sacrifice was a must. Mengzi dragged a castrated ram to the future site of their pit. The animal, obviously aware of its fate, dug its hooves in and pulled with all its might in the other direction. It was just a ram, after all, and no amount of struggle would let it escape its destiny. With a shout, Mengzi used both arms to lift it into the air, where it cried and kicked. Quickly Mengzi put his knees over the animal, got a knife from Huaqiu, and sent crimson blood spurting out of its neck.

"Please protect us, Earth God," Mengzi called out.

"We're protected," the others responded.

"Please give us lots of gold, Earth God," Mengzi called out again.

"Lots of gold," the others echoed.

The villagers came up, some with silk comforter covers and others with wool blankets to hang on the well frame. It was a sloppy-looking frame, made of a few crisscrossed horizontal beams. Without enough money to rent a hoist, they had to settle for a rope ladder and a water pump; the remaining money was reserved for other expenses. Luckily, the four of them were all young enough to be both owners and sand boys. Beizhou had worked for a while at Shuangfu's pit, so he had a good idea about how to go about it. With him giving instructions, the pit took shape.

Mengzi was first to dig. After surviving being buried alive, he was proof that "Great fortune comes to those who live through a major disaster." The villagers agreed.

His chest swelled as he dug his spade in, as if he could swallow up the sky or spit out the earth. This felt like his first major life endeavor. If he did it well, it would be a foundation that might change his fate. If he failed, no, he wouldn't fail. He flung the spadeful of dirt with so much force it was blown back into his face by the damned desert wind. "Is this a bad omen?" was the thought that crossed his mind.

Baigou was skinning the ram that was still twitching. After stripping the pelt off one leg, he pounded and pulled, quickly make the animal skinless, like a naked woman. It was handed to Fengxiang, who chopped it into pieces the size of a fist to feed the villagers who came to hang lucky red cloth on the frame.

Beizhou and Huaqiu took over the digging job.

Mengzi spotted his father. Laoshun had been standing far off, but slowly inched over, and draped a red object over the frame. Mengzi felt a warm current rise up. Despite his objection to Mengzi's risk taking, Laoshun still expressed his well-wishing in the unique, local style. Besides the villagers, family members of the four young men also came to "drape red." Opening a pit, like building a house, was a major event, and the more red drapes, the more auspicious.

The four young men did not mind hard work, so they hired only eight sand boys, who would work in two shifts, taking turns going down into the pit. The digging was easy, and soon a gaping, black hole appeared. Baigou tossed a few pieces of cooked mutton into the hole, as a sacrifice to the Earth God, and put the remaining pieces on platters he took to the well-wishers. With more people than mutton, none of them got much to eat, but fortunately there was plenty of liquor. They drank and shouted, their faces soon turning red.

The sun rose higher, so did the noise level along the Dasha River. At a glance, the bank was thronged with shouting people, like crazed ants. Noise from other sources were even more deafening—machines, workers, metal tools biting rocks, drinkers playing drinking games, cheers and curses—all gathered to form a whirlwind that rushed at people's heads.

Laoshun's face turned red after a few drinks; slurring his words, he staggered over, and Mengzi knew he was going to talk to him. It was the same every time his father got drunk. Tossing down his spade, Mengzi walked up to him and, sure enough, Laoshun began to mumble:

"Don't blame your old man, son. I have so little, but I have to support several people. I'm not like you. I lived through the sixties. Back then, corpses were piled in layers by the Dasha River. There was no grain in the warehouse, and we were all worried sick."

"I know," Mengzi said, "I know."

"What do you know? I can't sell the goats; I need them to give us kids."

"I know that."

"You don't know shit. The trees—"

"Watch out. Don't mess your pants when you fart," Mengzi said loudly before he finished, drawing laughter from observers. Laoshun shook his head and laughed with them.

Mengzi exhaled deeply and looked into the sky, a vast, blue expanse, where he could fly off into beautiful spots if he could sprout wings. The pit was his chance to do that; he had lots of ideas, big ideas, but no money. Any grand aspiration would be empty talk without it.

The hole got deeper. Baigou was getting the rope ladder set up so he and Huaqiu could start the first shift, which was less physically taxing, as the hole was still relatively shallow. Mengzi and Beizhou were busy building a hut; they dug a trough by the pit, piled on rocks, and laid a few logs before carting over wheat grass, which they spread out on the ground; they would be able to spend the night there after unrolling their bedding. Dust had yet to settle when Mengzi lay face-up on his blanket. He was keyed up, with limitless energy bouncing around inside him. The noise was thunderous, but he heard only his own heartbeat echoing in the sky. Thump, thump, loud and powerful.

Huaqiu carried sand with Fuqiangzi, recently out of school. Not particularly strong, he was drenched in sweat after a few rounds. He always wore a smile, which showed up brilliantly as he sweated. His favorite pastime was collecting Liangzhou folk songs. As a child, he'd spent time with the blind Minstrel Jia and learned quite a few tunes, though he hadn't mastered the longer narratives. When he had nothing to do, he hummed a tune or two. He had a very modest ambition: working as a sand boy to earn travel money so he could collect folk tunes from all over Liangzhou and publish a book. "The songs will be gone when this generation dies out, so I consider it saving our cultural heritage," he said. He'd be paid twenty yuan a day.

Mengzi sympathized with the sweat-soaked young man, who was panting like a cow. "Here, let me carry a few loads for you," he said.

"No thanks," Fuqiangzi said with a laugh. "I'll do it. I can't let you help when you're paying me. Besides, people are weird; the slower you go, the easier you tire yourself out. I'll get used to it in a few days."

"You're right, of course." Mengzi responded with a laugh.

Water had flowed down the Dasha River for thousands of years; beneath the top layer of sand were cobblestones that sent up a grating noise that set one's teeth on edge. Mengzi could not stand the sound, and his teeth hurt whenever he heard it. But another layer of sand lay several feet down, underneath which was dirt, followed by more pebbles. A dozen meters or more below that was a thin layer of sand where gold could be found. Continue digging and you hit something as hard as limestone, which could be rocks or clay. The crust stopped all digging for gold.

Mengzi began putting together a wooden framework when they dug past three meters or so. Without it, a rock could fall and open a gash on the diggers' heads, and the safety helmets they were wearing would be flattened if a big rock fell on them. Frames for such purpose were usually made of beams and rafters in a lattice pattern, with willow branches or shrub twigs filling up the middle. All the materials were readily available in the desert. You needed only to pick a dark night and take a camel-cart to Nanshan, where a few hours of illegal cutting would get you enough wood to use for a while.

5

Mengzi and Fuqiangzi took a camel cart to the desert to scrounge for birch branches. As they passed the dance hall, he spotted Yue'er and a few girls sunning themselves at the door. Picking up his pace, he pretended not to see her, but she called out to him:

"Hey, you're not too smug to recognize me, are you? You've just started a gold pit, but you already have your nose in the air. You promised to take me to Shawan, so what's happening now? You lied again, didn't you?"

"I'm going to gather branches." Mengzi said with a smile. "You can come along, but don't start crying when we're halfway there."

Yue'er laughed as she jumped onto the cart.

The sand boys hooted the moment she got on.

"Is that your bride, Mengzi?"

"Hell, no. She's a proper girl from a good family."

"These days, there's no standard for what's proper and what's not."

"That's right. Even if she's no longer a virgin, you can repair the maidenhead."

Mengzi glanced at Yue'er and saw she was squinting up at the clouds, so he breathed a sigh of relief as he whipped the camel to get it running like a gray dragon. The sand boys' voices came after them, but the rumbling cart made it impossible to make out what they were saying.

The camel cart turned into the desert, where the city, which was building an irrigation ditch, had paved a road by laying down dried wheat grass under rock and dirt. It was constantly being submerged by sand, but its outline was still visible. The cart did not sink as it went along. They kept running into sand boys heading the other direction with cartloads of birch branches.

After creaking along for two hours, they entered a sand trough deep enough to gather water from all around when it rained. Sometimes, runoff from neighboring hills would flow too fast to follow its original track and instead end up in the trough, where it stayed. As time passed, birch, red willow, needle grass, and yellow thorns made the trough their home. In earlier days, the villagers came to cut birch branches for the roofs or houses they were building; wriggling little worms soon sent down bran-like wood dust. Later, the county's forestry station put tree groves under its jurisdiction and sent a crooked-necked old man to guard against illegal logging. He appeared to be drunk all the time. Anyone who wanted birch would encounter no objection; he'd call anyone daddy for a bottle of swill.

The sun hanging above the trough spewed out its heat. Yue'er's nose was beaded with sweat, each sparkling drop adding an uncommon charm to her looks. Something strange softened in Mengzi's heart, but he was too lazy to pursue the thought. In his eyes, Yue'er was an immortal fairy who would one day fly into the celestial realm. He could pine for her all he wanted, but that would bring only frustration. Your heart is harmless if you leave it alone, but if you stir something up, it can turn into a ferocious beast and tear you to pieces, leaving you at a loss. Which was why most of the time Mengzi left it alone.

Fuqiangzi made an arc with his chopper and began cutting, littering the ground with felled branches, which Yue'er gathered and piled onto the cart. She moved in a lively, alluring manner; Mengzi felt heat rise up and his heart fluttered. He knew, however, that women are a mixture of happiness and trouble. Oftentimes, just when you feel happy, trouble follows. Take Shuangfu's wife, for example. All together he'd had several hours of pleasurable moments with her, but trouble came in rounds; his heart went into action, jabbing here and poking there, and before long he was a mass of scars.

He swallowed and walked up to tidy the branches and make room for more. With constant logging by sand boys, the shrubbery was thinning out. Mengzi realized that the growth would be gone in no time at this rate. Meng Baye was always talking about environmental protection, so Mengzi knew something about the issue, but it was more like frost, which turns to vapor under the unrelenting sun called survival.

Suddenly he heard someone screaming curses. He turned his head to see the old man with a crooked neck coming at them with a switch. Fuqiangzi was prepared; he took out a bottle of liquor from a cloth sack and handed it over. It was a common practice among the sand boys, so it should have worked, but to their surprise, the old man's switch whizzed in the air and lopped off the bottle's narrow neck. Fuqiangzi was too stunned to react when the next branch whizzed at his calf.

"Thieves. You're all thieves." He screamed at them, brandishing the switch while mouthing cheeky comments about their mothers.

It was clear to Mengzi that no sweet talk would work on the old man, who must have been reprimanded by the forestry station and was unhappy with the illegal loggers. If he went up, he'd be rewarded with a lashing, so he took out a rope he'd used on wild horses, made a lasso, and flung it. With a flick of the wrist, the old man fell and rolled into the sand trough, where his bound body loosened his tongue more, as he spewed even worse expletives against their mothers.

Yue'er blanched at first, but started laughing when the old man rolled down like a ball of meat. Fuqiangzi pulled up his pant leg to reveal ugly welts on his calf; he gave them a few quick rubs and spat at the old man. Instead of revenge, he hurried to load the branches.

The old man rolled into a sitting position, flailing and kicking. Afraid the lasso might come off, Mengzi looped it until the old man turned into a wrapped zongzi. Yet that only made him fill the trough with loud, colorful expressions.

"Hurry, load the cart," Mengzi shouted as he tugged at the lasso. He didn't want anyone from the forestry station to catch them red-handed. Fuqiangzi and Yue'er hastily loaded the cart, too harried to make a neat pile, so the branches were already teetering before the cart started moving.

"Hurry up, let him go," Fuqiangzi shouted.

Mengzi flipped his hand over to untie the old man. After what I did, the old guy ought to behave himself, Mengzi thought, so he was surprised to see him run at him, yelling and cursing. He was a tough old goat, he realized, so he tossed the rope at Fuqiangzi while dodging to the side and tripped the old man, who ran headlong into a sandy slope.

"Hurry!" Mengzi was sitting on the old man, like riding a tiger. If he let go, the old guy would fight, but Mengzi couldn't sit on him forever. He was still cursing, with three generations of Laoshun's ancestors his added target.

"Show him how an old man watches over melons," Fuqiangzi laughed.

That ought to work. Mengzi cut off a section of the rope to tie the old man's hands behind his back, then removed his pant cord, pushed his head down and stuck the angry face into the crotch of his own pants before wrapping the cord around it. The guard turned into a ball that rolled around the trough. His voice was muffled by his pants, so they could hear but not understand his angry shouts.

The three of them fled on their cart. The old man's smothered curses were still audible after they'd traveled a long way. Yue'er was holding her belly, laughing and rolling in the cart.

Not wanting the man to bake into a dry corpse under the hot sun, Mengzi sent someone to set him free as soon as he reached the pit. He immediately came after them at White Tiger Pass, cursing all the way, grabbed Mengzi, and was about to jump into the pit. After lots of sweet talk, Baigou and the others gave him fifty yuan and treated him to four *jin* of liquor. In the end, they had to turn Mengzi into "an old man watching over melons."

Looking at Mengzi rolling on his bedding, his head stuffed in his pants' crotch, the man said:

"I've never seen anyone that bad." He burst out laughing before he finished.

6

More than two weeks of hard work later, they had a pit heading down to the center of the earth. At first glance, it looked like Shuangfu's. Mengzi felt like being a boss, and the others were acting cocky, too, guzzling beer and shouting out their drinking games, until their faces were as red as roosters.

Yue'er came often to the pit. She always smiled sweetly and gave him a pensive look. One night, Mengzi walked her back; when they reached a dark spot, she was frightened. When she took his hand, he pulled her close and kissed her, wanting to do more.

"No," she said. "I'm saving myself for my husband."

"Then I'll be your husband." He was breathing hard.

She laughed and poked his forehead.

"You're the ugly toad drooling over a swan."

Mengzi rued his rash action when he got back to the pit. He thought she would be upset with him, but she returned the next day, with the same gaze, something shiny flickering in her eyes.

He was falling for her and, without realizing it, Ying'er had receded to the back of his mind. Nothing he could do about that. Ying'er would be a good wife, he knew, but still he longed for Yue'er. Ying'er felt cold, distant to him, while Yue'er was like fire, and something in her eyes could set him aflame even if she just looked at him quietly. There were pretty girls everywhere around White Tiger Pass, but Yue'er was the only one he wanted. When he thought about it, he became aware that he'd had a crush on her for a long time, but had kept the feeling to himself. Everyone in his village thought she would marry a city man, and never expected she'd flee back home.

Yue'er had come back a different person; she no longer talked about her aspirations, and seemed weighed down by something, as she was often lost in thought. She was more affectionate with Mengzi, without prompting, as if she had her eye on him. It puzzled Mengzi, who even thought it was on account of the pit. One night, under the effects of alcohol, he told her that once they found gold, he'd ask the Shaman to make a marriage proposal to her father.

"Do you really think I'm after your gold?" She smiled with her lips pressed.

Shuangfu had opened a pit next to theirs. His hoist rumbled insolently, taking the wind out of their sails. No matter how they looked at it, they really ought to buy a hoist, for it would save time and energy. But they were too expensive. Mengzi had to swallow his frustration. Baigou and others weren't pleased either, but they raised a racket as they played drinking games, loud enough to compete with the sound of the thundering hoist. Luckily, Shuangfu did not come often, showing up only when the bottom needed to be flushed out. Wherever a pit reached the bottom, wherever there was a gold strike, that was where you'd find Shuangfu.

Water dripped down the side walls, truly worthless, trouble-making pussy. They never saw a drop when there was a drought and water was urgently needed, but when they had no use for it, it found cracks to squeeze through, trickling here and dribbling there to pool at the bottom of the pit. At times like this, they flipped on a switch and the pump roared into life taking the water out.

Mengzi had woven the frame carefully. He had not been bold enough to go back to the desert after the logging incident. The old man's sons had suffered a great loss of face when Mengzi used the "old man watching over melons" on him, and had spread the word that they'd get even. Mengzi didn't scare easily, unlike some who freaked out at the first sign of a threat, but a smart man never willingly stands under a falling wall. Instead, he went to Nanshan to cut willow branches, which weren't as sturdy as birch, but strong enough to block falling rocks. With the beams and rafters chipped in by all of them, they got a frame that looked more ungainly than most.

Mengzi grew more apprehensive as they neared the bottom. Quite a few people had lost everything in recent days. Some had gotten rich, but more had suffered losses. He was sure that at some point in the past someone had panned gold around the area, because people kept digging up "worn pits," which were filled-in mines after gold had been panned. When you ran into a "worn pit," you'd never get your investment back, let alone strike it rich. Some that did not look like "worn pits" only produced bits of "gold chaff" when they bottomed out. The gold mines at White Tiger Pass were oddly and unevenly distributed, and tended to concentrate in spots. Lucky ones could dig up large chunks, gold nuggets called garlic cloves by the locals. Those with average luck managed to pan placer gold at most, while the unlucky never saw even a sliver. Everyone said that gold was an ass-kisser. It turns into iron when you're unlucky, and iron turns into gold when luck is with you. It all depended on your fortune.

God of Fortune, please bless me! Mengzi prayed silently.

Chapter Twenty-Five

A lone wild goose circles the sky, calls out to its flock
No compassionate response from anywhere

1

On that terrifying night in the desert, Ying'er saw that the monster lit up by her flashlight turned out to be her camel.

"Camel, it's our camel!" She shouted and nudged Lanlan, who sat up at once. The camel was snorting. What wonderful news. They'd thought they'd lost it for good, but, to their joyfully surprise, it had come back on its own. Lanlan stumbled over to the camel and untied a rope to remove their water jug. They were in luck, for it was still more than half full.

"Water!" Ying'er cried out, the word more refreshing than anything else.

Lanlan twisted open the plastic cap and handed her the jug, "Don't drink too much. Just a little for now, or your stomach will burst."

Ying'er took a pleasing sip and swallowed little by little. She'd expected a coolness to slide down her throat, but to her surprise, it felt like it was on fire. Maybe her esophagus was cracked. The thirst was even more unbearable after she swallowed a few times.

Lanlan took the jug away so she wouldn't drink more. Someone in her village had died from too much water after suffering from serious thirst. A stomach at a time like this had probably shrunk to the size of a fist.

After taking a small sip, Lanlan picked up the flashlight to shine on the camel. Quite a few items it carried had been lost. Their flour sack was in tatters, its contents gone; the goat pelt flask had cracked, so there was no more water in it. But at least the jug was undamaged and retained enough liquid for their survival. The gauzy scarf was there, still wrapped around two steamed buns. There had been more than a dozen when the camel left, but obviously they'd fallen off as it ran.

Their bedding remained on the litter, so did a canvas sack with ball bearings, a pack of gunpowder, and a roll of twine. Ying'er naturally wished that the flask was undamaged, so she could drink to her heart's content, but that was a pipe dream and would only make her unhappy, so she put it out of her mind.

The reins had been trampled and broken and were now only ten feet long. Lanlan took a length of the twine and divided it into pieces that she attached to the reins. They were overjoyed by the surprised return of the camel. Laoshun had told them that camels had a great sense of smell and could detect an odor ten *li* away if the wind was blowing in their direction. If the camel felt like it, it would have no trouble catching up with them. It had not lost much of its body fat, so obviously, it had enough to eat.

What had gone on in the camel's mind was a mystery. It wasn't hard coming up with reasons why it had fled, such as the threat of the jackals or the sweltering heat. They could also explain why it came back; it might have felt bad about abandoning the two women, for instance. But they could not fathom the internal struggle it had fought, though it it must have been as violent as battling jackals.

Having their hands on the reins, they finally felt better. Ying'er felt sorry for the animal: after escaping human control and experiencing an internal struggle, it had returned, only to be rewarded with the gift of the reins. That must mean that the humans didn't trust it, an unhappy thought, Ying'er assumed. She shone the flashlight into its eyes and saw only kindness and compliance. There was no sign of guilt over fleeing or happiness about its sudden arrival; it looked as composed as ever.

Their hunger intensified after a few mouthfuls of the buns and water. Despite the urge, neither of them dared to have more, for they did not want to die of bloating. Being hungry ghosts was bad, and bloating death wasn't much better.

The return of the camel fortified their minds, but fatigue sneaked in to take over their body. Lanlan made the camel lie down for them to lean against its side and doze off. It was a brief respite, but the most peaceful sleep they'd had in days.

It was bright and light when they woke up. They nibbled more of the steamed buns and felt their strength returning.

"Let's not go east now that we have our camel back," Lanlan said. "We'll head north again, which will take us to the salt lakes. We'd have to turn north after we reached the herders in the east anyway, and that would cost us more time."

She could not have imagined that her idea would cast them into the boundless desert, where the sword of death would again hang over their heads.

The sun was visible in the east, where a faint red glow showed in the sky. A striking contrast formed between the shady sand hollow and the luminous eastern sky, like a woodblock painting with clear gradations. Waves of sand rippled in undulating patterns, rising up to become dunes. The texture of the nearby patterns looked like wavelets, so delicate they hated to trample on them.

Ying'er shivered in the cold desert wind, though her jacket blocked some of the wind's force. Lanlan's face had a greenish hue and was covered in goose bumps. They'd been too tired to take down the bedding from the litter, so, not long after they fell sleep, they were awakened by an early morning chill typical of the desert. That was fine with them, as they could take advantage of the coolness and get moving again. The desert was such a weird place, a freezer in the morning and a Donkey Roaster at noon, Ying'er thought.

They got settled behind the camel's humps, solid, warm spots that gave them the feeling of climbing back into a small boat after falling into the water. Camels were great; now they had something to depend upon.

The camel's back rose and fell gently, slow but confident, making the sand ridge sway from their vantage point. The sun that had forced its way off the horizon was pitching too, but it to appeared to be carrying a heavy load. Ying'er's face was warmed by the sunlight, and she felt alive again. The sun would show its power in a few hours, but now that they had their camel, she was reassured. She couldn't help it; she was a woman, after all. Pain knifed through her feet and legs, after traveling all these nights; she ached all over. Without the camel, she could not have taken another step. She was too weak, too thin to have the strength that would take her to the sand sea's far shore. But the camel could. A large, steady animal, it seemed always deep in thought, like a philosopher. Though it said nothing, the force brimming from its body penetrated deep into her soul.

From the way the camels had shaken their heads and flicked their ears when they first entered the desert, Ying'er knew that was a sign of their reluctance. She recalled how Laoshun had said he'd had to repeatedly lash the camel's back until its fur flew. Sometimes his whip went for its tenderest spot—its nose—for the camel to obey his command. Camels obviously knew their backs would be used either for humans or for cargo once they were in the desert. Its destiny was to be a beast of burden, just as waiting was Ying'er's destiny. No animal would suffer willingly, so the camel she was riding had earned her respect for returning after its flight. If you'd decided not to come back, she said silently to the camel, you could be having an easy time now, either lying down in a sand trough to chew your cud, feasting on desert rice or, enjoying tender grass. Now you have to carry two women who have had a tough life, just like you, and set off again for an unknown future.

How could I not admire and respect you, camel?

Lanlan looked around to get her bearings. She knew a route to the salt lakes, but the jackals had ruined her sense of familiarity. Facing the surging sand waves, she felt that she had been cast into unfamiliar territory again by fate, a feeling that plagued her often, as she felt confronted by immense strangeness. From childhood to this moment, she came up against it again and again; she put up with it, and yet there was always more, endless unfamiliarity. The world was getting stranger by the day, and she felt unmoored, not knowing what to do.

"Have you figured out where we're headed?" Ying'er asked.

"I'm not sure. I'm kind of lost, but for now we'll just accept our fate, like a whipped lizard. Let's get on the road. If we're headed in the right direction, at some point we'll know for sure."

That's what we'll do then, Ying'er said to herself.

The sun rose higher and the heat began to attack them again. They had to conserve their water, since neither knew where they might find more of it. It was the source of their survival. Their thirst was nearly unbearable, but they mustn't drink too much, taking small sips only when they couldn't focus.

"Anyone who knows how to make use of water will never take too big a drink," Lanlan said. "Once it enters your body, it turns into urine. Every mouthful you take has to be converted into nutrients to support you, so pace yourself."

They got down off the camel after a couple of hours. it was foaming at the mouth and panting like a bellows, clearly exhausted. Lanlan said they had to let it rest. They picked a spot with desert stalks and unloaded the litter. Lanlan was stunned to see the animal's back festering and emitting a stench. It was obviously caused by the litter, which had rubbed it raw, bumping up and down when it ran. The festering spot looked horrible. Ying'er felt terrible that they'd sat on the camel's wound and made it travel for so long.

Lanlan took out some salt from the canvas bag, and mixed it with water to wash the wound. "Why didn't you make a sound? We wouldn't have ridden if we'd known you were hurt."

The camel called out, as if to say, it's all right, it's nothing.

The sun rose higher and the heat got worse.

"We'll have to do the same thing, lie down in a damp pit when it's hot and get on the move," Lanlan said. "We should have enough water to last us to the salt lakes if we're careful."

Ying'er knew Lanlan was trying to make her feel better. They'd have been able to travel on the planned route to the salt lakes if not for the attack of the jackals. Now it was hard to say if they would ever get there, after heading east for so long before turning north. She kept the thought to herself. When facing a dead end, you have to keep your morale high and refrain from being self-defeating.

"Heaven will always leave us a way out," she said to Lanlan. "We'll be fine now that we have our camel back."

Lanlan was happily surprised when she found in a small bag on the litter a bottle that was more than half filled with sesame oil. They'd packed it in a separate bag so it wouldn't break if it bumped against pots, and it had been saved from being jettisoned. It wouldn't taste good but it would supply them with the nutrition they needed; as plant-based, it would give them more energy than the steamed buns.

"Let's not touch the oil yet," Lanlan said. "The buns are so dry we need to eat them with water so they'll go down easily. We'll make do with them and the water for a few meals and drink the vegetable oil as a last resort."

The sight of the oil sent a coolness into Ying'er's heart.

They found a shaded hollow and dug two holes until they saw dampness in the sand; they let the camel have the larger one. It had an internal water reservoir, but prolonged exposure to the hot sun was still hard on it. They made it lie down in the pit to take in moisture while keeping it from losing more. Experience taught them not to dig too close to a steep slope. Lanlan cut down some desert stalks and carried them into the pit for the camel to chew on while it stayed out of the sun.

Thirst and hunger continued to torment them, but they felt much better than when the camel had fled. Back then, they'd run out of ammunition and provisions, so thirst and hunger were clawing at their insides. Now with food and water, they were able to put up with the two needs. They had little of the wonderful necessities, but at least it was something they could look forward to.

Lanlan kept mixing salt with water on the cap of the plastic jug to wash the camel's wound. She asked Ying'er to hold the jug between her legs while she made the solution. Ying'er was on tenterhooks, fearing the jug would break away from her grasp and spill the life-saving liquid over the sand; there seemed to be hands in the air trying to snatch it away from her. Her arms ached from the effort to secure the jug, and she got increasingly tense, to the point that she was exhausted by the time Lanlan finished.

After rinsing the wound, Lanlan poured the remaining solution into her palm and showed it to the camel, which then stuck out its tongue to lick the cool liquid. Camels love salt, and the saline water could be considered its reward even if the coolness had little effect. In the end, the camel actually had more water than they did, but that was fine with them. Neither of them wanted the wound to get infected, and both hoped it would scab soon. They needed the camel as their ride, but, more importantly, they felt reassured by its presence.

2

Two more days passed as they traveled by night and rested by day. They should have reached the salt lakes, judging by the progress they'd made. Instead, to their surprise, they found themselves in a rock-strewn gobi. Lanlan panicked at the sight, as she did not recall seeing rocks on her earlier trip. That could only mean they'd taken a wrong turn. The buns were long gone and they had little water left; they hadn't touched the oil, which would not last them long anyway. The camel's wound was scabbing, but neither had the heart to get back on. When fatigue overtook them, one of them led the camel while the other held onto its tail to conserve strength. Their legs felt like they belonged to someone else, so after a while they took turns to ride the camel, two hours each.

The camel's humps had caved in, a sign that it was losing its reserve energy. They hadn't walked past much vegetation; Lanlan had always tried to stop at grassy spots to rest for the day, for the camel's sake, but its humps sagged anyway. She recalled what her father had said about the humps as emergency energy storage; a camel must have enough water and feed, particularly the former. She remembered that, along the path to the salt lakes, there were several sites specially designated as camel supply stations. Obviously, the animal had missed its chance when they took the wrong turn. Lanlan unloaded the litter and removed the grass padding under the saddle to feed to the camel. She replaced it with a blanket. The little bit of grass was of scant use to a hungry camel.

Camels prefer to eat at night, which is the best time to travel. It grazed in the day, to be sure, but the sand troughs turned into a furnace when they stopped, and it could graze only for a short while before the sun forced it into the pit. Besides, they couldn't always rest in spots with vegetation. So naturally its humps had to cave in.

At least its wound was healing fast, likely due to its nature as quick healers. They are used to carrying loads that rub their backs raw, and, as time passes, a callous forms. The saline solution aided the scabbing process. The camel would be able to carry them as long as it had the energy.

Before leaving for the desert, her father had told them to crush a steamed bun to feed the camel if it was too tired to walk. But at the moment, they didn't even buns for themselves, let alone to feed the camel. To replenish its energy, they stopped for the camel to graze whenever they walked by a grassy spot. But, because of dehydration, it had lost interest in stalks that were dryer than the desert. Humans weren't much different. Try swallowing some fried flour after being baked in the sun for three days and see what happens.

In the past they had walked by a *magang* when they weren't looking for one. They had tender grass that was good to chew on for camels or humans. But they were nowhere in sight when they needed one. One day Ying'er finally noticed one around noontime, where water and livestock appeared. But Lanlan told her it was a mirage, and, sure enough, the enticing scene evaporated. It would be like a fly chasing after a fart if they'd headed its way.

The gobi was actually dotted with grassy spots here and there for the camel to enjoy. Lanlan was convinced that its humps would grow back up if it could eat like that for a month. But they hadn't come out to the desert to graze the camel; they were here for the salt lakes. She knitted her brows and retraced their steps before finally concluding that they'd missed their target. They had to have, she said. It was nothing but an oasis, and not a particularly large one, so they could easily have missed it if they'd been only one li off course somewhere along the route.

Now what?

"We have to turn around and travel west, back into in the desert. If we're lucky, we may walk right into it," Lanlan said.

They tied the camel to a desert shrub when they retraced their steps and began climbing up the highest dune in sight. It would take some effort, but the vantage point would let them see far, and they might even spot the shiny white salt lakes once they were on top. Dragging their leaden legs, they slowly headed upward, taking a break every few steps. It took them at least two hours, and they were spent when they reached the top. They gasped for air for a while before they could get up to look around. The dune had seemed to be the highest in the area, and they thought they'd see smaller ones down below. They were disheartened to see soaring mounds of sand, one higher than the next, all around them. Just looking at them drove any thoughts of more climbing out of them.

"Oh, no," Ying'er cried out and slumped to the ground, where she remained silent for a long time.

Lanlan was quiet too, looking glum. They felt like crying, but no tears came, and their minds were a blank. They would have crawled over if they'd seen a patch of white—the salt lakes—even if it had been on the horizon. But there were only dunes as far as they could see; maybe they would never reach the salt lakes.

"Let's go back down," Lanlan said.

"I don't feel like moving," Ying'er said. "I'd rather die up here and turn into a pile of bones."

"Let's go. We've got to keep going and see where it takes us."

With her eyes on the camel, a yellow dot, down below, Ying'er told herself that he wouldn't have bothered climbing if she'd known. It drained them of energy and was demoralizing.

Too tired to walk, she didn't feel like going down a gentle slope; instead she found a steep spot, sat on the sand, and slid down. Surprisingly, she felt like she'd sprouted wings as she glided down, the wind whipping past her ears, light as air. When she reached a flatter area, she heard Lanlan call out, "Be careful with your pants. You'll tear a hole in them if you keep going like that."

Ying'er did not want that, but the sensation felt too good. I don't even know if I'll live, so why worry about a pair of pants? She jumped back onto the slope, where the sand carried her along like water. Exhilarating. She hadn't felt so relaxed in a long time. She shouted happily, enlivening the silen trough. Infected by her excitement, Lanlan sat down on the sand, no longer worried about her pants either, and glided down. They yelled out joyfully, releasing long pent-up feelings.

After a while, Ying'er started to worry that the seat of her pants would be ruined. If that happened, she would not be able to face people when they reached the salt lakes. So, she turned over, and began swimming in the sand. Every stroke propelled her a distance; sand drifted into her collar, ticklish but pleasant. Lanlan copied her, and they filled the sand trough with their cheerful shouts. The unexpected delight erased all their worries.

When they reached the bottom, they spat out sand and laughed themselves silly. For years, they'd lived under the gaze of others; this was the first time they were able to let go, and were surprised to rediscover their inner girlhood at a time and in a spot where they were about to abandon all hope.

They each took a sip of the sesame oil, to celebrate their good mood.

3

The merriment had taken everything out of them. Worry stole into their hearts after the brief carefree indulgence. They wondered how far they would be able to travel, and whether or not they'd ever reach the salt lakes. The more they reflected, the deeper the funk into which they sent themselves, so they had to put the questions out of their minds. As the sun's power lessened, they got on the camel and headed west. It wasn't clear if they'd reach their destination, but moving meant they would not be trapped and die in the ocean of sand. Getting on the road was the better option. Even a blind donkey runs into a haystack sometimes, so they might happen upon someone going to the salt lakes or a herder. Whoever it might be would have a mouth under his nose, and would supply an answer if asked. They might even get some food and water, if it was a good person.

They walked by a camel carcass at dusk; it was lying by a sand eddy. Their startled camel shook its head so violently they nearly fell off. Lanlan was gladdened by the sight, for it signaled human traces in the area. Two black holes in the ghastly skull stared back at them. It must have been staring blankly for a long time. The bones were relatively intact, and its teeth and ribs remained attached. Clearly, it hadn't been attacked by wild animals either before or after it died. The bones of its own kind had their camel shake its head, flick its ears, and spit loudly. Laoshun would say it had seen a ghost, which feared spittle. Could the soul of the dead camel still be hanging around its carcass? They had heard about a corpse-guarding ghost that stayed by the bones until they were interred. Though frightened, Ying'er did not believe a ghost would be guarding its carcass in broad daylight.

"Look. It was on its way to carry salt," Lanlan said, pointing to the bits of fabric by the carcass. "It must have belonged to a Mongol and died of exhaustion on the road."

Ying'er saw no sign of salt transport, but was pleased to hear that. It was good news to see something like that on the road; they had seen only sand, gobis, and some desert vegetation, nothing with human connections. The carcass at least meant human traffic.

But it occurred to her that it could have been a wild camel. She didn't say anything, however, afraid of dampening Lanlan's mood. When you are at the end of your rope, you desperately need something to look forward to; even an illusion is better than despair.

If the camel died on its way to transport salt, Ying'er told herself, it could mean that the lakes were still far off; if not, the camel might have struggled to reach its destination. Her despondency increased as she speculated the reason behind the camel's death. If nothing else, it meant there was neither a water source nor edible grass nearby. What other than thirst or illness could have killed the camel? It must have given up hope before it died, as dispassionate as a meditative monk in his last moments. Lying quietly in a sand trough, it must have meekly met its fate. She let out a long sigh, as she thought about her own fate.

Lanlan had the camel kneel so they could climb back on its back. It rocked and swayed before finally getting to its feet.

"So long," Ying'er turned to say to the carcass. "You had a tough life." The sad possibility occurred to her that she might turn into a carcass down the road.

No visible path appeared as they traveled on, but they encountered bones, either a whole carcass or leg bones sticking up out of the sand. This could be camel path or a pasture, Ying'er said to herself. Otherwise, where did all the bones come from? She felt better now.

Lanlan hoped to shoot a rabbit, but oddly, the only live animal either of them had seen was the rabbit Ying'er had frightened off.

"Even a desert rat would be good," Lanlan said with a sigh. As a child, she'd roasted and eaten desert rats, which tasted better than chicken. When her hunger got the better of her, Lanlan wouldn't have minded seeing a jackal, though the mere thought of the scary beasts made her jittery. If they happened upon a lone jackal, one shot would produce a delectable treat. Some villagers said jackal was as tasty as dog, others said it was dry and bland, like fox, and there were still others who claimed it was sour, like crow. It didn't matter what it was like; it was meat, and it would keep them alive. But it was hopeless. The jackals dogged them when they wanted them gone, but now that one would be welcome, it was nowhere to be seen.

A single sip of the good oil provided as much energy as a whole meal. But less than half the bottle remained, even though they had taken only small sips each time. It was hopeless. Lanlan said they must have been followed by a hungry ghost that sneaked their oil. That had happened in the village. If you encountered one, even a fat ram would last no more than a few meals—mutton jinxed by a hungry ghost never lasted long. There was, naturally, another explanation: anyone whose food did not last long was born to be poor. Lanlan's father appraised guests this way: if the meat they bought for a guest did not get eaten right away, then the visitor was born to be rich. But if the meat seemed to disappear in no time, it would appear that the guest was destined to be poor. Based on his theory, Lanlan and Ying'er would live lives of poverty, since they could not even hold onto their food and water, and what they had left was disappearing rapidly. Ying'er did not believe in fate, but her conviction wavered, because with every incident she encountered, she seemed under the control of an unknown force.

Finally, they saw what appeared to be a camel path: a litter beside a carcass provided sufficient evidence. The wood on the rack had largely disintegrated in the wind; next to it was a pile of droppings that had been left who knows when. Lanlan was in high spirits, for, no matter how they looked at it, they were finally on the right track. Ying'er was happy, but somewhat dubious, though her mood also brightened. Why were there so many camel carcasses along the way? It not only meant that many salt transporters had passed through, but also signaled that the camels had reached the end of their lives after a long trek. She knew that they faced a fearful fate similar to the white bones littering their route. Did the path really lead to the salt lakes? If so, how far away were they? And could their energy sustain them until they found water? All this was unknown. Lanlan must have been aware of the doubts, she just didn't want to point them out.

What worried Ying'er most was the camel. The two of them could rely on vegetable oil, but the camel's humps were sunken now. How long would it last? It was carrying two adult humans, who weighed at least two hundred *jin*. When it tried to stand up with them on its back, it swayed and rocked before it made it. It wobbled when going uphill, as if it was about to fall. So, they climbed down whenever they were on an upslope and held the animal's tail to help them along. Obviously, it had just about exhausted its strength; otherwise it would not have reacted so strongly when it saw the carcasses.

4

After a break, they each took a sip of the oil and water before they set off for their nighttime journey. The camel carcasses infused the night with a sinister gloom, but also indicated that they were headed in the right direction. We'll be fine once we get on the road, Ying'er said to herself. Far worse to run around like headless flies.

"Moving slowly is always better than standing still. Every step takes us closer, so long as we're heading the right direction," Lanlan said.

"Down, down." They called out for the camel to kneel.

The camel hesitated briefly before kneeling slowly.

"It's too tired," Lanlan said with a sigh.

After they got on the camel's back, Lanlan flicked the rein and shouted "Dei, dei," a few times. The animal swayed as it tried to get up, but only managed to raise its rear legs once before lying down again. It cried out and struggled fruitlessly a few times.

"You stay and I'll get down," Lanlan said as she got down off the camel. She called out to their ride and pulled its tail, but it heaved a sigh and lay motionlessly.

Ying'er knew it did not have the strength to do what it wanted, so she got down too. She saw the camel flaring its nostrils, breathing slowly and laboriously. There were dry desert stalks on the surrounding sand dunes, but it ignored them. It was clear that its throat was too parched from thirst to swallow stalks more arid than the sun. She was grateful to the animal, without whom they would surely be slumped over in some sand trough. I can't ride on it any longer, no matter what, she thought. It isn't made of steel.

Lanlan called out to the camel a few more times, but it just cried piteously, as if to say, You go on. I'm done for. Ying'er remembered what Lingguan had said about camels, how, as long as they have any energy left, they will do what they are supposed to do even if that costs them their lives. In the past, camels in caravans often dropped dead along the way. She wondered if it had been hit hard by the sight of the carcass. It was possible. For older folks with a terminal illness, the news of a friend's death will strike them like a whip and make them lose the will to live. Ying'er patted its head and said:

"Don't be afraid. You're not them, you're different."

The camel cried out again, as if to say it wasn't afraid, but simply couldn't take another step.

Its humps had sagged and turned into leather pouches, and its ribs showed. It was breathing hard and kept sticking out its tongue, which had a thick, yellow and black coating. Its sudden collapse was clearly due to malnutrition, but there had to be non-physical reasons, but Ying'er did not know how to help lessen its mental problems. Impossible—she could not suddenly acquire an ability to communicate with the camel or get into its head. We can't leave it behind, we just can't, she said to herself, not only because it's worth two or three thousand yuan, but also because it has become a member of the team.

It then dawned on her why there had been so many camel carcasses around here. They were telling camels that came after them that they were dead, and now it was the newcomers' turn to die. What a horrific warning. Ying'er recalled how, after falling ill, Hantou had held on to an illusion of getting better. At the time, the flame of his life had continued to burn, though feebly, always on the brink of going out. He died soon after he learned the true state of his illness. Apparently, camels were the same; they thought they would never get out alive after seeing how many camels had died here. Some of them might have still been strong enough to go on, but the suggestion of death destroyed what little hope they had left. She told herself not to follow their example. I'll live as long as my heart isn't dead.

But how to save a camel that had lost the last bit of hope? Since she couldn't get into its head, she had to think of something else. After a brainstorm, she realized that there was nothing they could do but give it some of their sesame oil.

"But that's all we have left," Lanlan said with a knitted brow when Ying'er broached the subject. "And we may have far to travel."

"We can't leave it behind," Ying'er said. "It came back to us after running off."

"All right. Worst case, we die together," Lanlan said.

"That's right. If we live, we make it together. If we have to die, then we'll go with the camel."

Lanlan brought out the bottle and gave it a shake; the oil swirled around, leaving lovely patterns on the side. Ying'er's heart tightened at the sight of the shapeless liquid; Lanlan must have felt the same. There was enough left for them to take a few sips each; it wasn't much but it was the only food they had.

The camel looked at the liquid with greedy eyes, which it had done every time they took a sip. It surely knew how tasty the oil was. In the past, its owner would always reward it with some sticky dregs when a new batch of sesame oil arrived. It was nothing like a desert stalk, which, though good enough to stave off hunger, was repulsive to a tongue that was as dry as the sole of a straw sandal, and a throat that was as parched as sandpaper. The liquid was different; it was smooth and had a wonderful hint of coolness. It had only looked at it greedily, watching the movements around the two women's throats as they swallowed. It could even hear gurgling sounds when the syrupy, shiny, sweet dew slid down their throats. Every cell in bodies that were as dry as smoke cried out joyfully, like a goat that has quenched its thirst at a fresh well. But the camel knew it could only look. To be sure, it was lucky to have something like that to look at; it was painful and yet exciting to see the brief swirl of moist coolness on the inside of the bottle, after the monotonous view of the arid desert.

Naturally, the camel had not expected the woman—lovely, though her lips were covered in dry, dark skin—to tip the bottle toward it, and it thought she was merely teasing. It had been teased like often by villagers. The locals had a saying about hanging alfalfa on the skylight to make an old donkey yearn in vain. They did something similar to camels too. Village children often held up tender grass in front of the camel but snatched it away when it opened its mouth, then laughed over their prank. Humans were like that. In the past, it would close its eyes with a haughtiness when confronted with such teasing, but it was clear how great a temptation the whirl of coolness was at that moment. Even a single glance brought enjoyment. It must have felt both agony and exhilaration, for the enjoyment was painful, like a bachelor burning with lust when watching an erotic movie. His face would be flushed and he would breathe heavily, and yet his lively eyes would not miss a single scene that tormented and titillated him.

The same for the camel.

To its surprise, the bottle's opening was pointed at its own mouth, something it had not expected. Knowing well what the marvelous contents meant to the two women, it looked into their eyes and tried to apprehend the implication. But it saw only eyes brimming with concern. It remembered how once as a young camel it had stumbled into a rat's nest and broken one of its hind legs. Its mother had the same look in her eyes, an unforgettable sight. One should never underestimate a camel's memory; it can remember someone teasing it a decade before and never forgets a handful of fresh grass from someone eight years earlier. It has a better memory than most other animals, better than a horse. Like a horse, a camel has a commonly recognized ability to relate to humans, but with more kindness.

The camel was moved; it did not doubt the message from those eyes and knew she did really want to share the coolness. It did not know that was all they had left, but, from the way the women behaved, was aware of how valuable the liquid was—they took a small sip only every few hours. When they did, they shut their eyes to savor it, obviously trying to instill the flavor deep into their souls. Obviously.

"You go ahead and drink it," the camel felt like saying. It had learned manners from its owner, who behaved like that. He'd want to drink, but would say something similar when offered liquor. His politeness was apparently feigned and insincere, the camel's was genuine. What it meant was clear and straightforward, but humans could never understand, and it could do nothing about it. The camel also knew that changing the human heart was the toughest project in the world, so it had remained silent. Now it could not bring itself to drink the delicious liquid; all it sought was a basin of water. It would close its eyes and drink it all down, even if insects, bits of grass, or tadpoles swam in it. That would not do for the women, who had so little left to drink. The camel gave its head a determined shake.

It could not have imagined that she would tip the bottle into its mouth, or that the smooth liquid would spread over its tongue. It heard its taste buds cry out deliriously, as riotous as cicadas chirping under a hot sun. An unusual taste seeped into the depth of its soul, a sensation it would remember till the day it died. It could hardly be called a taste, for it was more like a vortex of happiness, or a tsunami of divine flavor. There were other analogies for what it was feeling, but it could not think of any. Its greedy taste buds opened feverishly, like farm-raised fish begging for food. The liquid was smooth and viscous, but he lapped it up to moisten its tongue. Now it could eat grass again. After that, it would be able to carry the two pretty women once more. It was unaware of human aesthetic standards, but from the looks by male humans, it knew they were real beauties; it remembered the adolescent gazes by the two herders they'd encountered along the way. They wouldn't really rip the clothes of the women, but their eyes did it for them.

As the liquid in the bottle continued to flow, its mouth took in more of the smooth delicacy, more than its taste buds could favor. The coolness slid down its throat, which moved happily, like entering a female camel. Owing to dehydration, its throat sounded like a snake that had yet to completely molt. Like a rattlesnake. Its throat must have cracked in many places, like a dry riverbed with crisscrossing fissures. The camel had deduced it from the lacerating sensation every time it swallowed dry grass. The throat should be smooth, with a mucous membrane, but now it had turned into an arid riverbed. Thirst was terrible, worse than the village camel with a split nose bridge. Split Nose was an awful camel that would chase after pretty female camels when they were in heat; it bit their hind legs when they tried to get away. They waged a real struggle, not a feigned one, but it was like biting themselves when their hind legs were in the male camel's mouth. One would eventually be pushed to the ground, with unthinkable outcome. So many young females squirmed and cried out sadly under Split Nose. But others of them were equally wicked, choosing to stick with Split Nose after he'd abused them. The camel felt an overwhelming disgust whenever it thought about it. But the unbearable thirst was worse than Split Nose, because the assault of thirst drove even the thought of the evil camel out of its mind.

The camel felt its throat writhe frantically; it was clearly elated, for nothing felt better than the sensation of oil slithering down an esophagus that had cracked like potato skin. It could even hear it moaning happily, like the sound it had made the first time it entered a "fresh" female camel. Male camels were similar to men, both favoring virgins, which in the camel world were called "fresh" camels. But the oil was more gratifying than a fresh camel, a sensation likely shared by its esophagus, for, if not, it wouldn't have writhed and moaned. Not everyone has heard an esophagus moan, but it was like heavenly music. The camel had not heard the expression that the greatest music is silence, but it was able to understand the great tones of happiness roaring silently inside. Imagine yourself under a sweltering sky, where even the air seems to be on fire; a thread of smooth coolness in your body would surely be powerful enough to penetrate deep into your soul. The camel was grateful to the woman for giving it something so marvelous. If I were a man, the camel thought, I'd chase after her. But of course, it was just a thought; daydreaming, a bad habit, based on a camel's natural inclination.

The coolness was slipping into its stomach, making it move joyfully. When the stomach moved, it was like a monster. Normally dark red, it had turned black and hardened, like partially tanned cowhide. It hadn't just stiffened, but had shrunk, like the face of an eighty-year-old woman, or the bark of a desert date tree, or a pig's bladder that had been hung under an eave to dry for three days, or a placenta that has soaked in brine and soy sauce for ten hours. All these images surely would give the stomach the look of a monster. It was making a crunching noise, as if three hundred rats were sharpening their teeth in unison, and the stomach was quickly filled with tiny particles like dust motes. They had settled in the creases of the stomach and, when the gastric juices left without saying good-bye, they took the opportunity to rise and float, limbering up and getting energized. They, too, were happily surprised to discover the oil sliding down the esophagus. No window had opened up in the stomach— that was the jackals' job—so the chamber was dim and the dust motes could not see the semi-transparent material slowly coming their way. The cells along its way had looted what they could get, thus slowing down its progress, but the smell was a vanguard that reached their noses before the liquid itself. No one should underestimate a stomach, which is not just your average sack, but a whole world that will, of course, die when you turn it into cured meat, leaving only a tasty fossil. The brain is the same. When one is alive, it cares about many things, exhibits a multitude of emotions, and develops countless affecting love stories. When it dies, it feels like odorous mush when you put it in your mouth; it can still be tasty, but you will never be able to taste all the stories it produced. The same is true with the stomach.

The sound made by a stomach monster is terrifying. You can exhaust all the adjectives in the world, but they will be woefully anemic. You can make the same noise when you see a ripple of cool, refreshing lake water after you have gone without water for three days in the desert; your breathing will be weak and your soul will be ready to fly off into the sky. It comes not from your vocal cords, but from your soul. Roaring like a whirlwind that fills the worlds beyond, the sound turns into clusters of flailing and grabbing hands, impossible to be represented on a musical score. The camel disliked those thrashing hands, which were, to him, robbers that wanted to seize the little bit of smoothness, shouting noisily to charge and grab, sounding like frenzied footsteps. The camel was ashamed for their sake, as it looked sheepishly at the woman holding the bottle. It wanted to explain, but could not find the words.

The crazed hands took away all the thick, smooth liquid flowing into the stomach, like a sponge soaking up water, or a spring rain irrigating a limestone sandbar, or tadpoles entering a whale's mouth. In any case, it was a silent process that left not a drop behind. Not completely satisfied, they waited for more to come, as did the camel. The mouth of the bottle knocked loudly against its teeth. To make sure it got the oil on the sides, she shook the bottle and the camel felt its teeth clatter.

She tossed the empty bottle into a sand trough. The camel wanted to tell her to keep it for water. She'd be able to fill it if they ran into herders or camel teams. It cried out, but naturally the woman did not understand what it was trying to say. Does she think I've dirtied the bottle?

It looked sadly at the sand trough. She can do what she wants, it thought. It's her bottle, not yours. So why worry about it?

Then it saw the other woman pick up the bottle, wipe its opening with her lapel, and put it in sack hanging on its back.

5

The women and their camel set off at dusk. The camel was able to get up and walk, but was still too weak to carry them. Another disaster. Riding a camel was tiring, their tailbones, bruised by the camel's backbone, burned as if on fire, and their backs were unbearably sore, but that used up less energy than walking. The small sips of oil appeared to have supplied them with energy, though it did nothing to lessen their thirst. Now they had to climb dunes that seemed to reach to the sky. They were not made to walk on sand, and had not gone through the transformation of body fat being converted into muscle for easy desert travel. Pain knifed through Ying'er's calves. Her feet sank with every step she took, and each time the pain worsened, erupting from her soles, causing her to limp.

Each step takes us closer to our destination, she comforted herself. But when she looked around, she saw only dark, soaring dunes. As usual, stars hung low, but they no longer interested her, lost along with the poetic sentiments she'd felt when they entered the desert. Finally, she realized that poetic sentiments are a luxury, something you can enjoy only when you have enough to eat and drink and your survival is not in jeopardy. It hadn't occurred to her to sing a folk tune since they started their journey. It now became clear to her why, unlike her, so many women weren't fans of the tunes; they likely faced the same sort of situation. Under the pressure of basic survival, poetic thoughts are an extravagance and a kind of mood. They require suffering, but when that suffering presses down like a towering mountain, there is no room for them.

So, just keep walking.

Dragging her painful legs, she gazed at the blurry vista ahead under a dusty setting sun. She jellified her thoughts, froze poetic sentiments, stilled her heart, and kept her hopes alive. She held onto the camel's tail, but pulled hard only when going uphill. On level ground, she strove to quicken her steps on leaden legs so as not to be a burden to the camel.

Holding the halter in her right hand, Lanlan looked to be leading the animal forward, but was actually helping herself along. Her father had made a point of putting on the halter before they left home. It wasn't necessary for a camel, which could be controlled by the nose ring tethered to the reins, but it would hurt the animal if she used the rein to support herself, since, as we've seen, a camel's nose is its most vulnerable spot.

There are two effective means of controlling a camel that is acting up. One is to yank on the reins, pulling on the nose to draw tears—if you want to know how that feels, give your nose a hard slap. Two, flog the camel's nose with a whip. It won't take much to make any unruly camel meek. When she tugged at the halter, which was woven of leather strips, that put pressure on the head, and would not hurt the animal even if she pulled hard enough to propel herself forward.

Ying'er held onto the tail to keep moving, made easier with the camel's help. Both women relied on their animal, but with little strain, compared to riding it.

The pain in Ying'er's legs never let up, but she shut her eyes every now and again. She was so exhausted she'd have fallen into a deep sleep if the sand had not tripped her up from time to time. It was beyond her control. Her exhaustion was like liquor in a cellar, the longer it is kept, the stronger it gets. At one point, she thought she was sleeping on her bed, let go of the camel's tail, and slumped to the ground. Luckily, Lanlan turned to check on her when they rounded a bend.

"You're lucky there was no wind. Otherwise, I wouldn't have been able to find you," Lanlan said.

The wind would have blown away all traces and howl strangely to carry off Lanlan's voice when she called out to Ying'er. That would have let other noises lead Ying'er astray, for it would have appeared that Lanlan was calling out to her and she would have followed it until she'd gotten to a place where Lanlan would never find her. That was how many people stranded in the desert died.

To prevent Ying'er from dozing off again, Lanlan tied one end of a rope to Ying'er waist and the other end to the litter. The rope was long enough that it would be slack if Ying'er kept her hand on the camel's tail, but would tighten if she let go. Lanlan, who held onto the rope, would stop and wake Ying'er up. To make it work, Lanlan had to keep the camel under control; otherwise, the animal would drag Ying'er along if startled. That would be like falling off a horse with your foot in the stirrup. As a precaution against that danger, Lanlan made a slip knot on the end of the rope tied to the halter so she could release it if something happened.

They stumbled along among sand hills, half asleep. There had been a bell on the camel when they set off, but it was lost when they escaped from the jackals. Now all they heard was the rustling of their feet on the sand, in addition to the occasional sneeze from the camel, which was loud enough to rouse a sleepy Ying'er.

Their flashlight batteries were running low. They had tried to conserve, but idle consumption can use up a great fortune. Lanlan turned it on only to check the path ahead. Sometimes a frightening carcass came into view under the column of light, a sight that would have sent them shrieking in the past, but was nothing unusual now. If they'd gone a long time without seeing one, Lanlan would even grumble silently, afraid they'd taken a wrong turn again. They weren't all camel carcasses either. Some looked like dogs, but could be foxes; they could not tell them apart. The flowing sand was supposed to bury the carcasses, but strangely, it hadn't, probably because the dunes to the north had blocked the gusting wind. That was just a guess. So many things in Nature defy explanation; something that should be wasn't, like the Crescent Lake in Dunhuang. Instead of being buried in sand it was still there, after centuries.

By midnight, they could not take another step, so they stopped to rest. Ying'er fell asleep the moment she sat down, while Lanlan remained standing to stay awake. She knew they'd be baked alive if they didn't cover more distance at night. But they were so thirsty, and the water in the jug was barely enough for a few more sips. A perilous situation. Thirst, like a fire, scorched her throat and her heart, but she didn't dare touch the water. We have so little left, she said to herself, we'll use it only to save a life. If one of us passes out from the heat, the other will revive her with the water. The few drops were not to be undervalued, for sometimes a tiny amount can delay a looming death.

She was overcome by engulfing sleepiness, which was impossible to resist, like dark nights or death. So, she leaned against the camel and squinted. She kept the camel standing, because she would sink uncontrollably deep into a dream world if it lay down. No, not a dream world. She was too tired to even dream now. She rested against the camel, thinking she would wake up the moment it moved, be it walking off or just lying down.

Then she shut her eyes and plunged into a colossal darkness.

6

Lanlan was still asleep when Ying'er woke up. The camel was down on the ground, with Lanlan resting against its side. It was sleeping, in a cautious manner. It could have lain down and stretched out its limbs, the usual way a camel slept. Experienced camel transporters would never lie down next to a camel, for fear that they would be crushed when the animal turned. But this was a smart camel that knelt to sleep. It was clear it did not want to crush Lanlan or startle her awake.

Dawn had arrived, bringing everything clearly into view. Off to the side was a human skull with bared teeth, staring at Ying'er. She ignored it. She wanted Lanlan to get more sleep, but knew it would be best to get on the road in the early morning cool. She had to nudge her sister-in-law to rouse her. Lanlan was startled when she woke up, her eyes open wide, as if she couldn't believe it was daytime again.

"Look at me. I slept like the dead," Lanlan said.

"Sometimes we just can't control ourselves." Ying'er replied.

The fatigue abated, but thirst returned with a vengeance. Hunger receded to the background when thirst raged. Lanlan had wanted to keep the water to save one of them later, but the thirst was too powerful to ignore, so powerful that she changed her mind. She poured some water into the cap of the jug and handed it to Ying'er, after which she drank a capful herself. They tried to moisten their lips with their tongues, but that was futile, for their lips were like dried potato skins, and could not be rehydrated. Lanlan's lips were badly swollen. It was odd how they had the idea and the strength to swell up while she was dying of thirst.

They got the camel up and got on their way again. The body should never be pampered. If you keep moving, even if there are aches and pains, your body will get used to them. But take a break, and the fatigue and pain will be aroused, which was how Ying'er felt at the moment. The soreness felt much worse than it had at night. Now that she was sore all over, she should not feel the thirst so much, but no such luck. Thirst and aches enveloped her like two whirlwinds. She wasn't as tired, however, so she was able to walk in relative wakefulness. It was hard to say whether that was good or bad, because extreme fatigue can overwhelm aches and thirst. And now, when exhaustion was lessened, thirst and aches reared their ugly heads, and they had fangs, tearing at her with every step she took. Ying'er had no time to worry about the path they were taking; just resisting the thirst and bearing the aches and pains used up all her mental energy.

The hill was less steep as they walked on, but became a dune. There was still little vegetation, and when they saw some, it was mainly desert stalks, which even the camel ignored. They started seeing camel droppings. Lanlan crushed a few of them, and they all looked ancient. Clumps of a thorny plant on which camel hair had snagged appeared near a sand eddy. The plants were long dead, meaning there was not enough underground water to sustain their growth.

In Ying'er's eyes, the salt lakes were no longer just a body of salt water. Many things in life were like that. If you search all over for something you've set your mind on, its importance will grow when you fail to find it, like her *yuanjia*, or the salt lakes. At this moment, the salt lakes were more or less like a holy land to them. She had yet to meet a religious practitioner who had conducted a similar search for a pure land in the heart. This grueling trek was meaningful precisely because of the importance of the "salt lakes" in their hearts, she said to herself.

She focused on certain things to divert her attention from the maddening thirst and aches. The first was her *yuanjia*. Had he also been tempered by life and death when he left Shawan for the wide world? she wondered. Lingguan's face appeared before her, sweating, his lips as swollen as Lanlan's. The image had been partially transplanted from Lanlan, who looked a bit like her brother. He must have suffered too, she thought. There had to be pain, hunger, thirst, and despair. He must have gone through what she'd been through. A warm feeling rose at that thought, as she felt she was not suffering alone. "They" were together in hardship. That was good, she thought. She would tell him about this life journey when they met again. He'd lie down on a sand hill at the outskirt of the village, his arm around her. A cool, gentle breeze would come from the desert, tussle her hair, which would brush against his face. She would close her eyes in happy contentment, as she slowly recounted the long, danger-filled trek through the desert. He would be surprised, but not frightened. He wouldn't be. He would just look at her with eyes filled with admiration, tender affection, and a force that could suck her deep into his soul. Though he looked calm, he must be feeling emotional turbulence, for he could not imagine how two frail women could take on ferocious jackals, and put up with thirst, pain, despair and loneliness.

I did all this for you, *Yuanjia*. She said silently.

He would look at her with a tender, loving gaze. She could almost see his eyes. Ying'er was convinced that this journey would be a testimony to her love.

Her thoughts turned to the salt lakes after that. To be sure, she could not imagine what the place looked like, but it had a mystique about it precisely because she could not conjure up an image. The lakes had become a kind of totem, after so much suffering, hardship, and searching. She hoped the trip would change her destiny, at least change her present life. When the family was hard up, she recalled, Laoshun would take a camel to the salt lakes and bring back hope each time. But what did the real salt lakes look like? The more they traveled, the more concerned she grew. It would sadden her if the place turned out to be disappointing after all the pain and suffering. She'd had many things to look forward to in her life, with a different one for each period. In the end, all had turned into soap bubbles, bright and colorful as they floated, but leaving unbearable disappointment and emptiness when they burst. She hoped it would be different this time with the salt lakes. Her heart was so weary it could not take another blow.

The power of aches and thirst was so overwhelming that she was frequently distracted from her musing. Her eyes could not keep from seeing the burnt yellow in front of her. The sun was showing its power again, but the sand continued to ripple into the distance, no end in sight. For all she knew, the salt lakes could be tucked into a furrow of the slope. She was afraid to look into the distance, for that only brought fright and despair.

They stopped to take a break and swallow the last sips of water. It had been two days since they'd last relieved themselves, meaning the water they took in remained in their bodies. Neither said a word as they drank, for they knew what it meant.

"Let's get going," Lanlan said.

They walked with the camel until noon. Ying'er wished they could resume traveling at night, but the flashlight batteries had died and they could not afford to make a wrong turn. Besides, their bodies would continue to use up energy even if they lay in a deep pit when they ran out of everything.

"Maybe we're close," Lanlan said. She was always saying maybe: maybe we'll run into someone, maybe we'll find water, maybe we'll get some food. They were hopes, these maybes, and all they needed was one to deliver them from privation.

But noontime closed in on them before they met a maybe.

The sun would not stop spewing its flames just because they lacked water, and their bodies would not retain moisture simply because of all the maybes. Dehydration showed its first sign in their heads; they started to doze off and began seeing things. Hallucinations were not a problem, unlike dozing off, which was a maw ready to swallow them up. Lanlan kept telling her not to fall asleep. Stay awake. Ying'er knew she would never wake up once she succumbed to sleep. So, they kept reminding each other, though the raging thirst was gluing their eyelids shut.

The camel was the first casualty. With its eyes half open, it flared its nostrils, breathing heavily, as if a gigantic bellows were moving slowly inside. It had done well, Ying'er thought. The energy from the little bit of oil had sustained the animal enough to help them over several ranges. She did not want it to collapse, because they were helpless to save it. The salt lakes weren't far, she thought—of course they weren't, at least in her mind, so the camel mustn't die. Lanlan stared woodenly at the camel and let out a long sigh.

The camel shuddered and slowly lay down. It stretched out its neck and limbs, its breath drawn out. They would have to pay the owner if it died, but money was the least of their concerns. Ying'er worried about the camel's survival in the same way she'd watched over her husband during his last moments. But her mind wasn't clear enough for her to feel too sad, even though she knew the camel was dying and that the two of them would be next. She was too muddle-headed to think about anything, only some faint regrets over dying.

She sat down, not because she wanted to, but because her legs made her do it. It was hopeless. If the camel had remained standing, she'd have been reassured. Now that it had fallen, she could not climb over the dune by herself; besides, what good would that do? There would be more dunes. She couldn't be bothered with thoughts of death or survival; all she wanted was to close her eyes and have a good sleep. She knew she'd leave the world for another if she fell asleep now, but she couldn't help it. Her brain wanted to sleep, and there was nothing she could do about it.

Gritting her teeth, Lanlan glanced at the camel and then at Ying'er. Lanlan's gaunt and shriveled face was sweat-stained, and black dust and dirt lined the sides of her nose. From her face, Ying'er could see that she too was in a sorry state, but it no longer bothered her.

"Hang in there," Lanlan said. "I'll go look for water."

"Where are you going to find water?" Ying'er felt like saying, but she knew looking for it was better than doing nothing. Lanlan might not find it, but giving up searching meant accepting death.

Without waiting for her response, Lanlan took the bottle and dragged her feet over to a sand trough in the north. Her progress was painfully slow, her joints creaking noisily, almost like a moving skeleton to a dazed Ying'er. She might not make it back, Ying'er said to herself.

Lanlan trudged around a sand hill and vanished from sight, leaving Ying'er the impression of a drop of water soaked up by the sand.

Don't leave me out here all alone, Ying'er wanted to say. A mild sense of sadness stole up on her and she felt like telling Lanlan, We have to die together if that's how it will end.

With its eyes nearly closed, the camel breathed heavily, the hollow spot on its belly rising and falling erratically. Could there be a jackal in there swallowing its intestines? Ying'er wondered. The terrifying creature could have wormed its way in through the camel's rear while the two of them were asleep. Oddly however, the thought did not frighten Ying'er. Go ahead, eat it. Finish it off and then come for me.

All was quiet. She remembered how the sun would shriek at noon, like thousands of cicadas chirping at once. But now the sun was silent. Not a sound to be heard in the sand trough; even the camel's puffs were fading. Its belly continued to rise and fall, but it wasn't making any noise. Ying'er could not hear her own heart beating, as she was dissolved by an enormous quietude. She wondered if she was still alive. She looked up at a sky so blue that it took on the quality of satin, against which shreds of silky clouds were either racing each other or vying to look stupid. She decided not to worry about it.

Again it seemed to her that Lanlan had lied. She wasn't off looking for water; she'd discarded her body and gone to another world, a terrific one, of course. It wasn't nice for Lanlan to do that; they should have left together. Ying'er was too tired to be resentful, for lethargy had woven a large net and cast it into the air, ready to drop down on her. It had done that many times already; once it was like a spider's web, at another time a fishing net, increasingly dense and tight. She knew that this time it would capture her soul. In the past she'd never worried about a soul. What she'd felt more was the involvement of her body when she was in love; only after separation had her soul become prominent in her consciousness. Now that her body no longer had a role to play, her soul was left to suffer the agony of longing. It wouldn't be terrible if the net of drowsiness took hold of her soul.

The camel stretched out its legs and lay down on its side, its usual pose when sleeping. It could mean that it lacked the energy to kneel. Its blood must be sticky, just like hers. When the sun stuck out its tongue, it would surely lick away moisture, and there was nothing she could do about it, because it was the sun. She didn't feel the heat, though, even if no clouds were out to block its white rays. The drowsiness had even dulled her sense of thirst, and soon it would submerge her soul. Go ahead and do what you want, she thought.

She wanted to think more about Lingguan before the drowsiness took over, but lethargy was a powerful force that overwhelmed everything, including scenes she wanted to revisit. In her recollection, Lingguan had been a handsome man, but she could no longer remember in what way. Her brain was working against her; the scenes kept intruding into her thoughts to set her mind and body aflame when she didn't want to think about him, but vanished without a trace when she wanted to.

A crow landed on a nearby sand dune, where it cawed. Ying'er knew she was dying. She had heard that crows loved the flesh of dead humans and, with a superb sense of smell, could detect the scent of death on a living person. It always cawed when someone was dying, which was why people thought it brought bad luck. According to Lingguan, however, crows were supernatural birds, underlings working for Mahakala, the protector of the Buddha dharma. I'll feed myself to the bird, then, if you say it's supernatural. She'd give herself willingly to the crow, but not to the jackals, certainly because of what he'd said. Her only wish was for the bird not to start on her before she died. She'd heard that a crow will go first for human eyeballs, which greatly disturbed her. How could it eat the eyeballs first? Before she breathed her last, she said to herself, she would crouch down and bury her face in the sand if she had to. She could not bear the thought of a black bird's beak reaching for her beautiful eyes.

More crows landed, all cawing and fixing their gaze on her. The camel opened its eyes when it heard the caws, the implication not lost on the animal. It looked at Ying'er, who looked back, tacitly sharing a sense of helplessness. Her eyes felt even drier, and a rumbling noise echoed in her head.

The birds must have pecked clean those white bones she'd seen along the way. They couldn't have found more delectable food in the desert than human flesh; no other animal had the same silkiness. So, they certainly hoped a human would die of thirst in their territory. Let me fulfill your wish, then, she said to the crows. But, could they have already gotten to Lanlan's eyeballs before coming for mine? She could almost see Lanlan, keeled over in the desert, her face a bloody mess. See, that was how her brain worked now; it would not show a picture she wanted to see, but instead gave her bloody scenes she abhorred.

Ying'er shook her head with great difficulty.

In her haze, she saw a few of the crows fly down and circle above her head. They were in such a hurry; they must have thought she was already dead. Or, maybe they wanted the fresh meat of a living creature, like humans feasting on live monkey brains. That had to be it. She was willing to feed herself to them, but not before she breathed her last. She waved the dead flashlight, but it was a poor weapon, so she snapped the whip off the camel's halter. It was a spare whip to lash the camel's nose if it refused to obey an order. Neither of them had had any use for the whip, for they'd had two docile camels. A black shadow swooped down on her just as she had the whip in hand. Quietly she mustered her strength, swinging it as best she could. Obviously, the crow thought she was dead, and had not expected an object to strike out. It also did not know it was flying so fast that it would be stunned when it smashed into a waiting whip. Imagine the force as the whip sped toward it.

With a muffled thud, the crow fell and rolled into a sand trough.

The other crows cawed and flew back to a nearby hill.

It twitched a few times and went still.

It felt so unreal to Ying'er. How strange, she thought. She knew how to wield a whip, but only so as to not wrap it around herself. The odds of her actually hitting something was like that of a blind donkey bumping into a haystack, or noodles falling into a blind man's mouth. What a surprise that she'd hit her target.

She crawled over to the dead crow and saw it was smaller than a full-grown chicken. With its wings spread, it had looked like a real bird, but on the ground it was a scrawny chick. On the sand were a few drops of its blood. Maybe the blood could keep her going a while longer. A timid person by nature, she was emboldened by her dazed, sleepy state, and grabbed the bird. Rationally, she wanted to twist its head off and suck on its blood. But she couldn't break it off, no matter how hard she tried. She began to retch when she imagined her mouth smeared in blood. Nothing came but dry heaves, but her stomach and esophagus went into a frenzy of action and drove away her sleepiness. I'll die before I eat this, she told herself. She flung the bird away; it made a dark but short arc in the air before falling into a sand trough.

I won't drink its blood, even if I die of thirst. She'd have hated to be like one of those blood-sucking monsters in movies.

I'd rather die than survive like a monster.

As she recovered her breath, she squinted at the crows in the distance, which were staring back at her. A mutual fear had developed between them. She was afraid they would fly over to peck her eyes out; powerless to fight them off, she'd sink into the dark night feeling sharp pains in her eyes. What's your hurry, she wanted to say to the crows. Even if you don't eat it now, the food will still be there. It dawned on her that she'd said something like that to Mengzi once, but it seemed so long ago. If she'd accepted his advances, she wondered, would it have been as disgusting as drinking the crow's blood? She had no idea.

The human and the crows faced off. The camel seemed above it. It had seen her feat, but showed no surprise; after all it had been through on this trip, nothing would surprise it, obviously.

Ying'er was dead to herself. She would die sooner or later, and would be crow's food. When the jackals attacked that night, she hadn't wanted to be eaten by them, but she no longer felt that way. It was all the same, no matter which one got to her first, she thought, as long as they didn't start while she was alive.

Any time now. You won't have to wait long. She sensed her soul drifting away from her body, which meant that drowsiness was overwhelming her wakefulness. Once lethargy took over, her soul would be gone. Where would it go? Would it go to see Lingguan? She'd heard that the soul acquired magical skills when one died, such as powerful hearing and eyesight, materializing anywhere, even thousands of *li* away. That wouldn't be bad. But she was afraid Lingguan would repulse her, just as she dreaded the disappointment she might feel once she found the sought-after salt lakes.

What she didn't want most was to see Lingguan flirting with a barbershop girl when her soul showed up. She had no idea why it couldn't be a different kind of girl. She didn't know, but she would hate to see that happen. Her soul would be heartbroken. Can a soul shed tears? She didn't know that either, but she was sure it would burst out crying. When a woman in the village hanged herself after being mistreated, quite a few people heard her sobbing late at night when all was quiet. Would she cry like that? She didn't know. While alive she'd had no control over her life, so how could she be sure of what happened after she died?

Stop thinking about him. A barbershop girl it is then. I can't do anything about what's in his heart.

She was crestfallen. All right, then I know what you're like while I'm still alive, and I won't cry myself silly after I die. What she'd imagined now became real. Abandoned by hope, she said to the crows silently, Come on now, why don't you?

The crows cawed loudly, too eager to wait, though none was bold enough to challenge the whip. The camel continued to pant like a bellows. When it opened its mouth, Ying'er could see its tongue, dark as a strip of tanned leather. It was nearing death too, she knew. That would be good;

they'd be each other's company, and she wouldn't be a lonely ghost. She could not count on Lanlan, who aspired to the Dakini Buddha Land of the Vajravārāhī, where her last thought would send her soul before she died. Ying'er would not be able to follow her, for she was not a true believer, thus the mortal enemy of a true practitioner. She could not catch up with Lanlan, but she had the camel. Camels surely did not know about the Dakini Buddha Land, which was fine with her. If it were convinced that it could reach the Buddha Land and had even made a vow to go there, then Ying'er would have to become a lonely, wandering ghost, since she did not want to see him flirt with a barbershop girl.

Don't go too fast, camel, she wanted to say.

But no sound came. She was cocooned in a thick, dense, strong net woven by drowsiness. Something like fur in the air was filling up her mouth, ears, and eyes. The crows had stopped cawing. She felt that the large birds were swooping down and that the wind beaten up by their flapping wings had formed another net. Large nets were descending on her.

Heavy darkness fell.

7

A faint sound came from faraway, much like her grandmother calling back her soul when Ying'er was little. Back then Grandma would say that her soul had strayed, and she would call it back whenever Ying'er looked dazed and confused.

Grandma's voice was coming from a great distance,

"Ying'er—ai—your soul was frightened far away but come back now—"

"Come back now—" someone would echo.

"Ying'er—ai—your soul was frightened high up but come down

now—"

"Come down now—"

"Ying'er—ai—your soul was frightened in the heat but come back cool—"

"Come back cool—"

"Ying'er—ai—your soul was frightened when hungry but come back full—"

"Come back full—"

"Ying'er—ai—the three souls and seven mortal forms return now—"

"Return now—"

Grandma could come up with more similar incantations. Starting from a relatively distant place, she called all the way back to their kitchen, where she put flour in a porcelain bowl and wrapped it in a piece of red cloth to press against her chest, back, and shoulders. A dent would appear in the bowl after a while, and Grandma would say:

"See that great loss?" She would add more flour and repeat the incantation, pressing until the flour was even in the bowl to conclude the soul-recalling rite.

Her mother was usually the one who echoed Grandma, who would not let Bai Fu do it. Her brother, a prankster, would invalidate the effort by saying the opposite of "come back," and they would have to find another auspicious date to start over.

Grandma's drawn-out voice was as sweet as rice broth and went straight to Ying'er's heart. Later when Grandma died, there was no one to perform the rite for Ying'er.

But the voice appeared again. It gave her a warm, cozy feeling in her hazy state of mind; she thought she was dead, because people said you can only meet dead relatives when you are in the underworld. How nice, I'll see Grandma again. Grandma had doted on her, her arms a safe harbor. When she was little, Grandma often held Ying'er in her arms, calling her "My sweet little girl" and giving her loud kisses. Magical as an old witch, Grandma always had something rare on her, like sesame candy or peanuts. She had endless ghost stories to tell, usually at night after turning out the light, scaring Ying'er so much she hid in Grandma's arms.

To her, the drawn-out voice sounded like silkworm threads that wrapped themselves around her and tugged at her, like a kite-runner. The wind of life was taking her forcefully to a bottomless abyss, while the voice, an audio string, tied her down. She was tugged closer and closer toward the person calling out to her, when she sensed a change in the voice; it sounded more like Lanlan.

She struggled to open her eyes; it felt like turning a rusty door latch. A blinding light splashed into her eyes when she forced them open, but it was too bright to see what was before her.

"Hurry and eat some of these." Lanlan sounded surprised and happy.

Finally, Ying'er could see Lanlan, who was holding a black stick. Ying'er didn't move, so Lanlan scraped the stick with the whip handle to rub off the black surface and reveal a watery whiteness underneath. Ying'er had seen it before. In winter time, after slaughtering a goat, the villagers would slow-cook it with mutton. What was it called? Oh, right, it was called suoyang.

Lanlan broke off a small piece and put it in Ying'er mouth. When she bit down gently, Ying'er felt sweet juice spread in her mouth. She had only seen dry ones, so she was surprised by its juicy content.

Lanlan gave her the whole piece she'd scraped clean, telling her to eat it all, while taking out another piece from her head scarf. Ying'er could not believe how much Lanlan had gathered in the scarf.

Lanlan chewed a piece and fed it to the camel. Still breathing hard, the animal stuck out its dark tongue and labored to move the juicy pulp Lanlan put in its mouth.

To Ying'er, this plant root was the best thing she'd ever had. A gentle bite sent its juice oozing between her teeth to be lapped up by greedy taste buds. They were ecstatic, like starving sparrow chicks seeing their mother return with a worm, their mouths opened wide as they chirped loudly. The sweet, aromatic juice summoned back her stomach's lost memory and sent it into a frenzy of movement.

Able to eat the black sticks on its own, the camel crunched away, and white juice flowed down the corners of its mouth, making Ying'er feel bad about the waste.

"Finish yours now," Lanlan said spiritedly. "We'll go dig more after some rest. There are loads of them in a sand trough over there."

Lanlan stopped her from having another one after she finished the first. She tried to pull up the camel; it struggled to its feet on shaky legs. It had eaten the piece Lanlan had given it. It was the best remedy for thirst and hunger, and a great tonic. After eating them, the camel's lifeline that had hung by a thread returned. Ying'er still had a headache, but her drowsiness was gone.

"That's enough," Lanlan said. "Don't eat too much. We'll have more later."

They took the camel to the sand trough, which was just around a bend in the sand, not too far, actually. There was soil in the sand, a perfect home for the plant. Lanlan located a crease in the ground and stomped on it, making a hollow sound.

"There are lots of suoyang down here," Lanlan said. "I dug those we just ate from just one spot."

Ying'er could see creases all around her, similar to the ground surface broken by potatoes. Some of the roots had poked through the sandy soil.

"Heaven never seals off all the exits," Ying'er said emotionally.

"It's the Vajravārāhī who saved us. Believe it or not. After I walked past the bend, I knelt down in the sand trough and prayed. I said,

Vajravārāhī, please help me leave the desert alive. If I do, I'll renovate your temple and gild your statue. I prayed for a while and then I saw a red figure nearby. I thought it was a herder and I chased after him all the way here, where I discovered suoyang instead. When I go back, I'll collect donations to repair her temple. I can't deceive the Vajravārāhī, can I?"

Lanlan was earnest and sincere. Ying'er wondered, however, if Lanlan had simply been seeing things, but she quickly chided herself for blasphemy. If the Vajravārāhī had in fact shown Lanlan the way here, the deity would be hurt by her doubts. "Then we should thank the Vajravārāhī," she replied.

Lanlan dug into a crack to reveal the stems inside. Suoyang is a parasitic plant in the shape of male organ, which can grow to about a foot long. Dark red in color, it thrives in sandy soil and is rumored to be a great tonic for impotence. It usually grows in clusters, the larger of which could weigh dozens of *jin*. They didn't have to work hard; digging and pushing away the sandy dirt revealed a cluster underneath. Lanlan scraped off the dirt with her whip handle before tossing it over to the camel. It cried out in great excitement, no longer looking tired and miserable.

They unloaded the litter and dug a pit on the shady side of the sand dune. After eating some more of the plant, they tethered the camel, climbed into the pit, and fell asleep. When they woke up, they had some more and went back to sleep, and did the same when they woke up. With enough sleep, aided by plenty of nutritious suoyang, they soon regained their vitality.

The following morning Ying'er saw seashells on gobi rocks. Obviously, there had been water at the spot. Perhaps the desert had once been a big ocean, she said to herself. Even an ocean can turn into a desert. Human life is so fragile. Indeed, she could be old in the blink of an eye; Lingguan too. What was the point in striving for a brighter future if we're both old? She couldn't help but feel resentful.

Putting her resentment aside, she dug up more of the fleshy stems. They would have the camel carry as many as possible, even if they had to walk. Once done, they would keep traveling in the direction they'd chosen.

Chapter Twenty-Six

A hawk wheels above a rabbit warren
A snake steals eggs in a sparrow's nest

1

In Laoshun's view, White Tiger Pass had ruined everything. Many of the positive aspects about the village vanished as the place thrived.

The first to go was tranquility of the mind. No one in the village had seen so many novelties. In the past, their most common meal was potato millet slurry, with hand-made noodles as a step up, and it would feel like the New Year's celebration if they had a bit of pork. After filling their bellies, they sunned themselves at a spot with the south-facing wall, where they chatted and enjoyed themselves. Now it seemed that White Tiger Pass had amassed all the good things in the world, some of which were beyond the dreams of old landlords and rich men. And there were also lots of pretty young girls to confound and distract the villagers.

Everything is different when one's mind undergoes a change. Take desert dates, for example. Laoshun had always given some of the tasty fresh fruit to every family in the village. His tree produced large, meaty, sweet dates, earning praise from everyone. But now Mengzi would not let him give any away, saying he wanted to sell them to the sand boys. Laoshun rebuked his son:

"Is money more important than face these days?"

He was surprised when he gave away the dates this time. The villagers reacted differently, with questioning gaze as if to ask:

"Why are you giving me dates? What do you want from me?"

Some had even turned him down, politely, as if afraid they'd be in his debt.

Laoshun was incensed.

He felt that so many good things were changing. In the past, everyone would lend a hand any time you needed help, but not anymore. Now their first thought was how much they could earn a day as a sand boy. No one would waste time for anyone else. For the first time the autumn harvest saw "helpers" who demanded pay, twenty yuan a day picking corn.

"Money was more important than face" to all of them. It was hopeless.

Of course, White Tiger Pass was buzzing with even greater activity, attracting more and more commerce. A wasteland had turned into a cornucopia, and more buildings were going up. He'd heard that even the county government office would be moving there. Shawan had become a typical city. All these did not concern him, because typical or not, the villagers still wanted their share of the good times.

There was only thing that frightened people like Laoshun, and that was land expropriation. It had happened already, when the county government-built offices for banks. The villagers waged a protest, but to no avail, so they recalled Goubao, "the traitor" chief, and replaced him as team leader with Baigou, an acknowledged hardliner. But Laoshun was not convinced that a small locust like him could keep cart wheels from moving forward.

Sure enough, Baigou was barely in office when they heard his raspy voice:

"A meeting. We're going to have a meeting. All adults must attend."

Laoshun knew that something was up, for things had been happening all too often lately.

In groups of twos and threes, the villagers arrived at the clan shrine. Baigou was squatting silently on a millstone under the tree, frowning to show his displeasure. The villagers did not mind when Baigou cursed them, because he was foul-mouthed. But if his face was clouded, then he was really angry. Why was he upset? Laoshun could not fathom a guess.

Baigou ignored the villagers, still with a dark look, his eyes narrowed and the muscles on his face twitching. He abruptly jumped off the stone roller and cursed in a voice so hoarse he sounded like someone else altogether.

"What's happening now, Baigou?" Laoshun asked unhurriedly.

"They've gone too far. The county office wants to sell Xihupo, six thousand yuan an acre."

"What?" A loud buzz erupted.

"Says who?"

"They're about to sign a contract."

"On what grounds?"

"On no grounds," Baigou said. "They said the land belongs to the government. Someone wants to build an amusement park or something."

"Incredible," Laoshun exclaimed. "White Tiger Pass is thriving, and everyone around it suffers. If Xihupo is sold, that will be the end of us."

"Not if we take the long view. We can't hold out much hope for farming now," exclaimed Meng Baye.

"We can at least fill our bellies, even if there isn't much hope. With no land, what'll we eat, the wind?" Laoshun demanded.

"Are you aware that they'll get sixty thousand yuan an acre, but will only give us six," Baigou fumed. "That's unacceptable. They have to give market value if they want to sell. You know the county office is profiting from the price difference. I know no one gets rich from farming, but we can't let them feed us a crock of shit like that. We have to raise hell over this. The developers give money and women to the county officials, and we're no match for them. But we're not going to take it lying down. We're going to go all out today. They've got money, we're got pigs, horses, cows, and goats. They go to saunas, but we've got plenty of women."

"Horse shit." Meng Baye said, wrinkling his nose. "How can you come up with that kind of rubbish."

"He's right." The men wanted to hear him out. "Listen to him."

"That's not what I meant," said a red-faced Baigou. "We won't really send them women. I just want to shame them. We'll take everything with us, money, pigs, goats, and women. We don't want to sell the land, but if we have to, then we set the price. That's what we'll do. You take what you want and choose any woman you like. We'll see if these jackasses are real donkeys or not."

The men all breathed a sigh of relief.

"But what if they are real donkeys? Then what do we do?" Huaqiu asked.

"Don't worry," Baigou said. "What can they do? They'll bite off more than they can chew if they try something." He grinned and continued, "What are you worried about, Huaqiu? Do you think they'll want that cabbage head of yours when even the pigs won't have her? She'd scare them off, sure as hell. Nothing to be afraid of."

"Hard to say," Mengzi said. "Cows eat spinach and pigs love what dogs won't eat. Maybe she'd strike their fancy and they'd want to have her."

The men laughed, including Huaqiu, who shook his head, and said, "She can't even make me hard. But watch out and see they don't want your wives, or you'll be wearing the green hats of cuckolds."

"Stop the bullshit and get serious." Baigou snapped. "Do you want to do it? If you say yes, we'll show them what we can do. If not, we'll have to come up with something else. Speak up, all of you. Don't call me a turncoat if they end up selling the land. What do you say?"

"Sure, we'll do it."

"It's not going to work," announced Goubao, who opposed anything suggested by Baigou, since he had taken his place as leader. Raising his voice, he continued, "Do you think they're sparrows that'll be scared off when you shout at them? Who are they? They're lizards. They've been shot at before, and won't be scared by a few firecrackers. Shame them? Like hell, they'll shame you, is more likely. If they were some of those infantile teachers, they might care about being shamed. But they're jackasses, a whole herd of them, and they don't give a damn about face. They're so thick-skinned their faces are like the callouses on your heels. Go ahead, try to pry them off, they won't care."

"He's right." The men went quiet.

"If playing soft doesn't work, we'll play hard. The world's different now. It's useless to be civilized and polite." Baigou continued, "When I bought a tire pump in town and wanted to exchange it, the shrew ignored me the whole time I called out to her. She even called me a hick. I decided she was asking for it, so I picked up the pump and called her a whore. Guess what happened? She exchanged it. In this day and age, you're wasting your time being civil. If you're afraid of this and that, they'll piss on your head."

"He's right. Let's smash their bones, the asses," the men said.

Meng Baye tugged at his beard pensively. "That's not the way to go about it. You'll have to take responsibility if something goes wrong."

"It's not to cause trouble, it's to shame them," Baigou explained when he saw the incomprehension on their faces. "Women shame them and men pretend to use their fists. You raise your fist like you really mean it, but just enough to scare them. Some of you act tough, and some of you sweet-talk them. Just don't cause your old dad any trouble."

"Whose old dad are you?" Meng asked with his eyes half-closed, with a glance at Baigou.

"The jackass officials', of course," Baigou replied with a smile.

2

Baigou handed out assignments and gathered donkey collars along with other items. Meng Baye cautioned them several times not to do it for real. Then the men, the women, and their livestock took off in tractors, an impressive caravan heading to the county government office.

Laoshun was worried most about Mengzi, who was a bit of a hothead and wouldn't think twice about tossing a baby down a well if he was provoked. He kept telling his son not to show off.

"All right, all right." Mengzi said impatiently. "Don't treat me like a baby."

The men were keyed up over the prospect of venting their anger. That did not sit well with Laoshun, for they were no longer their old selves. He cast a worried glance at his son, who he saw was whispering to Baigou.

"Nothing good will come out of it when these two get together." Laoshun frowned, worry-laden.

The county government office had a high, intimidating gate. They're the law, after all, Laoshun thought.

Baigou and the others unloaded the tractors with pigs, goats, and cows grunting, bleating, and moo-ing unhappily, lending a comical atmosphere to the compound. People there on official business stared wide-eyed at all the uninvited guests.

"Get them out of here. It looks terrible," a young man in a white shirt cried out in alarm.

"Tell the county chief to come out here," Baigou shouted.

After a quick look, the young man slunk back inside.

"Come out, County Chief!" Baigou shouted.

"Come out!" Mengzi echoed.

The fat county chief waddled out. With his hair combed back and his hands behind his back, he exuded authority. Wordlessly, he surveyed the area with a cold gaze, and Laoshun felt a chill run down his spine. He feared government officials, especially rotund ones with their hair combed back. His knees buckled, his spirit abandoned him. To be sure, if he had nothing to live for, he'd have enjoyed chopping off a head or two, but that was just a thought. He'd never do that as long as he had his potato millet slurry.

The county chief coldly focused his shiny, beady eyes on the villagers, not saying a word. Laoshun wished he'd say something, even scold them. But he didn't. Silence was more lethal than speech. Words are like a fuse to set off explosives. Maybe the chief knew that. Laoshun saw some of the villagers looking lost, not knowing what to do next.

Baigou chuckled, an inappropriate yet strangely fitting reaction. It loosened the rope stretched taut around Laoshun's heart.

"Don't worry," Baigou said in a measured way. "We're just here to deliver some gifts to you. You can have anything you want, goats, pigs, cows, everything. Women too. All we ask is for you not to sell our land. All right? That's all we have left." He unsheathed a knife and continued, "We're here today to thank the county chief for all his hard work."

"What are you doing?" The county chief backed off. "Is this a rebellion?"

Laoshun was pleased to see how the chief's posturing vanished the moment he opened his mouth; he now looked almost cowardly. What did he resemble? A big donkey dick, Laoshun told himself. It might appear big, but cannot withstand poking, and will go soft from a single jab. He smiled, pleased with his analogy.

Baigou waved his knife again, and the chief took another step back. "Don't worry," Baigou said with a chortle. "Nothing to worry about. I'd lose if I swapped my lamb's pelt for your old sheep skin." He walked up to a castrated ram, grabbed its neck, and plunged the knife in. Blood gurgled out. The ram silently took the knife; its kind eyes filled with liquid that slowly disappeared. They glazed over as it stared wide-eyed at the ground.

"Skin the goat so we can cook it and win Mister Official over." Baigou carried the knife between his teeth as he flung the goat at the chief; it kicked up dirt when it landed. The sun was heating up, giving off a burnt odor amid the smell of blood. The goat kicked its hind legs helplessly. Laoshun's throat dried up.

Drops of blood had speckled the chief's pant legs. He stamped his foot unhappily. He wanted to say something, but managed only to mumble as he gaped at the blood-smeared, crimson mouth holding a knife. He turned to renter his office.

Mengzi came up and grabbed him. Laoshun felt his heart rise up to his throat. Why the hell do you always have to be a hero? Laoshun asked silently. Why? He stared daggers at his son, whose gaze was fixed on the fat chief. "Not so fast. There's more."

Baigou walked up to a pig. The animal screeched, broke off the tether, and ran around the compound. The men gave chase. It had a dry, shrill cry, like jamming a sharpened corncob into your ear. Laoshun could not stand that noise, nor could the chief, he thought. Sweat covered his forehead and the tip of his nose on a bright red face. He mopped his forehead, his hand coming away with a sheen.

Mengzi and other young men caught the pig. Pigs are smarter than goats, and this one knew what lay ahead, which was why it was squealing, fleeing, and fighting. The men stumbled as they tried to grab it, cutting a sorry sight. But then Laoshun had second thoughts: maybe goats are smarter than pigs, for the goat knew it was useless to screech or fight. No matter how hard it fought, it would never get free, so what was the point in fighting? Fight all you want, but in the end you're going to die. Why not follow the goat's example and calmly submit to your fate?

The pig's angry squeals pierced the sky. The air seemed to cool, making Laoshun shiver. Baigou gritted his teeth, his blood-stained lips a scary sight. As if the pig personally affronted him, he twisted the knife, making the pig squeal pitifully, its blood gushing. Laoshun shuddered and the women shut their eyes, tolerating it as best they could. Laoshun realized why the pig was crying like that: it wanted to pass its suffering onto the people. That must be it, for his heart ached from the shrieks. The others probably felt the same, all but the butchers, of course, who derived pleasure from the painful cries of the slaughtered. "Slaughtering a pig is fun," he'd heard them say, "but not a goat."

The squeal slowly faded into their memories. Laoshun felt the stifling heat again, along with the heavy stench of blood. The pig's dark red blood was bubbling in the hot sun, where it dried up and hardened. Waving his knife, Baigou directed the men to carry the pig to the office entrance. Sweat was pouring down the chief's head; he wiped constantly, flinging sparkles of water each time.

More people gathered, including residents of neighboring villages who came to enjoy the festivities. The gawkers formed a wall against the wind. The sun rose higher, following its own trajectory, sending down blistering white heat, as if wanting to roast the people down below.

"There's still the cow," Baigou said. "Let's kill that one too for the chief's enjoyment, so he won't sell our land."

The chief waved both arms as he opened his mouth. But it took a moment for him to say in a raspy voice, "Don't be hold-outs. Why not sell the land? It doesn't give you much of a harvest anyway. There will be many jobs at the amusement park. Besides—"

"Horse shit." Mengzi snatched the knife from Baigou and grabbed the man. "The land is our livelihood. Why only six thousand per acre? Why? You think you can do anything you want to us, don't you? "

Laoshun realized that his son and Baigou had a two-man act going, but still he was tense.

"He's right. I'm going to beat the shit out of this jackass." Baigou grabbed the chief by his lapel and waved his balled fist as if to strike him in the face.

"Let's talk this over." Beizhu came up and dragged them away. "He's a reasonable man, we can talk it over with him. He'll listen." Beizhu the peacemaker.

"What's there to talk about with an animal like this?" Baigou screamed. "Did your conscience go into hiding when you sat in the sauna or when you screwed all your women? You women, come over here and lie down for the old jackass to enjoy himself. We'll see how long his old dick is."

"Watch your mouth, Baigou," Beizhu drawled.

"What do you mean, my mouth? I'm not educated, and when I talk, I like to be straightforward, like sticking a club in and out of a shirt sleeve. What else would you like? We've slaughtered a goat and a pig. What else? You want women, well, here they are, you jackass. Come on, come over here." Baigou yelled at the women, acting the part of a rabid dog.

The women blushed and hung their heads, remaining where they were.

"What are you scared of?" Baigou roared. "Come on, let this jackass have a go at you, and we'll see how long his tongue is."

The women were too shy to move. Baigou was outraged. "You're worthless."

Fengxiang looked up and walked over, clenching her teeth. "Who are you calling worthless? Watch your mouth." With a toss of her head, she went up to the chief and said, "Will I do? I'm not pretty but I'm clean, unlike those girls with syphilis."

"Of course, you'll do," Baigou said. "You all have the same twat. Some are pretty and some aren't, but all women look the same with a towel over their face."

A handkerchief had appeared in the chief's hand, which he used to mop his forehead. "What's this? What are you doing?"

Throwing modesty to the wind, Fengxiang grabbed the chief's arm, while a few women came up around him and looped a donkey collar around his neck. With some dragging and some pulling, they propelled the chief toward his office. He tried to fight them off, kicking up columns of dust.

"He thinks it's too much trouble to go inside. Let's do it here, then Come on, take off your clothes," Baigou directed.

"All right, all right." The chief finally spoke up. "We won't sign the contract, for now."

3

They laughed their way back to the village. It was certainly something worth celebrating. They were proud of what they'd done, but that was secondary. The most important accomplishment was saving their land, which meant saving their lives. That was enough for them. What else could they want, so long as they had something to eat? They asked only for enough to clothe themselves and fill their bellies. What else would they want if they could manage to survive? Even doing just that had required paying a price by losing their dignity. They'd done well. Without the farcical performance, someone else would own Xihupo, the largest, flattest, and most fertile land in the village. Most of what the villagers relied on to survive had come from there.

So, they had to laugh.

The women savored the comical sight of the chief wearing a donkey collar; they laughed until they had to hold their bellies and cry out. The men were laughing at the chief for not having seen a woman's big twat. They heaped praise on Mengzi and Baigou for their courage and brains. The two young men strutted like roosters.

"You're celebrating too soon," Goubao said frostily. "Shit-eaters can't overpower whoever dumped on you. He can work on the sly and have the water management station give you eighty percent of the water you should have. You can't count it by the bucketful, so you'll suffer silently, like a mute taking a beating. Besides, do you honestly believe he won't sign the contract? Why would he listen to you?"

The laughter came to an abrupt stop, like pouring cold water into a boiling pot. That was the truth. Who was the county chief, if not someone who had plenty of other schemes to strangle you? All their effort, elation, and self-satisfaction were nothing but ephemeral frost. When you open your eyes, even just a tiny crack, you'll see helplessness pour into you like hot soup. Laoshun was having trouble breathing. The air around him seemed to have thickened. The sun was a noisy heat wave, and the stifled air came crashing down. It had been like that for years. The helplessness he felt about life were like dark clouds, and when they appeared, they blotted out the palm-sized sky over his head.

Their feet stamped noisily on the ground as they walked in silence. Goubao's words were like rocks hitting painfully at their hearts. Their self-congratulation evaporated like moisture in the sun. Dust motes rose at the clatter of footsteps and spread over their mood. Someone would sigh occasionally, but only when he couldn't hold back, like a thief with a guilty conscience.

"Shit. All you get if you lose your head is a bowl-size scar," someone said.

"He's right. I wish we'd beaten that jackass. That'd be something."

"I agree. Let him have a taste of our fists and feet. We'll pound the crap out of him, like a pestle in a mortar."

"Actually, we'll cut him up if he really pisses us off. The worse that could happen is a bullet in the back of the head."

"The law can't deal with a mob. We'll slice him up if we feel like it."

"Enough," Fengxiang said with a laugh. "You show your fists when the fight is over. What kind of heroes are you? What were you all doing back there? You didn't even dare to fart, and wished you could hide your heads in your pants. Now you're talking like real heroes?"

The men stopped bragging about their courage, and their footsteps sounded spiritless. Someone heaved a sigh, an expression of all their helplessness.

"In fact," Goubao said. "It's not that we can't be heroes; it's just he has us in a chokehold. We're like little chicks, and there's nothing heroic about that."

"You're lying if you think he won't get his revenge. We played him for a fool today, and soon he'll pay us back. It'll be as easy as a dog biting into pig's bladder for him to play a dirty trick on us. The Monkey King was powerful, wasn't he? But all his magical skills couldn't get him out of the Buddha's palm. In the end, we're the ones who will suffer, and he'll still get his pay."

"He's right. Everyone knows to use a knife. The problem is, it's easy to pick one up but hard to put it down. Just think about Baldy Wang."

"Great plans mean nothing if you can't deal with small matters. The character for patience is a knife over the heart. A man's gotta be able to do that."

The men were talking among themselves, spewing enough reasons to justify retreat. Baigou looked glum as he picked up a rock and flung it into the distance.

"So, it's all your old dad's fault, is that it? Do you think I did all that for fun? The land doesn't belong to me alone."

"Watch your mouth. Don't call yourself old dad all the time. You're not our old dad," Goubao said, and the other men started in on Baigou, chiding him for calling himself their old dad.

"Fuck your ancestors." Baigou barked like a mad dog. "Go vent your anger on the official, don't take it out on me. The cat under your blanket bites your dick. I'd rather be a real man's horse groom than a councilor to a coward. It makes me want to throw up, working with you guys." He squatted down on the side of a ditch.

Mengzi smiled and walked off with Baigou.

4

Baigou took some men along to keep up the pressure several times after that, but their land was still expropriated and sold off. Outraged, Laoshun and others cursed the chief's mother. That changed nothing, while gold-panning pits continued to appear, spreading like a skin disease.

Rumors about the end of the world grew stronger. They heard that if a man went to a remote spot in the desert at midnight, sat on a stool, and practiced magic with a winnowing pan for a hundred nights, according to legend, the stool and winnowing pan would lift him into the air to escape the calamity of the end of the world. Years before, Big Head's father had done this for ninety-nine days. His bench made it to midair, when, unexpectedly, Mao Dan's mother shrieked:

"Aren't you afraid you'll fall, Third Uncle?"

Thud! Her words were like magic. He dropped to the ground and hurt his back.

Laoshun would not have believed something so outlandish if it hadn't happened near him.

The sun was barely out when he saw the Daoist Master, his forehead bathed in sweat, come out from deep in the desert with a stool over his shoulder and a winnowing pan under his arm.

"Did you manage to fly into the air, Master?" Laoshun said in jest.

"Soon, very soon," the man replied.

"I've heard you need to count on your fingers while reciting the incantation. How can you practice the magic when you're holding a pan?"

"Use your hand if you can, but if you can't, try visualizing it."

"The way I see it, instead of practicing magical skills, you should enjoy beef and turnips until the day you die, and you won't have lived your life in vain. I don't believe the world will end."

"You get your pleasure from eating beef stew, I get mine from practicing magic. We're different people, with different views. Like you married a woman who could work like a cow, but your son prefers Yue'er, a pretty but useless flower."

Laoshun's mood clouded over at the mention of Yue'er. He didn't like the girl. Ever since Mengzi and Yue'er went public with their relationship, Laoshun felt a thorn had formed in his heart to prick him every time the topic arose. He wanted his son to marry a hard-working woman, but Mengzi would not have anyone else. What was odd to Laoshun was how fast the girl's family had agreed, and that they hadn't asked for much in the way of betrothal gifts. They only had to spend ten thousand yuan for all the engagement and wedding presents. It was a large amount for Laoshun, but not so much that he couldn't come up with it.

Grannie Shaman had worked hard to make this happen, even though she'd criticized Yue'er in the past. The engagement and gift delivery were speeded up because Yue'er's family wanted it that way. Laoshun thought they should have had more time, but his wife disagreed, saying sooner or later the wool on a sheep's head has to be singed. She'd made up her mind to forget about marrying Ying'er to her son. One, she'd suspected that Ying'er could jinx her, given Hantou's death. She was dubious, but decided not to disregard the possibility, since every fortuneteller she'd gone to said the same thing. Two, the rumor that Ying'er was a "white tiger" had spread like the wind; Laoshun's wife believed it, which in turn made her uneasy. She was on edge because of her suspicion, making life hard. Three, she was afraid that Ying'er would find an opportunity to take the baby back to her parents. She was on tenterhooks whenever she was reminded of how something like that had happened in the village before. Moreover, Mengzi wanted it done as soon as possible. He liked Yue'er and, if he waited, another man could steal her away. He felt sheepish around Ying'er. Getting married while she was away would help avoid the awkwardness.

The world had surely changed, Laoshun mused. What was once considered a major event in life was now treated as something as trivial as catching a piglet. At least the two families knew each other well, and there was no fear of a scam.

Carrying a stool over his shoulder and a winnowing pan under his arm, the Daoist Master waddled off, like a strange big bird. Laoshun was amused by the receding figure. Human hearts were truly odd. When you're being stubborn, you can be tougher than granite. TV programs promoted changes in attitude, but decades had passed, and no serious changes had occurred. Yet one could accept new things at a shocking speed, and many he knew had been reborn as new people in no time.

Laoshun did not believe in the idea of the end of the world, and treated predictions of catastrophic winds, floods, or fires as bizarre. Where would the wind come from, he wondered. There surely wasn't a God of Wind, who opened his sack and let out the wind inside. If there were one, he could take it back in if he wanted. As for a flood, was it rain from the sky or water gushing from the ground. Actually, he wished there could be a flood to submerge the desert and bring forth greenery. And the fire? That was even more outlandish. He refused to accept that sand and soil can burst into flames. If there were to be a flood or a fire storm, reciting incantations could not stop it or put it out. Back when his wife had a cold, she had recited plenty of incantations, and yet her nose ran like a waterfall. No one would know how to fix a flood or a firestorm.

Besides, what was there to fear if a calamity really did occur? You'd live a few more days or you'd experience a form of deliverance from suffering. What was so great about life anyway? Being alive one day meant two half days of suffering and living for a year was toiling like an ox for twelve months. How was that supposed to be good? Being washed away by a flood, burned up in a fire, or blown off by a wind, leaving nothing behind, that would save a lot of trouble. He saw no need for self-cultivation, reciting sutras or incantations, or worshiping deities. While he was still alive, he'd rather train a few more rabbit hawks, sip a little more liquor, eat his share of rabbit, and listen to the storyteller. When the King of Hell wanted you, you kicked out your legs, and, ha-ha, that was the end of you.

Watching the Daoist Master walk off like a big bird, Laoshun thought that everyone was acting like a little donkey frightened by its own farts.

People said that Baldy Wang took over Huilanzi's body one night to send a message: the end of the world was on its way. The few who had died were just the advance guards, like a mouse dragging a shovel by the handle, and no one could hope to be spared. When the time came, nine out of ten men would perish and not a single woman would survive; there'd be no more cooking smoke from any villages and no family would have a man left; houses would be emptied out, and there'd be no survivors to wear the clothes in them; land would lie fallow and no one would live to enjoy the harvest. In any case, corpses would pile up like mountains and blood would flow like rivers.

Laoshun was dubious about Baldy Wang's prediction.

"It's odd. Baldy Wang didn't know how to read, but he sounded so literate after taking over Huilanzi's body," he said.

"We're humans when we're alive," his wife said, "but we're deities after we die. He might not have been very smart when he was alive, but he must be clever now that he's a deity."

"Hell would be empty if all the murderers became deities," Laoshun sneered.

"Not necessarily. Shakyamuni, the Buddha, once killed people. He killed five hundred bandits to save a boatload of merchants, and the bandits later became the five hundred arhats."

"Well, then why don't you kill someone, like Baldy did? That'd save you the trouble of burning incense."

"Fine. One of these days when I'm in the mood, I'll cut off your head when you're asleep and use it as a chamber pot," his wife said with a smile.

Her failure to complete the seven-day mediation was a great concern to her. She was worried that Laoshun's "evil deed" would bring calamity to the family. Since their oldest son's death, she had lived in fear, like a bird nearly shot with an arrow. The slightest sign of trouble would send her soul flying, disturb her mental state, render her helpless. As a result, when she kowtowed, she did it mainly to repent for Laoshun's sake and to pray for blessings for the whole family.

Laoshun did not appreciate her thoughts; he was intractable.

"Didn't you have your Guardian Deities? Why didn't they stop me? How could they prevent any calamity if they failed to block my way?" He added, "Huilanzi was sincere, I could tell. She offered incense and meditated, but bad things still happened to her. I hear she's gone mad. Where were your guardian deities when Baldy Wang attacked her?" He spouted contrarian ideas like this all the time.

All Mengzi's mother could do was redouble her effort in kowtowing, reciting incantations, praying in penitence, and offering sacrifices. She stopped trying to "convert" her husband, so he wouldn't offend further with his talk. Besides worrying about her grandson, she cared most about the Vajravārāhī.

Chapter Twenty-Seven

A golden phoenix from Lianhuashan
Lands on a sandy ocean shore

1

Mengzi and Yue'er were married. It was a festive, lively event. After eating and drinking their fill, the village men stormed the bridal chamber for the habitual pranks on the newlyweds, dramatically raising the level of the happy celebration.

But in his wildest dreams, Mengzi never dreamed that Yue'er would have syphilis. She would not let him touch her on their wedding night, explaining that she had used someone else's basin to wash up back in Lanzhou, where she'd contracted athlete's foot, and that the fungus was contagious. Mengzi did not quite believe her, so he forced her to get a checkup at the city hospital when they went back to visit her parents after the first month. The doctor sent her out after the examination and told Mengzi that she had syphilis.

The news nearly knocked him over. No wonder she wouldn't let him touch her. Thinking back about each time they had been together convinced him that she'd already known what she had.

Of course, he knew what syphilis was. A colossal trick and insult had been played on him, and, even before the doctor finished, a numbness spread from the back of his tongue throughout his body. His mind went blank.

"Have you had sex?" the doctor asked. Mengzi shook his head.

"Lucky for you." The doctor continued, "Don't worry though. Medical advancements these days can cure diseases like that."

Mengzi was quiet, but inside he was fuming.

"How could you? How could you deceive me like that?"

No wonder. No wonder. Scenes from the past came to him. Before they were married, she would say when he was aroused, "What's your hurry? I'll be yours after we're married."

He'd treated her demurral as a sign of chastity. He'd met too many loose women, and her refusal to give in had touched him. Having being around a few years, he'd learned a thing or two, personally and from others, and knew that love had become a luxury in his time. But how could his new wife have syphilis? He was thoroughly disillusioned.

"You should be grateful." The doctor tried to make him feel better. "She's flesh and blood, like you. She could be like cotton burning when it touches fire. You didn't get infected because she stopped herself."

Mengzi smiled unhappily. He was truly frightened now, which lessened his resentment toward her, but it didn't lessen the pain. He arrived at a decision—divorce. That helped vent his anger and took some of the weight off his mind. But on second thought, he wondered how she would survive after a divorce.

She was sitting on a bench at the other end of the hallway, her head down, waiting for whatever came. He walked over, but rather than look at him, she scooted to the side. "Let's go," he said woodenly and left without waiting for her.

It was bright and sunny outside. The brilliant day highlighted his gloom. He heaved a sigh. Hostility for Yue'er rose when he thought about his parents and all the money they'd spent for him to get married. He stopped and turned to look at Yue'er, who suddenly looked smaller and thinner, her clothes too big. A breeze blew over and sent hair flying over her pale face; helplessness, sadness, and worries oozed from her whole person. Mengzi's heart softened.

"She's fragile." He made his mind to have her illness cured before asking for a divorce. Even though they were husband and wife in name only, that did not mean he could just abandon her.

They walked side by side after she caught up with him, but neither spoke. It was quiet in the city; despite the countless sources of noise, the city was hushed. Loneliness reigned in their individual worlds, instilled in silence; a pale, sadness inundated them, and neither felt like talking.

Noticing her dry lips, Mengzi bought her an ice cream bar.

"Don't think too much," he said as he handed it over. "You're sick, so we'll take care of it."

She remained impassive until she burst into tears and told her story. In the beginning she'd made up her mind to leave the village, but when she went to the city she realized it was someone else's city, where she would always be a wanderer, unanchored, without her own place to settle down, like duckweed floating in a pond. She had tried many jobs and tried to keep her virginity. Later a businessman had promised to marry her, and that was how she got the disease. She'd gone through a lot before and since, Yue'er said. Finally, she realized that a simple, uncomplicated love of the countryside was more precious than anything. After her return, she'd set her mind on him; she underwent treatment while getting ready for the wedding, convinced that she'd be cured and would use her life to make up for his love for her.

Mengzi listened quietly, his mind filled with a strange tranquility. He understood what she was saying. He'd gone out for work too, and had felt the outsider's pain and displacement. One night, when he failed to find work, he roamed the streets, gnawed on by hunger and cold. He was surrounded by tall buildings with brightly lit windows that stared down at him like many eyes, but he could find no place to stay out of the cold. He could only walk back and forth on a broad avenue reflecting a pallid sheen, counting his steps and the minutes. He had no idea that a night could be so long, and the sense of being an outsider dogged him the whole time he was out there.

Mengzi shook his head and turned to see Yue'er looking at him with a gaze he knew too well. Back when his older brother had been terminally ill, he'd worn the same expression when he went to the doctor. A warm current rose up inside. He put his arm around her and gave her a squeeze. She sobbed.

Liangzhou streets were packed with noisy, shouting, cursing people, none of whom took notice of a girl and her tears or the man and his pain. No one noticed the tormented souls around them. They were rushing all around him, but to Mengzi they seemed too distant to make a difference to his suffering. With his arm around her, he kept walking. Yue'er was still sobbing, and he was gripped by tender feelings.

He knew that his fate was now bound up with this fragile girl.

To lift their spirits, they went window shopping and pretended to be in a good mood to please each other. But soon they realized it was phony and tiring. She stopped smiling and gazed into the distance, her eyes half-closed; with her face tinted with faint sadness, she looked unusually pretty. It would have been perfect if not for the disease, Mengzi thought, and his heart sank. The most beautiful thing was broken. He had had his aspirations, for a career and for love. Now, his wife—a person whom he'd imagined countless time—turned out to have such a shameful past. Her illness didn't bother him as much as her romantic past, and every time he thought about it he felt like he was drinking dirty water. He forced himself to avoid the thoughts, but the nauseating scene refused to vacate his mind. Then the idea of divorce would hit him like a bullet, and he'd feel the gratification of revenge.

"I don't want to be a spare ditch," he said to himself. In the eyes of Liangzhou residents, being a spare ditch was the worst; it originally meant to store extra water during irrigation. In Dream of the Red Chamber, Xue Baochai could not make it into the imperial palace, so she settled on Jia Baoyu, her spare ditch. It was humiliating to people in Liangzhou.

She had wanted but failed to stay in the city, so, next best, she'd marry him, Mengzi thought. He felt wronged, but his resolve weakened when he faced her, no matter how strong the thought of divorce. Her face was pale, white with helpless despair. He was reminded of his dead brother again; only those who had suffered great pain in life could understand helplessness. He sighed quietly and told himself to take each day as it came.

Neither said a word on the bus. He wanted to think of something nice to say, but he knew that at a time like this silence was best.

Yue'er was looking through the window at the scenery, her face impassive. Mengzi saw how the affairs in the human world, like the scenes outside, changed so swiftly that everything was different in an instant. Over the past few years, he'd gone through a lot; people were born and people had died, and what should be happy turned out to be sad. Yue'er, who had thought she could escape from the land, failed to sever the tether of fate, got infected, and wound up being the wife of a peasant. His heart ached at the notion of wife. That he would marry someone with such an affliction was unimaginable.

His heart felt squeezed when he thought about his mother, who had gloated over Yue'er's pretty face. "We have the prettiest daughter-in-law in the village," his mother could not stop saying. That was true, but Yue'er's disease was a slap in their ancestors' faces. His mother would not be able to hold her head up if she knew. Mengzi was outraged when he thought about how Yue'er and her family had pulled off such an insulting trick, like putting maggots in a person's eyes.

2

When they walked into her parents' house, her mother looked at him with concern. From her eyes, Mengzi could tell that she also knew, and a great sense of humiliation and anger rose up inside. They were in it together, he thought, and the target of their scheme was his parents. At this moment, her illness took a back seat as he fumed over their deception. You knew your girl was ill and yet you married her off, he said silently and decided to ignore the mother.

She looked at her daughter and then at Mengzi, wanting to say something, but nothing came out. Mengzi knew what she wanted to say. "You two talk," he said, "I'll go home to see if everything is all right there." Based on local custom, after spending three nights with her in-laws, Yue'er would spend another three days at her parents', the so-called "paired visits." He could certainly spend the three days with her, but he went home because he could not stomach the fact that they'd treated him like a fool.

He turned to look back after walking out the gate; Yue'er was leaning against a poplar tree, gazing at him silently. His heart softened at her despairing face and tears welled up in his eyes. He wanted to go back to be with her, but could not stand her mother's attitude, so he spun around the corner of the wall.

His mother was working by the gate.

"Have you eaten yet?" she asked.

"No."

"They didn't offer you anything to eat as a newlywed?" she asked in disbelief.

He couldn't tell her about the trip to the city, so he said:

"I don't like their food, too greasy. I'd like some plain noodles."

She put down her work and went into the kitchen.

He looked at her while he ate. She had lost weight, but seemed stronger than ever, and her sweaty face had a rosy glow. His heart ached when he was reminded of Yue'er's illness.

After he finished the noodles, he took to his bed, feeling depressed. Everything in the bridal chamber mocked him, and his pity for Yue'er vanished, replaced by humiliation and fury. "This is unforgivable," he said to himself. "I could overlook everything else, but not this. Not this. Nothing is more repugnant than this." Thoughts of divorce floated back into his mind.

A while later he was still downcast, so he got up and walked out into the field.

Many people who were out working their land teased him when he walked by. He gave perfunctory responses before walking up a sand ledge, where he could see White Tiger Pass in the distance. The place had gotten even bigger over the few days of his absence, with more new buildings and more red flags. He knew that a big developer wanted to buy up land to build an amusement park with many activities, including a camel racing ground, which attracted city folks. With enough to eat and drink, they had seen more than their share of interesting things, so they were looking for different pastimes. It might be a good thing, Mengzi was thinking, but what good would it do the villagers even if they built a big, splendid city? Since he didn't feel like walking any more, he found a spot to hunker down, his mind a jumble of thoughts that led nowhere.

Suddenly Yue'er appeared in his field of vision. She had gone home to look for him and followed him out here. Someone called out to her and she responded with her usual cheerfulness. He frowned at her voice.

"You heartless shit." Then he realized that she did not want anyone to know what she felt inside.

She stopped to chat with Fengxiang, who pointed in his direction. When Yue'er saw him, she trotted over happily, her face dazzling. He thought it was a put-on expression, but then saw that it was a genuinely bright look, like a lost child spotting her mother. Mengzi was touched; the warm feeling rose up again.

"I couldn't spend another minute there without you," she explained after catching her breath. "Don't laugh at me."

Warmed by her words, he took her hands and she held on tightly, as if afraid he might fly off.

"Hey, don't you even check where you are before getting so lovey-dovey?" Fengxiang called out from a distance. "How shameless."

Yue'er blushed and, sticking out her tongue, pulled back her hands and walked away from Mengzi. The sun was hanging above the hill in the west sky, where large clouds floated. Something pungent was carried on the wind, likely the stench of silt from pits at White Tiger Pass. He looked her, as a sensation of warm water filled up his heart. He realized that his resolve waned when she was with him.

They found a clean spot to sit down and make small talk, until he said, "You have to have that taken care of. Don't put it off any longer. You go to the hospital. I'll borrow money if we don't have enough."

Yue'er said she had some savings of her own and could ask her father for more. She'd pretend to be visiting relatives in the city and stay in a hospital for the treatment. She'd gone to a private clinic, but the doctors there all said it wasn't serious and simply wrote her a prescription. Despite the money she'd spent, it didn't work.

"Don't tell Ma and Pa," he cautioned her. He'd take care of it himself, no matter how serious.

"I'll truly be yours once I'm cured." She blushed. Her bright, pretty face excited him so much he held her and kissed her passionately.

Yue'er returned to her in-laws after the visit. A celebratory air lingered in the house, but Mengzi felt no cheer. Syphilis was curable, but it had broken something precious in him. He was upset and frightened; he resented Yue'er one moment and felt sorry for her the next. He reminded himself to smile, but still his mother sensed something weighing him down.

"What's wrong?" she asked. "Are you afraid you'll be tied down and can't run freely?"

Mengzi had been looking for an excuse to take Yue'er into the city, so he said:

"You're right. Yue'er plans to go visit her aunt in the city and she wants me to go with her."

"Go with her then, if you want. Don't stay shut up at home and get sick."

Mengzi went to White Tiger Pass the next morning. His pit would take at least three more weeks to reach the bottom, so he was free to take Yue'er into the city for her to check into Liangzhou Hospital.

3

Two weeks of treatment saw no visible improvement. The doctor said Yue'er was allergic to antibiotics, so he could not give her penicillin or cephalothin. He'd tried everything else, but nothing produced significant results. He was unhappy she hadn't sought treatment earlier; her condition was so serious they should try the larger hospital in Lanzhou.

"I did, but because I'm allergic to antibiotics, sometimes it just gets better and then it gets worse again. It just hangs on," she replied.

"Don't be scared. It's not AIDS. This isn't that serious an illness anymore," the doctor said, trying to comfort Mengzi when he saw his dejected look.

"He's right," Yue'er said. "I know people whose condition was worse, and were still cured. My father was told about an old Chinese herbal doctor who specializes in this. He can do magic."

After checking out of the hospital, Yue'er took Mengzi to see the herbal doctor. She told him that the doctor had learned ancient Chinese divination skills that gave him magical powers. Before Liberation, there was a Daoist Master in Liangzhou who was skilled in rain prayers. Even the county government sought him out during a drought. Before he started praying, a contract would be signed: the county would pay him five hundred bushels of grain if he brought them rain, but burn him at the stake if he failed. Each time before signing the contract, the Master would ask Old Mister Liang—that was what people called him, Yue'er said—who would pinch his fingers with his thumb to divine the particular date when rain would fall. The Master would enter the date on the contract. If no rain was forecast, he would not agree to pray for rain no matter how much he was offered. Even now, vendors who sold roasted chickens would come to see Old Mister Liang when they hadn't sold them all; he would divine an auspicious direction for them. If he said east, they would go east, and if he said west, they would head west. They would always sell every chicken, no matter how many were left. Old Mister Liang also made pills and potions to cure difficult and complicated illnesses. Illnesses worse than syphilis were nothing to him.

She looked confident.

But Mengzi was downcast. He could tell she was trying to cheer him up. Her eyes were often red-ringed, and he knew she must have been crying behind his back. He pretended to be convinced.

Old Mister Liang had an ancient face, which was oddly beardless. The only signs of his unusual talent were his large, fleshly ears, though they really could only be considered ear-shaped lumps. Mengzi was dubious of his abilities, in contrast to Yue'er's affectionate attitude.

With a blank expression and without asking questions, Old Mister Liang told Yue'er to take off her blouse before bringing out a tiny ball stuck with needles. A few rolls of the pin-cushion ball later, her back was covered with bloody beads. Mengzi asked if it hurt, she said it didn't. The old man repeated the procedure dozens of times before taking out a bottle and spreading its yellow, powdery contents over her back.

By then she was drenched in sweat, but her face brightened up. She took out some money; the old man snatched the bills and tossed them onto the table.

"You must keep at it if you want to be cured," he grumbled. "Don't come only when you feel like it." He grumbled.

"I used to be afraid of the pain," Yue'er said with a smile. "I'll come regularly from now on."

After taking packets of medicine and thanking him, they walked out the door. Yue'er was in a good mood as she told Mengzi that the treatments she'd had before had been effective, but she'd stopped because it had hurt too much.

"Otherwise I'd have been cured long ago," she said with a regretful sigh.

"Short-term pain is better than long-term suffering," Mengzi said. "This time you have to continue and finish. I'll get my hands on a motor scooter and bring you here every day."

"I don't need to come every day. Once a week will be enough, and I'll do the rest myself."

They took the bus back and headed to the dance hall in White Tiger Pass to store the things they'd bought during her hospitalization, so Mengzi's mother wouldn't be suspicious. Yue'er's father was chatting with someone when they arrived. The man was overly friendly with Yue'er, which irritated Mengzi, who thought he must have been in on the scheme. He gave the man the cold shoulder. That didn't seem to bother her father, who tossed Mengzi a soft drink.

"How's business?" Yue'er asked her father.

"Not as good as before. A few more places have opened, it's gotten more competitive. We have to have pretty girls to draw in customers."

Mengzi was disgusted by his reply. He set down the soft drink.

"I'll be off," he said as he spun around and walked out.

Bastard. Your daughter is ruined, and now you want to ruin other people's daughters. He felt like screaming at the old man, when Yue'er caught up with him.

"Did you hear that?" Mengzi barked at her. "He's looking for pretty girls."

Yue'er was quiet as they walked on, before she said:

"What happened to me wasn't Pa's fault. He never told me to do anything bad. I brought it on myself."

"Would you have done anything like that if he'd kept you here?"

"That's not how it is," she sighed and continued, "So many girls have gone astray in the city, and Pa has nothing to do with them. When I look back on those days, I realize I could've gone the wrong way many times. In Lanzhou, in the tea house, there were lots of temptations. The world is filled with traps, and you'll fall into one of them if you're not careful."

Mengzi had to agree with her, so he kept his mouth shut.

When they were back, Mengzi's mother whispered to Mengzi when she noticed Yue'er was thinner,

"Isn't she pregnant yet?"

Mengzi disguised the pain he felt with a smile. "What's your hurry?"

4

In the end, Mengzi's mother found out about Yue'er's illness.

The morning after their return, before heading out to the field, she went to their room to remind him of a something. He'd stopped locking their door since learning of her condition, afraid he'd lose control and do something he'd regret forever. She pushed the door open and saw Yue'er washing her private parts with the aid of a flashlight. Mengzi's mother knew something was off right away. Too startled to react, Yue'er froze before grabbing tissue paper to cover herself.

Mengzi's mother got him out of the room and asked in a low voice:

"Be honest with me. Does she have bayberry sores?" She looked as if she were seeing a ghost in broad daylight.

"What are you talking about, Ma?" he said with a forced laugh.

"Why me? What karmic sin did I commit?" she whimpered, her eyes staring straight ahead. Tears gushed, but she choked back her cries. She kept wiping off tears until her face was shiny wet.

"You must have been seeing things, Ma."

"I'm old enough to know what's what, son." She continued wiping and talking, "Yue'er's aunt, her father's second sister, had the same disease years ago. I've seen it; she looked just like her now. She's ruined you, son." She burst into sobs before she could finish.

Mengzi knew he couldn't hide it from her any longer. She must have thought that they'd had sex already, so he tried to make her feel better:

"I'm fine, Ma. I haven't touched her."

"Really?" She stopped crying to look at him. He nodded and she put her arm around him, as she cried even louder.

Mengzi felt a loud buzz in his head; he felt terrible and yet strangely relieved. He was glad the family would know, for it wasn't something he could keep in the dark for long.

"You know your situation better than me, son, and I won't tell you what to do." She wiped her tears and continued, "I'll just say this. Your life will be over if you come into contact with even a drop of that stuff that comes out."

She turned to rant, "The old bastards, they're worse than animals. They knew their daughter was sick, but they sent her over to ruin my son anyway."

"Don't say any more, Ma." Mengzi knew that Yue'er would feel terrible if she heard. "No one asked for a disease like that. She didn't get it on purpose." Yet he too was bitter and resentful over what Yue'er's parents had done.

Laoshun walked in and mistook the sight as another row his wife was having with someone. "What's the matter now, old hag? You're never up to any good, always complaining and arguing, and turning the house upside down."

"You got your son a wonderful wife," his wife said after blowing her nose. "She brought bayberry sores into our house."

Laoshun was shocked; he looked over at Mengzi, who gave him a brief explanation. He thought his father would fly into a rage, for Laoshun had been against the marriage from the start. To his surprise, his father cast a gloomy glance at the bridal chamber and then at him before wordlessly sitting down on the step to smoke woodenly.

It was quiet in the yard. The sun stuck half of its head out from behind the eastern side of the house to peer down on them. His mother kept blowing her nose.

Mengzi walked into his room, where Yue'er sat stiffly on the edge of the kang. He wished she would wail like his mother, for a good cry can bring relief sometimes. But she just sat there emotionlessly in a room thick with mournful, deadly silence. The wooden basin on the floor was an eyesore, with its yellow water, balled up tissue paper, and an empty glass bottle, and splotches of yellow medicinal powder, all of which felt oppressive.

Yue'er sat, rooted to the spot like a statue. Not knowing what to say,

Mengzi heaved a sigh. He understood how painful it was for his parents and how disheartened she was. They were all victims, but where was the victimizer?

He reached out to touch her shoulder. "They'd have known sooner or later."

His comforting words brought tears to her eyes, and she could no longer hold back. She was choking up despite the great effort to keep from crying out loud. Mengzi felt terrible. He put the cap back on the bottle, picked up the tissue, and pushed the basin back under a chair. He couldn't take the dirty water out yet; at a moment like this, he had to be careful not to further hurt his mother's feelings. She loved him, but she hadn't raised him to empty a chamber pot because of syphilis.

"It's not my parents' fault either." She wiped her tears and continued. "I was the one who wanted to marry you. I didn't expect the disease to be so stubborn."

"Don't say any more. I don't blame you." He gave her a hug and walked out. The yard dazzled under a brilliant sun. Chickens were pecking on the ground. Pipe in hand, his father sat motionlessly.

His mother was nowhere in sight. Mengzi tore out through the gate and headed to Yue'er's parents' house, where he feared his mother had gone.

5

Mengzi's mother indeed was on her way to see Yue'er's parents.

"Terrible, terrible people," she cursed along the way. Anger raged inside her, like a gusting wind looking for a way out. In contrast to the activities at White Tiger Pass, the village took on a desolate look. From the way she walked, some children sensed that something was up, something fun to watch, so they made faces at each other and quietly fell in behind her. A couple even stuck out their tongues as they mimicked her manner.

Terrible! She cursed Yue'er's mother for palming off a diseased daughter as a maiden, more abominable than selling fake medicine. Put aside the betrothal gifts they had accepted, wouldn't they become murderers if her son got infected? Terrible. Bastards. Animals. Scoundrels. She went through all the invectives she could think of, but none was enough to vent her hatred.

The road was dusty, but she was in too big a hurry to take another route. Her anxious feet kicked up clay dirt and stained her pants legs white. A few people she ran into asked where she was going, but she ignored them. They exchanged looks and fell in too. No one would pass up an opportunity to see a great show. Soon she was trailed by a line of would-be gawkers.

The gate at Yue'er's parents' house was not bolted. With one kick, Mengzi's mother burst through. Never in her life had she looked so formidable. The noise brought out Yue'er's mother, who upon seeing Mengzi's mother smiled, despite her awareness of something bad in the offing.

"Ah, it's you, *Qinjia*."

"You terrible old hag. You did real good, didn't you?" Mengzi's mother cursed as she took off one of her shoes. Yue'er's mother was slapped by the shoe sole before she could react.

"How dare you do that to us? Bayberry sores!" Mengzi's mother carried on with her cursing and shoe-slapping. Yue'er's mother tried to dodge at first, but the mention of bayberry sores took everything out of her, and she crumpled to the ground. The shoe-slaps kept coming, turning her face gray and then purple, with blood trickling out from the corners of her mouth.

Mengzi's mother might have gained more momentum in her assault had the other woman fought back. But instead, she kept her face up for her to continue her violent act. After a dozen slaps, Mengzi's mother knew she'd be laughed at if she kept at it, so she put the shoe back on, picked up a rock, and walked in the door.

"I'm going to smash the bayberry sores in this house." Sounds of glass breaking could be heard outside, followed by all sorts of noise, including wood breaking, and finally, her loud wails.

"You terrible old hag. Old hag. How could you deceive us like this?" She bawled and cursed, like a typical funeral crier.

Yue'er's mother sat at the door dully, covered in dust from head to toe. Her eyes were dry, like deep, parched wells. She'd been a proud, feisty woman all her life, and no one had ever seen her in such a sorry state. If this were her old self, she'd have fought back, with words and hands, and made a worthy opponent for Mengzi's mother. A good show develops only when two mighty forces meet. Though they failed to enjoy a good fight, the people heard something new and interesting.

"What are bayberry sores?" someone asked, to whom an explanation was given; imagination provided further details, and soon it was no longer a mystery.

Mengzi thought his mother had gone to the in-laws to demand an answer, and he had not expected her to raise such an uproar. When he got closer to Yue'er's parents' house, he stamped his foot when he saw the crowd. He hated his mother for what she was doing, for he knew that Yue're's reputation was ruined, as was her chance to live unaffected in the village. He pushed through the crowd to see his mother-in-law sitting in the yard, looking pitiable. He went to pull her to her feet.

"Come on, Mother, get up. We can talk inside."

She'd been sitting dumbly till then, and his gesture served to draw out a hell-raising wail from her. She bawled and banged her head against the ground; soon her forehead was covered in bruises and bumps.

"What are you looking at?" He glared at the gawkers. Two of them came up to grab her by the arms.

Mengzi walked in and saw pieces of a broken mirror on the floor and holes in the tea table that exposed raw wood. Knowing it was his mother's handiwork, he sighed.

She was sitting on the kang, wailing like a funeral crier and cursing every once in a while. "Bayberry sores." She had spread out a red satin blanket and put it under her. It was dirty from dust and filth. Mengzi was outraged and flabbergasted. How could she do that? He'd often seen similar acts used by other village women, but not his own mother. She'd resorted to the ploy once before, as far as he could recall: when he was little, Big Head had given him a bloody nose, so she'd taken him along to defile his house. She must have lost her head over her anger this time.

"It's shameful, what you did, Ma." Angry tears welled up in his eyes.

"Shameful? You think this is shameful? At least I didn't palm a sick daughter off as a virgin," she snapped shrewishly.

"Please don't talk like that." He pleaded with her. "She has to live here."

"She didn't worry about how you're going to live. We spent a pile of money and got bayberry sores in return."

Mengzi sighed deeply, suddenly feeling hostility toward his mother. Couldn't you at least think about me? he said silently. Yue'er is your daughter-in-law, so what you're doing has brought shame to the whole family. But she did not care about that now. There was nothing he could do about her unreasonable thoughts and actions, and could only sigh. When he thought about how Yue'er would be hurt, he began to worry: the spit from the villagers would drown her.

Baigou, who must have gotten wind of the commotion, stormed through the gate. Convinced that Mengzi was there to pick a fight, Baigou stared daggers at him. When Mengzi explained, he shouted angrily at his mother:

"I wish you were dead, all of you!"

Then he turned to scream at the gawkers, "What are you looking at?" That drove them away.

Baigou yelled at his mother again, "I thought you were whispering about something good. So, this was what you were keeping from me. You've shamed our ancestors so much they'll jump off the sacrificial table. Give it back to them. Return all the wedding gifts. Bring her back to cook and feed the dog."

The two women howled, one hoarse and the other full-throated, one loud and the other soft, their voices rising and falling. The gawkers were still gossiping. Mengzi was calm now that everyone knew their secret. It was actually better that it was out in the open, he said to himself. It was not all that serious when he thought about it. He felt so much better now.

But Yue'er would drown in the gossip.

How was she supposed to keep going?

Chapter Twenty-Eight

A camel's outstretched neck, a duck's long bill
Neither can reach the grass on another hill

1

Finally, a dazzling whiteness appeared before Ying'er and Lanlan.

It was harsh on the eyes after spending days in the yellow sand. As they got closer, they realized it was alkali soil, where nothing grew. The alkali had heated the ground and made it spongy. Even the air gave off a salty ocean smell.

"We're close," Lanlan said happily. "This is what the lakes edges look like."

Even the camel cried out cheerfully, like a celebratory note from a suona.

Ying'er's mood should have been buoyed as well, but instead she felt a strange calmness. She was afraid of another disappointment after such a long search.

As they walked on they saw towering salt hills. Lanlan told her those were mounds of salt crust dredged from the lakes. The sun shining down on them sent off countless reflecting rays. It felt like a dream to Ying'er.

Everywhere they looked was a brilliant white, like a crystal palace. Their camel cried out spiritedly.

There were people around the mounds, but from a distance they looked like ants. Ying'er spotted the salt lakes when they drew closer. They were a dozen or so meters wide and hundreds of meters in length. The water was a dark green, out of which workers scooped salt with metal ladles that allowed water to drip through holes when they were lifted out. Long stretches of dry land separated the lakes, where salt crystals were laid out in irregular patterns.

The men were wearing only underpants. It looked somewhat indecent to Ying'er, but they were "human beings," which the women hadn't seen in many days. She found it impossible to describe how she felt.

Lanlan walked up to ask one of the workers about water. He brought over a metal bucket and said:

"The metal cage is half full. You can have it all."

It amused Ying'er to hear the man call the bucket a metal cage.

The camel let out a long cry when it saw water. Lanlan dunked their bottle into the bucket. Air bubbles rose noisily as it took a long time to fill. She handed it to Ying'er, who drank despite knowing that it had once been in the camel's mouth. The water was tepid, but it was real water, much more satisfying than the juice of suoyang, though its roots had quenched their thirst. After finishing, she handed the bottle to Lanlan, who did the same. She was about to refill the bottle for the camel, but the worker set the bucket down so the camel could bury its mouth in the water.

Lanlan felt terrible about using up the water, but the man said:

"Don't worry. We've got plenty. Are you here to carry salt back or to work?"

That gave Lanlan the germ of an idea. "Work? We're not strong enough for what you're doing."

"There are plenty of things you can do," the man said, "like sewing hemp sacks or gleaning salt crystals. We could really use some help."

Lanlan glanced at Ying'er, who said:

"One of our camels died, and replacing it will cost a lot. It would be great, of course, if we could make some money here. We came to carry salt back for money, didn't we?"

"All right," Lanlan said to the man. "We'll try it out for a couple of days. We'll stay if we can manage the work."

"Let's go see the foreman."

"You can spend a few days here and give it a try," said the old foreman.

Ying'er had been worried they wouldn't see any women at the salt lakes. So, she was surprised to see quite a few of them. All with sunburned faces, they lived in a nearby rammed earth building.

"You can stay with them," the foreman said.

They led their camel over to the building and unloaded the litter. Its back was festering again and giving off a terrible stench. Lanlan scooped some salt water to wash the wound.

It was a small building without regular beds, just a row of railroad ties. Lanlan and Ying'er had set off with two mattress pads, but one had been torn into pieces and doused in kerosene to use as grenades. Their blankets were on the camel killed by the jackals, leaving them with only a pad. The railroad ties were uneven and the padding was thin, which would hurt their backs. But being away from home meant they couldn't be choosy. To earn enough to go home with dignity they had to put up with anything, even if it meant eating pig swill or working like dogs.

One of the women, Sansan, was big and strong, and very friendly. Not many women came out here to work in the desert, so whoever showed up was treated like visiting kin. Sansan dumped some noodles into boiling water and added salt. There were no vegetables, which were rare in the area. They were told that vegetables were carted over to the management station some eight *li* away, but the line was usually long, and the salt workers had no time to line up. Plain noodles were good enough. Their stomachs, shriveled by thirst, had been awakened by the suoyang plants, so now they could eat their fill until sweat poured down their foreheads. It was a wonderful sensation.

After they ate, Sansan found some hay for the camel, which she tethered to the door.

"Get some sleep. Your camel's safe. No one comes here but people with carts to transport salt. No thief would dare come."

Ying'er and Lanlan slept well.

2

That evening some workers came to Sansan for her to stitch the bloody wounds on their legs.

Ying'er was shocked to see skin on legs as hard as helmets, like callouses on an old cow's neck. The area was thick, grayish white, and covered in bloody cracks; the wounds were deep, a scary red, the size of an infant's mouth. They were not actually bleeding, but were still scary looking.

Sansan told them that the ladles weighed about thirty *jin*, too heavy for one man to pull out of the water, even with both hands. So they rested the handle on their thigh to use as a lever. Over time, a layer of skin as thick as a couple of coins formed on their legs. When they worked, the hard surface cracked and started to bleed, getting bigger and bigger. Luckily the wounds were bathed in salt water, so they hurt but without fear of infection.

Sansan threaded a needle to sew up the wounds.

Ying'er gasped. She hadn't expected her first sight at the sacred land to be such a sorry scene. She blanched and looked away, but could not escape the image of bloody wounds that seemed to bare their teeth and laugh frightfully. It was like a bad dream. She recalled how in the desert the salt lakes had always seemed like a cool dream. How disappointing that those disgusting wounds greeted her on her arrival.

Sansan asked Lanlan to help out. Lanlan was good at needlework, but on fabric not on bloody wounds. One of the workers chuckled as he took a threaded needle and put on a show of poking it through the thick skin to pull the gaping wound together. He was being playful, but the beads of sweat rolling down his forehead betrayed the pain.

They walked off cheerfully after the suturing. Sansan lit a kerosene lamp, for there was no electricity.

"The generator is reserved for the hoist," she told them.

The management station had electric lights that were turned off at ten at night.

"The man who gave you water is Daniu, the head of the workers. He's the best, he can scoop up ten tons of salt a day. The daily ration allotted by the management station is ten *jin* of flour per worker. They need to eat a lot to have enough energy to work."

Ying'er was surprised.

While they were talking, Daniu came, to say the foreman wanted them to pick *shagen*, one yuan per bucketful. They'd be paid at the end of the month. He also gave them canvas uniforms and dark glasses.

"Picking *shagen* is the lightest work around here. You're lucky. Someone just quit; otherwise you couldn't get the job even if you fought for it," Sansan told them.

Before they turned in, Lanlan gathered wheat stalks for the camel. There was needle grass on nearby sand dunes, but it was planted to shore up the sand, not for camel consumption. With plenty of water, the camel didn't mind the dry stalks and chewed away happily.

"The salt lakes were a dowry from a Mongolian lord to one of his daughters a hundred years ago," Sansan said late that night. "It was the best dowry any girl could hope for, like a treasure chest. The salt continues to grow no matter how much you scoop out. It really is an endless supply."

How could one woman be so much luckier than others? Ying'er wondered.

And yet what was so good about being lucky? The princess had a treasure chest, and still she ended up as a pile of bones.

3

After breakfast the next morning, they went up to the salt mounds. Mostly aged salt, the crystals were large, mined from recently dug pools, where they had steeped for years. After the aged salt was scooped out, new salt would grow in the alkali water in a few years, but the crystals would be smaller. Aged salt tasted better and fetched a higher price.

The salt crust—the hard ground surface—had to be removed before aged salt could be harvested, as the salt in alkali water was exposed. Grains of salt and sand fused to form crystals called *shagen* around the lake. Ying'er and Lanlan were to pick them out of the salt crystals.

It was a job for women, who were dressed in canvas work clothes and wore a scarf and dark glasses. Daniu told Ying'er and Lanlan to copy them.

The hoist transported a pile of salt and *shagen* and placed it on the mound. *Shagen* was black. Whenever Ying'er spotted a dark shape in the salt, she picked it up and tossed it into her bucket. The hoist made noise that seemed to drill its way into her head, and since loud noise bothered her, she felt she might lose her mind. Yet she had to ignore the din, as the salt poured down like water. *Shagen* rolled down the side of the mound, forcing her to work nonstop. She felt inundated by the racket.

"Dai! Are you blind?" Someone yelled as she lost herself in the work.

Ying'er turned and saw a menacing face staring at her. The man pointed at *shagen* still on the mound. She was not used to wearing dark glasses and did not know that *shagen* could get stuck on the side. She removed her glasses and gave the man an apologetic smile before climbing up to remove the shagen. Unexpectedly, salt flowed down with the cascading water. She'd barely straightened up when she was knocked to the ground by a great force, while thousands of needles shot into her eyes. With her hands over her eyes, she rolled to the side.

"Why did you take off your glasses?" The man chided her. "It's all right. The salt water stings, but it won't do any harm." He called over a worker to take her place and told her to get some fresh water from the bucket to rinse her eyes.

She did what she was told, and the pain subsided after a while. Wiping her face with a towel, she thanked the man and walked off, but he stopped her and asked where she was from. She answered, reluctantly, wondering if that was the rule around there.

It took a while, but she realized that picking *shagen* was not easy work. One reason was stress: as the salt flowed down, she had to stay focused and act quickly or the *shagen* would be buried in the salt. Another reason was a sore back from bending over. It felt as if it were broken. The long ride on their camel had already caused discomfort in her back, and now the pain was like a whirlwind ready to take her down. And there was the water that kept splashing into her eyes, stinging so much she was constantly in tears. The glasses were meant to prevent water seepage, but the water was like a sneak thief, impossible to guard against. When she was on the mound picking *shagen*, water would ride along the salt and splash in her face. Experience taught her to shut her eyes quickly; she was drenched head to toe, but her eyes managed to avoid direct contact with the water. Yet, the all-invasive water would always find a way to steal into her eyes and make them burn as if on fire.

She was feeling dizzy. And this was considered the easiest job, she thought. She had to agree, of course, when she recalled the sinister gaping wounds on the workers' legs. They were right about no free lunch, she said to herself. If she wanted to make some money, she'd have to put up with the hardship.

As the sun rose higher, the salt mound turned into a steamer. The smell of alkali grew stronger and spread around her, a pungent, acrid odor reminiscent of the ocean. The salt lakes might be a dead ocean, she thought. She recalled the sea shells she'd found when digging suoyang. A warm current like water rippled through her. Lingguan had promised to take her to see the ocean, which she'd only seen on TV, a trip to an azure blue stretched across the horizon. The ocean in her imagination would be cool, with breezes brushing her face, pleasantly ticklish, unlike the sweltering, stifling hot salt lakes. The work was tough, but she'd pretend it was the ocean he'd promised to show her. That would do, wouldn't it?

"Dai! Don't fall asleep on the job!" The man screamed at her again.

She woke up from her reverie to see all the *shagen* brought over by the hoist, sprinkled on salt, like pockmarks on a white face. She quickly picked them all out.

4

Ying'er discovered she was wearing a suit of armor; her clothes had stiffened when the sun licked off the water splashed on them. A layer of white salt obscured their original color.

She was wet one moment and dry the next. It felt awful being wet and sticky, either from sweat or the salt water, but it was equally uncomfortable being dry. When gusting wind and the hot sun dried her out, her armor-like underwear rubbed against her nipples. She could not tell which she preferred, wet or dry; all she could feel was the intensifying desire to have a shower.

Finally, noon came. The women went into a changing room made of grass mats. Ying'er took off her work clothes and saw it was indeed a suit of armor, for both the top and bottom could stand on their own. After changing, the women took their work clothes to rinse in buckets of fresh water and the salt dissolved, without any scrubbing. After spreading the uniforms out to dry, they made lunch.

Ying'er and Lanlan had flung their changes of clothes at the jackals, so they had nothing but the set they were wearing. New to the work, they hadn't known to take off their own clothes before putting on the uniform, so everything they were wearing turned as stiff as armor. They had no choice but to rinse their uniform and keep their clothes on, which rustled as they moved.

"What did the old dead baby want with you?" Sansan whispered to Ying'er.

"Who?" Ying'er asked.

"The foreman. The one talking to you."

"He's alive and well. Why do you call him that?" Ying'er was amused.

"We only call him that in private." Sansan giggled.

Sansan went on to tell her that the foreman was not in charge of the workers; he had a boss, but was himself quite powerful.

"We call him old dead baby because he likes a bit of you know what."

"No, what?"

"Well . . ." Sansan covered her mouth and giggled again. "What else could it be? He's always summoning female workers. But he does it out in the open; his wife died. You know what men like most, don't you?

A promotion, getting rich, and a dead wife. The old dead baby has all three. Naturally, he's quite eligible, and naturally, he's on the lookout for another wife."

The man entered in the middle of their conversation and dropped off two sets of gently used clothes for Ying'er and Lanlan. "How did he know we have no change of clothes?" Ying'er wondered aloud "I'm impressed."

He looked at Sansan, who said nothing until he left. When she finally recovered, she whispered to Ying'er:

"Do you think he heard what I said?"

"Probably not." Ying'er tried to reassure her.

"So what if he heard?" Lanlan said. "You can make money anywhere if you don't mind working as hard as a donkey."

"Then why are you here?" Sansan asked, and Lanlan had no answer.

"It's easy for a woman to make money, if you don't mind what you do." Sansan said. "If you want to keep your reputation, then you have to work like a donkey. You get to see your hard-earn money here. At some places, you work for nothing, because a dirty foreman will take it all from you."

Ying'er wondered if the foreman had given them his dead wife's clothes, which made her uneasy, but Lanlan had changed into one of the sets. Seeing her hesitation, Lanlan said:

"Go change. You gather firewood at the mountain where you are. Give me the old ones and I'll wash them."

Ying'er changed out of her stiffened undergarments and washed them in a bucket with Lanlan. After they laid the clothes out to dry, Sansan checked around before whispering:

"Don't underestimate the old dead baby. He's rich, and he has lots of ways to get more. Like he has a scheme going with a truck driver. With a load of four tons of salt, they chalk it up to six tons and split the money."

"How do you know?" Ying'er asked.

"You can't wrap a fire in paper." Sansan sneered. "It's an open secret. We don't own the salt lakes, so no one cares. In this day and age, anyone who can gets what he wants."

Lunch was ready, and they were about to eat when the foreman showed up again. With a glance at Ying'er, he dropped off bags of pickled mustard roots before walking out wordlessly. Looking at Ying'er, Sansan was about to say something, but decided against it.

It was still boiled noodles, but delicious; they were famished, and the addition of the pickled vegetables made for a good meal. Ying'er was sweating; it had been a while since she'd eaten her fill.

In the afternoon, when they knocked off for the day, someone came to weigh the *shagen* the women had collected. With only twelve buckets, Ying'er fared badly. Lanlan had fifteen, the best among them had more than twenty. If the hoist brought about the same amount of *shagen*, Ying'er reasoned silently, then she'd missed three bucketfuls, compared to Lanlan. She felt guilty. Whoever bought her portion of salt would have been shortchanged.

As she lay down on her railroad tie that night, she felt her thigh twitch, which bothered her. That always signaled something unexpected.

What could it be this time?

5

After working for several days, they had made a hundred yuan or so, but they'd have to wait till the end of the month to get their money. Sansan told them that they'd get everything they earned, with no unreasonable deductions.

"Even with that, not many people stay for long," Sansan said. "A wolf wouldn't pick a place like this to shit. Several people worked a month and left after they were paid."

Permanent workers never had their pay docked; in fact, the ones who scooped salt were very well treated. In the past, they had a monthly ration of three hundred *jin* of coarse grain, until a big shot arrived to tell the grain station to supply the workers with only fine grains like wheat and rice. They were also given a steady supply of meat. The others all had to pay for their food.

Daniu came to their room each night, either to chat or for Sansan to sew up the cracked wounds on his leg. He kept stealing glances at Ying'er, saying she was prettier than a woman in a painting. There were other women at the salt lakes, to be sure, but the elements had stained their faces a dung color. The men had never seen a woman with such a fresh, pretty face. Even someone with Lanlan's look was rare. She fared badly alongside Ying'er, who make her look average, even though she too was a pretty woman. But that didn't bother her. The events in the desert had convinced her to return to the Vajravārāhī. She'd begun recitations again, her heart filled with gratitude. The Vajravārāhī gave me back my life, she said to herself, I'd be unworthy of her if I didn't keep up with the practice.

Besides her religious practice, Lanlan constantly fretted over her parents back home. To ease their minds, she asked the foreman to place a call to the small shop in her village for them to tell her father that she and Ying'er were doing fine, working at the salt lakes, so they shouldn't worry. Lanlan found that parents were a contradiction; they seemed to always do or say something stupid when she was around them, but once she was away, she had only positive thoughts about them. She was guilt-ridden when she thought about their hard lives, with hardly a day of ease and comfort. Parents are like your hometown; you only feel its warmth when you're away.

Daniu was a model worker. He had a thin face, but was mostly ropy muscles, which rippled when he worked. The only flaw was his sunburned skin, and legs covered in callouses and gaping wounds. But he was like all the other workers, and Ying'er quickly got used to seeing them.

Daniu told stories, mostly about the permanent workers. To him, they were strange, and belonged to another world. For instance, he told them about a mother and daughter who had fallen for the same man, leading to a big blow-up. It sounded like a story from another world to Ying'er.

The old dead baby was another topic for Daniu, who called him Boss. The boss was a man of great importance to Daniu, who had been made into a sort of deputy. It wasn't much of a promotion, but he was in close proximity to power, and his status among the permanent workers was elevated. Whenever one of them had a problem, Daniu talked to the boss to get it resolved.

Besides his connection to the boss, Daniu stood to gain some benefits. After becoming a model worker who scooped ten tons of salt a day, he seemed to be on the receiving end of special treatment from the man who measured salt production. When the workers brought up the salt, it was piled up by the water in a prescribed shape; then the management station sent a man to measure the salt. Sometimes, when he was too lazy to do it himself, he had Daniu do it for him and double checked from time to time. So Daniu was vested with considerable authority, and whoever he favored would benefit. Naturally, he was mightily pleased with himself, and that was why he once thumped his chest and said to Ying'er:

"Come see me if you ever need anything."

He acted like he could swallow the sky and spit out the earth.

Ying'er thought that was funny.

6

There was to be a movie showing at the management station. The news spread like a whirlwind. After gobbling down their dinner, the women dressed up and got ready. Ying'er hadn't want to go, but Lanlan said:

"We're going. I don't really care what they're showing, but at least we get to see something different."

After feeding and watering the camel, they followed the crowd to the management station.

The road was paved with *shagen*, and flanked with bunchgrass and other desert vegetation. Daniu was attentive to Ying'er along the way, constantly checking on her; she ignored him as best she could. The other workers whispered back and forth, frequently roaring in feral laughter. Ying'er frowned and tugged Lanlan to drop far behind them. Daniu cursed the workers, who guffawed and walked off.

"Don't mind them," Daniu said. "That's just the way they are. If they don't see a woman for three days, they think every sow is a rare beauty."

"What are you talking about? Are you calling us sows?" Lanlan asked.

"No, no. what I meant was, there aren't many women around, and pretty women like you are especially hard to find, so of course they're acting like hungry wolves," Daniu explained anxiously.

"Do they plan to eat us?" Lanlan laughed.

"Don't worry. With me around, they wouldn't dare."

Lanlan pinched Ying'er and smiled with a hand over her mouth, "Listen to him. He wants to be our protector."

The management station was not large, just a few rows of single-story buildings. There were no chairs in the large room they called a movie theater, so the workers brought their own stools. Migrant workers were reduced to standing to the side, where they crowded into the women looking innocent. When Ying'er led Lanlan away, Daniu pushed his way out of the group to stand with them.

Old dead baby was there too. He handed two stools to Lanlan. Ying'er saw how a hostile look replaced Daniu's fawning smile when the boss turned his back. After the boss walked off, Daniu murmured:

"You'd better watch out, he's got his eye on you now. He's a lecher, always using the excuse of finding a wife to sleep with one woman after another. When he's finished, he tosses them aside."

"Why not follow his example if you can?" Lanlan teased.

"Women these days are all money crazed. There isn't a good one left." Daniu fumed.

He'd included Lanlan and Ying'er in his tirade, so Lanlan glared at him before pushing Ying'er up front to sit down.

The movie started, a story about a group of prisoners. Ying'er was turned off by some of the vulgar scenes behind them, so she looked around instead and saw that a large number of people had shown up. Commotions kept erupting among the migrant workers, followed by women cursing the men. She was grateful to the boss. He'd done them a favor by bringing the stools, she thought, so they could avoid the disgusting groping.

When the first reel was being changed, she saw Daniu shove his way up with a tree stump. He apologized right and left as he pushed his way through.

The movie started again, but his head blotted out half of the screen, incurring more complaints, so he crouched down. Ying'er was annoyed when she realized he wanted to sit next to them. Women like male attention, that's for sure, but it depends on who's giving it; it's obnoxious if it's someone not to their liking.

Daniu bored through the curses and arrived beside them. Lanlan scooted to make room for his stump. He sighed as if he'd accomplished something heroic. Ying'er frowned again, as she felt people pointing fingers at her back; it might be impossible to explain herself now.

Inevitably, affairs happened among migrant workers, but she didn't want any of that. For her, you have to hold onto something special, or you're just like an animal.

Daniu was breathing loudly, an irritating sound, a constant reminder that she was breathing in air that emerged from his nose. It repelled her, though she knew this was a character flaw. She couldn't help it, she'd been that way all her life. Even as a little girl she'd refused to drink from a glass someone had used, even if it meant going thirsty. The same went with bedding and clothes. Granted, there was an exception; she never minded anything Lingguan had used. Then again, reality had forced her to adjust. She'd put on used clothes the boss gave her and eaten from a metal bowl at the salt lakes.

Something scratched the back of her hand. Thinking it was unintentional, she ignored it. But the scratching got more insistent, and her face burned when she realized what was happening. She moved to the side to avoid the fingers, but her reaction only encouraged them to take her hand. She tried to free it, but the grip tightened. Outraged, she gave Daniu an angry glare and saw a lewd look on his face. If she hadn't worried about embarrassing him, she'd have screamed. Now that she couldn't free her hand or curse, he got bolder; he stuck a finger into her palm, which he then balled with another hand. The finger thrust back and forth, a gesture with meaning clear enough to humiliate her. Infuriated, she tried to pull her hand back, but no matter how hard she tried, she couldn't get loose. Helpless tears welled up in her eyes.

The finger was getting carried away, while the hand on hers was damp with sweat. She jerked her hand again but still failed to fling his away, so she jumped to her feet. Her head blotted out the screen, immediately drawing curses that felt like slaps across her face.

"I'll be back soon," she said. The hand was exposed as she got up, and finally she was free.

She walked away from Daniu at a crouch. Tears came the moment she was out of the crowd. She was reminded of the night when Pockmark Xu had tried to rape her; it felt equally nauseating now. I won't ever leave again after I get home, she vowed silently. The outside world was dreadful, and she was helpless out here. She recalled how she'd been ill-treated at her parents' house and how someone had poked her with a hammer handle at her in-laws'. She had no place to live in peace.

Many people were looking in her direction, so she pretended she was going to relieve herself. She hadn't had the urge, but once outside she actually did have to go. Looking around, she found a secluded place, but before she reached the spot, two large hands clamped down on her. She heard Daniu's heavy breathing.

"Let me go," she snapped at him.

"I want you so much I could die, dear little sister." He was panting. "Take pity on me and let me have it."

She struggled but could not get away. The hands were used to working with a metal ladle and might take her by force, so she changed her tone.

"Let me go and we can talk."

He did as she asked, but still tried to put his arm around her.

"Be a gentleman," she said as she dodged away.

"I'll be good to you; you can believe me. I mean it. If I'm lying, my ancestors are donkeys. Do you believe me? Do you?"

"Something like this can't be forced. I've already got someone."

"We can still do it, even if we're not married."

"How dare you say something like that!" she spat.

He went quiet, before surprising her by picking her up and walking into the dark. She struggled, but could not fight him off. She screamed, but got no response from anyone. His heavy breathing overwhelmed her senses. As she continued to struggle, she threatened:

"I'll kill myself if you don't stop."

"Women are all the same," he panted and said. "You fight at first, but soon you won't want to let me go."

She tried to bite his arm, but each time he blocked her. She started to cry.

"Daniu! Daniu!" A shadow came out of the theater.

Daniu let go of her and disappeared into the night.

Ying'er could tell it was the boss. Drying her tears, she walked out of the dark, not courageous enough to relieve herself.

"Is that you, Daniu?"

Ying'er said nothing.

Clearly, he had his eye on her too.

7

Daniu stayed away over the next few days, bold enough only to gaze at her from a distance. At night, Ying'er made sure the door was securely latched. Lanlan had misread everything; Ying'er had left ahead of her that night and Daniu had followed her out, which could only have meant that something was up. Something had happened, but not what Lanlan thought. Worried that it might cast a bad light on Daniu, Ying'er hadn't wanted to bring it up, but to clear herself with Lanlan, she had to tell her sister-in-law everything. Lanlan gnashed her teeth and said:

"I'll spit on him if he comes again."

Sansan was treating her differently too. Before Ying'er's arrival, she'd had something going with Daniu, enough to cause gossip. People were even saying that they'd slept together. Daniu had wanted to keep it a secret, but Sansan told others that he had tried to seduce her and that she'd turned him down. It was a loss of face for Daniu, who was so outraged he revealed their sexual relationship. Sansan liked him because he worked hard and made good wages. But now he had his eye on Ying'er, so Sansan turned cold toward her. She did not force them to set up their own kitchen, since they'd lost their cookware in the desert, but she no longer treated them as friends.

They had to see each other one way or the other, since they "dipped their ladle in the same pot," Lanlan thought. She didn't want to always try to figure out Sansan's mood, so she asked the boss where they could buy some cookware. He gave them some to use for the moment, saying it was left behind by migrant workers. He asked her if they wanted to move out. To Lanlan, it was still better to have someone around, so she told him they'd stay with Sansan. He thought that was a good idea.

After a few days at the salt lakes, some of the inconveniences became apparent to Ying'er: they did not have their own changes of clothes and no sanitary pads when they had their periods, and so on. Worst was the loss of the blanket on the dead camel. The desert baked in the day and froze at night; the heat was enough to cook a donkey and the cold could do a dog in. When the sun set, a desert wind began to howl, and the house felt like an ice cellar in the early morning. Sansan had shared a tattered wool blanket with them when they first arrived. It wasn't clean enough for Ying'er, who placed her blue jacket under it. Since the night of the movie, Sansan unobtrusively moved the blanket more to her side, and Ying'er knew that Sansan thought she had stolen her lover.

Ying'er could put up with all the inconveniences except for the unbearable chill before daybreak, which they tried to live with by not taking off their clothes before bedtime. Their work clothes were thick enough to ward off the cold. They'd rinse them off in the afternoon and by nighttime they'd be dry enough to spread out as a cover. Yet the chill always managed to bore through layers of clothes, and they had sore throats all the time.

And then there was their camel. It was a handy boat in the desert, but turned into a burden at the lake; they had to keep searching for food. The boss asked a Mongolian herder to graze the animal for a few days. They had borrowed it from a neighbor, who would be unhappy if it wasn't returned soon, even though it was fall and the camel wasn't needed until spring planting. Lanlan hoped to meet up with a Liangzhou man who would take it back with a load of salt. She'd done her math: she could earn something carrying salt back, but not as much as working at the lakes. Besides, she got paid cash here, while salt would be traded for grain that would then be sold for cash. It was too much trouble.

Lanlan asked workers to keep an eye out and let her know when someone came from Liangzhou for salt. But she soon discovered that her knowledge of the salt lakes was outdated by ten years. Back then, there hadn't been a highway, and people from her village crossed the desert for the salt. Now there was a highway; it was even farther from Liangzhou, but not too far away for motor vehicles. A truck could carry several tons, while a camel managed only several hundred *jin*. She felt like a fly in a bottle; the outside world had changed, but her understanding of it was stuck in what she remembered. If I'd known, I'd have just come to work here. After asking around, she learned that you can board a bus at Liangzhou to the salt lakes. She also heard that the truck drivers liked to give rides to women; all she had to do was wave and they'd stop for her. But a woman paid a terrible price if she ran into an immoral driver.

Now it became clear to Lanlan why there were so many jackals in the desert. In the past, salt carriers would travel with muskets, with which they picked off jackals, and that prevented them from forming packs. Now with the trucks rumbling down the highway, there were fewer camel caravans to shoot them.

She thought she'd been through a lot—marriage, beatings by her husband, asking for a divorce—enough for her to be dumbstruck by the changes in the world. If she hadn't come here, she'd have believed that the world hadn't changed from the time before her wedding.

The salt lakes had also changed. Manual excavation was a thing of the past, replaced by machines. A rabbit had been enough to exchange for a load of salt, but now it had to be paid for with cash. Other changes weren't such a big deal, except for the trucks that made the lumbering camels look pathetic. She finally understood why transporting salt on a camel's back had become a rare trade. To think how she had been so proud of her idea before they left!

With the outside world, you have to see it to believe it, but when you do see it, it will bowl you over.

She would work for a while, she figured. If they liked it here and someone could return the camel for them, they'd stay to work.

People can be buried anywhere, she said to herself.

<h1 style="text-align:center">8</h1>

The boss had heard from somewhere that the two women needed blankets, so he sent a worker over with a couple.

It felt like receiving coal on a snowy day to them, for they were good, thick wool.

Ying'er sensed that some workers were pointing fingers at and whispering about her. She was getting the hang of the work and was picking up more buckets of *shagen*. Starting on one particular day, she began gleaning more than everyone else, drawing odd looks from the women. That did not seem quite right to her either, as she discovered that her piles grew visibly larger every day after lunch break.

One day, instead of resting after lunch, she cracked the door open to keep an eye on the spot where her *shagen* piled up. Half an hour later, Daniu showed up. He walked up stealthily, with a fiber sack, and, after checking around to make sure no one was watching, dumped the sackful of *shagen* on her pile. Now she knew; he must have picked them up along the highway, where the road to the management station was paved with it.

Her face burned. How could he do that, she wondered. How could I face others if they found out?

She quietly nudged Lanlan and asked her to tell Daniu to stop. He looked supremely confident when he saw Lanlan.

"He said not to worry." Lanlan returned to tell Ying'er. "If anything happens, he'll take responsibility." She laughed and continued, "He said you're a fool. You'll get a couple of hundred more each month."

"What does he take me for?" Ying'er said unhappily. "I don't want that kind of dirty money."

When Daniu came for a repeat performance, she went up and, with a stern look, told him to stop making her look bad.

"Sure," he replied, convinced of her displeasure. "A cold kang greets my warm rear end. I just want you to know how I feel. I really do like you a lot and I want the best for you. Everyone knows how wonderful it is to nap after lunch. I don't mind going out there, as long as you can make a bit extra money."

"I'll tell the boss if you do it again." Ying'er threatened, afraid he wouldn't stop.

"Sure, all right. I'll stop." Finally, she'd put some fear into him and he slinked off quickly.

She was drenched in a cold sweat when she went back inside. She'd never be able to come clean, even if she jumped into the Yellow River, if people knew found out. It wasn't all that different from stealing the things herself, was it? Besides, they'd think I had something going on with him; otherwise, why would he do that instead of napping.

Sure enough, she overheard a worker say to another:

"See that pretty woman? She's Daniu's new flame."

The comment angered and humiliated her. There could only be two sources of the rumor, one of whom would be Daniu himself. She heard that the workers were all like that; the scarcity of woman had enriched them with fertile imaginations, and they enjoyed making up salacious stories. The other source might be Sansan, who acted as if Ying'er were a true love rival. Like women back in Liangzhou, she walked with an exaggerated flair whenever she saw Ying'er. "See, storming off like a thunderclap," in her mother's words.

Sansan rarely looked Ying'er in the eye now, nor did she talk to her, though they still shared quarters. Ying'er and Lanlan could not keep using her stove any longer, so Lanlan found some bricks to make a small stove by the door. The plants around the lake were reserved to shore up the sand and hence were off limits. After work, they went out to pick up camel droppings, which was great fuel, because it burned slowly. A few pieces lasted a long while. But the migrant workers had to cook their own meals, so they gathered camel droppings too, as did the permanent workers' children. With so many people gathering, the droppings were scarce. Sometimes it took an hour to find enough to cook a meal.

One day they went hunting during a lunch break. Lanlan wanted to gather more, so they borrowed a hand cart and set out for the herders' area. To their disappointment, there wasn't much left for them there either.

"If we'd known camel droppings could be so precious, we could have saved those from our own camels on the way," Lanlan said.

"Back then we had no control over our own lives. We couldn't have been thinking this far ahead," Ying'er replied, though she too felt bad about leaving the droppings on the way. Human hearts are remarkable, she thought. Sometimes the desire is as great as a bottomless pit, but at other times it is too easily satisfied. Now the sight of camel droppings would send them running ecstatically, their happiness as great as the joy of a scholar passing the imperial exam.

As they walked along pushing the cart, its wheels kept sinking into the sand, and soon they were sweating profusely. They'd sweat more than the droppings they gathered, Lanlan said. At work, they had to bend over constantly, so their backs were sore; they would have loved to lie down to rest, but there were things they had to do, even if they didn't feel like it. Eyes wide open, they searched for anything that could be used as fuel, the same way they had looked for the salt lakes. They had been so anxious and eager then, like now. It was sort of funny when they thought about it; the sacred land for them now was a sand trough with camel droppings.

Ying'er was dispirited an hour later.

"Let's go back, so we won't miss work," she said to Lanlan.

"Since we're here, why not keep looking? I don't believe the herders have plugged their animals' rear ends," Lanlan replied.

At that moment they spotted a pile in a nearby sand trough, seemingly smiling up at them. Overjoyed, they ran forward with the cart, feeling it was a dream, as if a fox fairy had cooked a meal for them. Part of the droppings were dry, other parts were still wet, but that didn't bother them. They scooped it all up, wet and dry, and tossed into the cart.

"What a strange camel. Why did it keep shitting at the same spot?" Lanlan wondered.

"We all have our habits, so maybe this camel is the same. It has a favorite spot to use as a toilet." Ying'er responded.

As they were leaving, they heard an aging voice cough; they jumped in surprise. An old man was rounding a corner of a sand hill where, Ying'er realized, a small house stood. It was tiny structure with walls made of salt slabs, and blended into the background; moreover, it was hidden mostly behind the eddy, which is why they'd missed it at first.

"Why are you stealing my fuel?" the old man demanded.

It dawned on them that he had collected the droppings. Their faces burned from shame. After Lanlan explained the situation to him, he said:

"Oh, so you're from Liangzhou. Then take the droppings. Consider it a gift."

"We can't do that. You have to cook too," Ying'er protested.

"Of course, you can." The man smiled and continued, "I'll just gather more. It's not like the animals' rear ends are sewn up."

He gave Lanlan two sacks and told them to dry the droppings before they used them. They had to keep the sacks in their room or the migrant workers would steal them at night.

They thanked him and pushed the cart back toward the lakes. After walking awhile, they noticed that the topography had changed, indication that they'd taken a wrong turn somewhere. It was a serious mistake, and they panicked when a quick check told them they had to be back at work soon. Then Lanlan found a solution: follow the ruts of their cart on their way in. The extra distance caused them to be an hour late for work.

The boss was about to send some migrant workers into the desert to look for them when they got back. They all breathed a sigh of relief when the women showed up. Lanlan thought they'd surely get a scolding from the boss, who, to her surprise, only told them not to go too far into the desert in the future.

They dried the camel droppings, stuffed them into the sacks, and placed them under their mats. Sansan was constantly short of fuel, so Ying'er gave her some any time she needed it, which softened the woman's attitude a bit. When her family came to see her, she shared some of the desert rice they brought for her.

The droppings from the old man weren't worth much, but the act warmed her heart every time Ying'er thought about it. There are still more good people than bad in the world.

In the meantime, the anecdote of the two women picking up the old man's fuel became a joke among the workers, who laughed when someone brought it up.

Chapter Twenty-Nine

A shot fired on a northern hill is heard in the south
The bullet now spent falls to the ground

1

The first real fight at White Tiger Pass broke out.

There had been disputes among the sand boys before, but they were minor arguments, such as clashing over panning leftovers. This time it was different, for even the municipal government got involved, which, to the villagers, was a big deal.

It was caused by the "big ox" found in Mengzi's pit.

The so-called "big ox" was a large boulder. All gold prospectors knew it was a good sign to see large boulders in a pit, for gold veins were often hidden beneath them. At White Tiger Pass there were mostly gold flakes, but oddly chunks of deposit shaped like real-life objects were often found. Rumor had it that Shuangfu had once dug up a gold boot that weighed over thirty *jin* and sold to a Hui. It was unverified, but everyone believed it, because shortly after that Shuangfu bought some more pits. Some of his new pits were next to Mengzi's. Mengzi felt his temper rise each time he heard the sound of Shuangfu's hoist; he had started more than three weeks after Mengzi, but had already made it down to hard rock.

Fortunately for Mengzi and his group, they spotted the boulder.

As a rule, they did not call a boulder by its name; it was an ox. Normally, what they removed was lots of sand or gravel, but when they saw a big ox, gold should appear. The larger the ox, the more gold they'd find, since that was where it was hidden. A brilliant yellow ought to come into view when the boulder was removed. A few days earlier, a teacher at a private school had come to Shuangfu's pit; that visit had been followed by the discovery of a big ox. Shuangfu said the teacher was a man who brought fortune with him, and kept him on to manage the pit. A pit manager had more authority than a pick-ax or shovel man, like an imperial commissioner, for he supervised every worker at the pit. Under most circumstances, a pit manager would not search the sand boys at quitting time, but he would if a big ox was unearthed. The one who would most likely see gold was the shovel man, who would cover it with loose sand when he noticed specks of yellow. He'd keep working until he sent the carriers away, and then pocket the gold. If the pick-ax man saw what had happened, convention dictated that they split the profits by cracking the piece into two. Which was why the pit manager frisked them whenever they dug up a big ox.

Mengzi and his friends took turns as pit manager, taking shifts. He was so traumatized by his experience at the collapsed pit that he envisioned the frame cracking and the earth closing in on him when he was at the bottom of the pit. His legs turned rubbery despite the knowledge that it was an illusion. Sometimes it did not feel like a job for any man, for he seemed to be holding his head in his hands and could lose it at any time. It was just a thought, however, since he needed to find gold to pay for Yue'er's treatment.

Finally, they saw a big ox.

The sand boys cheered loudly. Its back came into view first, the spine-like ridge exposed amid the sand and gravel. Keyed up by the sight, Mengzi dumped more sand into his basket than usual. The others were panting and sweating. They were so excited their feet worked doubly hard, one going up, the other coming down, back and forth to carry the gravely sand off the ox's back and out of the pit.

"We want a bonus when you find gold, Boss." Fuqiangzi shouted.

"Sure, you bet," Mengzi shouted back cheerfully.

Many heads gathered at the pit opening, all there too see the big ox. Mengzi wished he could see Shuangfu's face and the look of envy; the greater the man's envy, the happier it would make Mengzi. But he failed to spot the red glowing face among them.

"Move away," Mengzi shouted up. "You're blocking the light."

"Hey, don't you start acting like an ox. You're not flying up to heaven just because you spotted an ox," they shouted down at him.

Mengzi scrunched up his shoulders. He's right. How did I become so petty? he said to himself. But outwardly he refused to back down.

"Come down and see if you can dig one up."

"You'd better be sure. If it's a big ox, that's great, but watch out you're not riding a stone ass."

That made Mengzi's head buzz. He poked at the gravel. His spade hit something hard, a gritty sound, and his mouth went dry. Please let it not be a stone ass, he thought. Riding a stone ass meant two things to the sand boys. The boulder was bigger than the pit, making it impossible to move. Or, it might be so big it was part of an underground rock hill, which was small at the top, but had a base too large to know where it ended. Both spelled trouble. Even if there was gold beneath the big boulder, no one would know how to get to it, like a tiger trying to swallow the sky.

Don't worry. A big ox is better than nothing, Mengzi tried to buoy his spirits. Gold veins had a strange pattern. Long ago, a hole opened in the

God of Fortune's gold sack and sprinkled the ground with a long line of gold that might have started at Qingfeng Ridge. It was a common peak of the Qilian Range, the uppermost stream where gold could be found. From there, it traveled down to Moji Mount, Malu River, Shuanglong Gulch, before following the Dasha River down to White Tiger Pass. All the sand boys knew gold could travel along underground rivers. Besides following the flow of water, it could also move downward. With its heavy weight, it passed through gravely dirt all the way until it reached the bottom, commonly flagstone or hard yellow clay, which gold could not penetrate, so that was where it stayed, waiting for sand boys to dig it up centuries later.

Usually, they had reached bottom when a big ox came into view at a pit. Often the prospector removed the boulder to find glinting cloves of gold rising neatly out of the sand, shining brilliantly and making everyone dizzy. Sand, on the other hand, only produced common gold specks. That was why the whole of White Tiger Pass erupted with excitement when a big ox was discovered at Mengzi's pit.

"Those jackasses are going to be very rich," everyone was saying.

No one had expected it to be so big, however, bigger than the pit opening. How much bigger was anyone's guess. Sand boys loved encountering a big ox, but not one that was bigger than a pit site. That spelled trouble; pit managers all dreaded riding a stone ass.

As baskets of sand were cleared off the cow's back and carried up, Mengzi and his friends had their fears confirmed: their pit was indeed a stone ass.

They were deflated. It took little time for the elation over the discovery of a big ox to turn to the despair of riding a stone ass. It felt like falling from Paradise all the way down to Hell. They crouched by the opening to stare blankly, after a volley of curses, though they knew that even losing their voices would not change a thing.

The sand boys took a break after clearing the sand. Each pit was set at four square meters, and any farther than that either way would be encroaching upon others' territory. Mengzi was incensed over the fact that his pit was surrounded by Shuangfu's. He rued his own short-sightedness, for not buying more pits. He hadn't expected Shuangfu to buy up all the empty lots within three weeks. Spurred by his act, the other pit managers went into a buying frenzy, and there weren't many lots left at White Tiger Pass.

Mengzi was unaware of Shuangfu's purchases until he thought about expansion after finding the stone ass. In recent weeks, he had been preoccupied with starting the pit, getting married, taking his wife to treatment in the city. He and his friends had not realized that their pasty brains were no match for Shuangfu's, which the villagers had dubbed "chemistry brain." Worse yet, it was much harder to get a new pit, even if he'd wanted to. The city government had taken the mining rights at White Tiger Pass from Big Head and ordered the mining management station to inventory those that had been sold and were in operation. They could still buy a pit, but they had to apply to the management station, which would then send the request to the city government, where the mayor held sole authority to grant the rights. All this had happened in only two weeks.

The price of a pit went up dramatically. What had cost several hundred yuan to buy one from Big Head two weeks earlier went up to five thousand once the city took over. Which meant that Shuangfu didn't even have to dig; he could make millions by selling his sites.

The news was more depressing than finding a stone ass. They rued their loss until their tongues went numb.

"If we'd known, we'd have spent all our money on new pits," they said. Now they had nothing but a hard bone after others had gnawed off all the meat.

Regret was useless. What they needed to do was try to get off the ass's back.

And that was how the fight started.

2

Mengzi and his friends wanted to expand their pit.

At White Tiger Pass, gold prospectors dug straight down and tunneled outward when they reached the bottom. The tunnel had to be limited to one's pit site, in other words, not to exceed four square meters. Beyond that was someone else's turf. If one was a wolf, then the neighbor could be a jackal, the wolf eyeing the flesh, while the jackal hoped to drag out the intestines.

After rooting around, Mengzi and his friends failed to see the side of the big ox. But at least it was a real ox, not a rock hill, which was a consolation. The boulder surface was relatively flat, the type most likely to lie atop a gold cache, according to common belief.

Digging up a big ox was a wonderful omen, but regret rushed at Mengzi and the villagers like a tidal wave, and to the villagers. Everyone was heartsick over not buying more sites. If they had, they could see money falling into their laps whenever they turned around. Then they'd sell. No one had wanted sites back when Big Head had allocated one to every family in the village, giving it the grand-sounding name of "A pit to aid the poor." Mao Dan had even mocked Big Head's idea:

"White Tiger Pass has laid untouched for thousands of years. If I wanted to, I could stick out my tongue and slurp it up. Why would I need Big Head to give me a piece of it?"

Later they'd have had to pay several hundred to get a site, and the price kept going up until it cost five thousand, plus permission from the mayor. Who the hell was the mayor? A man more important than Heaven, that's who. As a result, the villagers could only thump their chests and stamp their feet in pitiful regret.

Now Mengzi believed the Daoist Master, who had said, "Riches will fly right past someone who's born to be poor." He was right. Through Big Head, the God of Fortune had given the villagers piles of gold, which they'd kicked away.

Maybe he was born to be poor, Mengzi thought. He'd heard about riding a stone ass, but hadn't seen it happen to many people, while he had barely started his first pit, and the stone ass came up and ducked under his ass. He couldn't get off it. It was hopeless. Baigou cursed, Beizhou swore, and Huaqiu prayed, but none of any of that made a difference. They were doomed to ride the stone ass.

Mengzi went down the pit himself to dig the horizontal path. The miners normally worked sideways only when clearing the bottom of the pit so they could dredge up more sand speckled with gold to pan. For Mengzi, though, it was to find where the big ox ended. No matter how big it was, if it's an ox, it must end somewhere, he thought. If he could expand their site, he might be able to find the end of the ox and he'd keep digging downward, clearing more sand, and, who knows, they might get to the gold cloves, if there were any, that is—no, there had to be some. When that happened, ha-ha, Mengzi laughed silently, he'd not only be able to cure Yue'er of syphilis, he could even root out AIDS. What disconcerted him was that when he reached the limits of their site, the big ox was all he saw—east, west, north, and south. He was so disappointed he didn't know what to do.

If he'd bought more pits, he could go farther in all directions, until he reached the edge of the ox, for it had to end somewhere. He'd asked someone to take a look for them; the stony surface was flat, not pointed, like a ridge. But unfortunately, their pit was surrounded by Shuangfu's. When had that ass learned the trick from Chairman Mao, who had ingeniously laid siege to cities from villages; Shuangfu the rich man had encircled the poor.

How could he not be furious?

Beizhu went to see Shuangfu with a request for the man to let them have a few of his pits. Guess what he said?

"Sure. Give me the money and I'll hand the pits over." What he meant by money covered both the mining costs and the rights to open a pit. The latter alone was so high it made their eyes pop. No gouging; Shuangu just wanted the current market price of five thousand, though he'd paid five hundred. To buy one pit in each direction they would need twenty thousand.

"Can't you sell them at your purchase price, Shuangfu?" Beizhu said. "Help out your poor pals."

"I'm helping you out by agreeing to sell." Shuangfu smiled. "Everyone knows the gold under the big ox would far exceed this amount. Besides, I'm not asking too much. The mining costs are based on machine operation. It would be an astronomical amount if it were based on human labor."

"How much altogether?" Beizhu asked.

Shuangfu showed him five fingers. When Beizhu returned with the news, Baigou erupted, "Damn him. He'll eat us up."

It was hopeless. This is the age of cannibalism, and he can do that to us, Mengzi thought.

Mengzi wielded his pickaxe with a savage force. The ground was hard, meaning it was new territory, unmined by anyone before. People were always complaining about digging into spots that had already been mined, but Mengzi didn't believe them. He'd asked his father and Meng Baye, and neither had heard about their ancestors panning gold at White Tiger Pass, except for a few prospectors during the Republican Era who had tried at Shuanglong Gulch. They had gotten so rich from the gold they oozed wealth, only to suffer terribly in struggle sessions later at the hands of the poor. Obviously, gold did not always bring good luck, but Mengzi still hoped to get his hands on some. He'd been poor too long. A saltless meal is tasteless, a penniless man is like a ghost. Poverty chills ambition and hair hangs loose on a skinny horse. Without money, a man can't stand tall and he makes no noise when he farts. Besides, he needed the money for Yue'er's treatment. His heart ached when he saw her gaunt figure.

"You've gone over the line," Huaqiu warned him.

The underground site started at the center of the pit, from where a rope with a set length was used to set the boundary. Crossing a boundary was an infringement upon other's rights. Pits were separated by a fifty-centimeter wide wall that neither owner could touch, in order to preserve order and prevent pit owners from digging into other's sites or taking someone else's gold. Safety was another concern. Without that wall, the pits could easily collapse. For now, however, Mengzi thought he could see the end of the ox if he continued. So, he kept digging, his pickaxe flying at the ground as if to vent his anger.

"He's not going to be happy if you don't stop now," Huaqiu said.

Mengzi mopped his sweaty face and took an angry breath. He tossed down his pickaxe and walked off. Fuqiangzi took over to shovel the gravelly sand into his basket. They had gone so deep the sand was water-logged, so a sand boy could only shovel three or four times before the basket was too heavy. Their neighbors, on the other hand, hooked a steel cable to willow baskets that were filled with gravely sand, and then turned on the hoist to bring them up and out. They had needed only a few days to reach the same depth that Mengzi and his gang had spent weeks digging. He could even hear them talking, and he was worried. He hoped the edge of the ox wasn't on their side, or he'd end up with nothing if they dug around it.

"What do we do now?" Mengzi asked Huaqiu.

"Why ask me?" Huaqiu said. "I don't know."

"Screw him. Let's keep digging." Mengzi spat.

And that was how the fight began.

3

"Watch what you're doing. This is our territory." They had barely started when an angry shout came from the other side.

"Your territory?" Baigou laughed. "Your territory is your women's belly. Even Shuangfu's woman's belly is fair game, and Mengzi works on that. This is nothing."

Beizhu and others roared laughing.

"Watch your mouth, Baigou." Mengzi cautioned.

Baigou bellowed like a wild animal. He'd been bored, now he wanted some action. Which was why he'd been the first to agree with Mengzi's decision to continue digging, forcing the others to go along.

A rock flew through the opening and hit the pickaxe without a crisp sound.

"Now you've done it," Baigou complained.

"So what? You're the one who's digging into our site," someone on the other side shouted. Before he finished, a shovel came flying over. Baigou dodged, and it just missed his leg.

"Get them!" Baigou yelled as he picked up a rock and flung it, followed by a scream from the other side. Mengzi kept digging silently; he wanted to enlarge the opening so they could storm through for close combat. The other side must have been doing the same thing, for soon a gaping hole soon appeared with a loud crash.

"Let's get them!" Baigou shouted as he shoveled sand at their opponents, who ducked and crawled toward their rope ladder.

"Go tell the boss," one of them yelled.

"Tell all you want. We'll screw his wife, and if he comes, we'll beat him up too." Baigou yelled back, his hand never stopping. The shovel was good at flinging sand, but its force was too diffuse to cause any real damage, despite the pained cries they heard from the other side.

"Get out of here. Go." Mengzi screamed at their opponents, who were smart enough to climb up the rope and split. Mengzi and his friends entered the other pit and took a good look to see a giant rock taking up the whole pit.

"Fuck," Baigou said. "They're riding a stone ass too."

Mengzi was stunned. Based on common belief, the size of the rock meant there would be plenty of gold underneath. He hadn't expected it to be so big that there didn't seem to be an end of it. He sighed secretly over their lousy luck, when suddenly a powerful stream of water shot at them. Turned out the other side had gotten out and turned their hose down at them.

"Dai! You want to drown us?" Baigou shouted up at them. Mengzi went back to his pit when the water began to rise.

Those on the other side were still cursing, louder and louder; obviously, they were coming down the rope ladder. The force of the water was also getting stronger, provoking Mengzi's desire to fight back.

"Go get a sack of desert stalks and some hot pepper powder." Fuqiangzi left and returned shortly. Mengzi lit the stalks with his cigarette lighter and, when thick smoke rose, placed the pile by the opening before sprinkling on the hot pepper powder. He then took off his shirt to fan the fire and send the smoke surging into the other pit, where their opponents began to cough.

"Oh, no. They're using poison gas," one of them yelped.

Baigou guffawed as he took off his shirt to fan the smoke. But he wasn't careful enough, and sent it right back at them. The strong, peppery smoke hit Mengzi in the face, making him tear up, sneeze, and cough.

Throwing down his shirt, he ran for the rope ladder, while his friends, racked by coughing fits, also clamored up.

Finally up and out, they were immediately aware of the power of the peppery smoke, and took in big gulps of fresh air. Their noses and chests hurt like hell and they were coughing like machine guns. The two sides seemed to be engaged in a coughing contest. It was so comical Mengzi felt like laughing, until he saw the other side picking up rocks. Revenge was on its way.

"Get back inside," he warned.

His friends also sensed the imminent attack and ran for cover. They were barely able to take a breath before rocks flew at them like crows.

The rocks landed on their shed and dirt ran down to fill the cramped space. Like a starving dog searching for a bone, Baigou looked around for a useful weapon, prompting Mengzi into action. "I'm not a man if I hide in a shed just because they're pelting us," he thought, as he grabbed a pickaxe. Afraid that the steel head might cause serious damage, he turned it upside down and knocked the head off. The handle was about the right length and thickness.

"Go for the legs, not the heads," he told the others as he stormed out.

They were met by their opponents, who also did not want to kill anyone and aimed their rocks low, at the legs and asses, with moderate force. Mengzi noticed that and jumped out of the way while advancing toward one of them. He used the handle on the man's thigh, a vulnerable spot, with only half the force, but the man fell to the ground, screaming like a slaughtered pig.

Baigou swung his birch switch indiscriminately. The branch was light and left a blue or red welt each time it hit, inflicting serous pain, but far from lethal. Two fell from his attack, while the others fled. Cowed by the force of his opponents, the fallen ones moaned piteously.

Bored by the easy victory, Mengzi didn't know what to do next. They were like mangy dogs now, so he couldn't continue the fight, but they might launch another attack if he went back to work. What worried him most were the sand boys Shuangfu hired to work at his many pits. If they all came at once, Mengzi and his friends wouldn't stand a chance. That possibility also occurred to Beizhu, who voiced similar concerns.

Sure enough, a loud commotion signaled a large gang of men heading their way. Disputes were common among sand boys, and gang fights occurred often. But such a large number was rare, and the sight made Mengzi's heart race. He knew he'd be beaten to a pulp if he fell into their hands; he wanted to run, but couldn't take the loss of face. He was still wavering when Beizhu shouted:

"Run. A wise man never fights against impossible odds." He turned back inside before finishing, followed by the others, all but Baigou. His face animated, Baigou hit the two downed men a few more times and went inside only when the enemy reinforcements were almost upon them.

Mengzi stopped and shouted into the shed, "This damned shed is useless. They could flatten it with their feet." He had to spin around and flee inside when they started throwing rocks at him.

Rocks rained down on the shed. Looking through the fanlight, Mengzi saw that the enemy was less than a few dozen meters away. "Let's run. We can't stay here." He picked up a pot and placed it over his head before racing out of the shed, followed by his friends, Baigou, wearing a pot lid, while the others covered their heads with blankets.

The other side sent rocks flying before they reached the shed, pelting them with rocks that rang out on their heads. Mengzi regretted the trouble he'd caused. None of the rocks that hit him really hurt, though the noise as they crashed against the pot was ear-splitting. Luckily for him, the pot withstood the assault.

He turned to look back when there was a break in the attack; the other side was cursing as they continued to charge. The sand boys had been under the thumb of their pit manager all this time, and that presented an opportunity to vent their pent-up anger; they wanted to turn the scuffle into a major battle. The curses, all aimed at their opponents' mothers, were lewd. Fuqiangzi had a blanket over his head, but his leg took a hit; he dropped the blanket and fell to the ground with a scream. Yet the assault did not lessen just because he'd been hurt, so he quickly picked up the blanket, folded it, and put it back on as he limped off.

Mengzi was in a terrible mood. The haphazardly flung missiles were like sparrows squawking during an autumn harvest, flying all over the place, and it was hard to say when one would land on him. He could tell that the other side was making an empty show, with the apparent intention of driving them out of their territory. Obviously, someone had told them to be careful, not to seriously hurt anyone. Mengzi knew they might not stop at taking over his pit. A few days earlier, when sand boys had a dispute, the winners had filled in the losers' pit. If Shuangfu's people did that, then all their hard work would be for nothing. He turned to Baigou.

"We have to fight back, or they'll fill in our pit."

Baigou agreed and ran back, one hand holding the lid, the other swinging his switch. "Let's beat these asses up."

Tossing down the pot, Mengzi picked up a shovel and charged. He tried to dodge the flying rocks, but several hit him in the chest, one so hard it made him cough, which enraged him. No longer caring what happened, he swung the shovel as he ran, shrieking like a wild beast.

Soon he'd fought his way into enemy lines. He aimed his shovel at the buttocks and thighs, an effective tactic that sent people to the ground with a pained cry.

"The ass is out to kill us," one of them yelled.

"He's going to kill someone."

Mengzi was startled; he wondered if he'd actually turned the shovel sideways to chop, not to smack. If it landed on the wrong spot, it could send someone's head flying. He stopped swatting with the shovel and used it to fling gravel and sand. To his surprise, it worked even better this way. The gravel lacked force but the sand flew straight into their eyes. Some were already crouching with their hands over their eyes and spitting sand, like so many injured mules.

Baigou's birch switch was a formidable weapon. Having learned some moves from Meng Baye, and kept up the practice, the trough was filled with the swish of his whirling weapon. A few of the opponents covered their legs and screamed. Beizhu and the others, on the other hand, picked up rocks and hurled them haphazardly; their aim was wide of the mark, but their shouts were terrifying.

"Get out of here!" Mengzi and his friends shouted.

The sand boys up front were intimidated. They wanted to keep up the fight, but were frightened by how recklessly Mengzi and his friends attacked. The timid ones ran off, the bold ones stood their ground.

"You don't care if you kill someone. Is that it? That'll cost you your life."

Mengzi could tell the other side was losing confidence, so he shouted back:

"I don't care. Anyone who comes this way is a dead man."

"We'll fill the pit with your bodies," Baigou shouted. The sand boys looked at each other, fear written on their faces.

"Who are you trying to scare?" someone shouted from a distance. "We're made of flesh and blood too. Pick up rocks and fight back."

It was Shuangfu's pit manager, on whose order the sand boys picked up rocks. This looks bad, Mengzi said to himself. They could beat me to death and I wouldn't know who did it. He took a few steps back. Rocks were already raining down on him.

"Run!" Fuqiangzi shouted.

Face be damned, Mengzi thought, I have to worry about my head first. He took off ahead of falling rocks that kicked up a storm of sand. The fight went out of Baigou once Mengzi ran off, so he used his lid as shield. Mengzi picked up the pot lid and held it over his head just in time. A rock hit with a clang, nearly braining him.

He managed to sneak a look behind him and saw men coming like a swarm of locusts, rocks flying. He gasped at the realization of the disparity between the two sides. They were no match for Shuangfu, in terms of money and number. Unwilling to swallow defeat, he knew there was nothing he could do. When he saw Beizhu running back to their shed, Mengzi yelled at him, "Don't go in there."

"Where should we go then?" Fuqiangzi asked.

"The village. Back to the village," Baigou said.

They ran back to the village. Beizhu shouting as they went:

"Demons are coming into the village, they're coming!"

The shouts drew women out of their houses. When they saw their own people being attacked, they showed their support by shouting at the enemy. At the sight of reinforcements, the pursuers stopped, but continued to throw rocks.

Everyone breathed a sigh of relief, having escaped a potential killing spree, despite the fact that they had all been hit by rocks. Then they saw the enemy race over to their shed.

"Fuck. They're going to fill in our pit," Mengzi said when muffled thuds came from their pit and their shed was reduced to rubble. The sand boys laughed and whooped as they stomped on the ruins.

Blood rushed to Mengzi's head. He threw down his shovel in dejection.

"Don't worry," Beizhu said. "They filled it in, and now they'll have to dig it up for us. Let's go see Big Head." That sent them off to Big Head's house.

4

Big Head handed down the same penalty for both sides. They'd all endured the pain for nothing. When dogs fight, they get nothing but mouthfuls of fur. The punishment was well-deserved. But Shuangfu's people should not have filled in the pit, so he told them to dig down to where it had been before. Shuangfu had to compensate the other side for the shed and everything else his people destroyed. He agreed to the judgment. His wealth had made him modest and amiable, oddly, and he reamed out his own sand boys, telling them not to cause him any more trouble. Then he sent a hoist to dig up Mengzi's pit.

Mengzi regretted his actions. The pits around his had all reached bottom; one was clearly riding a stone ass, while the status of the other three was unknown. If they were all in the same situation, fine. But if one wasn't, then they could dig down, skirt his pit, and his gold would belong to someone else. He had hoped to break through the wall to get ahead of the others, but that had ended in disappointment, like losing a piece of meat when failing to lure a dog to sleep. Beizhu could not stop complaining about Mengzi, who could only fume, unable to retort; he took his frustration out on the hoist and the sand boys, spewing filthy language.

The hoist and the sand boys who came along never talked back as they kept busy, though Mengzi felt they were dawdling. The hoist stalled constantly and usually required half a day for repairs. A sand boy, grease on his hands and sweat on his forehead, smiled apologetically to Mengzi, making it impossible to complain. He was making slow progress and Mengzi was in a hurry.

Sounds of rocks breaking came from the neighboring pit, where the drill thundered, each sound boring into Mengzi's heart. He could kick himself for not thinking about breaking up the boulder. He kept going over to ask about their progress in breaking it up, and drew consolation from each failure.

During a pause from boulder-breaking, Shuangfu sent someone over with a machine that made a strange noise. Mengzi had heard about something that sent waves fifty meters below ground. Electrical impulses would show if there was anything metal below. Mengzi studied the man's face, trying to glean information, but he remained impassive and emotionless. Disappointed, Mengzi sighed. This is not a world for the poor. Money gives you eyes to see and ears to hear. Without it you're blind and deaf.

There was no more empty land around, as Shuangfu's sand boys spread out and worked. They whistled, talked and bantered, throwing in a few unpleasant comments now and then, but Mengzi was in no mood to be bothered. He knew it wasn't worth it. It meant nothing to Shuangfu even if they filled ten pits, about as consequential as a single hair off nine cows. But their pit meant hope and survival; if they lost, they'd suffer so much it was hard to say if they could recover.

He suspected that the sand boy from Shuangfu was stalling, so he went to see Big Head. The man stank of alcohol and sprayed Mengzi with spittle,

"Enough already. I worked hard to get that for you, cleaving and hexing to carve out a deal. Tell me, who was the trouble maker? If you hadn't dug through the wall, why would he bother to get his hands dirty, playing with a little shit like you? If I were Shuangfu, I wouldn't even dig the pit up for you. If you complained about your pit, I'd say you injured my people. Do you know the injured sand boys have all gone into the city to be checked by the court's medical officer? They took pictures. If he decides to file a lawsuit, you'll be in more shit than you can handle. And you used smoke on them, smoke laced with hot pepper powder. The Nips did that to us. A few of them are claiming lung injuries and want to be compensated. It was me, Big Head said, who knows you're all too poor to even keep a fart in, who talked them out of it, like the rock on a pickle vat that keeps the bubbles down. If I hadn't said anything, you'd be in jail already, so don't come squawking to me."

Before Mengzi could defend himself, Big Head pushed him out and bolted the door behind him.

Mengzi blanched, as a cold sweat engulfed him. They might have been injured during the melee, but he'd taken hits too. He unbuttoned his shirt—no signs of injury. At first, he'd had bruises that turned yellow the next day, but were gone by the third day. The same was probably true for Baigou and the others. He hadn't expected the sand boys to go get checked by a court doctor. Mengzi raced over to tell his friends to have their injuries checked. Except for the bruise on Fuqiangzi's calf, their injured spots looked better than the rest of their bodies.

"Damn it. Even my body betrayed me. I was bruised all over and it hurt like hell that day. Now that I need evidence I've got nothing to show for it."

They sighed. Talk about the possible lawsuits sent them into a minor panic and regret over not having their injuries checked. Fuqiangzi said it would cost money, quite a lot of it, actually, and that shut them all up.

The way things were going, they had nothing worthwhile to say, and could only grumble about their worthless brains, about being blockheads. With a glum look, they hurled occasional shouts at the hoist, telling the sand boy to keep at it. He just smiled apologetically. No matter how much he dawdled, he made more progress than they would have by hand. They couldn't press him too much, for fear that he might stop working. Let Heaven and our fate decide then, they all said. Despite their verbal resignation, they still wore urgent looks as they checked on the other pit frequently to learn of the latest development. They were finally put at ease when they saw the borer spraying sparks without making a dent in the boulder.

There were crowds everywhere, as most of the village men had become pit managers or sand boys, and more had come from neighboring areas. White Tiger Pass was cramped, filled with pits, sheds, animal droppings, and trash. Most eye-catching were the small houses built by the river, with signs advertising dry-shampooing and massage services. Pretty girls of a certain type were spotted among the sand boys, a refreshing sight in a disquieted site.

Buildings rose straight out of the Dasha River bank, and more continued to sprout. Banks, credit unions, and shops opened up at White Tiger Pass. Whatever was available at Liangzhou could be found here. A rumor circulated about the potential of developing Shawan; besides gold prospecting there were desert tourism, culture tours, and more. A garrison dating to the Tang Dynasty was discovered slightly east of White Tiger Pass. It had been billeted by Tang soldiers but was later buried in the sand, which turned out to be good for the battlement, as the sand had preserved it well. Camps, a smoke beacon mound, military transport route, and armory were preserved and were very valuable. There was also a grotto from the Western Xia Empire, the Vajravārāhī Cave, which was even more valuable, for it was a sacred site that had been mentioned in Buddhist texts. The cave had been buried for a thousand years after an earthquake; now that it had been excavated, it was a rare treasure. They heard that a woman from the south wanted to develop the site, with an investment of tens of millions of yuan. Once a small city was created, the residents of Shawan would become urbanites.

A de facto city was already emerging, thanks to the buildings and the shops laid out in relatively fine order. It was no longer a township, but a town, a distinction that should not be taken lightly. The former meant the countryside, while the latter elevated it to the level of a city. They also heard that the town's government office would be moved to Shawan. A businessman with a long view planned to buy up a hundred acres of land to build a market, which, rumor had it, would be larger than the one in Liangzhou. What a boon. A good life was in store for Shawan residents.

Mengzi naturally welcomed news like this, but more than that, he wanted his pit to produce gold. He knew that money was the only thing that counted, be it in the countryside or in a city. Without money, country folk can make do, but an urbanite had to pay to pee or he'd die from holding it back. Besides, it didn't look as if Liangzhou residents were having such an easy life, with mounds of people being laid off. Except for government officials and civil servants, average citizens had it tough. If he were to become a city dweller, without money, he'd still live the life of a ghost. No one had food fall from the sky into their lap.

5

After being cooped up for days, Mengzi felt like going out for a walk for a change of scenery. What you can't see won't bother you. He told Baigou to keep watch before following the path among sheds for a stroll. None of the earlier scenes were visible along the way. The Dasha River had been turned upside down, while White Tiger Pass, like a magnet, attracted people, sheds, and buildings like buckshot. Well frames were erected at spots that he'd spurned, and flags were planted to lend a dazzling red to the sky above the river. When a desert wind blew, the flags flapped noisily and eerily. Everyone said red was a lucky color that drove away evil spirits. To Mengzi's eyes, the ocean of red was simply too jarring. He couldn't say why, it just felt that way.

After leaving his own shed, he discovered just how much and how astonishingly White Tiger Pass had changed, like day and night. Many buildings were rising out of the ground, with more on the way. A disquieting din permeated the area, driving away the tranquility and peacefulness of rural life. The world's gone mad, he said to himself.

When he stepped on the riverbank, noise from the hoist and the shouts of sand boys was replaced by different sounds, and he was in the thick of it. One strange girl after another came up to invite him in. Strange. This had been a corner of the desert where even wolves wouldn't shit, so where did all these pretty girls come from? It was the gold, he knew, but he had none, nor did he know if he ever would have any. Seducing a woman had required trickery before, but now it seemed pretty easy. With money, any of the girls would be happy to untie their pants.

He felt a rush of heat. He'd been preoccupied for days, his mind inundated with noise, so the women's voices felt cool and refreshing. He swallowed hard as he checked out each of the welcoming faces. Then he spotted the girl called Ju'er, so he whispered to her, "How much?" "Ten yuan for a dry-wash." She lowered her voice: "A hundred to get laid." Mengzi was stunned. He cast a frantic glance around, but only the women were looking at him; the men were tending to their business. The world didn't care whether he existed or not. "At least eighty," Ju'er whispered again, "can't be lower than that." Her voice was different too, soft and melodic. She was wearing a black skirt, her fleshy arms bared, and the mounds on her chest fanned the flames of desire in his heart. "I'll get my hair washed. It's filthy," he said in a loud voice, though even he could hear the sheepish undertone.

The "barbershop" wasn't big, with two chairs in the outer room. As a form of self-disclosure, he went straight for the chair and sat down. Now remorse crept in; he did have some money, but it was for the pit, not him. He was worried someone might snatch it away from him, and he felt that someone could be hiding in the inner room to do just that. Then there were the yellow-shirts from the police station who were watching him with sinister eyes, just waiting to pounce. He'd heard that anyone caught engaging in unhealthy behavior would be fined five thousand yuan, a scalp-numbing number. Ju'er could tell what he was thinking.

"Don't worry. We've paid them. They won't show up. It won't take long."

"But it'll cost me eighty yuan." Mengzi thought, while trying to find an excuse to leave, but his eyes were glued to her body.

"I promise you'll have a good time. You'll be well taken care of." She added, "I can play the flute too." When she saw his puzzled look, she rounded her lips and made a sucking sound.

He really wanted to leave, but his body wouldn't listen, nor his hands, which reached out for her. Recalling Yue'er's disease, he felt wronged. You didn't deserve that, he said silently. Then he wondered if Yue'er had been in Ju'er's place before, which upset him. He wanted revenge.

Mengzi pulled Ju'er close to kiss her, but she turned away. "I just had chin surgery." She reached out with one hand, "First things first." Mengzi knew she wanted to be paid, so he counted out the amount she asked. She put it away and called out to the door, "Keep an eye out for me."

After a girl at the door responded, Ju'er took him to the inner room, where he found two narrow beds.

She deftly took off her skirt, leaving only a strip of black cloth girding her lower belly. Mengzi wondered why she had that, but didn't feel like asking, because a loud noise was pounding at his head and a thirst tore inside her mouth.

"Take off your clothes." She said.

He was so nervous he shook. He felt like picking her up and throwing her down on the bed, but the thing that should show its prowess was sleeping quietly.

Her breasts swayed, a sight that aroused him. He grabbed and kneaded them, drawing a moan, which drowned his fears and brought up his manhood. She went and lay down on one of the beds.

He wanted to kiss her, but she kept turning away, likely not wanting to smear her nicely painted lips or perhaps put off by his bad breath. That made him unhappy. Yue'er was better, he thought. She was always fully engaged when kissing him. Her image floated up and he felt bad about what he was doing. Yue'er was sick; she was suffering, even if it was an illness that disturbed him. I'm worse than an animal, he said silently and gave himself a savage slap.

"I said take off your clothes." Ju'er was losing her patience.

Mengzi shook his head and closed his eyes, as something warm rose up inside. Yue'er, he called out silently. I won't betray you. With a flick of his sleeves, he walked out. The bright sun seemed weak. He felt bad about spending the money for nothing, but he knew he'd done the right thing.

The hoist was still roaring when he returned to the pit, and listless Baigou was staring at the neighboring one.

"Have they cracked the big ox yet?" Mengzi asked.

"Crack your dick is more like it. The boulder is harder than steel," a sand boy from the other side said.

After several days' hard work, they reached the bottom again and saw the boulder staring up at them mockingly. Mengzi found a hammer and started in on it; the crash of metal on stone continued all day and filled his head. They realized the boulder flaked easily, and they didn't need to strike too much to break a piece off. That was good news. They weren't large chunks, but if they could chip off one piece, they could whittle off a hundred. By aiming at a spot and working on it, they cracked a gaping hole. Mengzi and Baigou took turns and, each with a team, worked day and night, like a mouse nibbling at iron, gnawing on the boulder. Finally, one day a hammer struck and a large hole appeared, letting humid air rush into their faces.

It's open! They cheered.

A hammer struck again and again and the hole grew bigger. When it was finally large enough for a man to worm his way through, Mengzi grabbed a flashlight, tied a rope around his waist, and slipped down the hole. He was surprised by its size; water dripped and echoed in the vast expanse. Under his feet was limestone in the shape of a horse's teeth, so the locals called it a horse-tooth stone. He'd heard that gold formed on these stones. A powerful stream of underground water shot past and disappeared into the cracks.

Mengzi was flabbergasted. Where was the layer of gold-specked sand?

Chapter Thirty

A spider weaves a web
A moth falls on the hot kang

1

It was raining, so the women picking *shagen* got the day off. Ying'er wanted to go for a walk when some of the workers came for Lanlan to sew up their wounds. She'd seen enough that she could do the job now. It was too noisy and boisterous in the room, so Ying'er walked out.

They'd been here for some time now, but her job tied her to the salt mound, and she'd had no chance to be out and about. With the help of the weather, she left the room to take a stroll around to see the salt lakes.

The migrant workers were paid by their labor; the more salt they scooped up, the more they made. Some continued to work in the rain for that reason. A few of them were removing salt covers. As we've seen, salt covers were crusts formed over the salt lakes, a sort of tough shell. Explosives had to be used to blow away the hardest layer, and then drills were brought out to remove the softer ones before the sheet of sand and salt could be taken away to get at the aged salt steeped in alkali water.

The drill had a triangular tip fitted to a meter-long pole. Sansan once told them the drill weighed over forty *jin*. The workers raised the drill and brought it down hard, and when the tip got a purchase on the salt cover, they pried up a large chunk. The relatively uniform chunks of cover were used to build walls for houses, the irregular ones made excellent paving material in the desert.

"Ai—here's a salt stick for you," someone shouted from a distance.

Ying'er thought he was calling out to someone else until he repeated himself several times to assure her he was talking to her. To her a salt stick must be a *shagen*, so she said to herself, I pick those every day. I don't need you to give me one. Then she saw a shiny crystal in his hand. A quick glance told her it was nothing like the *shagen* she gathered. She walked over. The worker, a young man with fair skin and pleasant features, smiled and handed her the crystal. Her eyes lit up when she saw it. It was so beautiful, formed of a large salt crystal, glittering and translucent, as if carved. She loved it. She thanked him, earning a brilliant smile from him.

"No need to thank me. You can thank the salt lakes. They created it."

Ying'er spotted something familiar about him. After thinking hard, she realized that Lingguan had a similar look. The air of an intellectual.

"Have you been to college?" she asked.

"Baozi, he was a brilliant student." Another worker answered before the young man could open his mouth. "He's passed the college entrance exam, but his family couldn't afford to send him to college."

His face darkened. Ying'er didn't want to add to his misery, so she turned to gaze at the salt lakes.

The long strips of water resembled the wheat fields back in her village. They were about two meters wide, narrow enough for the workers to stand on land and still reach for the salt in the water. The length, however, could be as long as they could harvest, over a hundred meters long. The emerald green water had once stung her eyes. New salt crystals continued to form after the old ones were harvested.

Baozi went back to work. Lowering a board into the lake to push the salt a few times until the sand was washed away. Then he used a long metal scoop to scoop out the salt. When it was full, he anchored the handle on his thigh to pry the scoop out, but only managed to jiggle it, so he poured out some salt. Even half a scoop proved too hard, and soon he was panting from the labor. He won't make much money that way, Ying'er said to herself. Maybe in a few years. By then would he still retain his intellectual look? Or would he be as vulgar as Daniu?

Daniu must have been watching. For she had barely arrived when he came up to her. Seeing Ying'er's eyes on Baozi, he gave the young man a sullen look.

"Hey, see the way this guy works?" Daniu said after watching awhile. "Like a scrawny dog trying to pee. Here, I'll show you." He snatched the scoop from Baozi and in no time had produced a dozen scoops of salt, like a gust of wind chasing lingering clouds. Despite her antipathy, Ying'er had to admire his strength.

After a few more scoops, Daniu looked over at Baozi with a condescending, superior air.

"Give me a year, and I could be just like you."

"Like me?" Daniu guffawed. "In your next life, maybe. I was born with supernatural strength." He pulled Baozi over, lifted him up and flung him into the water. "Shut your eyes," Daniu said.

"Why did you do that?" Ying'er chided Daniu. Before she finished, Baozi floated to the surface, which made the others laugh. The salt water was heavier than a human body, so anyone who fell in would float.

He spat as he climbed ashore.

Ying'er was glad to see him unharmed. She knew Daniu would likely do something outrageous if she stayed, so she walked off and found a spot to sit to admire the crystal. Soon it seemed her heart was infused with its brilliant sparkles.

It was a fine rain, slightly heavier than a drizzle; when it fell on the lake, the rain made a shushing sound. She felt herself slowly taken in by the tranquil beauty. It had been a long time since she'd been disturbed by trivial affairs; she'd felt restless and hurried. Toiling away and rushing about all the time, she rarely had a moment of quiet to herself. It was wonderful here, taking in deep green water, a cooling rain, the waves of sand rippling imperceptibly away in the mist, and a world blurred by drizzles. When she was with people and their mundane affairs, she realized, she was often beset by a sense of helplessness and irritation, and her peace of mind suffered from the troubles and disputes. Now she faced Nature with simplicity, and it in turn gave her serenity, a cool regard for the world, and a transcendental grace.

Something sounded different in the rain, like the noise of ice melting in the spring. She was fearful, afraid that a monster might climb out of the green water to drag her down with it. She had to laugh at herself when she gave her fear some thought. After what she'd been through, she knew she was capable of rising above it all.

The sound grew louder as she listened carefully. She looked in its direction and saw something like ice cracking. Did the salt crystalize into a mirror before breaking into shiny pieces? She wondered. That must be it. She remembered what Sansan had said about the ratio of salt content in water; only the right ratio would produce salt, and only then would it crystalize.

She was sure the rain had altered the ratio of salt.

Soon she lost interest in the reason why salt water turned into salt crystals. Instead, she stared at the surface to see if chunks of salt might crack as she listened to the faint noise of them breaking off, until she forgot where she was.

Daniu had luckily stayed away, leaving her in peace. Ying'er sat in the fine rain until she heard Lanlan calling her back for dinner.

2

After they ate, Ying'er couldn't let go of the tranquility by the lakes, so she invited Lanlan to go with her. Sansan showed up with a woman before they walked out, however. They called the woman Wu Jie—Big Sister Wu—who was in charge of the workers collecting *shagen* and weighed their buckets every day. She'd treated Ying'er well, never filling the bucket to the brim when weighing hers and noting down more buckets than Ying'er had actually gathered. She got a little more money, though only a few yuan at most. Of course, she was grateful, since Wu Jie treated her so well despite a lack of kinship.

Wu Jie told Sansan and Lanlan to leave her alone with Ying'er so they could have a private chat. After the two women left, Wu Jie surveyed the room and said:

"I had no idea how hard you have it here. That's my fault. Just let me know when you need something, all right? What's mine is yours."

Ying'er knew she wanted something from her, or she wouldn't have braved the rain. But she had to wait for her to bring it up.

After some inconsequential chit-chat, Wu Jie finally brought up what she'd come for.

"What do you think of our boss?" She asked Ying'er.

"Which one?"

"The one they call old dead baby." Wu Jie laughed.

Ying'er had never called him that, and she felt sheepish. "He's fine. See this blanket? He lent it to us."

"He's really a very nice man, you know," Wu said emotionally. "Every worker has benefited from his kindness. They call him 'Timely Rain.'"

Ying'er had never heard the nickname, but she kept quiet.

"You probably didn't know that his wife died."

Now Ying'er got a sense of what the woman was about to say, and her heart raced. Sure enough, Wu came out with it, "He has his eye on you.

"He's been watching you for days. He thinks you're a fine woman.

"He's met many women, and he likes you more than all the others.

"If you say yes, you'll eat and drink only the best. No more hard work for you.

"There's a cart-load of women who want to fill the empty spot. If you're willing, he'll marry you right away."

On and on she went.

Ying'er was quiet the whole time, trying to think of an acceptable excuse that would turn him down without hurting his feelings. But she came up with nothing. I'll tell the truth, she thought.

"It sounds wonderful, but I'm afraid I'm not lucky enough to be that woman. I have someone already."

"Oh, where is he?"

"Working in the provincial capital."

Ying'er did not know where Lingguan was, but something prompted her to say that. "Working" was open to interpretation. Being the governor meant working, so did washing dishes. Wu would have to guess what work Lingguan was doing.

Wu Jie could not press the issue for now, so after more chit-chat she told Ying'er to give the matter some more thought before taking her leave.

Sansan walked in a new person, her cold demeanor gone instantly. She had been eavesdropping.

"Why didn't you say yes? He's like a golden nugget. Do you know how many women can only dream about filling in? If you're not sure, just go ahead and obtain a marriage certificate for now. Didn't you hear he wants to marry you right away? How could you turn down something so good?" Sansan wasn't done yet. "You think he's too old. Is that it? Actually, he's not that old. It's just the wind and sand here, so he has dark skin."

Lanlan was silent.

Ying'er asked her sister-in-law out for a walk. Holding an umbrella borrowed from Sansan, they went to the spot where Ying'er had sat earlier in the morning. Rain continued to fall. As the saying goes, "Morning rain falls light, but continues all day." That was so true. The rain was heavy enough to wet their clothes, but gave the world around them a charming beauty.

"That's a pretty good deal," Lanlan said. "You don't have to think too far into the future. Besides, you're thinking about him, but you have no idea what he's doing. I know I shouldn't be saying this, but have you ever given thought to how so many things are beyond your control?"

Ying'er's heart sank when she realized what Lanlan was getting at. With her eyes half shut, she looked into the distance. The workers were no longer out in the rain. The area around the lakes was quiet, but for the sounds of raindrops falling on their umbrella, and the occasional noise of salt cracking and breaking off.

"I want to tell you something. When I was little, my pa bought me a jade pendant. I loved it. One day my brother spat on it to spite me, because he knew I couldn't stand filthy things. It was soiled and I smashed it. You know what I'm saying? I know that living requires compromises. You have to go along with people and muddle through. But I can't do it. We're on earth for only a few decades, so why can't we lead a clean life? Something dirty can never be cleaned. Don't you agree?"

Lanlan heaved a sigh.

"Don't you have something in your heart that can't be soiled?" Ying'er asked. Well, I do, and if it's gone, life won't be worth living any longer.

"I don't want to give up my reasons to live for some good food and drink, or for some clothes.

"I can die for what I live for."

"Listen to you. What are you talking about?" Lanlan said, though she knew no one could change Ying'er's mind.

3

Sansan spread the word, and now everyone at the salt lakes knew what the boss was thinking, a loss of face for him. Men are like that; face matters more than anything. A stream of people came to see Ying'er, repeating what Wu Jie had said to her, with even more reasons for her to agree. Whatever they offered turned to dust when it encountered Ying'er's notion to die for what she lived for. But she never let on; she treated them all with silence, which, strangely, increased her appeal to the boss. Some even spread word that he would consider his life lived in vain if he could not make her his woman.

Now that everything was out in the open, the boss stepped up his pursuit, first by sending Wu Jie over with greens, the most enticing commodity at the lakes. Only once a week were vegetables trucked over from the city. To get them for their meals, family members of permanent workers were turned into full-time shoppers. They lined up early on the day the truck came. The migrant workers also sent someone to buy cheaper greens, though they were still many times more expensive than elsewhere. Ying'er naturally would like some too; the skin on her palms kept peeling, which, according to some, was caused by a lack of vegetables in her diet.

The boss had many trucker friends, who brought several sacks of greens each time they came. He then told Wu Jie to take some to Ying'er, who turned her down. She left them on the floor. Ying'er would not even let Lanlan touch the vegetables, which started out crispy green, but yellowed and wilted within a day. Sansan chided her for wasting food; After washing the rotting vegetables, she cooked and ate them herself. Ying'er let her be.

Wu Jie kept bringing more, and Ying'er kept saying no. Maybe the boss had a refrigerator, for everything Wu Jie brought was fresh. Once she left, Sansan went ahead and washed them. Ying'er did not want them, she would say, so it would be a waste if I didn't eat them. Soon the migrant workers heard about it and swarmed over to divide up that day's take once Wu Jie left after her delivery.

Everyone at the salt lakes now knew that Ying'er refused to eat vegetables from the boss. An admirable woman, they said. But those were fresh, crisp, lush greens. If she could turn down the boss's offer, then Daniu couldn't possibly get anything from her. They started to doubt rumors spread by Daniu himself. As they talked about her, Ying'er slowly became an almost mythical figure.

Daniu misread her intention, however. He thought Ying'er turned the boss down because she had fallen for him. The imagined scenario moved him so much he felt warm currents course through his body. Several times when he saw she was alone, he found an opportunity to walk up to her.

"I'll honestly treat you as well as you treat me." He added, "Just wait. I'll show you what I'm made of."

Ying'er was confused, with no idea what he meant by the way she treated him.

He was convinced she admired his strength. He could not forget the look she gave him when he scooped up salt like a gusty wind chasing lingering clouds. It was a look of astonishment, which he mistook as adoration. Day and night he thought of that look, which developed into more looks in his mind. Immersed in those imagined looks, he indulged himself and worked even harder, even scooping up eleven tons of salt one day.

Anyone who indulges in a world he has created can concoct many reasons why someone should be in love with him. She has no reason not to love me, he told himself. He was powerfully built, muscular, and energetic, and he made plenty of money. He came in second only to the boss in terms of income. But to him, the boss's money was dirty, from an illegal source. Who knew when the snow would melt to expose dead bodies, and the government would confiscate all the boss's money? His money, on the other hand, was hard earned, with blood and sweat; he was the rightful owner wherever he went. Besides, he'd heard that women liked strong men. The boss had passed his prime, and wasn't "strong" like Daniu.

He was forever humming a cheerful tune, which sounded like the song "Sunshine Fills Our Lives," but he was so out of tune it turned into a different song. It was an old tune, likely from a movie. There was an instrument in one of the workers' room, the kind you plucked with one hand and pressed the keys with the other. There was also a tattered book, where the song rested. One day when Baozi was bored to tears, he woke up the tune. At first it creaked and groaned, but came alive in a few days. It swirled everywhere accompanied by the instrument. Daniu listened along and slowly learned to hum it. He hummed when he walked and hummed when he worked.

You see, everyone who saw him said, Daniu is lovesick.

4

Wu Jie came again, but not to bring vegetables. She told them the two women had returned to pick *shagen*, so Ying'er and Lanlan would have a new job.

"Sure. We can do anything. If there's no work for us, we'll just go home," Ying'er replied with a smile.

"What are you talking about?" Wu Jie laughed too. "The new job isn't as dirty as picking *shagen*. It's still hard work, but no salt water."

Lanlan said they'd do it.

Their new job was to hold down blowing sand that would kill the salt lakes if it settled.

There were two ways to go about it: one, haul dirt up a dune to create dirt ridges, or two, press wheat stalks into the sand in a net-like pattern. Wheat stalks were scarce, so dirt was the common material. The management station had set the width and length for the ridge and paid by the meter. No matter which method they used, it was only temporary. Once the flowing sand buried the man-made barrier, the dune came alive again, so holding down the sand was an unending task.

Ying'er saw, once they got there, that holding down sand was harder than picking *shagen*, for they had to work under the scorching sun. There was no shelter to block the sun's harsh, relentless rays, but that wasn't the most difficult part. The more exhausting job was transporting the dirt in a canvas stretcher. Each holding one pole, they filled it with dirt before swaying their way up the dune. After each step forward they sank back half a step; walking empty-handed was hard enough, let alone carrying a heavy load.

Every time they moved a load up the dune, Ying'er felt the pole bite her hand as it pressed into her bones. The weight of the dirt dragged her down the slope. Her feet sank into the sand and the sand seeped into her shoes, where it cozied up to her feet, and she was a sorry sight after only a few steps. Gritting her teeth and holding her breath as if waging war, she managed to carry a load up to the top. She let go of the pole and slumped to the ground. When she noticed other women looking at her, she ignored them and their mocking stares, as she tried to catch her breath.

"Let's try it for one day," Lanlan mopped her sweaty forehead. "If it's too hard for you, we'll send word that we want to settle up and go home."

"What can we do back home?" Ying'er said. "Look at those women. They can do it, why can't we?"

They gritted their teeth and picked up the stretcher. Ying'er realized that her legs no longer belonged to her. Sweat oozed from her pores and her eye sockets. It proved the local saying, "The palms peel and the eyes sweat." The worst sensation came from pain knifing into her calves with each step. She wondered if her tendons were injured, but she didn't see any bruises.

By noon they'd sweated enough, but the ridge hadn't seemed to grow. After a rough calculation, Ying'er knew they wouldn't earn much the way their work had gone so far.

The spot was far enough from their room that they decided not to go back, as they had brought water and food for lunch. They'd thought they could work over the lunch break, but neither could manage to stand after a brief rest. Yet when they checked how others were doing, they were chagrined over their lack of progress.

They smiled bitterly at each other when Daniu came with Baozi to see them. Daniu hollered when he spotted them before running up the dune. Lanlan gave him a friendly greeting, while Ying'er smiled, making him feel welcome. He and Baozi picked up the stretcher and carried loads of dirt up the dune. Soon the ridge was much longer than before, after the women had worked all morning.

"You're foolish," Daniu said. "See this? Look how they did it." He went over to dig up the ridge someone else had built, and Ying'er saw the trick. Their neighbor had pushed sand together to form a ridge before covering it with dirt, which allowed her to build a long section with one load.

"But the work is wasted when the wind blows the dirt away," Lanlan said.

"Who cares how long the work lasts?" Daniu continued. "They're like cats covering their droppings. How much do you think you'll earn the way you do it?"

"But won't the management station find out?" Lanlan asked.

"Depends on how you go about it. Give the inspector a carton of cigarettes and he'll turn a blind eye. That should take care of it."

"That's cheating," Ying'er said. "We can't do that. We don't have to come all the way out to the desert to make that kind of ill-gotten money."

Daniu and Baozi continued to help the women until they were bathed in sweat. Before they went back to their own work, Daniu said to Ying'er:

"Let me go talk to the boss and ask him to give you lighter work. This is hard enough to kill a donkey."

The women got back to work after the break. Ying'er felt her body no longer listened to her, for she crumpled to the ground several times halfway up. The dirt was gone, of course. Lanlan was also panting from the tiring trek. Soon they were exhausted, not an ounce of energy left, but neither would consider cheating.

"Once there was a religious man who offered incense to the Buddha with profound sincerity, so the Buddha came to test him, in the disguise of a salt-peddler. The man used a rigged steelyard to get an additional half *jin* of salt. The Buddha smiled and said, three years of incense burning is no match for half of *jin* of salt." Lanlan continued, "The man had accumulated three years of good karma, but that was wiped out by half a *jin* of salt. The heart is the key to religious practice."

"I don't care about good karma. I just can't bring myself to do something like that. Being poor is nothing; we aren't worth that little," Ying'er said.

They kept building the ridge with real dirt, but had little to show for a day's work. They did not have to calculate to know that, if not for the dirt carried by Daniu and Baozi, they would have made less pressing the sand all day than picking *shagen* for one morning.

5

Daniu was in trouble.

When they returned to their room at dusk, Sansan told them he'd beaten the boss up. It was very simple. Believing he had a great personal relationship with the boss, Daniu went to speak on the women's behalf so they could continue collecting *shagen*. He forgot that he was still a worker, no matter how strong, and that "friendship" could only be applied to people with equal status. The boss just squinted at him.

"The old dead baby has been unhappy with Daniu for some time," Sansan said. "How could a mere worker dare fight him over a woman? The boss was looking for an excuse, and Daniu made it easy for him. He squinted at Daniu and said, 'Whose pants' crotch has rotted away to let you out? Who do you think you are?' That really pissed Daniu off."

They'd heard from Baozi that Daniu had been unhappy with the boss too. Ying'er recalled what Daniu had said, "Just wait. I'll show you what I'm made of." Baozi had told them that Daniu had wanted to slug the boss. When the boss wanted to marry Ying'er, Daniu had ground his teeth and said that the boss should take a piss to look at himself, that he was an old donkey salivating over tender alfalfa. He said more than that, which was then reported to the boss by some of the workers who wanted to butter him up. The boss then called Daniu an old dick.

Daniu was pissed off this time, but everything would have been all right if he had just slunk out of the boss's office. The boss liked to curse people, so it was no big deal, and Daniu should have just let him do it. But he'd promised Ying'er that he'd get her lighter work. He was a man of his word, and could not break his promise to a woman. This time he wanted to say what was on his mind. In the past, when the boss got drunk, it was always Daniu who carried him back to his room. The boss called him Brother and even got him involved in deals he couldn't ask other workers to do—they were watching him, their eyes on his position. As a result, Daniu was privy to some of the boss's secrets. A man of personal loyalty, Daniu never talked about them to anyone, except to Sansan, who once took care of him when he was drunk. Daniu had wailed and shouted, "The fucking world is so unfair. A few tricks and he rakes in so much money, like sweeping up leaves, while I work myself to death but barely manage to get by."

Daniu began to work on some people's behalf after learning some of the boss's secrets, which gave him plenty of face.

But this time the boss frowned when he mentioned Ying'er and told Daniu to get out. He'd have left if the boss had stopped there. But no, he shoved him and more than once, and Daniu shoved back.

"Just think how strong Daniu is," Sansan said. "The boss banged against his desk and nearly broke it."

"Even that would have been okay if it was just the desk that got flipped. But the boss picked up his chair, and when he did that, he was no longer the boss. He became someone who'd picked a fight with Daniu. Daniu did not want to fight, but his hands couldn't stop. He swung and the chair was in pieces. Then his fists went for the boss and knocked out two of his front teeth.

"Daniu broke the law. I heard that knocking out someone's teeth isn't a serious offense, but it's still personal injury. Serious or not, he hurt the boss. When the police went to arrest him, he fled into the desert.

"Daniu is done for. That single punch changed his fate. The management station docked his pay for the boss's medical expenses, so they said. The money was nothing. His greatest damage was, he was fired. He'll go to jail if he's caught, and running away makes his situation worse. Who knows how many years he'll have to spend in prison."

Women are nothing but trouble, the migrant workers said to each other.

6

Ying'er felt terrible. Daniu was in trouble because of them, no matter how she looked at it. If he hadn't tried to intercede for them, he'd still be the model worker. She heard that he'd put their salt lakes in such a good light that when provincial officials came to visit they all wanted to watch him work. The boss would surely have agreed to his request if not for Ying'er. But two male lions will fight to the death over a female, let alone two grown men. Besides, the boss had no plans to expand his career, so there was no need for him to lose face in order to make people like him.

Lanlan knitted her brows in silence. Sansan had made the situation sound serious, and the two women felt weighed down. It would have turned out all right if the police weren't involved; villagers were always getting into fights, causing nosebleeds or knocking out teeth, and no one mentioned personal injury. But the involvement of the police spelled trouble for Daniu. They'd heard that Liangzhou police had no trouble turning an innocent man into a murderer. Lanlan felt her heart pound when she tried to imagine the police going after Daniu.

It was late, but the three women were still awake, each with her own thoughts. The oil lamp flickered, its light revealing countless intrigues and the unknown. Outside, a wind howled, a common occurrence at night. They'd heard that Anxi was a world-famous wind tunnel, with a gale each year that could last from spring to winter. There were few trees to stand its way, so the wind could blow straight to where they were, bringing with it frightening sounds. All sorts of scary faces seemed to hide in the sounds, ghostly figures with disheveled hair and lips pursed to whistle hair-raising notes whenever they could. Ying'er could almost see the hair flying in the wind, sometimes like a horsetail, and a crazed snake at other times.

"Daniu was doing so well, why did he have to get into trouble?" Sansan sighed. "His sister depends on him for college. Now that he's in trouble, it'll be over for her."

Lanlan and Ying'er also sighed.

Suddenly there was a knock at the door, a cautious one that was barely audible in the gusty wind. They exchanged looks.

"Who is it?" Sansan asked.

Silence, except for another knock.

"Get lost if you don't want to tell us your name. I'll scream for help if you don't stop knocking. It's late, don't you know that?"

"Sansan." A voice from the outside.

Sansan cried out and jumped off the bed. The latch was off in the blink of an eye.

Daniu came in.

Ying'er was stunned. The police were looking for him, and yet here he was.

He was covered in dust. He found a bowl, filled it with water, and drank it down before smacking his lips and saying to Ying'er:

"I can't stay here. Come to Xinjiang with me."

Ying'er did not know what to say.

"Xinjiang is vast. I didn't kill anyone, so they'll give up chasing me. I can't stay here. You know the old dead baby bears grudges. Even if the police stop looking for me, he'll do something, so my days are numbered. Come with me. I'll be good to you for the rest of your life. I mean it."

Sansan looked at Ying'er with envy and indignation over Ying'er's failure to appreciate Daniu.

Ying'er smiled unhappily and glanced at Lanlan, who knew what her sister-in-law was thinking.

"She has someone already, didn't you know?" she said to Daniu. "Her heart belongs to him."

Daniu's face fell. "How come you've been so nice to me if you have someone else?"

Ying'er shook her head. She wanted to ask, "What did I do? What did I say? I never promised you anything. How was I 'nice' to you?" But she knew it would be a great loss of face for him if she told him that.

"What has she done?" Lanlan spoke up for her. "That's how she treats people and it's why everybody likes her. You let your imagination run wild, that's all."

He sat woodenly for a moment.

"I don't care who you like. I like you, and I'll make you mine even if it means my life."

It was terrible to hear him say "make you mine." That upset Ying'er, who felt like saying, "What do you take me for?"

"What did you say?" Lanlan objected. "You know a picked melon is never sweet, don't you? Look. Sansan has been so nice to you."

That brought a bright look to Sansan's face as she gazed at him.

But he frowned. "Let me think," he said after a moment. "I'll be back if I can't figure things out."

He was quiet, but then started sobbing. He reached up and his hand came away wet with tears. How could a strapping man, strong as an ox, weep like a little girl? This had hit him really hard. After wiping away more tears, he said with a grimace, "I'm done for. They'll beat me to death if they catch me. Don't you know those animals always try to kill their prisoners? The boss's son is a policeman himself. Besides, I'd be killed by other prisoners even if the police spared me. Prisoners are worse than the police. They have so many ways to make you suffer. They're called sixty-four dishes, and every dish can be fatal. You know the guy we called 'Bad Hip?' The guy who sews hemp sacks. A policeman's elbow ruined his kidneys."

He sucked in air through his teeth and fell silent.

"Even if I make it out, no one will want to hire me. How will I face my parents? They treat me like a money tree, and my sister relies on me. I can't think any more, I'll die if I do."

"How can a grown man say something like that?" Lanlan chided. "It's not going to cost you your life. You can go elsewhere if it doesn't work out here."

"That's easy for you say. In this day and age . . . I know it's my fate. A fortune-teller told me that I'd have a bump, a steel threshold, this year. I tried my best, but failed to avoid it. I'm not afraid of a beating. I just don't want to lose face. You may not know it, but anyone who's been in police custody is considered tainted in my village. No matter how hard you try, you can never wash off the stain."

"Then go apologize to the boss," Ying'er finally said. "Maybe he'll forgive you."

"No, he won't. I know what he's like. When everything's going good between us, he's great to be with. But if someone goes against his wishes, he'll bear a grudge for the rest of your life. He's lost a great deal of face this time, so how would he let me off easily? Besides, I know too many of his secrets, and he's wanted to get rid of me for a long time."

Then he turned to Sansan with a glum look. "Don't share what I told you with anyone. You'll lose your head if they knew." He finished with a long sigh.

"Make it all known to everyone," she said. "You'll be safer that way."

"It involves too many people. I don't know what to do." He turned to Ying'er, "Give it some thought, won't you? Xinjiang is really a great place."

Ying'er knew she had to stop him from having more fanciful thoughts, so she said, "I'd rather die than go with you. I've made up my mind, so leave me alone."

"I envy those bandits. If I could be one of them, I'd kidnap you to be my wife." He sighed and took down a leather flask from the wall—Lanlan had wrapped the opening with a thin hemp rope—and filled it with water before grabbing some steamed buns. He gave Ying'er a long, hard look before walking out with a sad smile.

7

Ying'er went to see the boss the next morning; she wanted to plead Daniu's case. Human hearts are all made of flesh, she thought. Some good words should warm his heart. She would say as much as she needed to help Daniu.

Without his front teeth, the boss looked older. She knew the teeth meant nothing, for they could be replaced with gold ones soon and make him look even more impressive. What mattered to the boss most was the great loss of face over being beaten up by a mere worker, and his rivals would make a big deal out of it. He didn't have a high-ranking position, but it had great monetary potential. No one could say for sure how much salt would come from Mother Nature; the amount was flexible, like a rubber band, and the elasticity meant a great source of fortune.

That was what they all said.

Ying'er took a good look at the boss, a first for her. She realized that, no matter who she saw, she found them all to be unfamiliar and odd, all but Lingguan. The boss had a similarly strange face, the kind she found least appealing. She wondered if it was an illness, an incurable one.

"I've come to plead Daniu's case," she said as she lowered her eyes.

"Fine," he replied unhesitatingly.

She looked up at him in surprise, for she'd expected him to come up with excuses to turn her down.

"Fine." His eyes glowed brightly as he stared at her. "The one who tied the bell has to untie it. He came to plead your case, and now you're pleading his. A favor for another favor."

"Thank you," Ying'er said.

"But you'll have to agree to it."

"What's it?"

"What do you think?" He continued, his bright eyes still on her, "Maybe I'm too impatient. How's this? We won't get married yet, because you need to get to know me. We'll try it out for a while. If it works, we'll tie the knot; if not, we won't."

The mention of "try it out" made her stomach turn. Naturally she understood what it entailed. She felt a hand clasping her throat and she had to fight for air. "No, that can't be done," she strained to say.

He walked out from behind his desk and came toward her. She backed to the door, afraid he might try brute force. With one foot in the room and one foot out, she planned to hold on to the door jamb and scream if he dared force himself upon her.

He knew what she was thinking and smiled as he said, "Then I'll have to let the law take care of it. Just think how many people work here. If everyone wanted to slug me, would I have any teeth left?"

Ying'er felt a pounding in her head as she struggled to continue, "I'm just here to do what I can. But, please don't be too harsh on him. Give him a way out and be lenient."

The boss chortled. Ying'er felt a powerful wave sweep through her head, so powerful she thought she might pass out. She quickly backed out the door, only to see some workers watching her. They knew why she was there, for sure, and she felt she'd let them down. "I'm worthless," she thought.

She headed back to her room. It was only a short distance, but it felt almost interminable. The pounding in her head continued. I did the best I could, she said to herself.

Men disgusted her. Why are they all like that?

8

"Hurry. A man's died." They heard shouts early the next morning.

Ying'er went out the door with Lanlan to see a large crowd clamoring around a pool. Sansan ran up with no regard for manners, and quickly let out a frightening howl. Baozi was sobbing.

Daniu's body was floating in the water. It was hard to see if he was injured. The dark green water submerged his blank stare. Ying'er felt a buzz in her head, as if trapped in a nightmare. Everything before her looked unreal. The other workers had blank expressions. Some would sigh now and then, drawn-out but hollow, like a breeze through a cave.

The pool was not far from where Ying'er was staying. She noticed signs of a struggle along the side, but not like there'd been a fight. The signs of struggle were clear to her, she was sure. Could he have fallen in accidentally? She wondered. But she knew he wouldn't have drowned if he'd fallen by accident. The salt water was heavier than a human body. Ying'er's heart was gripped by a large, invisible hand.

The police arrived, and the workers parted for them impassively. They were ordered to fish Daniu out; the coroner set about to examine the body by first telling the workers to strip him naked. Ying'er and the women left the scene.

Sansan had stopped crying, as Lanlan, her face ashen, laid her hand on Sansan's arm. Ying'er felt a great pressure on her chest, still puzzled by Daniu's death. Everyone would agree he died under unusual circumstances, she thought, but no one said a word. Daniu was such a simple, straightforward man. Could he have lost his life over a couple of teeth? She didn't know.

Sansan shuddered. She looked cold; she belched, as if she'd eaten too fast or too much. Ying'er realized that she had truly cared for him. Not a particularly good-looking women, she brimmed with vitality. Daniu, luck wasn't with you, Ying'er said silently. Her heart ached when she recalled how he'd felt about her. She'd been annoyed by the way he'd attached himself to her, and felt defiled by his attitude. When she thought back now, she was touched by his sincerity and devotion. The pain turned into something warm, which in turned made her nose ache so much that tears began to fall.

Everything felt unreal, as reality was negated by a strong sense of chimera. More and more she seemed caught in a nightmare, as she choked up. With her arm around Sansan, Ying'er shed silent tears, while Sansan stared blankly, her eyes sunken and dry. The desert wind and sun had sucked the moisture out of her skin and sprinkled her with sunspots. She did not like to spend her money on vegetables, but spared no expense on face cream. Ying'er knew the cream, no matter how good it was, would have no effect on the spots, which were caused by melanin. Sansan would never have fair skin so long as she worked under the blistering sun.

In the distance, the medical representative was dissecting the body, creating a whiteness among the onlookers. Ying'er avoided looking that way, reminded of the gray callouses and gaping bloody wounds, like babies' mouths, on his legs.

Baozi came over, wiping his tears, to squat by Sansan. He sobbed and said:

"Daniu has no visible wounds, but his shirt was in tattered, torn to pieces, actually. It looked like a monster had reached out from the water to drag him in." Baozi wiped his tears and continued, "His lungs and stomach were filled with water, so he'd drowned. But you have to agree, it's odd, because you can't kill yourself in that water. Daniu must have been forced under after he fell in. That has to be it.

"The boss is crying too. He said he called the police and told them to stop their investigation. He said it was only a couple of teeth . . . who could imagine Daniu would die like that.

"He could make it happen if he really wanted to kill himself. He could, like, grab a chunk of the salt crust before jumping in and he'd stay under. When he died and let go of the crust, the water would push him to the surface.

"When the poet, Qu Yuan, jumped into the river, he held a rock in his arms."

Ying'er did not feel like saying anything.

"Nothing serious will happen now, except that his sister has to quit school. He worked like a beast of burden for her."

9

Daniu was going to be cremated.

All the migrant workers went to see him off. His parents came, and howled like cows. Two shriveled people, like dehydrated eggplants. It was hard to imagine how they could have produced a son like a young ox. The old man howled, as tears dripped from his beard, while his wife wailed and banged her head against a salt crust over and over. When the management station sent for them, they were only told that Daniu had fallen ill, and were stunned to see that their ox of a son had already turned into a corpse covered in a red flannel sheet. To avoid saddening them more, the workers tried to keep them away from the body, which was the right thing to do, because the shriveled old woman would surely die of heartache if she saw how their son had been cut up during the dissection. The result was clear: no poison was found in his stomach and there were no visible wounds on his body. There were some scratches, but none were fatal. He had drowned, that was certain. The examiner believed it was a suicide, though the police held a different opinion.

There were various causes for his suicide. One of them claimed that Daniu hadn't wanted to be caught and tortured by the police. The second focused on his despair over the possible loss of his job at the salt lakes; he killed himself out of hopelessness. The third explanation maintained that he had nothing to live for after Ying'er's rejection. The last got the police interested in talking to Ying'er, who told them what Daniu had said the last night she saw him. Sansan was then called in.

After making a pile of dry kindling and cow dung, the migrant workers carried Daniu, wrapped in the red flannel sheet, and laid him on top, while a truck driver filled half a can of gasoline from his tank. Daniu's mother rushed up with outstretched arms, like a hen protecting her chicks. She wanted one last look at her son, but the workers were adamant about keeping her away. Her husband, on the other hand, was the practical type, who kept pestering the boss, grabbing at his legs whenever he could. It was the most effective tactic peasants used on officials.

"Your son killed himself," the boss said. "You can't ask us to pay for his life."

As if he hadn't heard, the old man held onto the boss's legs. Later the boss told the cashier to give the old man ten thousand yuan, to help the family out, not as compensation for the lost life, of course. They heard that the promise of money actually convinced the old man of the boss's guilt; if not, why would he have given so much?

The old man had objected to the cremation at first, for he wanted to fight for more money. Once the body was cremated, he wouldn't have any leverage to ask for more. But the body would begin to stink, so the workers came to plead with him, saying it would smell terrible. That changed his mind.

A pungent odor spread when the gasoline was splashed on the sheet. Daniu's mother wailed and rolled on the ground, creating a scene. Sansan and the other women wept along with her. Ying'er choked up, nearly suffocating her. Everything seemed to have turned into a thick and weighty dream, shadowy and unreal. One man held up a torch, its flame roaring in the wind, and slowly inched it toward the kindling under the sheet, where the impatient firewood burst into a blaze before the torch even touched it. Fire spread quickly, unrestrained and crazed as a whirlwind, quickly swallowing up the sheet.

The flames whooped cheerfully, like ecstatic crows, pecking away at the sheet and the clothes, and charring the fair skin. They seemed to favor the callouses and gaping wounds on his legs, for they kept licking at the spots; the hardened skin stubbornly guarded against changes of color, but the fire licked relentlessly until the gray skin whitened and started to crack.

The fire rose and spread, filling the air with its roar. Her mouth opened wide, Daniu's mother continued to wail and howl. His father had his mouth open too, as if crying or surprised that his son would last that long in the fire. That was true; it took time to cremate Daniu, who, unlike others with mostly fat, had muscle. Fat made the fire burn faster, while muscle needed help from the kindling to complete the final journey of the body. Gray spots began to appear on the skin and liquid oozed out but quickly evaporated in the fire.

Fire blanketed the sky, smoke began to vanish. The gasoline had done its job, and the rest was left to the kindling and cow dung. Daniu seemed embarrassed, for he twisted this way and that way in the fire, drawing surprised cries from the workers. Don't be afraid, one of them yelled out. It's his tendons. That shout calmed Daniu down; now he looked sheepishly quiet, like a magician whose trick had been exposed. As if to make up for its earlier misstep, his body produced a new kind of fuel, a bubbling liquid that seeped out of the rings of gray on the skin; it was a steam-like mist at first, but slowly gathered to form a drop that grew bigger and bigger until it rolled down the charred body and burst into brilliant flares.

With cooperation and help from Daniu, the fire took on a pure, clean look; the flames no longer spread wildly, even gained a degree of perfection. His flesh hardened and flattened out on the bones, meaning that fire had extinguished most of his body's moisture. His flesh and his bones congealed, though his body fat remained in the liquid stage. The workers watched, mouth agape, eyes glazed over.

The cries of Daniu's mother rose above the roaring fire, less the sound of weeping over the dead than the uncontrollable wail of someone who suffers from great pain. His father too was wailing, but he seemed capable of leaving his pain behind if he wanted, for he kept sneaking glances at the boss, whose face had a gray pall, maybe from sadness, but possibly from irritation.

The dry kindling was burned off, leaving only embers, but the cow dung continued to send up its unique flames. Daniu's body constricted. Cremation custom required that someone poke the charred body with a steel pole to make sure it burned completely. But no one came up, so he remained a black mess.

Dry kindling and cow dung worked differently from professional crematoria, and Daniu was not completely burned when the fire died. Someone said his mother wanted to take the charred body home, but his father objected; he wanted to bury Daniu in the desert instead, to avoid the hurt of seeing his grave back home. If Daniu had been burned into a pile bones, she'd have been able to go against her husband and take the bones with her. But the firewood worked to the old man's advantage; it wasn't powerful enough to burn everything off the bones and instead turned it into something like glaze. In the end, his mother had to let the workers bury him in a sand trough north of the salt lakes.

The day after Daniu's burial, Ying'er and the other women followed the local custom of making soupy rice as a send-off for Daniu. They didn't see the burial mound when they got there, and his remains were exposed. Animals had gnawed off whatever flesh was left on the bones, which, though darkened by the smoke, now showed rows of pristine white lines of teeth marks.

The women wept as they gathered the dispersed bones and buried them in the yellow sand.

Chapter Thirty-One

A snake hatches eggs in the coil of a neglected whip
The wheels of a horse cart crush peony flowers

1

Everyone in the village knew about Yue'er; they all expressed indignation toward her family and sympathy to Mengzi. In the beginning, Mengzi's mother felt vindicated and accepted their commiseration, but gradually she sensed her own blunder, though she never owned up to it. Yue'er's family sent over ten thousand yuan, the exact amount for the engagement; they made no mention of the gift, saying that the money would be used for Yue'er's treatment.

Mengzi's mother knew the money was the result of the fuss she'd raised, but it had come at the cost of harming Yue'er. People were talking so much about it that their spittle seemed to blanket the sky. It was the inevitable topic whenever the villagers gathered to chat, and they would invariably spit in the direction of Yue'er's house. Some even threatened to drag her over to the clan shrine to be struggled against, for bringing shame to the whole village. But that was just empty talk, since they were all afraid of her headstrong brother.

"It runs in the family," the villagers said. Yue'er's father's second sister had come down with the same disease. Before Liberation, she'd been a prostitute in a hotel in Hexi and received her just punishment when she got syphilis and died a horrible death. She was the only one they knew of to have been engaged in that profession. In recent years, quite a few of the young women from their village had left home to work, but they had changed their names and lived in far-flung cities. People were dubious about the source of the money wired home, but they had no proof to doubt the women's innocence. There was, however, iron-clad evidence of syphilis against Yue'er to nail her to the post of shame. The villagers even suspected that Mengzi was afflicted too, because they were convinced that cotton burns when it touches fire. They could not believe that he could manage to keep himself pure as jade when he had his arms around her alluring, shapely body. Now women avoided him, afraid he'd give them the same disease, even including filthy old hags whose faces were disgustingly ugly.

Finally, it dawned on Mengzi's mother that the fuss she'd raised had affected her son's reputation. No girl would want to marry him now, even if he were to get a divorce. She had to forget about that for now and agree to have Yue'er treated first. In her estimate, with the money from Yue'er's family, whatever the girl had could be rooted out by science.

In public she never admitted wrong, but her actions were a concession to her son and daughter-in-law. She convinced Laoshun to spend eight hundred yuan for a used motor scooter so Mengzi could take Yue'er to Liangzhou for regular treatments from Old Mister Liang.

Laoshun was insistent that Mengzi should stay away from White Tiger Pass, after fate had played a cruel trick on him and given him no gold. Luckily, it was a joint venture, so Mengzi paid something over three thousand yuan for his share of the loss. It was still too much for Laoshun, however, and he raged at his son several times until Mengzi stiffened his neck and said he'd take care of the debt himself. A father cannot control a grown son, so Laoshun had to keep his mouth shut, though he continued to sigh over the loss.

His parents began a frenzy of activity when Mengzi moved his bedding back home. They'd had nothing to worry about when he had been working at the pit and lived apart from Yue'er. Now the young couple would sleep on the same kang, turning Yue'er's disease into a sword hanging over their heads. They knew he had yet to touch her, but that was no guarantee that he wouldn't in the future. He was at a "combustible" age, and no one could say if he might lose control and go ahead with it. The trouble would be endless if he was touched by bayberry sores.

The old couple lived daily with their hearts in their throat. Besides telling him over and over to hold back, they set up a rule that the young couple were not allowed to lock their bedroom door. Mengzi's mother had a private agreement with her husband that they would take turns standing watch at night. When the light went out in the young couple's room, one of them would tiptoe over barefoot to squat by the door and listen. If anything unusual was detected, the sentry would sound the alarm. Laoshun didn't agree at first, for it seemed wrong, not something elders should be doing to the young. He agreed only when he saw how hard it was on his wife; she would take the first half of the night and he the second half.

Mengzi was in the dark about his parents' monitoring his every action at night.

One night, after her bath, Yue'er applied medicinal powder, put on her pants, and lay down on the kang. Her condition hadn't worsened, but there was no visible sign of improvement either. She and Mengzi talked about going to Lanzhou, though they heard that Lanzhou hospitals prescribed the same medicine she'd gotten from the one in Liangzhou. It would be a waste of money, and she was reluctant to go. Their conversation turned to something else, mostly amusing anecdotes from their school days. She looked to be in a good mood. She'd lost weight, but that did not affect her beauty; in fact, she looked prettier than ever in his compassionate eyes. He reached under the blanket to take her hand. Such a pretty girl could be looked at, but not touched; his heart ached and brought on a sad sigh.

"Don't sigh. You can do anything you want when I'm cured." Yue'er teased him. "By then maybe your heart will be willing, but not your body."

"By then you'll beg for mercy," he said. That made her giggle.

That went back and forth for a while. When he felt her palm getting wet, an exhilarating sensation, he tightened and then loosened his grip, the slippery feeling from that small hand leading to erotic thoughts. He leaned over to kiss her. Four lips came into contact and became inseparable, lips on lips, tongue twisting around tongue. The noise put Laoshun, who was on watch at the time, on alert. He sneaked back to the study to wake up his wife. "I heard something."

"Mengzi—" his wife threw something over her and walked out the door.

Mengzi answered her call. "Get your father some pain pills. He's got a headache."

Mengzi got up, turned on a flashlight, retrieved the pain pills, got some water, and handed them all to his father. Before he walked out, his mother cautioned:

"Don't get too close to her. You'd get the disease too if you're touched by what comes out."

"I know, I know."

His father felt reassured by his tone of voice, but not his mother. She put on a coat and went to stand guard.

The bodily contact had excited the young couple; just kissing had brought plenty of pleasure. When they were apart, they were two separate entities, but when they were in each other's arms, they became one. The tremendous sense of happiness drove out some of the unpleasantness. To avoid accidents, they kept their pants and undershirts on, but soon those got in the way, so they bared their chests and lay in each other's arms.

They were immersed in the special bliss of newlyweds. Mengzi felt himself falling: they started out holding hands, then kissing, then moving into each other's arms. As bodily contact grew more extensive, he felt greater bliss, and the temptation grew stronger.

His mother's heart fluttered anxiously when she detected activity. She told him to get medicine whenever she detected something unusual. Mengzi never wizened up about his parents' voyeuristic activities; he had no idea that the meager bliss he enjoyed had brought so much fear to them.

Temptation grew stronger, inducing pain. Yue'er's young body fanned long-lost sensations and feelings. Mengzi's body began to have a mind of its own, and it was hard to say when it would burst into flames. Kissing and touching were like pouring fuel on a fire. She was sensitive and responsive, making heavenly moans when they touched. Maybe she wanted to make him feel good, and maybe she couldn't control herself, but it brought both pleasure and agony. In the meantime, it also tortured Laoshun. "Slut. Slut," he kept muttering when he was on duty, fearful of the sound, but oddly eager to hear it too, so conflicted he was sweating.

The loving relationship between the young couple grew fast after the nightly bodily contact; they became inseparable, especially because they had to fight the demon of her disease together. Only when they were kissing did she feel the sweet tenderness of being a woman, but it was nothing like sexual pleasure, which would bring her down when it reached its height. Kissing and touching were exciting and the excitement could last forever. Temptation stoked by knowledge that they could not move beyond touching intensified the force to draw them closer.

One night they bantered and flirted as usual and continued touching like a young couple of lovers. They started out kissing. Then the moonlight stole into their room through the window curtains, infusing it with a dreamy quality. Mengzi discovered, seemingly for the first time, that Yue'er was beautiful beyond words. Her body emitted a wave of tenderness that set the flames of desire raging through him. She looked at him quietly, her gaze serene and sorrowful; her fingers danced playfully on his body, while she tried to calm her increasingly faster breathing. Mengzi sucked on her young breast, completely under the spell of the round, soft mound. He was able to force himself to stay calm at first, but soon a tidal wave took him under and he threw himself on her, kissing her madly. He'd die happy if he could become one with her, he thought. Yue'er tried to free herself, but she was quickly consumed by the fire of desire. He took out a condom and panted as he said, "I'll put this on. Just this once."

She shook her head nervously, "No, no." Her objection didn't last.

The desire raged, their blood roiled, an immense thirst tightened their throats, and their hearts beat like a drum with deafening sounds. Mengzi tore open the plastic cover and a soft object fell into his fingers, bringing with it an incredible sense of happiness and bliss.

"Mengzi—" They heard his mother's shrill shout. "There's a thief in the yard."

Yue'er was hit by the realization that her in-laws had been watching them. Like a child being burned, she burst into tears; so did Mengzi. With their arms around each other, they wept with abandon till dawn.

2

Yue'er continued to go for her treatment at Old Mister Liang's, while Mengzi's mother went on a search for home remedies. The people in their village had all heard about bayberry sores, but they had no idea what they looked like. Besides, Mengzi's mother could not tell everyone she met that her daughter-in-law was afflicted with the filthy disease. She could only ask people she knew well, people who had people they knew well, and so on, until everyone was aware of Yue'er's situation. Objectively speaking, her approach damaged her daughter-in-law's reputation, but it did serve the intended purpose. One day Pockmark Wang, the local doctor, gave her a remedy: smoking with burning cow dung. "In the old days, this worked on the newly infected." He explained that the cow dung had the essence of all vegetations, giving it medicinal efficacy.

Mengzi's mother did not know what essence was contained in cow dung, but it didn't cost anything. Many people in the village raised cows, and where there were cows, there was dung. When the sticky, wet droppings were slapped on a wall, they took only a few days to dry in the shape of cakes. Mengzi's mother collected many cakes of cow dung and piled them into a wash basin to smoke Yue'er. She refused at first, doubting that cow dung could be more effective than medicine. But her mother-in-law was too eager to say no to, so she sent Mengzi out—she'd rather die than let him see her festering privates.

After Mengzi left, she took off her pants to expose the afflicted spot. Mengzi's mother was stunned to see rotting flesh and yellow pus oozing from festering sores. Afraid she might embarrass the young woman, she held back the questions she'd planned to ask. She abhorred Yue'er's past behavior, but now she found herself filled with pity and compassion. She started to burn the dung, and a tiny spark began to spread; it was not an ordinary spark, but a spot of hope. The fire spread, and a plume of white smoke rose to waft over their heads. She moved the essence of vegetations to smoke the sores. Nothing much happened at first, but as the fire grew and the smoke thickened, yellow liquid began seeping out of the sores and gathering into a drop to fall into the fire, where it sizzled and moaned.

"Does it feel all right?" Mengzi's mother asked.

"It does."

Yue'er moved closer to the fire, the sizzle from the dripping yellow puss instilling a sense of vindication. It was the most detestable demon in the world, harming her after claiming so many victims. She could even feel the demon baring its fangs and screaming in the flames. It was a wonderful feeling. In the beginning, the warm fire felt good on the festering spots, but slowly it started to hurt, though not a normal pain, but a soothing, warming ache, comforting as it spread out. She wished she could melt into the fire and turn into a blue flame. "Go away," she said silently at the demon. "Or we'll die together."

As she lowered her body, more yellow liquid flowed along with a horrible stench. She now felt a burning pain, the fire no longer smoking, but baking her. She was eager to see results. It would be best if she could be cured after one or two treatments, so her beloved could have his way with her. Yue'er felt terrible every time she saw his tormented look.

When she saw that Yue'er was nearly pressing her sores into the fire, Mengzi's mother put a rolled-up towel behind her knee for her to stay higher. "It's meant to smoke, not bake," she said. She did not want the fire to burn Yue'er's skin, or they'd have to treat the burns on top of her current problem. As she added more cow dung, Mengzi's mother seemed to forget Yue'er's notorious past and treated her as her own child. A sick child doted over by her mother.

She removed the fire after a while. Yue'er put tissue on the sores, got dressed, and lay down on the bed. She was exhausted. A dull ache emanated from the smoked spot, but she was in high spirits, having found another treatment, a free one at that. To her a treatment meant a path. She often felt that all paths were closed off to her, that she'd come to a dead end, and she despaired. She had married Mengzi confident that it was curable and that scientific advancement would surely have some solution for this horrific disease. As she prepared for the wedding, she had started an intensive treatment, hoping to be cured before they were married. She never expected the festering spot to grow a tongue to lick at the area around it. Had she known, she'd have made different plans.

Lying on the kang, she gazed lazily up at the ceiling. The plastic wedding garland still exuded happiness, reminding her of their intimacy at night. She realized it all had to with the heart; she loved Mengzi, so a simple kiss brought her happiness. She could not imagine what kind of marital bliss they'd have when she was cured, but she was sure it would be a vortex of ecstasy to swallow him up. A smile danced around her lips.

"Feeling any better?" Mengzi asked when he walked in. Instead of replying, she just looked at him quietly. She noticed how he had lost weight and was seriously tanned. "Why are you in such a hurry?" she chided coyly. She pulled him over and pressed him against her chest, as an emotion unique to mothers rose up.

She touched his face over and over, feeling a soft, warm sensation. Mengzi felt that since the day he was nearly buried in the pit he'd changed; now he was always mulling over strange questions, such as the meaning of life. Life hadn't meant anything to him at first, but as he kept up his inquiry, including questions about the end of the universe, nothing meant anything to him anymore. He found that in the end everything become a colossal emptiness, a thought that extinguished all hope. But now, there was a woman in the boundless void to cry and laugh with him and accompany him in his lonely, sad life.

He kept asking himself about the meaning of life each time he recalled how helpless and lonely he'd felt down in the pit, how his rootless soul had drifted. These were meaningless questions, for there were no answers, just more to trouble him. He'd then envy his father and their generation for their lack of desire and needs, as well as a contentment that brought happiness. They were considered benighted, but who could say it wasn't wisdom on a higher plane?

The problem was, understanding something in a confused state was too difficult to achieve. Once one understood, however, it would be impossible to remain ignorant. Mengzi could not be like his parents, just as he could not go back to the womb. Moreover, he knew there was a kind of spiritual suffering that no one could cure. He was his only savior, but he did not know how to go about it. He longed for a hand of wisdom to soothe his soul, like Yue'er's hand comforting his body.

But where would he find that hand?

3

Mengzi's mother decided to send Yue'er back to her parents.

His parents were exhausted. They had sent messages to the salt lakes, telling Lanlan and Ying'er to return soon to share in their burden, but had not heard back. The old couple could not hold out any longer, working in the field during the day and standing sentry at night. The night watch was particularly tiring, for there were constant signs of trouble. Their nerves were stretched taut, and any more anguish would cause a nervous breakdown. In fact, they did not mind the taxing watch; what they feared most was the young couple going through with it when they lost control, or when they were half asleep. It would cause an irreversible mistake. Which was why they decided to send Yue'er back to her parents; she could come back to be Mengzi's real wife once she was cured.

Additionally, Laoshun planned to find something for Mengzi to do, so he wouldn't be bored and cause trouble. As luck would have it, the forestry bureau was about to start a wildlife conservation center. The officials had heard of Mengzi's experience at Pig's Belly Well and his familiarity with desert life forms, so they asked him to help out. It was like a sleepy head meeting a soft pillow. He was hesitant, but Laoshun accepted the offer for him; finally, the old couple could take a breather.

Yue'er could not stop weeping, as she was weighed down with worries. Mengzi's mother had explained over and over that they only wanted the young couple to live apart temporarily to avoid any accident, that was all. In earlier times, when a girl committed an inexcusable offense at her in-laws' house, she would be sent back home. Mengzi's mother told Yue'er it was different this time; it wasn't meant to be punitive. Now that it had come to this, she added, they had accepted the situation. No more angry words would come from them. All they wanted was for Mengzi to stay healthy. They would help with her treatment, as she was their daughter-in-law. On and on, Mengzi's mother offered comforting words, but still Yue'er continued to weep until she could hardly breathe.

So, Mengzi's mother sent for Fengxiang, who ended up weeping along with Yue'er. Yue'er knew what Fengxiang wanted to say, so there was no point in wagging her tongue. No matter how comforting Fengxiang meant her words to be, it would still amount to touching Yue'er's sore spot. When she had gone through hard times, Fengxiang had even envied Yue'er's freedom to roam free in the wild wide world like an unharnessed horse. Now she realized that roaming free had the danger of falling into traps, so she envied her no more.

They sat silently shedding tears side by side in Yue'er's bridal chamber, which seemed to mock her at the moment; the bright colors serving only to highlight her sorrow. Fengxiang dried her tears and said softly:

"Don't think too much. Get yourself cured first."

"I don't know why, but I have this terrible feeling, like once I leave, I'll never return."

"Of course, you will," Fengxiang said. "You'll be back."

Yue'er shook her head and sobbed.

Mengzi's mother could not stand the way Yue'er cried. She stamped her foot over and over. She herself was given to shedding tears and wailing, but she hated it when others cried. Whenever something didn't go right, she asked Grannie Shaman to conduct a divination, and she always said that the God of Tears was causing the trouble. Mengzi's mother had learned of the existence of this fierce demon, which appeared when someone stirred up trouble in that person's house. She wanted to go over and stop Yue'er, but Mengzi kept her back each time.

"Just let her cry. She'll feel better after a good cry."

She could cry all she wanted, but in the end, she had to do what the in-laws had planned for her.

After lunch, Mengzi left home with Yue'er, who did not want to go back. On his part, Mengzi knew his parents meant well for the young couple, besides his own realization that he was slipping into an unknown future. He was fearful that he might lose control at a critical moment. If his mother hadn't sounded the alarm that night, who knew what kind of trouble he'd have been in now. He shuddered every time he thought about that night. He knew their most important task now was to cure Yue'er's disease, and he'd been working hard to find money, behind his parents' back. He wanted to take Yue'er to Lanzhou for treatment; he'd do his best and leave the rest to fate.

They walked down a country path toward Yue'er's home. Along the way they saw villagers talking, but they turned away when the young couple drew closer. Mengzi said something to distract Yue'er, so she wouldn't feel bad, but a pained look appeared on her face nonetheless.

She didn't cry, though; instead she put on a brave face and walked with a firm step, seemingly to show her strength and to disappoint them. Mengzi understood her well, but decided against saying anything and talked about something else.

She dropped the façade of strength when she got home, as she threw herself into her mother's arms and burst out crying. Her mother wept along with her while Mengzi explained his parents' intention. He did his best to avoid using incendiary words, but his mother-in-law's face darkened, though she too refrained from saying anything provocative. Her family was in the wrong, and she'd have no right to even fart if the in-laws not only sent her back to stay for a while, but demanded a divorce.

Mengzi had a hard time taking his leave, however. Yue'er grabbed his hands and refused to let him go, looking more like grasping a life-saving straw than parting from her beloved. It was as if a demon would gobble her up as soon as he walked out. He was saddened by her insistence and her forlorn look, with the realization that he was her sole moral support. A young woman like her was too weak to confront a colossal demon of illness in an environment where everyone spat at her. He sighed deeply, hit by the cruelty of agreeing with his parents to send her home.

Yet it was quiet at her house. Her brother, Baigou, had left for White Tiger Pass. After losing all he had, he'd gone back to work as a sand boy, and her father was there to run the dance hall. The old and the very young were left with little to do, just as in Mengzi's own village. The yard was cheerless, pale-looking; a white lonely sun hung solitarily in the sky, infusing the yard with a sad whiteness. The world reflected what was in one's mind, and dejection changed everything.

Yue'er had gotten much thinner, her face a bloodless white. Alone with her mother, she shed the forced appearance of toughness and turned back to her frail self. Her hands were powerful, as if she'd put all her heart into keeping him around, and her eyes were imbued with deep longing tenderness.

Mengzi was so moved he wished he could pluck the disease from her body and plant it inside his own.

Chapter Thirty-Two

Clouds in the sky send down dewy rain
Darkness overhead wrecks a promising talent

1

Lanlan and Ying'er felt they were falling apart physically, after several days of working on the sand ridge. They did not want to cut corners, so their ridge was much shorter after three days than that which others had accomplished in one.

"The way we're going, we won't make any money after paying for our meals. This doesn't look like a place we can stay for long. Why don't we settle up and go home?" Lanlan said.

Ying'er felt terrible over what had happened to Daniu. People were pointing, she discovered, and that weighed heavily on her. The work was hard, and she did not feel like staying. They decided to hold out till the end of month, and leave for home after receiving their pay.

They turned their remaining flour into steamed buns, broke them into walnut-sized pieces, and fried them into crispy bread. They also pickled some scallions that were old but still edible. When their meals got boring, eating the fried bread with the pickled scallions would be particularly tasty.

Lanlan asked Wu Jie to return the wool blankets and cookware to the boss for them. Feeling bad about things, Wu Jie gave them three sacks of salt. According to convention, Mongolian herders got free salt for themselves and for their camels, so Lanlan accepted the gifts. They went looking for the herder, paid him for his effort, and got their camel back. The animal's hump had grown back after weeks of rest and food. But it didn't look quite right to Ying'er, though she couldn't say why. It was just a feeling.

Daniu had taken their leather flask that day, so Lanlan had to buy a plastic jug for water at the management station shop. The camel would carry the sacks of salt, so they would not be able to ride.

"We can walk," Ying'er said. "That's what legs are for."

Lanlan assured her that so long as no jackals came to bother them, they would travel in a straight line and would not get lost again.

Ying'er legs went soft at the mention of jackals. It was a problem of hers: whenever she was frightened by something, her legs would weaken any time it was brought up afterward. But she managed to hide her fear from Lanlan, for she knew that jackals scared her sister-in-law too. For now, they had to keep up their morale and avoid anything self-defeating. If she said she was afraid and Lanlan said the same thing, fright that had yet to become real would be enough to terrify them.

Lanlan checked their weapon supplies: they had half of a sack of gunpowder and some buckshot. She was afraid of jackals, but there was nothing she could do about it; they had to either traverse the desert or take a long detour. Traveling in a straight line meant they'd reach home in three or four days, if they didn't get lost. Taking a detour was harder to predict, but would require at least three weeks.

"Let's follow the short route taken by the ancestors," Lanlan said.

"That sounds good. We haven't run into any bad people so far."

When she was at the shop, Lanlan also bought kerosene, batteries, and other supplies. The kerosene was for the lantern, whose shade had been smashed during their encounter with the jackals. Luckily, the shop also carried glass shades. She bought bicycle ball bearings to use as ammuniction on wild animals, as well as firecrackers that would be more effective than her musket in scaring them off.

After returning the borrowed cookware, they did not feel like stocking up.

"It will cost money and add to the camel's load," Lanlan said. Ying'er agreed. They'd make do with the buns and water for the few days it would take to get home.

They got on the road. Ying'er felt a sense of emptiness. She recalled the high hopes they'd pinned on the lakes when they were searching in the desert; more eager, more earnest than an old Buddhist devotee hoping to reach nirvana. She hadn't realized that being close isn't always best. Imagining it to be a path for them, a turning point to change their destinies, it turned out to be no better than their villages. Now she knew that, unless she changed, she could not handle any hardship for long, not even making a sand ridge. These days, a three-legged donkey was hard to find, while there were more two-legged workers than ants. Once you offended the boss, you had to suffer.

She'd rather die than accept the kind of "change" the boss was hoping for. People were always saying that a woman can get rich if she succumbs to temptation, but would she still have her dignity if she walked down that route? To her, there was a line denoting human dignity; once you crossed it, you would no longer be human. Others could do what they wanted, but she would die before becoming the woman the boss wanted. She couldn't.

It was better to leave.

They entered the salt field. The camel clip-clopped across the spongy salted ground. Columns of dry, white dust rose, scorching and thirst-inducing. Thirst that had persecuted them must have been etched in their souls. Ying'er was tired. They had been hopeful on their way out, now their return trip was marked only by fatigue. It was time to leave, she told herself. Perhaps that was all the time she had been allotted to spend at the salt lakes; the time was up and there was nothing to hold her back. She realized that humans are lonely creatures, facing things alone, with no one to lend assistance. Be it pain or solitude, you have to suffer through it on your own. As their feet moved forward, the salt lakes eventually turned into a bright, whitish spot behind them. Looking at the waves of sand rippling into the distance, she had a feeling that she had again been tossed into the unknown, and she began to feel nostalgic about the lakes, where there were people, despite their differences.

Without meaning to, she thought of Daniu. A warm sensation filled her heart, followed by pangs of agony. No matter how she looked at it, Daniu had met his "steel threshold" because of her; if not to plead her case, he would not have gotten into a fight with the boss, and without the scuffle, he would still be a model worker. But so many things are hard to explain; sometimes personality determines your fate. Daniu would have run into trouble sooner or later if he could not control his temper.

When she thought about him, it seemed wrong not to feel something about the salt lakes, as if she were an ingrate, to borrow the word her mother had used on her when she was little. As a young girl, she'd been immersed in her own world and preferred to be alone with her thoughts. Sometimes, she treated lightly something that meant a great deal to her mother, who would then call her an ingrate. Thinking about her mother brought back sad memories of that rainy night. She shook her head and told herself to stop thinking.

In life, no effort is wasted, she had to say. Carrying the sand had been hard, but it had helped build up strength in her legs. When they started out, she recalled, pain had knifed through her calves. It had dulled after five or six days. And now, back in the desert, she walked with light, springy steps. The camel, however, looked to be straining. The load would be too heavy if they had a long way to go, but it should be able to carry a hundred kilos for a few days without trouble. To conserve the camel's strength, Lanlan chose gentle slopes, and yet the animal still panted hard and foamed at the mouth.

Luckily, it wasn't too hot. Dark, late autumn clouds blocked out the sun. The sky hadn't been so overcast when they left, only large puffy gray clouds. They would have waited a few days before taking off if there had been dark clouds like these, for large drops of rain could be hiding in them. That could spell trouble. Desert weather is as changeable as a baby's face. Likely, the dark clouds would be blown across the hills by the desert wind. Neither of them worried much about it.

Their steps were light, but not their hearts. Gone was the hope they'd had on their way out, and the salt lakes had not turned out to be the cool dream they'd wished for. The shiny broad road in their dream had darkened. What would they do when they got home? Lanlan said she'd come back if life got too hard back home.

"What would you do there? You could work yourself to make some blood money, and yet you'd still have to go against your conscience. When no one is bothered by their conscience but you, you'll be the outlier. Is that what you want?"

Lanlan did not respond.

"Say you could stay at the salt lakes forever, then what?" Lanlan had no answer. If they continued the line of questioning, they'd find that working in the salt lakes was pointless, merely earning sustenance by trading youth that was whittled away day by day. She could keep asking questions until she got to the disappearance of the body, but then everything would lose its meaning.

"When you look at it that way, self-cultivation and religious practice are still the best option," Lanlan said.

"What's the point of the practice if it's just the 'best option'?" Ying'er asked with a smile.

"I think I'll still go back to it when we return."

Compared with a host of other things in life, Ying'er discovered, what Lanlan wanted to do was still more meaningful. No matter what, the so-called accumulation of good karma would not vanish just because the body was gone. Could it be that the earliest practitioners had come up with the idea to look for meaning in a largely meaningless world after experiencing a sense of helplessness?

"You must travel down some paths in life whether they're meaningful or not," Ying'er said.

2

In the end, the rains came.

It started with muffled rumbles in the dark clouds, like a tiger's roar or a cow's low, even more like a grinding millstone. But a few dull thunderclaps bought down a surprising cascade of water. So many things in the world defy human wishes. Not a wet fart had come from the sky when they were parched. Now, with enough food and water, they were eager to go home, so there was a cloudburst. The rain came with full force; with no warning, a curtain of geysers was pulled straight down on them, and they were drenched before they could react.

Being the careful sort, Ying'er had put together enough provisions, including water, steamed buns and other staples, for ten days of travel, but she'd forgotten rainwear. Neither of them had expected to run into a deluge soon after leaving the salt lakes. It felt as if heaven were imitating their mothers-in-law by picking a fight with them or pulling a prank when they least expected it. This was a setback, a supernatural setback on their life's journey. Ying'er's mother would say that with fortune as an adversary, nothing they did would work out in their favor.

"It's must be our fate," Lanlan said.

"Some things really depend on how you look at them. You say this is our fate, but we could have made changes and done what the boss wanted. Then things might go our way. Which means that the setback was caused by an external force."

"But didn't you refuse to change? That refusal was your fate."

She has a point, Ying'er thought. Life will put up roadblocks if you try to adhere to an ideal while everything around you is changing.

The rain seeped into the sand. Their path wasn't muddy, but the wet sand stuck to their shoes and made them many times heavier than usual. It was tough going, but tolerable. The worst came from the rain itself, as it seemed to come at them from all directions, with water flowing down their hair and into their eyes. It was white as far as the eye could see, while the sounds of pelting rain filled their ears. Rainwear would have made things less stressful, though the going would still have been tough. The maddening thirst and extreme hunger on their way out remained visceral in their minds, pushing out the possibility of running into rain; otherwise, they would have gotten themselves some plastic sheets.

The raindrops were big and powerful, almost like whips. At first, their skin felt the pounding of each drop, but soon they were numbed by rain so cold their teeth clattered. It was, after all, late autumn. When the sun showed its face, the chill moved away, but then the dark clouds took over. Their faces were a pale white, their lips purple, and goosebumps covered their exposed arms. It was terrible.

A mist rose around them. Ying'er heard a loud crash, but knew it was an illusion, caused by the thump of rain on her eardrums. It was worse than the cold. She preferred peace and quiet, and found noisy places unbearable. Back when they were gathering *shagen*, what had bothered her most wasn't the stifling heat, but the noise. At the time, the concentration required for the work took her mind off it. Now, inundated by torrential rain, she thought she was on the brink of losing her mind.

Lanlan looked tiny as she walked along holding the camel's reins. Her clothes were plastered against her body. Gritting her teeth tautened the cheeks, an uncanny copy of her mother. Ying'er was fond of her sister-in-law and fearful of her mother-in-law, who was cunning and headstrong. A fleeting thought about Mengzi's mother was enough to make her knees weak. Ying'er realized that her mother-in-law was just like a jackal, capable of sending fear deep into her heart. She felt a harrowing terror when she thought about seeing her mother-in-law upon her return.

Would Lanlan become just like her mother? Ying'er wondered. Hard to say. She had found that so many pleasant girls unknowingly turned into severe mothers-in-law; they lost their femininity and gained the shrewish qualities of a battle-axe.

Please don't turn into your mother, Lanlan, Ying'er said silently. On second thought, she wondered if she herself would become her own mother, and her heart skipped a beat. She'd heard from villagers that her mother had been a beauty known far and wide. Yet life had turned her into a notorious shrew. Ying'er knew she had been forced to change. Lanlan's mother could have been like Lanlan now, and life had made her into a mother-in-law who made her knees buckle at the mere thought.

She felt something warm in her eyes. Please don't ever become your mother, Lanlan, she wanted to say. Then she realized that Lanlan would not want to change, but your clothes are tainted yellow when you walk through a rapeseed field. Change or not, oftentimes is not up to the individual. Then how about Lingguan? Would he become another Laoshun? That too was hard to say.

Even if they could actually spend the rest of their lives together, who could guarantee that they wouldn't become his parents, sniping at each other like poisonous spiders all the time? Ying'er knew she wouldn't want to become his mother, nor would Lingguan want to turn into his father. Yet there must have been a great force in life to change his parents into people they hadn't wanted to be. She despaired at the realization. I'd rather die than turn into someone like Lingguan's mother.

I'll die if one day I have to change and can't go on with life.

Her thoughts made the rain more bearable. The rainstorm would stop at some point, while the "change" she refused to accept might be something beyond human control. How awful. She took a closer look at Lanlan, who, she discovered, did look like her mother, but had something that was absent on her mother-in-law's face. Maybe it had to do with the Vajravārāhī. She'd heard you can hardly change your fate unless you have a religious belief, something that has the power to alter your destiny. Lanlan, for the sake of the Vajravārāhī, please don't become your mother.

Ying'er did not believe in the Vajravārāhī. If someone were to ask her about her belief, she would say love. When she was younger, she placed her love on the tender, poetic tunes. The problem was, she had learned most of the tunes from her mother, and they had done nothing to stop her mother from turning into a tigress.

The rain kept falling. She wiped the water off her face. She felt terrible. She should stop wasting mental energy on these thoughts. No amount of thinking would make any difference if life turned her into her mother, something that could occur without her awareness, like a baby falling into a wolf den and growing up as a wolf child. Death would be better than that.

The going was getting tougher. Their shoes were much heavier from the wet sand, compounded by the fact that they were climbing up a dune. They would have taken a break at the foothills and waited for the rain to pass if they'd known it was coming. But it had started after they were halfway up, when the slope was gentle and the climb was easier. Now as the slope grew steeper, they were having a hard time continuing. Ying'er wanted to call for a break and find a spot to rest, but she saw dark clouds gathering. The rain wasn't going to stop any time soon, she knew. They'd have to wait until they reached the other side to rest.

She put her hand on the litter to help her move forward. The camel was soaking wet. It had molted during the summer heat. When they first came into the desert, the camel had been molting, but not noticeably, and now it had shed all its hair, looking like a plucked chicken. It dawned on her then that the herder must have sheared the camel's hair, which was quite valuable. The man had gotten more than his fair share. She recalled how, when they'd first gotten the animal back, it had looked strange, but she hadn't tried to find out why, and it was too late now. There was nothing they could do. All she wanted was to sleep in a clean spot, and if she could have some steamy hot noodles that would be better than being an immortal.

Lanlan stopped when they reached a swirl in a flat area.

"Let's take a break to eat something," Lanlan said, as she opened the sack, only to see that the buns had turned mushy.

"I don't mind. Mushy's better than nothing." Ying'er commented.

They were sticky and not very tasty, but both women ate as much as they could, with the help of the pickled scallions.

The camel was huffing, stopping long enough to lick the rain dripping down its shoulder.

"The salt is melting," Lanlan said indifferently.

Sure enough, the salt sacks had lost some of their fullness. What a shame, Ying'er thought, but she said, "Let it melt. If Heaven wants it to melt, there's nothing we can do." The salt could not compare with camel hair that could fetch several hundred yuan, she felt like saying, but didn't. She didn't want Lanlan to feel bad, but to her surprise, Lanlan brought it up herself.

"Did you just find out?" Ying'er asked.

"I noticed there, but what could we do? We weren't strong enough. Besides, we asked him to graze our camel without getting a receipt. If we upset him, he could refuse to give us back the camel, and we couldn't do a thing about it." Lanlan sighed. "Worse case, we pay for the camel hair with the money we earned."

Ying'er wanted to reply, but realized there was nothing she could say, despite the heavy sense of helplessness. Could I have exhausted all my allotted fortune? Why is nothing going my way?

After having the camel lie down, Lanlan opened a sack, scooped out some salt and put it in a plastic bowl. The camel stretched out its lips and with a slurp, began to chew noisily and happily. Camels are fed salt daily, but mostly new salt, with nitre, which humans find bitter and feed to the animals. Naturally, it had never enjoyed old salt, and crunched away with delight.

The women, however, looked wretched, like chicks drenched by a winter rain. Their wet clothes came into seamless contact with their skin. Rain flowed down on hair plastered to their faces to wash their blue lips. The salt bowl quickly filled up with rain, but the camel screwed up its lips and slurped the wet salt, cheerful and unhurried. Ying'er felt a calmness when she looked at the animal. Camels are such good-natured animals, she thought. Come rain or wind, they always look unhurried; they must be aware that anxiety is useless when dealing with an outside world that is beyond their control. The world remains the same no matter how you feel; it will not change to fit your state of mind. Oftentimes it is your uncontrollable heart that is the source of your torment.

After slurping the salt like gusts of wind sweeping lingering clouds, the camel licked up the last of the salty water. Hoping for more, it looked over at Lanlan, who told it that slow-running water travels far. She got up and tied the sack. The salt continued to melt, but she wasn't in the mood to do anything about it. What they wanted most at that moment was not money, love, or high status, but a warm bed, which was beyond them. Humans are frail in certain ways. For instance, when Lanlan was well fed and warmly clad, what she treasured most was the Vajravārāhī. But at this moment, the Vajravārāhī was less attractive than a warm bed. The animal side of human nature demands creature comforts.

Ying'er discovered that their feet were becoming buried in flowing sand.

3

Shifting sand was coming their way.

They did not know that's what it was at first, for they'd only heard about shifting sand in stories, like Sandy, the monk in Journey to the West, who was born in it. They had no idea how sand shifted. When a gusty wind blew, they saw sand travel up the edge of a shady trough over to a sunny one, which was how a dune moved. The sand could bury houses and crops, but the villagers never called it shifting sand, for a dune moved at a glacial pace, a process mostly gone unnoticed by people. But this was sand that shifted before their eyes. Likely the surface of the dunes was too saturated to take in all the falling rain, so the water flowed down the slope, taking sand with it.

The dark, drab liquid spread slowly and rose above their feet without their noticing it. Ying'er froze in terror; she'd never seen anything quite like it. Oh, no, we're going to be buried by shifting sand, she thought. Death itself had not frightened her, but now she was terrified at the thought of being buried in sand. Obviously, not everyone can look death calmly in the face. Lanlan was less flustered, as she quickly freed her feet. The sand felt quite solid, unlike gooey mud. It had such a powerful pull, it took great effort to get her feet out, so she told Ying'er to move hers. By straining hard, Ying'er managed to get one foot out, and Lanlan had helped her with the other. "We'll be buried alive if we stay here," Lanlan said. She got the camel up and they slowly trudged up the slope, despite the rain.

Shifting sand does not occur everywhere. Since it follows the flow of water, it builds up in hollows. Lanlan avoided depressions, choosing to travel on prominent rises. They managed to skirt a few treacherous spots, but that made Ying'er dizzy. The sand seemed to encircle her and the sky was spinning. She thought she might pass out.

Her gaze traveled up the slope, but she could not see the top of the dune. The rain had blurred everything, spreading a gray pall over the horizon and the dunes. She had no idea what time it was, just that it was afternoon. Without the rain, they'd have been able to guess the hour, but rain had slowed time down. Had a few minutes passed, or a few hours? All they knew was they must crest the dune if they did not want to be buried by the shifting sand.

Lanlan kept to flatter areas and shaded troughs, following a zig-zag route to make the trek easier, but still sometimes they had to walk through shifting sand. Gradually, Ying'er realized that it wasn't as scary as she'd thought; she'd be safe if she moved her feet fast enough. The camel, on the other hand, was heavy, and its feet kept sinking into the sand, with a dull, unpleasant sucking sound. Its sides rose and fell as it breathed noisily.

The overcast sky pressed down like lead. Ying'er's sore, tired legs kept buckling. The farther up they went, the larger the area taken up by shifting sand. The rain had turned into rivulets that carried sand with it. Everywhere she looked, the surface shifted, covering her feet after each pause. The sand flowed down the slope to the desert below, so they were in no immediate danger of being buried. Eddies were the most treacherous spots, where the sand gathered like stagnant water. A careless step could send them tumbling into it and drown them.

It was much darker now, unclear whether that was because of the clouds or that dusk was descending. The jagged edges of lightning stung their eyes, and the rumble of thunder drew ever closer. Sometimes an explosive thunderclap would frighten the camel into tossing its head. Being struck by lightning might actually be liberating, Ying'er thought. She'd heard of people who self-immolated. It was too good a feat for everyone to be able to accomplish.

How odd that death had occupied her mind recently, imbuing her with a heavy sense of doom. According to villagers, that meant that the ghost of someone wrongfully killed was following her. Ghosts like that could not be easily reborn, so they must find a substitute, a common occurrence in the village. The Daoist Master said when that happened one must intone: "Everything originates in the heart, all religious teachings are illusory; seek salvation now, do not search for a substitute." The ghost would thus be liberated. Passed down by the ancients, the incantation was said to be very effective. Could Daniu be considered a victim? she wondered. The question conjured up the scary look on his face, and the rain took on a sad, gloomy feel. Reciting the four phrases seemed only to intensify the eerie feel of her surroundings.

The camel's feet were making louder sucking sounds, and the shifting sand appeared to be building. Her legs were sore and she was dead tired, but Ying'er did not dare slow down. Lanlan reminded her to take smaller steps to increase the pace of movement. The rain did not appear to be stopping and, worse yet, they still could not see the top of the dune. Ying'er felt drained of energy as she gasped for air, swallowing rain water constantly, and yet thirst dogged her. At least she didn't feel cold anymore, and she may have been sweating. Lanlan was swaying and stumbling on shaky feet, dragging the camel down with her movement.

Things did not look good, Ying'er knew; they'd be buried in the sand if they were too exhausted to move.

Suddenly, she saw Lanlan throw down the reins and sit on the sand, looking about to act up, or "play a dead dog," in the local term, a common ruse among Liangzhou women. Liangzhou had many well-known cases of miscarried justice; some had been rectified, thanks to a woman's "playing a dead dog." When all appeals had gone unheard, gone for all time, like a clay cow flung into the ocean, the women would wrap their arms around the municipal party secretary's legs and not let go until the grievance was redressed. Was Lanlan using the tactic on the gods? Ying'er was wondering when Lanlan called out to her, Hurry, lie down. Ying'er hesitated as she saw sand rising to her ankles. Lie down, Lanlan shouted again. Now Ying'er understood and lay down. The shifting sand surged under her, so with a twist of her body she began to float atop it.

Their camel stood dumbly. Lanlan called out to it, but it seemed not to have heard her. The sand quickly submerged its feet, then its calves. "Kneel, kneel," she shouted, but the animal was too frightened to move. Ying'er saw the sand rise up to its belly.

The camel is done, she thought.

The rain continued to fall, but the Western sky was brighter. When she looked in that direction, the sheets of rain looked more like columns of misty smoke rising from the desert into the sky. Elsewhere everything was hazy, as if the rain had turned to steam. Putting the scenery out of her mind, Ying'er felt somewhat relieved. It was a wonderful sensation to be carried along by the sand, almost like swimming. Drifting sand was not so scary, she found; it was heavier than salt water and would not easily claim you. On the other hand, it would be different if they ran into a flash flood, for the sand could swallow up houses and trees.

Ying'er wiped the rain from her face and turned to check on the camel. It was looking at them helplessly. She wondered if its legs were stuck in the sand. There was nothing she could do, now it was all up to fate. But she was happy to see the sky brighten and a hint of red appear in the West.

They stopped at a relatively level spot. Ying'er sat up gingerly and found she wasn't sinking, so she stayed put. Fright had driven the cold away earlier, but now it returned; her teeth clattered and her exposed arms were covered in goosebumps, with a greenish tint, like Lanlan's face. They'd freeze if the rain continued through the night. They had a lighter to start a fire, but where would they find kindling?

This had turned out to be the most harrowing journey of her life. On their way out, she'd had something to look forward to, but the vicious jackals and punishing sun had followed them everywhere, like their shadows. Their lives were soap bubbles fluttering in the wind, under constant danger of bursting. Now they were on the way home, with no more expectations, their dreams broken, their bodies weary, covered in scars. They were trailed by wailing wind and weeping rain. Their destination was a place the mere mention of which was enough to make her knees buckle. She really had nothing to look forward to.

She sat up after her prolonged reverie. The red had disappeared from the western sky, but the rain had died down a bit and the sand had stopped moving. Lanlan had fallen asleep in a heap. Ying'er woke her up so she wouldn't catch cold. They sat blankly, wordlessly before crawling over to the camel. Its legs were buried. When Lanlan tugged at the reins, it moved to get up, but couldn't quite make it.

They shouted a few times; the camel stuck its neck out, but its legs remained immobile. It had taken nearly all their energy to fend off the chill, so they were too exhausted to do more.

"Forget it for now. We'll spend the night here and dig its legs out tomorrow," Lanlan said.

There was no place to rest. They'd have loved a fire, but could not find dry kindling, so they ate water-soaked buns and fed the camel some salt. As the camel crunched the salt, they leaned against their ride and fell asleep.

4

The chill woke Ying'er up. Wind coming off the hilltop cut like ice water; the rain had not stopped, though it had lessened. Wet clothes against their skin was hard to endure; the part of her body against the camel was warm, but the rest was chilled to the bone. Her throat hurt and she was racked by shivers. This was not a good time to catch cold, she thought, as she rubbed the pressure points on her hand between the thumb and the index finger, then her temples, and finally her knuckles. I can't get sick, I'd be a burden to Lanlan. Please, Heaven, if you want me to die, wait till I'm home. If something happens to me now, I'll wear Lanlan out. She prayed to the Vajravārāhī, despite her lack of faith in the deity.

Lanlan sneezed and woke up. She groped her way over to sit on Ying'er's lap and held her tightly. Ying'er felt bad when she realized that Lanlan was trying to block the chill for her. "Someone has to take the headwind, so it might as well be me," Lanlan said.

"We'll take turns," Ying'er replied, feeling warmer now, with Lanlan in front and the camel in back. She tightened her arms around Lanlan, like a mother holding her baby, to lend some warmth to Lanlan's back.

It was too dark to see stars. The raindrops were smaller, but denser, giving their faces no chance to dry. Ying'er was grateful for the warmth from the camel. After a while, she made Lanlan turn to lean against the camel and put her arms around her. Lanlan said no, but Ying'er insisted. This must be what people mean when they say "depending on each other for survival," Ying'er thought.

Lightning continued to crackle in the distance, accompanied by the faint sound of thunder. The camel was snorting comfortably, yet like a dying old man. They managed to keep their fronts and backs warm by switching around, but their bottoms remained icy. "I won't ask for a hot kang now. Just a bale of wheat stalks would be enough," Lanlan said. Ying'er smiled wistfully.

"I realize that you're closer to me than anyone else in my life. I feel close to my parents, but we're so different they can never understand or be with me. But you and I have looked death in the face together. You can't go on without me, and I can't live without you. We're inseparable."

"I feel the same way. You have to agree that heaven was kind by giving each us a companion we can rely on. We won't be lonely ghosts if we die. Who knows how many have died a lonely death, all alone when alive and with no one around as they died?" Ying'er said.

"Would you stop talking about death?" Lanlan protested. "You may think that body of yours is a burden, but in fact it's a great treasure. You need it to become a Buddha or to have offspring. Without it, you are nothing but a gust of wind, unable to accomplish a thing."

"But sometimes the body is corrupted, and so is the person. If you don't want to be corrupted, you must abandon the body."

"What kind of talk is that?" Lanlan sighed. "Promise me one thing, Ying'er. After what you and I have gone through, even the ruthless jackals failed to claim our lives, so we must keep on going, no matter what we run into. Don't ever think about ending your life, all right?"

Ying'er sighed, but did not reply.

"Sometimes I do think life is pointless," finally she said. "If we live a few decades more, that only means to toil like an ox for that long. In the end, we turn from sweet, lovely girls into nagging old women no one likes."

"Well, it depends on how you look at it." Lanlan said, "Life is pointless if you just muddle through. But it's different for a practitioner.

Have you heard of a Lama called Tang Dong? He was a master of the Shangba Kagyu, who spent his whole life building a bridge. Back in his time, everyone had to walk across a rope bridge to cross a particular river, and each year about a hundred fell in and drowned. Before the bridge was built, Tang Dong was a common Lama, but what he did with his bridge made him the peer of the sun and the moon in people's eyes."

"He did all that because he could," Ying'er said. "You and I are alive, but are not even the equal of a kite. I don't want to accomplish an enormous good deed. All I ever wanted was to live like a real person, with the freedom to think my own thoughts and do what I felt like doing, with something to look forward to in life. I never expected to fall among a pack of jackals, each of them wanting a piece of me. Everyone wants to drag me down into a cesspool, to stain and turn me black. If I let down my guard for a moment, my heart, not just my body, would be stained black too. You can't always do something just because you want to. When you're next to a massive millstone, if you carelessly fall into it, you will be ground into powder."

Lanlan had nothing to say in response.

They changed positions again, and Ying'er felt plunged into an ice cellar. The wind blew against her chest, without anything to block its path. She shivered, wondering when dawn would arrive. "Why don't you take my place?" Lanlan said. "I'm used to staying on the outside."

Ying'er wouldn't have it. "You're flesh and blood too, like me."

Lanlan tightened her arms around her and said, "Let's keep talking. At a time like this, if we can't stay awake, we might die in our sleep."

Ying'er thought that was a good idea, but neither of them could find anything to say. The few things they forced themselves to talk about quickly bored them.

Darkness all around, even their hearts seemed black. The rain lessened noticeably.

"Let's light the lantern," Lanlan suggested. She took off her vest and told Ying'er to use it to block the rain, concerned that the heated shade might explode if it came in contact with the rain. She groped around to find the lantern and then the lighter. The gas-filled lighter was wonderful—it lit with a single flick to light up the darkness. But lighting the lantern required a great deal of effort, since the lighter was too big to reach the wick. Ying'er rolled up some camel hair and dipped it into the kerosene; finally, the lantern was lit.

It was fantastic to see all the light. Ying'er felt warm right away. She laid down the vest and leaned forward to shelter the lantern from the rain with her body. The kerosene had a penetrating smell, but it did not dampen her spirits. Besides bringing light, she discovered, a lantern was a good heating device. When she laid her hands on the metal grill of the glass shade, she felt a warm current come alive to worm into her palms then into her heart through her arms. Lanlan, come warm yourself, she called out.

The lantern was fantastic. Its heat was limited, but it was heat. They bent forward to shelter it and warm themselves. Then they realized that their hands were warm, but they were shivering now that they weren't leaning against the camel. By accident Ying'er noticed that when a raindrop fell on the shade, it wetted the spot briefly before evaporating.

"It's okay," she said to Lanlan. "The shade isn't too hot, it won't explode."

Lanlan could not bring herself to remove her hands after testing the shade. Now they could both comfortably lean against the camel, with Ying'er's hands on the metal grill and Lanlan's the shade. It was a taste of Heaven.

Lanlan adjusted the flame, depending upon the amount of heat their hands could take. When the shade lost heat, she turned up the flame, and when it was too hot, she turned it down. They were happy to have the limited heat the lantern gave off.

It was getting light out. They ate more squishy buns with pickled scallions. Then they tried to dislodge the camel. The wet sand still had too much pull for it to free its legs on its own. "If we don't do this, it'll die of thirst or hunger," Lanlan said. The shifting sand wasn't such a menace, after all, only if one's legs are stuck in it under the baking rays of the sun.

They started digging, scooping out wet sand that held the camel's legs. A few shouts and the camel managed to escape the trap. It cried out happily the moment it was free. Ying'er saw that most of the salt on its back had melted in the rain and that the sacks were flat. That did not bother her. So many things mattered so little to her now that she'd flirted with death, the wind and the rain. She could not tell if the feeling came from her weary heart or if it was part of the aging process. But it made no difference. She felt nothing, even earth-shattering events lost their significance. It was better this way. So often the mind is tormented because it cannot change a thing around it. Better that it should feel nothing.

Afterward, Lanlan said, the lantern had saved them from dying in their sleep on that cold, wet night.

Chapter Thirty-Three

The pain of longing punctures the liver
No way to ease the ache, a needle finds no resting place

1

Yue'er walked out the door and headed toward the Dasha River. There were many sand boys at White Tiger Pass, and she was sure they all knew about the village girl with syphilis, might even point fingers at her. But she didn't care. She was going to wait for Mengzi, who would be coming on this day. He came home every other day, bringing medicine and news from the city, as well as the blissful happiness she pined for.

She was increasingly attached to Mengzi. To be fair, she had only been fond of him at first. He was a rare gem, compared with the feckless men in the city, but she had not been in love with him. It came as a surprise that her feelings for him grew rapidly after they got married; maybe her guilt worked as the catalyst or maybe they had developed a deep emotional bond. Since she had been sick, she learned that she had come to care little about things that had once mattered a great deal to her, and Mengzi, who was by her side at her loneliest moment, was now her sole source of comfort. When the pain made her gasp, the muscles on

Mengzi's face twitched until his forehead was bathed in sweat. She was immensely touched by the sight.

The good health she'd longed for took second place in her mind; she yearned most to see him. She suffered through every minute, waiting for him, and an hour went by like a year. It was dull and depressing at home. They had few visitors; likely afraid of coming into contact with her "diseased fluids," they were scared just talking about it. Their house reeked of dung, because it had been a long time since they'd taken the kang apart to clean it out, though it served as an excuse to go outside. She smoked her afflicted parts several times, with encouraging results, for some spots were scabbing. Except for going into the city once a week for Old Mister Liang to puncture her back, she did nothing but smoke herself and swallow handfuls of pills. At least it seemed the attack from the Disease Demon had been halted and the fire of hope was burning ever brightly.

As usual, people avoided her when she was out, mostly women, who looked at her with intense loathing. They were afraid the "slut" would seduce their husbands and pass the disease on to them. She found them amusing. She ran into men too. Those from her clan kept a wide berth, obviously unhappy that she had disgraced their name. That was understandable; when the men quarreled with others from a different clan, they were deflated as soon as the other said "bayberry sores." But men from other clans, instead of avoiding her, actually walked up and examined her face carefully, either to detect wantonness in her face or to discover signs of sores. Yue'er never flinched; gallantly she let them look, and when necessary she would even nod and smile politely. She'd been scared to death that the villagers might find out; now that they knew, there was really nothing to fear.

What she did fear was losing Mengzi, who had become a kind of religion to her. She'd had so many things to look forward to, but one by one they vanished, until only love was left. If not for the threat of death, she might never have felt her love so strongly. With the Angel of Death lurking, her love raged like surging waves; the tide of love often swept away her fear of death, sometimes even drowned the Angel of Death. It was true, her desire to see Mengzi overwhelmed the pain of her illness.

She got up early on the days Mengzi was due back at the village. She made herself up nicely and went to wait for him at the corner he had to walk by, leaned against a desert date tree at the spot, and gazed to the far end of the path. She often fantasized that he was chugging up on that lovely, beat-up old motor scooter. It would become reality after a thousand fantasies. Her heart raced when he appeared, and a tidal wave of happiness swept her away. She ran up to meet the approaching spot of color. She ran and ran, and then jumped up to hug and kiss him. Sometimes she inadvertently pushed him over with the scooter. They would giggle and roll around in the dirt, getting up only when they saw gasoline spill out from the dislodged cap of the tank. They'd pick up the scooter and rock their way back to the village, her hands wrapped tightly around his waist.

That was her greatest moment of happiness. By then it was usually just before dusk, when the sun was hanging on the tip of the sand hills. Cooking smoke rose everywhere in the village, and at White Tiger Pass. On windless days, the smoke would not disperse, but would rise higher and higher until it drifted down on the village and the path. That gave her the feeling that she was part of a fairy tale. The motor scooter made a soft, sputtering noise, like a gentle tongue licking at her heart. Sometimes a flock of homecoming sheep would dawdle and linger by their scooter. Mengzi had to shout and honk. The sheep then turned their foolish faces to stare at her, eyes brimming with envy, oblivious to the wheels that were coming at them. It was such a comical sight to Yue'er, who usually made a face at them and "baa-baa-ed." She did such a great imitation that they would call back, "baa-baa," making Mengzi laugh.

"You must have been a sheep in your previous life," he often said.

She would savor the scene after he left for the city, and each recollection brought a rosy glow and an enchanted smile to her face.

The sand boys would whoop every time she walked by White Tiger Pass by herself. Drawing their voice out, they hollered, Ow—Ow, but instead of malice, they meant only affection. When Mengzi walked her home, they didn't shout; they turned to watch them silently, highlighting the roar of the monotonous hoists.

The wait seemed endless, the only flaw in an otherwise perfect day. She appeared at the spot just as the sun poked its head out, though Mengzi would not return to the village until it was about to set. She took steamed buns, water, and her medication with her. "Why go so early?" her mother sometimes asked before she left, but she did not bother to explain. She just couldn't stay in the house. When she was out by the path, she had something to look forward to. Her heart fluttered whenever a black dot emerged from the far end, and she craned her neck to see. If the dot, which was Mengzi at first, turned into someone else, a man or a woman, that didn't bother her. She just swallowed dryly and kept her eyes on the path.

The sun had a halo on one windy day, so her mother told her to stay in, saying there would be a desert storm and that he probably would not come home. Yue'er wouldn't listen; she wrapped a scarf around her head and went out. A storm did rise by noontime, a sandstorm whipping up waves of desert sand to swirl and lash at her. Soon the wind would not let her lean against the date tree, so she crouched down and covered her nose and mouth with the scarf, leaving a slit for her eyes, so she could watch the path, which disappeared when the wind blew; everything between heaven and earth was a blur, nothing but wind and sand. Even the sun was gone. "Stay back. The wind's too strong; don't come home," she mumbled, though deep down she hoped he'd be back. She was worried it was too dangerous on the motor scooter in the strong wind, and yet she wanted to see him. One minute she hoped he'd come, the next she'd hope he wouldn't, back and forth, on and on, until she was oblivious to the wind swirling around her.

Some villagers were coming home from the city. They knew it was Yue'er when they spotted a red dot in the wind. Since she'd begun coming to wait for Mengzi, criticism of her had begun to die down; tender-hearted villagers would even tell her to go home when they saw her waiting faithfully. "He'll see you at the house." But she kept her watch.

The sky disappeared when the wind reached the zenith of its power, as sand blanketed the sky like a curtain; the path vanished. The descending curtain created the image of hell she'd heard in stories. She'd been born near the desert, but did not know the wind could be so powerful. She'd always been inside when a wind blew in the past, so to her a wind storm was just sound, that of sand splashing against windows, the wind whipping past treetops, a howling that could be shua-shua, ou-ou, or some other eerie, scary racket. At this moment, all the sounds mingled into an uproar. Her face stung when sand found its way through the scarf.

The path, obscured by the sandstorm, had all but disappeared, like the tiny orb of light hanging in the western sky, dim and hazy, but with a powerful message. The wind raked across bunchgrass, obviously intending to uproot it, but the grass followed the will of the wind, its roots holding tenaciously. Yue'er peered at the grass over the edge of the scarf and the sight moved her. That's it, I should live like the bunchgrass.

Black dots were heading her way. A jolt of happy surprise spread through her. It has to be him this time, she thought. Despite repeated disappointments, she was full of hope; and everyone coming into view was Mengzi to her. It was better this way; the wind brought her hope.

The dots were getting closer; there were two of them, a man pushing a bicycle and a woman helping from behind. There was also a baby on the bike. Their clothes puffed up in the wind, and the bike reeled each time the wind billowed, but they managed to stay on the path. When they were close enough for her to see they were from her village, Yue'er shouted:

"Auntie, have you seen Mengzi?" Her words were barely out when the wind blew them away. She repeated herself several times before they heard her.

"No. Not even a ghost on the path. Go home. He won't come in this weather."

Dejection stole into her heart, but Yue'er perked up. "It's good he's not coming. Riding a scooter on a day like this could be dangerous."

They walked off, and Yue'er crouched back down against the date tree. The wind caused the tree to bump against her back again and again, and she swayed along with it, but feeling a sense of warmth. At the moment this was the only living creature that showed affection. The power of the swaying tree trunk was strong, but pliably tender, as if to say, "Go home. Go home. The wind is too strong for you to stay." A warm current spread through her nose and tears blurred her eyes.

She did not want to go home just yet. In recent days, her home, bereft of familial warmth, was depressing. The path, however, was filled with loving care, for only it could bring her happiness and fulfill her longing. The wind continued to toss sand around her and frequently obscured her view of the path, but the figure she yearned to see might appear. And so she waited. Whether he would show or not seemed to become secondary; what warmed her heart was the process of waiting.

The sun slowly edged down the sand trough and the wind died down; the sand meekly stayed where it was. You might not come. The wind is too strong. I won't fault you if you don't. Yet she kept her eyes trained at the end of the path. Finally a tiny dot appeared in her sore eyes. It grew bigger and bigger until she could see it was a familiar one. Surprised, she ran up joyfully.

It was Mengzi.

Happy tears flowed freely when she ran into his arms. He held her tightly, his tears mingling with hers to wash his dusty face. They both knew that they could not live without the other.

The sand boys cheered loudly when Mengzi came back with Yue'er, as if they too had been waiting all day. She closed her eyes and pressed her face against his back, crying happily.

2

She could not say when, but one day she realized that her condition had worsened. The scabs began to fester again and pain came in non-ending waves. Ulcerating abscesses appeared on her legs; neither the medication from the hospital nor the remedy from Old Mister Liang had any effect, and even the cow dung failed to work. A great pall loomed over her heart.

Her mother found another home remedy: she was to sit in a basin of distilled liquor. Contact with the alcohol brought terrible pain that spread through her body along nerve paths. But she gritted her teeth and remained seated, sweating from the pain. She said through clenched teeth, "I'm going to drown you." She thought she could see the Disease Demon crying out for help in the liquid, and she grinned with satisfaction.

But the sitz-bath wasn't as effective as the smoking cow dung. After putting up with torturous agony, she had yet to see any healing. The alcohol only killed off the virus on the surface, while more were in her blood. She knew that.

Her father was worried now. He scraped together enough money to send her to a hospital in Lanzhou, where various medicines were dripped into her vein, all but the antibiotics that caused allergic reactions. They saw no improvement. She could see clearly now that the Angel of Death was smiling smugly.

Her world was overcast when "death" began to plague her mind. All colors disappeared, leaving a ghostly whiteness like a shroud. Death had always felt distant to her, associated only with other people, but now it edged closer, with bared fangs. Yue'er felt gripped by a helpless panic and terror. Her mind went blank for a long time, a void except for a dismal emptiness, like an invisible shield separating her from the rest of the world. The world was out there, and she was inside, where everything else was far away, all but helplessness, fear, and an unsettling sense of bleakness. She often found herself in a nightmarish state, a dream, despite the assault of pain. If only it was a dream, she thought, the doubt removing her from the dreamy state; she felt a stabbing pain from the notion of death.

Was she really dying? She couldn't stop asking herself. Her life had barely begun, and she was already dying. She had yet to enjoy a full life; when she thought back, she realized that she had only lived a few brief instants, and everything else was a blur. Her life experience wasn't all that different from the path obscured by a desert sand storm, so ill-defined it might not have existed. Those brief instants, on the other hand, were quite clear: her aspiration as a school girl, learning to sing the tunes with Ying'er, kissing Mengzi wrapped in his arms . . . more or less only these images. Was that the total worth of her twenty-some years in the world?

Abstruse questions took over her mind. She'd always found the mention of death dispiriting, but now it pressed down on her, and she had to face it. What happens after death? What happens to the person called Yue'er when the body is gone? And so on. She had no answers. Sometimes she would ask her father, but he did his best to avoid the topic. Yue'er knew he didn't want her to feel bad. Luckily, these were fleeting questions skimming the surface of her mind, and they were quickly drowned out by wretched despair.

The Disease Demon was merciful enough to limit its ravaging effects to parts of her body that could be covered by clothes. No damage was detectable on her face, which, she could see in the mirror, was still pretty. The sight brightened and saddened her at the same time; a beautiful face like that would be gone in the end.

She wanted so much to live. When she thought about that, she realized that she'd lived only a matter of days. As a child she knew nothing, later her mind was occupied with school work. She had truly lived for herself only after she'd turned eighteen. Take away the sleeping hours, the time spent on making a living, and scenes that weren't worth recalling, and she had very limited life experience. What truly mattered to her were the days she'd spent with Mengzi. She really hadn't lived her life well. If she were to die like this, it was as if she hadn't lived at all.

Her face was often tear-streaked.

Sometimes she wished she'd fallen in love with Mengzi earlier; they could have started shortly after middle school, when she still had a clean, healthy body. If they'd had been in love back then, they could kiss and hug and even make love—her heart ached at the term—what a great pleasure that would have been. If they had, she might have . . . not might have, but definitely would have been free of the disease. What had happened over those days that she could not bring herself to recall had been caused more by her own emptiness than by the trick the man had played on her. There had been something to look forward to, but it was so far away it felt like soap bubbles drifting in a dream; they popped whenever she managed to catch one. Each pop brought disappointment, and after too many disappointments, a void developed in her heart; she wanted an outlet for the emptiness, prodded by an urge to sink into degeneration. Even if the man hadn't seduced her, she'd have fallen for some other man. She felt so empty inside she would not have been able to resist temptation. If she and Mengzi had started earlier, it would have been different. She was racked by remorse, though she knew that belated regrets would not help matters. But regret took the place of thoughts of death and drove out everything else; her pain and despair were swept away by remorse.

Did that mean she could only blame her fate? When she was younger, several fortunetellers had given her similar predictions of a good life, so exceptionally good, in fact, that she could marry an emperor. These predictions gave rise to many fantasies; she waited for a prince to appear, which was why she'd passed up Mengzi before. Then she left home to search, but failed to find the one, and instead found "syphilis." She could not understand why, with her kind of great fortune, predicted by several brilliant fortunetellers, she would end up like this. Had she ruined her own good fortune or was it caused by intervention from a mighty external force? She did not know, and no one could tell her.

She recalled Lanlan's mantra that your heart determines your fate. Lanlan had said that a compassionate heart brought a good life, and an evil mind led to a terrible fate, supporting her claim with examples that seemed to made sense at first. The theory collapsed when Yue'er applied the idea to her own life. She considered herself a big-hearted person who never held ill will toward anyone—though surely, she hadn't done her best to help all forms of life, as advocated by Lanlan. She had never once done anything evil, so why such a terrible fate? Something must have interfered with her life, Yue'er thought. She tried to figure out what that was, only to find her mind enmeshed in a jumble of thoughts.

What remained clear was her desire to live, a powerful thought like giant waves in a surging sea, especially when she thought of Mengzi. Kept busy with work at the forestry bureau, he could not come to be with her in Lanzhou, and she found it tough going after a few days. In the beginning, her desire to live remained strong, but slowly her longing for him reared its head and took over. At moments when her need to see him was unbearable, she had to suppress the urge to rip out the IV needle, and jump onto a bus to Liangzhou, where she could wrap her arms around him and bite his clothes—she no longer dared kiss him on the lips, for the doctor in Lanzhou said even saliva was contagious. She'd called him and told him to get a penicillin shot—at least they could hold hands and look at each other through teary eyes, which was a hundred times better than staying in a hospital room that was paler than a shroud. Sometimes, when the tidal waves of her longing for him managed to overwhelm her fear of death, she wanted to persuade her father to let her check out as soon as possible.

After large sums of money had been spent and large vials of medicine had been injected into her body, antibiotics that did not provoke allergic reactions could no longer defeat the raging virus. Worse yet, her liver, kidneys, and heart were threatened, something the doctor had told her father secretly and made him dry tears behind her back. But she sensed that something was wrong. A black festering spot on her leg gave off a horrible stench; the Angel of Death poked its head from the spot and made faces at her. To her the Angel of Death was a gossipy old mother hen whose beak peeked out from a wrapped scarf. It was that beak that had pecked her leg open. Sometimes, when she was in a daze, she would stare at it; she had tried hard to stay alert, but seemed to be losing her focus more and more frequently for longer periods. She knew that the net of death had been cast in her direction, like a hawk caught under a net with no chance to escape, no matter how frantically it beats its wings.

She could almost see the jaws closing in on her, a scene she'd often seen in fantasy movies. In her delusional state, she was always on the run, but her frail legs could not shake off a specter that was as long as a dark night. She dreamed a lot, but her dream was no different from her hallucination, in which she was on the run, chased by a shapeless monster that was getting ever closer. The shadow flowed up like water from behind and clamped its teeth on her shadow to slowly drag her into its mouth. At moments like this, she would cry out, "Help me, Mengzi!" Like reciting a magical incantation, she could be startled awake when she shouted his name. Then an intoxicating longing would sneak in and grab hold of her.

She counted each day of suffering; she heard seconds ticking away at a snail-like speed, the tick-tock creating a dull feeling in her heart. Pain slowed the passage of time unbearably, like a dark night that would not see light, with no shred of hope. When she was back home, she had been at least able to walk down the path to wait for the black dot emerging at the end, and she had that to look forward to, whether it was Mengzi or someone else. Now, besides pain, the shadow of death, and her father's worry-laden, sad face, she saw nothing to brighten her mood.

She knew she would soon be dead.

Oddly though, her fear of death was losing its sharp edge. She believed in the existence of the soul after death, and was afraid only of the loneliness she'd encounter. Sometimes at moments of selfish weakness, she wanted Mengzi to die with her. How wonderful it would be to die with the one she loved! When her pain abated, she would continue on the same train of thought. She liked to begin her fantasy from the time before they were married; the most beautiful shots were of them in each other's arms, kissing, and making love, followed by a scene of them lying side by side on a large, clean white bed. They were both infected, but neither felt despondent; instead they got more active—the most frequent images she had were naturally all about sex—and then they died one day, together. Their death occurred in the form of two alluring figures floating out of bodies that retained their beauty and fluttered in a butterfly dance. They would travel to scenic spots around the world, where they'd find flowers, grass, and clear, flowing water. Those were her only images. At such moments, she regretted not making love with Mengzi, but that was only a fleeting thought, because pain soon reminded her how ridiculous the idea was. She could never bring herself to make him suffer too.

Beyond a dread of loneliness, her greatest fear was that Mengzi would marry someone else. For her that was worse than death. She found herself suffocating whenever she imagined a wedding in which, instead of her, another woman took center stage—oddly the woman had Ying'er's face. Only at a time like this would she keenly feel the terror of death. What truly frightened her about death was taking Mengzi from her and giving him to a different woman. And she—if there was indeed a soul— could only weep helplessly; she could even conjure up the image of her soul, only a shadow now, crying. Like a motherless child, she would crouch by the bed in their bridal chamber and watch them lose themselves in their titillating act. She absolutely did not want to see that, but the scene stuck and played out in her head. She felt an enormous hand grip her throat so tightly she couldn't breathe; in a way, that wasn't all that bad, for it helped diffuse her bodily suffering. I don't want to die, she moaned.

The imagined future would often give rise to resentment toward Mengzi, even if she knew it was irrational; she couldn't talk herself out of it. In fact, she even found reasons to convince herself that she was justified to resent him. She knew well that he could not come to Lanzhou to be with her, since he was busy with work at the forestry bureau. Yet she skewed the fact and claimed he was avoiding her, planning to abandon her. She even blamed him for his mother's idea for their divorce. To prove her point, she found cases from her village where the man had someone new when his wife was barely in the ground. When she thought about this, she would despair, plagued by the idea that she'd lost the one she could count on. Everything appeared to be a sham, and nothing meant anything anymore. Love would vanish along with her perished body, so would the tunes she'd learned, as well as money, houses, parents, sibling, her youth and beauty. Everything was meaningless. She realized that all of life was part of a colossal scam, which was finally exposed as death approached.

It's a sham, all of it. She moaned.

A pair of teardrops slid out of her eyes and she choked up. Her father came up to ask how she felt, but she turned away, in no mood to say anything or see anyone. A despondent pall shrouded her heart.

Now everything is showing its true colors, she said to herself.

Chapter Thirty-Four

A black crow perches atop a chimney
A loud crash wakes one up from a dream

1

For helping out at the forestry bureau at rate of twenty-five yuan a day, Mengzi drew his pay once a month. On this day he got his monthly pay and sent the money to Yue'er's cash card. He wanted to send more, but had little luck borrowing any after asking around. Maybe I should be thick-skinned enough to ask Shuangfu's wife, he said to himself. He had to yet to pay back what he'd borrowed earlier, which made him somewhat sheepish, but for Yue'er he wouldn't mind if she gave him a humiliating tongue-lashing. There's nothing more important than medical help, he told himself. Maybe she'd be big-hearted enough to help out.

He was stunned when he returned home and heard about Shuangfu's troubles.

No one had expected him, if all people, to be in trouble, but it had happened. It was beyond human control; when trouble comes, no one can stop it.

Ordinarily, he should have been fine; though he had plenty of opportunities, trouble had never found him. Not a big deal, and yet it eventually got him. "It was a shitty little thing that got that ass. He's had his taste of the loose ones, the coquettish ones, the old and the young. And in the end, he got his hands on a student," Beizhu said. "He was working on a school building and got involved with a girl there. If he hadn't been found out, it would just have been a romantic flirtation, but now that it was out, the girl accused him of rape. I heard her homeroom teacher brokered a deal, but then kept the money, so the girl raised a stink, and the incident blew up in Shuangfu's face. He's not going to get out of this easily.

"It worked." He winked at Mengzi, who recalled what they'd done at the man's ancestral gravesite. Thrown into a minor panic, Mengzi looked around and felt better when he saw that no one was the wiser. "Why did I do something so shameless?" he rued.

"The workers at the site said she was very pretty, with fair skin and red lips, eyes that could talk, brows like willow leaves, and skin so tender it oozed water when you pinched it. That ass really knew what to pick. But now, hei . . ."

Mengzi was disgusted by his tone, what Liangzhou residents called "watching and laughing": watching others in trouble and laughing at them. Strange, however, how he'd been disgusted then by how Shuangfu had swaggered after striking it rich and was disgusted now by the "watching and laughing" of others when Shuangfu was in trouble. Mengzi couldn't explain himself, so he snapped, "What are you so happy about? He's in trouble, but that doesn't mean you're going to get his money."

"But it makes me feel great." Beizhu smiled. "Now Shuangfu's wife will be a rich widow. She went to the city to take care of things. She just got back, and I have no idea what she's done."

No wonder the 'iron general' was guarding the gate each time I went to her house. So Shuangfu is in big trouble, Mengzi said to himself. A serious matter like this, and she decided not to tell me, like I'm a stranger. The slight upset him.

He'd stopped going to Shuangfu's house after learning about Yue'er's illness. He didn't trust himself not to let her down.

"I knew something was up." Beizhu continued, "That day when the police came, they put on an act to cover it up. But can paper contain fire? A wind can go through even the thickest wall. Ai, if you know how to behave, you'll never get rich. The rich are never righteous and the righteous will never be rich. A car came for his wife at night, and I knew something was up. Sure enough, hei. Working the field is still the most solid option. Look at Shuangfu, an earthen mound on a piece of flat land, and he swaggered around when everything was going his way. If something bad happens, he crumples." Beizhu looked at Huilanzi, who was singing and mumbling something unintelligible nearby, and whispered, "Big Head's in trouble too. Who knows, one day everything could come out, and that mad woman will be another rich widow."

Unable to stand any more of his friend's talk, Mengzi frowned and headed to Shuangfu's house, trailed by Beizhu's snickering.

It was an annoying sound. Mengzi felt like slugging him. How odd. He'd hated Shuangfu so much not long ago that he wanted the man to suffer a serious setback. But now that he actually was in trouble, Mengzi could not bring himself to gloat. Could it really have something to do with what they'd done to the grave? He didn't think so, after giving the matter some consideration. Shuangfu had a long history of being a lecher, even before he and Beizhu dug up the grave. He was already well known for his sexual escapades with young women. Everyone knew he was always looking for pretty women to satisfy his needs. That meant he'd get into trouble sooner or later. On second thought, Shuangfu was not the only man engaged in that kind of behavior, so why was he in trouble, and not someone else? Maybe the grave desecration had ruined his good fortune. Who knows? When luck is with you, a major incident is nothing, but when you're on the losing end, a trivial matter can do you in. Mengzi turned the matter over and over, only to get even more confused.

No matter how hard he tried to absolve himself, he couldn't shake the suspicion that Shuangfu's trouble was connected to the grave incident, which bothered him a great deal. At that moment, Shuangfu took on the appearance of a man worthy of respect in Mengzi's mind. It was true, Mengzi thought. Shuangfu had been starving when he stole some corn, but the village had waged a harsh struggle session against him and given him a bloody head. He could not survive there, so he'd fled the village and turned everything around to become a prominent entrepreneur. Mengzi had heard the story from his mother many times; Shuangfu was brought up as a model. Later, Shuangfu's money and influence had made Mengzi feel inferior, which led to his agreement to dig up the man's ancestral grave, in hopes of turning his luck around. Mengzi hadn't expected Shuangfu's luck to actually run aground. Now instead of being vindicated, he felt even lower. He couldn't understand what was going on in his head and why it was rebelling.

Mengzi never truly believed in the kind of fengshui that his elders talked about; it all depended on how he felt at the moment. He had been dubious when he defiled the grave, but now he was more inclined to believe, and that made him feel bad. He was reminded of all the positives: Shuangfu was generous with aid to the needy, capable and accomplished, he built schools, made donations, and so on. The man's action scrolled through Mengzi's mind and made him feel terrible. Strange. He hadn't been like this before. He'd been the type to enjoy his drink when there was some and so what if he had to drink water the next day. His mother had called him a "blockhead" and his father said there was a basin of chaff sitting on his shoulders. Had he actually grown a brain, as his parents had hoped? Yet now that he was thinking, there was so much to annoy him, to make him feel terrible, to make life hard. He wished he could go back to the past. But once a mind is open, it is all but impossible to close it again. One thing led to another, and now his head was full of stuff, a jumbled mess of stuff he couldn't straighten out matter how hard he tried.

Mengzi walked to Shuangfu's house, with the intention of consoling his wife and feeling an urge to help. Unfortunately, He knew no important people; the only one who seemed important enough was the party secretary in town, who, to his dismay, had often confused him with Baigou. Yet his impulse to save Shuangfu was like a rising tide. He had no idea what to do and yet he was ready to offer ideas to Shuangfu's wife.

When he got there, he was surprised to see the building dull and dreary, its imposing grandeur gone. He walked into the yard, without sensing the height of the arch over the entryway. Some women in the yard were consoling Xiuxiu with pointless, empty words they all knew were phony. The speakers were weary, and so was the listener. They found an excuse to take their leave when he walked in.

The house went quiet.

The woman tossed a pack of cigarettes at him. Never a heavy smoker, he did not have to smoke all the time, but he took one anyway. He lit it and looked at her. She seemed unchanged, calm as usual, showing no sign of sorrow nor gloating expression. What is she thinking? He recalled she'd said once, "No one can avoid a line drawn by Heaven. The higher you rise the harder you fall."

"You were right. He's really come down hard this time."

She looked up and glanced at him. "I never wished that on anyone. That no-good man brought it on himself. There are repercussions for everything you do, you know. When the snow melts, the bodies are exposed. But don't you start watching and laughing. He's down, but still a man, so much better than those worthless shits."

"I agree." Mengzi smiled sheepishly. He suspected the last phrase was meant for him, and felt awkward when he thought about the grave again. He'd felt a sense of righteousness, somehow manly, but now that the feeling was gone, he could not speak with confidence. Ai, why did I do that? Mengzi was racked with remorse.

"You must be wondering why I look the same." A faint smile appeared on her face. "Tell me, how should I look? Should I gloat over his downfall? I haven't sunk that low. Wailing and complaining about the injustice? I don't feel that kind of affection for him. But I'm still his wife in the eyes of the law. After what's happened, that no-good man finally realized that none of his flings were reliable; they were the ones who exposed him, took advantage of his misfortune. I may be old and ugly, but I'm not the type to hit someone when he's down."

"Where is he now?"

"In custody."

"Is it serious?"

"If he gets to keep his puny life, I'll burn a ton of the best incense for him."

Mengzi was shaken. He wondered what to say when she continued, "Now he's finally learned who's good and who's not. He won't die in the dark, even if he takes a bullet, unlike some people who never see the light when alive and die an ignorant ghost."

"What happened?"

"The same old problem. When you pull up a turnip, dirt comes out with it. Put those aside, just this thing with the student is enough to seal his doom. She swore he raped her. Something like this could be no big deal, but it could also be big enough to summon an executioner."

"What about all his business dealings?"

"I'm supposed to take care of them. At least some of his people are reliable. I thought that in his eyes I was a ghost, but at least I'm still legally recognized as his wife." She laughed grimly. "You know, everything in the world is like a stage play. A man is a good guy one moment and bad the next, hot-tempered now and scheming later. People who are desperate to be rich fail to see a cent, while those who don't care for it have gold bars drop into their laps. Heaven is a real magician." She laughed again, but slowly she began to sob.

She was virtually wailing, and Mengzi was unnerved. What kind of ugly things will people say if they hear? He got up to close the door and windows.

After a while, she dried her tears and composed her face. "I've been pent up for so long. Now, finally I can have a good cry. Over the past few days, I've been wondering what it is a woman wants in life. When she has an honest and reliable husband by her side, she thinks he's worthless. She wants him to make a name for himself, to be a big shot, but she'll lose him if he becomes one. That no-good husband of mine said if given a choice to start over, he'd be happy to be a peasant, he wouldn't fight for anything or with anyone, he would have no ambition but to live a simple life and quietly work on a few acres of land and raise our child together. He even apologized to me, saying he'd hurt me and that I've done nothing wrong. Finally, he saw the light. If I could start over, I wouldn't let him go for anything big, looking for business opportunities, or an official position. I'd want him to be a good husband and a decent father." She teared up again.

Finally, Mengzi realized that Shuangfu was the one she held in her heart. He had to admit that he was a remarkable man, more astute and determined than many, so, naturally, he had a more serious woman problem than others. On the other hand, which man wouldn't if he could? Wasn't fooling around with women an important benefit of being an emperor? Who knows, maybe he'll be okay if some money changes hands.

"The problem is, everyone knows about it now. It would have been easier to deal with if it had been covered up. The main player won't relent. An official can talk in such a way that he could bite a nail in two. What we fear most is public anger. I've been smooth-talking the peasants who sold their grain and the workers who put up their money, so I came up with tens of millions and paid them back their investment. But when the public is angered, the officials can't help him if they want to."

"Was it really rape?"

"That's what everyone says now, but who knows. I heard the homeroom teacher talked her into it, but then refused to hand over her share, so she raised a fuss. It's disgusting, don't you think? I said to him, Shuangfu, you're such an animal. There are women all over the place, so why must you get involved with a student? If you're really that good, you should have tried to make her fall in love with you. Then, if anything happened, you could say it was just an affair. Now the girl is mad at him too; she's permanently tainted, since everyone knows about it. What could she say if not rape? I heard that many of the students want to transfer to another school, and the parents are complaining loudly. The homeroom teacher has been arrested. To be honest, that man is an animal too. They were drinking and he mentioned it in jest, but the teacher took it seriously and brokered the deal. He loves money like his life, no wonder it all blew up like this."

Mengzi was thinking about the grave again. The Daoist Master had said one is "driven" into something like this; the ghosts or spirits drive you to do things you might not want to do. And the "drive" usually changes someone's fate. If the ancestral grave is in good condition, your ancestors will harvest all the magical essences between heaven and earth and can protect you. With ancestral protection, the ghosts and spirits who try to "drive" you into doing something bad will not be able to get near you. But if the grave is ruined, the essences disperse. Humans need energy and ghosts need these essences; your ancestors will lose the ability to protect without them. Moreover, the chaff or red millet and the blood of a black dog are potent amulets that work like magic where you put them. With the amulets on his ancestral graves, Shuangfu's ancestors could not protect him, and it would have been a wonder if nothing happened to him.

"A dog never stops eating shit," she was saying. "I've heard this wasn't his first time. He's always had his eyes on pretty girls when he's working on a school construction."

Mengzi found he could breathe more easily after what she'd said. He was relieved. A thief isn't caught just because he hasn't stolen often enough. Shuangfu, you were bored with bold, loose women and wanted to try young ones, sink your teeth into tender new gourds. You did it once and nothing happened, so you were emboldened to do it again and again. There came a time something would happen, and once it did, your little life was no longer in your hands. It was indeed as your wife said, "You dug your own grave."

"Men are all like that. Some have the desire, but lack the nerve. Some have the desire and the nerve, but lack the opportunity. Some lechers are too timid and don't want to spend the money. Every man has the desire. You can't say you understand men until you see that."

She's right, Mengzi thought. But it's not worth sacrificing your life. "You need to save him. Money comes and goes, but not a human life," he said to her.

"I tried, of course." She sighed. "I've run around so much my tendons are about to snap in two. In this day and age, everyone is a blood-sucking lizard. They can have my blood if they want it. Water comes from the river and returns to it. I've done my best, so whatever happens is what's going to be." She was sobbing.

The woman had sounded so determined a few days earlier, when she talked about waiting for the line drawn by Heaven. Now the line was drawn and everything changed and she was feeling sorry for him. Is this what women are like? Mengzi wondered.

Only when she was sobbing did she show her feminine side. Usually she was more masculine than he was. He touched her shoulder and said, "Keep doing what you can. Money can make a spirit turn a millstone. Besides, Shuangfu is quite a man."

She threw herself into his arms and wailed, pouring out years of pent up bitterness with her flowing tears.

2

She had just dried her tears after a good cry when the principal of Shawan Elementary School and some of his teachers came to see her.

Shuangfu had just given the school two hundred thousand yuan to set up a scholarship under his name; it was meant to aid poor village children who could not afford school. The school had delivered a plaque to his house, accompanied by banging gongs and beating drums. The school still had the money, but now they could not keep his name attached to the scholarship; it would be shameful and humiliating to name a scholarship after a rapist. They'd use the village name. The principle said the town had weighed in on it.

"Call it anything you want. You decide. I don't care what it's called as long as the children benefit from the money."

The principle prattled on.

"Fine with me." She was indifferent. "Do what you want. Change it. I don't care."

After more clarification, the principal left with his teachers.

The house fell silent again. The smell of cigarettes was so strong she opened a window, sprinkled water on the floor and gave it a sweep, and then burned some incense. She sat, lost in thought for a while before saying, "See how things work these days? A while ago they felt so honored to have something to do with his name. And now they can't run fast enough. It's the same money, but the name is different. Tell me, which is more important, money or name?"

"We really ought to think of something," Mengzi said.

"I've gone everywhere, so have the people helping me. I'm happy you're thinking about me. Everybody else can't run away from me fast enough. Never fast enough."

Tears fell from Mengzi's eyes as he said impulsively, "I'm a beast. You don't know it, but the grave, it was me."

She squinted at him. "When I heard what happened, I knew it had to be you. When someone is doomed, grave digging won't do him in, and if he's going to be fine, you can dig all you want and he'll still be fine. I've heard that people who practice qigong can get into trouble if their bodies are overburdened with pure qi. It's the same with money. When you're on a higher plane of existence, you remain true to yourself no matter how great your wealth, but if you're not, you lose your head over money. It's like giving a bowl of liquor to someone with the capacity of one cup. Of course, he'll get drunk." She continued, "A thief doesn't get caught just because he hasn't stolen often enough. If the mind can't change, problems persist, and when that happens, sooner or later he'll be in trouble. When you think about it, it all seems to have been predestined. Only when the mind is changed can the destiny be different."

"It's like fate."

"Fate? What is that? Fate is in the heart. A kind of heart breeds a kind of fate. When your heart is impoverished, you're fated to be poor. When you're narrow-minded, you live a narrow sort of life. If you have the heart of a hawk, you live like a hawk and if you have the heart of a rabbit, you live like a rabbit. A terrible man has the ability to start a business, but hasn't the mind to keep it going. When a mound of sand rises up on level land, a gust of wind will level it. I've spent whatever money I've needed to spend. That money was the fruit of thousands of workers' labor, and I hated using it to bribe those hungry ghosts and mad fleas. You give them ten thousand and they'll want a hundred thousand. Like a lion with a big mouth, no matter how much you give them, it'll never be enough. The court can do what it wants. I asked him what he wanted, and he agreed to sell the company. I can't run the business for him, and I'd want to stay clear of it even if I could manage. They're like poisonous spiders in a jar fighting over something as small as a fly until they're all a bloody mess. It disgusts me just thinking about it. I'll deal with his shares, and they can fight if they want."

"But you need to save him, even if you have to spend all you have."

"Spend it all?" She smiled faintly. "You think that would get him off? If a wolf's mouth isn't sealed, you can't keep it shut with a few pieces of meat. It gets greedier the more it eats."

"So, you're giving up? That's no good." Mengzi looked unhappy. "What's money? When the person is around, there will always be money."

She smiled, but the smile vanished when she noticed the earnest look on his face. Her face was quickly awash in tears. She sobbed and said, "I can tell you mean it. You really want to help him."

"Don't worry. He'll live." She dried her tears and continued, "Maybe he'll get twenty years. Don't worry. There'll be corrupt associates even if he dies. He's kept a record over these years. He has a detailed account of who got what, and I have it now. When you pull up a turnip, dirt comes out with it. I'll be a wolf with its mouth sealed if he lives, but if he dies, I'm going to expose them all. I've given them money and said what I needed to say, and they're all aware of what will happen. This is what they call fighting poison with poison." She tried to console Mengzi when she noticed the tense look on his face. "Don't worry. They eat what they can and will do what they can too. All these years, he fed these scrawny dogs until they turned into fat wolves, and he kept a detailed record of everything. That no-good man let money go to his head, but he still has a brain. He entrusted me with important matters like this, he . . . he . . . he still has a heart." Tears welled up in her eyes again.

Mengzi was finally reassured, but still he thought he ought to do something. He knitted his brows, racked his brain, but had no idea what he could do.

"I'm worthless. I realize I'm a stupid pig when something like this happens."

She was touched. After some consideration, she went out and latched the gate before stepping on a stool to push on a spot on the ceiling. An opening showed, and she reached in to retrieve several packets. She gave him one and said, "This is the lifesaver. I made ten copies. You keep one, but don't ever let anyone see it."

It was neatly tied and could not be opened, even had a waxed seal. "Don't worry. I'll bury it in a dry spot and no one will know."

She gazed at him for a long time. "I've given copies to people I consider reliable. The original is in the safest place I could find. It's his record. Probably that no-good man could never imagine that only the woman he wanted to abandon and the man who desecrated his ancestral grave truly want to help him. That's weird, isn't it?" She squinted at the ceiling. "There's still some money and a few antiques, enough for you to live on for several lifetimes. If something happens to me, you make more copies and send them to the various offices in the provincial government. You can use the money up there."

Mengzi was unnerved. She sounded as if she were preparing for her death.

"You can never tell with matters like this," she continued. "I can't guarantee they won't kill me to stop me from talking. With one in jail and the other dead, they'll think they've cover it up seamlessly. But there

are others. As long as there's one left, they can't cover up all their evil
deeds." She laughed coldly.

Mengzi was moved by her trust in him for sharing such an important
matter. He felt an elevated sense of self and responsibility for the first
time in his life; he wouldn't hesitate if he were asked to give his life for
Shuangfu to get out.

"If you want to do more, you can ask someone to write a piece about
his contribution to the school renovation and ask people in the village to
sign."

"Will that work?"

"It's better than nothing. It'll be something to argue his case."

Mengzi was energized, for it was something within his ability. He
had come to borrow money, but couldn't bring up it now, not when her
family was in trouble. She, on the other hand, asked about Yue'er and
before he said a word about a loan, gave him ten thousand, saying he
could always come back for more if he needed it.

When he got home, he buried the package in the old wall behind
their house and then went to ask Fuqiangzi to write a petition that
listed Shuangfu's charitable contributions and sought leniency from the
government. Fuqiangzi read it out, and it sounded touching. Petition in
hand, Mengzi started from the east of the village, asking for signatures or
thumb prints. He'd thought it would require a great deal of explanation
and persuasion, so he was surprised that everyone had only good things to
say about Shuangfu, and all hoped to save him. They also praised Mengzi
for his action. He was impressed.

Night had fallen and the wind turned cold when he was finished.
He was sweaty from the task, and now felt a chill; but he was keyed up.
It was odd how worldly affairs and the human heart can change so fast.
He'd been eager to see Shuangfu suffer a defeat, and now he was equally
anxious to save the man. The urgency was the same, but the purposes

could not have been more different. Obviously, there were no everlasting friends or eternal enemies. When something is over and the circumstances change, everything else is different too.

Mengzi was grateful to the villagers. He'd thought they would gloat over Shuangfu's misfortune. They'd worn fawning smiles whenever they saw him, while they wished they could plunge a knife into his back. Now Shuangfu's fortunes had suffered a downturn and his wealth was seeping out like water in a sieve; yet they were focused on his positive aspects. When they added their thumb prints, they were sincere as they heaped praise on Shuangfu. Someone even asked if they should personally lodge an appeal. If necessary, they'd get on their three-wheelers and drive all the way to see those in charge; they'd beg or stage a sit-in, even a hunger strike. Mengzi didn't know if a group appeal was needed, but he appreciated their offer. That was odd, he thought. He "appreciated their offer," like Shuangfu was family? Back when his older brother had been sick, he'd offered his appreciation to the villagers for their help. Now he felt he was doing the same thing.

That was unexpected.

3

Several people appeared around a corner. "Is that you, Mengzi?" one of them asked. He barely acknowledged when his leg was hit. With a scream he fell to the ground, Oh, no. They're going to kill me to shut me up.

Several blows followed. He gasped. He could tell they were using clubs.

He thought they wanted the petition, but instead of searching they just kept hitting him. Suddenly something dropped over his head and dust filled his nose. It was a hemp sack, he knew. Oh, no, they're going to kidnap me, Mengzi grumbled when he felt himself suspended. His life was in their hands now, but he was more worried about Xiuxiu. They laid him on the ground after a long while.

This time he heard slapping sounds; they were using a belt.

He struggled in the sack and turned it taut to take some of the force from the belt, so it wasn't too hard to take. He screamed anyway, as a way to draw help.

"Now this will really make you scream," one of them yelled as he felt a sharp pain on his face. He howled like a crazed cow, which in turn unnerved his attackers enough that they went off like a wind.

All was quiet around and the pain subsided a bit.

"Help!" He shouted but heard nothing in response.

The sack was tied at its opening, forcing him to stay rolled up. He touched his chest and felt reassured when he could feel the petition there. Only his legs and face hurt, so maybe they hadn't planned to kill him. They could have turned him into a meat patty with the clubs if they'd wanted.

Or maybe they'd be back soon to kill him. Mengzi panicked and started kicking at the sack, but it was tied securely. He only kicked up dust to fill his nose; the smell told him it had once been used for vegetable seeds.

He kicked and kicked but it was a waste of energy. Anxious and flustered, he just kept kicking, and the hemp sack rolled with each kick. It was rolling faster and faster, and he could tell he was rolling down a slope.

It took a while before the sack stopped. He was too dizzy to fight his way out. His back was sore from bending over, so he changed positions. His nose felt terrible with all the dust; they were probably two dirt holes by now.

"What do they have in mind? If they wanted to kill me, then why use the belt? Oh, no. They left to kill her. They'll come back to finish me off after killing her. He was thrown into a panic. He could almost see her screaming under the attack of their clubs. He could imagine them falling on her, but not her screams. She looked like someone who wouldn't scream even when she was being beaten to death. All she'd do was snicker with her eyes half shut on a bloodied face, her hair disheveled.

He stopped sweating after the brief pause. "Help!" he let out another long shout and pricked his eyes to listen.

First, he heard the wind, then the sparkling stars, followed by an eerie howl, a familiar, sinister, cold and drawn-out sound infused with despair. What was that? He tried to figure it out, but his brain felt gummed up. He listened quietly for a long time and then his mouth went dry.

Oh, no. That's a wolf's howl.

His soul and spirits took flight. He recalled killing a wolf cub at Pig's Belly Well. Could the mother wolf be coming for revenge? Possible. Wolves had a sharp enough nose to differentiate all kinds of smells, even from a great distance. Was it coming for his life? But he hadn't finished what Xiuxiu asked him to do. And then there was Yue'er. What would happen to her if he died?

A long time passed, but the wolf didn't howl again. Mengzi wondered if he had been hallucinating, something that had happened quite frequently. Over the first month after his brother's death, he'd heard his mother crying at the bier all the time. Maybe it was the same with the howl. His brain must have "recorded" the sounds of a baying wolf back at Pig's Belly Well, and it played back at certain times. It was possible. He felt better now and started thinking about ways to get out of the sack. He was reminded of something the Monkey King on TV used all the time. Taking out his key, he started to work on the fiber on the sack one strand at a time. Finally, he picked open a large enough hole.

The air felt so fresh outside the sack, he breathed in deeply.

Everything looked blurred, but he could tell he was at Wolf's Tongue Bend, where dead babies were cremated, where wolves and feral dogs came to feast. Now he knew what those people had in store for him.

His legs hurt. They'd used full force with their clubs, and there must be bruises all over. His face felt numb and swollen when he touched it. That didn't bother him, for he had a thick, fleshy face, strong enough to take some hitting.

"They let me live and walked off without the petition. That's strange." Mengzi was convinced they'd gone after the woman. That must be it, but then again, maybe not. He changed his conclusions based on his hopes, when, finally, he shook his head and told himself not to waste any mental energy. Go take a look and he'd know.

A sudden wolf howl sounded. Now he was certain he hadn't been hearing things. It was indeed a wolf baying earlier, but this time it sounded closer.

His scalp tingled. He had to find a weapon, he told himself. He groped and found nothing but sand until he felt something like a stick, though it could be a human leg bone. He recalled that was where Baldy Wang had been cremated. The man's grim face appeared before his eyes, making him shudder. He wanted to toss the bone, but he had nothing better to use as a weapon against a wolf. It had the right thickness when he felt it with his hands.

He sensed that he was surrounded by flickering green eyes, like will-o-the-wisps, flashing greedy, cruel, sinister glares unique to wolves. But there was only the dark night when he looked around. He'd been like this at night ever since his close-combat with a wolf. He'd been scared witless, according to his mother.

The wind whipped past his ears, like a howling wolf. He was sure it wasn't the wind, but a wolf that he'd just heard. It was deep, gloomy, and cold, a real howl. He could tell it was an old wolf, like an old woman weeping at a tomb, one who had experienced all the suffering and despair in life, her heart hardened, and, having seen through the illusory world, wanting only to wail alone, no longer wishing to share her intimate thoughts.

Another howl. It grew into thousands of howls that seeped into his pores. Their eyes shone bright in the dark, their mouths drooled, their jaws moved back and forth and pulled toward each ear to form a gaping hole. He turned to check; there was nothing but the dark night.

He shuddered. Wolf eyes filled the night sky, flickering in an eerie green.

Strangely though, they all looked like Shuangfu's eyes.

4

The wolf just howled, never made an appearance.

Mengzi walked into the village and arrived at Shuangfu's house, where he banged on the copper ring on the gate. "Open the gate, open up."

"Who is it?" The woman asked from the yard.

"A wolf."

"If you're a wolf, then I'm Grannie Wolf." She laughed. The gate opened and a light from a fire rushed at Mengzi. He felt his heart drop down to his gut.

She was smashing the plaques, with inscriptions like "Benevolence to his hometown." She kept throwing the pieces into the fire to send the flames rushing into the sky. Fengxiang was bemoaning the activity, sorry to see them burn.

"Hey, what's all that dirt on your face?" the woman asked after a look at him. "What happened?" He mumbled a reply, wary of Fengxiang's presence.

"You came at the right time. Come, help me smash these."

"Why?"

"Why not?" She laughed, an easy laugh that displayed a rare cheerfulness. "These are all phony, useless. I'll feel better when I destroy them all." She raised a hammer and brought it down hard, making a cracking noise. Then she tossed more pieces onto the fire to make it crackle.

"Bring me the banners on the kang, Yatou. All of them," she called out to her daughter.

The girl walked out with a long face. She'd grown a lot since Mengzi had last seen her only a few months earlier. She was skinny, had a pale, sad face; obviously, what happened to her father had scarred her.

Xiuxiu grabbed the banners from her daughter and threw some onto the fire. Flames jumped up. "My god, would you stop that already? Let me have some of those," Fengxiang pleaded. "They're perfect for patching holes, making shoe soles, things like that. It's a waste to burn them. Look at this, such fine satin."

Xiuxiu bit her lip and frowned, and then walked inside and brought out a pair of scissors. With a few snips, she cut the remaining banners into small squares, piled them up, and handed them to Fengxiang. "Here. They make sturdy shoe soles that'll last years." Fengxiang took the squares and walked out happily.

The girl went back inside wordlessly with a grim face.

"Why the long face?" the woman shouted at her. "Everyone makes mistakes. It's okay as long as they change. I don't believe your father is a dope who will fail to see the light after twenty years. Besides, he may not get twenty years. He can get his sentence reduced for good behavior. You didn't do anything, so there's no reason for you to feel ashamed."

"I'm not like you, with skin as thick as the city wall," the girl replied.

Xiuxiu laughed. "Why should I feel ashamed? You eat the food you cook and you deal with the consequences of your own actions. He'll suffer for what he did and for me, I'll wait twenty years. Isn't that enough? He's lucky if he's be sent to prison, and I'll wait for him because it's my duty."

"You'll be an old woman in twenty years," Mengzi said. "With gray hair and a face like a walnut."

"So what if I'm old? I'll be with him when he's out. We'll plant corn and grow potatoes. When we work hard, we'll sweat happily, and when we take a break, we'll gaze at the stars and the moon. Won't that be nice? We were like that before. Later, when there was money, trouble followed. Too much of that is no good for you."

The fire died down, so she broke up another plaque and tossed it in. She went inside to mix a basin of warm water and brought it into the yard. Mengzi told her what had happened as he washed up. She frowned and said, "They're not the ones who did that. It's people who have a grudge against you."

Mengzi couldn't think of anyone with a grudge against him. He was hot-headed; he angered easily, but cooled off quickly. If it was someone seeking revenge, that didn't bother him; he'd taken a beating, but he'd live. They hadn't wanted to shut him up. Reassured, he took out the sheets of paper filled with signatures and thumb prints and handed them to her. "Good thing they didn't ruin these. I thought these were what they were after."

She spread them out, checked the contents, and carefully folded them back up to lay down on the window sill. Then she looked over to gaze at him until tears welled up again. Pulling him over she planted kisses all over him, something she'd never done on her own, as she had usually said the opposite of what her body was doing. Mengzi tried to dodge her lips, which touched his sore spots and made him wince, despite their tenderness.

Sobbing and kissing, she clung to him, while he bared his teeth to suck in air, whenever a kiss landed on a spot that hurt. Suddenly he yelped when her foot banged against his leg.

He rolled up his pant leg to see a long bruise on his calf. It had been a savage blow from the club, but luckily it had hit the fleshy area; if it had hit a bone, he'd have a broken leg. She yelped too, wiped her tears and went to a cupboard to unearth a bottle of iodine to dab carefully.

"Who could be so nasty? They could have killed you."

When she was done, she stared at him through teary eyes. "Don't come here at night, all right? You can come during the day, like visiting, you know, but that other thing, I don't feel like doing it again."

"What thing?"

"What do you think? In fact, sometimes I say to myself, I'm a woman, and I think about it too when all is quiet, late at night. I'd like to have you spend a night with me, but I have to live with dignity. I want to show him who I really am. There's nothing I can't do, but there are things I won't do."

"A tiger gets a reputation even if it decides not to eat people." He laughed. "Who will believe you if you remain true to your word?"

"How should I put it?" She shook her head and continued, "Let me tell you a story I read at school. I don't remember its title. A hero offended God, who made him push a boulder up a hill. He pushed and pushed, and when the boulder reached the top he was so exhausted it rolled all the way back down. He pushed and it rolled down, and that was what he did all his life. He never loafed on the job nor did he compromise. Don't you think that's a great story?"

"What's so great about it?"

"He was insignificant before God, but he maintained human dignity while repeating monotonous, fruitless labor. God was such a boring figure in the story, the man was so much more admirable. It's been years now, but the image of hero has stayed with me."

She sounded unhinged. She did that a lot, but strangely, whenever that happened, a shard of light would shine into his heart. He echoed her sentiment and said, "You're right. Like my Pa says, he can take whatever Heaven doles out to him."

"That's so true!" she said excitedly. This was the best response he'd ever given her. She gave him a serious look and saw something different in him. "That's right. Heaven can dole out whatever it wants because it can, but I can take it because I have my dignity. I won't complain about heaven or about people around me. I'll just silence my heart and receive all the calamities He wants me to have. I'll close my eyes halfway and smile. It's nothing. When you've tasted sweet, it's time to try something bitter. That's what life is all about."

She was sounding more and more like his father, Mengzi thought, except his father was always cursing heaven. When he thought about it, his father cursed because of how it bothered him. But just close your eyes halfway, smile, take the boulder, and roll it uphill again and again. If it rolls down, you just roll it back up.

At last he thought he understood her. Obviously, she was no longer interested in "their old relationship." In her eyes, God was her fate, Shuangfu too. Something hot rose up in him; he turned around and wiped it off before it could roll down his cheeks.

"I'll be off then," he said hoarsely.

"All right," she responded, also in a hoarse voice.

Chapter Thirty-Five

The Qilian Mountains have stood tall for a thousand years
The blue sky has remained overhead for ten thousand years

1

Ying'er and Lanlan returned to the village without attracting much attention. The villagers' minds were preoccupied with gold. Shuangfu's wife was said to have announced that she wanted to sell all the pits, which drew crowds of "money chasers." The hoists continued to roar, stirring with stories about gold and the city.

Laoshun rued the loss of his camel for days. What a shame that such a fine camel, good enough to be a stud, ended up in the bellies of jackals. He choked up every time he thought about it. But not openly. He kept it to himself. He told the two women to pay for the camel hair and never mentioned his camel again. In his eyes, it was another disaster the heavens cast his way, and he'd just have to take it. He could not bring himself to fault two frail women who had actually escaped from jackals.

Lanlan returned to the Vajravārāhī Cave. She planned to spend more time in there, hoping to achieve the kind of enlightenment she'd longed for.

Ying'er's status in the family changed significantly, now that Mengzi was married. She was no longer the Chen's daughter-in-law, but a substitute for the Bai family. Her mother-in-law put everything owed by the Bai family on her. She felt eyes on her back, staring daggers. There were no arguments, but her mother-in-law was so polite it was disconcerting. In fact, it started to take on a different meaning.

It was late, and her baby was still awake. Her mother-in-law asked for the baby a few times, but the boy cried each time. He would let the grandparents hold him during the day, but when night fell, no one but his mother would work. With her baby in her arms, Ying'er returned to her room. She felt terrible about Yue'er and her disease.

She had a belly ache; it wasn't too bad but the rumbling was uncomfortable. She got down off the kang, put on her shoes, and went out to relieve herself in the yard. It was quiet, the night blurring everything familiar. The warmth she'd felt was gone, as a chill seeped into her heart.

Lingguan had once said that love was a feeling. The comment had saddened her for a long time. How could sacred, sweet love be just a feeling? Now, when she gave it some thought, it could only be feeling, nothing else. The yard was the same, so was the house. The lovely sun had always shone down on the yard, where people talked and laughed, a place infused with peace, plenitude, liveliness. Now it was all gone, as if Lingguan taken the soul of the place with him, leaving only an old and ugly, stinking shell.

The room felt desolate, filled with a gloomy chill. She heated the kang, but failed to drive away the cold, which bored into her bones. She was no longer the Ying'er of yesterday, and this was not the same house anymore. Could one's whole life be only a feeling? Yes, life and death are feelings, she realized. What her body had that a corpse lacked was the feeling, just that.

She returned to her room and touched her baby's tender face.

A warmth rippled in her heart; the sensation had helped her through many lonely nights. A woman had to have something to look forward to, sometimes a lover, sometimes a baby, and sometimes other things. Without that something, life isn't worth living.

Suddenly she heard stirring in the next room. Someone was cautiously shuffling out the door. Ying'er knew it had to be her mother-in-law, who, she was sure, was checking to see that the lock on the gate had not been pried open and that the ladder was still leaning against the house. She knew her mother-in-law was afraid she'd run off with the baby.

The footsteps were indeed heading toward the gate, where the lock rang out, followed by more footsteps, and finally all was quiet again.

Tears fell. She tried to hold back, but the disappointing tears always came. Life really was not worth living any longer. No one had ever treated her like a thief before. She recalled how she had run back here, full of hope, on that stormy night, upsetting her parents, just to hold onto that miniscule dream of hers. Now her mother-in-law guarded against her as if she were a thief. What was there to live for?

Someone had rifled through her chest and walked off with rolls of fabric. That was all right with her. She didn't care; she was the daughter-in-law, and it was within her mother-in-law's right to expect something from her. But she ought to have asked first. She could have opened the chest while Ying'er was home; instead she waited until Ying'er was visiting her parents. That was wrong. Her own mother had crossed the line, and now so had her mother-in-law. How could they be so petty, acting so unlike mothers over something that small? They gave "mother" a bad name.

She looked up at the dust cover in the ceiling. It didn't look like anything had been disturbed. In a cut-out up there was a chunk of opium, procured when Hantou had been gravely ill. They'd planned to use it when he ran out of painkillers. She had dreamed about swallowing it many times, but each time her baby brought her back to reality.

Tearing apart the paper, she took down the small packet and stashed it inside her undergarment. Maybe it'll come in handy one day. Love was the reason for her to stay alive, and for that, she could also die. If she couldn't live an unsoiled life, she'd rather die a spotless death.

Her heart felt congested, which made her aware that she was alive. It had been a while since she'd felt like a specter drifting in a dream world. The dark night seemed to have dissolved her body and her soul. Nighttime had completed a cycle in her life; at first the night was just a night and had nothing to do with her, a separate entity. Later when she met Lingguan, the night had brought her dizzying happiness and stirred a warm sensation in her. Much later, the night was once again just a night, and so she lingered. It became extraordinarily long; she did her best to endure the unending hours, but the eastern sky seemed never to light up.

In her dreams, she drifted in unfamiliar places, with an inky sky, dark land, and a black heart. She no longer dreamed of her *yuanjia*. How she wished to see him again, but he refused to enter her dreams. There was nothing she could do about it. A lonely person has lonely dreams, bereft of a companion. In her dream there was no road, no sun, no wind, no rain, only dusty strangeness and a murky sensation. She drifted in the murkiness, to the east and then to the west, rising up and then wafting down, turning into a specter. His image took shape, but was blurred, no longer clear, as before. It was fine with her for everything, including her, to be blurred. But her loneliness was as intense as ever, tearing at her heart, in the company of the two mothers' actions.

Life really was not worth living.

Her heart was weary, as if it had been traveling down an endless road in a dark night, with no light to shine on the path nor stars to point the way. There was no wind or rain, just dead silence; not even footsteps. She had heard that after you died, you had to pick up all the footprints you left behind in this world before you could be reborn. She felt like a ghost walking down a winding road at night, searching for footprints buried in the passing of time. Many of her mental pictures had yellowed, like water-logged old paintings. What excited her had ceased to exist; what made her ache no longer caused her pain. It was like flipping through someone else's photo album; few things stirred her heart now, as it was steeped in loneliness.

One thing was clear to her: eventually she had to leave the room, the yard, and the feeling that was already fading. But she didn't want to leave.

2

Bai Fu came, looking embarrassed and awkward. This was his first visit after the time he kidnapped his sister.

To avoid arousing suspicion, he went to the study first to greet the in-laws and said to Mengzi's mother, "Auntie, my mother isn't feeling well, and she wants my sister home. I'll bring her back in a few days." Mengzi's mother knew he wanted to put her mind at rest when he said "bring her back," but decided to go along. "What's the problem?" she asked.

"We don't know. There's a lump in her stomach, but she doesn't want to have a checkup."

Mengzi sneered. He should have made up a better illness if he wanted to lie; "a lump in her stomach" sounded as empty as a fart. When she forced Lanlan into the exchange marriage, she'd used the same excuse. It would be cursing herself if she'd mentioned a real illness, while "the lump" was open to interpretation. The heart was a lump, so was a full belly or cancer; it all depended on how it was understood. She felt like sneering, but decided to go along,

"Oh, that sounds terrible. My uncle had one of those, and he howled in pain for a month before he died. I hope that's not what your mother has." She silently cursed maliciously: It's what the old witch deserves.

"I don't think so." Bai Fu was too simple-minded to see through her ruse. "She's the happy-go-lucky type and she hasn't done bad things, so she won't get a terrible illness like that."

Without meaning to he'd touched her sore spot. Her oldest son, Hantou, had died of liver cancer, the terrible illness that had given him a large lump. Based on Bai Fu's reasoning, Hantou must have done something bad, but she could not display anger, so she continued, "With illness it's hard to say. Good people can die of horrible diseases while evil people never get anything bad. It's really hard to say."

Bai Fu was no match for her kind of social interactions, so he asked:

"Auntie, will you let my sister go home for a visit?"

"Of—course." She gave a drawn-out reply. "She doesn't shit gold or pee silver, so why should I keep her here?"

With Ying'er around, she was always on edge, afraid the young woman would find an opportunity to run back home with her baby. Every time Mengzi's mother went out, she had to remind her husband and son to be on guard and assigned them sentry duty, and still her heart was in her throat the whole time. She hardly slept at night; when a wind blew or the gate creaked, she'd think Ying'er was sneaking out. Ying'er was the baby's mother, and trying to get the boy back after she'd taken him home would be harder than climbing into the sky. She was exhausted after being on tenterhooks since Ying'er returned from the desert. Sometimes she thought she'd just send her back to her parents. But she couldn't get rid of her like that, not after the formal wedding ceremony. She'd tried to use a ghost to scare her into running back home, but Laoshun had given her a tongue-lashing when she brought it up. Obviously, the human heart is the least constant; she'd been afraid that Ying'er wanted to go and had done everything she could to keep her, and now she couldn't wait for her daughter-in-law to leave.

Bai Fu was relieved, for he'd thought the Chen family would make it hard on him. He'd been worried ever since the kidnapping; afraid that Mengzi might seek revenge, he'd made himself scarce. But this time he couldn't say no to his mother. She'd said that Mengzi had hit him in the heat of the moment, but now that it had blown over, Mengzi wouldn't do that again even if he wanted to. Besides, Ying'er's mother couldn't send anyone else. Pockmark Xu could do it, but Laoshun might have a fight with him. If she were to come, an argument could easily break out between the two women, since they were like a needle against a wheat awn. She mulled it over and decided that Bai Fu was the best choice, for he was still Lanlan's legally married husband. He had every right and reason to come. Without telling his mother, Bai Fu brought along a knife. If Mengzi caused trouble, he'd let his knife do the talking. He was surprised by how smoothly it went. He'd no sooner opened his mouth than his mother-in-law agreed to his request. "My mother also said for Ying'er to bring the baby with her," he said at last. "She misses him."

"I have no say over her daughter, but she has no say over the baby." Mengzi's mother smiled coldly. "The baby stays."

"But my mother misses him. That's all, nothing more." Just hearing that put Mengzi's mother on her guard. She sneered. "Pack your things, Ying'er," she said. "Your mother has sent your brother to take you home." She turned to Bai Fu, "Not another word about the baby. She can't take the baby even if her head hurts from thinking about it. I won't be nice if you say another word."

Tears fell from Ying'er eyes.

She'd known what was in store for her the moment her brother showed up. She also knew her mother-in-law had been waiting for this day. It hadn't taken her long to realize she was superfluous in this family.

Everything changed so fast, like a magician's slight-of-hand.

Panpan looked at his mother with his large, black-pea like eyes, as if he had sensed something. Separation by death had already occurred and, it was time to be parted from the living. It was clear as day that she couldn't take the baby along. Her heart ached, for it was like cutting off a piece of it. She dried her tears.

Her mother's illness could be real or not; it was immaterial, just an excuse. They made up something to get her back home and here they had an excuse to send her away. Everyone needed the excuse, a tacit understanding between them. It was finally clear to Ying'er that she could no longer stay.

How she wished she could spend the rest of her life in this room. She didn't want to part with the familiar yard, the familiar environment, and the familiar feeling, which always reminded her of what she'd hoped for in life. Her wish was so pitifully small, and yet fulfilling it was harder than climbing into the sky.

What had brought her dizzying happiness was long gone, what remained was the baby. He'd become her whole life, but she knew that separation was inevitable.

Greedily, her eyes feasted on the baby, her lips kissed his face; greedily she watched him look at her with a smile; greedily, she gazed at him and shed tears. Being able to cry was a kind of blessing.

Panpan, the panpan of my life. I've hoped that the name would bring me what I looked forward to in life, but in the end it all comes to nothing. In her short life, she had been disappointed many times: she'd hoped to pass an exam and leave for the big world outside; she'd yearned for true love and a sweet outcome; she'd longed to wait in peace and to live a quiet life. All these had gone up in smoke. Now she had to leave her baby.

Cradling the boy, she kissed him over and over, her tears wetting his face.

She strained to look around her; she had to leave the familiar room that had brought such wonderful memories. She would like to take along the sky-blue blouse and her head scarf, but she tore her eyes from the objects. Her mother-in-law was a petty woman who placed great importance on such trivial things. She would leave them behind, but then she changed into the blouse. It wasn't made of fine material, but it was the best thing in her life.

Bai Fu came in and said in a low voice, "Ma wants you to take whatever is yours. Bring along everything that looks good to you."

Ying'er frowned in disgust. Both mothers were the same, placing more importance on objects than on people. Everything that looks good to me? she said. Could I take what I like best? Love of my life, how I wished I could take you with me to wander the world. We would live an enchanted life even if we became beggars. But where are you now? I'd choose you if there was a God and God gave me a chance. I don't want glory, wealth, fame or anything like that. But not once in her life was she able to choose what she wanted, not once. She'd be content if she could just once. But no, not a chance. She'd lived a wasted life.

A wasted life. Tears blurred her eyes.

"Ma said put on all the clothes you can, and wrap the fabric around you too."

The tears flowed. She realized that her mother was referring to the fabric from her chest, her wedding presents. Those were what her own mother thought about, and what her mother-in-law cared for. She meant nothing to either of them. One should value a person most. Lingguan, you're just like them, you know that? What future can compare with a real, lively person? This body will soon perish, *Yuanjia*, and where is the future you're searching for? Where are your ideals? Why didn't you take this youthful body, this beating heart, to create a lovely, romantic life?

Don't think about that anymore. It's all in the past, gone.

She brushed her hair hastily. In the mirror, a haggard face looked back at her. With a sigh, she threw down the brush and mirror and kissed the baby. "Let's go then," she said through clenched teeth.

"Just like that? What about what Ma said?" Bai Fu asked.

But she was already outside.

Her mother-in-law stood tenaciously guarding the door. She breathed a sigh of relief when she saw Ying'er come out empty-handed.

"I'll be off now, Ma," Ying'er said.

"Yes, go on home," her mother-in-law responded.

Why didn't you say that earlier? Ying'er wondered. But her mother-in-law must have had her reason. Ying'er brushed away wind-blown hair from her face and walked to the gate.

Good-bye, yard; good-bye, my little room.

Her face was awash in tears when she was barely outside. Bai Fu followed from behind, pushing a bicycle, clanging along the way and drawing curious stares. "Going home to see your parents, Ying'er?" One of them asked. "Why aren't you taking the baby along?" She muttered a reply and walked on.

The remote village and its clay soil looked the same now as it had when she arrived. But she was a different person. She'd been a young maiden when she came, and was now a widow. She'd known nothing when she came, and was time-worn as she left. Only one thing remained constant: coming or going, she had no choice.

She recalled it had also been an autumn day when the rickety vehicle had brought her here, turning a girl into a woman. It had been a windy day, with dust in the air and above the road ahead. She recalled how it had felt like a dream. It felt like that to her now. The village, the sand, and the date tree were already turning into dreamy impressions. What remained clear was the wound in her heart, which she would pick at when she wasn't paying attention.

Her flight on the stormy night came to mind. She'd thought she'd managed to escape her fate, never expecting that she'd have to return. She'd run away on her own and now she had to go back on her own. Are you happy now, Ma? You didn't have to kidnap me this time. I'm coming back, that should make you smile.

"Hop on," her brother said.

She jumped onto the rear rack of the bicycle. The wind sent hair blowing in her face. She ignored it. She must look like what her mother called a scruffy ghost. Why not? I can be anything so long as it makes you happy, Ma. Life had no set form; things came and went in an instant and you could be human one minute and a ghost the next. It doesn't matter, Ma. I could be anything.

It felt great not to have the baby, for there was nothing to tie her down now. He'd become a tethering rope. Her mother-in-law cherished the baby like he was part of her, so she needn't worry about him. Her mother had suggested going to court, but she couldn't bring herself to do that. The Chen family had suffered the death of their son, and she could not make them go through the heartache of losing the baby. The law was on her side, she knew, but she couldn't do it. Besides, with the baby in the care of her mother-in-law, she had nothing to worry about.

Undulating vast desert that had given birth to boundless mysteries; mild desert wind that carried all the familiar smells; cramped, squat but pretty village houses; twisted desert date trees with endless vitality, good-bye to you all.

3

Ying'er was getting married.

Like a rock rolling downhill, she had no control over her life. She'd sketched out a beautiful future, but the wind of fate made a mess of it.

Her mother bought two large satin comforters and two red-lacquered chests. She also asked village women to make shoe soles and pillow cases. These would be Ying'er's dowry to accompany her to the Zhao family.

What people considered major events in life were easy to carry out: chopping meat, buying food, inviting guests, applying for a marriage license—to the Zhaos, the license was immaterial, but they got one for her sake—hiring a car to take her over, and sending her into the bridal chamber to make it a done deal, like cooking rice to make a meal.

Her mother knew that was the best approach, which was why they'd taken care of all the required steps while she was still at her in-laws'. The engagement ceremony and delivery of betrothal gifts were carried out at the same time; Zhao sent over ten thousand yuan in cash.

It was a fine day, a puffy white cloud floated above distance hills, highlighting the clear sky without blotting out the sun. All their relatives came, in high spirits, pleased with the outcome of her "moving on." Zhao San was, after all, a wealthy man, and the relatives felt they gained plenty of face by association. They began arriving at the crack of dawn, and each offered a wedding gift that was usually about a hundred yuan. The gifts alone netted her family several thousands, and the smile on her mother's face all but crowded her eyes shut.

Her eyes dry, Ying'er sat woodenly on the edge of the kang, her face a blank, her heart a void.

She shed tears only when was by herself; they belonged to her alone. She swallowed the tears when they flowed into her mouth, and when they reached her heart, she choked up alone. If she fell sick from choking on her tears, she would deal with it herself. In front of people, she had nothing to say, for words were useless; nothing could express the helplessness and reluctance she felt inside.

Helpless, truly helpless. Fate was too powerful to resist. Inertia took control of her, no, swept her up and rushed her along; in no time she was on another hill, where she would roll off once again.

She was no longer in the mood to sing her favorite tunes, for they felt right only when her heart brimmed with emotion. Now there was nothing but a total blank, and helplessness—not even despair now. Her indifference was so intense it consumed everything.

Her mother was busy running around, mightily pleased, treating her indifference as silent agreement. But that was just her. Their relatives were surprised by her composure, but that was just them. The chests for her dowry were a dazzling red, but they were just two chests. The world and Ying'er were two entities; they were incompatible. The world could carry her body along, but her heart belonged to her alone.

As they ate, the relatives talked and laughed imprudently. Her family had put out simple dishes to tide them over. When the vehicles from the Zhao family came, they would all climb in grandly. The groom's family would treat them like gods and put on an impressive array of dishes, encouraging them to eat to their hearts' content.

Her father brought Ying'er a bowl of stewed vegetables, handed it to her, and told her to eat as much as she could; once over there, she wouldn't have time to eat, what with the ceremony, toasting guests, and the bridal chamber pranks. She did not reply; wordlessly and timidly he laid the bowl on a side table and walked out.

Her mother was talking loudly: "Come, have something. We're all family, let's not be strangers. Don't be shy. If you don't enjoy the food, at least fill your bellies. I don't want you to go hungry."

"What do you mean, fill my belly? If my belly is full, where will I put all the good food when I get there? They're going to treat us to sea cucumbers and squid," one of them said.

"Of course, we're no match for our son-in-law. A strand of his hair is thicker than my waist. You can't fill a plate with all my hair, I tell you."

Her mother laughed.

"What do you mean? Your girl will take charge once she's married, and with a little help from her, you'll have a big, fat rear end."

"That's right. When the time comes, don't forget us, your poor relatives."

They laughed and the talk continued.

Ying'er took up a mirror to look at herself. Her face was sallow, but had a little more glow, thanks to the red bridal outfit. She was surprised not to feel a heartrending pain, only a numbing sensation, something she hadn't experienced before. It was okay to feel numb. What felt odd was how the image of Lingguan had dimmed. Only the chunk of opium felt solid, smiling at her from under her clothes.

The bridal caravan arrived, a bus, a van, and a car. Thick red fabric draped the side mirrors and dazzled the eye. It was her first time in a car. It had been a bus when she married Hantou; she'd had to sit with the driver because of the passengers he took on. But the feeling had been no different; it was a major event in her life, and yet she felt it had nothing to do with her.

She got in. The seat was so soft she sank into it. Everyone in the village came to watch; children were running around, whooping up a storm. Everyone, young and old, was in high-spirits. This was a happy event, so naturally, people were smiling. Her mother greeted them joyfully and brought Ying'er a handful of dried noodles. "This is an 'old cooked meal' and you must remember to eat it when you're there."

Ying'er knew the noodles represented her lifetime fortune, an essential item for such an occasion. A woman from the Zhao family who'd come to welcome the bride accepted the noodles for her and said, "We know. Don't worry."

The caravan started moving, and villagers parted to let them pass. Columns of dust rose from behind the vehicles and seemingly veiled the village and everyone in it, but not the sun, which continued to scream down at them. They turned onto a main road under the hot sun. The caravan took a different route from the one they'd taken coming over; a bridal sedan must not travel the same route, nor could it stop midway. With her marriage to Hantou, the bus had broken down on the road, and later Hantou had left her behind. That seemed to have happened ages ago, it also seemed to be happening right now. She had been a young maiden then and now she was a widow moving on. How many years had passed in between? She wasn't sure, but it felt like no time at all. Everything was a blank, except for the brief dalliance with her *yuanjia* and the grief and pain after Hantou's death. Life was odd; when she thought back, only fragments remained of the long, critical part of her life.

A cheerful tune was playing in the car; a woman was singing, "So many memories in life, and I want to be in yours." So what if that happened? Better still that there was nothing in the heart, that she felt nothing. Otherwise, it might look ugly. Best to be indifferent.

A crowd waiting at the Zhao's door had set off firecrackers when they saw the car. There was also a bonfire, something missing in her first marriage. There had been only a brazier and a bucket of water. The bus had turned to face east. When she'd gotten off, she'd walked into the fire, then into water, and then into the house. That had not worked to avert misfortune, and the fire and water had failed to bring good luck.

The woman welcoming the bride took Ying'er by the hand and made three turns around the fire before walking through the gate. She was barely through when someone sprinkled flour on her head—"being together until the hair turns gray." The flour spotted her red bridal costume. She ignored it.

The yard was packed with people, tables, chairs, voices and eyes. The gazes formed a net through which she entered the bridal chamber, trailed by Bai Fu's voice, "So little money, like sending off a beggar." He hadn't sounded this forceful and self-confident in years. She knew her brother was talking about the money he'd been handed as he sat on the dowry chest. Before the chest was carried into the room, they had to pay him. He would not get up if there wasn't enough; they had to keep giving until he was satisfied with the amount. He then got to his feet, a signal for the bride's side of guests to get off the bus and van.

The bridal chamber was lavish, with far more elaborate furnishing than Hantou's family had supplied. Overhead, the ceiling was draped in colorful plastic flowers, on the walls were colorful paintings, and on the bed was colorful bedding. There were also tables and sofas, giving off an air of wealth. A cassette player was squawking on one of the tables, deafeningly loud. Normally, she couldn't stand loud noises, but on this day, she was too indifferent to care.

The fat guy in a blue outfit must be Zhao San. A quick glance told Ying'er the man had a greasy face and a bulbous nose, but nothing more, oh, wait, and a booming voice, even louder than Bai Fu's bragging when he won at the gambling table. It was nothing unusual; rich people were all loud. Her mother had abhorred a voice like that, complaining about the aggressiveness, but now she couldn't have enough of it, thanks to the masculine sound.

He could be manly for all she cared. It only made her want to throw up. She felt dizzy, as if she'd overdosed on cold medicine. The dizziness overwhelmed her, and everything before her felt like a dream.

The ceremony was more festive than the first time. Lots of fawning guests, joking guests, gawking guests, and cheering guests. Those in charge of the ceremony folded a felt blanket for the bride and the groom to stand on. She did what she was told, while Zhao San acted shy, drawing load guffaws from the villagers. A school friend of hers was in the crowd. She'd had such an ethereal personality that food hadn't seemed necessary to her, but now she was laughing like a country woman. The school friend's face blurred, and in her daze, Ying'er thought she saw countless gaping mouths, countless wide-open eyes, and heard countless guffaws, even the sun was abuzz.

She wished the show would be over soon. She was exhausted, as if she'd traveled a long road; weariness took over her body, and she wanted to lie down to sleep for a thousand years. See how her eye lids kept coming together.

Everything was a blur, all but the chunk of opium she'd swallowed before coming out of the bridal chamber, wide awake and smiling at her.

4

Afterward, Lanlan often wondered what the dying Ying'er was thinking on that afternoon.

. . . Obviously, exhaustion has woven itself into a tangled web, underneath which was sinister laughter. And there must have been also the howl of fate . . . despair . . . dazed. Breath as thin as gossamer from a silkworm, a thread, a thread and another thread, slowly in and out, ready to snap off any time . . . dark clouds must have trundled in the sky outside the window. Heaven, are you so vexed that you wish to pour down endlessly sorrowful rain? How can I send my despair and desolation to you?

The heart was mired in a cheerless funk. Everything took on a gray pall, illusory, unreal, seemingly nonexistent.

Tears continued to fall, faster and faster. She kept calling the name that made her heart ache.

Was this dark, cruel environment the hell? Black flies sniggered in the dark; thin demons danced in the wind; at the end of a chilled current was a cave, the cave of a jealous witch.

. . . Mother, why must you force me like that? I wish I could tear my body into pieces and give back my flesh and my blood, like the boy called Nezha. Would you let me off when you saw bright red blood and flesh staining the ground? Or would you continue to nag me?

Life has reached its end.

My heart will rest in eternal silence and you can keep on with your sinister laugh. I can hear blood dripping . . . let it drip. . . my soul is slowly dying, my body cooling, but I will die without closing my eyes, like God's lamb, where there are no fresh flowers. Why is the love of spring always so frail?

Look, the devil is nailing my coffin. It's painted red . . . they say it's made of cypress, valuable and long-lasting. Fine, then I'll smile. See, the muscles are moving on my cheeks. . . don't worry about my tears, and focus on the twitching muscles on my face . . . I'll just wipe them away. They're gone with a swipe of a hand or a sleeve. Cypress coffins are the best, better than poplar . . . better by far than being tossed into a cremation fire. A cypress coffin is still a coffin. It is once it's painted red or sketched with dragons or phoenixes. When you're dead, there's no need to worry about a coffin. Beauty and love can both be put aside. Coffins are just coffins; they carry nothing but piles of bones.

Ah, she heard the creaking of a heavy coffin board being removed.

Mother jumped out. Is that you, mother? Is that figure staggering under the force of a wind truly you? Are you really the gray-haired woman who often made me cry? Are you actually the weariness of life that carelessly poured into my heart? Are you indeed the crooked, old desert date tree? Are you the mother whose face is crisscrossed with wrinkles, but who could still call out brightly, "Ying'er?"

You are dancing barefoot, calling out to me, "Come in. My sweet girl. In here is a spring day I personally decorated for you."

Yes, Mother. I know it's made of cypress, painted red, valuable, long-lasting, warm, and pretty. I'll smile, then, Mother. See, the muscles on my face are moving again. Don't worry about my tears, and just focus on the twitching muscles. A swipe of my hand will erase the tears. Cypress coffins are wonderful. Mother. Since I can't carve the flesh off my bones, like Nezha, I'll just have to climb into the coffin. Thank you, my long-suffering Mother. You've gone through great trouble over my coffin.

I'll go happily, even though I know it's the lowest level of hell. Mother, I believe you; I know you're doing it for my own good. So, let my soul curse me.

I know I'll have to vanish, since nirvana is beyond my reach. I'll die another death at the lowest level of hell.

. . . Why is an angel's shadow so rare? Why is the devil's smile everywhere?

Why doesn't anyone bring me spring, knowing that I love fresh flowers? Why am I doomed to play the moon to the devil? Why was Cao Xueqin, who had to eat thin gruel, born to live in solitude? Why did old Tolstoy have to walk toward that small station? *Yuanjia*, my *yuanjia*. You'll tell me in our next life.

The coffin is almost here now.

Come on in, Devil.

5

Many stories about Ying'er circulated in Liangzhou.

Some said she'd died, had failed to live even through that autumn. No matter how many people hoped she'd lived, they knew that someone like her could not have stayed in this world too long. Many people hoped that she'd lived, but they all knew it was impossible for a perfectionist like her to survive in this day and age. There was strong evidence to support this version: No one in Shawan saw Ying'er again after that day, though no one saw her grave either. Naturally, her parents would not have a grave for her if she'd died that way.

Someone said Ying'er had been saved and that the marriage had been dissolved. On a dusty afternoon, Ying'er, who had gone through so many hardships in life, finally walked out under a pallid twilight sky, and out of a small village tucked in the crease of the desert. It was everyone's favorite version, the happiest possible ending of the time. They were convinced that she could defy her fate. They said she had taken her baby and the fabric from the chest after her mother-in-law returned it—how odd that so many people had noticed this detail—as she went in search of what she had been looking forward to. They refused to believe that if she searched the wide world, she would not find Lingguan. But some were worried, for even if she found him, would it still be the same Lingguan she'd longed to see? People agreed that everything was different now. A girl left home a maiden and came back a whore. Could Lingguan have remained unchanged?

By then, except for White Tiger Pass, with little for "everyone to talk about," in Liangzhou, everyone was talking about Ying'er, talk that spread like the wind, as if they all had something to do with it.

Lanlan found a piece of paper in the room where Ying'er had lived. It was Ying'er's handwriting, but she wasn't sure if her sister-in-law had written it or copied it from somewhere—

I know I can no longer see your familiar figure under the window where we once arranged to meet, but I can't help myself. I stand there to watch the wind and people passing by, because maybe, just maybe I'll spot you passing by.

You're not a wind that comes and goes without a trace, nor are you faint, misty clouds; you are a coral tree deeply rooted in my heart. I water you with the sweet dew of my longing every afternoon, hoping you will be infused with lush green and meet me again in the little room.

I said long ago that I wanted to plant a tree beneath that window.

You laughed with such free abandon, said it was a beautiful idea, but a tree cannot grow on a path people walk down. Now it has happened, for I have planted myself securely in this spot, quietly guarding the window and waiting for you to show up.

Why don't you appear as promised, following the lingering rays of a setting sun that shine deep into the lane? You know that around this time I wait for you on the street corner, gazing far off to the end of the world, waiting for your heartwarming smile and the comforting light under the window on a rainy night.

. . . How I wish I could run over on a breezy, rainy evening so we could talk all night, about how to return to see you a thousand years down the road. I'd tell you how, in search of a kind of mood, I wore out five hundred rush mats, fulfilled a dream a thousand times, and traveled once around the world.

Lanlan choked up and leaned up against the wall.

The room was shabby, its walls peeling, looking weatherworn, sitting silently amid noises.

Everything remained, including the room, the walls, and the desert date tree, but not Ying'er. . . the Ying'er who worked so cheerfully, the Ying'er who stood in the wind waiting for the man of her heart, the Ying'er who had a common pose but presented a unique sight, the Ying'er who slowly came up from the end of the lane . . . Weariness from all the tribulations rushed at her, and she wept silently.

Lanlan lamented in silent tears . . . Can't I go with you, Ying'er? I know I'm not gentle enough. I can't keep you here, so I must cover my heart with regret. The road leading out is too dark. I wanted to share in your sorrow, but I could not say so. Leave your sadness, then, and take your hopes with you. But in this life there will always be reasons for concern.

She continued to weep . . . little room, the fated little room. Was it ever decorated with tenderness? Has it retained the loving feelings? Did it preserve your loneliness? Has it settled your solitude?

Little room, the room of extreme longing . . . the wooden clapper of destiny, the cassock in the heart, the grotto from a previous life.

6

That night Lanlan strolled alone down the path to the desert, recalling the autumn of their trek and all that had happened in the desert. Everything seemed far away and hazy, as she felt an intense world-weariness.

Everything was indeed like a dream.

What remained was a faint trace the dream behind.

Other than that, time alone clattered to somewhere, starting in the primordial past and continuing on forever. Where is your destination, Father Time?

Is it true that, other than some dazzling sparks, you leave only a giant void in the human world? And that even the sparks will turn into deadly silence?

Ying'er, where in the world has your search taken you? Who lingers in your dream? Do you still remember that rainy night in the desert? Have you revisited the secrets in your heart? Do you recall the spot called salt lakes and the many stories that took place there?

On that night when all was quiet, only the footsteps of ever-changing time were distinct. How many stories took place at that moment? How many stories have now been concluded? Gazing ahead, one sees no precursors; looking back, one spots no followers. When you consider how vast and endless heaven and earth are, you cannot help but shed emotional tears.

What is life? Is it truly a dream? Is it really a spring dream that leaves no trace?

Is life really a giant void? What constitutes relatively enduring eternity?

Who will show me the way out?

Who will be my Master?

Who can give me clarity?

Chapter Thirty-Six

I'd rather see trouble in the Jade Emperor's land
Than have the path between us blocked for eternity

1

Yue'er checked out of the hospital on the doctor's suggestion. The medicine had stopped working, after damaging her liver and kidneys and causing other complications. The outcome was clear, and it would be a waste of money for her to spend more time in the hospital. The treatment had used up more than twenty thousand from her father and ten thousand Mengzi had deposited to her cash card. Her father wanted to continue the treatment, like trying to cure a dead horse. But Yue'er disagreed, "I want to leave. I don't want to spend another day here. If I have to die soon, then let me enjoy one pleasant day."

Villagers showed up when she got home. Many were moved by how she had waited for Mengzi at the path, and no one criticized her anymore. Some even shed compassionate tears. They all knew she'd been a fine girl, with a pretty face and a good heart. She had contracted a filthy disease, but everyone except the dead and the Buddha makes mistakes. They felt sorry for a young girl who had been like a flower. Lanlan had sought out many home remedies for her.

She saw Mengzi again. No matter how many reasons she had outlined to hate him, her heart still raced when he came. She didn't have to worry, now that he'd had penicillin shots. They no longer had to worry that he'd be affected by the virus passed on through kissing. She wanted to put her arms tightly around him and to kiss him like they used to do. Yue'er loved the sensation of their tongues doing combat, and that posed a great temptation; but she knew that even her saliva was contaminated. They could only hold hands and gaze into each other's eyes, either tearfully or with a smile. That was all right with her, for it felt like heaven compared to the enduring loneliness of a sick bed in Lanzhou.

The sight of Mengzi had made her desire to live swell, until it surpassed all existence. Her stomach turned into a laboratory for home remedies the moment he went to the city—his daily pay was barely enough to pay for her treatment. In addition to swallowing pile after pile of pills that were certainly harmful to her liver and kidneys, she continued with the smoking cow dung, suffering burns, and spent hours sitting in alcohol, causing festering wounds. She often dragged her weakened body to the field to gather weeds said to be antidotes; she chomped them down raw after rinsing them in water. Yet no matter how much she suffered, she continued to project the image of a pretty girl. Before she left the house each time, she carefully made herself up. She stopped wearing shorts and cropped tops so her infected spots would not be exposed; despite fatigue and aches, she applied light makeup, brightening her sickly face with a dab of rouge. Lip balm was a must. When she was alone, she checked her face in her little mirror and reapplied makeup when necessary. What she showed the outside world was always her prettiest face, so no one but her parents knew how terribly ill she was.

I'm Mengzi's wife, that's all. She said to herself. That was one of the reasons she had to make herself look good.

Every day she tried the remedies supplied by Lanlan, all but one, swallowing a live toad. She was told it was a magical cure someone had reluctantly offered. Yue'er had always been afraid of the creature covered in tumor-like lumps. When she put one up to her mouth and shut her eyes—she would swallow it if it meant more time with Mengzi— it croaked. The sound reminded her that it was a life form; it might even have a family that would suffer if she swallowed it. She could not take another life in order to continue to live. So, she bent down and gently lowered it into a stream. It even turned and croaked at her, as if to say thank you. That sent tears down her face. She sensed the little toad understood her heart; she'd never forget the compassionate look in its eyes.

Even the most obtuse villagers could sense her desire to live. Many wept when they spotted her waiting at the path outside the village, which she still did from time to time.

When no one was around, she knelt in the sand and prayed to the sun, to the Vajravārāhī, and to all the deities she could think of. She asked them to help tame the Disease Demons. She would be happy just to have a few healthy days to be a true wife to Mengzi. She was even willing to suffer after death—walk across a mountain of knives or leap into a cauldron of boiling oil. But she could pray all she wanted, and the ravages of the Disease Demon grew more intense. The festering spread fast and soon her clothes could no longer cover the spots.

She and Mengzi cried in each other's arms when they were alone. She had been resentful toward him when she was in Lanzhou, but her complaints were rooted in profound love. As the countdown started for her time on earth, their love grew even stronger, though more often than not they could only hold hands and gaze at each other in silence.

Besides his temporary work, Mengzi secretly sold blood several times. He searched for doctors and medicine he coaxed her into swallowing—she didn't want him to owe any more money. He had asked everyone he knew, but the money he managed to borrow was still not enough. The painkillers alone were a major expense. He decided that when Shuangfu's wife returned to the village he'd borrow more money from her and take Yue'er to Beijing for treatment. No matter how much it cost, he thought, as long as Yue'er could be cured. At most he'd work like a beast of burden for the rest of his life.

2

On this afternoon, the solitary sun hung above the sand hills, neither red nor bright but a lethargic pale white. Yue'er wanted to go see the desert, so Mengzi took her out on his motor scooter. They rode down the small path the villagers took to gather desert rice and into the desert. The scooter's low speed engine sounds were monotonous and weak, like old sighs. With a pack on her back, she sat sideways on the scooter, prevented by the bodily pain from sitting like before. She had taken care to apply light makeup and powder her face; on her hands were a pair of white gloves and on her face a saintly look. The desert wasn't far, but Mengzi purposefully made a circle around the village first; he was shrouded in a pall of overwhelming sorrow, his heart steeped in profound sadness.

Under a gentle breeze, he parked his scooter and walked with Yue'er to a sand dune. In recent years, the distance between people had grown greater, but the desert was moving closer to the village by the day, with great plots of land vanishing. Many desert plants, like bunchgrass and other vegetation, had been cut down to make supporting frames for the gold prospecting pits at White Tiger Pass. The shorn sand dunes looked forlorn. He knew that they were working like Yue'er's disease, eating away the good skin day after day. It wouldn't be long before the whole village was lapped up.

He chased away spying desert rats and sat on a hill for Yue'er to lean against him. The sun splashed its warm rays all over them, making them feel that they were truly alive. A faint noise like that of a city came from White Tiger Pass. It would lick its way into their village, like the desert. But Mengzi knew that eventually White Tiger Pass too would be buried in the sand, swallowed by the changing of time, or turned into a dispersing mist years later, when the universe died.

Everything felt airy and misty, like an illusion, nothing seemed solid, except for their embrace. Under the warm sun, he had his arms around Yue'er as they lay on the sand to savor the feeling of being alive. It was a fleeting sensation, rushing away like a floodwater the moment they felt it. He could sense it receding, a rapid and substantial change in an instant and yet seemingly eternal. Maybe this moment together would freeze-frame in certain way; let it freeze in his heart, he thought.

They spoke little, knowing that words were meaningless, as was thinking. Instead, they focused on enjoying each other's presence. No more looking forward to the future, for it was ill-defined, and looking forward to it would only damage the present. No more reminiscing about the past, for that was gone, and looking back on it wrecked the present. Just an embrace to wordlessly share the secrets in their hearts. They both knew that as noise encroached, silence was the greatest pleasure. It might not take long for the world to roil like a pot of boiling water, and when that happened, not even the word "silence" would remain in people's vocabulary.

Stop thinking about the disease, even if they knew the virus continued to eat away at her body. Best to put it out of their mind. In careful consideration, no one was completely healthy. From the moment one is born, the Grim Reaper starts to eat away at one's life, as cruelly as the syphilis virus. The only difference is that people are not aware of its progress. Obliviously and blithely, a baby grows into a teenager, and a middle-aged man gets old, getting closer and closer to the grave. So, ignore it and don't think about anything; just savor the sensation of being alive at one rare moment of tranquility.

Calm the mind and gaze out at the vast desert. The waves of sand rippled out into the unknown. No one knew where they came from or where they would end. There had to be many creatures in its folds, and like him, they must have suffered illness and pain, felt thirst, and held out hopes, but in the end, all vanished like smoke, and no traces were left in the desert. Many years later tens of thousands of people would still be living here, doing things the dead had done before: suffering pain and tempering their souls with eyes on the future. But would they know there was once a couple called Mengzi and Yue'er? Or, could the existence that they cared so much about only be a small part of a giant void?

Mengzi tightened his arm around Yue'er, feeling her supple, solid presence. He could hear her gentle breathing and her healthy heartbeat. Her heart seemed to be unaware of the corroding virus and continued to beat with confidence and ease. He also felt the young girl's resilient gentleness, but it failed to dispel the heavy sense of illusiveness. He did clearly feel death's presence. Illusory images flying past like flood discharge flashed by her heart and made all his sharp pain feel unreal. He could feel her pain, but he also knew it would be gone soon, thousands of times faster than the speed of the birth and death of a body.

Mengzi thought he'd let her down. He should be suffering like her, he thought, he should be so grief-stricken that he wanted to die, but he couldn't. The pain never left him, but soon it was effaced by a sense of illusiveness. All he could do was love her with all his heart.

She gazed out at the undulating sand ridges through half-open eyes. A ghostly white sun shone down from behind and gave the fine hair on her face a fuzzy glow. Yue'er slowly turned to look at him. "Do you think I'm pretty?" she asked softly. He tightened his grip on her hands, but said nothing.

With a sorrowful smile, she removed her backpack, took out a box of sandalwood incense, lit a few sticks and stuck them in the sand. Then she had Mengzi kneel down with her. He thought she was about to pray to some god, when she said, "Promise me we'll be husband and wife in our next life."

Warm currents rushed into his eyes as he said robotically, "We'll be husband and wife in our next life."

"Not just the next life but for three lifetimes."

"For three lifetimes."

"No, forever."

"Forever."

Gazing at him with tenderness and love, she gentle combed her fingers through his hair, straightened his collar, brushed off a few kernels of sand on his shoulders, and cupped his face to stare into his eyes. "Remember the promise you made today," she said slowly. Then she turned her face, aglow, to look at the setting sun with a corner bitten off by the sand dune.

3

Yue'er wanted to leave.

The festering had spread to her neck, and she knew that the pretty Yue'er would disappear if she stayed. She put a letter and a pair of shoe soles she made under her mother's blanket. They were for Mengzi. Besides the letter, the envelope also contained eight thousand yuan that his mother had just sent over. She wouldn't be using it now. In the letter she expressed gratitude to her mother-in-law, telling her that the real function of the money was to show that she had another mother.

As usual, she put on light makeup, picked up the prettiest and brightest outfit, and added earrings and a necklace before heading to a photo studio at White Tiger Pass to have pictures taken. She then told the photographer to give Mengzi the pictures. The man said those were his best portraits; he would like to hang them in the window. She didn't say no.

With all she would need, Yue'er followed the route Mengzi had taken that other day on the motor scooter. She enjoyed everything along the way and savored the scenes from the earlier trip, a sweet, happy smile blossoming on her face. The villagers who were out and about looked at her from a distance; no one disturbed her. She felt the compassion in their looks, which sent a warm current rippling in her heart.

She walked out of the village and into the desert.

She wished she could turn into a drop of cool, refreshing water and seep into the boundless desert.

Before she left, she'd burned off everything she'd used, for she knew they had all been tainted by the Demon's saliva. She had been doing that on and off ever since she knew what she had. Her mother had left for White Tiger Pass, so there was no one around. She was meticulous. Fire was the best thing in the world, she thought. However dirty it might be, everything could be cleansed in a fire bath. She hated the idea of anyone being hurt by the virus.

Fire is wonderful, she said to herself.

As usual, the waves of sand extended into the horizon, toward the unknown. Yue'er knew it would be same with her soul; she had no idea where she would drift to once her soul left the disease-ridden body. It was beyond her control. All she could do was leave her lasting beauty to the world. She could not keep changing the course of her life, so she would leave her beauty, and the best way to freeze beauty was death.

Nothing mattered more to her than beauty, especially to leave it in the mind of the one she loved. She would leave and merge into the spot where the yellow heaven and yellow earth were, where her beauty would freeze into eternality.

The image of a raging fire kept flashing before her eyes. It roared between heaven and earth, capable of burning away all worries. She'd heard how a phoenix reached nirvana in a fire.

A desert wind licked at her gently, the only thing close to her at that moment, no, there were also her memories. But memories leaped around like an unruly monkey. Let them be then. No one can freeze memories.

Before her was the spot where they'd taken the vow. The desert wind and sand had erased the traces they'd left, but the tenderness remained. The wind seemed to murmur the vow, which was why she felt herself enveloped in an enormous sense of happiness. She would stay quietly waiting for the arrival of "the next life." Don't forget your promise, Mengzi.

She smiled. It was high noon, but the sand trough wasn't hot, because of the clouds overhead. The kernels of sand were warm, and she felt herself in the arms of her beloved when she sat down. Taking out her hand mirror, she took one last look at herself and saw no sign of wreckage left by the Disease Demon. She stuck out her tongue. She would like Mengzi to be the last thought on her mind, but he had slunk off to somewhere. It had been like this over the past few days; it was hopeless. I'll deal with you in our next life.

A tiny creature came up to look at her through its round eyes. It was a small lizard, what the villagers called a sand baby. A baby of the desert, it can survive here no matter how hot or dry. She wished she could be a sand baby. It was wonderful to be alive, she thought. She didn't know what the world after death would look like; she wasn't afraid of transmigration or Hell, but she did not want to be reduced to nothing. Even being a sand baby was better than nothing, she thought.

That thought brought tears to her eyes, and she felt a sense of bitter resentment creep into her heart and begin to gnaw . . . She really hadn't lived well, she thought. She rued her life; she did not want to accept what was happening. Slowly the bitter resentment expanded and overtook her despair, agony, and a great many other things. A spark of fire burst out from deep inside and slowly spread.

With her eyes nearly closed, she gazed at the sand baby. The two porcelain gray dots in its eyes seemed to send out ripples to transmit a force to her.

After recovering her breath and calming down, she shifted her gaze to the sky and let the its liquidy blue trickle into her heart until she felt she had become a part of the sky.

A long time passed.

Faintly she heard someone calling; it sounded like Mengzi's voice, though she heard nothing but the wind when she listened carefully.

How I wish I could be a phoenix, she said to herself.

Yue'er sighed deeply, wondering if she should do something else. She thought long and hard, and finally hit upon an idea: she should sing a tune. She had yet to sing one for herself after doing it for others. In one's lifetime, one must sing a tune for oneself, so she licked her lips and started softly—

Three thunderclaps sounded to shake the ground.

All major deities worried and thought it unsound.

I'd rather see trouble in the Jade Emperor's land,

Than have the path between us blocked for eternity.

出 版 人	陈亦新	
责任编辑	梦 馨	
特约编辑	胡 丹	
装帧排版	陈 盼	
营销策划	雷贻婷　袁春梅　蒋毅华　葛万军	
出　　版	中华国际传媒出版集团	
地　　址	香港金钟道 89 号力宝中心第 1 座 10 楼 1003 室	
电　　话	(0852)35888733	
传　　真	(0852)35888717	
销售电话	(86)13434375544	
E-mail	xuemo1963@163.com	
印　　刷	阳信县卓越盛达印务有限公司	
版　　次	2021 年 8 月第 1 版	
印　　次	2021 年 8 月第 1 版第 1 次印刷	
规　　格	145×210mm	
字　　数	540 千字	
I S B N	978-988-79930-7-0	
定　　价	178.00HK$	

读者服务邮箱: 417825705@qq.com　　service@xuemo.hk

(版权所有　翻印必究)